# Soul Bond

By Blake Severson

## Book Two of The Dimensional Wars Series



To my family. I love you all for the continued support.

# Prologue



Alicia ran down the street, dodging in and out of the crowd. Today was a market day, which meant her favorite person would be out. The large stone buildings passed by as she charged through the city. The people she passed all had smiles on their faces, and the market was bustling with energy.

Her flight took her past the enchanter's shop, and she jumped out of the way of a patron exiting the building. In her stumble, her cotton dress snagged on the hinge on the sign and unraveled a line of thread. *Mom will kill me if I keep messing up my clothes.* She fiddled with the string of light blue fabric, attempting to smooth it down.

The summer day sent sweat trickling down her neck and caused her to stop at a nearby water faucet. She reached over and twisted the small valve to allow water to flow. Her hand brushed the flow, and she quickly snatched it back. *Who would need scalding water on a day like today?* A twist of the small dial on the side fixed the issue, and chilly water flowed in a steady stream. She brushed aside her shoulder-length raven hair and drank. The icy water against her lips sent a feeling of relief through her.

She approached the corner of the market and jumped onto a short stone wall. Her target wasn't visible as she scanned the faces in the crowd. With her search unsuccessful, her spirits dropped. One last look yielded the sight of a small group that gave her joy. With her new goal in sight, she hopped from the wall and dashed off.

It didn't take long to weave through the last of the crowd until she ran into a small street corner with a circle of kids seated around a bald man. His gentle, aged features gave him a kindly appearance. He wore long brown robes with no ornamentation, but the fabric was sturdy and well made.

"...and the brave knight vanquished the foe with a roar!" the storyteller bellowed out dramatically.

The crowd of kids cheered enthusiastically at his display. They all started up a chant asking for another story.

"Calm down, calm down," the storyteller called with a chuckle. "Do we have any suggestions for a story?"

Alicia stood up and yelled, "Tell us about the lost prince!"

The storyteller's gaze swung toward her, and he smiled gently.

"Ah, young Alicia, back to hear the courageous tale again? Fine, fine, I'll indulge you."

Alicia giggled in excitement and quickly took her seat with the other children gathered around. The storyteller was a popular figure in the market with the children of the city.

"One evil day in our kingdom, our illustrious king and queen fell to betrayal. Some of their advisors hatched a devious plot and assassinated Tristan and Violet Firebrand. Alas, fate had other ideas. The Holy Lady Lianna saw fit to shelter their son, Arthur, and return him in our hour of need.

"The usurper King Wailyn was steadily destroying our once grand country and driving the people into famine. It's rumored it was at the behest of an evil Goddess named Isabell," the storyteller whispered conspiratorially and sent them a wink, "but you didn't hear that from me.

"Our young Arthur returned to the world and took up residence in the village of Alem's Crossing. He developed a fast friendship with the locals and quickly made a name for himself as a champion of the people. A true adventurer at heart, he worked to keep them fed and even used magic to help rebuild the city.

"One day he ran afoul of a group of bandits. The nobles of the land used these thugs to harass the populace and steal food and goods. He valiantly trounced the fools, but nobly let them leave without further bloodshed. That was a mistake," the storyteller said in a low tone.

"Our young prince banded together with his group of five loyal friends, and they fortified the small wall around Alem's Crossing from the retaliatory attack of the bandits. The famous Paladin Samson single-handedly defended the opening in the wall while Arthur and his group fought off the rest. At the end of the day, Arthur's group defeated all forty of the bandits!"

"That can't be true! No group that small could ever defeat that many people by themselves," one older boy said.

"Well, over the long years, the numbers may have changed in the telling. I can promise you it was over twenty people, though, no matter what the exact number was," the storyteller confessed. "This battle was the key turning point in our story. You see, up until then, Arthur didn't understand he was the lost prince of our kingdom. His loyal companion, the dragon, Calfuray, found him, and she imparted the knowledge of his situation to him."

"But Mr. Storyteller, there isn't a village in the country called Alem's Crossing," one young boy told the old man.

The old man smiled and winked. "There isn't one anymore. What city do we live in now, son?"

The boy looked confused but answered anyway. "Alurian."

"Very good. Do you know how this city got its name?"

"Not really," the boy mumbled.

"That's because they originally called this city Alem's Crossing," the storyteller pronounced with a wicked gleam in his eye.

# Chapter 1

*The Power of a Bond*

The wind danced through the rolling field as Arthur stood in confused shock. *Calm down. Don't freak out. It's just an enormous lizard with wings. She seems nice,* he told himself as the dragon's purple scales shimmered in the sunlight. She shuffled on her claws, adjusting her weight, and Arthur flinched unconsciously.

"Calfuray is a beautiful name, and it's a pleasure to meet you, but I'm sorry to say I don't remember you. I also do not understand what you mean by a soul bond," Arthur told the dragon. His mind swam with the implications of her statement. *How was I once bonded with a creature of legend?*

First, he'd discovered he was the lost son, Arturian Firebrand. They presumed him dead since King Wailyn, the current seated king, murdered his parents during a coup he led. He found out that his parents sent him through a dimensional portal before King Wailyn killed them. With his bloodline power of Dragonfire awakening in the last fight, he wondered how they even pulled that off.

"Arthur, when a member of your family is born, they bond with a dragon for their lifetime. This soul bond allowed the person and their dragon to share benefits and abilities. It also helped each of them grow stronger and watch out for one another," Calfuray told him.

"If my parents were each bonded to a dragon, how were they murdered without the dragon interfering?" Arthur asked her.

She adopted a sad look on her scaled face. With her eyes downcast, she told him, "Your father was the only one bonded to a dragon. Your mother married into the family and therefore had no dragon bond of her own. Your father was born of the bloodline and had a dragon companion by the name of Draelon. When the attack came against your parents, Draelon was away visiting the dragon homeland. As soon as he detected the threat through their link, he tried to return to Tristan, but the betrayal happened too quickly, and he couldn't make it back in time to save them."

"Could I talk to him? I'd like to know more about my family. I wasn't even aware they were my family until yesterday and know almost nothing about them."

Her face fell even further as she shifted again. His instinct pushed him to the side a step, and she swung her long neck to follow his movement. "You can't talk to him, Arthur. He's dead. If one member of the soul bond dies, the other will die. This is why I thought you might still be alive, even though I couldn't sense our bond anymore when you disappeared. I was still a young dragon and didn't understand the situation. Even now, I don't know how you're here and looking as young as you do one-hundred years later, but I'm sure you are Arturian. I recognize your bloodline anywhere, even without our bond."

Arthur was crestfallen. He hoped she could lead him to someone who knew his parents. He needed to do some digging on his own but would have to keep it quiet as to not alert anyone of his true parentage.

"I'm sorry, this is all just as confusing for me as it is for you. I'm here because my parents sent me to another dimension. When my mother sent me there, it was under immense stress and she completed the spell in haste. It unknowingly sent me to not only another dimension but also further along the timeline. The Goddess Lianna brought me back to this dimension and to this world to help her gain influence here," he told her.

Calfuray snorted and little tendrils of smoke curled from her nostrils. "Lianna up to her old tricks again? Guess she's trying to make a move against Bell. Figures she would locate the lost son to make this happen. She lost control of this world when your parents fell from power."

"I don't mean to sound rude but is there a reason you came here? Don't get me wrong, taking to a majestic creature is an amazing experience but I can't figure out where this conversation is heading. I know you sensed me, and I appreciate you seeking me out, but I feel there should be more to it than that. Does it have to do with the bond we had?" he asked.

"Somewhat. We were soul bonded, and it was because of an accord between the dragons and your bloodline. With your unique circumstances, though, it has caused a bit of strife in the ranks. We could always soul bond again, but some dragons don't wish to get involved in human affairs once more. They believe it breaks our agreement. I'm not one of these myself, but I can't go against the others without reason. I came to offer a proposal to you instead," she told him.

"Well, I'm willing to listen to the proposal, and thank you for being open and honest with me," Arthur said.

"I'm willing to soul bond with you again, but I will require certain things from you first."

"Hold on a second, sorry to interrupt, but can you elaborate on what comes with a soul bond? I know you said it allows us to share benefits and abilities, but that's very vague. I wouldn't want to agree to a soul bond unless it had excellent benefits for us both since it's also putting your life on the line."

Her enormous mouth pulled back in a toothy grin as Arthur gulped and ran thoughts through his head. *She's not going to eat you. Everything has been fine. She's here to help. Good lord, look at the size of those teeth.*

"I appreciate that Arthur, and I'm pleased to see you're a smart man with morals. The benefits are worth the bond, though. We can share mana pools and spells between each of us. We can also assist each other in combat, both physically and magically, and gain new abilities. Dragons can learn magic, but we can't retain the knowledge of the spells. Magic is inherent in our bodies, but we can't focus it into spells without a human conduit. When bonded, I'd have access to spells you know for any magic skill I possess and meet the level for. The exception is our base magical abilities, such as our breath. You're also able to invest skill points into the bond as it levels up. It works similar to your talent trees for your other skills, and there are many options to choose from. As with your other skills, the options are random and unique to each person, but the abilities are usually rare."

"Wow, that really makes the bond seem worthwhile for both of us. I'm convinced that it's worth pursuing, at least. What are your conditions?" he asked nervously.

"Well, most revolve around you proving you can survive here. I want you to grow in strength and gain levels. I'll agree to the bond if you can reach level 20 and learn your first combat class. I'll also require you to reach level 10 in each of the four elemental magics, Earth, Fire, Air, Water, and finally, you must reach at least level 10 in Dimensional Magic. If you can meet these requirements, I'll be happy to renew our soul bond and help you in your endeavor here."

Arthur stood in shock. *She couldn't ask for something simple, could she? Luckily, I've got two of those requirements for the Earth and Fire Magic finished, but I haven't even learned Air and Water yet. I definitely must convince Allendria to show me Water Magic. That only leaves me with finding a source for Air Magic.* The thing that threw him for a loop was the Dimensional Magic. He knew his mother must have known it since she sent him away, but he did not understand how he could learn it himself. His parents couldn't show it to him, and, as far as he knew, no one else even knew about that magic anymore. *How am I supposed to learn lost magic? Much less level it to ten?*

"I can agree to those terms but must warn you there's an excellent chance I may never attain them. Almost everything on that list is obtainable, except for the Air and Dimensional Magic. I have met no one with Air yet, but I'm sure after enough time I could find someone. Dimensional Magic, on the other hand, is a lost art. As far as I know, my bloodline was one of the few to practice it, and since I'm the only survivor, I have no one to teach me the pattern for it," Arthur told her sadly.

"Luckily for you, your father strongly believed in being prepared for the worst-case scenario. He entrusted a tome of Dimensional Magic to my mother upon our bond for safekeeping. If you accept this quest, I will give it to you as your father intended," she told him with a big-toothed, feral grin.

*Really wish she'd stop flashing those daggers at me,* he thought nervously before his mind registered what she'd said.

*Can it really be that simple? The skill itself has to be special since it's so rare, but she is willing to just hand over a tome? Surely there is a catch?*

"So, just accept the deal? No catch? No monumental task I have to complete?" he asked.

"You humans sure are odd. I am a dragon and give my word. That should suffice."

"I formally accept your offer and agree to your terms," he told her seriously.

| Power of a Bond | |
|---|---|
| Requirements: Gain Level 20, Learn One Combat Class, Reach Level 10 in Earth, Fire, Air, and Water Magics. Reach Level 10 in Dimensional Magic.<br>Rewards: 10,000 experience, Unlock Dragon Bond Skill. | Description: Calfuray has agreed to renew your Soul Bond with her if you can meet the requirements. |
| You have accepted this quest. | |

She craned her long neck back toward her front right claw and carefully pulled off a compact leather bundle attached with a strap. Arthur couldn't guess how it ended up there, but would not question her about it. She brought her neck back around and held the bundle out in front of her, suspended at his chest level. Arthur took the few steps to reach her and carefully reached out to grab the package.

After taking a firm grip on the package, he told Calfuray, "Thank you", and reached up and gently caressed her snout. She seemed shocked by the action, but a tingle passed between them when he did. It was a sense of familiarity between them. She pulled back and looked at him.

"I shall keep my eyes on you, Arthur. I'll sense when you've fulfilled your commitment to me, and I'll return to you. Until then, keep safe." She turned but stopped as her eye fixed on something.

She looked back toward him, but Arthur noticed she was looking off to his right instead of directly at him. Calfuray made a slight snorting noise, which sounded like the dragon equivalent of a chuckle, and then she addressed the creature that caught her eye.

"Balair, you worthless little devil. How've you been?" Calfuray asked the small dragon who joined them at some unknown point in time.

"Good to see you, Calfuray. I'm back on this plane of existence, as you can tell," he told her.

"Of all the crimson dragonlings he could've summoned, he ended up with your worthless ass? I feel sorry for him," she said, then her eyes narrowed in thought.

"Hold on, if he already summoned you, then you should have known who he was and already told him. How is it he just found out?" She asked in an angry tone.

Balair backed up, a look of fear in his eyes. "I had no way of knowing who he truly was. His hair wasn't the color it is now because he hadn't awakened his bloodline yet. I knew he could speak with me through our bond, but I believed that Arturian died as did the rest of the world. Once he awakened, it all made sense."

She looked at him for long moments in silence before turning back to Arthur.

"Keep an eye on that troublemaker. He's looking rather scrawny, though, so try to level him up with you. He may be borderline worthless most of the time, but occasionally, he can be useful."

She turned to stare at Balair. "You keep an eye on him. I don't care if you die and get sent back to your plane. He can always summon you back. He will not return if he dies."

Balair cowered for a moment and stuttered, "Of course, I'll protect him."

She turned away from them, took two great strides, and leaped into the air while stretching out her wings and pumping them furiously to get airborne. Arthur felt her power as the air buffeted his face when she lifted off the ground.

He turned to head back toward the village and saw his party slowly approaching him as the dragon left. They all looked on with wonder on their faces as he met up with them.

"What was that about?" Allendria asked.

"That was the dragon, Calfuray. Apparently, she and I were soul bonded prior to me being sent to another dimension to escape King Wailyn. Our soul bond dissolved, but she has agreed to renew the bond if I can meet her requirements," Arthur told her.

"The soul bond was real…" she whispered under her breath.

"Apparently so. Calfuray told me it was something all members born of my bloodline received. It broke my bond with her when I disappeared from this dimension. Her requirements will be difficult, though," Arthur told her seriously.

"So, what does she require of you?" Samson asked.

"Well, she said I have to reach level twenty, gain my first combat class, reach level ten in all four of the primary magic skills, and finally reach level ten in Dimensional Magic," Arthur told them all.

They each looked at him in shock.

"How does she expect you to learn a lost art, much less gain level ten in it? I'm unaware of anyone living who knows Dimensional Magic. It seems she's leading you on a wild chase for no reason," Allendria said in a reserved fury.

Arthur chuckled for a moment. "Calm down, she predicted this problem and had a solution," he said as he raised the bundle in front of him. He opened it and showed them the tome that rested inside the package. They could each see the item description, and another gasp spread through those with him.

| Item:<br>Tome of Dimensional Power | **Durability:** 110/110 |
|---|---|
| | **Rarity:** Artifact |
| | **Quality:** Unrivaled |
| | **Weight:** 0.8 kg |

| | **Traits**: This book contains the knowledge to harness the legendary art of Dimensional Magic. |
| --- | --- |

"An artifact rarity item…" they all whispered in quiet awe.

"Arthur," Allendria whispered in shaking tones, "that book is probably the most valuable item in the history of this world. The art of Dimensional Magic doesn't exist anymore, and only a handful of items are still around that still use that kind of magic. Losing the magic was a hard blow to this world," she told him reverently.

"I understand that it's a lost art and a scarce one, but I can't see how Dimensional Magic would've been of much use. From what I've heard, the only thing they used it for was creating portals to other dimensions. That seems more dangerous than useful," he said in a tone that everyone else could tell sounded disappointed.

Allendria shook her head and giggled. "It goes to show how little you truly know. They made many of the best and most useful items made in this world with Dimensional Magic. Tell me, do the words 'Dimensional Bag' ring a bell to you?"

Arthur thought about it for a few moments, and then a smile spread across his face. "You mean Dimensional Magic was used to create Bags of Holding? I can use it to create pockets of space, linked to items, to make impossibly large storage containers?" he asked, excitedly.

"They're usually just called Dimensional Bags, but your description is correct. Few exist anymore. Most that do are owned only by royalty in different nations. I'm sure, with your imagination, you can think of many other uses for Dimensional Magic," she said to him.

Arthur was now giddy with excitement. He would eventually figure out how to make Bags of Holding. Learning some smaller spells would need to take precedence. The tome would probably only teach him the skill itself like his Earth Magic tome had, which meant he would be on his own to create spells using the magic. This meant he'd have to discover smaller spells for the magic to build up his skill level. He was sure that this ability, combined with Enchanting, would unlock his ability to make Dimensional Bags, eventually.

"Well, that's fantastic news. Looks like I've got my work cut out for me for a while. I definitely need to start grinding more experience for my skills," he said as he turned to look at all of them.

"I realized something just before the fight. I've been trying to make this a better place but forgot to share one of the most important things with you guys, knowledge. If any of you wish to learn any of the magic skills I have access to, please let me know, and I'll be more than happy to teach you how to harness them. We're in this together and we'll all grow stronger together. I've already agreed to teach Rowan Earth and Fire Magic and then help him unlock the Arcane Forging skill. I'm more than willing to do the same for any of you," he told them all.

He saw more looks of surprise, quickly followed by looks of determination. The feeling of his schedule magically filling up hit him, but he was perfectly fine with that. He didn't think any enemies made it away from the fight, so he wasn't expecting trouble soon.

They all gathered around as Arthur wrapped the bundle back up, and they headed back into the village. Arthur's first stop would be his room to unlock the skill for the book. Last time it took a long time and being exposed while standing in the middle of a field wasn't a smart decision. They all made it straight back to the inn and found seats to relax from the excitement of the morning.

"Everything all right, Arthur?" Daniel asked, concerned.

"Yeah, I talked to the dragon, and she's agreed to leave the village alone. She flew off and won't harm us," Arthur told the man.

Daniel let out a big sigh. "Thank the Goddess for that. The thought of that thing swooping down and destroying the village worried me. So it was a dragon after all? They still live in the world?" he asked.

"Yes, they do. The dragons have been avoiding us, but I think the battle drew her attention. I explained what happened, and she said she'd leave us in peace."

"That's splendid news!" Daniel exclaimed.

"I will run up to my room and relax for a bit. The excitement of the morning has me exhausted," Arthur told Daniel.

"Go relax. I'm sure we can take care of things."

Arthur stood and nodded to the group. He turned and headed for the stairs when he noticed Allendria was walking beside him. She had a smile on her face and grabbed his arm as they continued upstairs. They entered his room, and he turned to lock the door.

"You didn't have to come, you know? This will probably just involve me sitting here with a blank stare for a while as I absorb everything," he told her.

"I know, but I'll stay here to keep watch over you."

"Fine with me. It just means I'll be in enjoyable company when I return to normal," he said with a smile in her direction. She smiled back at him, and he sat on the bed and pulled out the book.

*You have opened Tome of Dimensional Power. Do you wish to consume this book to learn this ability? Yes/No.*

Arthur selected *Yes,* and a black vortex appeared over the book and started sucking the letters into it as the tome flashed through pages. He vaguely heard Allendria gasp as he watched the action. The vortex itself was the darkest black he'd ever seen, with tiny pinpricks of white. It reminded him of open space with the stars dotting the expanse. The vortex swirled until it absorbed all the letters, and the book crumbled to nothing. He stared at the vortex as it spun up and then slammed into his face. Darkness was being forced into his eyes, nose, and mouth as the information was being processed by his brain.

He saw flashes of portals being used to travel from place to place, dimensional pockets being used for many purposes. He even saw a talented mage use a small portal to get a strike into someone's back by stabbing through a portal, causing his blade and hand to emerge from an identical portal behind his enemy. It looked like this ability was far more useful than he originally believed. Learning how to build the spells would be the tricky part. Luckily, he already had a sizable mana pool so that could help him get past some of the challenges he faced with the other magics.

The visions stopped, and he was sitting back in his room, panting and sweating. He glanced around and saw Allendria staring at him with a look of concern on her face as she held his hand. He looked up to her and smiled.

"It's over now," he told her in reassuring tones. He heard the familiar chime he knew and loved and looked to his notification.

*Congratulations, you have learned the lost art of Dimensional Magic for a 1,000 experience bonus. Huzzah and be merry!*

Arthur was beyond pleased. Now to come up with spells to use. The problem was, he couldn't think of anything possible at such a low level. There were many ideas, but most required more magical ability than he had without additional skill levels. Looking to Allendria, the problem resolved itself in his mind, and he grinned. He would cheat a little to get this skill started. He knew if he could gain enough levels to get his talents, there was an excellent chance they'd teach him something he could use. He also had a glorious seventy-five hundred skill points from his quest he still hadn't used.

Allendria saw the look on his face and frowned. "Why do I feel you're about to do something stupid?" she asked him.

"Not stupid, this time. I realized that trying to find a dimensional spell I could use to help improve my skill at level one would be almost impossible. It was at that same time, I also realized I have seventy-five hundred skill points I can dump into it and get myself some talent points. I should easily be able to unlock at least one useful spell by the second tier of talents," he explained to her excitedly.

She smiled at him. "That's probably your best option for those skill points right now. I would suggest you use them in your combat skills since they're lacking, but you can always grind those up. Dimensional Magic isn't something you'll really be able to use until you learn a spell."

He nodded to her and thought of using his skill points.

*Do you wish to allocate any of your available skill experience? Y/N.*

Arthur thought of *Yes*, and when prompted, he selected all 7,500 to go into Dimensional Magic.

*Congratulations, you have reached levels 2, 3, 4, 5, and 6 in Dimensional Magic. Decreases the mana draw of Dimensional spells by 15%. End of your free ride.*

The results of his investment pleased him. That would give him four skill points to work with, and he hoped there would be a useful spell in there for him. He pulled up the first tier of talents.

*You have 4 unused Talent Points.*

| Talent | Description |
| --- | --- |
| Tier 1 | |
| Bend it to Your Will (0/10) | Increases spell power with Dimensional Magic by 4% per point. |
| Dimensional Drawer (0/1) | Teaches you how to create a Dimensional Drawer. This anchors a small, empty space to you for use as storage that is accessible from anywhere. |
| Power of the Void (0/10) | Reduces the mana needed to cast Dimensional Spells by 4% per level. |

Arthur was excited to see the option he
needed. He couldn't pick Dimensional Drawer
fast enough. That spell would unlock a way for
him to gain experience, but most of all it was
a spell he desperately wanted. The knowledge
from the skill, combined with the skill
increases in Dimensional Magic, should allow
him to almost immediately increase his base
size of the spell. He hoped to create a
dimensional space that would be like a
cabinet, but that would depend on what he
could accomplish. With a thought, he pulled
the menu back up and focused on the Tier 2
options.

*Congratulations, you have discovered the
Dimensional Magic Spell: Create Dimensional
Drawer. You have gained 250 experience in
Dimensional Magic for discovering a known
spell.*

| Create Dimensional Drawer | |
|---|---|
| Requirements:<br>Dimensional Magic<br>Mana Cost: 250 MP<br>Cast Time: 10 seconds | Description: Create a small, empty pocket in space that the caster can access from anywhere to store or retrieve items. Casting this spell will teach the spell Access Dimensional Drawer.<br><br>Dimensions: 1' x 1' x 2' |
| Mastery Level: 1 | |

| Talent | Description |
| --- | --- |
| **Tier 2** | |
| Spatial Work (0/10) | All spells that deal with creating spatial pockets are now capable of 5% more size per point in this skill. |
| Unlock Portals (0/8) | Portals are complex things that require a lot of knowledge. This skill will teach you how to summon small portals within 100 feet of yourself that connect to each other upon investing all 8 skill points. |

*Holy shit, that small Dimensional Drawer spell is rather expensive to create.* He assumed the Access spell it taught would be much cheaper when he finally created the space. The tier two options were fantastic, but it looked like he would need to specialize. He liked the idea of using small portals to get tactical advantages, but it was a significant skill investment. His mind drifted toward specializing in pocket spells instead. There was an idea he hoped would work that he thought would be invaluable, but he needed to be a higher level in Dimensional Magic to see it realized.

With these thoughts in mind, he dumped the remaining 3 points into Spatial Work. It was at this point he also remembered he had ten free talent points from the title he gained. He capped Spatial Work out at 10/10 with seven of those points. He saved the last three points.

He wanted to try out his recent spell to see what it would do. He cast the spell and watched as a square in the air in front of him, a foot and a half wide and a foot and a half tall, gained a dark black outline. The air in this space swung open. Behind it was a solid void in space. It looked like a massive black hole that didn't seem to have a definable end. Arthur was almost scared to reach into it but gave it a shot. He extended his hand, and after three feet of space, it stopped. The darkness felt solid and wouldn't continue. He moved his hand around and touched all the sides to see they were solid despite appearances. He also saw the spell he expected pop up.

*You have gained 550 experience in Dimensional Magic for successfully casting Create Dimensional Drawer.*

*Congratulations, you have reached level 7 in Dimensional Magic. Decreases the mana draw of Dimensional spells by 18%. Walk in the shadows.*

*Congratulations, you have discovered the Dimensional Magic Spell: Access Dimensional Drawer. You have gained 250 experience in Dimensional Magic for discovering a known spell.*

| Access Dimensional Drawer |
| --- |

<table>
<tr><td>Requirements:<br>Dimensional Magic<br>Mana Cost: 25 MP<br>Cast Time: 2 seconds</td><td>Description: Access a<br>Dimensional Drawer<br>you have already<br>created.</td></tr>
<tr><td colspan="2" align="center">Mastery Level: 1</td></tr>
</table>

Allendria watched him with a look of glee on her face.

"Is that a dimensional pocket?" she asked him excitedly.

"It sure is," he responded, smiling. "My personal storage locker. I must work with it until I can make larger ones. It could be invaluable for hiding special and sensitive items that I don't want people to mess with. Once I get them larger, I can also use it as a suitable storage area to fill up while out on our gathering trips instead of lugging a cart around. It would be nice to create a pocket the size of a room and just open it and toss in our spoils as we travel and then deal with it all when we get back," he explained.

She lit up with that explanation. "That sounds marvelous."

"I know you taught me Fire Magic as a favor for saving your life, which was a major step for you since it required you to defy your teachings, but is there any way I could convince you to teach me Water Magic as well? It's a skill I require and will have to level," he asked, sheepishly.

She giggled. "Of course, silly. I'd be happy to show you. You picked up the last one so fast. I think you'll have the pattern in no time. The method you used to teach me Earth was outstanding, so I can apply that same concept to help me teach you Water Magic. This should help you catch on much faster."

"Thank you," he told her sincerely.

"Thank you," he told her sincerely.

# Chapter 2



Allendria decided it was as good a time as any, so she sat next to Arthur on the bed. She had him lay his hand out, palm side up, and laid hers on top of his. She pushed the power into him that represented Water Magic. As with the other magics, this one comprised three distinct feelings intertwined. He felt the rush of an icy stream on an early spring day that then progressed into a rolling set of rapids and ended in a roaring waterfall of power.

This magical power differed from the others. The others had been all wrapped together to create one scene. The forces for Water Magic seemed linear and formed in the flow of a line when visualizing them. She separated the streams for him as he had for her, and he quickly mimicked each one.

"Combine them for me, please?" he asked her.

She nodded her head, and he felt the shift. He realized the error in his earlier thoughts. He thought this would signify a linear line for the powers but, when she combined them, they were a continuous circle instead. He mimicked the patterns and received a notification.

*Congratulations, you have learned Water Magic for a 100 experience bonus.*

"That's much quicker to learn when splitting like that. I wonder why the other mages don't teach it that way. Would probably make things go faster for them," Arthur said, amused.

"That would defeat the purpose. Those mages are there to make money from their profession. The longer they take to teach, the more money they can milk from the rich families."

"Such a waste. No wonder this entire world is going down the drain," Arthur said.

"Not sure what a drain is, but I agree with the sentiment."

"So, what spell do you recommend I use to level up Water Magic?"

She looked up, concentrating for a moment before she gazed back to his eyes.

"I'd say your best option would be Gentle Rain. It's a simple spell that lets you summon a tiny cloud to rain over a specific spot. It's best for you because you can cast it anywhere and don't have to be near a water source. The spell draws in latent water from the air to power itself," she told him.

"That sounds like a plan. I work outside a lot anyway, so it would be a quick way to burn off excess mana. Can you show it to me later when we're outside?" he asked.

"Of course, now let's get back downstairs. Even though your trance lasted about an hour, the day is still young, so let's go find our friends," she told him.

They walked downstairs together and found Rowan talking to Samson, but Vana was nowhere in sight.

"What are you guys up to?" Arthur asked them as they sat down.

"Just discussing priorities. Trying to figure out how to shift focus now that the bandits aren't an immediate threat," Rowan told them.

"That's a good question. I plan on spending the next couple of days doing some skill training. I need to teach you Earth and Fire Magic so you can start grinding your levels, and then I can show you the hidden skill you want. I can work with you on that tomorrow if you'd like," Arthur told him.

"I appreciate that, Arthur. I look forward to it."

"Arthur, I'm aware you offered before, but would you be willing to teach me tomorrow also?" Samson asked.

"Sure. You want to learn both skills, right? I'm sure Earth would be beneficial to you with your tanking."

"Yes, I'd like to learn Earth first, but I'd also like to learn Fire Magic. It would make for an excellent distraction when needed. I saw the attacks you launched with your Fire Magic to surprise people and knock them off guard." He laughed.

"Can't argue with you there. I'll start with both of you tomorrow morning. We can go to Rowan's shop so no one will bother us."

Rowan nodded at the suggestion.

"I'd like to get the important figures together for a meeting if possible. Can someone send out some runners to gather those needed? It's time to develop a long-term plan here," Arthur told them.

"I'll see to it," Rowan said as he walked off to pass the word.

Arthur, Allendria, and Samson sat in the common room, discussing mundane things as the rest of the village leaders walked in and took a seat. Vana was one of the first to pop up, but Dalia quickly followed her. Daniel proceeded to the front of the inn as people shuffled in along with Rowan. Arthur watched as more familiar faces filed through the door.

Corianne walked in with Zeke and James not far behind. It also surprised Arthur to see Noah and Toren enter. He had seen little of them since they volunteered to guard the inn during the fight.

They all gathered in the inn and pushed a couple of tables together for an impromptu village meeting. They needed to decide on a direction for the village.

"Thank you all for coming," Arthur called out over the conversations.

"Our initial fight was a success, but we all know that this isn't the end. There are way too many bandits roaming the land for the lords. We need a plan to help the village thrive."

"It seems to be an issue of time," Daniel stated. "We've bought ourselves a reprieve, but there's only so much possible in the limited time we will have. We know this fight isn't over, but, even worse, we don't know how long until they return. It's possible they sent a runner from the primary group to alert local guilds of the problem before coming to attack. They also may have said nothing to save face. Our true situation is unknown."

"I wholeheartedly agree with your assessment," Arthur responded. "We still need to set a course for the village, though. We cannot let it fall back into complacency. I believe we need to focus on the defense of the village, so working on the wall will be key for me until I can get it up to a suitable size. It worked well to delay them during the attack, but the fight would've been easier with a better wall that wasn't scalable from the ground. The primary problem is the workforce. I know we have a decent amount of villagers here, but let's be honest, I can do more in an hour with my magic than they can accomplish in multiple days' work. There's only a handful of us who have any access to magic."

"That's true, but there isn't much that we can do," Dalia said to the group.

"That isn't necessarily true. While it is a problem to address, there are ways to fix it. I know we have many people gunning for us, but more who would want us to succeed if they were aware of what we were doing. I'd like to end as much of this fight as possible without having to do any real fighting. I have no problem fighting to defend this village and the people in it, but I don't care to go looking for more problems."

"How do you plan on doing that? You truly believe you can make enough of a difference without fighting off these bandits?" Dalia asked in disbelief.

"I think we can make it happen, but it will rely on our village improving. I think we should focus on the walls, but at the same time, I believe it's time we work on the village Quality. If we can increase the village Quality level, it should help us bring others to the cause," Arthur told her.

"How are we supposed to do that? As you said before, it'll take a sizeable amount of work, and you're uniquely qualified to do it," Dalia said.

"Dalia's right. Even if I assist with my magic, there's only so much ground we can cover at a time," Allendria chimed in.

"I propose we create groups of people in the village responsible for specific services. For instance, we can create a group responsible for building and maintaining roads, another responsible for upkeep and building of necessary city services, even another for residential construction," Arthur explained.

"That gives everyone a purpose but still doesn't solve our problem," Dalia argued.

Arthur smiled at her. "That's why I'll offer to teach them magic."

Everyone froze, and then multiple people began talking all at once.

"What do you mean you'll teach magic? That's highly regulated and not allowed," Daniel blurted out.

"That might end up causing more issues than it helps with," Dalia agreed.

"Are you sure you should do that? You might invite more trouble than necessary," Vana exclaimed.

"Everyone calm down!" Arthur yelled over the group. "I understand your concerns but let's face it. The current leadership won't tolerate what we're doing regardless. We've already firmly drawn the lines, and it will only get worse. The best chance we have is to move forward as quickly as possible. We need to draw people to us to help us weather this storm. I'm proposing we offer to teach magic necessary for them to do their jobs. For this, I'd have them work directly for the village for a set amount of time. If they agree to that, I'll teach them the different elemental magics they need to know, and we can also help them learn the spells necessary for those tasks. This allows us to expand much faster and to grow our village. Teaching our unskilled villagers would be beneficial to our village and is the perfect solution."

"The idea sounds crazy, but at the same time, it makes sense. I've seen how much you've accomplished by yourself in the brief time you've been here and can't argue that having more people able to work in the same way would be fantastic. The trick is doing it right and attracting the people. It'll be a big initial investment with much of that being time," Daniel told him.

"By investing the time now, it will greatly increase the village production in the future. We need to have people who specialize in each aspect of the city, though. I don't plan on teaching everyone all the elemental magics I know, but I'll teach them what they need for their chosen job. Is it possible to teach Talent skills as well?" Arthur asked as he looked around the room.

Everyone looked a little lost at the question and couldn't decide on an answer. Finally, Allendria spoke up. "I believe it is, but you have to know the distinct forms of magic required to do the spell natively. It'd be something that would require a bit of trial and error, I believe."

"One more thing to add to the list. So how should we approach this?" Daniel asked.

"I'm guessing we can decide the primary groups we need and then work toward recruiting for them," Rowan said.

"Sounds like a plan to me. We know we will need a group dedicated to farming and monitoring the crops. These will need to know Earth and Water Magic for best use. We'll need a construction group that will have to focus on Earth and Fire Magic. I'm working with Rowan on training him to become a second Arcane Smith to assist with that aspect of the village. We shouldn't require too many in that role, at least not yet. We can discuss his apprentices reaching this goal as their levels increase," Arthur told them confidently.

"That sounds like an excellent start. What terms do we want them to accept in this offer? Something like this is extremely valuable, but we don't want them to feel like prisoners here," Vana said cautiously.

"You have a point, Vana. I'd suggest we offer a two-year employment term. Require them to work for the village for two years, and then they're free to do whatever they'd like, anywhere they wish. They'll still be free to do what they please within the village while employed here. They just won't be able to use their skills to help another village during that period. Anyone object to that?" Arthur asked.

"That sounds reasonable. What are we going to use to pay for their labor?" Dalia asked, concern evident on her face.

"That leads directly to our next issue. We need to establish fair market values for goods and services in the village. We can't rely on prices from other places because of their struggles, but we should be able to establish new prices for what we consider appropriate. I coined some silver and copper using my unique smithing skills, so we have currency to work with to get the process started. We must make sure we regulate prices here to prevent a crisis," Arthur told them.

"What funds are available? We need to know how much coin may be in play at one time," Dalia asked.

Everyone turned to look at Arthur.

"I've minted one thousand, two hundred and sixty copper coins and three-hundred silver coins. I'd like to keep old currency out of the system. The coinage I made is all mage-crafted quality and much harder for someone to fake."

"That's a wonderful start. The standard exchange rate is fifty to one, so we've got plenty to work with for now. We can always hope you find some more raw materials to make more. We can also convert the old currency to the new style as we find it," Daniel said thoughtfully.

"Daniel, any suggestions for standard prices that'd be fair?" Samson asked him.

Daniel contemplated. "I'd suggest keeping prices low and starting the economy from the bottom. As you said, we can't operate based on prices in other parts of the kingdom. None of those are realistic. The key things will be labor and food. Everything else will settle itself based on those two prices. I propose we set the food price at a standard two copper per serving. With that in place, we can offer to pay civil servants five copper per day. We can guarantee them two meals a day as a bonus for working under the employment of the village. This would allow them to spend their extra on family members or trade skills."

"That sounds fair," Dalia remarked. "We can always adjust that as circumstances change. I think Daniel is correct, though. People will set their prices on other goods as long as the price of food and labor remain steady."

Vana chimed in too. "It sounds like we need to get the word out then. How many workers do we want to allocate for each of the different jobs?"

"I'd suggest we find four people to tend the fields, four to be our construction team, and two for sanitation services," Arthur told them.

"Sanitation services?" Daniel asked.

"They'll need Earth, Fire, and Water Magic because disposal will be their business. It'll be their job to keep the city clean of refuse and garbage. They can use magic to clean the streets and buildings, while also incinerating garbage to keep it off the streets. I eventually plan to install a water and sewer system in the village, so we'll need workers to maintain these services," Arthur explained.

"What's a sewer system, and what do you mean by a water system?" Dalia asked.

"A sewer system is an underground network of tunnels that carry human waste away from a city for disposal. Initially, its purpose is to dispose of waste from the principal businesses such as the inn, but will eventually expand to encompass all buildings. That'll be part of our overall plan to rebuild the village. The current buildings won't do, and we need to replace them with stone housing that we can build quickly and efficiently. When designing these new buildings, I can ensure these necessary improvements are standard features," Arthur told them.

Rowan whistled at that. "It sounds like an extensive project to take on by yourself, Arthur."

"That's exactly why I want this construction group trained quickly. I'm confident I can get them trained to stone fast, and that'll allow them to work together to build these structures. It may take some time for them to learn magic skills, but once they do, it should progress quickly. I don't want our village to be one that hoards knowledge for individual greed and power. This information should be available to those who can use it. Rest assured, I'm not foolish enough to teach people without there being a reason for it, though."

"Is tomorrow morning too early to start? We can search the village this evening for candidates, and they can report to you in the morning so we can get these projects moving," Vana said.

"Sounds great to me. We can start tomorrow if you find me suitable people. Just make sure they're motivated and trustworthy. We'll announce the revised pay structure for the village, and I'll adjust the work order rewards to reflect copper instead of meal tokens. We'll gradually phase out the meal tokens until the economy is back on its feet," Arthur said with finality.

Their meeting adjourned, and everyone began leaving when Dalia motioned for him to join her.

"Can we speak privately for a moment?" she asked him.

"Sure," he replied. They walked over to the edge of the room, out of earshot of everyone else.

"Arthur, I can't help but notice the change in your hair color… the others may not remember what that signifies, but I do. You're not supposed to be alive, and it shouldn't be possible," Dalia said carefully.

Arthur sighed. "You're correct. I don't want the word out on who I am until we've established a solid footing here and necessary defenses. I guess it shouldn't surprise me that you know the significance of my recent hair color change since you're a descended of a family of nobles."

"The Flamekissed and Firebrand families were always allies. Your great grandfather was the one who granted my family their title of nobility over Alem's Crossing. Our great grandfathers were practically best friends when your family took the throne. We sided with your family in the war, and our reward was the title here," she explained to him.

"I appreciate you letting me know and would also appreciate it if you kept this quiet. I believe that our enemy knows I'm here, but I also don't think they know my true identity yet. If they did, I know we would've faced a far superior force that we wouldn't have had a chance against."

"I won't say a word to anyone about it. It's good to see your family back, though. Does this mean the dragons will return?" she asked.

"That's hard to say. The dragons are on the fence about returning. I just learned from Calfuray that they can't decide whether they will honor the agreement with my family. I'm working to fix that," he told her.

"As long as you have a plan, that's fine with me. I also want to help the village, so would you be willing to teach me magic as well?" she asked.

"What magic do you think would be most useful to you?"

"I think Water and Fire Magic would be the most useful. I'd be able to handle a lot of the minor things around town with those two," Dalia told him.

"We can do that. Meet me in the morning, and I'll work with you when I work with Samson and Rowan. It can be one large training session."

She nodded her head in thanks and moved back to the middle of the room to talk with Daniel.

Not wanting to waste any more time, Arthur walked outside. It was time for him to focus on the wall again. Defense would be their primary strength. Everything they'd come up against so far was relatively weak when isolated, and a wall did that perfectly.

He was heading toward the wall when Balair interrupted his thoughts.

*What are you up to?*

*Just going to work on the wall for a while. Can't you find something useful to do?*

*Not really… I can't do much on my own. My Fire Magic doesn't seem to be very useful in the village unless we're going to burn down those sad excuses for houses,* Balair told him.

*So instead, I'm stuck with you?* Arthur sighed.

*Cheer up. I'm sure it isn't the worst thing that's happened to you.*

Arthur just huffed and continued to the wall. When he reached the gatehouse where the battle had taken place, he took notice of the area. The battle had left no damage to the wall itself. They cleaned the battlefield of human remains, but the ground was bare and torn up where the villagers removed the gore.

Directing his attention back on the wall, Arthur focused on expanding the structure. Now that the initial barrier was complete, it was time to begin the next phase. He momentarily glanced at the large opening in the gatehouse and determined they'd need to address that soon. He took in a deep breath and got to work. He spent the next three hours in methodical casting and relaxation for mana recovery.

*You have gained 11,400 total experience in Earth and Fire Magic.*

Arthur considered doing some Leatherworking but, since his group all had a set already, using excess leather right now wouldn't do anyone any good until he could find a way to increase its quality. Some of that was sure to come from leveling Leatherworking, but there had to be a way to do it magically.

Allendria found him during his last resting period while he waited on his mana to regenerate.

"You ran off before I could show you the Gentle Rain spell for you to work on your Water Magic. Do you want to do that now, or would you rather wait?" she asked him.

"Now would be fine. I'm almost back to full mana again and was about to wrap up for the day, anyway. Guess you got bored sitting around town?"

"It sounded like you had a specific vision for what you wanted to accomplish with the village, so I didn't want to start randomly making changes that might not match your goals," she explained.

"I appreciate that. Once we have the construction crew running, I plan on creating a new design for the entire village. I want to ensure the villagers all have adequate space for their families and ease overcrowding. We can start building and moving people to new houses while salvaging the old houses for usable material and comforts. I also want to find a spot in town where I can build a house for myself. I'd like my house to be the model we base the others on. It gives me time to work out the exact way to create them and develop the spells to teach the construction crew," he said thoughtfully.

"This place could use it. That should also greatly improve the overall quality of the village. I'm assuming the rank will require you to bring in more people. That's one downfall of our success not spreading. It won't draw attention to us from those we want to join us."

"That's true, but it's imperative we weigh the pros and cons for each side of the deal. I've got an odd feeling that more villagers will make their way here as time goes on," Arthur told her.

They both sat down, and Allendria explained the spell to him.

"Gentle Rain is relatively easy to do. You must create a small swirl of Water Magic like you did for the Fire Magic during the incinerate spell. This will gather water in the air, and when a sufficient amount collects, it'll fall to the ground below the designated area. This is a small area spell, meaning it requires a lot of casting to be useful, so it's best used to water plants individually. I'd suggest you try to make the swirl around two meters in diameter. Much more than that is a waste. The key element here is the swirl. Just remember, as it gets wider you need the magic channels to start slowly sloping downward. This allows the water to collect along the spiral and gradually move downward until it falls," Allendria explained.

Arthur nodded his head and focused on his Water Magic. He felt the magic build in power as he directed his spell at eye level in front of him. Starting with a central spiral, he gradually spun it outward while slowly dropping its height. The spell reached a diameter of about five feet, and he determined that was large enough. The notification popped up immediately after cutting the magic flow.

*Congratulations, you have discovered the Water Magic Spell: Gentle Rain. You have gained 250 experience in Water Magic for discovering a known spell.*
*You have gained 50 experience in Water Magic for successfully casting Gentle Rain.*

| Spell: Gentle Rain | |
| --- | --- |
| Requirements: Water Magic<br>Mana Cost: 30 MP<br>Cast Time: 3 seconds | Description: This spell summons a vortex of water that draws moisture from the air to cause a gentle rain on the selected area for five minutes. |
| Mastery Level: 1 | |

*Not a terrible spell to work with.* Arthur thought to himself. The experience was decent for a base spell, he could cast it with no specific target, and he could cast it as often as he wished to grind experience.

"Thank you, that was easy with your explanation. It's definitely easier to learn spells when someone can talk you through it," he told her sincerely.

"It's my pleasure. I admire the work you're trying to accomplish here. I'm also pleased to hear you're trying to develop a plan to avoid fighting and still triumph. I know fighting is inevitable, but the fact you're trying to avoid it is refreshing. I imagine things will get worse as we get closer to the larger cities," Allendria told him.

"I think you're right. I was fortunate to end up on the edge of civilization, allowing me to avoid some of the rougher elements of life, but it will come back to haunt us eventually. How about we head back to the inn? It's getting dark, and I'd like to get cleaned up and grab some food. I'm starving!" Arthur emphasized with a pat on his stomach.

"Lead the way," she told him.

"Why? Just so you can stare at my ass on the way back to the village?" He laughed at her.

"You only wish. Hey Balair! Wake up, you lazy bum. Let's go," Allendria yelled at the sleepy dragonling nestled in the middle of the field, basking in the sunshine.

*Can you tell her to shut her mouth for me? I' enjoying the sunshine, and she's welcome to keep her loud mouth closed,* Balair grumbled at him.

*You really don't want me to tell her that. She won't be happy if I do,* Arthur told him cautiously.

*Pfft, what do I care? She's just a Dark Elf. I'm superior to her in every way,* he told Arthur with disdain.

*Your funeral,* Arthur chuckled at him.

Arthur turned toward Allendria and relayed the little dragon's words. Her face grew red as he recited what Balair told him. When he repeated the last part about being superior, he could see the fire in her eyes and would've killed for some popcorn to watch this show. She took off in a dead sprint for the dragonling.

As the distance melted between them, she reared back and slammed her foot into the dragon's side. She could've kicked for a pro football team with that boot. Arthur swore he heard the grinding of rib bones, and then the dragon flew ten feet and landed in a heap, choking and spluttering to regain his breath.

"You ever talk to me like that again, and I'll skin your worthless little hide and turn you into undergarments so you can permanently kiss my ass at all times of the day," Allendria yelled at him with a fiery temper still burning in her eyes.

Balair eyed her carefully and cowered away as he struggled to recover from the ordeal. He bowed his head to her and talked to Arthur mentally.

*Please tell her I'm sorry, and from now on I'll be respectful,* Balair choked out. Even his mental voice sounded pained.

Arthur relayed the message, and she calmed down a little.

"Fine, let's go, it's time to find some food," Allendria said.

*I tried to warn you.*

*Walking* back to the village, Arthur cast his new Water Magic spell multiple times to use up his mana.

*You have gained 600 experience in Water Magic for successfully casting Gentle Rain (x12).*

*Congratulations, you have reached level 2 in Water Magic. Increases the effect of your Water Magic spells by 3%. Playing with the rain now?*


Upon entering the inn, they found an empty table and laughed as Balair tried to scurry into a chair without falling out. Arthur needed to figure out a better way for him to eat, but he didn't want to be rude and suggest he eat on the floor.

Daniel brought out the food, and they ate in silence. Arthur enjoyed the chance to sit and listen to the crowd. The sound of laughter coming from the other patrons warmed his heart and firmed his resolve to see this through.

After supper, Arthur and Allendria went to the bathhouse while Balair wandered off up to their room. After a quick scrub in the refreshing water, they returned to the inn, and Arthur collapsed into bed. They quickly fell asleep in each other's arms.

# Chapter 3


*A Happy Accident*

Rayne crept through the hallway as quietly as he could manage. The gaudy decorations in the place further solidified his resolve in his mission. They'd been suffering, and the time spent taking the abuse of Lord Preston Wayne was over.

Lord Preston's family had been the overlords of Seora since King Wailyn overthrew the Firebrand family. The city was now a horrible mess of starvation and crime. Rayne spent most of his time using his stealth and thievery to stay alive. There were many close calls with the local bandits masquerading as city enforcers. Still, he was alive and surviving.

The last few months had gotten worse if that was even possible, and it convinced Rayne to go all-in and infiltrate the Lord's manor. Lord Preston should be a much easier target than trying to go to the regional capital and infiltrating Lord Golgara's home.

He shuffled up to the corner of the hallway and carefully peered around. The area looked clear of anything dangerous, so he quickly ducked around the corner and kept up his pace of skulking through the hallway. Paintings adorned the halls as he went. Many of the pieces looked like a six-year-old with a paintbrush, and a lousy temper created them. He wasn't an art man himself, but they must be valuable to someone.

An older woman had given Rayne the layout for this place as part of a vague job. The situation was odd, but he was desperate enough to give it a shot. The treasury was his target. It was a compact room, located in the basement level of the building, furthest from the stairs. The main floor had been a breeze to get through, and the guards here were laughable. They were poor excuses for human beings, and their appearances testified to that fact.

Their cast-off finery showed signs of misuse, and the stains testified to the lack of cleaning. Most of them didn't even wear the pieces of clothing correctly, attesting to their lack of sophistication. With his stealth skill as high as it was, he could quickly sneak past them and continue to the basement.

Rayne was taking a slower approach in the basement. He couldn't rely on the hope that all the bandits and guards would be worthless here. Getting complacent was the best way to end up dead in this city. Most of the time, you couldn't even sleep without trouble finding you.

At the next hallway intersection, he peeked around the corner. As fast as he looked around, he quickly whipped his head back. The sight of a man in serviceable mail armor standing in the hallway next to the corridor he needed to get through surprised him. If his information was correct, he was only a few halls away from the treasury. A lone guard here didn't bode well. He'd bet money there were at least two more guards by the room if there was a solo guard this far away.

Rayne sucked in a deep breath and steeled his nerves. He didn't care much for the art of assassination, but he was past the breaking point now. He typically tried to steal or resorted to spying missions, but his skills were ample enough to fight if needed. The armor on this man would be a problem. Luckily, Rayne was familiar with weak points in chain armor, and his stiletto dagger was a narrow blade, in the shape of a thin triangular prism, explicitly designed to get through the chain.

Rayne took a deep breath and slowly counted down in his mind. This would be a quick attack from stealth and would require him to activate two of his abilities to work. When he reached zero, he quickly rounded the corner and threw out his hand. A small stone flew down the hall and to the other side of his target.

*Your Distract on Bandit Guard (Level 14) was successful.*

Rayne breathed a small sigh of relief as he used a burst of raw Air Magic to push him faster. His footsteps were silent as the space melted away. He took his dagger and plunged it directly into the man's kidney while reaching his left hand around the man's face and covering his mouth. He clamped down hard to prevent the man's stifled cry from escaping and quickly ripped the blade out of his side.

*You have dealt 200 damage to Bandit Guard (Level 14) with Iron Stiletto Dagger (Stealth Attack) (Critical Hit) (Mortal Blow).*

Before the man could react any further, Rayne reversed the blade and drove it into the side of his throat.

*You have dealt 150 damage to Bandit Guard (Level 14) with Gag Order.*
*Bandit Guard (Level 14) has died.*

Rayne caught the guard's weight as he fell to the floor, dead. He lowered him quietly and checked the man's pockets. A few coppers were all he collected, but he bagged a little experience in his skills. Rayne rarely bothered to examine his skills or level anymore. Lately, it was rare to gain experience in anything but his thievery skills.

The Gag Order ability was one of his favorites to use in a pinch and was a recent acquisition from his talents. The skill had a five-minute cooldown, but it would sever the vocal cords in the throat. If it didn't kill the target with its damage, it would silence them permanently without specialized healing. Here, it quickly finished the man off after his massive initial HP loss.

The mail the guard wore was garbage. Rust dotted the suit, and it had no chance of stopping his stiletto dagger. He cleaned his blade off on the guard's ragged clothing and put it back in its sheath. He couldn't afford the gleam of metal on the knife to give him away.

Rayne found a door a short way down a relatively empty hallway, which looked to be a storage room. He dumped the body in the closet to keep it out of easy sight.

    With the body secured, he continued his mission. He quickly shuffled into the hallway that his source had described and regained focus. He crept down the hallway, checked the next, and continued his trek. These winding hallways were an absolute pain in the ass.

    Rayne reached the end of the last hallway and peered around the corner. The treasury room was at the very end of this last hallway. It had a heavy wooden door banded in iron. As he feared, there was a guard on each side of the door and these appeared better trained than the other guards. A quick scan of them showed their classification as City Guards and sitting at Level 15.

    Although Rayne did not understand what their skill set would be, he was past the point of no return now. His only option was to finish this and get out of town before retaliation could happen. The scenario would challenge him, though. He didn't want to use his hidden ability unless absolutely necessary. Keeping it in reserve for his escape would be his best option, but these two guys were far better armed than anyone he'd already dispatched.

    Distract probably wouldn't work on them, at least not without somewhere behind them to target. This would require him to use more misdirection abilities. He went through his breathing again and steadied his nerves. This would be another quick dash followed by an encounter.

    The end of his countdown approached quicker than he expected, but he dashed around the corner and tossed a small cloth bag at the guards. His skill activated, and the powder swirled into the air.

Rayne pulled both of his blades for this fight. His style used two blades, but one was a rare sight. Commonly known as a swordbreaker, narrow grooves covered the backside of the knife designed to catch sword blades in them. Once a blade became trapped, the wielder could quickly twist the dagger, and it could rip the weapon out of their opponent's hand. If they had a good grip, it was even common to snap a blade from the extreme force exerted by the twist. Most weapons only had so much flex in them before they'd break. Iron blades would commonly bend to unnatural angles since they weren't as hard as steel.

Rayne dashed in and punched into the first guard's side with his stiletto dagger and quickly followed with a slash from his swordbreaker to the man's helmet. He didn't expect to do much damage with the second hit, but he wanted to knock the guy off balance.

The guard stumbled backward, but before Rayne could pursue the stunned man, the other guard raced in and took a wild swing. Rayne quickly danced out of the way and ran back in to close the distance to the new target. Before the guy could stop his swing and recover, Rayne punched his dagger into his left side. The man fell back before Rayne could get a follow-up swing in.

*You have dealt 100 damage to City Guard (2) (Level 15) with Iron Stiletto Dagger (Critical Hit).*

As quickly as Rayne felt he'd secured the fight, he felt a sense of dread fall over him. His street senses screamed danger to him. He heard footsteps closing in, and before he could react, two unfamiliar faces came at him through the smoke. These two were the Bandit Guard style of fighters.

The first came in with a high swing while the second used a side sweep toward him. This scenario offered few options, so he sidestepped the downward slash and stepped directly into the sideways slash from the second man. He caught this blade in his Swordbreaker and used the momentum of the edge to twist the knife and quickly ripped it out of the man's hand. His Stiletto dagger came around in a quick motion and stabbed the man under his left armpit and directly into his heart. The guy crumpled to the ground.

*You have successfully Parried Bandit Guard (2) (Level 15).*
*You have dealt 250 damage to Bandit Guard (2) (Level 15) with Iron Stiletto Dagger (Heart Strike).*

*Bandit Guard (2) (Level 15) has died.*

The first bandit closed on him after
recovering from his missed swing, but to his
dismay, the initial guards were charging him
from behind. His smoke bomb was dissipating,
so their visibility was quickly returning.
There wasn't much room on either side of him
to work, and his space to move was rapidly
shrinking along with his window of time. His
mana was low because he'd been burning it in
bursts to increase his movement and swing
speed using his Air Magic. As much as he
didn't want to, it was time for him to
activate his hidden ability.

*Are you ready for blood?* Rayne asked the
voice in his head.

*Always,* was the response he received.
Rayne focused on the ability and triggered it.
Black smoke flowed from his clothing and
poured out of the sleeves of his shirt and
wrapped around his hands. Another cloud of the
black smoke poured from the bottom of his
pants and shrouded his feet while a final mask
of smoke billowed from the neck of his shirt
to fill his hood and obscure his face. The
smoke covering his face had jagged blue,
glowing representations for his eyes and
mouth.

*You have activated Shadow Form. Your
movement and attack speed has been increased
by 40%. Enemies find it 50% more difficult to
target you accurately.*

Rayne felt a smile come to his face, and
the gruesome blue visage mirrored a jagged
smile within the smoke. The Bandit Guard in
front of him stepped back with fear and
despair on his face. Rayne dashed in and
smashed his Swordbreaker into the man's neck
and punched his dagger into the man's chest
with a heavy thud. The man crumpled to the
ground and was out of the fight.

*You have dealt 100 damage to Bandit Guard
(1) (Level 15) with Iron Swordbreaker
(Critical Strike).*
*You have dealt 150 Damage to Bandit Guard
(1) (Level 15) with Iron Stiletto Dagger
(Heart Strike).*
*Bandit Guard (1) (Level 15) has died.*

Rayne turned to face the remaining two City
Guards. Their faces quickly morphed into
shocked fear as they saw what he'd become.
Since his ability was short-lived, he had no
time for hesitation and advanced. His enhanced
speed almost allowed him to run circles around
the men, so he punched two quick strikes into
the first guard. One in his side and the
second in his back, directly into his lung.
With momentum still on his side, he ducked
under the second guard's swing and stabbed the
stiletto dagger into the man's armpit to watch
both guards fall to the ground.

*You have dealt 100 damage to City Guard (1)
(Level 15) with Iron Stiletto Dagger (Critical
Strike).*
*You have dealt 75 damage to City Guard (1)
(Level 15) with Iron Stiletto Dagger (Critical
Strike).*

*You have dealt 200 damage to City Guard (2)
(Level 15) with Iron Stiletto Dagger (Heart
Strike).*
*City Guard (1) (Level 15) has died (x2).*

Rayne let out a breath he hadn't realized
he was holding and surveyed the room. There
was absolute silence, and he heard no cries of
alarm. Before he could start checking the men,
he fell to a knee. The shadow energy fled back
into him, and with it came the standard debuff
he received when he used that ability.

*You have been inflicted with Soul Weakness.
Your health and mana regen rates have been
decreased by 40% for the next hour.*

*Damn that debuff hurts.* Rayne thought to
himself. He couldn't afford to sit around and
do nothing, though, so he quickly set to work
searching each of the men. Each of the two
Bandit Guards had a few coppers on them, while
the City Guards carried one silver each. That
alone made this trip worth it. That was more
money than Rayne had seen in months.
There wasn't any time to worry about hiding
these bodies, so he finished searching the two
City Guards, and, to his disappointment,
neither had a key to the treasury. It didn't
surprise him too much. All of them worked for
criminals, so why would they ever try to trust
them with access.
Approaching the door, he smiled when he saw
the lock. It was pretty standard and obviously
not designed as much of a deterrent. He pulled
out his slim pieces of metal and set to work,
manipulating the tiny pins inside the device.
After a few minutes, he heard the satisfying
click and opened the door.

Rayne entered the room with a massive grin on his face at his apparent triumph, but after a moment of looking around, it quickly morphed to confusion. The room was almost bare. Cobwebs covered parts of the room and it looked abandoned. *How could the treasury be this barren?* The Lord here had done nothing but hoard his wealth… unless it was all a hoax, and they really didn't have the resources anymore. That would make sense with the absolute lack of food and production in the cities.  Making money required trade goods to buy and sell, and due to the incompetent fools in charge, the town was as destitute as the people that inhabited it.

Rayne looked crestfallen as he scanned the room. Instead of being set for life, he ended up almost empty-handed. Sure, he had two silvers to his name now, but those wouldn't last very long. To top it off, his body count from this adventure would make him a heavily hunted target if they ever found out who was responsible. His previous escapades had caused no lasting attention to him since no one knew exactly who he was.

His despair was climbing when he thought he saw something shimmer in the room's corner. He approached it carefully and discovered a tiny slip of paper sticking out of a crack in a wooden shelf. The paper exuded a sense of destiny as though it was for him alone. He opened up the letter, and his eyes grew wide at the contents.

*Valiant Rayne,*

*I'm sorry your journey led you here to receive, what seems like, no reward. I promise that your prize will be much more fabulous than you know. I have a higher purpose for you, and there's a friend of mine who will need your help, although he may not know it yet. Your ability to pass this test proves you're worthy of this quest.*

*I can only promise your life will change forever if you listen to my guidance. Please gather as many trustworthy people as you can, not affiliated with the local lords or gangs, and escort them to Alem's Crossing. The new mayor there is causing quite a stir, and I think you'll get along nicely. I'm proud of your unwavering strength to overcome the circumstances you've been through, but I pray you heed my words and make the journey. It'll be the best option for you and your sister.*

*With Love,*
*The Goddess Lianna*

Rayne's jaw almost hit the floor. The fact it mentioned his sister was the only reason he took it seriously. It was his mission in life to protect his sister, so much so that there wasn't a soul here who knew the two of them were related. There was no doubt this was a mandate from a Goddess. The name Lianna was familiar to him. Rose had mentioned it before, and he vaguely recalled she was a popular Goddess during the time of the Firebrands. He also remembered it from some of the discussions amongst the Shadows of the Flame. *What in the world was happening here?* Before his train of thought spiraled out of control, an unexpected notification appeared.

| A New Start | |
| --- | --- |
| Requirements: Hidden<br>Rewards: 15,000<br>experience, 2,500<br>skill experience. | Description: The Goddess Lianna has tasked you with escorting the citizens who are tired of the oppressive lords to Alem's Crossing. Completing this quest will offer great rewards. Your experience bonus will be increased based on the number of people delivered on the journey.<br><br><ul><li><10 people - Base experience</li><li>10-20 people - 10% experience bonus</li><li>21-30 people - 25% experience bonus</li><li>Over 31 people - 40% experience bonus</li></ul> |
| Do you wish to accept this quest? Y/N. | |

*Damn*, Rayne thought. He'd never seen an Epic level quest before. Scalable rewards were also uncommon in quests, and he'd never even heard of a quest that offered unassigned skill experience to use. That quickly quelled any doubt he had, so he promptly accepted the quest. Getting out of there should be quick, and he could quietly search the city for people to join him. He typically would've scoffed at the promise of something better as hearsay, but with the situation as dire as it was now, many would follow him. It would take him close to three weeks to get to the tiny village of Alem's Crossing, but he'd be happy to make the trip if it meant a better life for his sister. His resolve hardened, and he decided they'd leave first thing in the morning. That would give him the rest of the day to scout for potential travelers to join him.

Rayne quickly took off through the manor and back to the city proper. It would take some work, but he was more determined than ever to finish the quest entrusted to him.

# Chapter 4

*Magical Instruction*

Arthur exited the inn and soaked in the sun's warmth on his face. His morning felt like every other so far. Daniel's cooking skill ensured breakfast was always a delight. With his belly full, it was time to head over to Rowan's shop to teach some magic. Daniel and Dalia were confident they'd have a group of people ready for training a little later in the morning, so it gave him time to work with the others first. Dalia informed him she'd be working with interviewing the candidates for the crews instead of their training and opted for a rain check.

As the smithy came into view, he saw both Rowan and Samson. The gruff-looking warrior watched Rowan work the forge with keen interest.

When Arthur got close, Rowan ceased his work and began putting some of his tools away.

"Give me just a second to get some of this cleaned up, and we can get started."

Rowan quickly cleared out the work area, and everyone grabbed a small stool from Rowan's stash around the shop.

"All right guys, this process is fairly straightforward, but it will probably take some time. I've found a better method of teaching, so I'm hoping it'll help you all pick it up more quickly. Luckily, once you've learned one magic skill, it becomes easier to learn additional ones."

"Let's get started then," Rowan said
eagerly.

"Hold your horses. A bit of explanation is
in order first. One at a time, I will have
each of you place a hand on mine. Then I'll
begin pushing magic into each of your hands.
You'll feel the magic as it leaves me and
enters your hand, but it'll be difficult to
determine what it is. Fire Magic and Earth
Magic are both similar and made up of three
separate bands of power. I'll separate these
for you as they enter your hand. Your job is
to manipulate your mana inside yourself to
create three identical bands of energy. Once
you've matched your bands of power to mine, I
can slowly demonstrate how to combine these
threads to complete your magical training.
We'll be starting with Fire Magic," Arthur
explained.

Both men stared at him with absolute
attention etched on their faces. He extended a
hand to each man and felt their hands settle
on top of his. From that point on, most of his
morning became a very long and tedious test of
patience. It was apparent they were actively
trying to manipulate the energy, but with
mixed success. After three hours of sitting,
Rowan got two of the three bands of power, and
Samson only solidified the first.

Arthur hoped the attention to detail from military life and the work of a craftsman would help them progress quickly, but he imagined a strange idea like this was more challenging to grasp. He couldn't fault them for how things were going. Allendria had told him it usually took a while for people to understand the concepts of magic the first time. Arthur had the distinct advantage of learning his first magical skill from a tome, so the feeling of the power allowed him to familiarize himself with unknown magics even faster. These two men had no familiarity to work with and were reliant purely on their ability. After many hours of work, Arthur called for a break.

"Let's stop for a while, guys. I need to get up and stretch. Sitting here for this long is killing me," Arthur told them.

They both looked around for a moment before they came to the same realization with a grimace. They'd been focusing so much on their work, that they hadn't noticed their stiff joints. All three men stood up and began stretching out their legs. While they were taking a break, Arthur decided it'd be the perfect time to burn some mana and work on some Arcane Smithing. He wanted to make some pieces that Rowan and his apprentices could finish.

"Hey Rowan, I'm going to burn some mana while we wait. Is there anything specific y'all need made? I'd like to make a handful of items with enchantments that I can leave for you and the apprentices to finish."

Rowan thought on the problem before answering. "Some sets of armor for the city guards would be good. I know we don't have any currently, and before long, they'll be necessary. It'll also help to have some set aside in an emergency to arm people for defense."

"Sounds perfect. I think I can mass produce the armor that Samson is using for the city guard. I'd like to keep them all the same style as a symbol of our village," Arthur told him.

Samson looked slightly downtrodden at the news that his armor wouldn't be unique anymore.

Arthur chuckled. "Don't worry Samson, I plan on upgrading your set to steel soon. I've already unlocked its use with my talents. I believe that by combining that knowledge with my Arcane Furnace spell, I'll be able to get the correct mix of carbon in the iron to create the steel that we need."

Rowan perked up at that. "You think you can transform our iron into steel?"

"I think I can. I already know that it's all about the carbon content in the iron and the proper way to heat treat steel after forging, so it shouldn't be terribly hard to make it happen," Arthur said confidently.

"Well, hurry and get to work then. If I can ask, though, why wouldn't you create the steel first and then just make everything from that steel? It will be better all-around and is much more durable," Samson said.

"I could do that, but wouldn't steel armor and weapons have higher requirements that might prevent our lower level villagers from using them?" Arthur asked, confused.

Rowan and Samson both gave each other odd looks. "Why would there be different requirements? A sword is a sword, no matter the material that comprises it. Hell, a steel sword is lighter and typically more flexible than iron, so if anything, it should have fewer requirements. The only items I've heard of that have specific criteria to wield them are usually anything of a magical or religious nature. Even those are typically absent of level requirements. They just require a specific skill or alignment," Rowan explained.

Arthur looked at him in disbelief for a moment, but the more he thought about it, the more it made sense. It always rubbed him the wrong way when it magically required a higher level to wield a weapon or armor. It was the same damn tool and just made out of a different material. Unless it was inherently magical or substantially heavier, he couldn't think of a valid reason it would have more demanding requirements. Also, as Rowan had mentioned, switching to better materials would decrease weight and increase the weapon's natural strength, so they'd require less work than subpar equipment.

Considering this information, Arthur changed his plan. There was also an excellent chance if he jumped to steel first, he'd be able to pack more enchanting power into the items. Since he discovered he could incorporate the enchanting runes into his Arcane Smithing spell, it was a perfect choice.

"I'll shift focus then and instead work on modifying the iron into steel with my Arcane Furnace. I agree it would be the best option for our situation," Arthur conceded.

He walked over to the pile of iron ingots and grabbed a couple. He was afraid this would require some trial and error to get right. The best chance he had would need charcoal, though.

"Rowan, do you have any charcoal around the forge? I know you mentioned you kept some around from time to time," Arthur asked.

"Yeah, there's a bucket around here somewhere," Rowan responded as he began looking around the shop for the container. After a few moments, he came back to Arthur carrying a bucket of the black briquettes.

"Thank you. I need this to introduce the additional carbon into the iron."

Arthur grabbed a couple of chunks of charcoal along with an iron ingot and tossed them into the fire. He wanted to get a jump start by getting the metal into the heat and, after a brief delay, he pulled it out with tongs. Using his magic, he levitated the metal and then tossed the charcoal into the mix. Building up a layer of protective Fire Magic, he activated his Arcane Furnace spell.

The temperature gradually increased, but instead of letting it settle at the heat he had for iron, he kept raising it. He needed the metal to melt so it would absorb the carbon from the charcoal. The process proceeded quickly, and the metal started flowing. Arthur began to moving the charcoal through the metal in slow circular movements with the hope it'd absorb evenly through the granular structure.

His mana continued to fall since he was changing the spell and not casting the typical Arcane Furnace. When he felt the spell ran its course, he pulled the charcoal lumps out and re-solidified the bar into a single chunk. He pulled the heat from the spell and examined the bar in his hand with trepidation.

*You have gained 80 experience in Earth and Fire Magic for successfully casting Arcane Furnace.*

<table>
<tr><td>Item:<br>Iron Ingot</td><td>**Durability**: 30/30<br><br>**Rarity**: Common<br><br>**Quality**: Good<br><br>**Weight**: 4.0 kg<br><br>**Slot**: Crafting Item<br><br>**Traits**: An Iron Ingot for metalwork.</td></tr>
</table>

*Well damn*, he thought to himself. It didn't work, and he wasn't sure why. After a few minutes of thinking about the problem, he decided that his method of cycling the coal through the molten iron wasn't sufficient to allow it to absorb the carbon.

*There has to be a better way to do this.* He wracked his brain for a solution before finally walking over to one of the tool racks and grabbing one of the larger hammers. A piece of charcoal clanked to the metal bar near his feet, and he slammed the hammer onto it over and over until the charcoal was primarily dust.

Arthur also decided to use one lump of charcoal in the process this time. If he added too much, the carbon content would be too high and create pig iron instead of pure useful steel. The dust version of the charcoal should absorb into the metal more efficiently. With his mana pool still over halfway full, he immediately tried the process again.

The process started the same way, and when the metal reached the molten level, he pushed the dust into the mixture. Instead of it floating through the metal and around the space, it seemed to absorb into the melted mixture. He kept the metal swirling and folding in the air for a few minutes to allow any necessary chemical reactions to take place, then molded it back into the brick style used for the ingots. To prevent the destruction of the grain structure of the steel, he slowly drew the heat from the metal. The bar fell into his hands and notifications popped up.

*Congratulations, you have learned the Crafting Spell: Arcane Furnace (Steel). You have gained 350 experience in Fire and Earth Magic for discovering a known spell.*

*Congratulations, you have reached level 18 in Fire Magic. Fire Magic spells now have a 51% increased effect. I'm a little disappointed you haven't tried whistling while you work.*

*You have gained 100 experience in Earth and Fire Magic for successfully casting Arcane Furnace (Steel).*

*Congratulations, you have successfully created Steel Ingot. You have gained 120 experience in Arcane Smithing and Blacksmithing for creating this item.*

| Spell: Arcane Furnace (Steel) | |
|---|---|
| **Requirements:** Fire Magic and Earth Magic<br>**Mana Cost:** 40 MP<br>**Cast Time:** 5 seconds | **Description:** Cast a spell to melt iron and introduce carbon to create steel. The initial cast takes 5 seconds, but the time required to complete the item depends on the amount of metal.<br><br>**Special Traits:** Using this spell increases the base Quality by one rank as long as the item and materials used are within your skill range. |
| **Mastery Level:** 1 | |

| Item:<br>Steel Ingot | **Durability:** 30/30<br><br>**Rarity:** Uncommon<br><br>**Quality:** Good<br><br>**Weight:** 4.0 kg<br><br>**Slot:** Crafting Item<br><br>**Traits:** A solid ingot of steel. Used in metalworking. |
|---|---|

"Hell yeah!" Arthur exclaimed as he celebrated his success. The best part was, he now understood the ratios needed to make this happen every time, and he wouldn't have to influence the spell directly. In his glee, he saw Rowan and Samson standing nearby in anticipation, and he tossed the ingot to Rowan.

The sizeable man caught it and looked at it. His face morphed into an enormous grin, and he looked back to Arthur.

"You did it! This changes everything for us. We're now officially more industrial than ninety percent of the country. You know, if you plan on rebuilding the village with stone, we really shouldn't need to keep this much iron around. You could transform all of this iron into steel, and it would give us a large stockpile," Rowan told him.

"Sounds good, but we must find more iron. The gatehouses will need wooden doors made for them, and I want those doors banded in iron for strength and flexibility," Arthur responded.

"I'll see it done. I also need to talk to our woodcutting duo to get some larger logs that can stretch that height, and we can work on getting them cut into lumber style pieces."

"I guess that means it's time to get back to work with your magical practice for a while. I'm essentially out of mana anyway from modifying that spell, so it's a perfect chance for us to continue while I regenerate," Arthur told them.

They all went back to their respective seats and resumed their magical training. Another hour went by, and Rowan got all three bands of power to match while Samson still struggled at two. He sent Rowan off to work on his own for a while as Samson continued working toward getting his three to match. Arthur considered letting Rowan attempt to blend them, but he didn't want to explain the process multiple times and end up distracting Samson in his current task for no reason.

It took Samson another hour and a half, but the man got the last band of power solidified in his mind. Arthur called Rowan back over to resume the final part of the training.

"Okay guys, the last part of this is crucial, and you must follow it the exact way I show you. The first part is tough, but it still requires one more step. You must combine the three bands in the exact pattern necessary. I will show you the first step to weave them together, and then when I detect you get it right, I'll weave the last one for you. Manipulate your magic to work in the same way, and you'll succeed," Arthur explained.

Both men nodded their heads and reached out to Arthur. He pushed the power back in with the separated strands and let them quickly solidify their beams of energy. When they each had their three bands complete, he showed the first step and kept slowly repeating it. To his surprise, Samson had this part in less than a quarter of an hour. He showed him the last portion of the pattern immediately after. Rowan finished his first mixing of power after half an hour. Coincidentally it was at this same time that Samson succeeded and unlocked his Fire Magic.

Samson jumped up with glee and, out of exhilaration, sent a stream of flame out of one hand into the air. It was a short blast, but the man hooted in excitement.

Rowan concentrated harder and did his best to avoid being distracted by Samson's glee. It took him another ten minutes, but he smiled as the last piece snapped into place, and Rowan received the Fire Magic skill.

"Damn, that was tough but, oh man was it worth it," Samson exclaimed.

"The best part now is you two get to work on burning your mana. You'll first need to grind some levels in Fire Magic. Luckily, I know the perfect spell for you guys to learn. You need Weak Flame. Samson, it's the same spell I usually use to distract enemies during a fight. More importantly, it will allow you to survive anywhere with access to fire for cooking. Rowan, it's the spell I used to heat the rivets in place so we could avoid marring the armor Samson wears by throwing it back in the fire. It'll be even more important to use on steel where we don't want to soften the finished areas to attach the lining."

"Since you mention that, I suggest all of our city guards receive Fire Magic if you agree with it. Any military man needs to harness fire to survive. Especially when traveling on a campaign," Samson chimed in.

"Outstanding idea. I prefer to avoid a large fighting campaign, but I'd much rather have our people prepared for anything. I plan on heading back to the inn for some food, and then I'll train the construction workers for Earth Magic. You two need to keep burning your mana on the Weak Flame spell every chance you get to level up. To learn it, just heat a chunk of metal for a handful of seconds, and the spell should activate. Picture the flame about a foot long as it exits your hand," Arthur told them.

"Will do," both said in unison as Arthur turned to head for the inn. He stopped himself and diverted back to the shop. His mana pool was full, so he grabbed iron ingots and charcoal and set to work. He cast his Arcane Furnace (Steel) spell eleven times and stacked the new steel ingots to the side. As he left the shop, he waved at Rowan and Samson and chuckled as they both huddled over chunks of iron and channeled flames into them.

*You have gained 100 experience in Earth and Fire Magic for successfully casting Arcane Furnace (Steel).*
*Congratulations, you have successfully created Steel Ingot (x11). You have gained 1320 experience in Arcane Smithing and Blacksmithing for creating this item.*

Upon entering the inn, Daniel immediately approached him.

"Welcome back, Arthur. How'd everything go with Samson and Rowan?"

"Good. Both now have access to Fire Magic and are eagerly burning mana to level it up. Looks like two kids playing with a new toy."

"Doesn't surprise me. We located the first wave of candidates for you. We found four volunteers for the construction crew, six for the fields, and two for the city work. We had to turn away some for now since I knew it'd take time to get these guys trained," Daniel told him.

"I had a feeling we'd have a good turnout for this. When I get the current crews trained, it'll be up to them to train any future groups we establish, so that'll save me some time in that regard. I think I'll start them all with Earth Magic, though. Most of their work will involve the walls and roadways. My Fire Magic skill was lower than my Earth Magic when I learned the trick to transform earth to stone, so I want them to have a better base in Earth than Fire when I attempt to teach them the spell," Arthur said.

Daniel led him to a gathering of people near the back of the inn. Twelve people stood in front of him. Each had a look of eager anticipation on their face. He decided they'd find a space outside to work in the shade. Being outside would allow him to take frequent breaks to use his mana. Grinding some experience in his Dimensional Magic would be necessary, but he didn't want to show that power off to the villagers. It might alert someone to his true identity.

"Let's head outside so we can get this started," Arthur called over the milling voices in the room.

They all diligently followed Arthur out of
the building and ended up settling in a shaded
area beside the inn. Arthur spoke briefly
about his expectations for them and what their
jobs would entail. Everyone confirmed their
two-year commitment, but the news that they'd
earn wages in coin and receive two meals a day
at the inn brought smiles to their faces. Now
they'd have a guarantee of food and some money
to spend, which was a new experience.

Arthur explained the teaching process to
them in the same way he'd explained it to
Rowan and Samson. This would be tricky with so
many people, but he wanted to avoid breaking
them into smaller training groups. It'd take
forever to teach everyone that way. Instead,
he had them sit in two groups of six on either
side of him and stack their hands in a pile.
His hands found their way to the stacks on
either side of him, and he pushed magic into
the two groups.

After diligently working at this for a
solid hour, Arthur thought it'd be an
excellent time for everyone to take a break.
Only a handful had got the first band of
power, and everyone needed a chance to
stretch. While on their break, Arthur walked
farther away from the inn and began burning
mana. He cast his Gentle Rain spell seventeen
times to burn all of his mana and help him
with some Water Magic experience. If he
couldn't work on his Dimensional Magic, he
might as well work on Water Magic.

*You have gained 850 experience in Water
Magic for successfully casting Gentle Rain
(x17).*

*Congratulations, you have reached level 3 in Water Magic. Increases the effect of your Water Magic spells by 6%. You know you'll get wet, right?*

Everyone resumed their positions when Arthur returned to the group, and they repeated the process. An hour of training with a brief break in between seemed to be a good pace for them to balance learning the skill and basic muscle comfort. They did this for three more cycles of training and rest. At the end of those four cycles, six of the twelve progressed enough to have the three bands of power solidified. The other six had two of the three complete. Arthur also got his Gentle Rain spells cast during the breaks.

*You have gained 2,550 experience in Water Magic for successfully casting Gentle Rain (x51).*
*Congratulations, you have reached levels 4 and 5 in Water Magic. Increases the effect of your Water Magic spells by 12%. Taking this seriously, huh?*

To avoid dragging this process out too long, he split them, so the ones who had all three of the lines of power complete were on one side of him. He pulled them to the side and explained combining the bands in the same way he did for Samson and Rowan.

They resumed their training while he kept the bands split on one side and demonstrated combining the power with his other hand. While doing that, Arthur zoned out a bit to get a glimpse of his Water Magic talents.

*You have 2 unused Talent Points.*

<table>
<tr><th colspan="2" align="center">Tier 1</th></tr>
<tr><th>Talent</th><th>Description</th></tr>
<tr><td>Flow With It (0/10)</td><td>Increases spell power with Water Magic by 3% per point.</td></tr>
<tr><td>Purify Water (0/1)</td><td>Teaches you the spell to purify any water source and remove contaminants.</td></tr>
<tr><td>Conserve to Preserve (0/10)</td><td>Reduces the mana needed to cast Water Spells by 3% per level.</td></tr>
</table>

The options seemed to be standard from what he was used to seeing. The talent of Purify Water was the obvious choice and could be invaluable to survival, especially in the wild. He committed that point and pulled up the Tier 2 options.

*You have 1 unused Talent Point.*

<table>
<tr><th colspan="2" align="center">Tier 2</th></tr>
<tr><th>Talent</th><th>Description</th></tr>
<tr><td>Summon Basic Water Elemental (0/1)</td><td>Summons a small water elemental that can be used as seen fit. Helpful for routing water flow and cleaning.</td></tr>
</table>

| Waterlogged (0/10) | Each point increases Water Magic Spell power by 2%, and every 2 points increase your base Intellect by 1. |
| --- | --- |
| Irrigation (0/10) | Water magic spells cast for plant growth have a 5% greater effect per point invested. |
| (Hidden Ability) Water Enchantrix Matrix (0/1)<br><br>This ability will only become available if you have the following prerequisites:<br><br>• Water Magic > Level 5<br>• Enchanting Skill > Level 5<br>• Have created Enchanted armor that resulted in a set bonus | Gives you the knowledge to create an Enchantrix Matrix for the Water Element. This is the basic structure for advanced Enchanting patterns. |

Water Magic would definitely need some quality time grinding with those options. The talents that granted Intellect were immensely helpful. There was no way he was passing up the Enchantrix Matrix, though. This one may teach the water style matrix, but since he could naturally read the language, it meant he could quickly adapt it for every element.

Arthur's attention snapped back to the trainees as one of them stood up in excitement. The man unlocked his Earth Magic. In the next half hour, all but one trainee that had all three bands complete gained the skill. Arthur was confident the last man wasn't far behind. There was only one woman left trying to discover the secret to solidifying the last band of power.

Fifteen minutes later, they both achieved their goal. Allendria came by to check on the progress and looked around in amusement.

"What are you up to?" Arthur asked as all the trainees got up for their respective breaks.

"Just seeing how things are going. Any luck?" Allendria asked.

"Funny you should mention it. I could use your help," Arthur said with a sweet smile in her direction.

Allendria glanced at him and frowned. "What hell did I just walk into?"

"It's not that bad. I was hoping you'd be willing to teach the base Earthen Wall spell to the trainees that learned the skill while I help the last achieve their success," Arthur told her.

"Some already learned the skill? That's very rare for people to take less than a day to learn their first magic skill. How's that possible?" She asked.

"I've been using the same method I used to teach you by splitting the power and then showing them how to combine it. It seems to speed up the training," Arthur told her.

Allendria contemplated that for a few moments and then nodded. "It was effortless to adjust to the new magic you taught me when you split it. I suppose that would also make it easier for others to learn it for the first time."

"So, do you have time to help?" Arthur asked.

She sighed. "I'll help."

Arthur led her over to the group that unlocked the skill and introduced her to them. It was important they listened to her and did exactly as she said. Some villagers were still cautious about a Dark Elf being there.

Arthur quickly scampered off to the side to burn his mana by making it rain and then returned to the remaining six trainees.

*You have gained 850 experience in Water Magic for successfully casting Gentle Rain (x17).*

He explained the process to combine the bands of power in the same way he had to the previous group, and they returned to work. The second group was much faster, and within half an hour, the entire group learned the skill. It took Arthur and Allendria another hour to teach them the Earthen Wall spell. Most of her group completed the spell, and the couple remaining joined the rest with Arthur.

Arthur breathed a sigh of relief when the last person finished with a triumphant cheer.

"Impressive work, everyone. You guys and gals did a fantastic job with this. Tomorrow we'll task you with working around the village. I want you to use your magic every moment you can. You all learned the Earthen Wall spell. Your best option is to cast the Earthen Wall spell and then use your magic to flatten it back out. That'll help you also learn the Flatten Earth spell. That one will be important, especially if you're on the construction team. After a day or two of skill work, I can start teaching another school of magic you need for your job. I hope to get all of you working on your own within a week to turn our village around," Arthur told them all.

"Get some food for the evening and get ready for work tomorrow. Don't let your mana go to waste," he continued.

They slowly started moving from the building and talking animatedly. Arthur turned to Allendria.

"Fancy a bath?" Arthur asked. "I've been sitting around all day sweating and working with trainees."

Allendria smiled and nodded her head. Arthur grabbed her hand, and they headed for the bathhouse. On the way, Arthur decided a little more irrigation was in order and emptied his mana pool again.

*You have gained 850 experience in Water Magic for successfully casting Gentle Rain (x17).*

*Congratulations, you have reached level 6 in Water Magic. Increases the effect of your Water Magic spells by 16%. Waterlogged isn't a pleasant look on anyone.*

Arthur didn't even need to examine the talents again to know he wanted those two points to go into Waterlogged. That would bump his Intellect up one and boost his total mana up to 580.

The bathhouse water was a welcome comfort after the long day. Arthur sat on a bench in the shallow water while Allendria leaned against him. He slowly ran his hand through her hair and enjoyed the moment.

"You should take a break more often. If you keep this up, you'll wear yourself out," Allendria told him.

"I can't. We're running on an unknown deadline, and there just isn't enough time in the day. Mana reserves also inhibit some of my work. If I didn't waste so much of my mana regen while sleeping and doing other tasks, it wouldn't be as bad but…" Arthur trailed off on the statement.

*Surely it couldn't be that easy? There had to be a way to store mana, and if I can figure that out, I could stockpile our excess mana. Something like a necklace or bracelet would be a great focal point to draw in unused mana, so it doesn't go to waste. With enough resources, I could even get people in town without magic skills to wear them to build up a reserve.*

Arthur looked at the information the Water Enchantrix talent granted him. After a handful of minutes examining the structure, he smiled. There was a way to do it. Allendria was right when she said he just needed a better set of instructions. The new matrix showed him an example and even had the benefit of showing him how the correct arrangement of the structure. It should be easy for him to adapt it to the principles of mana. The mana collection would require a separate matrix structure that linked with the mana storage, similar to the different enchantments he used on the bathhouse filter.

Arthur considered jumping out of the bath and immediately running to the inn to start work on his idea, but when he looked over at Allendria's smiling face, all of those thoughts fled. *It can wait until tomorrow.* They remained in each other's arms while he continued his smooth caress on her hair. He ran a finger along her cheek and then lifted her chin for a soft kiss. Finally, looking like a prune and thoroughly waterlogged, they got dressed and headed back to the inn.

They entered the inn and spotted Balair. To their amusement, he was running around the room and dodging swings from a long wooden stirring spoon Trisha wielded like a sword.

"What in the world is going on here?" Arthur called above the commotion.

Both Trisha and Balair stopped running around and were panting.

"That insignificant foul creature crawled up behind me, stuck his nose against my butt, and licked the back of my leg. If I catch him, I'm going to kill him. I might get to see if dragonling tastes any good," Trisha told Arthur in anger.

"Why the hell would you do that?" Arthur called to the little dragon.

*What do you mean? Have you looked at her body? I was only trying to admire the woman's curves.* He snorted toward Arthur.

"What in the world is wrong with you? You can't act that way around other people. You better figure out how to act with civility before I send you away. You're useless as it is, and so far, I can't find a reason to let you stay," Arthur told him hotly.

*I'm sorry. I guess it's just my nature. I'll try to work on that and am sure I ca…* Arthur would never know what he would say because Allendria ran around him and, with a boot to his side, launched the dragon across the room in an impressive replay of their earlier interaction.

Once again, the dragonling rose sputtering and wobbly.

"Did you think my threat was just for how you acted toward me? If you don't straighten yourself up, I'll be the death of you," she yelled at him.

The little dragon did the smartest thing Arthur had ever seen him do and ran outside and hid.

"I'm sorry about that, Trisha. He isn't used to human interactions and customs. I think Allendria solved the problem for you, though, and I doubt he'll bother you again," Arthur explained to her.

She sent Allendria a grateful smile. "Thank you, and thank you as well, Allendria. I better get back to work."

Arthur shook his head at the events of the evening and ate with Allendria in the room before they made their way upstairs to bed.

# Chapter 5

*Advances in Enchanting*

It was time for Arthur to change things up. He rolled to his side and gazed at Allendria. Reaching out, he caressed her cheek to wake her.

"Good Morning," he told her softly.

"Is it morning already? I feel like I just fell asleep," she grumbled.

Arthur laughed. "Fine, go back to sleep. I'm off to breakfast."

He rolled from the bed, got dressed, and quickly scarfed down his meal. Instead of going straight to work on something for the village, he did some work for himself today. There were no pressing matters that needed his attention. The new crews they trained yesterday required time to gain some levels. The focus could swing back to them tomorrow.

Arthur decided to work on his Enchanting today. With the new matrix he learned, he wanted the chance to explore his options and see what he could come up with. Hopefully, he could figure out a way to make his Enchanting skill useful, not only for fighting but also for the general populace.

Ensuring he had a large sample of items to work with was vital, though. He checked the storage room in the inn before he left. While looking around, he gathered smaller pieces of the yew wood that Rowan had cut since it had a higher capacity for magic than ordinary wood. There were still plenty of sapphire chips stored in his bag, and he didn't see the point of bothering with the coins. It might be necessary to enchant them, but worrying about them now wasn't.

A few pieces of leather slipped into his bag. It was primarily some of the smaller pieces that he took just to test out unique combinations on. There was no point in using higher quality pieces in case he destroyed something on accident.

Arthur carried the wood under an arm and walked toward the forge.

His thoughts drifted to Balair. *You find anything useful to do today?*

*Yep, hiding from Allendria. I'll find something to eat when she leaves the inn. Until then, I'm avoiding notice.*

Arthur could only laugh at that. She must've finally put genuine fear into him after kicking him twice. Arthur was confident Allendria would spend the day with the construction crew. She'd taken a keen interest in their progress.

The forge was his go-to spot for any work, so he went directly there. Rowan was usually comfortable with him working there, and it was the place least likely to take damage if something went wrong. Samson was watching Rowan work when Arthur arrived. The warrior in him inexplicably drawn to the creation of his tools. Rowan didn't appear bothered by the audience.

Arthur sat off to the side and ensured he was far enough away to avoid causing any damage to either of the men if something went sideways on him. His priority was to examine his new matrix.

This matrix seemed familiar to him, but he couldn't quite place it. The script snaked down in an undulating line as it continued its path. The benefit to this example was he could see how the wording reacted. The enchantment itself didn't mimic what a typical English sentence would be. Instead, it mirrored how he previously did his enchantments by using keywords that caused the desired effect.

The only difference between what he'd done previously and this was the slight up and down curve to the writing. It seemed to have a tight curvy pattern to it, but it never got wider or narrowed. Without further clues, he couldn't think of any way to change it, so he took a shot at some enchanting with the new structure.

He could practice his writing on the leather, and it would help him in his precision for picturing the effect with his Arcane Smithing. He laid out a small scrap and envisioned a pattern in his mind with the desired runes. A thin piece of coal slid from his bag into his hand and settled on the leather.

Since he wasn't in a rush, he wanted to try an Earth Spell. He believed Earth and leather would mix well for effects. When he unlocked the Hard as Stone ability with his talents, he thought it'd be a good utility spell, but, as the previous fight taught him, mana was always at a premium. Naturally incorporating it into the armor, and having it activate on command with stored mana, would save him resources in a fight.

If he could figure out the enchantment to inlay an active spell on leather, he could focus on developing a modified version of the matrix powerful enough to fuel the enchantment. For now, he'd burn his own mana for the activation.

He wrote the script down, so the effect was a shell of stone extending to cover the leather scrap. The complicated script was a challenge to alter, but he knew it should be more than sufficient to contain the power when he imbued it.

This enchantment would take multiple parts for it to function as he wished. That first part would contain the spell itself. The second part, he wrote parallel to the first and included the activation effect. He tied this activation to the word 'Encase.' These two should be enough to test this piece on its own. If he could get it to work, he could add a third part for the storage of power.

With the symbols set in the leather, he
pushed in the necessary Earth Magic. He
pictured the effect as a person saying the
word 'Encase' and the leather gaining a layer
of stone that increased the hardness of the
item. The mana draw pulled an initial rush of
150 mana out of his mana pool. Knowing that
his enchantments usually pulled out half
upfront, he was confident he'd complete this
enchantment. When it climbed to the 220 mana
point, the leather caught on fire and burned
to ash in moments.

*Well, that wasn't what I planned,* Arthur
thought to himself. There shouldn't have been
anything to cause the spell to do that. Arthur
supposed too much mana infused in the material
caused it, but he would imagine leather could
hold more than that. The only other things he
believed were that the script style was wrong,
or his spiral design wasn't working correctly.

*It's time for some trial and error.* Using
another scrap of leather, he wrote the
original spell again without the activation
and imbued it by itself. This would eliminate
a problem with this enchantment.

He pictured the same effect of stone
covering the leather but without the
activation word. The mana flowed out of him,
and to his surprise, it only pulled out 50
mana. Another 50 mana later and the
enchantment completed. The results weren't
what he expected, though. The leather itself
didn't gain a shell of stone. Instead, it
gained a trait that blocked a percentage of
physical damage. It was still a great
enchantment to have, but it wasn't what he'd
hoped for.

*Congratulations, you have successfully enchanted Leather Scrap. You have gained 75 experience in Enchanting.*

Something itched at the back of his mind. That enchantment cost much less than he expected, and he thought he knew why. Using another small scrap of leather, he did the same scripting, but this time in his old straight-line style. Pushing in the mana and picturing the exact effect he had last time, it confirmed his thoughts. The initial draw was 100 mana. It appeared that the design of the pattern increased the efficiency of the enchantment in terms of magic usage. The enchantment was complete, and the leather had the same effect as the last, but the bonus was lower. The new matrix dropped the mana needed and increased the base effect. The original piece gave an 8% decrease to physical damage while the one using his old style gave only 4%.

*Congratulations, you have successfully enchanted Leather Scrap. You have gained 85 experience in Enchanting.*

    This told him the structure was the problem that caused the failure of the first one. He assumed it wasn't possible to combine the matrix designs the way he had. This led him to study the waving lines as he pictured them side by side. There was still a familiar look to them that he couldn't place. His eyes roamed up and down the line, and then he did the same while picturing the second one he'd done. When envisioning them side by side, his eyes started playing tricks on him. The lines shifted, so they didn't look like a wavy line on a graph. Instead, they looked like a spiral line. When he considered both together, he laughed to himself.

    That was why he thought they looked familiar. When you intertwined them and looked at them just right, they mirrored the structure of DNA. He was sure that was the problem. The structure needed to weave together to look like a DNA model. There was an excellent chance that correctly intertwining these would result in the Advanced Matrix Structure. If that were true, his enchantments should be more efficient and more powerful.

Taking this recent knowledge, he tried his original enchantment again, only this time, he intertwined the script, so the two sets of instructions crossed each other in a 2D representation of a DNA helix. When he finished, he took a deep breath and hesitantly fed it mana while picturing his original intent. The initial mana draw came out and shocked him. Either he did something very right or very wrong. To power both enchantments at once, it pulled only 80 mana from him. Another 80 trickled from him as he watched the process in anticipation and the spell completed. The results were just what he'd hoped for.

*Congratulations, you have successfully enchanted Leather Scrap. You have gained 180 experience in Enchanting.*
*You have discovered the Enchanting Art of Advanced Matrix. You have gained 3 bonus talent points in Enchanting.*

| Item:<br>Leather Scrap of<br>Stone Shell | **Durability:** 75/75<br><br>**Rarity:** Uncommon<br><br>**Quality:** Good<br><br>**Weight:** 0.1 kg<br><br>**Traits:** A scrap of leather, enchanted with the ability Stone Shell. |
|---|---|

| | Stone Shell: Upon activation, a layer of stone will encase this item and increase resistance to physical attacks by 25%, any wearer suffers a 15% penalty to speed. This ability requires 30 mana to activate.<br><br>• Activated by the word "Encase".<br>• Speed reduction penalty decreases by 5% for every 10 Agility or Strength the wearer possesses. |
|---|---|

Giddy with excitement, Arthur picked up the scrap and said, "Encase." He felt a pull as it drained 30 mana from him, causing a layer of stone to crawl across the leather. Oddly enough, Arthur felt a bit of the slowness creep over him. It wasn't much with his Strength and Agility stats, but it was noticeable. This was precisely the breakthrough he needed. This was something even a non-magic user should be able to use.

The validation that he'd successfully figured out the advanced structure was also rewarding. It'd definitely help him with his efficiency. Now it was time for him to solve his mana issue. With his new understanding of Enchanting, he should be able to create some kind of mana storage that'd actively siphon excess mana for later use.

For this to work, he needed to make the container item first and then figure out the script. His initial design would be for him, and it'd incorporate a sapphire chip inside of a steel case with an iron chain.

Arthur found one of the steel ingots he'd made in the workshop and tossed it in the fire. He pictured a slight indentation on the front to hold a sapphire chip. His would be the only one with an embedded gem for now, but eventually, he wanted them all to have that capability. He was sure they could store more mana with a gem than the steel could do naturally. With the mage-crafted quality they'd have upon completion, it should be sufficient.

He pictured the emblems as a teardrop with an indention in the front for the gem. The trinkets themselves were only a couple of inches in diameter so, when he cast his Arcane Forge spell, the ingot melted and formed twelve individual teardrops with a smooth and shiny appearance. The top of the teardrop had a small hole through it for a chain he'd add later.

*You have increased 50 experience in Earth Magic and Fire Magic for successfully casting Crafting Spell: Arcane Forging.*

*Congratulations, you have successfully created Intricate Mage-crafted Steel Amulet (Unfinished). You have gained 720 experience in Arcane Smithing and Blacksmithing for creating this item (x12).*

Now it was time to sort the enchantment. Weaving these lines of power together would be interesting. He wrote the first one to store any excess mana over the wearer's maximum. Still, he ensured that he put a cutoff on the enchantment so it would stop absorbing mana after reaching its maximum capacity. The second enchantment was the one that'd allow the wearer to draw on the stored mana at will. After some time, he lined the two structures up and combined them. The mana flowed from him as he pictured the desired effect and activated the enchantment. It pulled 100 Mana from him in a rush, and he held the power while the rest slowly trickled out.

*Congratulations, you have successfully enchanted Intricate Mage-crafted Steel Mana Amulet (Unfinished). You have gained 180 experience in Enchanting.*

| Item:<br>Intricate Mage-<br>crafted Steel Mana<br>Amulet (Unfinished) | **Durability:** 100/100<br><br>**Rarity:** Rare<br><br>**Quality:** Excellent<br><br>**Weight:** 0.1 kg<br><br>**Mana Capacity:** 0/500 |
| --- | --- |

| | |
|---|---|
| | **Traits**: An Intricate Steel Amulet, created using magical techniques. This item will have more capacity for absorbing magical power. Combine with a chain to create Intricate Mage-crafted Steel Amulet.<br><br>Mana Storage: Captures excess mana regeneration from the wearer that can be accessed for use upon need. |

*Not bad at all.* 500 mana wasn't an enormous amount, but it wasn't anything to sneeze at. For Arthur, it wouldn't be of much use since his mana regen was so uncommonly high. He could fill this in less than half an hour. It'd work perfectly for the everyday villager, though.

That brought up another problem for him. These would fill up rather quickly, and he needed them to keep recharging. He'd have to create a large storage container that they could dump the excess mana into, but that problem would have to wait for now. Instead, he shifted his focus back to the necklace to add the Sapphire Chip. His original addition of a Sapphire Chip to the bathhouse filter increased its charges by a little over fifteen times. He hoped that using the advanced structure of enchantment on the amulet would increase the capacity on this necklace even more.

Arthur considered trying to put an advanced script on the sapphire chip but, as small as the piece was, it'd be almost impossible to put more than a single storage symbol on it. With the last chip he worked with, he used a watered-down version of charcoal to paint the symbol onto the gem, and then he fed it mana to etch the symbol into it, so he repeated the process here. Using Fire Magic, he heated the face of the amulet enough to embed the gem and secured it with the edges of the surrounding metal. To his surprise, the mana capacity jumped up to 10,000. The advanced structure increased the bonus to twenty times more.

Arthur forged thin, iron chains for all the necklaces with his Arcane Forging. The chain design included a small fold-over clasp to hold the jewelry on the wearer. When finished, he enchanted them one at a time and then attached chains to them all.

*Congratulations, you have successfully enchanted Sapphire Chip. You have gained 20 experience in Enchanting.*

*Congratulations, you have learned Jeweler for a 100 experience bonus.*

*You have gained 50 experience in Earth Magic and Fire Magic for successfully casting Crafting Spell: Arcane Forging.*

*Congratulations, you have successfully created Basic Iron Accessory Chain (Unfinished). You have gained 240 experience in Arcane Smithing and Blacksmithing for creating this item (x12).*

*Congratulations, you have reached level 8 in Arcane Smithing. Increases the stats on items created using this ability by 14%. Pretty little baubles.*

*Congratulations, you have successfully created Intricate Mage-crafted Steel Mana Amulet. You have gained 1200 experience in Jeweler for creating these items (x12).*

*Congratulations, you have reached level 2 in Jeweler. Increases the stats on Jewelry you make by 2%. Ooh, shiny.*

| Item:<br>Intricate Mage-crafted Steel Mana Amulet (Sapphire Storage) | **Durability:** 100/100<br><br>**Rarity:** Rare<br><br>**Quality:** Excellent<br><br>**Weight:** 0.1 kg<br><br>**Mana Capacity:** 0/10000<br><br>**Traits:** A magical amulet made using mage-crafted steel for the purpose of storing mana. |
| --- | --- |

| | Mana Storage: Captures excess mana regeneration from the wearer that can be accessed for use upon need. |
| --- | --- |

That'd be immensely helpful. The number of things he could get done with that amount mana would be phenomenal. With his insane amount of mana regen, it'd take him a little less than seven hours to fill the amulet to maximum capacity. Thinking of his wall project, he ran calculations and found that he'd be able to cast his Raise Stone Wall spell over three-hundred and fifty times first thing in the morning. The protective wall would be complete in no time with the additions he wanted.

Arthur slipped the amulet over his neck and tucked it under his shirt. He'd need to keep it on him at all times. He approached Rowan and Samson, carrying the necklaces as they dangled from his hands. They stopped what they were doing and turned their attention over to him.

"What have you got there, Arthur?" Samson asked with a nod toward the necklaces.

"I've got a bit of a surprise. I think you'll both enjoy these, especially with your new magical skills," Arthur explained with a smile as he handed an amulet to each of them.

"These are fantastic!" Rowan exclaimed as he slipped one over his head.

"It'll greatly increase my fighting ability. My chief concern with learning magic as a fighter was having to waste points on attributes for my mana pool. If I could just save up mana in these items, I can ignore those stats and draw from the excess here during a fight," Samson said in a thoughtful tone.

The implications of that statement swirled in his mind. "I honestly hadn't thought about that. My key concern was to get these to the villagers for stockpiling extensive amounts of mana for the work we need to complete in the village. I hadn't considered the challenge the warriors would have with stat allocation. I should have, but I'm so used to balancing my stats that it hadn't occurred to me. It should also allow you to use better spells than your normal mana pool would allow for in an emergency."

"Exactly, but how would we put these to use for the entire village?" Rowan asked.

"I plan on making many more and having the other villagers wear them. When they're full, we can take a charged amulet from someone and give them an empty one, especially if they didn't need the mana for magical skills. Eventually, I plan on making a large storage that we can dump the accumulated mana into from all of them. We can have everyone stop by once their amulets are full, and transfer the mana into the new storage," Arthur explained.

Samson considered the plan and nodded. "That should work, especially short term. Do you think we have a chance for magical defenses anytime soon? I know you have some skill in Enchanting, but not sure what you've discovered. If we could create a magical network to link this power from the centralized storage you hope to make, so it feeds directly into the village defenses, it'd make this place a verifiable fortress."

"Ha, spoken like a true military man! Yes, I hope to get to that point eventually. There are a few different projects I still need to figure out, but the village layout will be a major one. I'll need help with that and also rely on you to ensure I miss nothing from a military perspective, Samson. Rowan will need to assist me with the production and commerce side of things. As soon as the wall is complete, I plan on finding some land in the village to claim and build myself a house. After that, I want to rebuild the village. This time we'll do it correctly from the start," Arthur said with enthusiasm.

The two nodded in agreement.

"What are your plans for the rest of the day?" Samson asked.

"I'll stick around here for a little longer and start turning the iron into steel. Then I'll probably head over to the inn around midday, grab something to eat, and find something else to focus on. I have some other magical training I need to do," Arthur told them. He planned on spending the afternoon grinding experience in Dimensional Magic by himself, but he didn't want to say too much about that around them yet. They knew about him and his magic, but he was trying to keep it out of sight, out of mind.

Arthur excused himself to get back to work, and Rowan resumed his smithing. A smile formed on his lips when he saw Samson also pick up a hammer to help. The stockpile of iron ingots was still rather large, but Arthur had patience. It only took him half an hour to regenerate his mana, so there was never a lot of downtime with his work. He spent the next three hours of his time turning iron ingots into steel.

*You have gained 8,700 experience in Earth and Fire Magic for successfully casting Arcane Furnace (Steel) (x87).*
*Congratulations, you have successfully created Steel Ingot. You have gained 10,440 experience in Arcane Smithing and Blacksmithing for creating this item (x87).*
*Congratulations, you have reached levels 9 and 10 in Arcane Smithing. Increases the stats on items created using this ability by 18%. Sweat is worth the effort.*
*Congratulations, you have reached levels 10 and 11 in Blacksmithing. You are granted a 30% bonus to forging speed. You should try swinging a hammer sometime.*

Arthur quickly checked on his Arcane Smithing tree and realized he had far more points than he thought. Reflecting, he realized he never invested in his talents at levels 6 or 7. *A mistake like that will be the death of me someday.*

You have 10 unused Talent Points.

| Talent | Description |
| --- | --- |
| *Tier 1* | |

| | |
|---|---|
| *Eye for Quality (0/5)* | *Each point increases the chance of the quality of the items you create advancing one level by 5%.* |
| *Unlock Steel (1/1)* | *Teaches you the secrets of forging steel with magic.* |
| *Granular Structure (0/5)* | *Each point increases the amount of armor on items you create by 4%.* |
| | *Tier 2* |
| *Material Savings (0/10)* | *Each point decreases the material needed to make items by 3%.* |
| *Will of the Many (1/5)* | *Each point increases the amount of items made when forging multiple items at once by 10%.* |

With his idea for necklaces, the Will of the Many talent became even more critical. He put 4 points into it and then put 4 into Granular Structure. Now that they had access to steel and his Enchanting skill was much better, Samson would need a new suit of armor. Tier 3 should be open for his Blacksmithing, so he eagerly pulled it up next.

*You have 10 unused Talent Points*

| **Talent** | **Description** |
|---|---|
| | **Tier 1** |

| In the Flame (0/5) | Allows greater control of the flame while smithing. This gives you a 2% chance per talent to increase the Rarity level by one. |
| --- | --- |
| Weight Reduction (3/5) | Decreases the weight of finished materials by 5% per talent |
| Material Savings (0/5) | Every item you create uses 5% less metal per talent |
| **Tier 2** | |
| Weapons of War (0/5) | Weapons you create have 5% increased attack and durability. |
| Power of Defense (1/5) | Armor you create has 5% increased armor and durability. |
| **Tier 3** | |
| By Grabthar's Hammer (0/5) | The art of Blacksmithing and the art of war are not too dissimilar. Each point invested in this skill reduces the forging time of items by 5% and also increases damage with melee weapons by 2%. |

| Molten Core (0/10) | For every 1 point invested in this skill, you gain a 1% increase to final stats on an item. When you invest all 10 points, you will unlock the art of core inlays. |
| --- | --- |
| (Hidden Skill) Blast Furnace (0/10)<br><br>This skill will only become available if you have the following prerequisites:<br><br>• Blacksmithing > 10<br>• Arcane Smithing > 8<br>• Ability to Forge Steel | Each point invested in this skill increases the efficiency of the Arcane Furnace skill when creating Steel and future metals. There is a 4% chance per point invested for items made with Arcane Furnace to increase in Rarity by 1 level. |

Arthur needed some kind of reminder to keep him from forgetting to use his points. *Where was a smartphone when you needed one?* The skill By Grabthar's Hammer made him chuckle a bit for the reference, but he focused on the options. All of them were useful in their own way, but he had limited points to use, so he decided to go big or go home. Hidden talents had paid off so far, and he'd love to bump up some of his work another quality level. All ten points went into Blast Furnace.

With the arrival of midday, Arthur strolled out of the forge. Rowan and Samson waved their goodbyes as he left, and he returned to the inn. He walked into a flurry of activity as people bustled about. Some had shown up for a midday meal, while others were there to visit. Arthur even saw some of the new work crew talking amongst themselves. Daniel walked into the room, and Arthur met him at the bar.

"Your place is getting busy lately. Before long, we'll have to rebuild it and make it larger," Arthur said with a grin.

Daniel glanced around the room. "I like the place. I'm just not sure I'd welcome a lot of change, but it may be necessary."

"We could always keep wood flooring and tables. Hell, we could even line the walls with wood as well to give it that comfortable feeling in the common area. The top floor with the rooms would be the stone style, though, with wood floors," Arthur told him confidently.

"I suppose I could live with that. What do you have planned for the rest of the day?" Daniel asked, looking at Arthur.

"A little magical training by myself. I also have something for you to hand out," Arthur said mysteriously. Eight necklaces slid free from his bag, and he handed them over to Daniel.

"Are you sure?" Daniel asked.

Arthur laughed. "Of course I'm sure. They'll be the key to our village building efforts. I'll make some more later."

"I'm not sure we could afford to hand them out. They're worth an absolute fortune. There were a few relics like these in older generations, and the prices on the remaining ones are enough to buy a village," Daniel told him quietly.

"They base those prices on Rarity. These are relatively cheap for me to produce, and we're working to reset the market. We need to make luxurious items more commonplace. There'll be many other things like this. As the village grows, we must rely on commerce to draw in the operating costs of the village, so selling items like these will be a staple for us. Until we need that money, though, they stay with us and no one else," Arthur said firmly.

"Fine." Daniel breathed out. "You test my patience sometimes, but I can see the logic in your actions."

"Besides, I kept the best one for myself," Arthur told him with a sly grin. He leaned over the bar and pulled out his necklace to show Daniel. As soon as the man looked at the stats, Arthur stowed it back in his shirt while Daniel looked like he would faint.

"Dear Goddess, Arthur, you could've just kept that to your damn self. I don't want to end up in an early grave because some local lord decides he wants an item of yours that's fit for a king," Daniel said as he shook his head.

"Nothing special." Arthur waved off. "I'm confident I can make ones that are even better than that before long."

Daniel spluttered for a moment and then spoke. "Keep it to yourself, then. Between those trinkets and Samson's armor, there will already be enough reasons for us to become quick targets."

Arthur waved the comment off. "Oh, that old armor. Now that I have unlocked steel, I plan on remaking it, even better this time. It's irrelevant, though. We already have a target on us, so our best hope is to get as many advantages as we can manage before the enemies return."

Daniel sighed in agreement, and Arthur walked to the entrance and exited the building. On his way to find a quiet spot to work on his Dimensional Magic, he realized he was yet again wasting opportunities. All the work he'd done on the steel ingots and necklaces was technically classified as work for the village. As such, he could assign work orders for it. He quickly made a work order for 99 steel ingots and one for the 12 necklaces. A reward of 10 copper finalized the orders. He needed to get a little coin in his pocket but also wanted to keep the rewards low to allow higher experience gains. His experience shot up as he accepted each work order.

*Congratulations, you have completed the Work Order: 99 Steel Ingots for Alem's Crossing for the following rewards: 10 Copper Coins, 9900 Arcane Smithing Experience, 9900 Blacksmithing Experience, and 2500 Character Experience.*

*Congratulations, you have reached level 11 in Arcane Smithing. Increases the stats on items created using this ability by 20%. Cheater.*

*Congratulations, you have reached level 12 in Blacksmithing. You are granted a 33% bonus to forging speed. The simple way is not always the best way.*

*Congratulations, you have reached level 16! You now have 5 available skill points. About time you made some progress.*

*Congratulations, you have completed the Work Order: 12 Steel Mana Amulets for Alem's Crossing for the following rewards: 10 Copper Coins, 2400 Enchanting Experience, 400 Jeweler Experience, and 700 Character Experience.*

*Congratulations, you have reached level 8 in Enchanting. Your enchantments have a 21% decreased mana cost. Can I get one of those?*

*Congratulations, you have reached level 3 in Jeweler. Increases the stats on Jewelry you make by 4%. Ooh, shiny.*

*That's more like it.* The bonus character experience was a crucial part. Gaining experience in his magic and crafting skills just took some time in the village, but his character experience was only going up from fighting and the work orders. It was best to avoid fighting, if possible, but they'd need to forage some more before long. He needed to see if he could find some more hunters in the village to take with them. It was doubtful they'd get any more meat than usual, but it'd help train some of them to be self-sufficient later.

With his additional levels, he invested his
talent points before he forgot again. For
Arcane Smithing, he put 1 point into Granular
Structure, and he used the remaining 5 to max
out Eye for Quality. Both of his Blacksmithing
points went into In the Flame. For his skill
points, 4 went into Agility to bring it to 24,
and 1 went into Intellect to bring it to 25.
This gave him an even 600 total mana.

It was at this point he realized he missed
another major item he could claim for an
order. Arthur claimed most of the wall when he
built it, but he never did a work order for
the bathhouse he created. He could issue a
work order for anything explicitly created for
the village. He made the order, specifying a
magical bathhouse, and set the reward for 10
copper coins.

*Congratulations, you have completed the
Work Order: Magical Bathhouse for Alem's
Crossing for the following rewards: 10 Copper
Coins, 10000 Earth Magic Experience, 10000
Fire Magic Experience, 3000 Enchanting
Experience, and 4500 Character Experience.*

Seeing that much experience eased some of
Arthur's tension. There was still a long way
to go, and the experience requirements were
getting higher, but he needed to strive for
the level twenty mark. Unlocking a class would
help him reach his quest goal for Calfuray.

Arthur settled in a secluded spot in the shade of the village wall. He wanted to spend the afternoon burning mana and leveling up his Dimensional Magic skill. With some luck, he might even come up with more ideas for spells. The immense cost of the Create Dimensional Drawer spell limited him to only two casts at a time, but the experience gained from them wasn't too bad.

*You have gained 1100 experience in Dimensional Magic for successfully casting Create Dimensional Drawer (x2). Do you wish to assign these spaces a unique identification? Y/N.*

*Interesting: a spell option.* Arthur thought. It made sense. *How else would you keep track of what you were accessing with the access spell if you didn't have the spaces labeled?* Arthur didn't label these casts because he had no current use for them. The experience was what he wanted. There was a draw to the idea of making individual spaces to hold distinct types of items. *So much for inventory limits.*

Arthur leaned back against the wall enjoying the quiet and the breeze when a familiar face showed up. Opening his eyes, he saw Balair huddled on the ground in front of him, looking like a cat getting ready to pounce.

*What are you up to, lazy dragon?* Arthur asked him.

*Whatever I want to be up to. I wanted to see what you were doing. All the experience you were raking in today made me curious.* Balair responded.

It confused him for a moment, then realized that Balair also gained experience when he did. Those couple of work orders had boosted him nicely and, looking at Balair, he saw the dragon had gone up to level 12.

*You really are nothing but a freeloader. Is there anything useful you can do?* Arthur asked.

*Sometimes, yes. Most of my use is around Fire Magic, and there isn't much of that needed around the village.* Balair informed him.

*Is fire the only magic you're capable of learning because of your nature, or is it merely the only one you know?*

Balair eyed him cautiously. *Fire Magic is the only one I know, but I'm capable of using any of the others except Water Magic.*

*So how about I teach you Earth Magic, and maybe you can be of use around the village? If you can get your level high enough to make stone, you'd be even more useful.* Arthur thought cheerfully.

Balair became very still for a moment and eyed him thoughtfully. *I don't think I should. It's typically not allowed for familiar style dragonlings to learn other magics. The other dragons of the world wouldn't agree with that idea if they ever got wind of it.*

*Why do you care what they think? They've all but abandoned the part of this world inhabited by humans from what I can tell. To top it off, it appears at least some of them are trying to go back out on the deal my family had with them, so why would I care about their customs?*

*I suppose it'd be all right as long as I don't show the ability to other dragons. I just don't want you to invite more trouble than you already have.* Balair told him wearily.

*Trouble seems to follow me everywhere in this world. Come over here, and I can show you the magic of Earth. Do dragons use the forces of magic the same way as humans? Do you mimic the power to gain use of the skill?* Arthur asked.

*Yes. We can learn with that method, but we tend to adapt the magics to our own use once learned.*

Arthur nodded at that, and the little dragonling came and sat next to him. Arthur put a hand on the creature's scaly hide and pushed the split energies of Earth into the beast. Balair turned toward him in surprise.

*What made you split them?* Balair asked.

*I found that everyone I teach learns much faster in this method. I split the powers until they can replicate all three and then show them how they combine.* Arthur explained as he leaned back to relax.

Barely fifteen minutes later, Balair told him to combine them, and within less than half an hour, Balair learned the Earth Magic ability.

*You should work on nothing but Earth Magic for a while. After you get around level five, I can show you how to change dirt into stone.*

Balair nodded in agreement and moved to the side. Arthur watched as the dragon cast an Earthen Wall spell and then cast Flatten immediately after.  It confused Arthur. He hadn't seen the little guy learn those spells, so how could he cast something from a skill he'd just taught him?

*How'd you cast that without discovering it
first?* Arthur asked him.

*I can cast anything you can as long as I
have the skill prerequisites. As soon as I hit
the required level in Earth Magic, I'll be
able to cast the Stone Wall spell so you won't
have to show me. I gain the same benefits of
shared magic from you that Calfuray and the
dragons do from their bond since I'm a
familiar.*

Arthur forgot about that part of his
conversation with Calfuray. It only made sense
that he and Balair would share a similar bond
due to him being a familiar. That also meant
it would save Arthur a lot of time training
the creature.

Arthur sat with Balair as each took turns
casting spells and regenerating mana. During
the next round of spells, Arthur discovered a
flaw in his plan. He'd used the Create
Dimensional Drawer spell when he should use
the access one. When his mana filled, he cast
the Access Dimensional Drawer spell on a whim
because he'd never cast it. The cabinet-like
space he'd made previously appeared, but the
experience was the important part. He gained
50 experience from the cast of the spell, and
with it only costing 25 mana, he could cast it
24 times in one sitting. With his regen and
bonuses, it was closer to 27 times per mana
pool since it took time to cast the spell and
dismiss the spell door with each cast. They
spent the next four hours enjoying the time in
peace together and leveling their skills.

*You have gained 10,800 experience in
Dimensional Magic for successfully casting
Access Dimensional Drawer (x216).*

*Congratulations, you have reached levels 8, 9, and 10 in Dimensional Magic. Decreases the mana draw of Dimensional spells by 27%. Just stuff it all in the closet and close the door.*

It was time to invest his new points in his talents. He hoped to make it to level 10 today, so he saved the talents from each level to give him more to work with. Arthur chose to only pull up the new Tier 3 talents for Dimensional Magic since he knew the others.

*You have 8 unused Talent Points*

| Tier 3 | |
|---|---|
| Dimensional Disposal (0/1) | Teaches a spell that opens a Dimensional portal that will remain until dismissed. Anything placed in the portal will be lost to the void. |
| Through Time and Space (0/10) | Grants understanding of basic Dimensional transport upon investing all 10 points. |
| Expansion (0/10) | Increases the maximum size of your Dimensional spaces by 15% per point. |
| Enchantment Weaving (0/1) | This talent teaches you how to use Dimensional Magic on Items and Accessories. |

The options were intriguing, but there was
no way he would pass up Dimensional Disposal
or Enchantment Weaving. The disposal portal
may sound useless, but it would be a terrific
boon for waste disposal in the village and
could drastically improve health. There was
also the hope his Enchantment Weaving would
yield the secrets to bags of holding.

He dumped his other 6 points into
Expansion. There was something he was hoping
to make with his Dimensional Magic, but he had
a long way to go for it. That would require a
sizeable dimensional space. With the current
talents he had for maximum size, it was about
time for him to make a new storage container
that was large enough to be useful.

Arthur reviewed what he learned from his
Enchantment Weaving and decided there was no
way he would've figured out the trick to it.
It required a semi-complex set of instructions
to allow the pocket to stay anchored to the
device. To top it off, the control elements of
it were just as complex. Arthur would have to
invest some time into making storage
containers. His control of Dimensional Magic
allowed him to use the spells while the
villagers would need better storage options.

Balair walked with a majestic gait,
confident with his recent accomplishments, as
he trotted beside Arthur back to the inn. They
met with Allendria for dinner, and then a
quick trip to the bathhouse followed shortly
after. Balair also got in the water, and the
warmth pleasantly surprised him. He was even
more elated at the buff he received. The 10%
bonus to experience worked for him as well.
After a long productive day, they returned to
the inn and turned in for the night.

# Chapter 6



*Moving Forward*

The next couple of days proceeded in a similar pattern. They started the morning with breakfast together and discussed any vital business for the day. Arthur tasked Samson with recruiting guards for the village. Samson did his best to level his Fire Magic and scoured the village to find people to volunteer. Noah and Toren, who volunteered as guards during the attack, agreed to take up spots on the village guard. Arthur wanted five people to help supplement the force.

Allendria worked with the trainees and ensured their training progressed. Arthur was sure by the third day of their work they'd be ready to unlock Fire Magic. The crew was doing an excellent job of scouring the village and cleaning the place up. They leveled many places around the village to prepare for the upcoming construction. Allendria also had the foresight to get the crews into the fields. She showed them how to harness their Earth Magic to sift through the dirt, removing rocks and debris. It also allowed them to learn spells for plowing fields and softening soil for better growth.

Arthur tasked Vana with finding at least two more people who would act as rangers for the village. He needed a couple more that would be capable of foraging the surrounding area for food. With the handful of monsters they'd spotted in the forest, a three-person team should be more than sufficient to deal with them. Vana convinced James, the village woodcutter, to join her, but she was still searching for one more person. The next time the group went hunting, the new rangers would travel with them for training.

Arthur's morning comprised working on the walls. With the large surplus of mana from his necklace, he made substantial strides on the wall's progress. Instead of spending all morning out in the fields, he reduced the time spent to only two hours. His regen gained him 2,400 additional mana during that time. When combined with the 10,000 surplus from the necklace, he had 12,400 total to work with. Between his bonuses and his reduced mana cost from mastery, he could cast the Stone Wall spell four-hundred and twenty times in two hours. Arthur also got the work order experience for the wall.

*You have gained 42,000 experience in Earth Magic and Fire Magic for successfully casting Combination Spell: Raise Stone Wall (x420).*

*Congratulations, you have reached level 19 in Fire Magic. Fire Magic spells now have a 54% increased effect. Is it hot in here or is it just me?*

*Congratulations, you have unlocked Mastery level 4 for Combination Spell: Raise Stone Wall. The base mana cost for the spell has been decreased by 5 and the base length has been increased by 50%.*

*Congratulations, you have completed the Work Order: Expand Stone Wall Thickness for Alem's Crossing for the following rewards: 10 Copper Coins, 15,000 Earth Magic Experience, 15,000 Fire Magic Experience, and 5000 Character Experience.*

*Congratulations, you have reached levels 19 and 20 in Earth Magic. Increases the effect of your Earth Magic spells by 57%.*

Reaching level 20 in Earth Magic was welcoming to him though. The class system in this world seemed to favor that level, but he'd still need to reach a personal level of 20 to take advantage of those benefits.  With two additional levels, he checked his Earth Magic talents. He hoped there'd be a new tier of options to choose from. Instead, an unexpected message greeted him.

*Congratulations, you have reached level 20 in Earth Magic and been promoted to Journeyman in the skill. Please choose one of the following as a bonus for this achievement:*

| Spell: Earthquake | |
|---|---|
| Requirements: Earth Magic<br>Mana Cost: 50 MP<br>Cast Time: 7 seconds | Description: Harness the power of Earth to cause the ground to shake at the target area. Anyone occupying the space will be disoriented. Those with low resistances will be knocked to the ground. |
| Mastery Level: 1 | |

| Spell: Mineral Compression | |
| --- | --- |
| Requirements: Earth Magic<br>Mana Cost: 80 MP<br>Cast Time: 15 seconds | Description: Use the extraordinary force of the Earth to compress materials into gems. Gems gained are based on the original material used. |
| Mastery Level: 1 | |

| Spell: Transform Soil | |
| --- | --- |
| Requirements: Earth Magic<br>Mana Cost: 120 MP<br>Cast Time: 20 seconds | Description: Transform a designated space that is 20' x 20' x 50' into arid farmland. This ability will sort out all rocks and stones from the area and increase the latent nutrients in the ground to encourage plant growth.<br><br>Increases crop yield in the designated area by 25%. |
| Mastery Level: 1 | |

*That was unexpected.* The level 20 bonus didn't appear to be a new talent tree, but rather an option to choose a special spell. Arthur felt the mechanics for the three options were difficult to understand, even though they sounded relatively simple. The Earthquake spell seemed tantalizing just for the sheer confusion it could cause on a battlefield. Being able to move the ground beneath the enemy and knock them from their feet would be amazing. Arthur was familiar with how earthquakes worked from back on Earth, though. Being in a couple when he had briefly lived in California gave him an excuse to do some research on them. Since he understood many of the mechanics, he was confident he could figure that spell out on his own.

The Mineral Compression spell could be invaluable. He had some Sapphire chips left from his early expeditions but if he wanted to push his Enchanting, he'd need many more. It was sporadic to find gems when mining. This meant he'd need another source instead.

The last option to Transform Soil was a spell he hadn't even considered before but might be worth taking. The food shortage was an immense problem here, and being able to clear an area for planting, while also increasing the yield of that area, would prove to be a significant boon.

After some contemplation, Arthur chose the Mineral Compression spell. His confidence led him to believe he'd eventually be able to learn the other two on his own. Not being very fluent in geology and physics, he wasn't sure he'd figure out the compression spell.

His 4 extra talent points went into Power of the World to decrease his mana cost further and to increase his Intellect by 2. His mana pool was growing nicely as it now reached 640. He dumped his two recent Fire Magic talent points into Familiar Growth, bringing that up to 4 total points. Balair had done an admirable job of helping since Arthur taught him Earth Magic, so it seemed a reward was in order.

With the work on the wall completed for the morning, he returned to the village. Members of the new civil service teams waved at him as he passed. Arthur observed as they used their newfound Earth Magic to move dirt and level out many areas around town. They were also putting their power to use by clearing the ground of obstructions. He nodded back at them as he continued past.

Arthur spent the rest of the morning by the wall working on his Dimensional Magic. Three hours' worth of work allowed him to use his Dimensional Access spell 155 times.

*You have gained 7,750 experience in Dimensional Magic for successfully casting Access Dimensional Drawer (x155).*

*Congratulations, you have unlocked Mastery level 2 for Access Dimensional Drawer. The base mana cost for the spell has been decreased by 5.*

*Congratulations, you have reached level 11 in Dimensional Magic. Decreases the mana draw of Dimensional spells by 30%. Enchanting would be nice.*

Arthur let his mana fill one last time before leaving, but instead of casting Access Dimensional Drawer again, he created a new spell with larger dimensions. The power of Dimensional Magic wove in front of him as he focused on the desired outcome. A line appeared in mid-air, and he carved out a doorway with his will. He created the door to match the size of a standard house door on Earth. Once the outline was complete, he tugged on the magic, and the doorway burst open to a solid wall of nothingness. He used only 100 of his mana on the doorway, so he focused on the shape of the door and started building a storage area directly behind it. The space reached a depth of twenty feet, and the strain on his mana increased. Pushing it that far drained 200 more mana from his reserves, but he needed to push his threshold here. Focusing on the left side wall of the void, he pushed his power in that direction to widen the room through the door. He could only expand it ten more feet before his mana dropped to 40. With his reserves so low, he completed the spell with this extra size.

*Congratulations, you have discovered the Dimensional Magic Spell: Create Dimensional Storage. You have gained 250 experience in Dimensional Magic for discovering a known spell.*
*You have gained 450 experience in Dimensional Magic for successfully casting Create Dimensional Storage.*

| Create Dimensional Storage | |
| --- | --- |
| Requirements:<br>Dimensional Magic<br>Mana Cost: 350 MP<br>Cast Time: 10 seconds | Description: Create a space that is 8' x 20' x 10' that can be used to store items.<br><br>Caution: This space is deadly to any living beings if they are inside when the space is closed. |
| Mastery Level: 1 | |

*Congratulations, you have discovered the Dimensional Magic Spell: Access Dimensional Storage. You have gained 250 experience in Dimensional Magic for discovering a known spell.*

| Access Dimensional Storage | |
| --- | --- |
| Requirements:<br>Dimensional Magic<br>Mana Cost: 25 MP<br>Cast Time: 2 seconds | Description: Access a Dimensional Storage you have already created. |
| Mastery Level: 1 | |

That was what he was hoping for. It was good to know it included the warning about living beings. This storage space would be invaluable for their missions when they traveled. It would be the perfect ability if he could open it up, throw in their kills and loot, and keep moving. *No more hauling that infernal cart through the forest*. Arthur would bet he could put in storage containers or shelving if he wanted. He could also customize unique storage rooms for different items. Since he could identify the spaces, it'd make it easy to organize the things they found. For now, he didn't need more than one storage room.

Happy with himself for his latest accomplishment, he walked over to the inn for some lunch. There, he met with Allendria and Vana, which allowed him to get an update on progress around the village. Vana thought she found her last ranger but was still trying to convince them to take the job. The growth of the construction crews pleased Allendria, and she thought they'd be ready for their Fire Magic as soon as tomorrow. She was so excited about being able to do something useful that she even volunteered to train them in Fire Magic herself. That was a welcome development since he didn't fancy wasting half a day sitting in one spot and watching people attempt to learn an ability.

After they finished eating, Arthur left and waved goodbye over his shoulder. His trip to the blacksmith shop was quiet and uneventful. Rowan and Samson were milling around the area but didn't look to be working on anything. Arthur assumed they'd just finished with lunch and were killing some time.

"What's up, guys?" Arthur asked as he approached.

"Not much. Stretching the legs after our lunch break. Didn't quite feel up to starting back at the forge yet," Rowan told him with a wave.

"Care to learn your Earth Magic? I only plan to do some work here in the forge this afternoon, so it'd be the perfect chance to take advantage of the time," Arthur told them.

"Like you even have to ask," Rowan said with a smile.

"It would be an honor, my liege," Samson said with all seriousness.

Arthur frowned at that. "We've had this discussion before. I know it's hard to break from the military mindset, but when it's just us, no need for the formalities."

Samson looked a little uncomfortable but nodded his head in agreement. Arthur spent the next two hours working with them to unlock their Earth Magic. As he suspected, they both picked it up quicker than they had Fire Magic. After he taught them the basic Earth Wall spell, he focused his efforts on Smithing.

Getting the iron ingots turned to steel had been his primary focus lately, so he continued the work for the next couple hours.

*You have gained 6,400 experience in Earth and Fire Magic for successfully casting Arcane Furnace (Steel) (x64).*

*Congratulations, you have successfully created Steel Ingot. You have gained 7,680 experience in Arcane Smithing and Blacksmithing for creating this item (x64).*

*Congratulations, you have reached level 12 in Arcane Smithing. Increases the stats on items created using this ability by 22%. Do some actual work for once!*

*Congratulations, you have reached level 13 in Blacksmithing. You are granted a 36% bonus to forging speed. Steadily pounding is nice, but sometimes you need to speed it up.*

As much as Arthur enjoyed seeing the experience and level ups, one could only continue making the same thing so many times before needing to change to something else. Arthur switched to making some mana necklaces. Now that he'd made a dozen of them, he could include the advanced script during the forging process. Since he didn't need to waste time engraving the runes, he started brainstorming ideas for Samson's new armor. There were a few scraps of leather lying around that he used to sketch out some of his ideas. He did this while waiting for his mana to recover enough to enchant the necklaces.

*Congratulations, you have completed the Work Order: 64 Steel Ingots for Alem's Crossing for the following rewards: 10 Copper Coins, 6,400 Arcane Smithing Experience, 6,400 Blacksmithing Experience, and 1,900 Character Experience.*

*Congratulations, you have reached level 13 in Arcane Smithing. Increases the stats on items created using this ability by 24%. Cheater.*

*Congratulations, you have reached level 14 in Blacksmithing. You are granted a 39% bonus to forging speed. The easy way isn't always the best way.*

*You have gained 400 experience in Earth
Magic and Fire Magic for successfully casting
Crafting Spell: Arcane Forging (x8).*

*Congratulations, you have successfully
created Intricate Mage-crafted Steel Amulet
(Unfinished). You have gained 2,880 experience
in Arcane Smithing and Blacksmithing for
creating this item (x48).*

*Congratulations, you have successfully
enchanted Intricate Mage-crafted Steel Mana
Amulet (Unfinished) (x48). You have gained
8,640 experience in Enchanting.*

*Congratulations, you have successfully
created Basic Iron Accessory Chain
(Unfinished). You have gained 960 experience
in Arcane Smithing and Blacksmithing for
creating this item (x48).*

*Congratulations, you have completed the
Work Order: 48 Steel Mana Amulets for Alem's
Crossing for the following rewards: 10 Copper
Coins, 8000 Enchanting Experience, and 2800
Character Experience.*

*Congratulations, you have reached levels 9,
10, and 11 in Enchanting. Your enchantments
have a 30% decreased mana cost. You know you
can't just wave your hands to fix everything,
right?*

Arthur chose to assign his two extra talent
points to Arcane Smithing. The last levels he
gained, he just dumped them into known
talents, but he never checked his new Tier 3
talents. He pulled up the new Tier 3 options.

*You have 2 unused Talent Points.*

| **_Tier 3_** |
| --- |

| Embellishments (0/10) | Allows the smith to embellish items created using different materials. These embellishments will grant additional bonuses to the pieces made. Each point invested in this skill increases the bonus granted by embellishing by 5%. |
| --- | --- |
| Mana Saturated (0/20) | Teaches you how to infuse mana into your work to increase latent magical ability and increase set bonus attributes. When you have invested all 20 talent points, you will unlock the talent to make Magesteel. |
| (Hidden Talent) Soulbound (0/1)<br><br>Requirements:<br><br>• Blacksmithing > 10<br>• Arcane Smithing > 10<br>• A Familiar Bond | Teaches a smith the ability to soul bind a suit of armor with a wearer. This soul bind enhances the natural skills of the wearer to further enhance the armor. Soul bound armor can only be worn by the one bound. A smith with this talent may remove the bond from a wielder. |

*Damn it.* Now is when he truly needed a ton of excess talent points. The talent to unlock Magesteel had shown itself, and he would have a while to wait for it. That said, he wouldn't pass up Soul Bond. One talent point to help lock a set of armor to one person's use and granting bonuses to the pieces was not something he could pass up. Embellishments sounded great, but he wanted Mana Saturated first. With the one point in Soul Bond and the other in Mana Saturated, he remembered the three bonus points he still had floating around and added them to Mana Saturated. From there, he moved on to his Blacksmithing talents.

His 4 points available in Blacksmithing went into Molten Core, giving all his items 4% increased stats. Inlaying cores sounded interesting, although Arthur wasn't sure what that meant yet. From here, he pulled up his Enchanting talents for Tier 3.

*You have 6 unused Talent Points.*

| Tier 3 | |
| --- | --- |
| *Blessing of the Ancients (0/10)* | *This talent increases the chance any item you create will be Blessed by the Ancients. Each point invested increases this chance by 1%.*<br><br>*Blessing of the Ancients:* |

| | *Divine inspiration influences the item to change its properties and improve it. The possibilities are endless and unpredictable.* |
| --- | --- |
| *Power Overwhelming (0/10)* | *Each point invested in this talent increases the base charges on an item by 10%.* |
| *Enchantment Mend (0/1)* | *Allows you to repair damaged items with enchantments on them without damaging the enchantment itself.* |

The Enchantment Mend was a simple decision. His items would eventually lose durability, and he didn't want to lose the enchantments on them due to the damage. If he could repair items and ensure the enchantment stayed intact, it would save him a lot of time and resources. One point went into Enchantment Mend, and he dropped the other five into Blessing of the Ancients. The ability didn't seem like much, but typically something with such a low chance of success had terrific results.

It felt good for Arthur to just make things. The satisfaction of making things that were useful and appreciated was a unique feeling. When they finally finished the wall he'd feel much better about their defense, but it still needed a lot of work. If Allendria could get the construction teams trained in Fire Magic and get them to stone, he could leave much of that work to them.

Arthur called it a night and waved his goodbyes to Samson and Rowan. On his way back to the inn, he ran into Dalia.

"Hey, Arthur. How's your evening going?" she asked.

"Pretty good. It's been a long day of work. There never seems to be an end to it all," he told her.

Dalia smiled at him devilishly. "I can think of a way you might take your mind off work. It was fun last time, and I imagine it'd be again. Fancy a little action with a noblewoman?"

Arthur chuckled at that. "I truly appreciate the offer, but I'm in a relationship, and I'm almost 100% sure that wouldn't be in my best interest. I agree it was fun, but that's all it was. You even made a point of stressing that it was a one-time thing yourself."

She narrowed her eyes at him. "You're going to deny me? That doesn't sound like what you truly want," she told him as she slowly parted the front of her blouse to reveal ever-increasing amounts of cleavage.

"Oh, I'm sure, and my decision is final. I appreciate the offer, but no thanks. Have a good evening, Dalia," Arthur said as he continued the rest of the way into the inn.

Dalia's simmering rage pierced into him as he brushed past. Who was he to deny her what she wanted? After all, she was the noblewoman of this village.

* * *

The next day followed an almost identical pattern. The wall was the first item on the agenda. He spent the morning extending the face of the wall up to fifteen feet and adding crenellations on it. Since he spent the previous day doubling the width of the wall, there was a slight lip that someone could stand on, but it was so narrow that it was almost dangerous. The next task would be to widen it again to allow for a true wall-walk behind the crenellations.

His magic had come a long way, and between his mana regen and his overnight stockpile, he could add a section of wall around the entire perimeter in a couple of hours. He made the crenellations around the wall as the whole before walking back to the forge. The last of the iron ingots were on the list for today. Arthur planned to make himself a set of armor after he finished with the set for Samson. His current set of leather was useful, but he thought a suitable set of sturdy mail would better suit his fighting style. Since he would be a melee fighter that used magic, the mail should give him enough protection without hindering his movement too much. It was a delicate balancing game.

Rather than working on pendants after he worked on the steel conversion, he used the time to practice on his Water Magic. Just wandering around the village and casting the spell seemed a little wasteful, so he traveled to the fields outside of town and kept casting his spells on them. Most of them were still unplanted and unused, but keeping them wet and healthy would make future growth better. Daniel found some volunteers to plant the seeds he brought back from their gathering trips, and there were a few fields with green sprouts popping up in them. If the crops worked like all the other skills in this world, they'd grow and produce faster than he'd normally expect. He took a quick glance at the experience gained for the day.

*You have gained 48,400 total experience in Earth Magic and Fire Magic.*
*Congratulations, you have completed the Work Order: Expand Stone Wall Height for Alem's Crossing for the following rewards: 10 Copper Coins, 15,000 Earth Magic Experience, 15,000 Fire Magic Experience, and 5,000 Character Experience.*
*Congratulations, you have reached level 21 in Earth Magic. Increases the effect of your earth magic spells by 60%. One day you might finish that wall.*
*Congratulations, you have reached levels 20 and 21 in Fire Magic. Fire Magic spells now have a 60% increased effect. Maybe try cooking?*
*You have gained 7,680 total experience in Arcane Smithing and Blacksmithing.*

*Congratulations, you have reached level 14 in Arcane Smithing. Increases the stats on items created using this ability by 26%. Hurry and make Samson's armor. I want to see it.*

*Congratulations, you have reached level 15 in Blacksmithing. You are granted a 42% bonus to forging speed. You should really find some more hobbies. Not sure you have enough already.*

*Congratulations, for reaching level 15 in Blacksmithing, you have been granted 1500 bonus character experience.*

*You have gained 5,100 total experience in Water Magic.*

*Congratulations, you have reached level 7 in Water Magic. Increases the effect of your Water Magic spells by 18%. You finally did something useful with your Water Magic.*

Seeing his Fire Magic surpassed level twenty, he opened up the talent page to see his new choices.

*Congratulations, you have reached level 20 in Fire Magic and been promoted to Journeyman in the skill. Please choose one of the following as a bonus for this achievement:*

| |
|---|
| Spell: Sheathe in Flame |

| Requirements: Fire Magic<br>Mana Cost: 40 MP<br>Cast Time: 2 seconds | Description: Wrap your weapon in a layer of flames. This causes an additional 4-7 Fire damage per strike and has the chance to inflict a burning ailment causing an additional 5 damage every 3 seconds for 2 minutes.<br><br>This heat of this spell causes your weapon to lose 1 durability every 20 seconds in addition to normal durability loss. |
| --- | --- |
| Mastery Level: 1 | |

| Spell: Elements of Heat | |
| --- | --- |
| Requirements: Fire Magic<br>Mana Cost: 75 MP<br>Cast Time: 5 seconds | Description: Create heating elements out of your supplied materials that to regulate heat in associated areas. Better materials allow for better control. |
| Mastery Level: 1 | |

| Spell: Perfect Temperature |
| --- |

| Requirements: Fire Magic<br>Mana Cost: 100 MP<br>Cast Time: 30 seconds/channeled | Description: Channel flame into a nearby object to reach a perfect temperature.<br><br>Want your bath water at a specific temperature? How about cooking your food to an exact measurement of heat? All is possible with this spell. |
| --- | --- |
| Mastery Level: 1 ||

The options were intriguing. The funny thing was, with a bit of thought, Arthur was sure he could figure out the last two with minor trouble. The first one would be tricky to pull off. The durability drawback sucked, but Arthur was sure there'd be a way around it. With these thoughts in mind, he chose Sheathe in Flame.

As he arrived back at the inn that evening, he spotted Samson, Vana, Allendria, Daniel, and Balair all sitting together in the corner. Arthur joined them and took a seat.

"Hey guys, how are things going?" Arthur asked.

"So far, so good. Business is booming, and we're seeing a lot of interest in the workforces. I don't think we'll have any issues when we choose to create more teams. Most people never gained useful skills and would welcome the chance," Daniel told them.

"That's good to hear. Vana, any luck on the rangers?" Arthur asked.

"As a matter of fact, I have both of my candidates ready to go. When do you think we'll get them some action?" Vana asked him.

"We'd have to make sure they have weapons and possibly some light armor, but do you want to set something up for tomorrow?"

"Tomorrow would be fine. We have a handful of bows in the village storage that Zeke has been turning in for work orders. They don't have armor, but neither did we when we started. If it's just an outing into the forest and not us going on a dungeon dive, they should be fine. Rowan, would you happen to have two spare iron daggers they could use?" Vana asked as she faced the burly blacksmith.

"I think I have a couple lying around the shop they could use. Nothing fancy like Arthur makes, but they should get the job done. You could always swing by and see for yourself," Rowan told her with a wink.

She blushed a deep red, and everyone around the table chuckled.

"Wow, I wasn't aware Vana could blush," Daniel said with a laugh.

"Now, if we could get her to be more civilized instead of always playing in the trees, there might be hope for her yet," Arthur added.

Vana turned a narrow gaze in his direction. "You know I can make that healing ointment burn much worse than it already does next time you get injured, don't you?"

Arthur gulped at that. He remembered the burning pain from the dungeon they'd been in.

"Forget what I said," Arthur quickly amended.

Everyone at the table laughed even louder at his uncomfortable look. Arthur turned his gaze to Samson.

"How's the search for guards going?" Arthur asked the stern man.

"Not bad at all. I found five people to help round out the guard force. Toren and Noah remained on after the fight with the bandits, and I've recruited three others. Noah and Toren have the armor we outfitted them with during the assault and a dagger each, but not much else. The other three have no gear to speak of," Samson told him.

"Do any of them have any useful skills?" Arthur asked.

"A couple have some skill in unarmed, and three of them are proficient in cooking. It should help them maintain the guard force itself. Nothing with blades or armor, though."

"How about archery? That'll need to be their primary focus for now. With the wall now at a respectable height, defending it with archery is a priority."

"None of them have enough skill in archery to be useful, but I'll start training with them tomorrow. Archery will become our focus," Samson promised.

"Perfect. Vana, can you talk to Zeke and have him stockpile completed arrow shafts, minus the heads. I'll need to find some time to make some more heads, but it's a quick process for me. If he needs any supplies, we can use our trip tomorrow to search for them."

"I'll let him know," Vana agreed.

"That reminds me," Arthur began as he turned toward Rowan. "Your mission for tomorrow is to work on getting the gates together. You should have enough iron left over to band the wood. James and his son have been working on gathering the needed logs. As quickly as they work, I assume they have most of it already done. I'll speak to James, but I'm sure since he'll be working with us as a ranger tomorrow, you could have Jack help work on the gates. When you get the doors assembled, let me know, and I can help you get them mounted. We'll need to bring plenty of iron with us to make proper hinges."

"I'll see it's done. The extra help will be useful. Do you suppose I could find a few other hands to help?"

"I don't care if you have to enlist the help of half the village as long as you can get them done. Those gates should be everyone's priority right now. The redesign of the village and expansion of the wall, combined with sturdy gates, makes this place much safer," Arthur told him genuinely.

"Then I'll devote all my resources to it until we finish," Rowan agreed.

"Daniel, anything you need around here? I know you appear to be pretty busy, but it looks like you're handling it well," Arthur observed.

"No, I'm doing all right. If we get a greater influx of people, then I may need some help, but the workload here is pretty well-balanced," Daniel told him.

"Awesome. Sounds like everything's set. Vana, meet me here with your people early in the morning. Samson, feel free to bring your recruits. Sometimes a trial by fire is the best way to learn. It's time to dust off your armor and get back to work," Arthur told him with a smile.

Samson's mustache curled up as he smiled, and he gave a solemn nod. "See you in the morning."

# Chapter 7

*Unexpected Encounters*

Arthur opened his eyes to the gray nothingness he had seen once before. He wasn't sure what to make of these experiences. The previous one had left him with a rather disturbing image of his parents in conversation and talking about his death.

With trepidation, Arthur thought of them again, and to his surprise and dismay, a small window appeared a scant distance away. Worried about what he might see, he approached the window cautiously. Peering through the window, tears came to his eyes, seeing his mom and dad again. To his disappointment, it looked like they were in a hospital room.

His mother was lying in bed with an IV pump attached to her. His father sat in the crappy recliner near the bed and looked like he had slept little.

"Things will get better hun, don't worry about it. This situation sucks, and I hate that you're stuck here for the treatment, but if we can get it out of the way, things can go back to normal," he said.

"You keep saying that, but it isn't feeling any better. The doctors always sound so downtrodden when they come in here as if the treatment isn't working, and the numbers don't seem to act as they should. I fear I may not beat this despite our best efforts," Eve said in quiet tones.

Jon's eyes watered as he spoke to her. "You can't lose hope. You need to keep your strength up if you want to beat this. We'll make it through this and get back to our time together. Maybe we should plan a vacation for when you've recovered? Give us a goal to shoot for. You always wanted to go to Europe, and we've never had the chance. How about we plan a week there and travel the entire area?"

Her eyes watered to match his. "That sounds great, my love. I'll keep fighting this so we can make our trip."

Jon moved his chair a little closer to her bed. He sat in the chair with his head lying over the edge and onto her bed with her. They lay there holding hands. Tears streamed down Arthur's face despite his attempt to keep them back. What happened to her, and what were they doing? Was this even real, or was his mind playing tricks on him? The window faded from his view, and he closed his eyes to darkness.

***

Rayne crept in front of the caravan. He found thirty-five people who wanted to make the trek with him out of the city. It honestly wasn't a hard task, and many more probably would've joined him, but he had a brief window of time to escape. Alarm bells sounded moments after they left the city and echoed as they traveled down the road.

Luckily, their trip progressed swiftly and was uneventful. His focus returned to their journey as he ducked into a set of trees along the road. Rayne took a position as a scout for the group. He and two others ranged ahead to keep the path clear for the others traveling with them. They didn't want to run into something dangerous that could harm their friends and family. With Rayne's sister in the group, he wouldn't take any chances.

They'd been on the road for weeks and weren't too far from their destination. He traveled through the forest as quietly as possible, hoping to get lucky enough to encounter some game to kill for food. There was almost nothing to eat, but it wasn't much different from living in the city.

Rayne rounded what felt like the thousandth tree and came to a quick stop. Guttural noises echoed off the trees around him and sounded like they originated somewhere in front of him. He hadn't traveled outside of the cities much, but the noises didn't seem like animals. There was no way to understand what they said, but there were multiple distinct sounds that he attributed to voices, and they'd each respond after one another.

Finding concealment in some bushes, he slunk his way forward. He would need his stealth skill to kick into overdrive here. The distance between him and the noises closed as he crept forward. When he felt like he was next to the sounds, he came to a stop and peeked through the bush in front of him.

There were three large, green-skinned creatures sitting around a small fire with their weapons nearby. Rayne hadn't seen one of these creatures before, but he recognized them from their description. Many parents used stories of orcs as a scare tactic for their children. The infamous green monster who'd come and eat you if you didn't behave, wash up thoroughly, or go to bed when told. Any number of reasons could cause the threat of orcs to materialize.

These three were muscular and, judging by their posture, he was sure they knew how to fight. They were wearing scraps of leather armor on distinct parts of them, but none wore a full set of armor. Each wore poorly maintained iron weapons. Confronting them would be a terrible idea, so Rayne crept backward slowly. His luck worked against him, and he backed right into the leg of a fourth orc and ended up scaring both himself and the orc. The orc jumped back like something tried to bite him, and Rayne jumped to his feet and drew his stiletto dagger.

The orc bellowed in rage and charged at him with a heavy iron sword. Rayne had the advantage of speed and quickly sidestepped the attack while plunging his dagger into the orc's side.

*You have dealt 75 damage to Orc (1) (Level 14) with Iron Stiletto Dagger (Critical Strike).*

Rayne couldn't afford to take his time here. There were at least three more of these on the other side of the bushes next to him, and this orc's roar would've drawn their attention. He activated one of his skills.

Rayne rounded the orc and punched his dagger into the creature's back, directly into his kidney. The orc reared backward in pain with another yell, but Rayne was faster and took the blade out only to slam it into the orc's back on the other side. His swordbreaker appeared in his hand with a quick motion, and he used it to slit the orc's throat. The creature fell to the ground.

*Orc (1) (Level 14) has died.*

The encounter limited his options. He could hear the other orcs crashing through the brush near him. It was stupid for him to go toe to toe with these larger beasts. He was an excellent fighter, but no one was infallible. Turning on his heels, he took off in a mad dash. He dropped a small pouch and used a skill as he fled to throw off his enemies.

*You have activated Smoke Bomb. Enemy visibility reduced by 35%. Enemy accuracy reduced by 35%.*

Billowing white clouds of smoke poured from the pouch as he ran. The sound of trees and branches snapping were easy to make out as he fled from the creatures. His stealth skill helped him avoid leaving too much in the way of tracks, and he hoped none of them were skilled in tracking.

With his speed boost, he quickly gained ground on the noises coming from behind him. After ten minutes of running, he slowed to a walk to regain some of his Stamina. He reflected on the problem with the orcs but wasn't sure how to proceed. He'd killed one of the four he spotted. There was no way to know what to expect from them. It could just be a small roving band looking for food or something to steal, but it could also be a scouting party. From what he'd heard, orcs were the smarter of the subspecies and did a lot of the scouting and made tactical decisions while goblins were their ground fodder.

Figuring there was nothing he could do about it now, he rejoined the traveling group. He would talk to the other scouts to see if there was any cause for concern. After an hour of quick travel, the caravan came back into view. When he arrived, he spotted one of the other scouts and wandered over to him.

"See anything?" Rayne asked.

"Ran into some trouble." The man named Howard responded in hushed tones to avoid the others hearing him.

"Did it happen to be of the ugly green kind?" Rayne asked him.

Howard gave him a troubled look and nodded. "I found a camp of the damn things southeast of us in the direction I traveled. They were directly between us and our destination. To make matters worse, they appear to be traveling toward Alem's Crossing."

"Shit!" Rayne exclaimed. "As if things weren't bad enough. I ran into four of them in the forest on the western side of the road. Since you saw them on the eastern side, I'm assuming the ones I saw were a scouting party. You must've encountered the primary force. Were you able to see how many there were?"

"I saw at least a hundred of the ugly little goblins and a couple dozen orcs, but there was no way I could get close enough to see all of them."

"So, what do you think we should do?" Rayne asked the man.

Howard thought for a moment and came to an answer.

"The group I saw was moving toward our destination, so I think it'll be a chance for us to see what's happening. We can follow them at a distance and keep track of their progress. If they attack the village and it looks like there's no hope, we have time to turn and run for it. If they attack the village and it looks like the village will prevail, we can step in and help when the battle turns in our favor."

That was some well thought out logic that Rayne couldn't argue with. They continued at a slower pace, and two hours later the third scout, Uriel, showed up with bloody marks on him. He'd stumbled into a pair of orcs and barely got away with his life. The man and the orcs came face to face as they rounded a tree and surprised each other. The surprise of the encounter caused the orcs to freeze for a moment, and Uriel used that chance to get in a few preemptive strikes. He took a few hits trying to flee but managed to get away safely.

After talking with the final scout, their plan remained the same. There wasn't any chance they could get around this force, and turning back seemed pointless now. They shadowed the army from a distance and hoped for the best. Rayne wasn't a very optimistic person, but he felt confident the Goddess Lianna wouldn't have given him this quest if it wasn't possible to complete.

The group continued their way down the road cautiously, hoping for a chance at a fresh start and praying the army ahead of them didn't change directions. Rayne and the two scouts monitored the force and ensured they traveled at the right pace to avoid an encounter. Within a few days, they saw the orcs and goblins get more animated. Rayne could get a good enough angle from the top of a tree to know that they weren't far from the village. Oddly enough, he could see a decent size wall in the distance with some sturdy looking gates mounted in it. This might just work out in their favor.

*** 

Arthur woke with a start and reached for his face. The puddles of liquid on his face confirmed the tears he suspected. The dream was so vivid that it felt like he was truly there with his parents. This was the second dream regarding them, and they oddly seemed to be linear in how they occurred. The experience was an odd feeling.

"You okay?" Allendria asked as she sat up in bed beside him and put her hand on his back.

Arthur shook his head. "It's only an unpleasant dream. I just can't seem to shake how it felt. They seem so real."

She eyed him for a moment. "This isn't the first dream like this?"

"No, it's not. I really don't know what it means, but this is the second dream I've had like this. They start the same, but what I see in the dreams is different. It also feels like I'm seeing real events as they happen," he told her carefully.

"Don't dismiss dreams. They're said to be a window into your soul. Maybe you're conflicted because of some inner conflict?" she asked.

"Hard to tell," he told her noncommittally. "We have too much to do today to get caught up on this. You ready for a trip through the woods with a lot of untrained people?" he asked with all the false cheer he could muster.

"That sounds like loads of fun," she said with a sarcastic tone in her voice. "You sure this is a smart idea?"

"Absolutely not, but they've got to start somewhere. We just need to take it easy and let them get a feel for things."

"Well, we better get started. It'll take most of the day to do this correctly," she said in resignation.

They both grabbed their gear and walked downstairs. The inn was full of people getting prepared for the morning work. Arthur saw a handful of the people that would join them this morning. Balair tromped over and ate with them. The little dragon was somewhat reclusive, but you never knew how his attitude would be from day to day.

*Ready for the hunt?* Arthur thought to Balair.

*As ready as I can be. Why does everyone hate sleep so much around here? Can't this wait until later in the morning?*

*Nonsense. Need to get started now. Early bird gets the worm and all that.*

*The damn bird can have the worm. Why the hell would I want a worm, anyway? I'd much rather sleep longer.*

*You'll be fine. It'll give you a chance to flex some of your Fire Magic you haven't been using.*

*I've been using it much more now that I have Earth Magic to make stone. I've been keeping myself busy around town,* Balair said with a hint of pride.

*The villagers could only be so lucky to have such a majestic being grace them with his magical powers.* Arthur said in mock sincerity.

Balair puffed up his chest at the praise until he caught the sarcasm in the tone and turned a glare at Arthur.

*You're an ass sometimes. You know that?*

*Yep,* Arthur sent him cheerfully. *Now you know how it feels when I have to hear it from you.*

The group finished their meal and walked outside. A small crowd gathered around Samson. He assembled his new trainees for the guard, and all five of them were waiting and visibly anxious.

"No need to worry, guys. We'll be there with you for the entire trip. Vana will work with her new scouts as they travel ahead of us, and we'll be identifying targets for you to take out. Our primary goal today is to work on your archery skills. I'll need some time to make proper weapons and armor for everyone," Arthur told them.

They all nodded in agreement. Noah and Toren stood in the armor they'd received during the bandit attack. Arthur waved both of them over to him, and the two approached Arthur nervously.

"Don't worry, fellas. I just wanted to set some expectations. I plan to keep this very simple and safe, but if anything happens, I expect you two to step up and protect the others. You two have armor and they don't. Samson will do his best to counter serious threats, but you two have the added duty of protecting the other three trainees. Understand?" Arthur asked them in a severe tone.

"Yes," they both said in unison.

Arthur nodded and walked to Vana, who was gathering her scouts. He waved as he approached and saw the two scouts she chose. James smiled as he spotted the man, and Arthur's grin grew more prominent as he realized the second trainee was Zeke. Both men had a respectable competency with Archery already, so it'd be up to Vana to train them on the other essential aspects of being a scout.

"Arthur, I've been able to stockpile a decent amount of arrow shafts, but without some feathers for fletching, I can't make anymore. I've also got three more bows completed and have them with me," Zeke told him.

"Can't ask for any more than that. We'll keep our eyes open for feathered animals while out today to get the fletching you need," Arthur told him and turned to face James.

"Good to see you, James. Is Jack working with Rowan?" Arthur asked.

"Yes sir, sent him over first thing this morning to get to work. The lad likes Rowan anyway, so there shouldn't be an issue," James told him.

"Good. You two will stick to Vana like glue. Learn everything she can teach you while we're out today. Also, keep an eye out for anything that may be of use to us while we're in the forest. We're hoping to train, but gathering resources is also important. Plants are a priority, and ensuring you don't damage them before I get to gather their seeds is vital," Arthur told them.

"Sure thing," James said. Zeke just nodded his head in agreement.

The group gathered together, and they handed weapons out. Each of them got a basic bow and a quiver of arrows. Arthur even made sure he had a bow for this trip. The only person who didn't have a bow was Allendria, but she was proficient with her magic and her small dagger.

Samson gathered his forces into a small marching formation while Vana took Zeke and James and headed out of town slightly ahead of the group. She'd work on the basics of picking a path and scouting for game while Samson kept his forces in order. Arthur and Allendria walked on one side of the formation together to monitor the group.

He could see Balair circling overhead, and the dragonling would occasionally swoop down to scare some of the new guards. They weren't used to the flying creature yet. Arthur just hoped Balair didn't push his luck enough to piss one of them off and get an arrow in him.

The trip to the forest was quick, but the moment they entered, Arthur saw the anxiety on the trainees' faces. As with his other trips, the outskirts of the forest remained empty and barren. James and Zeke took alternating shifts running back to deliver scout reports. Vana was doing an impressive job of training them so far. It wasn't too far into the forest when one of them brought back some useful information.

"We've found a spot to hunt. Vana said it's full of smaller creatures that are perfect for the group," Zeke told him.

Arthur nodded in acknowledgment. He turned to address Samson and the guards.

"The scouts have found an ideal hunting ground ahead of us. Everyone get your bows out and arrows ready. I don't care what the animal is, if you see something, shoot it. We're here for experience first and foremost. There isn't much you can kill here that we can't find some use for," Arthur explained.

Everyone nodded, and Arthur turned back to Zeke. "Lead the way."

They crept through the trees, and Arthur spotted Vana. He held his hand up to show they were close, and everyone slowed down while trying to be as quiet as they could. They weren't very successful, judging by the look on Vana's face every time she heard a branch crack or leaves crunch, but they tried.

She motioned for the trainees to split into two groups. Three took one side, and two took the other as they left the cover of the trees. Arthur, Samson, and Allendria came out behind them to keep an eye out for dangers as the trainees walked through the clearing. Arrows flew in all directions as Arthur watched small creatures run away in a panic.

Two squirrels fell from the trees with arrows in them, while quite a few arrows found nothing and fell to the ground or embedded in a tree. A small gaggle of geese took off from the center of the clearing near a small pond of water. Arthur tried not to laugh as the men fired arrows at them. One of them scored a hit and took down a goose. As the geese rose higher, Arthur expected the shots to stop, but to his surprise, he watched three arrows fly up, and each took a bird down. Immediately following that, another three fell from the sky.

Arthur checked his surroundings and spotted Vana, James, and Zeke with their bows out. Apparently, Zeke was serious about his need for feathers. The geese rose out of arrow range and Arthur had just turned his attention away when two more fell from the sky and hit the ground beside him. He looked up to see Balair circling above him with a look of pleasure on his face.

*You have gained 60 experience for your familiar killing Goose (Level 8) (x2).*

*Magnificent job.*
*Those things were just a warm-up. I hope we can find something worthy of a hunt,* Balair sent back.

When they finished searching the entire clearing for smaller game, Arthur told everyone to gather all the dead creatures and pile them in the center. He also instructed them to gather all the fallen arrows they could find. They could salvage the tips from the broken bolts.

Arthur smiled at the thought of what he was about to do. None of them had seen this ability yet, so he expected this to be an enjoyable show. He cast his Access Dimensional Storage spell, and the air in front of him shimmered before the outline of the doorway became visible. The air in front of him seemed to open in his direction, and he could see the door to his dimensional storage room hanging a couple of feet off of the ground.

He started picking up the dead animals and tossing them into the storage area. They flew through the empty blackness and landed in the room. They appeared to be floating in what he could only describe as a never-ending void. Arthur kept tossing animals in for a few seconds until he picked his head up and looked around.

All the people surrounding him looked at him in stunned silence. Some stared at the open dimensional doorway in abject fear. Arthur couldn't blame them. It seemed a little unnerving. He needed to snap them out of their trance, though.

"Enough gawking! Everyone get to work. Get these animals into the storage room. We don't want to have to carry them all back by hand, do we?" Arthur asked.

They all jumped at his initial statement, and then slowly began hauling corpses. Arthur could see some of them casting untrusting glances toward the doorway as they worked, but most got used to it quickly. The haul wasn't too bad. Arthur spotted six squirrels, eight rabbits, and nine geese as they flew to land in a pile in the room. It probably would've been more if not for the new trainees' inexperience in Archery, and the sheer number of shots missed. If nothing else, they should all have a basic skill level in Archery· now.

The group salvaged everything they could and got back into formation. Vana, James, and Zeke left to scout ahead while the rest followed at a distance. This pattern continued twice more through the morning. The next clearing they found yielded similar results.

It comprised more minor game. Seeing their previous kills still perfectly preserved as they left them in the room eased some of their tension regarding the dimensional storage. Another six rabbits, four squirrels, and even a deer found their way in from the second clearing.

The third clearing was where things changed. They divided into their two teams to sweep the clearing as they emerged from the trees. Their paths led them along the edges of the space as they picked off small animals. Arthur saw many more animals fall this time than last. The guards were quickly gaining ground in their Archery skill. With sufficient targets, it was quick to level the skill.

Everything was going smoothly until there was a rumbling that Arthur felt more than he heard. The forest shook, and Arthur glanced in the direction of the rumbling. He saw Zeke running his way, waving wildly.

"Arthur!" he yelled. "An enormous group of boars is charging directly at us! Something must've spooked them!"

"Samson!" Arthur yelled. "Get all the men into formation in the center of the clearing. We need to prepare to defend against a charging sounder."

Arthur heard Samson bellow out commands as the men raced to do as ordered. Samson took the front of the formation in his intricate set of armor while Noah and Toren lined up on either side of him. The unarmored recruits held a position behind this new wall of metal armor. Arthur and Allendria each took a side of the formation behind Toren and Noah.

Not three seconds after they'd gotten into position, the first of the pigs charged from the trees in a full-speed dash. Arthur hoped they'd avoid their group and take the simple route through since they weren't being overly threatening. The creatures may be hefty, but anyone who'd ever seen a charging boar could tell you they could move fast.

The first few boars in the group came close to them and then veered around their position. A collection of sows came trundling by, with some piglets following nearby. After about twenty passed, there was finally one that wanted to challenge their strength.

The boar in question must have weighed a hefty three hundred pounds and was hauling ass when it charged at Samson. Luckily, Samson saw the charge coming and thrust the bottom of the shield into the ground as hard as he could and braced behind it for the assault. Arthur wasn't sure that was the best idea, but there wasn't time to do anything about it.

When the boar hit the shield, a metallic
shriek resounded as one of its tusks scraped
across the face of the metal, and it pushed
the shield backward. The force was significant
enough to cause Samson to stumble back. His
natural weight, combined with the weight of
his armor, wasn't an easy amount to move.

The charge stunned Samson, and he looked
like he'd have a nasty bruise on his arm from
the impact. The boar seemed to be in worse
shape as it looked drunk and stumbled around.
Its nose jutted from its face at an odd angle,
obviously broken. Before it could react, Toren
and Noah dove toward it and drove their iron
daggers into its neck. The creature squealed
and fell to the ground.

Toren and Noah helped Samson back to his
feet, and they resumed their positions. The
pigs were still charging through the clearing,
and a few skirted the edge of the group.
Arthur drew his sword and held it in his left
hand. One boar got too close to him, so he
slashed into its neck.

*You have dealt 100 damage to Boar (1)
(Level 10) with Steel Longsword of Minor
Beastslaying (Critical Hit) (Mortal Blow).*

The pig squealed as it stumbled away and
left a bloody trail. They could hunt it down
later if needed. More came their way and
skirted them, but a few more charged the group
head-on. Noah fell beneath one's charge, and
it gouged him in the leg with one of its giant
tusks. Arthur was behind him and jumped
forward to run his sword through the beast's
side before it could do any further damage.

The boar fell dead, and Arthur helped Noah back to his feet. The inexperienced man was a little shaky with the damage to his leg but held his ground. Another charged at Toren, but he kicked at it and spooked it, causing the beast to turn at the last minute. The side of its body still hit him and caused him to stumble, but he stayed on his feet and got back into place.

Rowan stepped forward into one as it approached and took his shield in both hands by the arm straps and swung the thing full force. The shield bash of epic proportions slammed into the pig's face, causing it to squeal and roll twice before it came to a stop on the ground. It landed in front of Noah, and he wasted no time plunging his knife into the stunned creature's neck to ensure it didn't get back up.

The last of the pigs passed their position, and Arthur turned to watch them pass. To his surprise, there were more pigs on the ground behind them with multiple arrows protruding from their bodies. His gaze moved to the trainees and saw they had their bows in hand and were shooting at the hogs as they passed. The men were smart enough to not waste an excellent opportunity at stockpiling food. The meat would go far when it came to feeding the village.

They were taking stock of their surroundings when Vana and James came crashing out of the trees where the hogs just emerged. The look on Vana's face did nothing to help Arthur's mood.

"What's wrong?" he asked.

She pulled up, out of breath, and turned to him. "Another group chased the pigs, and we got caught in between the two. I hope you have some arrows. We now get to deal with their pursuers, and they won't pass us up. Have you ever had to kill a harpy?" she asked with a smile.

A chill went down Arthur's spine as he pictured what he remembered about harpies in the games he played and the books he read on earth. The thought of facing any version of them worried him.

"Everyone get your bows out and arrows nocked, right now!" Arthur yelled over the group.

They looked confused, but everyone scrambled to do as told. As the noise intensified from the direction the pigs had come from, the first feathers came into sight.

# Chapter 8

*Impending Raid*

A flurry of feathers emerged from the tree line and resolved itself into a humanoid figure. Well, it was somewhat humanoid anyway. The creature had the body structure and basic shape of a human. Small feathers covered it from head to claw, and it was close to five feet tall. Large talons, resembling that of an eagle, stood in dark contrast to their lighter feathers.

Bat-like wings, with a spike at the top of the arch, sprouted from its back while feathers layered the bottom of its wing. Most of the creature was white, but there were occasional splashes of brown amongst the feathers. Their faces looked like someone had taken a human, glued feathers over their entire face and head, and slapped a sharp eagle's beak on them.

A moment after it emerged, Arthur saw more feathers behind it. The lead creature slowed its pace as it exited the trees and more filed in behind it. Arthur took this time to activate his Scan ability.

| **Name:** Forest Harpy | |
|---|---|
| **Level:** 12 | |
| **Type:** Sentient | |
| **Rarity:** Uncommon | |
| **HP:** 240/240 | |
| **Stamina:** 160/160 | |
| **Strength:** 8 | **Experience:** N/A |
| **Agility:** 12 | **Skills** |

| **Endurance:** 10 | **Combat Skills:**<br><br>Whirlwind: ? (???/???)<br>Rake: ? (???/???)<br>Swoop: ? (???/???) |
| --- | --- |

*You have gained 120 experience in Scan for use against Forest Harpy (Level 12).*

*Well, it could be worse.* The harpies kept filing out of the forest until eight hovered in front of them. He breathed a sigh of relief, seeing only eight. They may have been small, but they could fly, and their talons looked deadly.

Arthur was about to issue orders when he saw a teal color through the trees. Some harpies turned to look at what approached. Another hag emerged from the trees, but this one was brown, where the others were white. Instead of the splashes of brown the others had, teal stripes decorated its face and legs while its wings were almost solid teal. Arthur had an unpleasant feeling about this one and activated Scan.

*You have gained 150 experience in Scan for use against Mystical Harpy (Level 15).*

| | |
| --- | --- |
| **Name:** Mystical Harpy<br>**Level:** 15<br>**Type:** Sentient<br>**Rarity:** Rare<br>**HP:** 250/250<br>**Mana:** 300/300<br>**Stamina:** 150/150 | |
| **Strength:** 8 | **Experience:** N/A |

| Agility: 15<br>Intellect: 10<br>Wisdom: 6<br>Endurance: 9 | Skills<br>Combat Skills:<br><br>Whirlwind: ?<br>(???/???)<br>Lightning Ball: ?<br>(???/???)<br>Static Discharge: ?<br>(???/???) |
| --- | --- |

*Dear sweet baby Jesus. This was the last thing we needed. I've never faced a caster before, so this could be bad.*

"Be on your toes!" Arthur told them. "The teal one is a caster and looks like it deals in lightning. Samson, you hold what you can in front of us. They seem to stay close to the ground, but it doesn't mean they can't fly above us. Trainees, you're all on archery duty. Take shots when you are clear and try to stay in the formation."

"Should we split up?" Allendria asked.

Arthur thought about that for a moment. If the caster were indeed electricity-based, they'd need to spread out to prevent it from taking them all out in one hit.

"Samson, keep the guards in formation. Vana spread your scouts out to shoot from different directions. Use the trees if you can. Allendria, you're with me," Arthur called to them.

*Balair, watch our backs, please,* Arthur sent to him.

Balair's voice took on a serious tone as he responded. *I've got you.*

Arthur pulled his bow over his shoulder and nocked an arrow.

"Fire at will!" he yelled.

As arrows flew across the field from the guards, Arthur let an arrow fly for the Mystical Harpy. The arrow zipped across the clearing but, right before it hit, a spark of lighting raced from the creature and zapped the shaft. The arrow wobbled and flew off course before digging into the ground. Confused, Arthur checked his notification.

*Mystical Harpy's Static Discharge deflected your Simple Iron Arrow.*

"The Mystical Harpy can deflect arrows with one of its skills. Vana, your team is responsible for keeping it occupied until we can clear out some of the rest. Keep firing at it to keep it distracted."

"Oh, sure! Let's just distract the thing that can supposedly throw electricity with some lousy arrows it can deflect. Do you even think about what you say before it comes out of your mouth? Never mind, woman to the rescue! I'll keep it busy," she called as she whistled in a high shrieking noise and ran for the trees.

She disappeared behind one tree, and Arthur wasn't sure where she went. The normal harpies started their advance, and a few of them sported arrows embedded in different limbs. Two of them stirred up a big gust of wind that caused ranged attacks to miss their marks. Arthur assumed this was their Whirlwind ability.

One of the Forest Harpies launched itself high into the air, furiously beating its wings. It came diving for the group, and Samson ran to intercept it. He heaved his shield above his head, and the claws raked along the face, causing narrow furrows deep into the metal and emitting a high-pitched shriek.

As soon as it passed, two of the trainees launched arrows at its back. One arrow pierced through its right wing, while the other sunk into its right leg. It let out a squawk of pain as it circled back toward the front of the group. Its altitude started dropping as it flew around, and by the time it reached the front of Arthur's party, it could barely hover off of the ground anymore.

Two more Forest Harpies charged at them from the front while another two tried attacking from the side. Arthur saw Allendria launch a blast of fire at the one on her side, but the creature flapped its wings with extreme force and caused the fire to dissipate in the wind.

Arthur took on one that approached on his side as it closed with him. Instead of waiting for it to come to him, he charged toward it, creating some space between himself and the rest of the group. The creature hovered off the ground, causing its head to be a little taller than Arthur. Unfortunately, the dangerous part was its claws. With its right claw headed directly for his face, Arthur brought his sword up to catch it.

The claw ricocheted off of the blade, which
led to a burning feeling in Arthur's hand from
the impact. He kept his hold despite the pain.
He could've sworn he'd just hit a baseball too
high on the neck of an aluminum bat with the
way his hand stung.

Arthur lunged at the creature, but it was
agile enough to twist out of the way. He
stayed on the offensive as he kept pursuing
the beast. His constant barrage of attacks
allowed him to keep the harpy off balance, and
a few of his attacks even scored minor hits.

*You have dealt 45 damage to Forest Harpy
(1) (Level 12) with Steel Longsword of Minor
Beastslaying (Glancing Blow) (x3).*

Wanting to mix things up a little, he
closed the distance and acted as if he would
swing. When he saw the direction the harpy
would dodge, he sent a blast of Weak Flame
directly into its face. The beast flapped its
wings and squawked in protest. With it
stunned, Arthur brought a heavy slash down and
into its left shoulder. The weight of the
blade and his force sheared clear through the
creature and split it in half diagonally.
*These things must have bones that are light
and hollow like a bird.*

*You have dealt 10 damage to Forest Harpy
(1) (Level 12) with Weak Flame.*
*You have dealt 185 damage to Forest Harpy
(1) (Level 12) with Steel Longsword of Minor
Beastslaying (Cleaving Strike).*
*Forest Harpy (1) (Level 12) has died.*
*You have gained 150 experience in Swords
for defeating Harpy (1) (Level 12).*

*You have gained 250 experience for
defeating Harpy (1) (Level 12).*

The entire group of harpies rushed the
guards and Noah, Toren, and Samson did
everything they could to help block the talon
strikes from the unarmored fighters. Some of
the unarmored group suffered cuts on their
arms despite the effort. An audible snapping
sound drew his attention, and he watched one
trainee swing both halves of his now broken
bow at a harpy to drive it away.

The Mystical Harpy scanned the trees and
emitted static discharges to deflect numerous
arrows as they flew in. Vana must've had Zeke
and James working to circle the beast with her
to keep it distracted. Arthur saw arrows fly
from three separate directions as he ran to
assist the guards with their struggle. *As long
as Vana can keep it up, there's hope we can
win this fight.*

Two of the harpies around the guards took
to the air, and one of them swooped down at
one of the unarmored guards. One man lifted
his bow up and barely deflected the claws, but
received a deep cut on his arm. The harpy went
to lash out again when a blur of red barreled
into its face, causing it to elicit a shriek
of pain.

Balair arrived on the scene and clamped
down hard on the harpy's face with his teeth
firmly planted in each side of its head. Blood
flowed from the teeth wounds, and Balair upped
the ante. A torrent of flame erupted from his
throat, and he cooked the creature's face as
he held on. Its wings beat frantically as it
tried to kick its talons up high enough to
dislodge him, but the design of its body
wouldn't allow it to reach him.

The harpy collapsed on the ground as Balair continued his relentless assault. He finally stopped breathing fire when the creature ceased moving. Another hag closed on Balair's position, but he spotted it, darted directly into the air, and took off in a flash. *The little bastard sure is fast.* Arthur thought to himself.

*Excellent work, Balair. Keep it up,* Arthur sent to him.

Balair didn't respond with words. Instead, a smug feeling of satisfaction permeated Arthur's mind. Arthur reached the guards and took a high swing at the closest harpy. Another guard distracted it and it didn't see Arthur as he approached. The blade sheared through the creature, splitting it in two.

*You have dealt 220 damage to Forest Harpy (2) (Level 12) with Steel Longsword of Minor Beastslaying (Cleaving Strike).*
*Forest Harpy (2) (Level 12) has died.*
*You have gained 150 experience in Swords.*
*You have gained 250 experience.*

The other flying harpy darted down and slashed Arthur across the back. Fortunately, his armor blocked some of the damage, but it still stung as the claw raked his skin.

*Forest Harpy (3) (Level 12) has dealt 25 HP damage to you with Swoop.*

Arthur turned to face it when an arrow hit the thing in the side of the neck. The arrow went clean through, burst out of the other side of its neck, and kept flying. Arthur glanced to the side and saw one guard nod his way with their bow up. He nodded back at the man and ran for the next harpy. Samson, Noah, and Toren took out three of the regular harpies while Allendria killed another.

"Samson, you guys handle the last two of these Forest Harpies. I'm going for the Mystical one before it shakes off our rangers," Arthur called to the armored man.

"I've got them. Take Allendria with you. You'll probably need her," Samson called back.

"Allendria! Let's go after the Mystical Harpy. The guards can handle the two remaining Forest Harpies," he yelled to her as he spotted her on the other side of the group. They both headed toward the Mystical Harpy at the edge of the woods.

"Vana, what's the status?" Arthur called to the woods.

Her voice came from behind the Mystical Harpy. "Well if the goal was to piss it off, I think we succeeded. Otherwise, we haven't accomplished a damn thing."

Arthur charged directly at the creature. It faced the woods, looking for the source of Vana's voice while Arthur approached it from behind. As he brought his sword down, an arc of static shot from the harpy and sizzled throughout his blade. The pain of the shock caused him to drop the weapon. "Son of a bitch!" Arthur hollered as he shook his hand.

*Mystical Harpy (Level 15) has dealt 15 HP damage to you with Static Discharge.*

Arthur spotted a flash of red diving for the harpy and sent to Balair. *Don't charge it! It has a shield of electricity.*

The speed that Balair flew didn't give him time to adjust course. He slammed into the static shield, but his body continued through and hit the harpy in the chest. Balair bounced off of it and tumbled away with his scales looking scorched. The impact threw the hag off balance, and it frantically flapped its wings, trying to steady itself.

The creature righted itself and looked around in anger. It flapped its wings and gained altitude. Arthur eyed it warily as it rose from the ground.

*Thanks for the late notice!* Balair sent to him.

*Hey, don't get pissy with me. I just found out myself doing the same thing with my sword.*

Balair huffed at him, and Arthur saw the pile of scales rise from the ground again.

*This damn thing is annoying me. We can't seem to attack it with anything. That static shield is preventing us from doing any damage,* Arthur vented to the red dragon.

*Hey, I did ten damage to it when I crashed into it.* Balair sent as he smiled a toothy grin in Arthur's direction.

*Oh, forgive me all mighty one and your combat prowess. You care to do that twenty-four more times? I'm willing to let you try,* Arthur asked him.

Balair gave him a sheepish look. *Yeah, excellent point. Not gonna work.*

As they stood there arguing, Arthur suddenly felt a stinging pain hit him in the back of his left shoulder. The burning pain caused him to turn and look at the spot. To his immense surprise, he saw an arrow sticking out of his shoulder.

*Guard (Level 8) has dealt 25 HP damage to you with Simple Iron Arrow.*

"Who the fuck shot me with a damn arrow?" he yelled at the guards behind him.

The group of guards slowly shuffled apart until one man remained standing by himself in the middle of the group, looking terrified. Arthur's eyes burrowed into the guard, and he watched him squirm under the gaze.

"Sorry, M'lord. I was trying to shoot the flying harpy but missed," the man told him.

"What's your name?" Arthur asked as the man continued to look nervous.

"P… Paul, M'lord," he responded.

"All right, Paul, new rule. We do not allow trainees to shoot arrows at anything when a friendly fighter is in the same direction. Do we all understand?" Arthur called over them all.

They all nodded in agreement, and he saw a few of them covering their laughter as they stared at Paul with a look of pity. Arthur reached over and tugged the arrow out of his shoulder. His leather armor prevented it from sinking in too deep, but it still hurt pulling it out.

The Mystical Harpy was now roughly fifteen feet off the ground and staring straight at the group of guards. Arthur saw lighting gather along its wings.

"Everyone spread out!" he yelled as he
realized what was coming.

The Mystical Harpy finished gathering the
electricity, and a ball of lighting formed in
front of its chest. The ball shot forward and
bounced along a path just like a lightning
bolt. It zipped within two feet of Arthur and
caused every hair on his body to stand
straight up. An arc of electricity bounced off
of the ball and hit him in his left arm,
sending a stinging pain shooting down his side
and into his left leg. The shock sent him to
his knee as it felt like his nerves blazed
with fire.

*Mystical Harpy (Level 15) has dealt 75 HP
damage to you with Lightning Ball.*

The ball of lighting continued forward and
shot straight for the pile of guards. They
tried to spread out but didn't have enough
time to make it far. The ball of lightning
would hit directly in the center of the
guards. Fear spread over Arthur as he realized
the damage would be catastrophic. Before the
ball hit the ground, a chunk of earth quickly
lifted from the field and sped to intercept
the lightning. The two missiles hit each
other, and the piece of dirt exploded into
dust while the orb of lightning burst and arcs
of electricity shot straight down into the
ground, avoiding their men.

Arthur breathed a sigh of relief and looked over to see Allendria with her arms out and panting from her quick reaction. His mind finally caught up to what happened as he realized the solution. His stupidity would be the death of him one day if he weren't careful. They just needed to ground the lightning, and it typically couldn't affect earth. It was time for some more flair.

Arthur clapped his hands together and activated Summon: Stone Spear. The weapon started rising from the ground as Arthur grabbed the shaft and gradually lifted it. As soon as the stone blade emerged, he hefted it up over his shoulder. Arthur took two quick steps forward and launched it, using his best javelin throw, directly into the Mystical Harpy. The projectile soared the scant distance and was perfectly on the mark. The static shield arced as the spear passed through, but it couldn't affect the spear's path in any way. It punched through the harpy's chest, and it screeched as it tumbled to the ground and came to a stop.

*You have gained 80 experience in Earth Magic and Fire Magic for successfully casting Summon: Stone Spear.*
*You have dealt 240 damage to Mystical Harpy (Level 15) with Stone Spear (Critical Hit) (Fatal Blow).*
*Mystical Harpy (Level 15) has died.*

    Arthur looked around and surveyed the
damage. The group of guards looked battered
from the fight, but none received severe
injuries. Allendria looked around the area,
checking for more enemies. Samson checked on
the status of his men and got them back in
fighting shape and then into formation. Arthur
saw Vana talking to James and Zeke by the tree
line. He walked over to the group of rangers.
    "You guys okay?" Arthur asked the group of
scouts.
    "Pretty much bottomed out on stamina and
will need to recover my arrows, but not
injured," James said through his heavy
breathing.
    "My stamina isn't terrible, but I'm
completely out of arrows. I'll need to scour
the field to find some more," Zeke told him.
    "We'll be fine. I'll get these two to clean
up and retrieve arrows, then we'll set off to
search for any dangers," Vana told him.
    "Fantastic work, Vana. Looks like you have
a solid group of scouts. James and Zeke, I saw
you two moving around the harpy to keep it
distracted as well. Magnificent work."
    They all beamed at the praise and nodded.
    "Enough lollygagging, you two. Get to work
finding your arrows. I'm getting back to
work," Vana told them. She sent Arthur a smile
as she ran into the woods. The woman must have
incredible stamina to still be going at that
speed after the fight she just had. Arthur
walked back to the group of guardsmen.
    "Impressive work Samson, minus one nameless
guard shooting me," Arthur said as he cocked
his gaze at the offending man in question.
Paul had the grace to hide behind another
guard out of Arthur's sight.

"I'll work with them, sir. They're still green, and most of them just learned Archery today," Samson said with a quick salute.

"Make sure you work on group tactics with them. They'll primarily be fighting in the village, but they also need to work as a team if tasked with investigating issues outside the village. This training should include learning not to shoot your teammates," Arthur told him with a smile.

"I don't think they'll make that mistake again, sir," Samson told him with a gruff laugh.

"Well fought, Sir Samson. Your men are coming along well," Allendria told him as she approached.

"Thank you for the timely save. I'm pretty sure the knight should save the damsel in distress, so maybe I need to find a skirt," Samson said with uncharacteristic mirth.

Allendria smiled at the joke. "I'm not sure we have enough fabric in town, but I'll keep it in mind."

"I'll get the storage room opened. I want these corpses thrown in it. We have the boars that'll be good for meat, and I'm sure the harpies will be of some use. If nothing else, they'll provide a hefty supply of high-quality feathers for fletching." Samson nodded and walked to his men to issue orders.

A ball of crimson floated down to hover next to Allendria, and Arthur smiled at the little creature. The lack of scorch marks on the dragon's hide shocked him.

*Thought you were injured?* Arthur sent to the dragonling.

*I was injured, but the level I gained from the fight fixed me up,* Balair told him.

Arthur checked on the remaining experience gains he'd ignored during the fight.

*You have gained 250 total experience in Archery.*
*You have gained 400 total experience in Light Armor.*
*You have gained 250 total experience in Spears.*
*You have gained 650 total experience in Swords.*
*You have gained 2,300 total experience.*
*Congratulations, you have reached level 17! You now have 5 available skill points. Getting closer to your goal.*

*That's not a bad haul,* Arthur thought. It was the combined experience from the boar fight and the harpies. He took those five points he'd gained and put two into Strength, bringing him to 14. The next two went into Agility, bringing it up to 26. The last point went into Luck, bringing it to an even 10.

Luck played a significant role in many of his previous fights, so he felt obliged to dump a point there. A slip at an inopportune moment could easily kill him. There was no reason to tempt fate any more than necessary.

The guards scrambled around the field, gathering carcasses. Arthur cast his Access Dimensional Storage spell again and allowed them to throw carcasses in. Some guards even found some of the injured boar not far into the trees and brought them back out. Samson wouldn't allow them to venture far, and Arthur ultimately agreed with the decision.

By the time the guards finished dumping in carcasses, they'd totaled up ten hogs and the nine harpy carcasses. The forethought of the trainees to shoot the pigs as they passed had helped reel in more of those. The men continued to round up anything of use. Zeke and James even found some plants that Arthur could cast his Germination ability on.

*You have gained a total of 3,160 Farming experience for assorted plants.*
*You have gained 32 Rosemary Seeds.*
*You have gained 22 Thyme Seeds.*
*You have gained 15 Mint Seeds.*
*You have gained 55 Peppercorn Seeds.*
*You have gained 22 Okra Seeds.*
*You have gained 12 Cucumber Seeds.*

Arthur's attention shifted to the trees when he heard rustling, and a distressed-looking Vana emerged. *It's odd for her to make that much noise in the forest.* She prided herself in her ability to travel swiftly and quietly, so something must've really rattled her for her to act like that. Arthur hurried over to her.

"What's wrong?" he asked in a low tone.

She looked up at him with fear in her eyes. "Orcs and goblins. Lots of orcs and goblins."

"Samson, Allendria, Zeke, and James, can you meet us over here for a moment?" Arthur yelled over the clearing.

All those he identified made their way to them at the edge of the clearing. He wanted this to stay quiet for the moment until he knew more about what they were dealing with.

"Vana, please repeat what you just told me," Arthur said as the others gathered around.

"I just spotted a force of orcs and goblins in the forest," she told them nervously.

"How many orcs were in the group? How many goblins? Were they armed? Did they spot you? Where were they headed?" Samson started frantically asking.

"Whoa, slow down Samson," Arthur interjected. He could see the look of bewilderment on Vana's face as the stream of questions was going on.

"I… I'm not sure. I ran across two smaller groups of them. They weren't large parties since each had one orc and five goblins in them. The fact that I found two of them so close to each other spooked me," she said as she calmed herself.

"That's not too bad," James said as he heard Vana's tale. "Twelve enemies isn't a problem for us. Hell, Arthur could take them by himself."

Samson hit James across the back of the head with an open hand.

"You idiot," Samson spat. "A single orc and band of five goblins is a standard size scouting party. If there were two of them that close together, they have a much larger force in the area. We need more information."

James rubbed the back of his head but went silent at Samson's words. They all looked at each other in confusion for a moment. None of them were entirely sure about the best course of action.

"Fine," Arthur said. "This is getting us nowhere. Samson, James, and Zeke, you take the other guards and get back to the village as fast as you can. We don't know if that's their destination, but I have a terrible feeling it is. As soon as you get there, ready the place for war. Zeke, make every arrow you can. You can steal anyone you need in the village to help you with labor. Samson, get the guards into shifts and have them watch the walls. Ask the construction team to expand some sections of the wall, allowing them to be wide enough for archer crews to stand on them at intervals. James, help Samson get those gates ready. I want them finished and ready to hang by the time I return. Allendria, return with them and organize the women of the village. Get supplies ready to provide food for the fighters. We also need to find any scraps we can that would make suitable bandages for wounds."

*Go with them and protect them.* Arthur sent to Balair. *If possible, try to scout the path to the village from the air to make sure they run into no resistance. When they make it back, come find us. We may need your eyes.*

He felt a firm resolve from Balair at his statement and knew the little guy had entered serious mode.

"Vana and I will do some in-depth scouting and get a better idea of their numbers and intentions. As soon as we know more, we'll return to the village. Also, Allendria, use any magic you need to get the tasks done. If you or the construction crew need more mana, you have the authority of the Mayor to draw from the mana amulets around the village."

"We'll take care of it," Allendria resolved.

"Hurry and get going. I'll help get the gatehouse doors mounted as soon as I return, but get them completed and to the gates by then," Arthur told them.

Samson saluted and returned to his men. Zeke and James followed right behind him, while Allendria stepped forward and gave him a tender kiss.

"Stay safe and come back," she told him quietly.

"You can't get rid of me that easily," he told her with a cocky half-smile.

She shook her head at his antics, then turned and chased after the others. Samson yelled orders, and the guards frantically tried to get ready to move. Arthur turned his attention back to Vana.

"Let's go hunting," he said with a feral grin.

# Chapter 9


*Reinforcing the Village*

Arthur and Vana sped through the forest. He easily kept up with her as they weaved through the trees and undergrowth. After a good half mile, she slowed her pace. Arthur slowed to match her and followed as quietly as he could.

Vana crept through the trees and came to a halt. She motioned with her hand for Arthur to come to her. When he was even with her, she motioned for him to look around the tree and through the brush. Arthur did as suggested and saw what she found. It was one of the scouting groups. As she described, there was an orc and five goblins with him. They weren't wearing much in terms of armor, but they each had an iron weapon or a stout wooden club. The iron weapons weren't in very good shape, but they'd kill you if hit with one.

The group camped in this clearing but hadn't been here long. They had a fire going, but there wasn't much ash in it yet. The goblins were all eating and drinking as they sat around the fire, while the orc watched each of them.

Vana tapped Arthur on the shoulder and motioned for him to follow her. He turned from the group and slowly backed away. Spotting Vana, he crept to her new position. They both worked their way through the trees as silently as possible and headed further into the woods. After a couple of hundred yards, Vana stopped again.

*You have gained 250 experience in Stealth.*
*Congratulations, you have reached level 2
in Stealth. You are 3% more difficult to
detect by enemies.*

"That was one of the groups I saw earlier,"
she told him.

"I figured. They don't look like they've
been there long."

"That's because they haven't. We almost ran
right up to them, but I sensed something off
and slowed down. When I spotted them last,
they were farther away than here. They were
also slowly moving at the time," Vana told
him.

Arthur dreaded the answer but knew he
needed to hear it. "Are they headed toward the
village then?"

Vana sighed and nodded. *Damn.* This was not
what they needed. He'd hoped for some peace
and quiet so they could build up their
strength before he needed to deal with the
corrupt lords in this land. The last thing he
needed was a goblin raid.

"Let's keep going. I'll stick to you like a
shadow and see if we can get an idea of
numbers," Arthur told her.

She nodded and dashed into the forest
again. The trees blurred by as they kept a
quick pace. Vana went a few hundred more yards
and then slowed again. They crept up to the
edge of another clearing, and Arthur saw spots
of green in it. He took a quick look and his
stomach fell a little.

Five full scouting parties congregated in the clearing, amounting to twenty-five goblins. Most of them sat on the ground to take a break while a few wandered around aimlessly, waiting for orders. Five orcs were all gathered around a sixth orc. The sixth orc wore iron armor. A red cloth attached to his shoulder plates, draped down across the front of his armor, directly below the neckline.

The orcs were all making guttural grunts and assorted noises that made Arthur feel uneasy. After a few moments, his ability to understand languages activated, and he could understand what they were saying.

"We've only spotted a few animals," he heard the first orc saying.

"Look careful. These creatures sneaky," said the second.

"Bah, filthy humans can't stop," another chimed in.

"Enough! Follow orders. Return scout teams to forest. Search all way to village. We want none escape," the orc with the red sash said.

They all grumbled something that was a vague agreement and went back to their squads. Arthur could hear them barking their orders for the goblins to get back to their scout leader. He motioned for Vana to back up, and they quickly left the area.

*You have gained 350 experience in Stealth.*

"The one in the red was some type of leader. Maybe something equivalent to a sergeant. The different scouting parties reported to him. They're all about to head back out, and their target is the village," he told her.

"How the hell do you know that?" she asked him with an odd look.

Arthur thought about that for a moment and realized Vana didn't really know about his ability to understand other languages. "I heard them speaking."

"They were speaking? You could understand those noises?" she asked, bewildered.

"Yes. Long story short, I have an ability that lets me understand any language. Well, any I've heard or seen so far," he quickly amended.

Vana chuckled at that. "Works for writing as well? Man, would some of the old scholars love to get their hands on that skill."

"I bet they would, but I'll keep it for myself. It's part of the reason I can do Enchanting with relative ease. That being said, we don't have time for further discussion. They're about to be on the move again, and based on the conversation, this is still a paltry scouting force compared to the primary force. We can't afford to wander through the forest any longer. We need to get back to the village and quickly. I'll see if Balair can fly over and do a little scouting from the air. It'll be safer than us running into a group of scouts, or goddess forbid, the main army," he told her quickly.

She nodded and motioned for him to follow her. She ran through the forest and barely left a mark on the ground as she passed. Arthur wasn't terrible himself, but she still outdid him with ease. The trip back to the edge of the trees was uneventful. As soon as they exited the forest, Arthur could see the village. It looked like a kicked over anthill. People scurried all over the place, but Arthur was thankful the preparations seemed to be underway.

*Find anything?* Balair asked. Arthur looked up and spotted the little dragon hovering overhead.

*About thirty goblins and seven orcs so far, and there's no doubt they're headed for the village. I have a feeling there are many more, but the forest seemed a little too crowded to hang around. Could you scout along the edge of the trees and follow them back toward the road to Seora? I have a feeling that's the direction the primary army is coming from,* Arthur sent to him.

*Fine, fine. I'll go check.* Balair told him as he turned and glided the direction Arthur mentioned.

"Balair will scout from the air and try to find the bulk of their force. We need to get the village ready for attack," Arthur told Vana.

She nodded to him in agreement, and they both left the forest and headed directly for the northeastern gate. This gate helped repel the bandits, and now it looked like the improved version would get to test its strength against a force of orcs and goblins.

As they reached the gatehouse, Arthur spotted the new gatehouse doors headed toward them. A sizeable group of people carried both doors as they walked side to side. The wood on them was as thick as a person, and metal bands crisscrossed the front and back of them for further strength. Arthur waited patiently for them to arrive.

"Thank you all. We need to get the other gates up as well. If you still have the strength, please help with those," Arthur told them.

"Already done, Mayor," one villager piped up. "This was the last to deliver."

With that, the group of people turned and headed back into town. Arthur shook his head and saw Rowan approaching. His path led directly to the gate, and steel ingots reflected a greyish light from the cart.

"Hey, Rowan. You got all the gate doors finished?" Arthur asked.

"We did indeed. Most of the village chipped in to help prepare the wood and get the metal bands in place. Now we just need to hang them. I brought the metal I thought you may need. You ready to do your part?" Rowan responded.

"Perfect. Time to get to work," Arthur said as he examined the opening.

Walking to the cart, he grabbed two of the steel ingots and poured raw Fire Magic into them. Without a forge present, he needed to heat them himself. He pictured the large barrel hinges he wanted to make and even put some runes on them. His design incorporated a rune set of moderate, power, resist, and corrosion to prevent rust. Moderate, power, and durability to give them more durability, and finally moderate, power, and flex to allow them more freedom of movement so they wouldn't snap under pressure.

With the first piece complete, he started pouring in mana for the enchantment. His immediate reaction was one of shock as 500 mana flowed out of him in a flash. He quickly siphoned mana from his amulet into his mana pool to top it back off as the rest of the spell consumed another 500 mana. He took a quick look at the resulting hinge.

| Item:<br>Enchanted Mage-<br>crafted Steel<br>Gatehouse Hinge | **Durability:** 400/400<br><br>**Rarity:** Rare<br><br>**Quality:** Excellent<br><br>**Weight:** 5.0 kg<br><br>**Traits:** A Steel Gatehouse Hinge, created using magical techniques.<br><br>Enchantments:<br>• Will not corrode or rust.<br>• Critical damage will not bend or |
| --- | --- |

| | distort this item. |
| --- | --- |

*Yep. That'll work.* The thing cost 1,000 mana to enchant, not counting the mana spent on creating it, but it'd be worth it with the durability it offered. He created five more identical hinges, and then they were ready to attach to the doors. The size and weight of the gates made him use three on each door. He took another steel ingot and heated it up. With it, he made large steel nails. He took some liberties with the design and made them shank nails. With his experience in construction, he knew the damn things were nearly impossible to get out. Rowan brought an assortment of hammers with him and eyed the nails as Arthur handed them over.

"Trust me. That style will hold better than anything," Arthur told him. *Well, short of screws or true bolts.* Rowan nodded at the statement and attached three to each door with the new nails. *Now was time for some magic.*

He told everyone to clear the area. He used raw Earth Magic to pick up the first door, and the weight of it sapped his mana quickly. He lined it up where it needed to go on the wall. The door drifted toward the wall until they touched the stone. He poured magic through the door, causing the rock to melt away at the point of impact. He kept channeling the magic as he slid the hinges until they were perfectly flush with the wall.

He let go of the door, and it sat perfectly on the hinges. Touching the wall, he sent a little power into it to make sure the stone was holding the hinges well. Everything worked as intended, so he moved to the next door. They repeated the process on this door, and soon enough, they were staring at a perfectly hung set of gate doors. Arthur spotted two long and thick chunks of wood near the gatehouse and knew what they were for. Rowan had the forethought of including metal "U" shaped brackets on the back to hang the wooden braces to keep the doors closed. Arthur used some quick magic to lift them both and set them in place.

"One gatehouse down and two more to go," Arthur said in a pleased tone. He looked around and spotted Samson admiring the new door.

"Guard Captain Samson!" Arthur hollered to the man. Out of reflex, Samson came to attention with a salute. "How are the preparations coming?"

"Moving along, Mayor. Each man has an assigned post with a bow and a hefty supply of arrows. A few have knives but not much else. We desperately need melee weapons," Samson answered.

Arthur thought about the situation. Their best bet was for them to each have a sword and a spear. The spears would be of best use repelling anyone who tried to make it up the wall, and the sword could dispatch any enemies who reached the top. The wood for the spears was the problem. Arthur could easily make everything needed to assemble a sword, except for the small handle, using his magic. The poles for spears were typically wood because of weight concerns. His mind caught up to the problem, and he hit himself on the forehead.

*I don't have to make the shafts out of wood. I just can't make them solid metal or they'd be too heavy. I can use my Arcane Smithing to make a hollow tube and incorporate a large spear point on the end. I could even design it with wings on the side like a boar spear to help push with. Not only would they be more durable and sturdier, but I can put enchantments on them.*

With his decision made, he turned to Samson. "Samson, I'll get you some weapons. Follow me while we get these two gates up, and we'll have it done in no time. Rowan! Set your apprentices to making as many sword handles as possible. Standard size. I will mass produce some swords and spears once these gates are up. I might need the amulets of the village gathered to ensure we have enough mana to do it," Arthur called to the men.

Both men nodded their understanding, and Arthur took off for the village. Rowan followed close behind while pushing the cart of steel ingots, and Samson held pace with him. When they came to the intersection in front of the inn, Arthur had them stop. Daniel stood outside the inn and looked nervous.

"Hey Daniel, don't worry. We'll take care of this problem. In the meantime, I have a problem for you and those without something to do in town," Arthur said with a grin as he turned away from the inn and cast Access Dimensional Storage. The doorway opened, revealing the mountain of corpses inside.

"What the hell is that, Arthur?" Daniel asked in shock.

"A recent spell," Arthur shrugged. "This is what we killed in our hunt. Do me a favor and gather some people to get working on this. You can take all the game animals to the inn for processing. The harpies… pluck them for their feathers and save anything on them that may be useful. We can burn the rest of the carcass. Set the feathers from the colorful one to the side for me." Arthur told the bewildered man.

"Are you sure it's safe to go in there?" Daniel asked him.

Arthur sighed at that but understood his caution. Without hesitation, Arthur walked into the dimensional space and grabbed a rabbit. He then walked back toward Daniel and tossed it his way. "Of course it's safe. I see plenty of people standing around with nothing to do, so let's get this meat processed."

"Fine, we'll take care of it," Daniel said in a resigned tone.

"Cheer up, Daniel, it's food for the table," Arthur told the man as he took off in a dash again headed for the gatehouse in the northern part of town. The trip was quick, and as last time, he made the hinges and nails and then immediately mount the door into the stone. A quick burst of magic lifted the two logs into place in the brackets to secure the doors. His excess mana in his amulet, combined with his regen, let him accomplish both doors, but his power reserve was practically empty. He made a quick stop at the inn on his way to the final gatehouse.

"Daniel, do you have anyone here with the charged amulets I asked you to hand out?" Arthur asked.

People stepped forward and took the amulets off their necks. Arthur received the necklaces and began pulling in their stored mana. The mana would fill his mana pool but, once his pool was full, it'd automatically dump the excess into his personal amulet. Twenty people later, both his mana pool and his amulet's mana reserve were full.

Arthur turned and continued his trek to the final gatehouse. He repeated the process one more time as the gates took their rightful places on the final gatehouse. They lowered the logs to secure the gates, and Arthur let out a small sigh of relief.

"All right, you two. We have to get to the smithy now. We have some work to do," Arthur told Samson and Rowan. Both men nodded, and they jogged back to the smithy.

As soon as they entered the area, Arthur saw people swarming the place and working on small wooden handles. Rowan sent a messenger from the first gate to his apprentices and they enlisted the help of others. Arthur immediately went to the large forge and tossed in a handful of steel bars. His first thought was to make the spears.

He wanted a long, slender tube that was hollow but capped on the end. It also had to be thick enough to get a good grip on, but not too thick so it wouldn't be cumbersome to hold. The blade would be a long point, and the wings would flare out on each side for roughly six inches. With the design in his mind, he added some runes to it. Along the blade, he placed weak, power, and sharp, while along the spine, he placed weak, power, and durability. For the staff itself, he only did weak, power, and flex. The blade needed to be sharp and stay sharp while it was important for the metal pole to remain straight and not bend on a significant impact.

Two ingots of steel floated out of the forge, and he cast his Arcane Forging spell. The metal flowed and melted together while the spear took shape. The hollow cylinder formed first, and as it reached to correct length, the blade took shape. When the blade and the wings were complete, the end capped off to cover the tube. The weight of the spear pleased Arthur as he hefted the weapon in his hand. He focused on the symbols and poured mana into it. The enchantment ended up taking 300 total mana, but the spear was worth it.

| Item:<br>Enchanted Mage-<br>crafted Steel Boar<br>Spear | **Attack**: 14-18 |
|---|---|
| | **Durability**: 120/120 |
| | **Rarity**: Rare |
| | **Quality**: Excellent |
| | **Weight**: 2.5 kg |
| | **Traits**: A Steel Boar Spear, created using magical techniques. |
| | Enchantments:<br>• This blade will not lose attack damage as the durability falls.<br>• This blade loses durability 10% slower.<br>• Critical damage will not bend or distort this item. |

*Just what I wanted.* He turned and saw Samson's face and frowned. The man had a look of disappointment on his face as he eyed the weapon Arthur was holding.

"What's wrong, Samson?" Arthur asked.

Samson looked hesitant to speak up. "Well, I don't know how well that'll work. A solid metal spear will be too heavy for the men to wield, and the metal pole will be hard to hold on to."

Arthur knew the weight wouldn't be a problem because of him making it hollow. Samson didn't know that yet, but he had a point about it being hard to hold on to, especially when they started sweating. The bar would be slick in their hands. The solution came to Arthur, and he set to work. He pictured the section on the bar he wanted to change and heated it up. He cast Arcane Forging on this specific section only. The metal changed, and instead of the smooth metal, now coarse knurling took its place. This was the same design commonly found on weightlifting bars back on Earth to help maintain a grip on the bar. They were crisscrossing diagonal lines. He put one set on a lower section of the rod and one up a little higher to space them where a soldier would place their hands. With the changes made, he nodded at the weapon and tossed it to Samson.

The man caught it and looked at it in surprise. His hands and eyes roamed the design as he realized the weight was ideal, and the spear point was sharp. His gaze settled on the knurling and placed his hands on the grips. He tried to pull his hands down the rod and found he could hold on to the pattern rather well.

"Well, I take back what I said. I don't know why I continue to doubt you," Samson said with a chuckle.

"Oh no, please continue to doubt me. I hadn't thought about the grip problem until you mentioned it, so I had to add the knurling on the rod to fix that problem. I'll make the rest of them with that part included," Arthur explained.

"That'll work. I like the boar spear design you used. Should work perfectly to repel a siege." Samson commented.

"Thought you'd appreciate that. The wings on there will help prevent the goblins from getting too close to the defenders once they're stabbed. Seemed like an excellent compromise for our inexperienced fighters," Arthur agreed.

"Might make a military man of you after all," Samson told Arthur.

"Doubt it. Back to work I go. I've got a lot to make and not much time to do it."

Arthur made nine more spears. He wanted to have extras to arm villagers in an emergency. When he finished the spears and enchanted each of them, he moved on to swords.

He stuck with the exact same enchantments that Samson had on his and made ten of the sword blades. He had one of Rowan's apprentices feeding the fire and warming the ingots for him while he worked. The process moved quickly as he raced against the clock.

When he finished the ten blades and their accompanying runes, he made the pommel caps and the guards for them. He could leave the handles and assembly to the apprentices. With the enchantments complete, he looked at the first sword blade to see how they would turn out when finished.

| Item:<br>Enchanted Mage-crafted Steel Short Sword (Unfinished) | **Attack:** 12-15 |
|---|---|
| | **Durability:** 90/90 |
| | **Rarity:** Rare |
| | **Quality:** Well Crafted |

| | |
|---|---|
| | **Weight:** 1.4 kg<br><br>**Slot:** Main Hand/Off Hand<br><br>**Traits:** A Steel Short Sword blade, created using magical techniques. Combine with the necessary handle materials to create an Enchanted Mage-crafted Steel Short Sword.<br><br>Enchantments:<br><br>• This blade will not lose attack damage as the durability falls.<br>• This blade loses durability 10% slower. |

*I've got to dedicate some time to making me a suitable weapon. I should also invest in some scale armor. If I intend to be a melee fighter, leather just won't cut it. Mail should provide the right protection without inhibiting my agility too much if I enchant it correctly. Arthur pondered.*

Arthur handed the pile of blades and sword components over to Rowan's apprentices, and they hurried to get them over to the shop for assembly. The apprentices began fit testing the pieces as soon as they arrived. To his surprise, he also saw one of Rowan's apprentices use Fire Magic to heat the tang and peen it over. Looked like Rowan had taken advantage of teaching his apprentices that useful skill.

With the weapons out of the way, he shifted focus to armor. The Arcane Forging spell was so cheap that his mana regenerated almost faster than he could cast it. Most of his mana usage was from the enchantments. Each of the spears cost 200 mana to enchant, and the swords took him 150 mana each. He was constantly regenerating mana, but he was using it far too fast to keep up. Between the final gatehouse and weapon enchantments, he was almost completely out of mana again.

"Samson, do me a favor and round up some more full amulets. I'm running out of mana and have more work to do," Arthur told the man. Samson nodded and jogged off. Arthur turned his focus back to the forge. He nodded to one assistant, and they kept tossing bars into the forge as he worked.

Samson arrived with the amulets he needed, so he quickly refilled his mana pool and asked the man to return them to their owners. The next thing he wanted to do was to help protect the guards a little. His decision settled on breastplates and helmets. Those would be the most effective pieces they could have. It also had the added effect of protecting most of the vulnerable spots from archery fire when on the wall. It cost him nothing extra to make the pieces more intricate, so he settled on a pattern that copied Samson's armor. Samson's next set would be even better when he could get to it.

With a vision of the breastplate in his head, he pictured the runes he wanted to be inlaid on the inside of the breastplate design and cast Arcane Forge. He created ten breastplates that mirrored Samson's, only in steel.

| Item:<br>Enchanted Intricate Mage-crafted Steel Breastplate<br>(Unfinished) | **Armor:** 110<br><br>**Durability:** 155/155<br><br>**Rarity:** Rare<br><br>**Quality:** Excellent<br><br>**Weight:** 4.0 kg<br><br>**Slot:** Chest |
| --- | --- |

| | **Traits**: An Intricate Steel Breastplate, created using magical techniques and enchanted with special magical power. Combine with leather lining to create Enchanted Intricate Mage-crafted Steel Breastplate.<br><br>Enchantments:<br><br>• Adds +1 Strength to wearer<br>• This breastplate loses durability 10% slower. |
|---|---|

Arthur handed these to the apprentices with instructions to get liners made for them and get them assembled. They nodded vigorously as they looked at the items. They knew they'd get extensive amounts of experience for the task, so they were excited to get to work. Ten helmets in the same style as Samson's followed. The design worked well for protecting the face while not obstructing the view more than necessary.

| Item:<br>Enchanted Intricate Mage-crafted Steel Barbute (Unfinished) | **Armor**: 45<br><br>**Durability**: 110/110<br><br>**Rarity**: Rare |
|---|---|

**Quality:** Exquisite

**Weight:** 2.3 kg

**Slot:** Head

**Traits:** An Intricate Steel Barbute, created using magical techniques and enchanted with special magical power. Combine with leather lining to create Enchanted Intricate Mage-crafted Steel Barbute.

Enchantments:

- 10% decreased chance to be blinded
- This helmet loses durability 10% slower.

Arthur also handed these over to the apprentices, and Samson had a look of deep longing when he laid eyes on them.

Arthur chuckled, "Feel free to swap your breastplate and helmet if you wish. They mirror your equipment, but in steel. When we can dedicate some time, I plan to make you a completely new set of armor with far better enchantments."

Samson sighed, "It'd be useful now, but I understand the time constraint is an issue. I'll use one of each of those when they finish assembling them. I've sent runners to take completed spears to our current guards. The extras are still in the smithy where the apprentices placed them, but I'll take one with me."

"I wouldn't expect any less. With the work here complete, we need to get back to the wall. I have to make some modifications for our defense," Arthur told him.

Samson nodded and walked inside to grab his new spear. He followed Arthur away from the smithy as they traveled back to the wall.

"Do you think we can win?" Samson asked.

"I don't know. You can bet we'll do everything possible to survive," Arthur told him with resolve.

Samson just nodded in response and they continued the rest of the trip in silence. As they neared the wall, Arthur received a message he was waiting on.

*Found the army,* Balair said.

*Army?* Arthur asked in dread.

*Uh, yeah. Can't classify it as less than that from the numbers I saw.* Balair said.

*Damn, how many?* Arthur asked as he continued walking.

*At least five hundred goblins and one hundred orcs,* Balair told him.

Arthur stumbled when he got that message. His eyes widened in fear and Samson saw the expression.

"What's wrong?" Samson asked.

It took Arthur a moment to compose himself when he finally answered. "Balair told me there are at least five hundred goblins and a hundred orcs in the army headed this way," Arthur told the man quietly.

Samson went white as a ghost at the news. "Oh, sweet Goddess, what shall we do?"

"We'll fight them with every underhanded thing I can think of if necessary. I've noticed you haven't used any special abilities or anything. Did you receive any special skills from Goddess Lianna for your Paladin status?" Arthur asked him.

Samson's face changed to a determined look as he answered. "I received two but haven't used them because they have a long cooldown and appear to be for emergencies. One allows me to lift the fighting spirits and capabilities of those near me for twenty minutes. This allows them to fight through minor wounds with ease. My second ability allows me to call divine light to the field of battle and heal those within range of the spell. That one is my most powerful, but it has a cooldown of a week."

"Well, it's good to know you bring some utility with your power. Hold it in reserve until you see fit," Arthur told him.

*How far out was the army?* Arthur asked Balair in his mind.

*At their current pace? I'd say you have a few hours at most.* Balair responded.

"We have to hurry. We only have a few hours until they arrive. I'll probably need the rest of the amulets in town," Arthur told Samson. The man nodded and hurried to find some people to help gather them.

Arthur made it to the gatehouse and a plan formed in his mind. The current wall was right around sixteen-feet high, so it wouldn't be easy for them to climb. The actual problem was the landing behind it was only four feet wide. That didn't give much room to maneuver. The archers needed wider areas they could stand on to focus on firing and not have to worry about falling off the wall.

Arthur also needed more archers but, to do that, he needed more bows. Zeke could only make them so fast, and soon he would need to fight. Arthur had the option of trying his hand at making a steel bow but, without knowing the exact properties required for the spring steel, it'd be almost impossible. The steel needed to have just the right amount of spring to it for a steel bow to work. He also didn't have the time to experiment with metallurgy or enchanting to tweak them until he found something that would work.

Magic would have to play a substantial part in this fight. There was no way around it with the limited weapons they had. He'd find as many volunteers as he could to help hold the village, but there was a chance it wouldn't be enough.

His mind snapped back to the problem at hand, and he considered the platform spacing. His mind settled on making a platform that was the same height as the walking space but was ten feet wide and six feet deep. This would create an area that was ten feet square for archers to work from. He could also incorporate stairs along the backside of the platform for easy access.

With this idea in mind, he started the spell. The stone rose in the designated space. It slowly built up to the correct height, and Arthur could see the stairs taking shape around the edge. When the spell completed, a notification he'd never seen before excited him. As a matter of fact, he'd ignored almost all of his notifications lately.

*You have gained 10,265 total experience in Arcane Smithing and Blacksmithing.*

*Congratulations, you have reached level 15 in Arcane Smithing. Increases the stats on items created using this ability by 28%. Nice mass production run.*

*Congratulations, for reaching level 15 in Arcane Smithing, you have been granted 1500 bonus character experience.*

*You have gained 7,900 total experience in Enchanting.*

*Congratulations, you have reached level 12 in Enchanting. Your enchantments have a 33% decreased mana cost. Impressive work there.*

*You have gained 4,100 total experience in Earth and Fire Magic.*

*You have gained 100 experience in Dimensional Magic.*

*Congratulations, you have created the Combination Spell: Raise Archer Platform. You have gained 500 experience in Earth and Fire Magic for creating an unknown spell.*

*Congratulations, you have created a new Combination Spell. Do you wish to name this new spell? Yes/No.*

*For creating the new Combination Spell: Raise Archer Platform, you have been granted a one-time bonus of 250 Earth and Fire Magic Experience, 250 Personal Experience, and 1 Intellect. Live and be merry.*

| Spell: Raise Archer Platform | |
| --- | --- |
| Requirements: Fire Magic and Earth Magic<br>Mana Cost: 80 MP<br>Cast Time: 10 seconds | Description: Raises a platform that is 10 feet wide, 6 feet deep, and 12 feet tall. This also has a staircase attached that allows access to the platform from the ground level. |
| Mastery Level: 1 | |

Arthur had never discovered a new spell before. The spell itself didn't seem like anything special, but he was sure adding the stairs to the side was something that no one else had included. Most others probably made the entire wall and then just added stairs later. He couldn't think of a reason to name the spell, so he selected *No*. The 1 bonus Intellect was fantastic.

After reviewing the gains he made in the different areas, Arthur decided it was time to pull out the big guns and abuse his power. He needed to create work orders for what he completed amplifying his experience. A work order for delivering the unique game animals, another for the feathers from the harpies, another for installing the gates on the three gatehouses, and then a final work order with the steel spears joined the list of active requests. He would have to wait to claim the rest of the weapons and armor until the apprentices completed them. He set each of these to the standard ten copper reward and turned them in.

*Congratulations, you have completed the Work Order: Game Animals for Alem's Crossing for the following rewards: 10 Copper Coins, 2,000 Sword experience, and 1200 Character experience. (Group Turn-in)*
*Congratulations, you have reached level 7 in Swords. Swing speed with swords increased by 18%. Like you really deserved that!*
*Congratulations, you have completed the Work Order: Feathers for Alem's Crossing for the following rewards: 10 Copper Coins, 2000 Archery experience, and 1200 Character experience. (Group Turn-in)*
*Congratulations, you have progressed to Level 7 in Archery. You are granted an 18% bonus to accuracy. Let it fly!*
*Congratulations, you have completed the Work Order: Complete the Gatehouses for Alem's Crossing for the following rewards: 10 Copper Coins, 2000 Enchanting experience, 2,000 Earth Magic experience, 2,000 Fire Magic experience, and 1400 Character experience.*

*Congratulations, you have reached level 13 in Enchanting. Your enchantments have a 36% decreased mana cost. Impressive work there.*

*Congratulations, you have completed the Work Order: Steel Spears for Alem's Crossing for the following rewards: 10 Copper Coins, 800 Enchanting experience, 800 Arcane Smithing experience, 800 Blacksmithing experience, and 600 Character Experience.*

After dealing with that business, Arthur turned his attention back to the wall. Samson returned to him and brought him more amulets, so he quickly sucked used them to restore the mana reserves of his necklace. He was back at full but also knew there weren't many left to use in an emergency.

He cast his new Raise Archer Platform spell on the other side of the gatehouse to match the original. He then walked down the wall and cast the spell every hundred feet. He did this ten times on each side of the gatehouse to have a good spread of defensive locations. This work netted him another 3,800 Earth and Fire Magic experience. A work order for the platforms netted him another 1,000 experience for Earth and Fire Magic and another 800 character experience. Arthur waved at Samson, and the man hurried over.

"We need to get back to the inn and address the village. They need to know what's coming, and I have to see if we can get any more volunteers," Arthur told him.

"Let's get going then," Samson said.

Returning to the village, Arthur told everyone they passed to meet at the inn. A crowd had already formed by the time they arrived. Arthur walked toward the entrance and saw Allendria standing there waiting for him. He gave her a quick smile and turned to address the village.

"Fellow villagers, I know we've had our share of trouble. The bandit attack is still a fresh memory, but I must call upon you to defend your homes again. Those of us who fought back last time won't be enough this time. A force of five hundred goblins and a hundred orcs are marching for us," Arthur said. As soon as Arthur finished, pandemonium erupted over the entire group.

"Where will we run to?" one person said.

"What will happen if they take the village?" another chimed in.

"Calm down," Arthur told them. "I know that number is alarming, but we have a defensive wall now. This will help us defend against assaults. I want to call for volunteers to defend our village. I've made a handful of weapons for the guards and have extras for any others who wish to fight. Make no mistake, this group of raiders appears to be on a mission and they would have been here regardless of what happened in the past."

Ten more people stepped forward to volunteer to fight. Four were women. Samson took them to the side to get them set up.

"I implore you all to show some faith. We succeeded once against overwhelming odds and shall do so again," Arthur told them confidently. He contemplated where the conversation was going and adjusted his speech a little. Now was the perfect time to push his goal in this world.

"Turn your faith to the Goddess Lianna. She is the one who helped us win the last fight, and she'll help us again. We have her first ordained Paladin, Sir Samson, with us in this fight. We won't lose."

Everyone started murmuring while looking at their fellow villagers. With those words of comfort, a few more people stepped forward and nodded in agreement. Arthur would never turn down a few more hands in a fight.

"Everyone make your way inside. If you can't or won't fight, there'll be plenty of things around the village for you to assist with to help support those who do. Please cooperate with Daniel and those who are coordinating the defensive effort," Arthur told them.

Arthur turned and headed inside. He motioned for the others to follow. Rowan, Samson, Vana, Allendria, Dalia, and Daniel all filed in behind him. The dominant group of decision-makers was present. To his surprise, Balair even squeezed his way into the building when Arthur wasn't paying attention.

"Okay, this could be bad if not handled correctly. I know from the scouting that Vana and I did that they're purposely targeting the village. I also know it's a force numbering around five hundred goblins and a hundred orcs. I know little more than that. Vana, anything to add?" Arthur asked as he looked to the ranger.

"Nothing. You pretty much summed up how screwed we are on your own," she nodded back to him.

"Not helping, Vana," Arthur told her with a huff. "Samson, what can you cover with what you now have?"

Samson considered the question. "I can cover most of the attacking side of the wall for a few hundred yards with ease. I'll need far more weapons and armor to make this work with our new volunteers, but I'll split them into distinct groups. I'll have one set designed to use the spears to push off the walls, another group to respond to any threats that reach the walls with swords, and the last group for archery. The archers can respond to melee combat when needed. I'll get helms to the pikemen since they'll be closest to the wall, and I'll give the sword carrying militia the breastplates for added defense in hand to hand. We sorely need more bows."

"Zeke, is there anything you can do for our bow and arrow problem? I have a feeling we'll need far more arrows and bows than we currently have," Arthur told Zeke.

"The arrows are simple enough to learn. I can teach a team of villagers to make them as long as you can keep a steady supply of arrowheads. The bows are a different matter. There's limited wood here that's suitable for bows. I can make them relatively quick, but I think my efforts are better focused on the walls to repel attackers," Zeke told him.

Arthur considered the problem before settling on a decision. "I have to agree with you, Zeke. We need you on the walls during the attack. I'd like for you to gather a group of people here in the inn first and show them how to make the arrows. Get them started on production and then get to the wall. If we can hold their assault and get a break, I'll need you to make more bows. Luckily, I have more of that yew wood that'd make a suitable candidate for bows. You can use all of it for this."

Zeke nodded his head and ducked away from the group. He walked directly for the door and Arthur assumed the man went to find his workers to make arrows.

"Rowan, preparations so far?" Arthur asked the Smith.

"I've a handful of iron arrowheads in storage that Zeke can use but, based on the numbers you just told me, they're not enough. Since you converted most of the iron to steel, we have had little time to make a lot of items. Our effort was on completing the gates," Rowan told him, sounding disappointed.

"Don't worry Rowan, we'll fix the problem and I don't blame you. None of us expected this to happen. You need to unlock Arcane Smithing sooner than later. If you've been keeping up with your magical training, you should be at a high enough level for me to teach you. We'll just need to wait for a window of time. Until then, I want you to churn out as many blades and arrowheads as possible. Have the apprentices moved to arrowheads and you get some knives and swords churned out. They don't need to be pretty, just functional. Enlist help from villagers to make more handles. We can always reforge them using Arcane Smithing after the fight," Arthur told the man assuredly.

"I'll take care of it," Rowan said as he turned and dashed for the door.

"Daniel, food, and supplies?" Arthur asked.

Daniel looked at his feet for a moment in shame.

"What's wrong?" Arthur asked.

"We have a big problem. We're out of salt," Daniel told him. The man sounded like he would burst into tears.

"No big deal, so we'll have some bland food for a while. Vana and the scouts found some more herbs while we were out, and I have some more seeds for you. We can offset the taste with some of those. It'll be fine," Arthur consoled the innkeeper.

Daniel looked up with confusion in his eyes. "I'm not worried about seasoning food. We can't preserve the meat you brought us because we are out of salt. Most of it will spoil before we can use it."

*That is quite the dilemma.* Salt was a staple here in this world. Food preservation hadn't developed to include freezers. There were multiple solutions he could come up with to solve this problem. One would be a short term and one a long term.

"Don't worry Daniel, get them cut up and processed into usable pieces. I can place them in a dimensional space and it will keep them preserved until we need to use them. It isn't ideal since it requires me to be present to open it for you, but it's a short-term solution. When I have some time, I'll build you a cold storage room to solve this issue," Arthur said.

"Cold storage room? What's that?" Daniel asked.

"Exactly as it sounds. I'll create a room that stays cold all the time and doesn't heat up. It's a common method of preserving food where I'm from. I can make one that just keeps things cool and will preserve them for shorter times. I can also make one that'll make them so cold they freeze and will preserve them for much longer. It'll solve the problem so don't worry. I'll even try to include the design in the new houses we'll be building so people can preserve their own food," Arthur said and quickly waved his hand, "We're getting off track. Long story short, get them ready for use, and let me know. I'll store them and fix the problem later. Keep out what you can use before it goes bad."

Daniel nodded and sighed in relief. "Thanks. I was worried all of your effort on that hunt was gonna go to waste. I'll get back to work so you can take care of the problem."

Arthur nodded as he walked off and turned to Samson and Vana.

"What are we working with Samson?" Arthur asked.

The grizzled man sighed. "A lot of unskilled people and some barely trained guards. I have a strange feeling that'll change in the next few hours."

"I'm sure you're right, but we can hope the enemy will delay when they see the wall. That's new and not something they'll be expecting. It may delay them enough for us to prepare some more. Until then, let's get everyone to the walls. We also need at least one person on the vacant walls to the northwest, south, and east. We don't want them trying to sneak people over the wall in an undefended area," Arthur told him.

"How will they alert people if someone tries? We need a warning signal of some kind," Samson told them.

"Assign a person with Fire Magic and they can send up a jet of flames. It's not the best option, but it should work for now. We'll have to add it to the list of problems to solve as we get some time," Arthur continued. To his amusement, he saw someone he hadn't previously noticed standing there writing exactly that.

Katherine was present for the meeting, and she was diligently noting what he said. She also included things to remind him about later.

"Hi, Kat! Sorry, I didn't see you there. Hope you can keep all this straight so we can address it as we find time," Arthur told her with a smile.

"Thanks. I am the Assistant Mayor after all," she said with a soft chuckle. "I plan on getting you back for that somehow, by the way."

Arthur was pleased to see the woman hadn't lost her humor in their current situation.

"Vana, you and the scouts will have to be on the wall and we'll ensure you three have the best arrows and bows available."

"We'll be ready, don't worry about us. Hopefully, Samson's new volunteers can swing a sword without killing each other," she said with a chuckle.

*She has a point.* Balair sent to him.

*Good to see you paying attention to the situation. Figured you'd have run off to hide by now.* Arthur said to the little guy.

*Psh, I'm not scared of some puny goblins. I also don't want Calfuray to kill me if she found out I abandoned you.* Balair sent with a shiver.

Arthur chuckled at that before Dalia entered the conversation.

"So what can the lady of the village do for you?" she asked with a smirk.

"I'm glad you asked. I need a figure of authority and grace next to me. I have a feeling we'll get a demand at some point in time and you'll need to be present to represent the people of our village. Until then, try to keep everyone calm and focused on their tasks. We need the population to stay close to the inn. If an emergency comes up, they need to retreat to the inn quickly," Arthur told Dalia.

"Just send word if you need me for negotiations. I'll try to keep them calm," she told him.

Arthur turned to the last person he hadn't addressed and smiled.

"Allendria, I think you'd be best suited to organizing our construction crews for quick repairs and changes to our defense. Naturally, you'll be fighting during the attacks, but your knowledge of magic would help keep them in line," Arthur told her.

"Of course, Lord Mayor," she said with a smirk and a mock bow.

As soon as the words left her mouth, another person came barreling into the room.

"Lord Mayor, the raiders are within sight of the wall!" he called as he spotted Arthur.

Arthur nodded at the messenger and turned to Samson.

"It's time to go," he told the burly man.

"They'll feel the wrath of a paladin," Samson said grimly.

# Chapter 10


*Raiders at the Door*

Arthur, Samson, and Allendria raced from the room, followed closely by Balair. As soon as Balair cleared the doors, he took to the air, dust swirling from the beat of his wings as he flew for the approaching army. The rest of them ran to the wall at a steady speed. The steady clomp of their feet sounded as they kept a pace that wouldn't drain their Stamina by the time they arrived.

As they neared the wall, Arthur noticed a lot of work was complete. Soldiers lined up along the wall, decked in the newly created gear. The first row carried steel spears and wore helmets while he saw the breastplates and short swords on the second set of guards. The combination of fighters should provide an excellent amount of coverage for the wall.

Arthur noticed more holding bows. He was sure that every bow in the village currently sat on top of the wall, minus his. His feet felt heavy as he ascended the stairs. The two other men at the top looked to him with surprise.

"Lord Mayor, what are you doing up here?" the first asked.

"It's just Arthur. None of this Lord Mayor nonsense. I'm up here to fight, what else would I be doing up here?" Arthur asked the man.

The man just stared at him with an open mouth and couldn't come up with a response. After a few moments, he just nodded and returned to his spot, awaiting a command. Arthur walked to the crenellations and looked through the open slot.

On the edge of the horizon, he could see a giant blob cresting the hill. It was definitely the raiders they were expecting. They watched as the force approached in the distance. Arthur glanced around and saw the nervous looks on the faces of those near him. Samson had a gruff look on his face as he waited on the archery platform on the other side of the gatehouse.

Arthur noticed the approaching army stopped shortly after cresting the ridge. He smiled inwardly as he knew it was from the surprise of finding the village walled off. Unless they planned on assaulting any of the major cities that had established walls already, there'd be no reason for them to consider scouting the targets. Tiny villages in the open countryside should be absolutely no challenge for a force of their size.

Their delay didn't last long, and within a quarter of an hour they were back on the march. Their speed was noticeably slower than before. They looked to be making a more cautious approach seeing there were unknown defenses in place.

*At least they're not complete idiots.* The raiders stopped when they reached a space roughly one hundred yards from the wall. Arthur heard some grunting and saw some of the larger orcs conferring with each other. Unfortunately, he was too far to make out what they were saying.

*They appear nervous,* Balair sent with a chuckle. *I guess their free conquest around the countryside wasn't supposed to include a defensive wall.*

Arthur giggled at the little dragon's comment. *I'd imagine you're correct.*

The volume of the argument increased but was distorted because of the distance. To his surprise, two more orcs approached, but these looked much different. They were not quite as large as the others, but they wore long robes made of a deep purple fabric. They didn't have hoods on, but dark purple paint streaked their faces. Arthur couldn't be sure, but he believed they were casters of some kind.

His gaze swept through the rest of the forces, looking for others he may have missed. Those were the only two he saw wearing purple robes, but other fighters showed signs of being casters. Arthur looked at weapons as an indicator. Anything that carried a small knife or staff, he mentally labeled as a caster instead of a fighter. Fighters loved their larger weapons. There were a couple that had dual blades that he marked as sneaky types instead of casters. In his quick sweep, he counted thirty goblins, and twenty additional orcs who he thought would be magic users.

Arthur turned to look around him. He spotted Samson and Vana near to him on the platforms across the gatehouse. To his left, he saw James on the platform next to him, preparing for the fight. Samson glanced his way and Arthur waved to get his attention. Samson looked confused for a moment until Arthur motioned for him to meet him behind the gate. Noticing Samson and Arthur meeting up, Vana joined them. They all raced to the ground behind the gate.

"What? They could attack at any moment!" Samson was furious.

"I know that, but they have two odd figures dressed in robes I have no doubt are casters. I also did a quick look through the army, and I believe there to be roughly thirty goblins and twenty orcs who also have magical abilities," Arthur told them.

Samson became quiet after that. To Arthur's relief, Allendria approached as they were talking.

"Allendria, what's the best way to counter other casters in a fight?" Arthur asked. "They seem to have a decent amount of them."

After a few moments, she settled on an answer.

"No one here really knows any warding or shielding spells, so the best way to counter their magic is by overpowering their element or negating it with an opposing element. I'm able to do this, and you should also," she said as she looked to Arthur. "I don't know about any of our others."

"So, countering?" Arthur asked.

Allendria let out a quick sigh. "It's what you unknowingly did with the harpy. Use an elemental weakness against the spell. In the case of the electricity, you used earth that would negate its effect. If they tried to throw a block of ice at you, then you could burn it away with a blast of fire before it reached you. Overpowering can be difficult and is more of a mana struggle. If they manipulated the earth somewhere, then you would influence the same space with your magic and override what they changed using your own mana. Those typically end when one person gives up, or one runs out of mana."

Arthur nodded at that. "That's fine. Allendria, gather any mana amulets are near that may have charged since I drained them earlier. You can use that excess mana to help you counter spells. I have decent capacity and have recharged a bit of my amulet in the time we've been planning. You and I are on spell duty, and I'll use my bow in between. Everyone else, focus on keeping them off the wall. Vana, I plan for you to take out their casters when you spot them. Look for any with odd colorings on them or wielding small daggers or staves."

Everyone nodded, and each raced back for their positions. Allendria ran for the platform on the other side of Vana. It would allow them to cover a larger space as long as they kept enough mana to fight back.

Arthur reached the top of the wall and saw the orcs still conferring while the goblins looked around, confused. One orc in a purple robe stepped into the middle and angrily slammed a staff to the ground. Shadows seeped from the site of impact and crawled toward the legs of the surrounding figures. All the nearby orcs started backing away from the shadows in fear. The creature said something in an angry tone, and all the rest just nodded while keeping their eyes down.

The orcs turned their attention to the robed figure as it gave commands. At least, Arthur thought they were commands. After half a minute, the orcs spread back out among their goblins. The units gathered around their orc commanders and listened carefully. It confused Arthur to see some of the forces of goblins leave the group and start preparing a campsite. Two of the units, which comprised two orcs and twenty-five goblins each, turned and lined up in formation, facing the city walls. A notification startled Arthur.

*You have entered an Active Raid Zone!*
*This raid zone comprises the Army of Darkness and the Defenders of Alem's Crossing. Aiding either side in this contest will offer rewards when the raid completes.*

| Repel the Raid | |
|---|---|
| Requirements: Participate in actions to directly or indirectly influence the outcome of the raid. Rewards: 15,000 experience, 3,000 Unassigned Skill Experience, 5 Talent Points | Description: A new raid has started near Alem's Crossing. Aid either side in the fight. If the side you assist survives the raid, you receive the rewards. |
| Do you wish to accept the quest? Yes/No. | |

*Another activated quest? It disturbed him since it left the option open to assist either side.* With no other choice, he selected *Yes*. The quest window dropped, and he saw the look of wonder in the eyes around him as they received the same message.

It was moments later that the realization hit him. If the quest activated and it listed the zone as a raid, that meant the goblins planned to attack. Arthur turned to Samson.

"Get them ready! They're about to charge!" he yelled.

"Everyone, look alive. Prepare for assault. Let arrows fly as soon as they're within your range," Samson yelled down the wall.

The force in front of them moved toward the wall. They started at a slow trot but quickly morphed into a full-speed dash across the grassy meadow. Arthur's bow was up with an arrow ready.

When the enemies entered his range, he activated Aim Shot, and his vision zoomed in. He picked the lead goblin and aimed for the base of its neck. The arrow raced forward as he released and punched through the bottom of the goblin's throat, continuing until it embedded itself into its spine. Its fellow fighters trampled it as if fell to the ground.

Arthur dismissed the damage notifications. There would be far too many to keep up with before this fight was over. He drew another arrow and activated Aim Shot again. This time he took a goblin directly in its heart. His speed was fast enough that by the time the shaft reached the target, he almost had the next one on the string and ready to fire.

He scanned the field in between shots while he mechanically pulled out the next arrow and nocked it. Arrows flew from multiple places. Vana, James, and Arthur were the only ones that could hit them at this distance. Some tried, but their arrows fell short or veered wide of the mark. As the goblins got closer, more arrows hit their intended targets. The inexperience of the defenders was showing, though. Many of the attacks were just hitting limbs or glancing off the enemy and only causing minor wounds.

As the goblins closed within thirty feet of the wall, more arrows found their targets. By the time the first goblin reached the wall, he guessed almost half lay dead on the field. Arthur killed four, and Vana took out five. James killed three, and Arthur saw that Zeke had also arrived at the wall and removed another two. The other guards accounted for the remainder of the kills

Before the goblins reached the wall, one orc bellowed a command. Arthur's mind registered the words and translated them for him.

"Fall back!"

Most of the army turned tail and ran for the main raiding force. A few foolish goblins kept charging in some kind of frenzy and launched themselves at the walls. To their disappointment, the walls were too tall and too smooth for them to climb using their natural abilities. They tried to scrabble along the face of the wall, but since they made it of solid, fused stone and not of individual stones mortared together, they couldn't find purchase on the face.

Arthur looked over the edge and sent an arrow with an Aim Shot into one of the scrabbling goblins. The other two fell with arrows from Zeke and Vana, respectively. Arthur took down two more as they retreated. All said and done, the village killed thirty-eight of the fifty goblins from the force.

A quick glance at his notifications showed something odd. He received 1,050 experience in Archery and Aim Shot for the kills of the five, level fifteen goblins bringing his Aim Shot to level 3. His personal experience was off, though. It showed he gained 3,850 total experience for the fight. He dug through the details to see what the issue was. His five personal kills awarded him the full experience, but it penalized the raid kills from those on his side of the fight. He only received 40% of the total experience from kills he didn't directly attack.

Arthur couldn't complain about that development too much. He couldn't expect it to let him keep all of that experience with so many fighting. If that was the case, he'd expect leaders to go to war just to mooch experience from their follower's kills. This world would be a never-ending war zone.

To Arthur's surprise, a group of orcs approached the forces fleeing the battle. Without a word, they drew swords and swiftly removed the heads of the orcs that led the retreat. The goblins that returned with them all looked frightened, but the orcs returned to what they were doing.

Arthur assumed they spared them since it was the orcs who gave the order to retreat. Apparently, losing wasn't acceptable to these creatures. As he watched, the raiders continued to spread out and set up their camp. A few haphazard-looking tents sprung into existence around the field and fires were lit throughout the camp.

The orcs stayed to one side of the camp while the goblins stayed on the other. The tents were all used by the orc commanders. As Arthur watched the events unfold, the entire group of orcs gathered together and formed a circle in their camp. They sat down in a cross-legged position and waited.

Their actions extremely confused Arthur and he couldn't figure out what exactly they were doing. While he waited, Samson approached him.

"Are they calling it quits?" the paladin called up.

"Looks like they are for now. I plan to monitor them for a little while to see if I can figure out what they're doing," Arthur told him.

Samson nodded and turned to leave. He issued orders and pulled most of the forces off of the wall. There was a guard force left behind but it was for quick response and alarm, not for a full-scale fight. Allendria walked up the stairs and joined Arthur on the platform.

"Any idea what's going on?" she asked him.

"Honestly, I was hoping you might," he told her.

"Not sure. I know they commonly gather and decide on actions as groups. It isn't uncommon for them to have nominated leaders among their fighters, but they'll still make major decisions as a group. The leaders are typically in charge of combat scenarios after they decide a strategy," she explained.

"I guess they're preparing to have a strategy meeting then," Arthur said.

They stayed on the wall and continued to observe the force. The orcs remained seated and were relatively quiet, while the goblin force was noisy and constantly scurrying around. After about fifteen minutes of nothing, Arthur heard Allendria let out a sharp hiss. He turned to look at her and saw her gaze directed toward the tree line.

Arthur followed her line of sight and his vision locked onto what she'd seen. Three figures approached the army on foot. They all had tall and lithe builds but, to Arthur's surprise, they all had the skin color of Allendria.

"Allendria, who are they?" Arthur asked in concern.

"I can't tell yet. Give me a few minutes," she told him.

They both watched as the group approached the orcs. None of the orcs or goblins moved to intercept them and merely continued to do nothing as they approached. The man in the lead continued walking, stepped over the shoulder of one of the orcs, and entered the center of the gathering. The other two waited outside the edge. To Arthur's surprise, the Dark Elf held his hand to the side and a chair of stone quickly sprouted from the ground where he stood. He then took a seat and looked at those around him.

"What in the name of the Fallen One is he doing here?" Allendria spat.

"Who is it?" Arthur asked the now furious woman.

"That's Lyrinth, the right-hand man of my uncle," she told him with venom in her voice.

"The same uncle that was attempting to overthrow your father?" Arthur asked in concern.

"The very same. Although, I fear they've probably succeeded by now. Especially if they're with this force."

"So he's a mage?" Arthur asked her to keep her talking. He didn't want her to spiral into a self-induced depression.

"Yes, he is. Primarily Earth and Fire Magic. He's fond of using that Earthen Chair spell to show off like it's some impressive feat," she said while smiling at Arthur. "You should make that spell with a fancier chair. If I know him, when we repel their next assault, he'll want to meet for negotiations. It'd be hilarious to see the look on his face when he tries to show off and you outdo him."

Arthur laughed wholeheartedly at that. "You can be truly devious when you want to be. I'll make it a priority."

*A flash of red caught his eye in the sky and drew his attention. Where were you during the fight?*

He got a sense of irritation from the little dragon as he answered. *I've been flying around the walls ensuring none of them try to sneak in.*

*Thank you, Balair. I'm pleased to see you taking some initiative.* Arthur told him.

*Meh was bored and needed to stretch the wings.* The little guy said as he tried to brush off the compliment.

Arthur turned to Allendria. "I can't hear what they're saying but I have a feeling it may take them a while. I'm sure he plans to ream them out because of their failures, and then they'll develop some kind of attack plan. Fortunately, they haven't seen our magic in use yet. As far as they know, we're just normal people, guarding their village with archers. I think they'll devise a plan with some small ladders and shields to get a force close enough to scale the walls. I also estimate they'll bring around a hundred, maybe two on the next assault. They won't commit the entire force to an unknown scenario, but they'll commit at least that much. We only killed them with arrows, so they'll believe themselves superior if they can counter them. We have work to do," Arthur told her.

Arthur and Allendria turned away from the force and walked off the wall. They traveled to a small gathering of people behind the gate. Samson and Vana were there, so Arthur waved them over. The two approached them with eager looks on their faces. He could tell they wanted to know the plan.

"We have a bit of an odd situation. I don't know if any of you saw, but there's a group of three Dark Elves conferring with the orcs out there," Arthur told them.

They both looked to Allendria quickly before realizing what they were doing and returned their focus to Arthur.

"Allendria told me that the Dark Elf in charge, named Lyrinth, has close ties with her uncle. I also know her uncle has been working to gain influence within the Dark Elven society, so he may have far more followers than she is aware of," Arthur continued.

They both nodded. "So… where does that leave us?" Vana asked.

Arthur raised his eyebrows and let out a breath of air. "That leaves us in a fight with a bunch of orcs and goblins. The Dark Elves may decide to fight, eventually. I anticipate them to come up with a plan to mitigate our effectiveness with arrows and try to attack again with a slightly larger force. We didn't show any of our magic, so they don't know our full capabilities. It's possible they'll just commit to an all-out attack, but I suspect the Dark Elves are controlling this situation closely. Keep in mind, that's all based on what I'd consider," Arthur told them.

"So… we have no idea what will happen is what you're saying," Samson said with a sigh.

"You got it," Arthur told him with a clap on the shoulder. "We just need to prepare for anything. I need to go check with Daniel to see how the villagers are doing, and also check on our arrow supply. I have a sneaking suspicion we'll need more, so I'll need to make more arrowheads while I'm there."

"What do we do about the field of battle?" Samson asked with concern.

Arthur considered the question. There were still plenty of excellent resources left out there on the dead goblins. Many of them used iron weapons, and he knew that their supply of iron and steel was dwindling. They could also recover some serviceable arrows from the field of battle.

"Let's wait for nightfall. A handful of us can go to the field to scavenge for useful materials. I'm hoping they don't stage a raid in the dark, but we'll know for sure as the day drags on," Arthur told them.

They nodded in agreement. A voice in his head interrupted any further conversation.

*Two groups are approaching. One is trying to sneak up to the southern wall while the other is launching for the northwestern wall. Neither are aiming at a gatehouse.* Balair told him.

As soon as the message went through, he turned to the others.

"Samson, get a group and head for the northwestern wall. A party of goblins is trying to launch a sneak attack. Vana and Allendria you come with me. Another group is headed for the southern wall. Samson, look for Balair in the sky, he'll guide you to where they're trying to assault," Arthur told them hurriedly.

"I need two archers who can run fast with me. Right now!" he yelled at the people milling around by the wall.

They all looked a little startled but two of them quickly stepped forward to follow them. To his surprise, Paul was one of them. Chuckling to himself, he turned and they headed for the southern wall. Samson issued orders and gathered his crew.

Arthur and his new group dashed across the open ground and stayed near the wall. The land was flat and even out near the wall so it made the travel easier. It also had the advantage of being pretty empty. There were a couple of fields inside the walls that were now showing plants in them from his adventures into the forest but nowhere near what they needed yet.

They sprinted as quickly as possible until
their Stamina was low and would then slow down
to a maintainable jog to let their Stamina
slowly trickle back up. Once it was close to
full they took off in the dash again. There
was a good amount of distance between the
trees and the wall, so Balair's warning gave
them some time. It also helped that the
goblins weren't aware they'd been spotted, so
they were still trying to sneak up to the
wall.

Arthur saw Balair circling the wall ahead
of them and continued in that direction.

*You're supposed to show Samson where the
attack is on the other wall*, Arthur said to
the dragonling.

*I can see his group. They still have some
distance to go. I wanted to alert you guys
first. I'll head to him when he gets closer*

As soon as he reached that section of the
wall, he cast his Raise Archer Platform spell
and climbed the newly made stairs to the wall.
Looking through the crenellations, he could
see the clumsy goblins as they comically
ducked from tiny spots of concealment to the
next.

*How many do you think there are?* Arthur
asked Balair.

*I see around twenty at a quick glance, but
they're staying close-packed. I don't want to
come down any closer. Up this high, I should
look like a normal bird and not set off
suspicion.* Balair told him.

*Thanks. Can you go to the other spot to
help Samson find his way? We'll take care of
these guys.* He told Balair.

*Sure thing. Hey, do I get a raise for my
services?* Balair asked with a grin.

*Why not? Tell you what, I'll double your pay.* Arthur told the little guy cheerfully.

*But I don't make anything…* Balair sent back, confused.

*Fine, I'll triple it.* Arthur said with an internal giggle.

The dragon preened at the comment for a moment, and then his mind caught up. *Hey wait, that's still the same thing!*

*Go help Samson and quit wasting time.* Arthur told the little guy.

*Sheesh, fine.* He responded and flew off in a huff.

*I probably should reward him for his help when all this is over.* Arthur thought to himself.

He walked back off of the platform and back to the ground. He went a hundred feet to each side of him and created more archery platforms. Returning to the group, he laid out the plan.

"This'll be pretty simple. Vana, you take the platform on the right. Allendria, you're with me in the middle. You two," Arthur said, looking at Paul and the other guard, "take the platform on the left. Wait for them to get within range, and I'll call the signal to fire. Fill them with arrows as quickly as possible. I plan on letting them get a little closer before signaling to shoot. I want them to commit to the attack and not have time to retreat before we kill them."

They all nodded in agreement and ran to their positions. Arthur returned to his lookout atop the wall, and Allendria joined beside him.

"Need me to do anything?" she asked him.

"Only in an emergency. I want to keep our magic concealed with these smaller groups. This shows we need our guards set up to watch the walls sooner than later. I know I tasked Samson with it, but we didn't have enough time prior to the attack to get them in place," Arthur explained.

They stood on the wall and leaned into each other for some quiet comfort. They remained there until Arthur noticed the group closing in. When they reached a hundred yards out, he looked to the groups on each side of him and signaled for them to get their bows ready and nock an arrow.

He studied the enemies as they approached and counted sixteen goblins and one orc. They tried to stay low and approach quietly but were doing a terrible job. They jumped from low spot to low spot, but the land itself was relatively flat. There wasn't much concealment by the time they were one hundred feet away, so they rose and sprinted full speed toward the wall.

"Fire at will!" Arthur yelled as he pulled back his arrow and activated Aim Shot.

His vision flew forward as he sighted on the nearest goblin. The arrow released and, without hesitation, another took its place. The motions were almost mechanical to him as he continued to fire off arrows at the attacking force. Goblins dropped quickly to the onslaught, and he got fed up with the nonsense of it all. He spotted the orc charging in, its eyes glowing red with what Arthur could only assume was some type of bloodlust ability. They were close enough now that Arthur felt like he was standing directly in front of the orc when activating Aim Shot. He released the arrow, and it found the mark he hoped for, directly in the orc's left eye. The bulky creature stiffened for a moment and then dropped to the ground, twitching.

The rest of the goblins near the orc panicked and began running in all directions. This made them even easier to pick off. Before long, only one of the ugly things remained alive. To Arthur's disappointment, the thing ran away from the village and was too far out of range. It may actually help them if it reported their total failure to the main army so they wouldn't try this tactic again. If they made an attack like this with the entire force from different directions, they could very well win the fight.

Arthur turned to look at the rest of the defenders and motioned for them all to meet on the ground. As they all made it to the bottom of their respective stairs, Arthur immediately started laying out a plan.

"Magnificent work on the defense. They were testing us, I'm sure of it. We have little time to waste. You," Arthur said, pointing at the guard with them whose name he didn't know, "Stay here on the wall and make sure none try to return. If you spot anything, send up a burst of flame. I'll have Balair keep an eye out for your signal. The rest of us will race for the other invasion point to help Samson. I'll have him send someone to relieve you once things have calmed down."

The guard nodded and the rest of them left at full speed, headed for the northwest section of the wall. Arthur saw Balair circling above their destination. They cut directly across the clearing and skirted the edge of the village to make the quickest time possible to reach their target location.

Their haste was unnecessary in the end. They arrived in time to find Samson and his group descending from the narrow walkway around the wall. Without Arthur here, they hadn't been able to take advantage of larger archery platforms. The walkway on the wall was still barely wide enough to stand on and shoot arrows. Samson saw their group coming and walked to meet them.

"You get them all or did they run?" Arthur asked Samson.

"Got most of them. Three made off during the attack before we could take them down. I mainly just watched the action. Hell, Vana did most of the killing. She's a damned impressive woman," the man said with a hint of admiration in his voice.

Vana walked up as he was making his statement and had the grace to blush at the compliment.

"Thanks, Samson. You're not so bad to watch yourself," she told him with a wink.

The look that Arthur saw on Samson's face almost made him burst with laughter. His face went slack at the surprise of her being near and started turning a little red himself. He still grinned at her before he turned his focus back to Arthur. Arthur noticed his gaze lingering before he turned back to him and knew Samson was interested in more than just her fighting skill.

"Let's regroup at the inn. We'll need something to eat and have to come up with a plan," he addressed the group and then turned to Samson. "I left one guard I took with me to watch the section of wall we defended. You should choose someone to stay here. I'll make some platforms for them to have a more comfortable watch."

The Paladin nodded and went about issuing orders while Arthur walked to the wall. Four spell casts later and this stretch of wall was the proud new owner of four archery platforms, each spaced roughly one-hundred feet apart. Between these four and the four he cast where his group fought, he netted an additional 1,520 experience in Earth and Fire Magic.

*Do me a favor and keep an eye on the surrounding area until we come up with a plan, will ya?* He asked Balair.

*Fine.* He answered in a huff. *Can't stay up here forever without a break, so hurry.*

Arthur and the group weaved through the village and made for the inn. Daniel waited outside for them as they approached.

"Just who I needed to see. We need the village leaders together for a strategy meeting. Can you get them?" Arthur asked the innkeeper.

He looked at Arthur for a moment, then replied, "Done."

Arthur gave him a confused look as Daniel gestured to the inn. Arthur let out a chuckle as he realized the leaders were already inside. A gathering of nervous faces confronted him as he entered the building.

# Chapter 11

*A Matter of Planning*

The small group of faces waited patiently as Arthur traipsed over to the table they all gathered around. Samson, Vana, and Allendria entered with him and took seats nearby. As soon as his butt touched the chair, the frantic questions peppered him all at once.

"How many are there?"

"Did they leave?"

"Are they still here?"

"Can we beat them?"

Arthur couldn't begin to guess which question came from who. He held up his hands for quiet and waited until everyone noticed the gesture and calmed down.

"Hold off on the questions until I've explained what happened," Arthur told them with a sigh.

Some of them jumped to their feet, eager for news, and now regained their composure and sat back down. Arthur stuck to the facts and explained the force they were facing. He described the initial attack and told them he was sure it was just to test their defenses. The two groups that attempted the sneak attack wrapped up his report. Their faces told him what he needed to know about their level of alarm.

"It's good that we've repelled them, but I believe they'll try to come up with a strategy to negate our arrows. Not sure how they would accomplish it, but my guess would be shields of some kind. Luckily, they don't know we have magic. We'll hold that back until absolutely necessary. Any ideas on how to deter the army? My biggest concern is them trying to sneak around to undefended portions of the walls," Arthur said.

"Decoys?" Dalia asked.

"What are you referring to?" Arthur asked.

"Set up decoys along the wall. We could set up fake people along the crenellations in hopes they'll avoid the surrounding walls. It doesn't even need to be very detailed. Just something that vaguely looks like a head in between a crenellation. Spread them out randomly along the wall, and maybe they'll all focus on the main gate instead."

"I like it! Samson, any idea on how to make it work?" Arthur asked the captain.

"Magic is the only way I can think of. We don't have enough spare resources to do it any other way. There's also not enough wood lying around for stakes to put anything on. Could you or our construction teams make something with stone? Maybe a long stem from the wall and then put a face shape on top. If their magic is good enough, they could probably make it look realistic," the big man responded.

"I think the construction crews can handle that. Their skill with stone has increased, and they were due to start wall expansion work soon, anyway. Having them work along the wall and make these decoys would be a perfect use of their talent," Allendria chimed in.

"Great. Allendria, can you set them up to start that right after we finish here? We can get mana necklaces to them as needed," Arthur said.

She nodded in confirmation, and he turned his attention to Daniel.

"How's the food prep going?"

"Good enough. I pulled in all the extra help I could find and got most of it done. We've set aside what we need for a while, but there's a lot you need to store."

Arthur nodded at that. "I'll take care of that as soon as we finish here."

"Dalia, how are people reacting so far?" Arthur asked.

"Better than I expected to be honest. I thought we'd have a few going crazy with the situation, but most seem to be eerily calm. I'll keep an eye on them."

"Thanks," Arthur told her as a thought came to mind.

*I don't suppose you have something to do with that?* Arthur thought toward the Goddess Lianna.

*Possibly… they are living in a village under my direct influence after all.* She said with a mischievous sound to her voice.

Her response startled him. Arthur breathed a sigh of relief that there was one less problem to worry about.

*Not that I'm complaining, but how can we talk directly?* Arthur asked her.

*Influence, silly. When you first arrived, my power here was almost nonexistent. As you further my goals, I gain more of a foothold and can do more directly.*

*Thank you.*

"Samson, can we get a few scavenging teams together? I'd like to go out after dark and see what weapons and items we can recover off the dead goblins and orcs by the walls. Preferably before the other goblins get the same idea."

"I'll get some men lined up."

"Let's take a break, get some food, and then get to work. I hope to use what time I can the rest of the day preparing for a siege. Rowan, we'll be working in the forge. I need to teach you how to forge with your magic," Arthur said with finality.

They all nodded agreement and took a seat. Paula and Trisha entered the room and brought in bowls of food. Another savory stew of some kind. Arthur was fond of stew but would love a nice steak and some fresh bread. In the meantime, he focused on eating so they could get to work.

The meal wrapped up quickly as everyone rushed to finish their food and filed out of the room to start their tasks. Arthur stood up and nodded to Rowan. The two men left the inn and walked toward the blacksmith shop. Arthur caught sight of Balair scurrying along behind them.

They passed Allendria as she gathered the construction teams to leave for the wall. When Arthur first met her, she was a secluded and antisocial person. She was coming into her own now, and her voice took on a more authoritative tone. Instead of getting caught up in his musings, they sped up their trip. Time was not on their side.

As soon as they arrived at the blacksmith shop, Rowan started issuing orders to the apprentices. They looked exhausted but jumped to work anyway. They brought stacks of metal ingots out, and the forges roared to life.

"What level are your Earth and Fire Magic skills up to now?" Arthur asked the sizeable man.

"My Earth is up to 10, and the Fire is at 12," he told him with a half-grin.

"That was awfully quick. How'd you manage that?" Arthur asked in surprise.

"I've been using them to augment my forging ability. Heating metals, using Weak Flame to help me shape, I'm honestly surprised I haven't accidentally discovered Arcane Smithing myself already. Can't figure out what I'm missing. That and I've been getting boosts to the experience with the bathhouse and from work orders."

Arthur considered all the information, and it all made sense. At least Rowan was smart enough to use every advantage he could think of.

"Based on what you told me, you're only missing one real element of the spell. If you already use your Fire Magic to heat the metal and Earth Magic to shape it, you're just missing the intent. My guess is, you heat the metal, then slowly push and pull the metal into shape, sometimes using your hammer for adjustments?" Arthur asked.

"That's about it. What'd I miss?"

"For Arcane Smithing, you don't just push the metal to shape, you have to focus on the exact outcome you wish to see. Picture the item you wish to make exactly as you want it made in your mind, then use the Earth Magic to make the item conform to that shape in one solid pass. When you accomplish that, the skill will become yours. Just like your other spells, it requires a specific goal to trigger the spell completion."

"Well, I'll be damned. Something that simple, and yet I never considered it. I'll try it," Rowan told him.

"Try making something simple like a basic dagger. After you do it a couple of times, it becomes easier. You also want something easier to unlock the skill and gain the spell, so you don't accidentally run out of mana for larger projects."

Rowan nodded at that and turned to the stack of metals. He grabbed one of the remaining iron ingots and tossed it into the fire. Burning mana early in the process to heat the metal wouldn't help him learn the forging spell and the subskill.

Arthur walked over to the pile, grabbed two ingots of steel, and tossed them in the fire. He was past due for an upgrade. His first item would be a new sword. His sword wasn't terrible, but compared to the level of things he could make now, it was a joke.

Settling on a new design took some thought. His current longsword wasn't an ideal design. It was hard to wield at its maximum effectiveness one-handed, and his fighting style used a longsword and a dagger together. If he truly hoped to become a Spell Blade when he reached level twenty, he'd need a weapon that'd work well with that style. With this information in mind, it caused him to settle on an arming sword. It was the standard style of old school knights back on Earth and designed for one-handed use. He wouldn't have as much reach as his current longsword, but he could live with that since it'd be easier for him to swing at higher speeds.

He pictured the blade at thirty inches long and then imagined the tang tapering to the correct size. A smile came to his face as he thought of the guard and pommel style he wanted to use for the blade. The design for the pommel made him change to focus on the tang itself. He would blend some old school and some new school forging here. Instead of relying on heat and peening the pommel on, he would put threads on it. Modern-day blacksmiths on Earth would use this method by cutting the threads on the tang with a die and then tapping the threads into their pommels. This design would also allow him to take the weapon apart if he needed to repair or replace anything. The last detail was the fuller along the middle of the blade on both sides. With the design in mind, he lifted the steel ingots from the fire with his magic and cast his Arcane Forging spell.

The metal flowed and stretched into the base shape. The familiar line of power moved over the blade, and Arthur watched in fascination. The tip quickly formed, and then cascaded down to show the bevels of the edge. The power worked to the end of the metal as the tang narrowed and the threads wound along the rod. His image was sharp in his mind, so the end of the tang looked like fine threads from a bolt. The piece cooled and fell into his hands. The sheen of the metal looked great, and the piece sported a smooth polish.

*You have gained 50 experience in Earth Magic and Fire Magic for successfully casting Combination Spell: Arcane Forging.*
*Congratulations, you have successfully created Intricate Mage-crafted Steel Arming Sword Blade. You have gained 225 experience in Arcane Smithing and Blacksmithing for creating this item.*

| Item:<br>Intricate Mage-crafted Steel Arming Sword Blade | **Attack:** 18-24<br><br>**Durability:** 150/150<br><br>**Rarity:** Uncommon<br><br>**Quality:** Exquisite<br><br>**Weight:** 0.7 kg<br><br>**Slot:** Crafting Item |
| --- | --- |

|  | **Traits:** An Intricate Steel Arming Sword Blade, created using magical techniques. This blade will have more capacity for absorbing magical power. Combine with handle components to assemble an Intricate Mage-crafted Steel Arming Sword. |
| --- | --- |

The base stats weren't bad, but he'd have to come up with a suitable set of enchantments for it. There was no point in half-assing the design this time. With an army at the wall, he needed the best weapon he could get his hands on. Instead of shifting his focus to enchanting the blade, he finished the pieces of the handle.

The next piece to work on was the guard. Arthur grabbed another ingot of steel and went over the design in his head, ironing out the details. With the picture in mind, he set to work. As soon as the steel was hot enough, he lifted it out of the fire and cast his Arcane Forging spell. The metal flowed and shifted to the general shape. This guard started as a rough "U," then the details filled in as the line moved across it. The power moved, and Arthur smiled as his design came to shape. The features on the piece were breathtaking as it dropped into his hand.

*You have gained 50 experience in Earth Magic and Fire Magic for successfully casting Combination Spell: Arcane Forging.*

*Congratulations, you have successfully
created Exceptional Mage-crafted Steel Wing
Guard. You have gained 80 experience in Arcane
Smithing and Blacksmithing for creating this
item.*

| Item:<br>Exceptional Mage-crafted Steel Wing Guard | **Durability:** 85/85<br><br>**Rarity:** Uncommon<br><br>**Quality:** Exquisite<br><br>**Weight:** 0.3 kg<br><br>**Slot:** Crafting Item<br><br>**Traits:** An Exceptional Steel Wing Guard, created using magical techniques. This guard will have more capacity for absorbing magical power. |
| --- | --- |

A smile came to Arthur's face as he marveled at the guard. It was a piece of intricate beauty. Dragon wings of steel extended away from the central slot for the blade to slide through. The centerpiece of the guard looked like the scaled hide of Calfuray. The only things that stood out were two slight depressions on each side of the guard near the center. Arthur left these to house gems to use to power enchantments. It was marvelous work that would've required a master crafter on Earth days to carve by hand. He reverently set the piece to the side.

The pommel was up next, so he tossed another ingot in the fire. This would match the guard, but instead of the dragon wings, he pictured a majestic dragon's head. The eyes remained empty spaces to house further jewels as he saw fit. The metal rose from the fire and the spell cast. The line of power flowed, and, again, the finished pommel fell into his eagerly waiting hand.

*You have gained 50 experience in Earth Magic and Fire Magic for successfully casting Combination Spell: Arcane Forging.*
*Congratulations, you have successfully created Exceptional Mage-crafted Steel Dragon-headed Pommel. You have gained 75 experience in Arcane Smithing and Blacksmithing for creating this item.*

| Item:<br>Exceptional Mage-crafted Steel Dragon-headed Pommel | **Durability:** 85/85 |
| --- | --- |
| | **Rarity:** Uncommon |
| | **Quality:** Exquisite |
| | **Weight:** 0.2 kg |

|  | **Slot:** Crafting Item<br><br>**Traits:** An Exceptional Steel Dragon-headed Pommel, created using magical techniques. This pommel will have more capacity for absorbing magical power. |
| --- | --- |

    The only remaining item on the agenda was the handle itself. Arthur would usually make it out of wood, but he didn't have the time or patience to carve one right now. His magic was useful in smithing, so there had to be a way to make it usable in the other crafts. He'd considered this problem for a while and was eager to try an idea he'd thought might work.

    Arthur walked around the blacksmith shop until he found a chunk of wood close to the correct size. He walked to the open area outside of the building and opened up his senses to his Earth Magic. His power searched through the dirt below his feet. It brushed across all the different dirt compositions until it found what he was looking for. With a force of will, Arthur pulled up with the power. Small bits of sand rose from multiple holes around the area and coalesced over his head.

His magic shifted, and the gathered material compressed itself into the shape of a funnel. The narrow end of the funnel was the size necessary for the diameter of his handle while the mouth was a little larger than the chunk of wood he held in his hand. He solidified the shape and left ridges of the pebbles of sand exposed on the inside of the cone. Arthur created a cone of sand that had the coarseness of sandpaper on the inside.

He brought the cone closer to his level and floated the wooden block to it. When the block closed the distance, his magic shifted again and caused the funnel to spin at incredible speed. As it continued to turn, he forced the wood into the funnel and slowly pushed. Sawdust flew out at a prodigious rate as the piece of wood disappeared into the mouth of the funnel. When most of the wooden block made it past the mouth of the funnel, he saw the wooden rod emerge from the narrow neck. His power stayed steady as he pushed the wood through and, before he knew it, a wooden rod, perfectly smooth, emerged from the end. Immense pride filled him, and he heard the expected chime. To his surprise, he received a notification he hadn't expected.

*Congratulations, you have learned the hidden subskill Arcane Woodworking for a 500 experience bonus.*
*Congratulations, you have created a new Earth Magic Spell. Do you wish to name this new spell? Yes/No.*

*Another new spell?* The subskill was an
existing skill, but the spell he used to learn
it was unknown. The proper question was, what
to name it? He passed on naming the last but
wanted to see how this one turned out. He went
with a simple name and called it Cone of
Sanding. A long and arduous name would be
worthless and confusing.

*For creating the new Earth Magic Spell:
Cone of Sanding, you have been granted a one-
time bonus of 250 Earth Magic Experience, 250
Personal Experience, and 1 Intellect. Use your
new power wisely.*

| Crafting Spell: Cone of Sanding | |
|---|---|
| Requirements: Earth Magic<br>Mana Cost: 60 MP<br>Cast Time: 5 seconds | Description: Summons a cone of spinning sand that can shape wood to your desired size. |
| Mastery Level: 1 | |

*You have gained 90 experience in Earth
Magic for successfully casting Crafting Spell:
Cone of Sanding.*
*Congratulations, you have successfully
created Smooth Wooden Rod. You have gained 75
experience in Arcane Woodworking and
Woodworking for creating this item.*

The bonus from that ensured Arthur would work toward discovering new spells in the future. A permanent boost to his Intellect was outstanding. The experience was delightful, but the stat boost was leaps and bounds better in terms of rewards. He was daydreaming about an unending stream of stat points from developing new spells when his mind snapped back to reality. He had a sword to finish.

The enchantments would be tricky on this piece. He also needed gems to complete this weapon. This thought caused his mind to sway toward a new ability he recently obtained but hadn't yet used. This would be the perfect chance to try out Mineral Compression. The spell would have limited use on just about any dirt around but, luckily for him, he was sitting in a blacksmith shop. There were piles of partially used and burned up coal outside. There were also rock chunks from the crushed ore as they separated it during purification. Coal was beneficial for its carbon content. Hopefully, his magic would allow the compression of this material into a useful gem.

Arthur moved to the closest pile of the cast-off rock and pulled out a double handful. With this new substance in hand, he concentrated on it and cast Mineral Compression. The spell completed after the necessary cast time and Arthur watched as the stone melded together into a solid ball. It flowed like mercury until one large glob existed and then started folding on itself. Arthur couldn't explain it in any other way. The material just seemed to fold into itself time after time and shrink. It kept compressing down until it was the size of his thumb and then a bright flash emitted. Arthur was momentarily blinded, and when his vision returned, a shining blue gem sat in his hand.

*You have gained 120 experience in Earth Magic for successfully casting Earth Magic Spell: Mineral Compression.*

| Item:<br>Manufactured Sapphire | **Durability:** 50/50<br><br>**Rarity:** Uncommon<br><br>**Quality:** Well Crafted<br><br>**Weight:** 0.02 kg<br><br>**Slot:** Crafting Item/<br>Magical Item<br><br>**Traits:** A man-made sapphire created using magical means. |
|---|---|

It would take him a while to get the engraving done for his enchantments. That would be enough time to refill his mana before he needed to empower them. Arthur cast the spell seven more times to make more of the artificial gems, using the rest of his mana pool with the spell taking 80 MP a cast. To his surprise, the results weren't always the same.

*You have gained 840 experience in Earth Magic for successfully casting Earth Magic Spell: Mineral Compression (x7).*
*You have received Manufactured Sapphire (x2), Manufactured Ruby (x3), and Manufactured Emerald (x2).*

Arthur couldn't tell if the spell made a random gem each time or if it had something to do with the composition of the specific handful of materials he used. Either way, the results of the spell satisfied his needs. Those gems would be useful for containing power. His attention turned toward Enchanting. It was time to figure out what to do with his weapon.

This weapon would be a work of art and, as such, each piece would work together with the enchantments complementing one another. The blade was the first on the agenda. Arthur worked out what he would need, and he used a durability enchantment mixed with a heat resistance effect. He wanted to use his new Sheath in Flame spell he learned but didn't want to risk damaging his weapons. If he added an enchantment to protect the blade from heat, it should allow him to use the spell without penalty.

Arthur would create this weapon correctly, so he expanded on the most advanced enchantment technique he knew. It was time to go for broke and see if he could discover the Expert tier Enchantment Matrix. If it was what he thought, it shouldn't be too difficult. The pommel would be his test piece, though. He wouldn't install gems until the base enchantment was working as intended.

He fetched his engraving tools from the shop and sat down to plan the design. The helix design for DNA structure would be his aim for the process. He also planned on adding in the crossbars, hoping they would activate the next matrix style. He wanted the end cap to be sturdy so his enchantment included the matrix for durability, but he also added symbols for blunt damage. His hopes were for it to increase damage when bashing enemies with the pommel of the weapon.

The matrices were in place and he used his best judgment on how to connect the crossbars in the structure. This comprised tying them together using basic word blocks for power. He chose this design and finished the engraving. When he finished, he walked a scant distance away from the forge and started infusing the mana into the piece to activate the enchantment. His surprise quickly morphed to fear as his mana steadily drained, but there wasn't the large initial pull he expected. The mana was a constant flow, and the pommel started to "feel" full. The piece emitted a faint glow and Arthur panicked. He threw it as far as he could and dove to the ground. Not three seconds after it left his hand, a loud *boom* rattled the clearing. Pieces of dirt peppered his back as he lay on the ground with his hands covering his head.

Arthur lifted his head to take in his surroundings. Dirt lay scattered all over the place but, most surprising of all, was the crater where the pommel landed. There was a charred hole in the ground that was five foot wide and three foot deep. The explosion from that enchantment would've killed him had he not thrown it when he did.

His body trembled from that realization as he got back to his feet. Rowan came running towards him while his gaze swept the field.

"Are you all right?" the blacksmith yelled as he approached.

Arthur waved at him and tried to put on a smile to hide his discomfort.

"Yep, perfectly fine. My enchantment overloaded and blew up. I felt it becoming unstable and threw it. Sure screwed up your yard though," Arthur said with a chuckle.

Rowan eyed him warily. It was obvious the man didn't fully believe Arthur was fine, but he also knew there was no point in trying to force it out of him. He merely nodded in acknowledgment.

"Need any help then?" the blacksmith asked.

"Nope. I'm good. We've got far too much to do and too little time. Thanks for checking on me, Rowan."

"Fine, fine, just don't blow yourself up or we're all screwed," he said as he walked back to his shop.

Arthur took a moment to compose himself and surveyed the area. His nerves were still raw, and he had to hold himself in check to keep the shakes from breaking out again. His focus turned to the ground around him and he cast Flatten Earth. A few casts of the spell allowed him to repair the surroundings to make them look like new. The healing of the land helped ease him slightly.

*You have gained 180 experience in Earth Magic for successfully casting Earth Magic Spell: Flatten Earth (x3).*

He pulled his attention back to the threat at hand and set his jaw. He didn't have time to sit here and feel bad for himself. It was time to fix the problem and get back to work. Walking over to the forge, he tossed in a chunk of steel and let it heat. A quick cast of his Arcane Smithing spell made him another identical dragon-headed pommel.

*You have gained 50 experience in Earth Magic and Fire Magic for successfully casting Combination Spell: Arcane Forging.*
*Congratulations, you have successfully created Exceptional Mage-crafted Steel Dragon-headed Pommel. You have gained 75 experience in Arcane Smithing and Blacksmithing for creating this item.*

He set it down and continued working. This
time he distinctly arranged his script.
Instead of doing the writing along the spiral
lines and interlocking them with random words
of power, he flowed the text through the
structure. He wrote one line and, when he
reached the cross bracket, kept flowing his
script across it. When entering the opposite
line, he followed it down and continued the
same pattern. This created writing that looked
like a spinning staircase. Two of these lines
formed a dance together to complete the spiral
structure that intertwined. Hopefully, this
would be the correct form. If not, he needed
to give up and use his Advanced Matrix
instead.

Walking back to his spot, he sent the mana
into the piece as he visualized the effect.
His mana dropped a prodigious 100 mana but
then slowed. Arthur kept his focus on the part
until the additional 100 mana trickled out,
and the spell settled into place. He let out a
grateful sigh as the process finished. His
notifications reassured him.

*Congratulations, you have successfully
enchanted Exceptional Mage-crafted Steel
Dragon-headed Pommel. You have gained 350
experience in Enchanting.*

*You have discovered the Enchanting Art of
Expert Matrix. You have gained 3 bonus talent
points in Enchanting.*

| Item: Enchanted Exceptional Mage-crafted Steel Dragon-headed Pommel | **Durability:** 110/110 |
| --- | --- |
| | **Rarity:** Rare |
| | **Quality:** Exquisite |

| | |
|---|---|
| | **Weight:** 0.2 kg<br><br>**Slot:** Crafting Item<br><br>**Traits:** An Exceptional Steel Dragon-headed Pommel, created using magical techniques. This pommel will have more capacity for absorbing magical power.<br><br>Enchantments:<br>   • Blunt damage increased by 15% |

The Enchantment worked and, from the looks of the experience, the higher quality matrix also increased the experience amount he gained. His mana usage was high, but it also increased the base durability more than expected. Two of his new rubies gained storage runes, and he melded them into the pommel. The pommel gained 2,000 mana storage in addition to its current enchantment. Arthur hoped for more, but he couldn't be too disappointed. The manufactured gems must not store as much as normal gems.

*Congratulations, you have successfully enchanted Manufactured Ruby (x2). You have gained 100 experience in Enchanting.*

His attention shifted to the blade. The patterns here would help it resist heat and increase its durability and sharpness. His old enchantments worked well on the current swords they used, so the heat one was the only fresh addition. Pushing his mana in, the magic settled into the metal with ease.

The wing guard was next on the list, and he took a careful look at it. The durability enchantment was an obvious choice, but instead of going with standard enchantments, he put a control aspect on this piece. This section would be a conduit for the power in the weapon. He would design one gem on the guard to power his spell on the blade and to harness the spell Sheathe in Flame. The other gem would draw in power to fill the pommel with mana. This would keep Arthur from needing to burn his mana to fuel the flame on the blade.

He put an enchantment structure on one of the manufactured sapphires to symbolize it gathering power, while another set channeled that gathered power to the pommel. He tied the other gem to the activation ability in the guard. When activated, this gem would impart the Sheath in Flame spell onto the blade and pull the needed mana from the pommel gems. With the ideas in mind, he bestowed the magic into the gemstones and the symbols permanently burned in. He lay the last of the gems in the sockets, and he looked at the finished product.

*Congratulations, you have successfully enchanted Exceptional Mage-crafted Steel Wing Guard. You have gained 350 experience in Enchanting.*

*Congratulations, you have successfully* enchanted Manufactured Sapphire (x2). *You have gained 100 experience in Enchanting.*

<table>
<tr><td>

Item:
Enchanted Exceptional
Mage-crafted Steel
Wing Guard

</td><td>

**Durability:** 100/100

**Rarity:** Rare

**Quality:** Exquisite

**Weight:** 0.3 kg

**Slot:** Crafting Item

**Traits:** An Exceptional Steel Wing Guard, created using magical techniques. This guard will have more capacity for absorbing magical power.

Enchantments:
- This guard draws in 8 mana per minute.
- Upon activation, the spell Sheathe in Flames will cover the blade of the weapon.

</td></tr>
</table>

The spells seemed to take hold as he intended based on the description. The last piece was the handle itself. Arthur kept it simple with durability and a grip enchantment.

*Congratulations, you have successfully enchanted* Smooth Wooden Rod. *You have gained 120 experience in Enchanting.*

He wanted this thing to last a long time, so the durability was necessary. It was also an enchantment he knew he could cast reliably. With all the pieces complete, he yelled for Rowan to join him. Rowan came running at this call.

"What's wrong?" he asked in concern.

"Nothing. I wanted you to be present to see my new sword when I assemble it. I also want to show you the design I have for the tang and pommel," Arthur said as he pointed to the threads on each. "These are threads and are used to connect pieces together quickly and firmly."

Arthur showed the use by screwing the pommel onto the tang and removing it again. Rowan's eyes widened at this.

"That's great, but wouldn't that take far longer to make than just peening it," Rowan said with skepticism.

"You forget about Arcane Forging. If you just picture them, they'll be part of the design," Arthur explained with a smile.

Rowan slapped his forehead with his hand. It was apparent the man was not considering his new skill.

"Now, let's put this together and see what we get," Arthur told him with glee.

Rowan nodded and helped him get the guard and handle fit tight up to the blade. Arthur held the piece in one hand while he attached the pommel with the other. As soon as the pommel was tight and wouldn't turn anymore, a loud gong sound rang in the clearing. He looked to Rowan, and the man looked frightened, obviously hearing the noise himself.

Before either could say anything, the sword floated from his grasp and spun in mid-air. A flash of light accompanied by a gust of air radiated from the blade and pushed them back a step. The sword stopped spinning and slowly floated back to him. The weapon in front of him now stunned him.

*Hark and Rejoice, a named weapon has been created! Ember joins the fray!*

*Congratulations, you have successfully created Ember. This is a unique named weapon. You have gained 1,000 experience in Arcane Smithing and Blacksmithing for this feat.*

*Congratulations, you have been granted a Class! You have gained the hidden class, Arcane Artificer. You have gained 5,000 experience for earning a hidden class.*

| Item:<br>Ember | **Attack:** 28-36 |
| --- | --- |
| | **Durability:** 215/215 |
| | **Rarity:** Unique |
| | **Quality:** Masterful |
| | **Weight:** 1.4 kg |

**Slot:** Main Hand/Off Hand

Mana Storage: 0/3,500

**Traits:** A named weapon created by an Arcane Artificer. This weapon is unique, and another like it has never existed in this world.

Enchantments:
- This weapon draws in 12 mana per minute and fills its internal mana storage.
- Upon activation, the spell Sheathe in Flame will cover the blade of this weapon. Drains 1 MP/second.
- Blunt Damage with Pommel increased by 18%.
- Reduces chance to be disarmed by 20%.

| Class: Arcane Artificer | An Arcane Artificer is capable of creating unique weapons and armor for the world. This class offers the following bonuses:<br><br>• Ability to create a unique item once every seven days. (This requires materials and craftsmanship of exquisite quality to activate)<br>• All weapons created by an Arcane Artificer will have 10% higher damage.<br>• All armor created by an Arcane Artificer will have 10% higher defense. |
| --- | --- |

"That's not possible…" Rowan whispered to himself as he saw the weapon. "Had I not seen it myself, I'd never believe it."

"I'm surprised myself. Still not sure I believe it either, but hard to argue when I'm holding the finished product," Arthur told him with finality.

The weapon was a piece of beauty, which is probably why it triggered the unique creation. Arthur marveled at the blade that looked sharp enough to cut through anything. The ruby eyes on the head of the pommel seemed to shine with rage, and the bright gem on the wing guard sparkled. A soft blue glow emanated from the gem on the guard. Arthur couldn't resist the chance to try it out. He pushed some mana into it to help charge it. Twenty mana would be enough to test it.

With a thought, he activated Sheathe in Flame on the sword. Brilliant blue flame shot from the guard and encased the entire blade. The fire only extended out an inch from the edge of the blade, but it was impressive as hell. He let the flames dance for a few seconds and then shut them off. Wasting mana would not help him in the long run. A sword this fine needed a scabbard to match it. Before he could worry about the sheath, he spotted a form dashing their direction.

"What the hell did you do now?" Allendria yelled at him angrily.

"Why do you always assume it was me that did something?" Arthur asked her.

"Well, what other idiot is constantly getting themselves into trouble around here?"

"Meh, good point. Either way, it wasn't trouble. I was making weapons. I made myself a sword."

Her eyes narrowed at him.

"You made a sword, and it caused the loud noise and a ripple of magical wind?" She said in disbelief.

"Uh… yeah," Arthur responded, ever so elegantly.

Her eyes fell to the sword he held and her words stopped as her mouth hung open. She held out her hands, and Arthur laid the sword in her grasp. Her eyes shot open as she looked at the blade. Arthur wasn't sure how they got wider, but he'd be damned if it hadn't happened.

"You made this?" she asked in astonishment.

"Yep."

"It says only an Arcane Artificer can make this style of weapon. I didn't think you unlocked a class yet?" she asked in disbelief.

"Technically, I hadn't, until I finished the weapon. I gained the class when I completed the sword."

"Figures. Only you would accidentally acquire another hidden secret. It's beautiful, though. Guess you wanted to play on the family heritage?" she asked as she motioned toward the wings and head on the weapon.

"That was the idea. The craftsmanship of the piece helped give it the bump it needed to create a unique and named item. My Arcane Artificer class allows me to create a unique item once every seven days. It still has to be an exceptionally well-made piece to qualify, but it can only trigger once in the time allotted," Arthur explained.

"That could prove useful, for sure. You'll be a force to be reckoned with if you can make a unique weapon once a week."

"Actually, it doesn't only apply to weapons. I can make armor as well with this skill. It just has the same limits. I was planning on making a new set of armor for myself. Now that I'm using a melee style, I want to protect myself better. I think with my Arcane Smithing, I can make an impressive set of scale armor that is lightweight and doesn't hinder my movement too much. I was hoping to get it done before we need to scavenge tonight," Arthur said as he gazed up at the sun.

"You may not have the time for that, but you could try. At least get the major pieces finished for now. It's not long until dark. We have to hope they don't try a night assault," Rowan chimed in from the side.

"I know I don't have enough time to make a full suit from scratch, but I plan on making the scales and attaching them to my leather armor. It'll help protect my skin from the metal and save me some time. Having to make the full set with lining would take far too long," Arthur told the smith.

Rowan nodded at that. "That should work. If you need any help, let me know."

"Thanks. Allendria, anything happening at the gate?" Arthur asked.

"They're still gathered in their meeting. From what I can tell, they haven't reached a decision yet."

*You see anything suspicious up there?* Arthur asked Balair.

*Nothing yet. I have to come down for a break and get some food to boost my Stamina back up before long.*

*I'll make sure Daniel is expecting you,* Arthur told the dragonling with a smile.

"Balair says the area is clear from the sky. Can you go let Daniel know that Balair will come down for a break soon and he'll need food ready?" he asked.

"I'm sure he already has plenty prepped and ready to hand out as needed but I'll let him know to expect the pile of scales. If anything comes up, I'll send a message. Everyone's working on preparing meals and making arrows right now. Any word on when we'll be getting some more arrowheads? We have the fletching and a decent amount of shafts but not nearly enough arrowheads. Luckily, Zeke's paranoid and keeps a lot of rough arrow shafts at his place," Allendria informed him.

"I'll make some soon. They don't take too long to create. Actually, Rowan, do you want to take a crack at them? They'd be easy with your Arcane Smithing. You'll just envision as many as you can within the confines of the metal you use when you cast the spell," Arthur said.

"I'll give it a shot. If I can't figure it out, I'll come find you," Rowan agreed.

"Let's get back to work then," Arthur said as he leaned forward and kissed Allendria on the cheek.

"Thank you for checking on me," he whispered to her.

"Stay out of trouble, will you?" she asked him as she grabbed his hand and smiled.

Rowan moved back to his anvil and Allendria bounded off toward the inn. Arthur returned to the forge. The most important thing was the scabbard for his new sword. He found two thin boards of wood that were the correct length and a small chunk of steel.

One of the easier methods to make scabbards was to take two thin boards, hollow out the shape of the blade inside each board, and glue the edges together. This could create the perfect channel to hold the blade inside the wood. The problem with the plan? Glue. They had nothing on hand strong enough to make that connection. You could always nail it together or use some other physical attachment, but it didn't look as good. That was where Arthur wanted to use the steel. He would make the wooden form to encase the sword and then he'd use his Arcane Smithing to make the metal flow around the wood and create a shell to hold it together.

He needed to find the best way to make the hollowed-out space within the pieces of wood. His mind drifted back to his previous spell for woodworking. Moving back to the space he used before, he reached out and found the rough sand piled on top of the ground. He pulled it up into a ball and shaped it into a wheel that was almost the same width as his sword blade. The wheel hovered about waist high and he spun it with his magic. He created a stationary sanding wheel and ran the board along the wheel to create the groove he needed. Sawdust filled the air and he could smell the familiar scent of wood shavings. When finished with the groove and sanding the edges into a round shape, he admired his work.

*Congratulations, you have created a new Earth Magic Spell. Do you wish to name this new spell? Yes/No.*

Arthur fist-pumped the air in excitement with another new spell created. Using magic to manipulate sand to do the sanding process on wood must be something unique. He'd seen Zeke use sand to smooth out wood with cloth, but no one must have considered doing it using magic. The funny thing was, Arcane Woodworking wasn't new. This meant there were other spells that work on wood, and he hadn't discovered them yet. He stuck with another easy name for this one.

*For creating the new Earth Magic Spell: Sanding Wheel, you have been granted a one-time bonus of 250 Earth Magic Experience, 250 Personal Experience, and 1 Wisdom. Strive to be better.*

| Crafting Spell: Sanding Wheel | |
| --- | --- |
| Requirements: Earth Magic<br>Mana Cost: 50 MP<br>Cast Time: 4 seconds | Description: Creates a wheel of sand that can be used to shape wood. |
| Mastery Level: 1 | |

*You have gained 80 experience in Earth Magic for successfully casting Crafting Spell: Cone of Sanding.*

*Congratulations, you have successfully created Wooden Scabbard Scale (x2). You have gained 80 experience in Arcane Woodworking and Woodworking for creating this item.*

The Wisdom was a welcome bonus. He
neglected it more than the other stats since
he naturally regenerated more mana than
others. With a new spell under his belt and
the scabbard pieces complete, he test-fit his
sword and it fit perfectly. He wanted to make
some adjustments to the scabbard before he put
it together, though.

It was time for some enchanting. Since it
was wood, he wanted to use a weaker
enchantment. He wouldn't use something of
greater power like he did for his sword and
risk destroying the sheathe. He used a small
chisel that Rowan had in the shop to cut a
narrow channel out of the bottom of the
scabbard. With some watered charcoal, he drew
an advanced matrix and set it up to be a
cleaning spell. *Why bother cleaning your sword
after killing things if you didn't need to?*

He placed the enchantment inside the groove
of the scabbard and infused it with mana. The
results were what he hoped for. The steel went
into the fire and within a few minutes, he had
it hovering in front of him while glowing an
almost white with heat. He envisioned the
design he wanted, moved the two pieces of the
scabbard into place, and cast the spell. The
metal stretched out into a thin sheet that
almost looked like foil. It flexed and wrapped
itself around the scabbard pieces and melded
itself into a solid metal case. The outside of
it sported a design of dragon scales. He left
a slight groove open on the bottom, while the
top edge had a thick sleeve of steel around it
that had a slot for a belt to slide through.
The piece was a fitting match for his blade.

*You have gained 50 experience in Earth Magic and Fire Magic for successfully casting Combination Spell: Arcane Forging.*

*Congratulations, you have successfully created Intricate Dragon Scale Scabbard of Cleansing. You have gained 200 experience in Arcane Smithing, Blacksmithing, Arcane Woodworking, and Woodworking for creating this item.*

| Item:<br>Intricate Dragon Scale Scabbard of Cleansing | **Durability:** 125/125<br><br>**Rarity:** Uncommon<br><br>**Quality:** Well Crafted<br><br>**Weight:** 0.4 kg<br><br>**Slot:** Container/Belt<br><br>**Traits:** A scabbard, wrapped in steel, and adorned with a dragon scale pattern.<br><br>Enchantments:<br>• It will remove all dirt and impurities on any blade placed in this scabbard. |
|---|---|

*Another jackpot.* The best part was, he received experience in all 4 skills associated with making that scabbard at the completion. Making items like that seemed the perfect way to bump up multiple skills at once. Instead of attaching the scabbard to his hip on his normal belt, Arthur fed a strap of leather through it and tied it onto his back. A sense of calm settled over him as the blade took up its new home. The access over his shoulder would be easy for him to reach, but more importantly, it wouldn't hamper his movement having the scabbard bouncing around his legs.

With a deep sigh, he looked to the sky. The sun crept ever lower to the horizon and his time was running out. He needed to get the scale made to fit on top of his leather, so he turned back to the forge and went in search of some more steel.

# Chapter 12



*Scavenging*

Navigating to the pile of steel, Arthur selected the pieces he would need and tossed them in the fire while his mind turned to design.

The critical piece to worry about was the breastplate. It offered the largest area of protection and would guard the more vital parts of his body. Arthur planned to go all out on the dragon motif, so the scales he made would look like dragon scales. For a bit of flair, he'd also make his spaulders on the shoulders look like dragon wings. The top claw of the wing would sit on the front of the shoulder, and the wing would look like it was laying backward. The bottom of the wing would cover the backside of his shoulder. He didn't want the design to stick up too far from his shoulder. Any significant dips or humps in armor, no matter how nice they looked, only caught weapons and allowed them to dig deeper.

The front of the suit would sit on a thin plate of metal while the back would be solely scaled, connected at the tops, and overlapping each other like shingles on a roof. Each scale was longer than it appeared, but the previous ones covered half of them in their pattern. That hidden part was where they connected. A suit like this would take forever to make with a standard style of smithing. It'd require you to make each scale individually and then painstakingly assemble it. With his imagination fueling it, he could do it in one pass.

He removed the metal from the fire and cast the spell. The wings formed as the magic took shape. The scales cascaded from the bottom of the wings. The front had a more rigid look to them with the reinforced plate, while the pieces on the back flexed more. It took almost two minutes for the section to complete due to the complexity of the attachments, but it looked great once completed. It registered as armor casing rather than simply armor since there wasn't lining.

He kept the enchantments simple on this one and chose a durability enchantment and also one for flexibility. He used the advanced matrix for all of them and hoped the flexibility enchantment would allow him to move easier.

*Congratulations, you have successfully enchanted Intricate Scale Mail Chestpiece Casing. You have gained 240 experience in Enchanting.*

Arthur pulled his leather chest piece off and held it to the new armor. He stuffed the leather piece into the scale casing, and when it was sitting inside correctly, he received an unexpected message.

*You have inserted Enchanted Basic Studded Leather Vest into Intricate Scale Mail Chestpiece Casing. If you combine these, the leather vest will no longer register as an individual piece of armor, even if removed and will instead be classified as a lining. Do you wish to complete this action? Yes/No.*

It made sense when Arthur considered it. It would be cheating if something damaged your mail, and you shucked it from the lining only to have your lining be its own set of armor. That would also be difficult for the stats to meld together. Arthur selected *Yes,* and the pieces merged into one.

*You have gained 50 experience in Earth Magic and Fire Magic for successfully casting Combination Spell: Arcane Forging.*
*Congratulations, you have successfully created Intricate Scale Mail Chestplate. You have gained 350 experience in Arcane Smithing, and Blacksmithing for creating this item.*

| Item:<br>Enchanted Intricate<br>Scale Mail Chestplate | **Defense:** 28 |
| --- | --- |
| | **Durability:** 180/180 |
| | **Rarity:** Rare |
| | **Quality:** Exquisite |
| | **Weight:** 2.8 kg |

<table>
<tr><td></td><td>

**Slot:** Chest

**Traits:** An Intricate Scale Mail Chestplate, created using magical techniques.

Enchantments:
- Adds 3 Agility to the wearer

</td></tr>
</table>

The Agility boost was a surprise. Arthur hoped it would allow him to move easier in the mail, but he hadn't expected it to just flat out increase his Agility. He wouldn't start complaining, though.

The rest of the pieces moved along in the same order. He sped up their production by just making the scales and including the enchantments for durability and defense with the spell. His familiarity with those allowed him to engrave them with his Arcane Forging skill as he made the pieces. His helm, gloves, and pants were this only pieces for him to complete since his bracers were already metal. They were all the same standard blue armor, but the gloves had 12 defense and 100 durability, while the helm had 14 defense and 120 durability. Finally, the pants had 22 defense and 150 durability. Overall, he was ready for a fight.

It took him some time to get his new armor on, but he eventually managed. The only thing he couldn't get on himself was the chest piece. He walked over to Rowan to get the man's help.

"Figure out the arrowheads?" Arthur asked.

"Actually, yes, I did. I failed the first try and made one large spearhead instead, but I figured it out," Rowan said as his eyes moved up to look at Arthur.

The look on his face was priceless as he took in the sight of Arthur with his new armor on.

"Impressive, huh?"

"You're damn right, it's impressive. I'm not sure any of those goblins will harm that armor with their shoddy weapons."

"I hope that's true. Would you mind helping me get this chest piece on? It's hard to maneuver over my head and get it on by myself."

Rowan waved him over and took the chest piece from Arthur. He looked at it for a moment and whistled in appreciation. It took some finagling, but they got the chest piece on Arthur. He completed the suit with his helm, and he looked regal.

"Had I not already known you were royalty, I'd sure believe it now," Rowan said in a whisper.

"Thanks for that," Arthur said with a chuckle, "but regardless of who I'm supposed to be, I'm still just a friend."

Arthur reached out and clasped arms with the burly smith, and they nodded at each other.

"I have to run. I need to see how things currently stand, and we'll be coordinating a resource run when we leave to scavenge the bodies for supplies. Nothing would please me more than to take their iron, re-smelt it into steel, and kill them with weapons made from their own materials," Arthur said with a maniacal fire in his eyes.

"Good luck and stay out of trouble."

Arthur nodded and left for the inn. He
approached the building and spotted two guards
standing outside the doors holding weapons.
One of them was Paul, and the other was Noah.
They both saluted Arthur but faltered as they
noticed what he wore.

"A… Arthur? Is that you?" Paul asked
hesitantly.

"Of course. I figured if I had some better
armor, it might prevent me from getting shot
in the back with an arrow again," Arthur told
him with a smile.

Paul grimaced, but then it morphed into a
smile at Arthur's levity. They nodded to him
as he walked through the doors. The room
contained the main people running the village.
At his arrival, the room became quiet as
everyone turned to admire his new armor. His
hood was back so they could easily identify
him in the light, but it was still a lot to
take in.

"Arthur… is that what you've been working
on this afternoon?" Daniel asked in awe.

"Yep. You like it?" Arthur asked. When he
did, he pulled out Ember, held it to the side,
and activated its Sheathe in Flame. The blue
fire poured over the blade, and everyone
gasped in surprise. He let the spell dissipate
quickly and returned to normal. It promptly
disappeared into the scabbard on his back.

"So, any news?" Arthur asked the room.

"The elves appear to have left. We have
seen the orcs walking around camp and talking
to the goblins. Teams have also been spotted
running into the woods and returning with
trees they chopped down. I don't think they'll
attempt to attack tonight. They seem to be
preparing for their assault. My guess is, they
will use the wood for shields or barriers,"
Samson summarized.

Arthur grinned at that. Fire was always fun
to play with, and he had just the idea to fix
it.

"I think we can fix that problem, but it'll
require us to show our hand with some of our
magic. That's of lesser concern at the moment,
since it'll take them some time to prepare. We
need to get our team arranged for scavenging.
I want to get the two areas they tried to
sneak up on us cleaned out first, and then
we'll try to skirt around the wall to scavenge
the front line. Did you see anything
resembling sentries set up?"

"I saw a handful, but most looked bored and
weren't paying attention," Vana chimed in.

"Even better. A night raid on them may be
in order," Arthur said. He saw Samson open his
mouth to object and continued "Nothing major.
We can send some arrows into their camp to
scatter them in disarray and pull back. Don't
want to expose ourselves to too much harm."

Samson's mouth closed at that, and he
nodded. Arthur could tell he still wasn't fond
of the idea, but he was a soldier and was used
to taking orders.

*It's still clear out here, but I'm about to
head in for the night.* Balair sent to him.

*You can't stay out to cover us while we
scavenge?* Arthur asked.

*I can barely see as it is. By the time you guys come out, there won't be much light to see by. You can probably manage with the moonlight, but there isn't enough of it for me to see at the distance I'm trying to scout from.*

*Dragons can't see in the dark? I thought you were supposed to be some all-powerful creature? Don't you have a night vision spell or something?* Arthur asked.

*Do you have a night vision spell?* Balair asked calmly.

*Uh… no.* Arthur answered hesitantly.

*Then how the fuck would I have a night vision spell, you idiot. I can only cast spells you know in schools of magic I'm trained in and have the appropriate level for.*

*Sheesh, no need to get all pissy about it. Wait, I've seen you shoot fire from your mouth a few times, and I definitely don't have that spell.* Arthur responded, confused.

*That's a racial ability and not a spell, you moron.*

*Forget what I said then. Come back in when you need to. Do you want to come with us on our brief trip? You could stay with us near the ground. Might even get to kill a goblin if they stray too close.*

*Fine, I'll tag along.*

*Come down and get something to eat before we head out.*

*On my way.*

Arthur turned to Daniel. "Can you bring out some food for us? Balair will join us soon. We'll need to eat before we leave on our merry adventure."

"Like digging through dead goblin bodies is a merry adventure," Arthur heard Vana mutter.

"Cheer up! Just remember we get to shoot some goblins tonight," Arthur told her.

A smile spread across her face, and they all sat down. The meal ended quicker than they hoped. Arthur was sore from all the standing he'd been doing throughout the day and didn't want to have to get back up, but there was no choice. Balair came in and wolfed down his meal in record time. Arthur, Vana, Allendria, and Samson walked outside. Samson motioned toward a group of guards outside and beckoned them over. He chose two of them, seemingly at random, and told them to gear up.

"I don't think we'll need them," Arthur told the Paladin.

"I doubt we need them, but the more goblins they have to search means the less of the nasty bastards I have to put my hands on. Rank has its privileges," the gruff man said with a twinkle in his eye.

Arthur laughed at the comment and clapped him on the shoulder. They checked their gear and gathered together. Their trip to the northern gate was quick, and Arthur used his magic to lift the bar. They opened it just enough to slip out one by one and closed the door again. Guards stood by on the other side to raise the heavy bar back in place.

The group made their way west as they skirted the wall. The goblins had assaulted the northwestern portion of the wall and avoided trying to attack the northern gate. It wasn't long before the bodies came into view. They'd been sitting in the sun all afternoon and didn't have a pleasant smell about them. Some buzzards and crows took off with a protesting squawk as they arrived to interrupt their meal.

"Fan out. Take anything of value you can find. We can use even the wooden weapons for something," Arthur said as he turned. He cast his Dimensional Storage spell, and the familiar doorway appeared.

"Toss everything in, and I'll close it up."

They all set to work as they searched through the bodies. It wasn't the easiest task in the dark, but there was just enough moonlight to outline the figures. They could see the occasional shine of iron as they searched. The trip to this first group of dead goblins yielded eight crude iron weapons, three wooden clubs, a scattering of copper coins that had unfamiliar markings on them, and a handful of serviceable pieces of leather and cloth. They'd be lucky to get the smell off of the fabric or leather for them to be usable, but time would tell. Some serviceable arrows joined the pile of goodies in the storage.

Arthur closed the door for his spell, and they continued their trek. They didn't want to go back into the village just yet, so they continued their stroll through the darkness. They circled the western side of the wall and then headed south. Following the wall back to the east, they found the site of the second ambush. Their pattern was the same as last. Arthur opened his storage, and they set to work.

This group's weaponry was like the last but less had iron weapons, and more were using the wooden variety. None of the odd-looking coins were present in this group, but they scavenged some more arrows, leather, and cloth. Every little bit would help. Their supply of metal in the village was dwindling quickly. With what they were gathering, it could stretch the amount they could work with.

The group headed for the gate with the encamped army. They were careful in their trip, and Arthur had Balair monitor the area ahead of them. The trip was overall uneventful, but they could see the fires of the army camped a few hundred yards from the site of the battle.

"I'm not going to open the magical storage until we have everything gathered. I don't know if their casters can detect my magic use. Let's gather everything and stack it near the wall. When we have all of it, I'll open the storage and we can quickly toss everything in," Arthur told them.

"If they're decent casters, they'd be able to detect it. Hopefully, by casting the spell near the wall, they'll think it's something inside the village and not become alarmed. Your Dimensional Magic also has a unique feel to it and they probably won't know what it means," Allendria supplied.

Arthur nodded, and they continued their
unpleasant task. The force that assaulted this
gate wore similar armor, but their numbers
were more extensive than the other forces.
This group held a little over 20 poor-quality
iron weapons, but they found a few good
quality pieces. The field was littered with
arrows, and they recovered almost fifty that
were still serviceable. More leather and cloth
pieces joined the pile of goods, and they also
found a handful of the odd copper coins. One
orc even had a ring of interest.

| Item:<br>Ring of Minor Health | **Durability**: 45/55<br><br>**Rarity**: Uncommon<br><br>**Quality**: Good<br><br>**Weight**: 0.05 kg<br><br>**Slot**: Finger<br><br>**Traits**: An iron ring enchanted with special properties.<br><br>Enchantments:<br>• Adds 20HP to the wearer's total health. |
| --- | --- |

Twenty health was nothing fantastic, but it was something he could use. Arthur immediately slipped that ring on. His gauntlets had enough room with the padding for it to sit under the gloves without issues. He'd examine it later to see if he could determine how to make another like it. Learning how it granted health with Enchanting would expand his knowledge and allow him to make similar items.

With everything piled up, Arthur quickly cast his Dimensional Storage, and everyone tossed in equipment as fast as possible. The metal clanged together, making a hell of a lot of racket as they landed on each other, but they had no guarantee taking it slow would be any quieter. If one of their mages detected the spell and sent people to investigate, it would cause a problem.

When all the items joined the pile in the storage room, Arthur dismissed the spell. Everyone sat in silence and listened to their surroundings. They could hear some of the guards shuffling above them on the wall, but they'd been told to hold fire unless commanded otherwise. Luckily, Samson had informed them of the mission before they left. The surroundings remained quiet, so Arthur decided it was time for some fun.

"Samson, you take everyone and head for the northern gate. Vana and I have some mischief to cause," Arthur whispered.

"I don't think we should leave you out here alone. If they charge you, there won't be time for you to escape without help," Samson said with concern.

"Thanks for the confidence. I think the two of us can shake off a group of goblins," he said while gesturing to Vana. "We'll rely on confusion and stealth. I don't plan on doing too much damage, though. More than anything, I just want them nervous and on their toes."

Samson huffed at that. "Fine, but I still think you're an idiot."

"Point taken. Let's get moving. Vana, time for some target practice," Arthur said as he waved her to follow.

*Keep an eye on us, will ya?* Arthur sent to Balair.

*Fine. You know this is stupid, right?*

*Well aware, but these assholes came knocking on our door without cause, so I'll make them pay for it.*

*Whatever, just don't die. I'm enjoying this plane again.*

*Yeah, yeah, I'd hate to disappoint you.* Arthur sent.

"You sure you don't want my help?" Allendria asked.

"I'd love your help to cause mayhem, but I don't want to tip our hand with the magic yet. You're not exactly sneaky and only have magic. Do me a favor and get forces to the wall here in case we stir up the hornets' nest. If you have to, unleash your magic to cover us if we get in trouble," Arthur explained.

"Can't argue with that logic, even if I don't agree with it," she said with a sigh.

His hand slipped into hers for a moment as he stared into her eyes. He lifted her hand up and pressed his lips to the back. Letting go of it, he slipped backward, and Vana followed. They slowly wove through the hills. Staying down low as they traveled reduced their speed but helped conceal them from sight.

When they were about forty yards from the edge of the camp, Vana held up her hand. "Patrols," she whispered.

"How many?"

"I saw two."

"Take them out together?" Arthur asked.

"I'll take the right. You get left," Vana told him.

He nodded, and they both pulled out their bows. Arthur spotted the two guards she mentioned and lifted his bow to take aim. Activating Aim Shot, he set his sight on the goblin's heart.

"Three, two, one, now," Vana softly muttered, and they both released.

The arrow zipped from the string and hit perfectly in the goblin's chest.

*You have dealt 230 damage to Goblin Sentry (1) (Level 14) with Steel Arrow (Heart Strike).*

*Goblin Sentry (1) (Level 14) has died.*

Arthur shifted his gaze and noticed Vana's target was dead on the ground. Between her skill and the fancy bow she got from the dungeon, she was a force to fear. They nodded to each other and proceeded forward. They pulled the two iron weapons off of the sentries and each put one in their belt. He wouldn't summon his storage this close to the enemies to toss the items in.

They didn't have any coins on them, so they crept forward. When they were twenty yards from the edge, they froze again.

"Any closer and they'll see us. They're night blind from staring at the campfires right now. How do you want to do this?" she asked.

"I'm open to suggestions. I'd like to cause as much panic as possible without painting a target directly on us."

She took on a thoughtful look as she considered ideas. Her eyes scanned the camp in front of her. They settled on a large stack of supplies and an evil grin came to her face.

"How fast can you enchant some arrowheads?" she asked.

"A few minutes. I can't enchant ones already on arrows and completed, though. I'd have to pull them off to enchant, and then we'd have to put them back on."

She looked to the sky for a moment and then motioned for them to back up. They made their way back to the bodies of the sentries. She took her dagger and cut strips off their clothing. With a practiced motion, she wrapped arrowheads in some of the cloth and cinched it down tight. Digging in her pouch, she pulled out something that looked like pine sap and smeared it on the fabric. She made four arrows and handed two to him.

| Item:<br>Steel Arrow of<br>Ignition | **Durability:** 25/25 |
| --- | --- |
| | **Rarity:** Common |
| | **Quality:** Good |
| | **Weight:** 0.2 kg |
| | **Slot:** Arrow |

<table>
<tr><td></td><td>Traits: A steel arrow, wrapped in flammable cloth. When set on fire, it can light objects it strikes on fire.</td></tr>
</table>

"I like your train of thought," Arthur told her.

"What's a train?" she asked in an odd tone.

"Never mind. I like your idea. Do you want me to light all four at once with my magic so we can shoot them off quickly?"

"Yes, I do. We'll aim at the base of that pile of supplies over there," she motioned at the stack, "the bottom looks to be some kind of oil."

Arthur nodded, and they moved closer to the target. They circled around the camp to get out of the line of sight of some of the goblins.

"After the fire starts, let's back up and circle around. When the goblins run up to put out the fire, start picking the stragglers off. We should be able to take out plenty on the edges before they figure out what's going on. Well, that is, if you make good shots," she said with a wry smile.

"Hey now, I can hold my own. Just because you're some badass archer, doesn't mean I can't perform when needed," Arthur retorted.

"Is that what Allendria told you?" she asked with a devilish grin.

"Ask her yourself. She might blush and hide, or she may slap the shit out of you. Either way, I'd love to see the outcome," Arthur told her with a wry grin of his own.

They nodded towards one another and
returned their attention to the business at
hand. Vana held out her two arrows near his
two, and with a quick burst of Weak Flame, he
lit all four on fire. They quickly brought up
the first arrow and fired into the crates. The
second followed almost as fast, and both
scurried backward.

They watched as the fire licked higher on
the crates, and within a minute, the blaze
gained strength. Cries of alarm came from the
nearby goblins, and Arthur and Vana prepared
their bows. Goblins ran around frantically,
kicking at barrels and trying to separate the
now burning materials from the ones yet to
catch fire.

As more charged to the fire, Arthur and
Vana started their target practice. They
initially thought to shoot those on the edge
of battling the flame, but it became apparent
the better targets were those secluded to
themselves and ignoring the fire. Arthur
picked his target, activated Aim Shot, and let
loose. The arrow flew from the string and
lodged into the goblin's neck. He crumbled
over to the ground and lay still.

*You have dealt 220 damage to Goblin Fighter
(1) (Level 13) with Steel Arrow (Severed
Spine).*
*Goblin Fighter (1) (Level 13) has died.*

He couldn't afford to delay, so he quickly
found another target and fired. Aim Shot was
paying dividends. This close to their enemies,
it almost guaranteed a perfect shot every
time. Vana picked her targets carefully, and
between the two of them, eight more goblins
fell to the ground without notice.

Arthur was getting ready to fire on another when a voice intruded in his mind.

*Some orc commanders are coming down to investigate.*

*Thanks,* He told the dragonling.

He held his hand up to Vana, who ceased firing and looked to him. He motioned to the orcs, and she nodded.

Both of them watched the orcs approach and waited for an opportunity to fire. They were doing their best to help get the goblins under control and get the fire contained. The orcs moved through the camp and kicked goblins that were lazing about and ignoring the commotion. Arthur watched one of them get close to one of the dead goblins and took aim.

The orc reared his leg back to kick and froze. His eyes spotted the arrow, and he turned to shout, but Arthur's arrow was faster. The arrow pierced his throat, and all thought of speech left him as he fell to the ground, holding his neck while blood seeped between his fingers.

"Fire away, they'll see the truth soon. Hit as many as you can, and we'll haul ass back to the wall," Arthur muttered to Vana.

Her bow snapped up, and she fired as quickly as she could draw arrows. Arthur was right behind her and aimed for every orc he saw. Five more enemies fell before the shouts of alarm changed to cries of anger. Their attention turned from the fire to the arrows slaying their comrades. Goblins ran around the camp and scrambled for weapons. It was then that Arthur decided enough was enough and touched Vana on the arm. They quickly scurried backward, staying low to the ground. When they reached a distance of roughly fifty yards, they stood and sprinted with all their might.

Their run went smoothly until Arthur spotted a flash of red heading their way.

*Look out!* Balair sent.

Before he could see what was happening, Vana grunted and fell. Arthur stopped in his dash and turned to look at her. She had dropped to the ground with a nasty burn on her right leg. One of the enemy casters must have hit her with a fire spell. Arthur bent down and hefted her over his shoulder. His pace resumed as he ran for the wall. He could barely make out the gatehouse in the night's gloom, but he wouldn't slow down.

"I appreciate the gesture and don't think I'm ungrateful, but your armor sure hurts with all the jarring," Vana grumbled as she jostled on his shoulder.

"My apologies, princess. Next time I'll summon a carriage," Arthur said in mocking tones as his breathing sped up.

It surprised them when Samson stood at the gate to greet them on their arrival. The gate was open just enough to squeeze through, so they all ushered inside. The door was quickly pulled shut, and a burst of magic lifted the bar back into place. He lay Vana down in front of him and collapsed to the ground, breathing heavily.

"You going to be okay?" he asked the injured woman.

She sat up and looked at her leg. "It looks worse than it is, I think. Most of the shock of it is over, so I think I can limp on it. I have some cream back in the village that can help numb burns and speed up the healing process. I should be fine."

Arthur let out a sigh of relief. "Take the time you need and get that taken care of. You," he said as he gestured toward one guard. "Assist Vana back to the inn and make sure she treats her wounds, then return to your captain for assignment."

The man came to attention, saluted, and walked over and held his hand down to Vana. She took his hand gratefully as he helped her to her feet. He held her arm as she leaned some of her weight on him. They left for the inn, and Arthur turned to see Samson watching in concern.

"I could've let you take her," Arthur told the captain.

His eyes turned to meet Arthur's, and they hardened in resolve.

"My place is here to defend the village."

"It's okay to care, Samson. We all need someone to keep us grounded. You don't have to be alone to fulfill your duty," Arthur said in sympathy.

Samson looked down for a moment, and then his eyes lifted back to Arthur. "I'll consider it. The military lifestyle in me has a tough time adjusting to that idea. Do you think she'd welcome the advance?"

Arthur chuckled. He'd seen this man hold his ground against a fearsome charging boar and take the charge head-on, but the idea of Vana rejecting him worried him. Women sure knew how to get to a man.

"There's no harm in trying. I think you've got an excellent shot," Arthur told him in all seriousness, "she's a fiery woman, but I think she'd welcome a strong man who's also a fighter himself."

"How are things looking past the wall?" Arthur asked.

"Honestly? Looks like you kicked over an anthill. We can see torches scurrying around the edge of the camp and one larger blaze that was easy to spot from here. I guess that was your doing?" Samson asked.

"Yep, sure was. We needed a distraction. Ended up killing an impressive amount of them too," Arthur told him as he did a quick check of his experience gains.

*Goblin Fighter (Level 13) has died (x5).*
*Orc Commander (Level 17) has died (x2).*
*You have gained 1,325 total Experience in Archery and the Subskill Aim Shot.*
*Congratulations, you have progressed to level 8 in Archery. You are granted a 21% bonus to accuracy. Aim first, then shoot.*
*Congratulations, you have reached level 5 in the Subskill Aim Shot. Increases firing speed and time dilation by 12%. Aim carefully and release.*
*You have gained 1,750 total experience in Stealth.*
*Congratulations, you have reached levels 3 and 4 in Stealth. You are 9% more difficult to detect by enemies.*
*You have gained 1,500 total experience.*
*You have gained 760 total experience due to raid member kills.*

He hadn't noticed Aim Shot was already past level four, but when he searched back through his notifications, he saw it happened during the initial assault on the wall. His shifted focus to a melee fighter had caused him to stop using the ability much.

"What's your assessment?" Arthur asked.

"Judging by the mayhem there? I'd say they'll get the mess cleaned up and turn in for the night again. I wouldn't expect an attack before daybreak," Samson told him.

"Sounds good. I'm headed to the inn to sleep. Send someone for me if things get interesting. Make sure you get some sleep yourself. We'll need you fresh in the morning," Arthur told him.

Samson nodded at him, and Arthur left for the inn. His walk back was calm and leisurely, but before he made it halfway, Allendria walked up beside him.

"Eventful evening?" she asked.

"It was. Couldn't do any less."

She turned to look at him with a hunger in her eyes. "Care to make it a little more eventful?"

His smile stretched ear to ear as she led him in the bathhouse's direction. He knew he needed the sleep, but he'd be damned if he was turning down a woman with that look in her eyes.

# Chapter 13



*Decisions, Decisions*

Rayne watched the attack with reserved glee. Not only had the tiny village of Alem's Crossing repelled the orc forces, but they also did it with almost no effort at all. Only a handful of the goblins reached the wall, and even those fell to the defender's arrows. The call to retreat was amusing to watch as they returned, though.

A wicked part of Rayne enjoyed the sight of the orc commanders executing the orc forces that called for the retreat. *Brutality could sure demonstrate a lesson when needed.*

Rayne was on the fence about sticking around and trying to get to the village or just turning tail and retreating for the nearest city. After what he witnessed, he now understood why the Goddess sent him. If the village was holding out this well, they could be a genuine force of change. Joining them may be the key to overthrowing some of the evil in the world, starting with a small army of goblins.

He cut his musings short as he watched the scene unfold. His hidden location on the northern side of the army kept him safe, but the sight of the three figures with purple skin emerging from the trees chilled him to the bone. The grace they exuded with their casual travel reminded him of only one other being he'd encountered.

The people of Alem's Crossing should be
able to hold off the goblins and orcs, but if
the Dark Elves joined the fight, the momentum
might swing the other way. Rayne continued to
watch as the forces met, and the orcs gathered
around the leader of the Dark Elves. From this
distance, he couldn't be sure, but he thought
the leader was none other than Lyrinth. He
strained his hearing to make out any part of
the conversation, but it was no use. With his
attempt at eavesdropping failing, he waited
for them to take action, instead.

The archery skills exhibited by the
defenders of the village looked impressive
unless you scrutinized them. Rayne spotted the
many missed shots and also knew they only had
a handful of people effective at a distance.
When the attackers got close, the story
changed, though. The goblins and orcs would
attack again, but there was a good chance they
were planning a way to negate the arrow fire.

Rayne backed away from the edge of the
trees and headed for their encampment. He
hadn't made it three steps before he heard a
noise in the brush ahead of him. Diving to the
side, he landed in a thick bush. Clinging to
the center stalk of the bush helped conceal
him as he wrapped his body around the small
shrub. He sat as still as possible and slowed
his breathing.

A group of three goblins walked past the bush he hid in. They followed the same game trail he'd been walking on. Judging by their odd grunts and grumbling, they weren't happy with their assigned duty. They continued past him without even stopping, and Rayne let out a sigh of relief. He could easily handle the three of them with the poor combat skills they displayed so far, but he didn't want the orcs to order more patrols around the area.

Drawing attention to their surroundings would only make it more difficult for him to sneak close enough to see what was happening. He extricated himself from the bush and plucked a few errant twigs from his outfit. The leather straps loved to reach out and grab things from time to time. *Damn forest doesn't agree with my city-style thief clothing.* He grumbled to himself.

The rest of the people with him camped a little over a mile behind the army, along the road. Upon arriving, the other scouts approached him.

"What's the verdict?" Howard asked.

"The village repelled the first attack without a single person being injured. I think they'll hold off the attack. Whether they can eradicate the force and give us a chance to get to the village, is an entirely different matter. I plan on going back tonight to see what I can discover," Rayne told them.

The third scout, George, looked to him. "Why ya doin' that? Seems like a good way to get shot or stabbed."

"I'll take care of myself. I need to see how this plays out. With luck, I'll be able to find an opening to get a message to someone in the village," Rayne told him.

Both men looked at him like he was a fool but didn't bother to argue. There was no point in trying to change his mind. They learned that shortly after this entire trip started. Rayne went from group to group, reassuring them that the village held and looked promising. These people needed every bit of hope he could give them. Their lives had been tough for a long span, and now that they uprooted everything for a chance of something better, their new salvation was under siege.

"How you holding up?" he asked Libby.

"Fine. Are you going to stop sneaking off to watch the fight? You're just one man. You can't fight them all yourself."

"You know I need to. Someone has to see what's happening. It may become important to step in and assist at a crucial turning point. This is our only hope," he told her quietly.

"Can't someone else do it?" she pleaded with him.

"You already know the answer to that. I'll be careful. I promised to take care of you, and I can only fulfill that promise while I'm living. Have some faith in me, little one," Rayne said with a chipper tone.

"I would, but you have a nasty habit of making stupid mistakes," she told him dryly.

"Psh, fair enough. I'll strive to be more careful."

They sat in silence together. She handed him her brush, one of the few belongings she'd brought with her from home. He sat down behind her and started brushing her hair. Rayne didn't mind, though, and it helped ease his sister. She needed every bit of help she could get lately. If it meant he had to sit there and brush her hair for hours, it was a sacrifice he'd gladly make.

When her nerves calmed, she finally laid
down to sleep. It was still midday, but Rayne
planned to be out again tonight. He laid next
to his sister and dozed off for some needed
rest.

* * *

Rayne's return trip through the woods was a
little rockier than he'd hoped. More patrols
were out, and he had to duck and hide more
times than he'd liked to admit. One time even
left him quickly scaling a tree to hide in its
branches because of the lack of underbrush. He
moved at a slower pace and kept an ear out for
the patrols, so he had plenty of time to find
a spot to hide.

He regained his previous hiding spot
shortly before dark and didn't see any sign of
the Dark Elves. The camp moved about again and
looked to be digging in for the night. Rayne
initially guessed they'd try a night assault,
but the arrows must've spooked them. He
watched as the goblins milled about for the
evening and did nothing more than cause a mess
of perfectly beautiful countryside.

Movement drew his attention to the woods on
the other side of the goblin camp. Teams of
goblins entered the forest and came back out
with small trees and wood of varying sizes.
While some of it was meant for firewood, the
sheer volume of timber leaving the forest told
Rayne they planned something.

Rayne alternated his view between the camp
and the village walls. Soldiers dotted the
walls, and he watched one shift rotation as he
observed the action. Right before dark, he
spotted a silhouette descend from the sky
toward the village. He thought it was merely a
bird at first, but the closer it came to the
ground, the more he was sure it was too big
for a bird. The creature landed somewhere in
the middle of the buildings and disappeared.
The odd sight perplexed him. His focus turned
back to the goblins, and he sat and watched.

The evening turned dark, and visibility
faded. He activated his Ring of Darksight, and
the night sky lit up in front of him. The best
part was, the ring didn't have a maximum
distance for its effect. Instead of just
illuminating the area in front of him, it
caused his eyes to change the way they
filtered light and allowed him to see as far
as his eyes usually would as if it were
daylight.

The evening moved on with little action
until Rayne noticed something suspicious. Near
the wall of the village, a small group of
people converged. They must have snuck around
from the southern side of the fence, but Rayne
was paying more attention to the goblin camp
than the village. He watched as the group
worked their way through the dead and grabbed
weapons and arrows, piling them up near the
wall. More than likely, they would tie them
into a big bundle and have someone lift them
over the wall.

Their work was far more interesting than what the goblins were doing, so his focus stayed on them. They all gathered by the piled up armaments, and Rayne almost fell over in surprise when a solid black doorway appeared near them. He watched as each person started throwing items in as fast as they could grab them. The loud clang of the weapons was barely audible to him, so he was sure the noisy goblins didn't hear a thing. When they finished, the doorway just vanished.

He expected the group to disappear back into the village now that they had the spoils of war. To his further surprise, two of them moved toward the goblins while the rest went back around the wall toward the northern gate. Rayne's eyes stayed glued on the two as they crept forward. He watched them close in on the closest sentries and stop. Rayne smiled with a bit of inner joy as he watched them silently drop both targets and move closer.

Rayne didn't want to miss what would happen, so he left his concealment and crept toward the camp himself. There were multiple camp areas, but he veered around the back and headed for the one the two unknown figures approached. Rayne had a feeling this would be interesting.

The two advanced and then retreated while Rayne crept forward, causing him to consider stopping and going back to his concealment. Since they stopped at the two dead sentries and didn't continue toward the village walls, he kept moving forward. The two skirted the side of the camp and took a position near an enormous pile of crates and supplies.

*I'm really starting to like these two if they're doing what I think they are.* As he watched events unfold, they were, in fact, doing what he thought. The surprising part was, Rayne watched the male figure set arrows on fire with his hands. This person was a magic-user and wore some fancy-looking armor.

The fire they started went up quickly, and they retreated farther along the edge of the enemies. Rayne held position on the backside of this group and watched. The goblins went into a frenzy and started trying to contain the fire to no avail. The two he was observing began firing into the camp. At first, he couldn't figure out what they were shooting at. He expected them to pick off people trying to fight the fire. After some careful observation, he decided he liked these two. They were picking off the lazy ones, sitting around the camp, and ignoring the fire.

Rayne saw movement out of the corner of his eye and shifted his gaze. A group of orcs moved toward the commotion. His vision flashed back to the two unknown figures, and then he glanced toward the night sky. He couldn't explain why he did, but in the air, he spotted the flying object he'd seen earlier in the day. To his utter shock, it was a small dragon-looking creature.

Rayne was only familiar with their basic description from the tales the members of the Shadows of the Flame used to tell. His old group of rebels were loyal to the Firebrand family, so stories of their blood and the dragons were popular ways to waste time when they weren't on a mission.

His gaze shot straight back to the two attackers, and he watched as an arrow struck one of the newly arrived orcs, and they collapsed. It wasn't long until the cries of alarm started for the actual attack that was happening. More enemies died, and Rayne saw the two turn to run off.

A glow of red caught his attention toward the back of the camp. His vision locked on one caster in the goblin army, building a small ball of fire in their hands. They reared back to launch it at the fleeing people. Rayne couldn't explain why, but he quickly snatched a small dagger from his belt and hurled it with all his strength.

The blade spun end over end until it impacted the caster. The knife hit the caster with the edge of the blade rather than the point.

*You have dealt 10 damage to Goblin Mage (Level 15) with Iron Throwing Knife (Glancing Blow).*

*Congratulations, you have learned the skill Throwing Knives for a 100 experience bonus.*

*Warning! You have joined an active raid. Your actions have caused you to join the side of Defenders of Alem's Crossing. Your actions have caused you to accept the Quest: Repel the Raid.*

| Repel the Raid |
| --- |

| Requirements: Participate in actions to directly or indirectly influence the outcome of the raid.<br>Rewards: 15,000 experience, 3,000 Unassigned Skill Experience, 5 Talent Points | Description: A new raid has started near Alem's Crossing. Aid either side in the fight. If the side you assist survives the raid, you receive the rewards. |
| --- | --- |

That wasn't part of his plan, but it could make for an extraordinary amount of experience if they could survive. Rayne admonished himself about never picking up Throwing Knives, but better late than never. It was enough to knock the caster's aim off and cause the small projectile to strike the woman in the leg instead of hitting one of them directly. Rayne sighed in relief at that, but he couldn't afford to sit here any longer. He scurried backward and quickly picked his way back to the tree line.

Looking back at the frenzied camp, he spotted the small flying creature hovering above the action. The beast was looking directly at him, so he turned to face it. He waved at it, gave it a quick salute, and turned to run for the trees again. The reaction may not be necessary, but it felt right.

When he reached the trees, he ran into two goblins. With the attack that just happened, he took the chance to dispatch them. Neither paid attention to anything, so a quick stab to each of their backs was all it took to take them out.

*You have dealt 180 damage to Goblin Scout
(1) (Level 12) with Iron Swordbreaker
(Critical Hit) (Mortal Blow).*
*You have dealt 180 damage to Goblin Scout
(2) (Level 12) with Iron Stiletto Dagger
(Critical Hit) (Mortal Blow).*
*Goblin Scout (Level 12) has died (x2).*

Rayne didn't bother checking the experience
notifications as he kept moving. He'd seen
notifications his entire life and had learned
to ignore any that weren't combat-related or
from recent skill acquisitions. Wasting no
time, he headed directly for camp. More sleep
would be welcome, but he needed to check on
the situation there first. There was a good
chance tomorrow would be interesting.

He wasn't far from camp when a shadow stood
up from the grass with an arrow pointed his
way. Holding up his hands, he came to a stop.

"Whoa, Howard. It's just me," he told the
ranger.

The bow dropped back down, and Howard
walked forward.

"Anything interesting happening at the
camp?"

"More than you know. I got to watch the
defenders pull a small night raid against the
orc forces. Set a large stack of supplies on
fire and even picked off around a dozen
goblins and a handful of the orc commanders.
The numbers weren't much, but it was only two
people doing it."

Howard whistled. "Wow, just two did that
much damage? Did they get caught?"

"Nope, they both made it back to the wall.
The orcs injured one, but it didn't look
serious."

"This might just turn out in our favor," Howard said with a glimmer of hope.

"We can only hope. I plan on getting some sleep for now. I'll watch the events unfold tomorrow. It's stacking up to be an interesting day," Rayne told him.

They nodded at each other, and Rayne continued toward the camp. He slowed his pace and enjoyed a leisurely walk. On the horizon, he spotted something that worried him. His speed increased, and before long, he was in a dead sprint to the camp. His course led him directly to one of the camp leaders. Her name was Tina, and she was a wild little thing. You didn't question her too much, or she'd bite your head off, but she had a heart of gold. She was always quick to help when needed. Rayne stood outside her small sleeping area and called for her. It took a minute, but she finally stumbled over to him.

"What the hell are you waking me up for?"

"I think we have trouble coming. I see light on the horizon and fear we may have another force marching this way. I need to go scout it to see what we're dealing with, but we need everyone hidden and out of the clearing. Smother all the fires as best you can and move them to the trees. We may not have a lot of time."

She nodded in agreement as her gaze swept the direction he pointed. Rayne dashed through the camp and found Libby. Arriving beside her, he gently shook her awake.

"You need to get our stuff together and
follow the others. I'm going to check out
something in the distance, but I fear more
soldiers may be heading this way, and we don't
know if they are friendly or not. Tina can
help if you need anything," Rayne told her
quietly.

She nodded her head as she rocked forward
and wrapped her arms around him.

"Stay safe and come back," she whispered.

"Always and forever," he answered her
softly. He wouldn't rush her hug and let her
take a few more moments. When she composed
herself and pulled back, he lifted her chin
with his finger and smiled at her.

"Keep your head up. We'll get through
this," Rayne said with every bit of cheer he
could muster.

A slight grin came to her face, and he got
to his feet. One last nod to his sister and he
was off at full speed again. He dodged through
the different people camped in the area,
trying to avoid making too much noise. The
approaching army may hear the commotion and
investigate. Tina would get them all up and
moving as quickly and quietly as possible.
This whole caravan would've fallen apart long
ago if not for her careful ministrations.

He sped across the field, making excellent
time. He'd deactivated the ring when in the
camp but now had it active again. Being able
to see clearly allowed him to maintain a quick
pace without danger of hurting himself. A
slight ridge marked the landscape in front of
him, so he slowed his pace. Running over the
edge and right into a sizeable force of
enemies would be a supremely awful idea.

He crouched low and crept to the edge. The
drop wasn't steep, and the sloped path to the
top was only a few hundred yards from here. He
caught sight of where the glow came from and
broke into a heavy sweat. Reinforcements had
arrived, and there may be no hope for the
people of the village now. With those
depressing thoughts, he dashed back to the
camp to help get them out of sight before this
group made it to them.

# Chapter 14

*Final Preparations*

banging noise reverberated in his head. The late night came back to hit him hard. His sheer drowsiness caused him to turn to his side to resume sleeping when clarity came to him. *The village is under siege.* He bolted upright in bed and hurried to get dressed.

"What is it?" he called from the room.

"The goblins and orcs have been in a frenzy since the sun came up. Paladin Samson thought you might want a chance to eat before they need you at the wall," a voice said through the door.

"Thanks for the heads up. You can go about your business. I'll head downstairs shortly."

Arthur heard the guard walk down the hall as he resumed getting ready. Allendria woke up during all the commotion and was now up and getting dressed as well. Arthur outfitted himself in his armor, and Allendria helped him slip the chest piece on.

The two entered the common room of the inn to a sizeable crowd. People ran everywhere carrying supplies, food, bundles of arrows, and everything else imaginable. Armored people sat around much of the room, eating. There was some good-natured joking filtering through the crowd, but it was a rather stoic atmosphere, all things considered.

Taking Samson's advice, Allendria and Arthur got a quick bite to eat. While they ate, Daniel came to the table and reminded Arthur of something he'd forgotten.

"When can you help me stash the meat we have so it doesn't go bad?"

"Forgot all about that. As soon as we finish eating, I'll open the dimensional storage behind the inn, and we can get that loaded before I return to the wall," Arthur told him.

Daniel nodded in agreement and went back to his work. The man never seemed to have the time to sit and relax. Arthur couldn't tell if it was because he stayed busy or if he was just one of those people that felt they always needed to be moving. They finished their food quickly, and Arthur went to the kitchen. He waved at Daniel as he passed and motioned out back.

The familiar Dimensional Storage door opened as he cast his spell. There was one enormous problem with the storage that he hadn't considered until recently. Throwing all the dead creatures in there was a marvelous way to haul them back to the village, but it left one hell of a mess to clean up with all the blood on the floor. You wouldn't want to store good food or supplies on something like that. When the door opened, the cleanliness of the space surprised him. Something inherent in the magic must clean unwanted fluids and grime from the floor. He honestly couldn't begin to describe why or how, but he wouldn't complain.

Arthur and Daniel hauled food into the storage room from the kitchen. Luckily, Daniel found some old crates and wooden barrels to store the meat in. He assured Arthur they'd thoroughly cleaned them before any food went in, but Arthur waved his explanation away. He'd seen Daniel prepare food and methodically clean his inn enough to know the man wouldn't take chances with the village food. It took them a good fifteen minutes, but they got all the food loaded into the storage.

"Do I just need to flag you down when we need more? I kept enough to last a day or two, but we have to cook all of it into longer-lasting stews. It'd spoil otherwise," Daniel said.

"Yeah, I can open it anytime you need. This is just a temporary solution. When this raid is out of the way, I plan on fixing this problem with a long-term solution. I'm sure you're aware this has the inherent flaw that only I can access it. I have a plan to make a room that can safely store food for longer periods without the need to salt it," Arthur explained.

Daniel nodded at that. "I remember you mentioning that. I can't say I understand what you're referring to, but I guess I'll take your word for it."

"You'll see when I'm done. I have to get to the wall. Samson said they're scurrying around this morning, and I want a status report on how things are going. I'll see you later," Arthur called as he walked back into the common room of the inn.

The crowd in here looked much the same. A few fresh faces peppered the room, but the mood remained constant. He continued past them all and out front while Allendria trailed right behind him.

"I'll check on the construction crews to see how their progress is going, and catch up with you on the wall when I'm done," Allendria told him.

Arthur nodded, and she darted off toward the primary staging area for the construction work. Arthur's mind wandered as he walked to the wall. These issues kept popping up, and it was always at the worst time. He just needed a stretch of peace to allow the village to build up and prosper, but instead, he kept getting assaulted by unknown forces. His construction crews could be put to much better use improving the village, and now they were being forced to help brace for the siege.

Arthur was never a violent man himself and had always been fond of making things more than destroying them. The fact that forces kept conspiring to destroy what he worked hard to rebuild angered him. *Why does everything in this world keep pushing me toward fighting?* Arthur thought to himself with a resigned feeling.

Before he realized it, he arrived at the gatehouse, and Samson came down from one of the archer platforms to talk to him. He shook himself out of his dark reverie and turned his attention to Samson.

"Status?" Arthur asked.

"They're preparing to assault the wall. It's probably best if you see for yourself," Samson told him.

Arthur nodded and followed him up the stairs to the archer platform he vacated minutes ago. When he reached the top, Arthur peeked through the crenellations to assess the situation. His gaze swept over the forces. Looking at the activity in the camp, Arthur wasn't sure if their preparations excited him or not. He knew they'd try to find some way to counteract their arrows. Based on what he saw, they were doing precisely what he hoped.

They were constructing large wooden shields. Some were for charging infantry, but others were so wide they'd need multiple units to carry. Looking at them closely, Arthur could see the strategy. They would creep the enormous walls forward with a sizeable force concealed behind them. When they were close enough, the enemy could come around the wall and attack. Well, that was his original thought, until he saw one wall from a different angle. There were stairs built into the back of the wall. The damn creatures had built a wall that acted as a siege tower.

This design would typically be useless because the defenders on the wall could use their height to shoot over the top of the wooden barricade and kill those behind it. Since the village wall wasn't very high yet, by the time the wall was close enough they could shoot over it, it'd also be close enough for the goblins to race up the stairs and assault those at the top of the wall.

As much as Arthur dreaded it, it was time to pull out their magic. He hoped to keep it a secret until he knew if they'd have to go toe to toe with the Dark Elves running this band, but without it, this fight would take a turn for the worse.

He motioned for Samson to come with him, and they descended the stone stairs. When they reached the bottom, he turned to the captain with a sigh.

"It's time for magic. We still have a little time before they finish those barriers. I'll run to the blacksmith and get busy making some new arrows. We'll need them to counteract their wooden defense," Arthur summarized.

Samson nodded along as Arthur spoke. The man was stalwart in his duty.

"I'll send someone for you if it looks like they're ready to attack."

*That delay could be costly.* With a flash of inspiration, he turned to look to the sky. He spotted the speck he hoped would be hovering up there.

*Keeping an eye on things?* Arthur sent to Balair.

*Pretty dull, unless you count watching goblins chop down trees.*

*I'll take dull. The longer they take, the more time we have to prepare. Can you do me a favor? Watch Samson. If he sees anything that makes him suspect an attack is coming soon, he'll signal you. You can relay the message to me much quicker than him sending a runner,* Arthur explained.

*Oh, so now I'm a glorified messenger? Do you know who I am? I am a member of a proud bloodline that dates back for countless years. My power will amaze despite my stature,* Balair sent.

Arthur chuckled to himself at the crazy little creature.

*Is that why you wouldn't fight Lazaru and his group? You were afraid it wouldn't have been a fair fight with all of your power and majesty?* Arthur said in a mocking tone.

*Had to test you somehow. Had to make sure you were worthy of my attention. I'll say you passed, albeit barely. I gave you a chance after that,* Balair told him with a sense of pride.

Arthur shook his head at the dragon's praise for himself. Lord help him if the little guy ever became more powerful. His ego would end up getting him killed.

*Fine, oh mighty one. Will you help me out?*

*Sure. Have Samson wave my way if he suspects something, and I'll relay the message,* Balair conceded.

"Samson, I just talked to Balair, and he's agreed to relay for you. If you need me, just find him in the sky and motion toward him. He can contact me mentally. It'll be much faster than sending a runner to the village."

"I always forget the little guy can communicate with you. Hard to imagine since he never talks. I'll signal to him. That idea is much better," Samson agreed.

Arthur turned and walked back to the village. His mind wandered again as he walked until Balair interrupted him.

*There was someone else there last night.* Balair sent him mind to mind.

Arthur stopped in his tracks. *What do you mean?*

*When you raided the goblin camp last night. I saw someone else during that fight. He saved either you or Vana from that caster.*

*What do you mean? That caster hit Vana with his spell,* Arthur sent in confusion.

*The caster hit her leg because the other person threw a knife and caused him to lose concentration. Otherwise, I'm sure either you or Vana would've been the recipient of a fireball directly to the back,* Balair told him solemnly.

*So another player in the game and we don't know if they're on our side or not?* Arthur sent.

*Well, I wouldn't say they were against us. He did attack the caster to help save you,* Balair said thoughtfully.

*True, but is it an enemy of my enemy type of scenario? Maybe he just used the chaos of our attack to get a hit on a target he was already hunting.*

*Be cautious, but I don't think that's what happened,* Balair told him.

*Why not?*

*He saw me. I watched him throw the knife, and then he retreated from the camp and headed back to the woods on the northern side of the army. He crossed part of the field and then stopped and looked right at me. He waved at me and then turned and kept running for the trees,* Balair told him.

*Odd. You sure he saw you and wasn't waving to someone on the ground?* Arthur asked.

*Yes, I'm sure, you fool. My sight isn't the best in the dark, but I was close enough to see him. He looked directly at me and waved. It's also important to note it was another human,* Balair told him.

*Interesting. This could open up a whole other host of problems, but for now, I need to focus on the assault. This will have to be a concern for another day.*

*Keep an eye out for him. I'd like to talk to him if the chance ever presented itself,* Arthur responded.

He received the mental equivalent of a grunt of agreement and resumed his trek. His feet took him to the blacksmith where Rowan was busy at the anvil. It gave Arthur a sense of pride to watch Rowan use his newfound Arcane Smithing to make weapons. Arthur stood by and observed the magical work. He'd rarely had time to watch the spell happen from an observer's point of view. The magic flowed, and the steel reshaped itself. Before long, Arthur watched a handful of steel arrowheads fall to the anvil with the tinkling sound of metal.

"You're getting the hang of that quickly," Arthur called to Rowan.

"Yeah, it's easy when I already understand the way to forge the items. Much easier to visualize how it should look when I'm familiar with the design. I struggle on unfamiliar concepts, though," Rowan confided in him.

Arthur clapped the big guy on the back. "You'll get the hang of it. Don't worry about it."

"How's the situation out there," Rowan said as he motioned toward the northeastern wall.

"They're preparing to assault the wall and are building large wooden shields in addition to moving wooden walls with stairs on the back. They appear simple, modified versions of siege towers."

"Damn. So why are you back here and not on the wall?"

"They're still preparing for their assault and aren't ready to attack yet. In the meantime, I've determined it's time to use magic. The next assault will require it," Arthur explained.

"Need any help?" Rowan asked.

"Not really. Going to make enchanted arrowheads that can do fire damage to the wooden shields and wall. If we can set them on fire, they can't use them as effectively. The wall could still be tricky. Even on fire, they can still push it and make it harder for us to see them. I'm still working on that one," Arthur told him.

"Well, holler if you need anything. I've got to get back to work. Sounds like we'll need many more arrows."

Arthur moved away from Rowan and found the steel he needed. The problem was, he wasn't sure how this enchantment would work. *I'd kill to have a good old-fashioned machine gun right now. Talk about a quick way to solve the problem.*

That thought faded almost as quickly as it came. The idea of creating a firearm popped up a few times, but it always came down to the same thing. Making the gun would probably be possible. With enough experimentation, he'd be able to create a steel alloy that'd be suitable to make springs from and eventually figure out all the pieces needed to make a gun, even if he had to resort to an old-style musket. The actual problem came with ammunition. Making the casings and the bullet itself was not an issue with his Arcane Forging. Gunpowder halted the process.

Arthur had a vague idea of how to make
gunpowder. Few people on Earth could actually
tell you how it's made, except by the
companies that produced it. It wasn't a
closely guarded secret or anything, it just
wasn't something people would try to figure
out often. Arthur had been adventurous in
attempting to make homemade fireworks with
some friends back on earth, so he knew they
made it with a combination of saltpeter,
charcoal, and sulfur. Sourcing those materials
was difficult.

The charcoal was simple. The other two
might be tricky to find in abundance. There
was the chance he could replicate the effect
of gunpowder using enchantments, but that
would require some serious experimentation,
and there wasn't time to mess with it.

The key would be figuring out this
enchantment. Arthur knew he wouldn't have any
problem making the arrowheads. Trying to find
the correct enchantment that would allow the
arrows to emit fire was the snag. He could add
the symbol for fire and imbue it into the
bolt, but he was afraid that would just add
points of fire damage to the arrowheads and
not make an actual flame come out. He needed
something that would cause the shields and
walls to ignite.

After some careful thought, he still
couldn't get past the problem. His mind kept
thinking of unorthodox ways to imbue the
enchantment and scribe the words, but there
was no way he could do it that could guarantee
it'd work as he needed. *I'm more likely to
blow myself up trying to imbue these,* Arthur
thought to himself and then froze.

*If I can't catch the pieces on fire, why not make them explode?* If he could enchant something with a sizeable amount of Fire Magic, and then create something that would quickly discharge all the energy at once, it should create an explosion of fire. With this idea in mind, he set to work.

Finding something to contain an extensive amount of fire energy was relatively easy. His Mineral Compression would work nicely for this. Seeing the familiar pile of cast-off coal, he cast the spell three times to get some material to experiment with.

*You have gained 360 experience in Earth Magic for successfully casting Earth Magic Spell: Mineral Compression (x3).*
*You have received Manufactured Sapphire (x1) and Manufactured Ruby (x2).*

With some components in hand, it was time to experiment. Filling a gem with the magic was easy. Detonating it was the tricky part. Arthur considered creating a compact disc that would look similar to a watch battery from Earth, placing it on the end of the arrow shaft, near the head, and having it discharge the gem on impact. His concern was, when the arrow released from the bow, the force of the launch would cause the shaft to hit it immediately instead of on impact with a target.

If he couldn't rely on an impact explosion, it would require him to make a timed one. The new arrow design would fill the gem with Fire Magic and set it in the middle of a bodkin style arrow. Arthur made a small steel collar to fit the arrow shafts that could hold the gem. This collar contained some advanced matrix runes that would trigger the Fire Magic. This enchantment had a ten-second delay. If someone channeled a tiny bit of Fire Magic into it, the collar would activate and start the timer. The collar sent a signal into the gem to release its energy after the specified time.

The design took a lot of trial and error. On one attempt, Arthur blew up the gem, and it was almost too close to him. It left him temporarily deaf until his ears recovered. Another try he didn't have the expend portion of the enchantment correct, so, although it released the power, it did so slowly and in a small flame. It looked like the arrow spewed a Weak Flame spell. A few adjustments made sure it would quickly expel its energy in all directions.

    To further complicate the entire process.
It required multiple pieces to make. Arthur
sent for a handful of fletched arrow shafts
while he worked. He created the bodkin head
and the steel sleeve to connect the gem to the
shaft. Assembly was another matter. It
required Arthur to heat the end of the sleeve
so he could form it to the gem, then heat the
back of the bodkin arrowhead to attach it to
the sleeve. Finally, he needed to attach this
to the shaft. This process caused him to
nearly kill himself. When he heated the metal
on one piece, the enchantment was too close to
the heat and set itself off. He was being
careful and noticed the flaw, so he got rid of
it before it damaged him. The explosion was
impressive and had he not tossed it as far as
he could and dove to lay prone on the ground,
it would have severely damaged him.

    This incident bothered him and made him
reevaluate how and where to place the
enchantments. All the mistakes aside, he
finally completed an arrow and smiled with
pride at how well it turned out. Being new, he
could even give it a name. Not only that, but
he also gained two additional skills with it.

    *Congratulations, you have learned the
subskill Metal Construction for a 250
experience bonus.*
    *Congratulations, you have learned the
hidden subskill Arcane Metal Construction for
a 500 experience bonus.*

    *You have created a new and never before
seen item. Do you wish to name this new item?
Yes/No.*

*You have named this new item Timed Hellfire Arrow. You have gained a 500 experience bonus in Enchanting, Arcane Metal Construction, and Metal Construction.*

*Congratulations, you have reached level 2 in Metal Construction. Decreases the time it takes to assemble metal constructions by 3%. Building with metal now, huh?*

*Congratulations, you have reached level 2 in Arcane Metal Construction. Increases the effectiveness of metal constructions created with magic by 3%. I see what you did there.*

<table>
<tr><td>

Item:
Timed Hellfire Arrow

</td><td>

**Attack:** +3

**Durability:** 30/30

**Rarity:** Rare

**Quality:** Well Crafted

**Weight:** 0.1 kg

**Slot:** Arrow

**Traits:** A specially enchanted steel arrow. 10 seconds after activation, arrow explodes and deals fire damage to any near it. Damage done is based on the distance from the explosion.

Explosion Damage:
- Deals 140 fire damage to any

</td></tr>
</table>

|  | <ul><li>within 5 yards of the blast.</li><li>Deals 80 fire damage to any between 6 and 20 yards of the blast.</li><li>Deals 40 fire damage to any between 21 and 30 yards of the blast.</li><li>Has a chance to inflict burn status on any enemies hit with the arrow's effect.</li></ul> |
| --- | --- |

Both of the subskills fell under the Blacksmithing skill. It made sense because of the metalworking. The arrow was precisely what he needed, though. It would not only be more than enough to catch anything on fire but, if his luck held, the explosion could break apart some of the siege walls. Only time would tell, but it was their best option. With the kinks worked out and the first piece made, he went to work.

    His Arcane Smithing helped create the
necessary pieces while his new subskills
helped him assemble them. The exciting part
was the Arcane Metal Construction. Since he
hadn't learned a new spell for his work, this
meant the arrows were possible to create with
mechanical devices and would still function.
He only received the arcane version of the
skill because of his magical manipulation of
the metals. It may be necessary to determine
the best way to make these in a purely
mechanical fashion.

    After three hours of grueling work in the
blacksmith and some failures, he was the proud
owner of six of the arrows. Even when he
discovered the method to make them, it still
took him a long time to make each piece,
enchant it, and then assemble it without
blowing himself up. He needed to use his
Mineral Compression spell six more times to
get enough gems to power the arrows he now
had. He would've kept going, but he received a
message he was dreading.

    *Samson believes the attack is coming soon.*
Balair sent.

    *Thanks. On my way.*

    Arthur grabbed the arrows and headed for
the wall. Allendria met him as he passed the
inn. She held his bow and joined him on the
trip. He'd left the bow at the inn earlier,
but luckily, Allendria had the foresight to
bring it for him.

    As they jogged for the wall, Arthur handed
over one arrow for her to examine. Her eyes
widened in shock as she saw it.

    "You can make more of these?" she asked in
disbelief.

    "Of course, they're just time consuming to
make."

"These are invaluable against a force like this. Not as useful against some of the well-armed forces in this world, but rabble like this, it's perfect," she said in admiration.

"Glad you approve," he told her with a chuckle.

Arthur did a quick inventory of the experience he gained while working in the blacksmith shop.

*You have gained 720 experience in Earth Magic for successfully casting Earth Magic Spell: Mineral Compression (x6).*

*You have gained 800 experience in Earth Magic and Fire Magic for successfully casting Combination Spell: Arcane Forging (x16).*

*Congratulations, you have successfully created Timed Hellfire Arrow. You have gained 1,050 experience in Arcane Smithing, Blacksmithing, Metal Construction, and Arcane Metal Construction for creating this item (x6).*

*Congratulations, you have reached level 16 in Blacksmithing. You are granted a 45% bonus to forging speed. Honestly? Found another secret?*

*Congratulations, you have reached level 3 in Metal Construction. Decreases the time it takes to assemble metal constructions by 6%. You really like new skills, don't you?*

*Congratulations, you have reached level 3 in Arcane Metal Construction. Increases the effectiveness of metal constructions created with magic by 6%. Can you do anything without magic?*

*You have gained 1,560 total experience in Enchanting for enchanting 25 items.*

Nearing the wall, Arthur was pleased to see Vana come his way. She was back on her feet and moved with no issues. Whatever ointment she had for burns must've done the trick. When she approached, he handed her three of the arrows. By the look on the woman's face, you'd think Arthur had proposed to her, and that he was a millionaire. The sheer glee in her eyes almost scared him.

"Use them wisely. They're primarily for the siege walls," Arthur said calmly.

She nodded. "It's always nice to get a gift from a handsome man," she giggled before turning to see Allendria's icy glare.

"Uh, sorry, force of habit," she quickly amended with an abashed look.

Arthur fought to suppress a laugh. He definitely didn't want Allendria's gaze to shift focus to him. Arthur leaned over and took his bow from Allendria and kissed her on the cheek.

"You'll probably have to open up with your magic this time. Use it however you see fit."

"You always know how to talk to a lady," she told him with a wink.

"You." Arthur pointed to a guard. "Gather all the filled mana necklaces you can find and bring them to the gate. I think we'll need them before this fight is over."

The guard nodded and darted off. Arthur turned and took the stairs two at a time to join Samson on his platform. Arthur was about to speak when he noticed the grim expression on Samson's face. He turned to the army and froze.

"Samson, is it just me, or is that army larger?" Arthur asked in a low tone.

"Yep, that's the problem. Reinforcements arrived recently. They don't even look that tired, which leads me to believe they arrived in the night and stayed back a distance to recover before making themselves known," Samson summarized.

"What's the count?"

"From what we can tell, our estimates put them at another thousand units. Mostly goblin," Samson said in a resigned voice.

"Well fuck," Arthur said under his breath. *One step forward and two steps back, as usual.*

"Plans?" Samson asked.

"We'll use every trick we can. A guard is bringing up our reserve mana necklaces for the attack. I want every platform armed with at least one archer and one mage. We'll burn them back to hell," Arthur said in an icy fury.

Samson nodded at that. The two stood there in silence, staring at the enemy army.

*Arthur, trust the shadow.* He heard the soft and familiar voice in his mind.

*What does that mean?* He sent in response.

*You will understand when the time comes.*

*Really, you can't give me a straight answer?* He asked.

*Well, that wouldn't be any fun. Plus, there are rules to adhere to,* the Goddess Lianna responded.

*So, any chance you could help with my situation?* Arthur asked.

*Oh, finally coming around, are you? Do you wish to formally invoke my help?*

*That sounds ominous. What does it entail?* Arthur asked in a reserved tone.

*It would entail you becoming my Champion and not just by reputation. I can only grant my favor and power to those who have formally requested it. Samson requested it officially, so he received it. Instead of a champion, he specifically asked to become a paladin. You're classified as a champion of mine on this world by the other gods, but you've never formally accepted my power. Because of this, you've none of the benefits that come with that power,* she explained.

*There has to be a catch in that somewhere. It can't be as simple as just ask for it. What's in it for you?*

*For most, it is some kind of bond to me, for you, not really anything since we're already bonded by an agreement.*

Arthur thought about the situation. He had a nagging feeling that there was a catch in this agreement somewhere but couldn't figure it out. It couldn't be that simple. Samson had dedicated his service to her, and, as far as he knew, there were no other requirements Samson had for his position. If that held true, his agreement with her already bonded him to her when he came here. As much as he didn't care to trust these divine forces, he needed help.

*I formally accept your aid as your champion,* Arthur intoned.

*Done!*

A beam of light seared into him from the sky. The entire landscape turned a stark white, and he felt power coursing through his veins as he rose off the ground. He didn't know it, but the surrounding area stilled. Even the orc and goblin army all stopped moving and turned to watch the beam of solid white with a dark, floating figure in it. After an unknown length of time swimming in a glow of warmth and comfort, Arthur felt his feet touch the ground again. The light faded, and notifications met him.

*You have gained the title Champion of Lianna. This has unlocked the Divine Power Skill Tree. You have gained 2 divine points to use.*

### Title: *Champion of Lianna*

*You have gained the title of Champion of Lianna for pledging loyalty to her and formally accepting her aid. With it comes the following bonuses:*

- *Your maximum mana is increased by 300.*
- *Unlock access to the Divine Power Skill Tree.*

*Do you wish to access your Divine Power Skill Tree? Yes/No.*

Arthur couldn't select *Yes* fast enough. As the window popped up, he heard Lianna issue a ladylike snort punctuated with a '*You're welcome*' and stared at his new skill tree.

### *Novice Skills*

| Divine Fury (0/1) | Channel a raging storm around your body that deals 25hp/s damage to enemies. Lasts for 30 seconds.<br><br>Mana cost: 600<br>Cooldown: 3 days |
|---|---|
| Nurtured Growth (0/1) | Infuse plant life in a 100 square yard space with the power of divinity. Plants will grow 150% faster and produce 100% more usable food.<br><br>Mana Cost: 800 Mana<br>Cooldown: 2 Weeks |
| Call Wrath (0/1) | Marks a target enemy for wrath. All damage you do to a marked enemy is increased by 100% for 5 minutes.<br><br>Mana Cost: 150<br>Cooldown: 1 Day |
| Retribution (0/1) | Call upon holy fire to bathe an area and deal damage to all enemies in the space. Cast range of 200 yards. Deals 50 hp/s damage for 10 seconds.<br><br>Mana Cost: 500 mana<br>Cooldown: 5 days |

| Blessing of Salvation (0/1) | Send out waves of healing energy to revitalize allies near you. This ability will restore the health, mana, and stamina of all nearby allies by 40%<br><br>Mana Cost: 200<br>Cooldown: 7 days |
| --- | --- |

The options were incredible. The only downfall was he only had two points to spend. It appeared his title as Champion gave him more flexibility in how he progressed with skills. Samson told him it merely granted him his specific powers. It also listed these as novice skills. If he could advance these the same as other talent trees, then the future options were unthinkable. Granted, he had no way to know how to improve these. The proper question was, could he earn more points to unlock more skills?

*Lianna, thank you for the gift. Is it possible to earn more skill points?*

*Of course, silly man. Defeating Champions of an opposing God can grant you more points. Completing quests and defeating Champions are also the ways you level up your Divine Champion skill,* she told him.

He immediately pulled up his status sheet and saw a new skill named Divine Champion listed.

*For every five levels you gain in the Divine Champion skill, it will grant you a skill point. Just like your other skills, you can unlock hidden talents with unique criteria.*

Arthur was about to ask her about that, but she preempted his question.

*And no. I won't tell you what the hidden skills might be or how to unlock them,* she told him in an exasperated tone. *Now go kill some goblins, my Champion.*

Arthur grinned at her dismissal, but his mind turned back to the problem at hand. He sorely wanted to stop fighting and take back this world through trade and economy, but the world kept stopping his plans. His current issue needed fighting skills, and he was just handed some wonderful ones. He had a handful of options to choose from.

Out of the gate, he dismissed Nurtured Growth and Call Wrath. Nurtured growth, although significant, wouldn't help him stop this army. Call Wrath was good against one person, but he was facing a massive horde. Three options left may have been challenging to weed past, but one thing helped make his decision easy, Samson.

He knew Samson already possessed a mass healing spell from his Paladin abilities. While it didn't restore mana and stamina, it was still very potent. Since he could rely on Samson to take that role, he put his points into Divine Fury and Retribution. With the two new spells in his arsenal, he felt a bit of calm wash over him. A quick assessment of himself showed he had very respectable stats. He condensed the stat page to give himself an overview of what he needed to know for the fight.

<table>
<tr><td>Name: Arthur Firebrand</td></tr>
<tr><td>Level: 17</td></tr>
<tr><td>Age: 26</td></tr>
<tr><td>Race: Human</td></tr>
</table>

HP: 430/430
MP: 990/990
Stamina: 410/410

Strength: 14
Agility: 26
Intellect: 29
Wisdom: 13
Endurance: 20
Charisma: 9
Luck: 10

Experience:
21150/30000 (0 stat
points available)

**Skills** (175% boost to
any skill for level
up)

**Combat Skills:**

Archery: 8 (920/3800)
  - Aim Shot: 5
(395/1900)
Block: 2 (380/750)
Dual Wield: 5
(975/1900)
Identify: 1 (75/500)
Light Armor: 6
(700/2500)
Parry: 3 (550/750)
Scan: 4 (370/1400)
Small Blades: 6
(795/2500)
Spears: 2 (450/750)
Stealth: 4 (470/1400)
      - Detect
    Hidden: 1
      (50/500)
Swords: 7 (1155/3200)
Unarmed: 1 (275/500)

**Magic:**

Dimensional Magic: **11**
(3750/7200)
Earth Magic: 21
(42965/57000)

| | **Fire Magic:** 21<br>(25165/57000)<br>**Water Magic: 7**<br>(3050/3200) |
| --- | --- |

His new and expanded mana pool made him feel warm and fuzzy inside. Too bad the spells he gained from the Divine Tree were still so incredibly expensive. The best part was he now had additional mana storage that he quickly checked.

*Ember: Stored Mana: 3500/3500*
*Intricate Mage-crafted Steel Mana Amulet (Sapphire Storage):     Stored Mana: 10,000/10,000*

That was much better. Sitting at an effective mana pool of 14,490 was almost insane to think of. Unfortunately, he knew that would disappear far faster than he'd hope when this fight started. He'd also need to make some new offensive spells when this fight started so that it would drain more mana than usual.

His gaze turned to the force. They would need a strategy for this one. He turned to face Samson and waved at the man. Someone near Samson tapped him when he saw Arthur waving their direction and motioned for the captain to look. Arthur motioned for them to meet on the ground behind the gate. He didn't want to yell. The sound would carry too far.

They both climbed down from their spots. A glance around showed Vana, Allendria, James, and Zeke also coming down to join them. That would work out nicely if everyone was on the same page. When all of them gathered around, Arthur turned to address them.

"We need a plan for this to work. I think we can hold them at the gate and prevent them from ever taking the wall. The problem with that strategy is, they're bound to move around the walls and try to attack from other locations. We don't have the manpower to hold them back at that point. Samson, do you think you can be my wall?" Arthur asked.

Samson looked uneasy for a moment and then smiled. "What do you need from me?"

"I propose we allow them to get one of the siege walls into place so they can scale the wall with the steps. I want you standing at the top to show them the folly of their ways," Arthur told him.

Samson's smile grew from there.

"It would be my pleasure."

"Allendria, Zeke, Vana, and James, I need y'all to focus on containing them to the front of this wall. If any of them try to veer around the walls, use everything you need to push them back. Their numbers are larger so they can afford to spread out. We can't let that happen. I know I told you those arrows were for the walls, but you may need to use a couple for crowd control."

Everyone nodded in agreement. Arthur was about to take his spot on the wall when Zeke spoke up.

"What do we do about the ladders?" Zeke asked.

Arthur thought for a moment.

"Let a couple through from time to time. I plan to unleash all levels of hell with my magic today. They need some hope. Make sure you only let ladders land when there are melee defenders near that area on the wall."

"Sounds good."

Everyone gave each other grave looks and turned for their spots on the wall. Arthur rushed up the steps and watched as the goblins and orcs spread out across the field. Wooden ladders, shields, and four of the portable walls stood throughout the group. A sea of green enemies lined up rank upon rank in the open field. Arthur let out a slow breath and tried to calm his nerves. A feral war cry rang out over the field and utterly shattered his attempt to calm himself. The sound of a thousand voices yelling in unison shook the stone wall. The army was charging.

# Chapter 15

*Furious Assault*

The ground rumbled as the force approached. The large and bulky walls moved slower, carried by scores of goblins and a handful of the orcs. A sizeable group of orcs dotted the top of the distant hill. They looked like the commanders of the army. If they were within range, Arthur wouldn't hesitate to use his new skill to kill them all. Hopefully, they would advance closer as the battle progressed.

Arthur pulled his bow over his shoulder and set an arrow on the string. Lifting it, he waited until the enemy closed into range. Activating Aim Shot, he sighted and released. The arrow sped forward and punched straight through a goblin's throat. With as thick as the enemy was, he didn't truly need to use Aim Shot, but he didn't want to waste arrows. Taking them out in one shot was much better than hitting a limb and just wounding them.

His rate of fire continued. The rhythm of drawing the arrow, fitting it to the string, and releasing it became second nature. When the enemy was within thirty yards of them, he stopped using Aim Shot. He kept unleashing hell on the enemies until he reached back to find his quiver empty. He was about to drop his bow and start casting spells when a young man ran up to him and dumped another bundle of arrows into the quiver on his back. Nodding in thanks, he resumed his assault.

Arrow after arrow found a mark in the goblin army. Not every shot was a kill, but most of them at least removed an enemy from the fight. More than once, he took someone down with a blow that wasn't fatal, but their fellow raiders trampled them to death as they fell. Arthur did his best to target those carrying shields or ladders, although a few caught his arrows on their shields. The closest siege wall was now forty yards away and slowly trudging forward. Luckily, it was heading for Samson's spot on the wall.

Arthur shifted his focus to the second wall, crawling another twenty yards behind the first. It was time for some fun. Pulling out the first Hellfire Arrow, he activated Aim Sight. While in the time dilation, he picked his thumb up off the bow and lightly touched the side plate on the arrowhead. Channeling a small tendril of mana into the arrow, he felt it activate. Picking a spot near where the stairs connected on the back, he released.

It quickly soared across the open air and thudded into the wall. The arrow stuck fast, but a little lower than where he aimed. He held his breath in anticipation as he counted the seconds in his head until a loud boom sounded. Arthur watched in glee as a giant ball of fire erupted from the arrow and crawled along the front of the siege wall. The force of the detonation caused the wall to crack where the stairs connected, and the forces holding it struggled to keep it aloft. They managed for a brief time until the wall flexed, and the crack expanded enough to let flame shoot through. The fire burned some of the goblins carrying the wall, which led them to drop their section. This caused a chain reaction that further strained the already weak point, causing the wall to break apart even more. Within a few minutes, the two pieces of the wall had collapsed entirely and burned merrily.

The soldiers were still coming in unending waves, but a glance around showed him his people were doing an admirable job. The best part was, magic was still being used sparingly on their side. A glance at his notifications filled him with a bit of excitement.

*You have gained 8,700 total experience in Archery for killing Goblin Raider (x58).*

*Congratulations, you have progressed to levels 9 and 10 in Archery. You are granted a 27% bonus to accuracy. The exploding one was a nice touch.*

*You have gained 5,700 total experience in the Subskill Aim Shot for killing Goblin Raider (x38).*

*Congratulations, you have reached levels 6 and 7 in the Subskill Aim Shot. Increases firing speed and time dilation by 18%.*

*You have gained 11,600 total experience for killing Goblin Raider (x58).*

*Congratulations, you have reached level 18! You now have 5 available skill points. Just keep swimming.*

He was so engrossed with the combat that he hadn't noticed the level gain. His first thought was the kill count was far too high, but a glance through his combat log showed him most of those deaths were from his Hellfire Arrow. The damage it caused to the goblins, coupled with the wall collapsing on many of them and archers finishing off the rest, quickly added to his total count. He wished he had time to look through his talents for Aim Shot, but the battle was still moving nonstop.

He glanced at his stats and dumped two points into Agility, two into Strength, and one into Wisdom, bringing him to 28, 16, and 14, respectively. He flexed his hand with his extra strength and increased reflexes. The power he felt was almost like a drug as it coursed through him. An arrow snapped to the string, and he released. He completed the motion in a noticeably faster time. It wasn't a groundbreaking difference, but it was a welcome change.

Arthur continued firing into the mass of goblins until he saw a problem. Three ladders butted against a portion of the wall near where Zeke stood. All three were being scaled by goblins. If they didn't do something quickly, they'd lose that part of the wall. He couldn't get a decent shot from his current position, so he used his new weapon. The wall wasn't very wide along the edge, but, with his Agility, he could skirt along it until he came to Zeke's position, two archery platforms over.

Ember came free of its sheath and, in one smooth motion, cleaved through the nearest goblin as if it wasn't even there. He barely even felt a tug as the blade passed through its shoulder, across its body, and out the other side near the hip.

*You have dealt 240 HP damage to Goblin Raider (1) (Level 14) with Ember (Cleaving Strike)*
*Goblin Raider (1) (Level 14) has died.*

*Holy shit!* He knew Ember was a fantastic weapon, but the sheer power of that strike was impressive. More goblins noticed his arrival and gathered near him. Zeke tried to get arrows off in the close-range combat, but he was struggling. Two guards were in varying states of injury along the section of the wall.

With a malicious grin, Arthur activated his sword's spell Sheathe in Flame. Snarling blue fire burst from the guard of the weapon and flowed to cover the entire blade. Nearby goblins flinched backward at the display. Some looked especially fearful, and one even soiled himself. The smell was atrocious, but the effect was satisfying.

Dashing forward, he laid into the enemies and rushed for the ladders. One goblin foolishly tried to jump in front of him with an upraised weapon. Ember came down and cleaved through the pathetic iron weapon and continued directly into the creature's skull. It dropped to the ground dead.

Two more goblins moved to intercept him. He brought his dagger out and caught one strike on his dagger and the other on Ember. The sword's flame burned the weapon it came in contact with, and the goblin's iron knife discolored and distorted as Arthur forced pressure onto it. He twisted Ember and pushed the opponent's knife away while bringing the blade back across the ugly thing's face. It shrieked in pain as the flaming sword burned a large gouge across its face and melted one of its eyes. The stench of burning flesh almost made Arthur gag.

He pivoted to the side, and the second goblin fell off balance. It was foolishly trying to force him off balance by adding weight to its blade. When Arthur spun his sword and moved out of the way, the goblin fell forward, and Arthur brought his dagger back around and slammed it into the creature's back. It fell to the ground, twitching.

His assault kept him moving forward. Goblin after goblin ran to stop him, but the fire from Ember and his quick attacks with his dagger worked in his favor. Within a few minutes, he reached the ladder. More orcs scaled the crude contraptions as quickly as possible. Now was the time for magic.

Arthur was new to his magic, and while he was comfortable using it around the village to help, he wasn't familiar with weaving it into his fighting. The rational part of his brain with his years of life on Earth told him it wasn't possible. This caused him to fall back on hand to hand martial skills. It was time to force himself from that mold.

Arthur swung his sword out and cleaved the head of the next goblin that crested the top of the ladder. The body and head both went backward and collapsed off the ladder, hitting some of its allies on the way down.

Arthur didn't have many offensive spells in his arsenal, but that was about to change. He leaned over the edge and pictured a large spray of flame flying from the end of Ember and engulfing the ladder and those on it. Pushing Fire Magic into the idea as quickly as he could, he watched in fascination as the flame built in intensity along the edge of Ember before spewing from the end like a flamethrower. The inferno was warm enough to make his face feel like he developed a slight sunburn.

He held the power and let it flow from him as his mana plummeted. Such a large spell taxed his normal mana, but he also knew he was creating a new spell. After twenty solid seconds of scorching flame, he cut off the magic and received a notification.

*Congratulations, you have discovered the Fire Magic Spell: Flamethrower. You have gained 250 experience in Fire Magic for discovering a known spell.*

*You have gained 300 experience in Fire Magic for successfully casting Flamethrower.*

| Spell: Flamethrower | |
| --- | --- |
| Requirements: Fire Magic<br>Mana Cost: 150 MP<br>Cast Time: 4 seconds<br>Cooldown: 2 Minutes | Description: Concentrate extreme heat in front of you and blast it out in a cone. This spell deals damage to anything in its AOE Path.<br><br>AOE Path Size: 8'x8'x30'<br>Damage: 25hp/s<br>Duration: 20 seconds<br>Additional Effect: Ignites any flammable material in its path. |
| Mastery Level: 1 | |

*You have dealt 1,440 HP damage to Goblin Raider (Level 14) (x6).*

*Goblin Raider (Level 14) (x6) has died.*

*You have gained 1,200 total experience for killing Goblin Raider (Level 14) (x6).*

One spell and six dead enemies to go with it. That didn't even count the experience he gained during the charge through goblins to reach the ladder. A glance showed the totals from it.

*Goblin Raider (Level 14) (x9) has died.*

*You have gained 1,050 total experience in Swords.*

*You have gained 1,225 total experience in Small Blades.*

*You have gained 525 total experience in Block.*

*Congratulations, you have reached level 3 in Block. Successful blocks grant you a 6% chance to stumble the opponent. Good job, Grasshopper.*

*You have gained 1,800 total experience for killing Goblin Raider (Level 14) (x9).*

The ladder hit by the Flamethrower spell was nothing more than a charred skeleton. There was no doubt it'd crumble into ashes as soon as someone touched it. His gaze moved to the remaining two ladders leaning against the wall. His Flamethrower spell was fantastic, but a high mana cost and a cooldown limited it. The mana cost wasn't an issue with his current setup, but the cooldown was surely killing him.

Running to a point between the two remaining ladders, he looked over his shoulder at the guard behind him. "Cover me while I take care of these two."

He bent over and placed his hands on the wall for direct contact. His mind reached into the ground and funneled up more rock into the wall itself. The magic pulled and condensed the surrounding stone until he had enough extra for what he wanted. With a quick force of will, he caused two pillars of solid rock to punch out, away from the wall, and send the two remaining ladders flying from the power of impact.

The amount of mana used in that spell startled him. Even his attempt to learn Flamethrower had only cost him around 400 mana. The cost to cast this last spell totaled 700 mana. He was subconsciously refilling his mana reserves from the surplus in his amulet. Since they removed the enemies from the wall, he had a bit of time to check and find out why the mana cost was so high.

*Congratulations, you have discovered the Earth Magic Spell: Stone Punch. You have gained 250 experience in Earth Magic for discovering a known spell.*
*You have gained 350 experience in Earth Magic for successfully dual casting Stone Punch.*

| Spell: Stone Punch | |
| --- | --- |
| Requirements: Earth Magic<br>Mana Cost: 80 MP<br>Cast Time: 2 seconds<br>Cooldown: 60 seconds | Description: Pull in dense concentrations of stone to force out in a column of stone. Only works in places stone or soil is present.<br><br>AOE Path Size: 3'x3'x8'.<br>Damage: 50 HP blunt damage. |
| Mastery Level: 1 | |

*Congratulations, you have learned Dual Casting for a 500 experience bonus.*
*Goblin Raider (Level 14) (x4) has died.*
*You have gained 800 total experience for killing Goblin Raider (Level 14) (x4).*

*So, I dual cast the spell. That would explain why the cost was so much higher.* Arthur wanted some more information on the rules of Dual Casting, so he called up the skill description.

*Dual Casting - Allows you to cast two spells at the same time. You can cast any two spells together. It allows you to dual cast two copies of the same spell by paying the spell cost for both abilities plus an additional 50%. If you dual cast a spell that has a cooldown, it increases the cooldown until next use by 200%. If you cast two spells from opposite elements together, there is a 50% chance of failure for both spells.*

*Well, that explained a lot.* He was also foolish enough to learn Dual Casting at the same time as a new spell, so it increased the already overly enormous mana cost of creating the new spell by 250%. He couldn't get caught up in this problem now. The fight was still moving around him, and he needed to get back into the fray.

A look around showed Samson standing in front of the stairs of the siege wall, assaulting anyone who dared to crest the top. Samson swung his shield and hit a goblin in the face that sent him tumbling over the edge of the wall and back into the crowd. Arthur turned and spotted Zeke. The man fired arrows as quickly as he could. Before Arthur shifted his focus, he saw a dark black arrow sprout from the man's left shoulder. Zeke fell to the ground and grabbed the shaft in pain. Arthur was about to run over and help the man, but he watched as a stern look spread over his face and then yanked. A gush of blood came out with a chunk of flesh. He yelled out and looked on the verge of collapse. Zeke still got back to his feet and looked out over the battlement.

Since it appeared Zeke would be okay, Arthur swept his gaze across the wall. The defenders were holding out well, but many showed injuries and looked exhausted. They were rotating melee fighters to the front when new ladders made it to the wall so the rest could get a momentary break. A ladder hit the wall near him, and he was back in the fight. He stood his ground at the wall and took his time systematically killing any who came up the ladder. The battlefield was still crawling with goblins, but almost none of the orcs joined the fight. To Arthur's dismay, another of the siege walls closed the distance to his portion of the wall. With no more time to waste, he cast Flamethrower at the ladder in front of him. He couldn't afford to let it stay there while he tried to deal with the siege wall.

*You have gained 300 experience in Fire Magic for successfully casting Flamethrower.*

*You have dealt 960 HP damage to Goblin Raider (Level 14) (x4).*
*Goblin Raider (Level 14) (x4) has died.*
*You have gained 800 total experience for killing Goblin Raider (Level 14) (x4).*

With the ladder a smoking ruin, his gaze shifted to the siege wall. It was forty yards away and closing quickly. He pulled another Hellfire Arrow from his quiver and set it to the string. Activating Aim Shot, he touched the side of the arrow and channeled the mana in to activate the timer. He was lining up the shot when something impacted the back of his left shoulder and sent the arrow flying. It missed its mark and hit a foot in front of the wall and stuck in the ground.

Arthur turned toward the direction of the strike and saw a goblin standing there. It had its iron dagger above its head and was getting ready to drive it in him again when Arthur sidestepped the attack and kicked the creature in the side. It stumbled and fell over the wall and back onto its fellow goblin attackers. Confused about the event, he looked at the log.

*You have taken 0 HP damage from Goblin Raider (Level 14) (Armor).*

The log didn't tell him much, but it appeared the goblin's weapon wasn't able to penetrate his armor. He didn't dwell on it any longer because he heard the explosion of his arrow. It drew his gaze to the field where his shaft landed. A fiery conflagration engulfed the center of the siege wall. His luck held and, although the arrow hadn't hit the wall, the forces had continued forward and walked past it. When it exploded, it did so directly under the marching forces and behind the wall. This caused the attacker's side of the wall to catch on fire, and the ones that survived the blast dropped it and scattered.

A glance down the wall surprised him. Zeke was up and firing his bow again. He didn't look like it had injured him at all. Some other soldiers along the wall that Arthur knew had been in terrible shape and now seemed as good as new. He had a tough time figuring out why until he saw a notification that was continually climbing.

*You have gained a 100 experience bonus for learning the Medium Armor skill.*
*You have gained 120 experience in Medium Armor.*
*You have gained 23,120 total experience from the raid kills for Goblin Raiders (Levels 12-14) (x289) (57,800 x 40%).*

*The damned experience!* Arthur thought. He hadn't realized the experience was adding up that fast. It seemed like it wasn't right, but he also guessed battles weren't nearly this one-sided. If both sides were killing large numbers of combatants, each army would have their people regularly refreshed by leveling up. His people were also starting at lower levels. They were essentially power leveling right now. The better gear was allowing them to stay alive long enough to reap the benefit of the experience.

Knowing it would take a blow that was almost instantly fatal to stop his defenders was a comfort, but the fight still had a long way to go. They'd taken out a good number of them but still hadn't killed the numbers in the original force, much less the extras that arrived recently.

*A group of them are trying to break off and circle to the right.* Balair sent to him.

Arthur turned toward the place Balair mentioned and saw them peeling off from the edge and heading further down the wall. They were too far down the wall to use an arrow from here, so Arthur dashed across the battlements toward their general direction. After a hundred yards of skirting the small wall-walk, Arthur was close enough to fire an arrow to cut them off. His last Hellfire Arrow came free, and Aim Shot magnified his vision. The arrow timer started, and he set his sights on the charging raiders. His aim focused on a spot ahead of them at a distance where the explosion should go off right as they arrived, and then he released the arrow.

It soared across the field and embedded into the ground in front of the advancing forces. Their charge continued, none the wiser until a ball of fire engulfed the front ranks of the goblins. Those not caught directly in the fire quickly backed away and stopped moving in that direction. Those who were trapped in the fire rolled on the ground in agony as their clothes continued to burn, and their skin bubbled.

The sound of another explosion drew Arthur's attention, and he turned to see one of the other siege walls go up in a ball of fire. He grinned in satisfaction when he saw Vana's attention on the large contraption. A glance at the field confused Arthur. Samson held his spot on the wall at the top of one of the siege walls, but he had destroyed two of them, and Vana just took out the fourth. Those were all that were visible when the fight started. Looking out over the field, he spotted another wall moving his direction. The bizarre part was the wall moved much quicker than the others.

*Is that another wall?* Arthur asked into his mind.

*Not exactly,* Balair said hesitantly.

*This is not the time to drag out the information I need,* Arthur grumbled.

*Sorry, I was trying to circle behind it. It isn't a wall. They took a bunch of the single ladders and put wooden boards on the back to make them look like a solid wall. It is actually a lot of individual ladders carried side by side in a line. Since each is only carrying a standard ladder, they are moving faster.*

*Well, damn. Time for something drastic.*

He slung his bow back onto his shoulder and held both hands out in front of him. Concentrating on the space, he started building a ball of fire between his hands. The power swirled, and the heat increased as it spun faster and faster. The ball grew in size and strength until it was the size of a soccer ball. He balanced the ball of energy on one hand and pictured the final aspect of the spell. Arthur was sure to include the time aspect he wanted to impart by imagining the spell flying forward and impacting the wall of ladders on the left edge. He hoped to force them to move more toward the center of the wall. If he attacked the middle, it was more likely they'd scatter, and it'd make matters worse.

He reared back and launched the spell forward, more for some added drama than anything, and watched as it flew in a quick line toward the wall. It splashed against the ladder he aimed for, and a torrent of flames burst from the impact.

*Congratulations, you have discovered the Fire Magic Spell: Fireball. You have gained 250 experience in Fire Magic for discovering a known spell.*

*You have gained 250 experience in Fire Magic for successfully casting Fireball.*

| Spell: Fireball | |
| --- | --- |
| Requirements: Fire Magic<br>Mana Cost: 125 MP<br>Cast Time: 6 seconds<br>Cooldown: 5 Minutes | Description: Condense a ball of Fire Magic into a sphere and launch it at enemies.<br><br>AOE Size: 15'x15'x15'. |

|  | Damage: 140 hp<br>Additional Effects:<br>    ● Ignites any flammable material it strikes.<br>    ● Inflicts burning damage on target enemies that causes 5 hp/s damage for 20 seconds. |
|---|---|
| Mastery Level: 1 ||

*You have dealt 700 HP damage to Goblin Raider (Level 14) (x5).*

*You have inflicted Burn to Goblin Raider (Level 14) (x5).*

The raiders quickly realized the big flaw in the design. Since they were standard ladders covered in wood, they didn't reach all the way to the ground as they ran with them. This allowed the explosion to ignite the surrounding ladders, but more importantly, it allowed the flames to flow underneath and burn the goblins carrying them. Since all wore ragged and oil-stained clothing, they lit up like a dry Christmas tree.

A few collapsed from the fire and to Arthur's amusement, they dropped their ladders. The ladders fell across the path of the goblins to their sides and caused them to fall onto the now burning ladders, further fueling the flame. Arthur wanted to laugh at the sight, but attackers were still coming in overwhelming numbers.

He needed to come up with an excellent spell to use that didn't have a pesky cooldown. There was more than enough mana he could burn, but nothing he could do with it. The fact that it seemed to get darker drew his attention. His eyes shot to the sky to see a thick layer of black clouds headed directly for them. Looking toward the enemy's command area, he spotted a mass of their casters in a circle making odd motions and appearing to chant, although he couldn't tell for sure from this far away.

This new storm front moved far faster than anything natural, and Arthur saw a wall of rain heading for the battlefield. Their casters tried to restrict the effectiveness of fire and the arrows at the same time. Heavy rain would usually knock arrows down and off course for anything but short shots.

Arthur looked up and down the wall and saw everyone still holding. Three bodies were lying on the ground behind the wall, though. Someone took the time to lay them together in the same area out of respect. Someone else had also taken it upon themselves to arm up with their weapons and armor, as the men were all in their essential clothing. Some support villagers must have seen them fall and taken their place.

The storm quickly doused the burning fires as it swept across the battlefield and toward the defenders. The sting of the icy rain pelted his face. He immediately felt drenched under his armor. His earth and water spells would need to take precedence in the fighting now. Looking down below him, he spotted puddles already beginning to form. A devious idea made him smile as he considered the best way to accomplish what he wanted.

He ran back down the wall-walk and
continued past the last of the attackers until
he reached an empty part of the wall. He
focused on the stone beneath him and followed
it to the ground in front of the wall. He
shifted the dirt in front of the wall with
Earth Magic and caused it to get deeper and
wider. This continued until the whole reached
a size he deemed sufficient for his plan.

*Congratulations, you have discovered the
Earth Magic Spell: Dig Moat Section. You have
gained 250 experience in Earth Magic for
discovering a known spell.*
*You have gained 125 experience in Earth
Magic for successfully casting Dig Moat
Section.*

| Spell: Dig Moat Section | |
|---|---|
| Requirements: Earth Magic<br>Mana Cost: 60 MP<br>Cast Time: 12 seconds | Description: Digs a hole in the ground to serve as a moat for protection<br><br>Dimensions: 50'x20'x8'. |
| Mastery Level: 1 | |

The spell had taken more mana than he
expected it to use, but it was because he made
the starting dimensions so large. Creating a
spell that stretched a fifty-foot area and was
twenty feet wide and eight feet deep was no
minor trick. The heavy rain filled the hole as
Arthur hoped. Now that the spell was in his
arsenal, it was time to use it everywhere he
could.
*Can you help?* Arthur asked Balair.

*Gotcha. I'll start at the opposite end of the wall as you. I don't have near the mana you do, but it'll be enough to make some of it.* Balair told him, and the ball of red scales dove toward the opposite end of the wall.

Arthur sped along the wall, stopping just long enough for his spell to form. It was humorous watching the confused goblins as they sunk in the disappearing earth. Arthur ran down the stretch of the wall and refused to stop his process. The work became methodical as he continued to walk down the wall and repeatedly cast his spell. He cast the spell twenty times before the moat spanned the front of the gatehouse and butted up against the siege wall that Samson fought to hold.

Arthur could honestly sit here and watch the man fight all day. The fluid motions he made as he swung his shield into his enemies, followed with a perfect stroke in retaliation, was mesmerizing. Arthur only needed some popcorn to top off the experience. Well, that, and a chair.

He joined Samson on his portion of the wall. Pulling his sword free, he took the time to repel a few goblins to break up the monotony of his spell casting.

*Goblin Raider (Level 14) has died (x5).*
*You have gained 1,000 total experience for killing Goblin Raider (Level 14) (x5).*
*You have gained 2,500 experience in Earth Magic for successfully casting Dig Moat Section (x20).*
*You have dealt 1,440 HP damage to Goblin Raider (Level 14) (x6).*
*Goblin Raider (Level 14) has died (x6).*

*You have gained 700 total experience in Swords.*

*You have gained 875 total experience in Small Blades.*

*Congratulations, you have reached level 7 in Small Blades. Swing speed with Small Blades increased by 18%. Keep stabbing them in the back!*

*You have gained 175 total experience in Block.*

*You have gained 175 total experience in Parry.*

*You have gained 1,200 total experience for killing Goblin Raider (Level 14) (x6).*

The first five goblin deaths confused him, and then he noticed they were the five his Fireball struck. They succumbed to the burn damage or took an arrow from a defender before the rain arrived.

"Nothing like a little rain to wash off the filth!" Samson called as they fought.

"All the sticky blood becomes annoying." Arthur smiled back.

As much as he wanted to remain in that spot and keep killing goblins, he needed to finish his spell casting. He nodded to Samson, sheathed Ember, and resumed his trek down the wall. The moat expanded quickly as he went. He passed Vana on her tower and waved at her.

"Doing impressive work," he told her.

"Ah, thanks. I knew you cared," she said with a laugh.

He kept his pace around the wall until he reached the next archery tower where Allendria stood. As soon as his feet touched her platform, he ran over and gave her a quick kiss on the cheek.

"Keep on your toes," he told her and
resumed his work.

"Keep your head down while you do that. I
know you think your armor is impenetrable, but
it isn't."

His pace continued, and he halted his
course another twenty spell casts in this
direction. All told, he had a thousand-foot
long moat on each side of the gatehouse. It
had only cost him a staggering 2,400 mana.

Between his amulet and Ember, he still had
just a hair over ten thousand mana left.
Looking at the rain falling, he frowned. The
moat filled up quickly and already rose to the
knees of those foolish enough to descend into
it. In some places, the goblins stood out of
the water, but that was because they were
standing on a pile of their fellow raiders'
corpses.

He could feel the mana swirling in the air
that fueled this storm. If he could get rid of
the rain, it would be an enormous help to his
archers. Allendria told him to fight a caster
you could cancel their spells by directly
influencing against it and overpowering them
by raw mana usage alone. With that thought in
mind, he ran back toward Allendria.

"I'll stand with you because I'm about to
do something really stupid. So… don't let me
die," he told her over his shoulder.

"What the hell does that mean? You've
really got to stop being so vague when you say
crap like that," she fumed.

Arthur just shook his head and raised his
arms. Pulling on his Water Magic, he started
accumulating all the water he could in front
of him. It was a staggering amount as it
swirled and gathered into a ball. He ended up
having to condense the water, and he swirled
it so he could store more in a smaller space.
This caused the water to become pressurized,
making it harder to control.

His effort was not in vain, though. He drew
in as much water as he could from the portion
of the storm that maintained the spell. As the
water siphoned away, the spell faltered. There
was only a finite amount of power fueling the
spell and, once it lost the ability to
circulate correctly, it fizzled.

The rain slowed considerably and Arthur
turned his focus on the ball of water in front
of him. In a flash of insight, he activated
his Fire Magic. Instead of heating the water,
though, he pulled all the heat out of it. The
ball of water crystalized and turned into a
very heavy ball of ice. This ball of ice was
ten feet in diameter of solidly condensed ice
and, with a force of will, Arthur sent it
flying into the enemy ranks in front of him.
He only needed to picture a sufficient
distance for it to travel, and its weight
would take it the rest of the way as it
crushed anything in its path.

*Congratulations, you have discovered the
Combination Spell: Ice Boulder. You have
gained 250 experience in Water Magic and Fire
Magic for discovering a known spell.*

*Congratulations, you have reached level 8 in Water Magic. Increases the effect of your Water Magic spells by 21%. That was a neat trick. Can you carve it into something next time?*

*You have gained 140 experience in Water Magic and Fire Magic for successfully casting Combination Spell: Ice Boulder.*

| Spell: Ice Boulder | |
|---|---|
| Requirements: Water and Fire Magic<br>Mana Cost: 200 MP<br>Cast Time: 20 seconds<br>Cooldown: 10 Minutes | Description: Condense a ball of water into a sphere and flash freeze it. Send the boulder flying at enemies.<br><br>Dimensions: 10' diameter<br>Damage: 200 hp (Crushing) |
| Mastery Level: 1 | |

*You have dealt 2,400 HP damage to Goblin Raider (Level 14) (x12).*

The clouds thinned, and his archers continued to fire. Light was finally visible at the end of the proverbial tunnel. The fight had been very one-sided since the start. His people's superior weaponry and defenses turned this into a slaughter. His gaze swept across the wall now that finished watching his ball of ice crush goblins with grim satisfaction. The sight that greeted him further down the wall instantly diminished his hope.

# Chapter 16

*Dire Situation*

The fight had been far too easy. Instinctively, Arthur knew this, but his hopes were high because of the low-level goblin raiders. Looking down the wall, he realized the truth. All along the wall, forces in black sprouted on the battlements and launched a massive assault on the defenders. Most of them were taking damage by the second as they were being pushed back from the edge of the wall. Arthur caught sight of ladders slamming into place over the side, and more forces rose to join. He used Scan on the nearest of the ominous figures.

*You have received 180 experience for successful use of Scan.*

| | |
|---|---|
| **Name:** Dark Infiltrator<br>**Level:** 20<br>**Type:** Human<br>**Class:** Rogue<br>**HP:** 320/320<br>**MP:** 140/140<br>**Stamina:** 300/300 | |
| **Strength:** 12<br>**Agility:** 28<br>**Intellect:** 8<br>**Wisdom:** 1<br>**Endurance:** 14<br>**Charisma:** 8<br>**Luck:** 8 | **Experience:** N/A<br><br>**Skills**<br>**Combat Skills:**<br><br>? (???/???) |

*Fuck. Not only were they a much higher level, but they also had a class. Sneaky bastards must have made it to the wall under stealth and scaled to the top before launching their assault.* Arthur prepared to launch into the nearest one when a strange sight caught his eye.

Samson glowed a bright white color. For a moment, Arthur could swear the man had wings of molten silver expand from his back, and then a wave of pure magical force swept across the field of battle. It harmed nothing it touched, but when it hit Arthur, he felt power infuse him.

*You have been blessed by the Paladin Samson. Increases your attack and defense by 15% for 20 minutes. You will be able to ignore minor wounds and continue fighting.*

The message washed over him, and he smiled. Samson finally used one of his divine abilities. Now fully reinvigorated, Arthur pulled Ember free from its scabbard while simultaneously pulling his dagger with his other hand. His stride brought him directly to the first of the infiltrators, and he slashed in a broad stroke with Ember.

The rogue spotted the attack and ducked beneath the blade. He tried to stab out with his dagger, but Arthur caught it on his own. Arthur kicked out and hit the man in the knee.

*You have dealt 20 HP damage to Dark Infiltrator (Level 20) with Kick.*

He stumbled but regained his footing before Arthur could take advantage. If it would take this much effort to kill these guys, he'd never make it across the wall before they did too much damage to the defenders. A glance behind and to the right of the man brought a devious grin to his face.

"Hey, what's small, red, and good at distraction?" Arthur asked the now confused man.

Before he could respond, Balair crashed into the back of the man's head and sunk his teeth in. Timing his attack just right, Arthur lunged forward and impaled the man on his sword. The rogue looked utterly shocked as he fell to the floor, unmoving.

*Balair has dealt 50 HP damage to Dark Infiltrator (Level 20) with Bite (Critical Hit) (Sneak Attack).*

*You have dealt 160 HP damage to Dark Infiltrator (Level 20) with Ember (Critical Hit) (Mortal Strike).*

*Did you just call me small, asshat?* Balair sent angrily.

*Don't worry about it.* Arthur replied. *I was just distracting the guy.*

*See if I help you again. I'll just go find someone else's ass to save instead.* The small dragon hissed as he launched himself from the stone wall.

The defenders on the wall made it difficult for him to utilize too many of his offensive spells, so instead, he activated Sheathe in Flame on Ember. The sword lit up with its eerie fire, and Arthur charged forward. The next Infiltrator wasn't nearly as lucky. This one never even saw him coming because he was too busy attacking one of his fellow defenders. The defender looked ragged and had more dings and gouges in his armor than Arthur thought was possible but was still on his feet. Arthur's sword swept out and cleanly separated the rogue's head from his shoulders as he kept running toward the next target.

*You have dealt 320 HP damage to Dark Infiltrator (Level 20) with Ember (Decapitation).*
*Dark Infiltrator (Level 20) has died.*

His next target met the same fate and quickly fell before him. He continued past those fighting and made it to Allendria's platform. She was busy fending off an Infiltrator of her own. She dodged out of the way and sent blasts of fire at the assassin to cause him to jump away. Arthur barreled onto the platform with an overhead chop, but the rogue somehow sensed or heard him. His blade came down but found nothing but air. It continued downward until it struck the stone wall, and sparks flew from the impact. The sword vibrated in his hand, but he tried to ignore the sting. Suddenly, a sharp pain in his arm caused him to jerk back and lift his weapon in defense.

*Dark Infiltrator (Level 20) has dealt 35 damage to you with Exquisite Iron Dagger.*

*Well, these guys can definitely do damage to me. I wonder if the knife can get through my armor, though.* He thought absentmindedly. His thoughts returned to real-time as he leaped forward with a high one-handed chop. The swing was a feint, though, as he brought his dagger around from a different angle in his off-hand. His enemy almost fell for it. Lifting his weapon to deflect the blow, he spotted the knife coming and jumped backward. To the rogue's dismay, he forgot about Allendria. A scorching blanket of flame slammed into the rogue from the side and caused him to screech in horror. He fell to the ground, writhing from his injuries and burns.

"Thanks for that. I just needed a distraction to kill him," Allendria yelled out.

"Any time. I've got to keep moving, though. You doing okay on mana?" Arthur yelled at her as he passed.

"For now. I've drained some of the necklaces they brought to the front, but I'm doing fine."

Arthur nodded and kept moving. He trusted her to do whatever she needed. Second-guessing everything his people did would only cause unnecessary worry. He continued methodically working his way down the line. Two infiltrators dealt damage to him, but only enough to piss him off but not debilitate him. He journeyed down the wall until only two of the infiltrators remained. A quick glance behind him showed his people were still holding their own repelling most of the ladders now that they had dealt with most of the infiltrators.

*We have a huge problem!* Balair yelled into his mind.

Arthur squinted his eyes at the pain from the volume of that yell in his head.

*Never do that again, you flying rat. What is it?*

*Look to the other side of the commanders.*

Arthur knew it had to be something serious because he didn't even give him shit about Arthur calling him a flying rat. His eyes found the spot Balair referred to, and a cold sweat sprung on his head.

*Well, damn. That'll require a change in my plans.* He ran down the steps of the archer platform he was on and dashed back toward the gate.

"Samson! Do you see them?" Arthur yelled.

Samson was quiet for a moment until Arthur heard him respond, "Dear Goddess."

"Yeah, my thoughts exactly. Can you hold the wall? I need to take Allendria and Vana. We'll go around the side of the army and take care of that problem."

"We'll hold them. If you guys can't fix the situation, nothing will save us," Samson intoned.

Arthur continued with his run and came up behind the platform with Vana.

"Get your ass down here! We have a crisis to fix," Arthur called up to the ranger. It was apparent she'd seen the threat as well because she came bounding down the stairs with no argument. They continued until they reached Allendria's platform.

"Come down, Allendria," Arthur called to her. "It's time to sneak behind enemy lines."

"Why in the name of all that is holy would we do that? We're holding the wall without an issue. Are you out of your damn mi…" she began but trailed off, "I'm coming down."

Arthur watched her scramble to the ground with a look of worry on her face.

"Finally spotted them, huh?" Arthur asked.

She nodded and looked back to him. "How the hell are we going to stop three full-sized siege catapults... and where the hell did they get them?"

"Doesn't matter where they got them. We have to sneak around and attack the catapults from the rear. Speed will be key here. It'll still take them some time to get them into place and ready to fire. This is a quick mission. Get behind them, burn the catapults, and get back to the wall," Arthur summed up.

Allendria and Vana nodded, then they all ran for the southern wall. Climbing the last archery platform, they skirted farther down the wall and out of sight. Each of them dropped over the edge with a thud. Their legs were shaky from exhaustion, but they continued. Dashing across the clearing as fast as they could, they stayed low to avoid detection. They made it to the forest without delay and then skirted the edge of the trees to circle behind the army.

Running so fast, they completely missed the band of goblin scouts they came face to face with. Arthur pulled his weapons. They caught the goblins flat-footed and not expecting to come across a group of defenders near the forest. Arthur charged the first three in a small group, and Ember made quick work of two of them. The last almost drew his knife when Arthur's dagger found its way into the creature's chest.

*You have dealt 200 HP damage to Goblin
Scout (Level 12) with Ember (Critical Hit)
(Mortal Blow) (x2).*
*You have dealt 200 HP damage to Goblin
Scout (Level 12) with Enchanted Basic Mage-
crafted Iron Dagger (Heart Strike).*
*Goblin Scout (Level 12) has died (x3).*

Vana finished the remaining two in the
group, then they continued as planned. Arthur
glanced at his reserves and cursed at himself.


*You have gained 38,800 total experience
from the raid kills for Goblin Raiders (Levels
12-14) (x485) (97,000 x 40%).*
*Congratulations, you have reached level 19!
You now have 5 available skill points. One
more step to go.*
*You have gained 2,500 total experience for
killing Dark Infiltrators (Level 20) (x10).*
*You have gained 1,300 total experience in
Swords.*
*Congratulations, you have reached level 8
in Swords. Swing speed with swords increased
by 21%. Stay sharp because a weapon will
eventually make it through your armor.*
*You have gained 390 total experience in
Small Blades.*
*You have gained 160 total experience in
Medium Armor.*
*You have gained 3,080 total experience from
the raid kills for Orc Commanders (Levels 16-
18) (x28) (7,700 x 40%).*

He'd neglected his notifications again and hadn't been watching his experience gains constantly adding up from the raid kills. Judging by the timeline of it and his other notifications, he leveled up around the time he cast his Ice Boulder spell. The distraction of the fight caused him to miss it all.

The battle was escalating, and he wasn't comfortable with his lower HP. Arthur dumped 4 points into Endurance and put the last into Charisma. This brought his Endurance to 24, which bumped his base HP and Stamina up to 490. His Charisma evened out at 10. He was missing 60 of that HP from his fight on the wall.

Continuing through the trees, they encountered no more resistance. The trip took a solid half-hour to get around the back. By the time they reached a location that they had deemed far enough behind the lines to attack, they saw they'd arrived later than hoped. Arthur watched as a catapult fired, and a boulder launched across the field. It hit short and rolled toward the wall. It lost most of its momentum, so the wall took minimal damage when the boulder finally hit it and came to a stop.

The catapults may be in position and firing, but they hadn't found their range yet. There was a window they could use here. Arthur turned to the ladies.

"This'll be a mad rush to cause as much damage as possible. I'll charge into the field. You two follow behind after a five-second count."

"Uh, yeah, not doing that. You aren't charging ahead without us," Vana told him.

"Calm down. I'm not planning on assaulting head-on solo. I need the time, so I can stop when in range, and launch a Fireball at the furthest catapult. That only leaves us having to deal with the first two up close," Arthur explained.

Some tension melted away in Vana's shoulders at his statement. She nodded to him in agreement at the plan. Arthur rose to his feet and left the cover of the trees at a full sprint. The first catapult was only a hundred yards away, but the third was twice that distance. He revised his earlier strategy. The spell didn't list a maximum cast distance for Fireball, but Arthur would bet the power of the spell waned the farther it traveled. He slowed his speed and motioned for the girls to catch up to him. They joined beside him, and all took off together at an increased pace.

"New plan," Arthur huffed as he ran. "The last catapult is so far away I need to reach the first catapult, if not the second before I can cast my spell. Allendria, you and I will assault the first catapult with a rush of fire while Vana covers us. As soon as it's on fire, we continue to the second. You work on taking down the second, and Vana will continue covering us while I throw a Fireball at the third."

Allendria nodded and he heard Vana grunt in
agreement. The woman could be very unladylike
when she wished. The distance melted quickly
as they neared a crew of six goblins and an
orc operating the first machine. Wasting no
time, Arthur and Allendria both halted and
held their hands up as they drew closer.
Allendria cast her Blazing Inferno spell
toward the group as Arthur unleashed
Flamethrower. All the enemies manning the
catapult immediately caught on fire and began
screaming.

"Get back," Arthur screamed as he saw the
ropes holding the tension on the catapult fray
and burn away. They took a few quick steps
away from the catapult before one line
snapped, and wood splintered. The arm popped
off of the machine and fell to the ground. The
heat pouring off of it was intense.

*You have dealt 900 HP damage to Goblin
Scout (Level 12) with Flamethrower (x6).*
*You have dealt 150 HP damage to Orc
Commander (Level 16) with Flamethrower.*
*Goblin Scout (Level 12) has died (x6).*
*Orc Commander (Level 16) has died.*
*Heavy Catapult (Raiders) has been
destroyed. 500 bonus Raid experience for all
on your side of the conflict.*

The group continued for the next catapult.
It sat almost directly between the first and
last. Another identical team of raiders
operated this one. Arthur couldn't use
Flamethrower yet because of the cooldown, so
he played it safe and dual cast his Blazing
Inferno into the group.

He took sight of the last catapult and started casting his Fireball spell. The power built and swirled until it threatened to fly free from its confines. Arthur flung the ball, visualizing the path it needed to take. When it was ten yards from the catapult, it exploded as an arrow zipped into it and triggered it early. Fire splashed all over the area and still ignited parts of the catapult's frame but not enough to be a threat to the machine.

Turning to see where the arrow had come from, Arthur spotted one of the Dark Elves with his bow drawn and an arrow aimed directly at him. The elf was only thirty yards away, so there was no chance he could dodge the incoming attack. *Or can I?* He thought to himself as he activated his sword skill talent ability Passata Sotto. He couldn't consciously move fast enough to dodge a projectile like that, but abilities worked by their own rules of speed.

His body moved on its own and quickly
dropped to perform the attack. He was sure he
looked like a fool standing in the open field
and striking upward at empty air, but the
arrow flew over his head and barely grazed his
helmet. He came back to his feet and charged
the elf. It wouldn't take long for the archer
to get another arrow ready to fire.

To his surprise, the elf didn't even bother
with the bow. Instead, he dropped it, pulled a
sword, and charged right back at Arthur.
Almost faster than he could see, the elf swung
the blade at him in a horizontal arc for his
midsection. Arthur took a quick hop back to
avoid the strike and lunged forward with the
point of his sword. The elf twisted in a way
Arthur wouldn't have believed possible, and
the blade found nothing but empty air.

If Arthur hadn't drawn his dagger during
the run, he would have died at that moment.
The elf was able to change the direction of
his blade and bring it back to slash at
Arthur. He pulled his dagger up, and the edge
reverberated as the elf's sword bounced off of
it. The weapon still gouged his armor on the
shoulder but didn't take away any health.

*You have taken 0 HP damage from Dark Elf
(Level 22) (Armor).*

An arrow flew past Arthur and the Dark Elf somehow knocked it out of the air with his sword. Arthur wasn't sure if he was naturally that fast or if it was an ability he used. Ember came down in an overhead slash at the enemy, but he easily countered the strike. Their blades met, and the elf twisted his sword around Ember until he knocked it to the side, and a backhanded slash caught Arthur in the chest.

*You have taken 15 HP damage from Dark Elf (Level 22) (Blunt Damage).*

The blade itself didn't deal damage to him, but the impact of the attack rattled his armor, and an ache spread across his chest. This elf was incredible. He could hit hard enough to damage him through armor. Stumbling back a few steps, Arthur reassessed the fight. It was obvious this man was far more skilled than he was. He was taking deep breaths and trying to slow his breathing while the elf didn't even appear winded. Before this went any farther, Arthur cast Scan.

*You have received 200 experience for successful use of Scan.*

<table>
<tr><td colspan="2">Name: Harlian</td></tr>
<tr><td colspan="2">Level: 22</td></tr>
<tr><td colspan="2">Type: Dark Elf</td></tr>
<tr><td colspan="2">Class: Swordmaster</td></tr>
<tr><td colspan="2">HP: 510/510</td></tr>
<tr><td colspan="2">MP: 100/100</td></tr>
<tr><td colspan="2">Stamina: 510/510</td></tr>
<tr><td>Strength: 28</td><td>Experience: N/A</td></tr>
<tr><td>Agility: 22</td><td>Skills</td></tr>
<tr><td>Intellect: 5</td><td>Combat Skills:</td></tr>
</table>

| **Wisdom:** 2<br>**Endurance:** 20<br>**Charisma:** 5<br>**Luck:** 5 | ? (???/???) |
| --- | --- |

*Well, son of a bitch. There's no way I can beat this guy in a one-on-one sword fight.* Arthur thought after seeing the man had the Swordmaster class.

"Arthur, I'm almost out of mana. You need to take out that catapult before it fires!" Allendria yelled.

*Shit, not enough time. I don't want to use this now, but I need to.*

Arthur lifted his hand and faced his palm toward Harlian. "Dragonfire."

The flame swirled in his palm and blasted out in incredible force. Harlian looked utterly astonished as the fire slammed into him. He held his sword in front of his face and attempted to thwart off the flame and protect his eyes. As the spell faded, it amazed Arthur to see the man still standing.

*You have dealt 450 HP damage to Harlian (Level 22) with Dragonfire (50 resisted).*

Horrible looking burns covered him from head to toe, but he was still on his feet. The Swordmaster tried to retaliate and moved to swing his sword at Arthur. As soon as he moved his arm, he screamed out in pain and dropped the blade. His skin had split where burned and it was bleeding profusely. Not wanting the man to suffer any longer, he swept Ember across his neck, and the elf dropped to the ground, dead.

*You have dealt 60 HP damage to Harlian (Level 22) with Ember (Critical Hit) (Mortal Blow).*

*Harlian (Level 22) has died.*
*You have gained 275 experience in Swords.*
*You have gained 275 experience in Small Blades.*
*You have gained 275 experience in Parry.*
*Congratulations, you have reached level 4 in Parry. Increased success chance with parry by 9%. That was a low blow.*
*You have gained 400 experience.*

A glance toward the catapult revealed a problem. Four of the goblins had peeled away from the contraption to attack Vana and Allendria. They had already dealt with two of the ugly creatures, and they were lying on the ground, but the other two were each attacking Vana and Allendria. Allendria was doing her best to dodge the swings of the small iron sword from her attacker. She would send short blasts of fire at it in between dodges and dash in to strike with her dagger. Vana was also dodging attacks directed her way. She had her knife out and used her bow to deflect the blows of her enemy. The goblin attacking her was only wielding a wooden club.

Arthur's eye caught the remaining orc and two goblins cranking the wooden wheel to bring the arm back. They'd recently fired a boulder while the fight happened. To Arthur's dismay, he saw the hole it had created in the wall. The arm was almost in place, and an enormous boulder sat next to it. The orc and goblins rolled the stone into place and readied to launch it. With no other choice, Arthur cast his Create Dimensional Storage spell. He envisioned it at the top of the catapult arm's arc and facing toward the boulder.

Arthur counted off the time as the spell power built inside him. He watched nervously as the goblins and orc scrambled over the machine to make the last few adjustments before they launched. His fear intensified as the orc grabbed the handle to release the arm. With a yank, the latch released, and the arm sprung forward. A moment before the boulder arrived, his spell completed, and the hole opened up, right at the top of the arc. The catapult arm slammed into the crossbeam, and the boulder took off flying. Less than two feet from its launch, the rock disappeared in midair, and a loud crashing noise reverberated. Arthur quickly closed the door before stone showered out.

*You have gained 450 experience in Dimensional Magic for successfully casting Create Dimensional Storage. Do you wish to give this space a unique identity? Yes/No.*

Arthur quickly assigned it as 'Storage Number 2' and focused on the task at hand. With the orc and goblins utterly confused by what had just transpired, Arthur took the opportunity and ran for Vana and Allendria. Their targets weren't paying attention to their surroundings, so he efficiently ran up behind them and skewered the first with his sword. Pulling it free, he crossed the distance to the other in seconds, and his dagger punched into its back. Spinning on his heel, he dashed for the catapult and repeated the same trick he used last time. Extending both hands, he dual cast Blazing Inferno.

*You have gained 240 experience in Fire Magic for successfully dual casting Blazing Inferno.*
*You have dealt 480 HP damage to Goblin Scout (Level 12) with Dual Blazing Inferno (x2).*
*You have dealt 240 HP damage to Orc Commander (Level 16) with Dual Blazing Inferno.*
*Goblin Scout (Level 12) has died (x6).*
*Orc Commander (Level 16) has died.*
*You have gained 150 experience in Swords.*
*You have gained 150 experience in Small Blades.*
*You have gained 1,450 experience.*
*Heavy Catapult (Raiders) has been destroyed. 500 bonus Raid experience for all on your side of the conflict.*
*Congratulations, you have reached level 20! You now have 5 available skill points.*
Finally, at the coveted level. Now the actual work begins.

Arthur quickly assigned 1 point into
Intellect, 2 into Endurance, and 2 into
Strength before a loud blast echoed across the
field and drew his attention back to the wall.
The siege wall that had been assaulting the
wall was now a burning wreck. Samson moved and
took a position at the breach in the wall. He
was holding the gap, like he had during the
bandit attack.

"Looks like he finally used it," Vana
quipped.

"What?" Arthur asked.

"I left one of the Hellfire Arrows with
Zeke before we left in case of this exact
scenario," she explained.

"Good thinking. We need to disrupt their
ranks. They still outnumber us by a large
margin."

"Take out their commanders?" Allendria
suggested.

"I love the way you think," Arthur told
her.

Early in the fight, he considered hitting
them with a new ability, but they never got
close enough. Some forces toward the back of
the army turned to fight those responsible for
destroying their siege weapons. Arthur didn't
want to spend too much time here, so he
focused on the area with the commanders. They
were only around 150 yards away, so he
activated one of his divine abilities.

A bright light shone down from the sky and enveloped him in pleasant warmth. He could feel the power build in him from his activated spell. The fiery glow of Retribution slammed into the command zone of the enemy army, and he could hear the screams of those affected. The beam of light seemed to pulse as waves of energy slammed into the ground of the affected area.

"We can't stick around much longer. They've spotted us, and there's a sizeable group already headed our way," Vana called.

Arthur nodded, and they ran for the tree line. They didn't make it far before a stream of fire flew in front of them. They came to an abrupt stop and turned to see the second dark elf standing there with a hand extended in their direction.

A black hood obscured their face, making it hard to distinguish features. Vana didn't wait for words and sent an arrow straight at the figure. The bolt slammed into an invisible barrier and splintered into pieces.

*Damn a mage.* Arthur activated his scan ability.

*You have received 220 experience for successful use of Scan.*

| Name: Syrosia | |
| --- | --- |
| Level: 24 | |
| Type: Dark Elf | |
| Class: Pyromancer | |
| HP: 380/380 | |
| MP: 600/650 | |
| Stamina: 380/380 | |
| Strength: 4 | Experience: N/A |
| Agility: 7 | Skills |
| Intellect: 29 | Combat Skills: |

| **Wisdom:** 23 <br> **Endurance:** 14 <br> **Charisma:** 10 <br> **Luck:** 9 | ? (???/???) |
| --- | --- |

Arthur couldn't tell for sure, but judging by the name and the delicate hands, this was a female Dark Elf. Seeing her class as a Pyromancer, his instinct was to pull on his Water Magic. His skill set with water was very limited, but now would be the perfect chance. Since Arthur had no way to make barriers like this elf, his only options were to counter her magic with water spells or overpower her mana with his own.

"You two cover our rear. Keep those goblins from getting to us before I can finish her," Arthur told the two ladies behind him.

Arthur felt her drawing in Fire Magic, so he pumped mana into his Water Magic and went on instinct. His magic swirled, and water formed in a large disc in front of him right as a small globe of flame jumped from the mage's hand.

The small globe of fire sizzled as it connected with the shield of water. Loud hissing noise emanated from the impact, and steam rose into the air. Both spells vanished, and he was staring at Syrosia again.

*Congratulations, you have discovered the Water Magic Spell: Water Shield. You have gained 250 experience in Water Magic for discovering a known spell.*

*You have gained 180 experience in Water Magic for successfully casting Water Shield.*

| Spell: Water Shield |
| --- |

| Requirements: Water Magic<br>Mana Cost: 60 MP<br>Cast Time: 2 seconds<br>Cooldown: 60 seconds | Description: Form a shield from pure elemental water.<br><br>• Can block a total of 80 physical damage before it dissipates.<br>• Can block up to 40 magical damage from any element but Fire.<br>• Will negate a Fire Magic spell that strikes it. |
| --- | --- |
| Mastery Level: 1 | |

*Syrosia's Fire Orb and your Water Shield have canceled each other.*

The elf didn't waste any time and immediately summoned more Fire Magic. This time, Arthur took a fresh approach. He poured mana into his Water Magic and formed multiple spikes of water with the points facing the mage. Using his Fire Magic, he pulled the heat from them and caused them to solidify. He focused his will on the projectiles and envisioned their path. They launched from his side and sped directly for the Pyromancer.

She saw them coming and lifted her hands toward them. A quick burst of flame stretched from her hands and engulfed the projectiles. They melted quickly and evaporated under her fire.

| Spell: Ice Spikes | |
|---|---|
| Requirements: Water and Fire Magic<br>Mana Cost: 40 MP<br>Cast Time: 4 seconds<br>Cooldown: 30 seconds | Description: Form spikes made of water and then flash freeze them into deadly projectiles. The projectiles launch forward to attack the target. Produces 8 spikes.<br><br>• Each spike deals 30 water damage upon impact. |
| Mastery Level: 1 | |



The flames didn't extend far enough to cause any harm to Arthur, so he focused on his next attack. This would be a battle of attrition. He had far more mana than she did, but she didn't know that. He heard Allendria cry out behind him and grew concerned. The goblins must be in melee range, and that meant time was running short. This back and forth with the mage wouldn't cut it.

Syrosia concentrated her Fire Magic again, so this time, Arthur directly opposed her. He focused his power on the building energy in front of her. His Fire Magic weaved into the ball of energy and counteracted her spell. He pushed his influence in the opposite motion of her so she couldn't build up the heat by circulating the flame. She threw her head back and her cowl flew from her head.

She was an odd sight with her lithe build and long brown hair, but the worst part was her face. Half of her face had a hideous scar that looked like it had been part of an unfortunate fire. Her eyes glinted red as she glared at him.

"You dare try to counter me, you filthy human?" she yelled in his direction.

"You're no match for me, give up before I finish that scar for you!" Arthur called back.

The statement had the exact effect he'd hoped for. Her rage grew even wilder, and Arthur saw all reason flee her eyes. If she had been smart enough to cancel the spell and try ones with quicker cast times, she might have stood a chance. Instead, her rage caused her to do everything to attempt to overpower him.

Arthur could feel her power as it fed into the spell, but just as quickly, he pushed his energy in to counter it. The struggle continued until Arthur saw sweat pour from her face. When the exhaustion was evident, he sent a massive burst of Fire Magic into her spell and caused it to swirl in the direction he was forcing it. Before she could react, he popped the barrier containing the energy, and it exploded in her hands.

Flames engulfed the poor woman as she screamed in rage and pain. Arthur didn't waste any time and immediately cast Ice Spikes again, aiming the spell for the center of her chest. The solid projectiles formed around him and zipped toward Syrosia. She was struggling to recover from the fire spell when the shards slammed into her chest. Her mouth opened to scream, but only a puff of white mist spewed forth. It reminded him of breathing outside on a chilly winter day. She fell backward to the ground and lay still.

*Congratulations, you have won a contest of magical strength. For being the victor in the struggle, you gain one free talent point in Fire Magic.*
*You have dealt 80 HP damage to Syrosia (Level 24) with Fire Overload.*
*You have gained 80 experience in Water Magic and Fire Magic for successfully casting Ice Spikes.*
*You have dealt 240 HP damage to Syrosia (Level 24) with Ice Spikes (Heart Strike).*
*Syrosia (Level 24) has died.*
*You have gained 425 experience.*

Arthur let out a sigh of relief until he heard a shout of pain. Spinning around, he caught sight of Allendria and Vana, surrounded by a large group of goblins. They were somehow holding their own but were taking minor injuries here and there. Four others broke from the group and charged Arthur. Growing tired of this fight, he decided it was time to put an end to it.

Both arms stretched to his sides as he summoned his other champion ability, Divine Fury. An almost imperceptible storm swirled around him, and he dashed forward. It was difficult to tell there was any danger until something was within the range of the spell. When he was close enough to the first goblin, an invisible wave of force slashed across one arm of the creature as it screamed in rage. This onslaught of invisible attacks continued as long as the enemy was in range.

Arthur wouldn't rely solely on the spell, though, and dove forward with his sword. Instead of aiming for pure killing attacks, he went through the group with quick and efficient slashes to cause damage but not kill. His spell would finish any left alive.

A goblin stepped in front of him and swung a dagger, but Arthur knocked it to the side and stabbed the creature in the shoulder using his knife. He pulled with all of his strength and tossed the goblin away from him while wrenching his dagger free. This charge continued as he worked his way through the edge of the battle. Vana and Allendria followed in his wake and avoided much of the fight. Occasionally Vana would finish one of the goblins when it tried to rise, but Arthur was so focused he barely noticed.

The charge continued until he broke past the last goblin and looked at an empty space in front of him. He checked behind him and only saw dying and injured goblins scattering the ground. A few of them were lucky enough to hit him, but none of them did any damage with his armor protecting him.

*You have gained 880 experience in Medium Armor.*

A scan of the field showed him the raiding force was scattering and in disarray. None of them could figure out what they should do or where they should be because they'd killed or injured the orcs in command.

"Well, well, you must be the leader of this rabble," a low and menacing voice sounded behind him.

# Chapter 17

*A Confrontation with Evil*

Arthur slowly turned to face the voice. A tall elf with raven black hair stood not thirty yards away. The only way Arthur could describe the style was a man bun. His dark purple skin and pointed ears stood out, but the most disturbing feature was his eyes. They were a solid black and looked like pools of darkness.

"You must be Lyrinth," Arthur said in hesitation.

The tall elf looked shocked for a moment at the statement.

"How do you know my name?" he asked.

Lyrinth's gaze shifted to a point behind Arthur, and his eyes widened at the sight. He let out a fit of raucous laughter.

"Not only has the Goddess blessed me with the chance to destroy your little pocket of resistance, but she's also delivered to me the princess of the Dark Elves. Princess Allendria, have you been hiding with these human vermin this whole time in this crappy little village?"

*Princess?* Arthur thought in confusion as he turned to look at her. Her face showed a mix of emotions, but when she looked at him, the only thing that came through was sorrow. Allendria's face turned back to Lyrinth, and a look of anger flashed onto her delicate features.

"I've stayed here with my friends while you and my uncle have perverted our way of life. I saw where things were headed and wanted nothing to do with the destruction of my people."

"So, you ran away? No wonder your father fell so easily. Looks like you take after him. Both of you are nothing but cowards. Had you just embraced the Goddess Isabell, none of this would be necessary," he told her with his arms stretched out to the side, condescending.

"I saw what your pathetic excuse for a Goddess calls worship, and I'd never demean myself to her," Allendria spat. "She'll ruin the entire world if she gets a chance."

"You'd better watch your tongue. I look forward to finishing this fight and taking you back home. I'll petition Glirin to let me have you for myself. I've been loyal to him all this time, after all. I doubt he'll sully himself with you."

"Awfully cocky of you to assume I'll let you take her anywhere," Arthur shot back. "She's here as an honored guest and can stay as long as she wishes, under my protection."

Lyrinth's eyes narrowed at the statement. "Surely you didn't, princess? You honestly sunk so low as to become intimate with some no-name human in a horrible excuse of a village? Had I known this, I wouldn't have needed to kill your father. He would've done it for me out of shame."

A massive gout of fire streamed past Arthur and slammed into Lyrinth. The heat from the flames radiated off Arthur's skin, and he had to bump up his natural fire protection with his magic to keep it from scorching him.

When the flames died, Lyrinth stood in the exact place he had before with one hand out in front of him, palm facing forward. Scorched and burned patches of land dotted the ground around the standing figure, but underneath his feet showed no signs of damage.

"That wasn't very polite," Lyrinth said with a dangerous tone to his voice.

Arthur chanced a quick look backward at the ladies. Allendria looked dead on her feet, and if he was a betting man, he'd say she used every last bit of her mana for that previous spell. Vana had an injured arm and a cut on one of her legs. The goblins ceased their charge for the party when they noticed Lyrinth joined the fight. They resumed their previous attack and charged for the village wall.

"You two get out of here, now. You're both too weak to do anything but distract me. I'll meet you back in the village. Keep each other safe."

"But Arthur…"

"No." He cut them off. "This isn't up for debate. Leave now, and I'll finish this."

Although visually upset by his words, they slowly nodded and headed back for the trees. Arthur's gaze swung back to Lyrinth, who stood with an amused smile on his face.

"You honestly think you can beat me, weakling?" he asked as he threw his hand to the side and a large stone chair lifted from the ground. He walked to the chair and sat in it with a smirk.

Arthur chuckled internally at his display. Allendria was correct about the man's arrogance, so to further poke the bear, Arthur upped the game. He focused his magic and extended his hand to his side. Picturing the effect he wanted, the piece rose out of the ground. Jagged edges lifted from the stone and coalesced into one large structure. The chair completed itself, and he smiled as he strode over and took a seat himself.

Surprise flashed over the dark elf's features as he took in the sight of the monstrosity. The jagged sword blades of the seat would surely inspire a hint of intimidation, even though they were merely stone and not metal. Arthur had always thought the Iron Throne was pretty badass himself. Granted, he'd also pictured it much larger, as intended in the books and not as shown in the television show. The elf narrowed his eyes as he quickly smothered his look of surprise from the spell.

"I wasn't aware many of the humans still had the knowledge to combine magics. Especially not one in some far-flung outskirt village. Who are you… exactly?" Lyrinth asked.

"Name's Arthur," he responded with a nod. "And you need to get the hell away from my village."

The ground in front of him shifted as he felt the elf push his magic into the spot. He quickly worked to counter the spell with his own mana and saw the man using a combination of Earth and Fire Magic to form a stone spike to shoot out and impale him.

Arthur used his magic to push against the elf and interrupted his flow of magic and broke down the structure of the spell. Both men stared daggers at each other while their contest of wills continued in the ground between them. Lyrinth's eyes twitched, and his hands clenched into fists as he released the spell. Arthur was sure he had far more mana to use than Lyrinth could afford. He doubted the man knew that, but it was apparent he wouldn't waste all his mana trying that approach.

Instead, he slowly stood from his chair and waved his hand behind himself. Lyrinth's chair shattered into dust and settled back on the ground. Arthur didn't bother dismissing his chair. It was nothing more than a waste of mana during a fight. He hoped this man's arrogance would be his downfall.

Lyrinth reached over his shoulder and pulled a sword free from its sheath. The blade was almost black in color and felt wrong to Arthur. He couldn't explain why, but it made him feel uneasy. Before he could dwell on it too much, Lyrinth sprung forward at full speed with a slash for Arthur's head.

Arthur ducked under the blow and followed it with a swing from Ember. The elf caught the blade on his own, and they stood there, staring at each other with hatred on their faces. Trying to get the upper hand, Arthur activated Sheathe in Flames on Ember, and the bright blue fire flashed. The moment of shock that registered on Lyrinth's face was just enough for Arthur to pull the sword back and swing again.

The blade inched past the elf's sword and struck him in the side. Lyrinth wore plain looking leather armor, but looks were definitely deceiving. Ember hit the leather and quickly slowed. It cut into the leather but didn't make it into flesh more than about an inch. Lyrinth jumped back in surprise as he looked to the wound.

*You have dealt 30 HP damage to Lyrinth (Level 28) with Ember (Armor).*

"Where'd you get that blade?" he asked.
"Oh, you like Ember here?" Arthur said as he ran an admiring hand down the flat of the blade, "I'm rather fond of it myself."
"Ember?" Lyrinth asked in confusion before his face morphed, "You're wielding a named weapon?"
Arthur only smiled and dashed at the elf. His sword whistled through the air in a flat arc aimed for the elf's midsection. Lyrinth recovered from his surprise and brought his own sword into the path with incredible speed. When the blades met, the force of Lyrinth's strike caused his sword to twist in his hand, and he almost dropped it.
"I look forward to taking that blade from you as well," he called with a sinister grin.

Trying to gain some separation, Arthur kicked toward the elf's midsection, but he twisted to the side, and the foot passed him. Lyrinth's hand whipped out and grabbed his leg as it passed, and he held it upright, causing Arthur to stumble and try to recover his balance. He summoned his magic to him and started the cast timer on Flamethrower. Before the spell cast time elapsed, Arthur saw the power of Fire Magic envelop the elf's hand and intense heat shot into his leg. The burning pain made him forget the entire situation as he fell to the ground.

*Lyrinth (Level 28) has dealt 50 HP damage to you with Burning Touch.*

The fall interrupted his spell cast, and the power that was building in his hand quickly dissipated. He landed hard on his back, and his breath left him for a moment. A sword blade came down for his head, but he rolled to the side to avoid it as dirt flew up from the impact. Still trying to get air back into himself, he kicked out blindly and felt his foot impact flesh.

*You have dealt 10 HP damage to Lyrinth (Level 28) with Kick.*

The sweet sound of the elf snarling in pain came to Arthur's ears, and he smiled as he rolled again and quickly made it to a crouched position. To his dismay, as his gaze came up, a sword was already on its way toward him. Without time to get his sword up to defend, he barreled forward to tackle the elf. The sword continued to fall, but the pommel hit the back of his shoulder before the blade could finish its swing. The impact jarred him and caused pain to flare, but he had the elf in a solid grip as they both tumbled to the ground in a heap.

*Lyrinth (Level 28) has dealt 60 HP damage to you with Steel Sword of the Dark Champion (Blunt Damage).*

Arthur didn't like the implications of the name of the sword Lyrinth wielded, but he didn't have time to dwell on that now. He brought himself up and straddled the elf. Being so close to him, he couldn't get a swing in with Ember, so he pulled his dagger with his left hand. He raised the blade and plunged it down but, before it landed in the elf's chest, a fist of stone smashed directly into his chest and launched him backward and off of his perch.

Bouncing back to his feet after the impact, he saw the fist that struck him still stuck in the ground at its origin. Lyrinth was also back on his feet and brushed off his clothing in disgust from the scuffle. Arthur activated his Dual Casting and started the cast time on Flamethrower as his power climbed.

"You fight like a backwater farmer yourself. I am a little ashamed that I even took a single hit from you. Your form is nonexistent, your attacks are sloppy, and you haven't stood in a proper sword form this entire fight. You are such an embarrassment to the art that…"

Before he could finish the statement, Arthur's dual cast spells flared to life and jumped toward the elf. The flame spiraled from him and battered at the elf. Heat from the fire almost overwhelmed Arthur's own defenses. When the flame cleared, it shocked Arthur to see Lyrinth standing in the same place he had been.

*You have gained 600 experience in Fire Magic for successfully dual casting Flamethrower.*

*You have dealt 300 HP Damage to Lyrinth (Level 28) with Dual Cast Flamethrower (700 HP Damage Resisted).*

The elf's eyes reflected the promise of Arthur's death, and smoke came off parts of his armor and his body. Besides the sizeable amount of damage the elf resisted, the most startling part was he still barely looked injured. Deathly worried about what he might see, he did what he should have done from the start and cast Scan on the elf.

*You have received 260 experience for the successful use of Scan.*

**Name**: Lyrinth
**Level**: 28
**Type**: Dark Elf
**Class**: Duelist, Geomancer

<table>
<tr><td colspan="2">Title: Champion of Isabell<br>HP: 540/880<br>MP: 600/1050<br>Stamina: 380/380</td></tr>
<tr><td>Strength: 26<br>Agility: 15<br>Intellect: 26<br>Wisdom: 16<br>Endurance: 27<br>Charisma: 15<br>Luck: 10</td><td>Experience: N/A<br><br>Skills<br>Combat Skills:<br><br>? (???/???)</td></tr>
</table>

Arthur gulped at the sight. Not only did the man have two classes, but he was also a Champion. There was no way to tell what bonuses or abilities he gained from his champion class. If his Champion abilities worked similar to Arthur's, he could be capable of terrible things.

*Arthur, trust the shadow,* drifted to him once again.

* * *

Rayne watched the action of the battle as it unfolded. Rayne followed the army as it passed their hiding group of refugees. His hope died in his heart as he saw the forces charge the wall of defenders. That was until they started handily repelling them. Arrows flew from the sky like rain, and he could hear the cries of dying goblins echo across the field.

    The first explosion startled him and caused
him to jump in his hiding spot. He watched as
the large wooden wall split and caught on
fire. A valiant figure in plate armor stood at
the top of the siege wall. He cut down goblins
as easily as a farmer cuts wheat while bashing
others in impressive feats of strength with a
heater shield.

    Rayne could see another figure laying waste
to any in his way as he ran along the
battlements. This one wore an armor Rayne
hadn't seen before, but looked like it had
wings on the shoulders. It was difficult to
tell for sure from a distance. The sight
confused him at first, but after some
observation, he was confident it was the same
person he saw in the raid the previous night.
Quick and decisive movements, coupled with the
man's stride pattern, solidified his thoughts
on the matter.

    The fight continued, and no matter how
hopeless it looked, the defenders held. The
storm that blew in had an ominous feel to it,
but the defenders turned the new downpour to
their advantage. The man in the winged armor
even pulled the moisture from it and created
an enormous ball of ice to launch at the
attackers.

    Rayne crept through the trees, trying to
avoid detection. He took a position in the
stand of trees directly behind the orc and
goblin army instead of his usual spot across
the field of battle. He needed to be within
striking distance if necessary. The loud
creaking of wood interrupted his concentration
and drew his attention to a location behind
the army. Multiple giant catapults appeared,
being pushed into position by large groups of
orcs and goblins.

The activity on the wall became a frenzy as they spotted the machines, but before long, Rayne noticed the man in the winged armor was missing from the wall. The catapults creaked to a stop in the field near the back of the army. They weren't far from his hiding spot in the trees. The orcs and goblins made more headway in the battle as the catapults began their barrage. More were cresting the wall. Without the winged figure laying waste to the attackers on the wall, their defense had significantly fallen.

Rayne had almost given up hope on the battle when movement near the edge of his vision caught his attention. To his surprise, not one hundred and fifty yards away, three figures dashed across the opening toward the catapults. The man in the winged armor led the dash, and they used Fire Magic to destroy the machines and operators.

Rayne was about to charge out and help when he spotted movement again to his other side. A Dark Elf strode from the forest line and moved straight for the group of ambushers. The team of three headed for the tree line when the elf cast a spell that blasted in front of them and stopped them in their tracks.

Rayne saw them talking, and the two women in the group left for the trees. The man in the armor remained in place, and a ferocious fight ensued. When the one in the winged armor blasted the elf with his powerful fire spell, Rayne wanted to cheer in excitement. Unfortunately, when the flame cleared, the elf stood there looking extremely pissed.

*Well, damn.* The battle was turning, and the defenders looked on the brink of winning but, Rayne knew without a doubt if this man died, the city would fall. *Time to save the day.*

***

The elf's gaze promised unending pain as it burned into Arthur. Arthur's fingers flexed on his sword handle as he prepared for the inevitable attack. Instead of an attack, maniacal laughter greeted him.

"Ah, haha, ha! It's going to be incredibly fun to kill you. I can already picture crushing your bones with my bare hands. I'm done playing this game, though," the elf yelled into the air.

Deep black energy swirled around Lyrinth and seemed to bleed from his eyes. The power felt like an extreme perversion of magic. It built up and spun faster as it condensed down onto Lyrinth. Before Arthur could react to stop the spell, the power exploded away from Lyrinth and caused Arthur to stagger backward.

Lyrinth sported a new appearance after it cleared. Inky black energy coated him like slime, as it moved across his body like a living creature. The blade he wielded also changed and glowed a deep purple. Before Arthur could comment on the change, Lyrinth charged forward.

His speed increased even further, and the elf's sword slammed into his left side, causing him to fly backward and land on his back.

*Lyrinth (Level 28) has dealt 50 damage to you with Steel Sword of the Dark Champion (Armor Shear).*

His hand touched the impact zone and felt the destroyed section of armor where the blade struck. It barely scratched his skin but the pain from the impact caused his ribs to ache. Sitting up, the purple blade flashed in his vision again. He lifted his dagger to intercept the attack, but as soon as the edges met, Lyrinth's sword snapped it at the guard and continued into Arthur's right side.

*Lyrinth (Level 28) has dealt 50 damage to you with Steel Sword of the Dark Champion (Armor Shear).*

He couldn't afford to take more hits like that. Arthur swung Ember up blindly, and the feeling of a semi-solid impact pleased him.

*You have dealt 40 HP damage to Lyrinth with Ember (Glancing Blow).*

Arthur's gamble paid off. His anticipation of the elf's attack allowed him to get a blind shot on the enemy. Sadly, his reaction was so quick the attack only glanced off him. Arthur never saw the follow-up attack, but he sure felt the impact as it jarred against his right shoulder guard.

*Lyrinth (Level 28) has dealt 40 damage to you with Steel Sword of the Dark Champion (Armor Shear).*

His hand instinctively rose to his shoulder, and he felt the rent in the armor. The power on the sword Lyrinth carried allowed it to cut through armor with ease. *It's just strange that it doesn't cut through flesh as well.*

The glowing blade slammed into his other
shoulder. The pain of the strike still hurt
immensely, even though it didn't break the
skin.

*Lyrinth (Level 28) has dealt 40 damage to
you with Steel Sword of the Dark Champion
(Armor Shear).*

Arthur almost resigned himself to death at
that point. A glance at his status showed he
was fading fast.

| HP: 235/550 |
| Mana: 1010/1010 |
| Stamina 270/530 |

His mana stayed full with him siphoning
from his sword and amulet as he tried to cast
spells, but the elf was so damned quick he
kept getting interrupted. Every time the power
built, the elf's attacks, mixed with the
strange magic on Lyrinth, interrupted the flow
of mana on his spells. Fate had cast him down,
and his second chance would be a failure in
this life.

Arthur's head swam at the hopelessness of
this fight. His health wasn't critical, but at
the rate this man attacked, it was only a
brief time until his end. Instead, he heard a
grunt of pain that surprised him, since it
didn't come from his lips. The blue flame from
his sword pushed a little light into the
surrounding fog, and Arthur couldn't believe
what he saw.

A man in dark leather with shadows bleeding from his cowl, hands, and feet fought toe to toe with Lyrinth. His anxiety spiked when he saw another person shrouded in shadows until he remembered Lianna's words. *Trust the shadow.*

The new character worried him, but he would trust Lianna in this. It also helped that the man, woman, creature, whatever it was, fought his enemy. Arthur slowly got back to his feet.

His armor barely held onto his frame with the large rents in parts of it, but if it blocked even one attack, it would still be useful. He mulled over the idea of joining the fight. Judging by the speed the two fighters attacked each other, he would only get himself killed. Instead, he waited on the sidelines and watched. If he could find an opening to exploit, he would.

The Shadow and Lyrinth traded blows back and forth, and it amazed Arthur to see him holding his own against the elf. Out of curiosity, he activated Scan on the new fighter.

*You have received 180 experience for the successful use of Scan.*

*Congratulations, you have reached level 5 in Scan. Those sweet talents are now available.*

| | |
|---|---|
| **Name:** Rayne | |
| **Level:** 17 | |
| **Type:** Human | |
| **HP:** 240/270 | |
| **MP:** 88/160 | |
| **Stamina:** 190/270 | |
| **Strength:** 15 | **Experience:** N/A |
| **Agility:** 28 | **Skills** |

| Intellect: 7<br>Wisdom: 2<br>Endurance: 21<br>Charisma: 12<br>Luck: 10 | Combat Skills:<br><br>? (???/???) |
| --- | --- |

*Rayne, huh? Might have to ask him to just go by Shadow. Seems more fitting anyway. How the hell was someone so low level holding off Lyrinth?* Arthur could barely get in a hit on the man, but this other guy held his ground, even if he didn't make much progress. Arthur spotted the opening he needed as Lyrinth kicked out and sent Rayne to the ground.

Arthur summoned his power and Dual Cast one of his newer spells. As righteous payback on Lyrinth, two fists of solid stone formed on each side of the elf and smashed into him.

*You have dealt 60 HP damage to Lyrinth (Level 28) with Dual Stone Punch (Crushing) (40 resisted).*

The Shadow leaped to his feet and slammed one of his blades into the elf's side. The attack injured Lyrinth, and the elf's teeth clenched in pain, but Rayne left himself wide open with his attack. Arthur watched the purple glow fade from Lyrinth's sword, and he slashed at Rayne. The edge sunk into his leather and blood welled around the wound. The blade in Rayne's left hand fell to the ground as he stumbled backward, and another slash from Lyrinth caught him in his right shoulder. Rayne dropped to a knee and looked to be barely holding onto his other weapon.

Arthur lifted his hand and dual cast his
Ice Spike spell. The razor-sharp shards of ice
crossed the distance and slammed into
Lyrinth's back. His back arched in pain, and a
feral scream escaped his open mouth. Sadly,
not all the spikes struck the man.

*You have dealt 150 HP damage to Lyrinth
(Level 28) with Dual Ice Spike.*

Lyrinth determined Rayne was no longer a
threat because he turned and ran toward
Arthur. He only traveled a few steps when the
slimy blackness faded along his body, and he
returned to normal. Feeling better about his
chances, Arthur readied himself for the
charge.

Arthur caught the sword on his own as it
came down and gritted his teeth against the
burning in his hand. Lyrinth's sword spun and
slashed across his body in a quick motion and
caught his breastplate. Luckily his strike hit
one of the few remaining pieces of armor, and
it blocked all the damage, but he felt
something snap.

Arthur caught another quick strike, but the
following swing found his armor again. As
before, it blocked the damage, but the armor
creaked and fell off him in pieces, its
durability destroyed.

Arthur's thoughts strayed to the people of the village. *Samson, Vana, Daniel, Dalia, I'm sorry I won't be able to keep my promise. I hope you stay strong and continue fighting for the village in my absence. I'll miss you, Allendria. I wish we had more time to see where this would go. Balair, I'm sorry you'll end up trapped in your own dimension again. I can't see any other way to end this fight, and I don't think I can survive my next attack.*

He sighed in resignation and waited for the right moment. Three more strikes flashed forward, and Arthur stumbled like a drunken fool before the elf reared his blade back for a hard overhanded attack, giving Arthur the shot he needed. Holding his ground, he thrust his sword forward as hard as he could. It punched into the elf's stomach as Lyrinth's sword came straight for his face. Closing his eyes in expectation of the end, he felt hot blood splash his face, and a heavy weight crashed into him and took him to the ground.

*You have dealt 260 HP damage to Lyrinth (Level 28) with Ember (Critical Hit) (Mortal Blow) (Burning).*

Opening his eyes, Arthur saw Balair lying on top of him. The little dragonling had a large gash across his body and bled profusely.

*I made it in time,* he sent weakly.

*Thank you, my friend.*

*Don't thank me, just make sure you summon me back when you can,* he snorted.

The little creature stilled and sagged in his grasp. Arthur's chest tightened with sorrow as he held the body of his friend. He ran his hands over the little dragon's face and closed his ruby eyes. His attention focused on a wet, coughing sound in front of him.

"If I'm to die here, I'm going to take you with me!"

Arthur looked up to see an incredible amount of power building in front of the elf. A spell that large significantly limited his options. He couldn't tell precisely what type of magic the man was using. Without knowing how to counter it, he could only think of one solution.

Pulling all the mana he could muster, he started pouring out Dimensional Magic in front of him. If he couldn't counter it, he planned to attempt to siphon it into another dimension. He pictured a funnel of swirling dimensional power with the mouth facing Lyrinth. The funnel snapped into place right as Lyrinth's spell launched forward.

The energies collided, and the spinning mass of power pulled the shadowy power in. They merged and spun faster. Arthur felt it tug at him as the power increased. It became so violent it pulled him forward and sucked him into the vortex himself.

His surroundings reminded him of going to warp speed in many of the sci-fi shows as white pins of light flew past him at incredible speed. His body came to an abrupt halt, and he looked at a solid white wall. The room itself felt familiar like he'd been there before.

"Arthur… is that you?" A weak voice came to his ears. The sound sent a chill up his spine and brought tears to his eyes.

# Chapter 18

*The Fall*

Arthur carefully turned toward the voice. His eyes scanning the room as he spun. The small chair that his father was in last time sat empty with a crumpled blanket on it. When he completed the turn and saw his mother, he could do nothing but cry.

"Mom," he said hesitantly.

Evelyn covered her mouth with her hand as she began crying at the sight of her lost son.

"I must be hallucinating. I guess my time must almost be up as I imagined. Are you here to take me to heaven?" she asked.

Arthur walked gingerly toward his mother and kneeled beside her bed. He reached out and took her delicate hand in his own. The last time he'd seen her, she wasn't this frail. Either his visions were real, and he somehow was back on Earth, or he was having another one of his visions. This felt so real though, and this time he was in the room interacting with her. Before he was only a passive observer and watching events unfold, similar to looking through a window.

"No mom, I'm not here to take you to heaven. I really can't even figure out exactly where to start." Arthur breathed as he shook his head. "I don't know if you'd believe any of it."

"It's okay. You can tell me anything, dear. I've been holding on for so long. I wanted to stay for your father, but I've realized I'm not destined to make it through this. Something's been telling me to hold on a little longer, and until now I couldn't figure out why," she told him as she cupped her other hand on his cheek.

Arthur stood and took a seat on the bed beside her. He explained the incident the night he died. When he mentioned the Goddess, his mother adopted a soft smile. He explained his time in the world of Dravincia. He told her about the odd way the world behaved like some of the video games on Earth.

"You should have no problem in that world then. Especially if it works like the video games you used to love to play. I bet you adapted to it quickly," she said with a chuckle.

He could only smile at his mother. He continued the story and explained that he was the village mayor and how he worked hard to protect it. Before the story made it any farther he had to send a quip his mom's way.

"I also finally found the woman you've been hounding me about. She's beautiful and makes me happy. We haven't had a lot of time together, but I'm hoping she'll be the one. You might find her appearance a little odd, though. She has purple skin after all," he told her with a laugh.

"Come now, you know I've never been one to judge anyone on color. If she's good enough for you, I'm sure I'd love her as well. What's her name?"

"Her name's Allendria. She's actually a princess, believe it or not," he said as his thoughts strayed to the recent information. "I just found that out earlier today."

"Figures, you could never find anyone on Earth worth your time, but you're sent to another world and enthrall a princess," she said with a huff.

A small coughing fit took over for a few moments and Arthur held onto her until it passed. A look of concern crossed his face as he looked into her tired eyes.

"I also found out something about myself. I know who my biological parents are," he whispered.

Her eyes welled with tears at the statement. Arthur wasn't sure if it was because of what he said or how he worded it. She lightly fanned at her eyes and spoke after a brief time.

"You found them? They were from Dravincia?"

"I didn't find them. They died a long time ago. I learned that they were the king and queen of the kingdom I'm in back on Dravincia."

Arthur explained the story he was told. He told her about how most of the kingdom loved and admired them and then they betrayed by ones they thought of as friends. He ended the telling with their escape and sending him to safety right before the usurpers killed them.

"We always knew you were special but now we know why we felt that way."

"Don't worry, Mom. It doesn't matter what I learned, you and dad will always be my parents. I was just able to find the biological ones. I'm sure they would've done a fine job raising me but that was something you two did for me. I'll always love you as my mother," he told her as he held her in a long embrace.

His mother began another coughing fit, and it took some time for it to calm back down. A moment later, Arthur the alarm on her monitor startled him. A glance at it showed an elevated pulse. Her face morphed into a grimace of pain and a soft moan escaped her lips. A few seconds later, her heart rate returned to normal, and the monitor was silent again.

"What's wrong?" He asked frantically.

"The cancer. I've been fighting it for so long, but I don't think I can do it anymore. I've tried for as long as possible and I'm glad I did. It allowed me to see you one last time before I leave this world. Arthur, I want you to live your life to the fullest. Never let anyone tell you what you can or can't accomplish. You know better than that. Your father and I did everything we could to prepare you, and I can only hope it was enough," her voice floated to him weakly.

"Mom, you can't leave. I just got back. I need you. Stay with me," he said as he held her tighter.

Struggling to hold herself up, she laid back against the bed. Her eyes closed and scrunched up as if in pain. Arthur wasn't a doctor, but he could see her health declining quickly. Panic set in and he brought his hands up in front of his face. A thought caused Fire Magic to move toward his hand. A slight smile reached his face as he realized his magic still worked.

Leaning over his mom, he gently placed his hand on her shoulders. He used his Water Magic to send out a sense of discovery through her body. The magic could detect the blood as it pumped throughout her body. He wasn't sure what he could do in this scenario. Using his power, he identified the composition of the blood as it swirled in her veins. Without medical knowledge, he wasn't sure what it should look like.

Turning his power inward, he examined his own. It had a similar feel, but there were slight differences. With this new knowledge in mind, he turned his thoughts back to her. Isolating the differences, some of them felt 'right' as if they needed to be there. One in particular had a very wrong feeling to it. Focusing on the power, he pictured a filter that would sift the blood and collect the impurities out of the bloodstream as it flowed through it.

He pulled the power in and envisioned the effect. The magic was on such a minuscule level, that it was hard to determine if it worked correctly. He saw the tiny filter pop into place with his magic.

*Congratulations, you have created a new Water Magic Spell. Do you wish to name this new spell? Yes/No.*

*For creating the new Water Magic Spell: Filter Minor Impurities (Blood), you have been granted a one time bonus of 250 Water Magic Experience, 250 Personal Experience, and 1 Intellect. Don't give up!*

*You have gained 80 experience in Water Magic for successfully casting Filter Minor Impurities (Blood).*

| Spell: Filter Minor Impurities (Blood) | |
| --- | --- |
| Requirements: Water Magic<br>Mana Cost: 40 MP<br>Cast Time: 3 seconds | Description: Create a filter in the specified part of a blood vein. Will filter weak and minor poisons or impurities out of the blood as it passes through. |
| Mastery Level: 1 | |

Arthur watched anxiously as the blood continued to filter, but it wasn't filtering fast enough. He cast the spell twelve more times throughout different large veins in her body. With it only being capable of filtering weak and minor impurities, it may not be strong enough to fix the problem.

*You have gained 960 experience in Water Magic for successfully casting Filter Minor Impurities (Blood) (x12).*

It seemed to help and he could see her bloodstream clearing of that odd-feeling impurity from before. It concerned him that her vitals weren't improving. He kept glancing from the machine back to his mom, and the only change was her vitals slowly got worse.

He panicked at the uncertainty of what was happening. He wasn't sure what to do, and his mind went blank with panic. His medical knowledge was very limited at best but he struggled to sift through any of it for a speck of hope. None of the spells he knew were of any use in this scenario.

"Mom, hang in there for me. I'm working to fix the problem. I just need more time. I've already been able to get most of the impurities out of your blood. You should be fine in no time," he told her reassuringly.

Her hand reached out and grabbed his. "Arthur, my dear, you can't fix this. I know you have great new powers but it's too late. The chemotherapy treatments combined with cancer has already wreaked more havoc on my body than you can fix."

She forced her eyes open and looked into his. "You have to let me go, sweetheart."

Tears sprang unbidden from Arthur's eyes as he looked at his mom. He gripped her hand as he cried.

"You can't leave me," he whispered. "I just got back to you."

"I'll never truly leave you," she said in a soothing voice. "Everything your father and I have ever taught you will stay with you throughout your entire life. We'll always be with you in spirit, no matter where we go."

"You can't go. You've taught me to fight my entire life and never give up."

"I've suffered for a long time with this, dear. It's by far the worst experience of my life. I'm tired, my body hurts, and everything on me is falling apart. My muscles have atrophied and I can't even get around on my own. Life has become an exercise in suffering. It's time to go. John and I have already made peace with it. I'll miss you two so much, but it's time to move on," she said with a voice laced in pain and sorrow.

Arthur couldn't respond to her statement. He could only stare at her as he cried. Her tears joined his as they held each other. With nothing else he could do, he spent the time he could holding his mom. His mind raced back to his early years. Time they spent cuddled on the couch together watching movies. She was always there to cheer him on at all his sporting events. She was there for everything in his life and he felt powerless not being able to do anything. For the love of God, he had magic now and still couldn't save her.

*Lianna, please help me. I can't lose her now,* he called into his mind. Only silence came back to him. Despair gripped him as the realization of his helplessness hit him. He wasn't sure how long they had held each other, but the sound of an alarm startled him.

Jumping to his feet and out of the bed, he looked around. The machine alarm blared, and the monitor revealed a flat line. He glanced back at his mom in the bed and reached down. He couldn't feel a pulse and stood there in a mixture of shock and panic. Pushing Water Magic into her, he tried everything he could to keep the blood circulating throughout her system. No matter how hard he tried, nothing changed.

He lay his head on hers as streams of tears
fell from his face. He spent more mana casting
more filters and burning mana to move the
blood around her body. Another glance at the
machines only confirmed his fear.

Arthur leaned over the bed and kissed his
mom on the forehead. "I'll always love you and
I'll miss you dearly."

Noise came from outside, and Arthur heard
the door open. The noise drew his attention to
the door just as his father walked through.

"Arthur… how…" was all the man could say.

"Dad, I couldn't save her. I'm sorry," was
all he managed to say before something pulled
at him and he flew backward. The earlier
sensation returned, and he felt like he was
flying through space. His feet touched down
and a familiar sight was in front of him. He
appeared back where he left, and he could see
the walls of the village in the distance.
Arthur sunk to his knees on the ground.

"He's over here," Allendria's voice rang
across the field.

Arthur heard the pounding of feet as they
came to him.

"He's alive and looks okay. The day is
won!" Vana yelled.

Arthur could do nothing but kneel on the
ground and cry. Allendria came up behind him
and slowed to a walk. She carefully picked her
way around him and kneeled down in front of
him.

"Arthur, what's wrong? We won the day. When
you defeated Lyrinth, the remaining orcs and
goblins fled."

Arthur struggled to find words to answer
her. His tears flowed down his face unabated.

"I couldn't save her, I just couldn't save her," he told her as he lifted his watery eyes to meet hers.
"Save who?"
"My mom."

# Chapter 19

*Picking up the Pieces*

Allendria meandered through the village. Construction moved along nicely on the new buildings. She smiled and waved at one of the construction groups. There were now three full groups of people working to build and restore the village.

The wall was the first thing addressed. When the goblins retreated a week ago, the crews worked throughout the night until the destroyed section of the wall stood once again. They cleared the field of battle of the larger boulders used by the catapults shortly after.

Instead of climbing into the new moat and pulling all the bodies out, the crews raised the dirt until they flattened the space and retrieved the partially rotten bodies. It took two days of work to gather the bodies and systematically burn them all.

The workers sorted the useful items to separate locations. The metal went to the blacksmith, while they stacked the cloth near the inn until they could determine if anything was worth trying to salvage.

To further complicate things, a group of refugees showed up shortly after the attack. Samson allowed them to shelter inside the wall and the village worked to feed them, but they weren't officially part of the population. Arthur fell into a deep depression and it was almost impossible to get him to take care of anything short of opening the food storage for Daniel when he needed it.

Allendria wasn't sure what to do. She felt deep sorrow for him. His world had collapsed around him and he'd lost the most important, loving, and encouraging woman in his life. She knew exactly what he was going through with losing her own mother. She knew there was nothing she could say or do to ease his pain. Time would be the only thing to heal his broken heart. His sorrow was so deep he hadn't even taken the time to discuss the revelation she was a princess. She didn't know if it was because of his overpowering grief or if he just didn't care about the news.

She had put her skills to heavy use during the cleanup and did much of the incineration work for trash and bodies. Now that the battlefield was clear, and the village was getting back to normal, she sorely hoped Arthur would come out of his mental anguish.

"Allendria, where are you off to today?" called Vana.

"Making my rounds," she replied while smiling at the ranger. "Seeing if I'm needed anywhere. Most of the work is settling back to normal, it seems."

Vana nodded. "How's Arthur?"

Allendria sighed, "Still lost in despair. You've seen him a few times, I'm sure. He doesn't focus on anything, really. The village is running on its own mostly, thank goodness."

"I hope he gets past this sooner rather than later. We need him to help lead. I'm thankful he had the forethought to set up our magical teams because they've been essential so far. I have an ominous feeling we'll need him soon and just can't shake it," Vana mumbled.

"We'll be fine. We vanquished the goblins and I still think we have time before the bandit crews make another attempt, if any still exist after the goblin raids. I just wish Arthur was himself. He always had so many ideas on how to make our village better and, now that we finally have the time, he can't focus."

"Just keep an eye on him, will ya? I've got to get going. I promised James and Zeke we'd take a quick trip around the edge of the tree line to work on some of our scouting skills. I'll catch ya later," Vana called as she turned and waved over her shoulder.

"Later," Allendria said with a wave.

Allendria resumed her previous walk toward the northeastern gatehouse. The weather was pleasant, and the sun felt good on her skin. Before she reached her destination, a voice called out to her.

"Lady Allendria, do you have a moment to talk?"

A smile spread across her face. After the battle, she took a little time to get to know the man named Rayne. He was the reason that Arthur survived the battle with Lyrinth after all. To her amazement, the boyish man was fulfilling a quest from the Goddess Lianna, and a group of people who wanted a fresh life accompanied him. Allendria couldn't blame them after speaking to some of them and learning of the hardships they faced in the city.

"Rayne, good to see you today. What can I do for you?"

"Sorry to bother you, Lady Allendria. I was hoping I'd get to talk to the mayor. The people I traveled with are appreciative that you've provided for them so far, but they're feeling more like prisoners instead of welcome guests. I was hoping to discuss formally joining the village population so we could do our part to help," Rayne told her politely.

"I'm terribly sorry. I understand it's a tense situation. The mayor experienced a terrible loss during the battle, as I'm sure you've heard. None want him to get past this struggle more than I, but it hasn't happened yet. Have you talked to Katherine? She's the assistant mayor and probably at least has the authority to grant you freedom inside the walls and give the blessing for your people to help around the village. I don't think she can officially name you as villagers, but she should get you started."

Rayne perked up at that. "Thank you, my lady."

"Enough of that. Allendria is fine." She waved him off.

Rayne grinned, "As you say, Allendria. Do you need assistance with anything? I tend to have plenty of time on my hands and nothing to do."

"I appreciate the offer but I'm just inspecting the work. The construction crews are the ones doing the heavy lifting, so to speak."

"That rather surprised me. Magic was very rare to see in the city. I didn't expect to see any of it this far away from civilization."

"Another, very correct, statement. The mayor is responsible for that. He sees a world where magic should help and be widely available. He doesn't care for the endless profiteering the nobles and mage guilds adhere to."

"I look forward to finally talking to him. If you'll excuse me, I'll go look for Katherine," Rayne said with a quick bow.

"You can probably find her at the inn," Allendria called to Rayne as he walked away.

Continuing her trip, Allendria finally walked up to the gatehouse. They had completed the repairs on the wall and she saw multiple members of the construction crew scrambling and working tirelessly to add on. After the battle, it was obvious they needed a walkway behind the wall. Arthur's archer platforms provided an excellent base for them, but the walkway between them was so narrow it was dangerous to traverse during a fight.

The workers now focused on expanding the wall and building up the walkway. It took some convincing, but Allendria coaxed Arthur to come to himself long enough to teach her how to use stone. She in turn taught the crews how to do it. Now they scurried along the wall like a small army of ants while small sections of stone rose to connect with existing walkways.

The workers didn't have the benefit of Arthur's enormous mana pool, so they focused on smaller sections at a time. After the attack, the villagers unanimously decided that the walls should take priority. With the additional crews, the work moved faster. *This initial expansion should only take a few more days with the use of the mana storage necklaces, although it would move so much faster if Arthur would assist,* Allendria mused.

She walked among the different workers and spoke to them personally. She'd grown fond of many of them. Several people in the village were still uncomfortable with her presence, but not this group. Working hand in hand with them made her feel more at home.

One of the crew members, a woman named Olivia from what Allendria recalled, worked to fill in a section on the wall. The dirt rose to fill the gap and stone formed from the top, working its way down. Allendria frowned as the woman stepped onto the still forming block to finish her spell. The ground continued to transform but, right as the spell completed, the stone beneath her feet crumbled, and she fell.

On instinct, Allendria's hand whipped out in front of her and the dirt swirled near the base of the now crumbling block. A flat section of soil quickly lifted in a small cylinder until it caught the stumbling woman. Olivia looked over the edge of the dirt platform in terror. Allendria allowed a quick breath to escape.

"Olivia, please be more careful in your work. A fall like that would've almost certainly broken a bone and, with the way you fell, might have broken your neck. Never walk on your work until the spell is complete," Allendria told her in lecturing tones.

"Yes, Lady Allendria. My apologies."

Allendria grimaced at the title that now followed her. As far as she knew, no one but her, Arthur, and possibly Vana, knew of her heritage in the village. That led her to believe the people were referring to her by Lady because of her relationship with Arthur.

She pulled her thoughts back and used more magic to move Olivia's new platform next to a stable portion of the wall so she could resume work. The young woman shakily vacated the platform and sunk to a seated position to regain her wits following the experience.

Allendria glanced to her mana count and grimaced. The spell took a sizable amount of mana. Mainly because it used raw magic and not an activated spell. An activated spell took far less mana, but they also had the downside of a cast time. One major benefit of using raw magic was the ability to make the effect instant, even if the mana cost was often prohibitive.

Allendria continued touring the wall and took the time to wave and give words of encouragement as she passed. Her focus was on their safety and helping them with their magic. Luckily, no other incidents happened, but she got the chance to help multiple people with their magic as they worked. The afternoon melted away while she worked side by side with the villagers to improve their home. *My home.*

***

Rayne strolled through the village. Arguably, there wasn't a lot to stroll, but he managed, anyway. His target was the best-looking building standing within sight. There wasn't a lot of competition, though, judging by the state of repair on display on most of the structures.

The quality of the streets shocked him for such a tiny village. They were better than most of the city streets he typically traversed. Villagers dotted the path, all seemingly busy with different tasks. The stark contrast between this village and Seora was a night and day difference. Industry in the cities was at a halt, yet here, everywhere he looked, he saw bundles of materials carried back and forth. He could hear the quiet hammering of metal from a blacksmith shop even though it was too far away to see.

He squeezed past a few people gathered near the entrance to the inn and walked into the building. The sight amazed him almost every time. Gerrard and Greta, his old friends and two people he regarded as family ran a respectable inn back in the city prior to their demise during the riots. They always kept the place in pristine cleanliness. The first time Rayne entered the inn in Alem's Crossing, he felt a sense of wonder that somewhere so far out would have the same cleanliness. Most of the inns in the cities he visited lacked basic cleanliness. Gerrard's inn was an exception to the rule. This one also seemed to be under that same exception.

Rayne wasn't sure what Katherine looked like. He was familiar with Daniel, however, so he took up the matter with him. The always smiling innkeeper was a welcome sight. His work was the reason the people who traveled with him ate so well.

"Hello, Daniel."

The innkeeper turned to face Rayne. "Well if it isn't the hero himself. How're you doing today? The people with you faring well?"

"Actually, that's why I'm here. We're doing fine, but after a week of nothing, it's taking a toll on us. We truly appreciate the help, but everyone is getting a little anxious about what our future here holds. I spoke to Allendria about it and she told me to talk to Katherine for permission for the refugees to work around here to do our part," Rayne told him.

"That sounds like a solid plan. So why are you talking to me instead of Katherine?" Daniel asked.

"Well, I don't know who Katherine is or what she looks like," Rayne replied sheepishly.

Daniel laughed out loud. "That sure explains it."

He motioned for Rayne to come closer and then pointed to a small woman at a corner table. She looked like she hadn't slept in a week and her hair was a wiry mess. Two books sat in front of her on the table and she appeared to be writing in one of them.

"That would be her," Daniel told him.

"Thanks, Daniel. If you'll excuse me I need to visit with her."

"Be careful with her. She's been driving
herself a little too hard without Arthur
around. The stress is slowly wearing her
down," Daniel told him quietly.

Rayne nodded to him, "Thanks for the heads
up."

Rayne walked over to the table and stood
nearby while the woman wrote in her book. The
silence dragged on as he stood waiting for her
to acknowledge him. The sound of the quill
scratching the page was almost painful. As
quiet as it was in the room, the writing
sounded like a charging army. After what
seemed like an eternity, Rayne lost his
patience and politely cleared his throat.

"Uh, what, someone say something?"
Katherine asked as she looked around in a
daze.

"Hello Lady Katherine, my name's Rayne. Can
I sit? I'd like to discuss something with
you."

"I guess I can spare some time. Have a
seat," she said and gestured toward the seat
across from her.

"Thank you. I'd like to request permission
for the city refugees to assist in the
village. I spoke with Lady Allendria, and she
told me you might be able to give us
permission to work and help earn our keep
instead of sitting around in boredom. We
appreciate the help the villagers have
offered, especially the food, but feel bad not
being able to contribute."

Katherine stared at him for a few moments.
She looked lost for words for a little while
as the gears appeared to turn in her sleep-
deprived brain.

"Do your people have any skills? What type
of work are they willing to do?"

"Some of them do, but it all varies. I don't know all the skills they have personally. I'm sure they're willing to help with anything, though."

"Well, without the mayor's approval I can't just let you guys take just any jobs. I can't allow any of you to work on the guard or rangers, but I might be able to allow some of you to work the fields and supplement the construction forces. I can't allow anyone to learn the magical training specific to those roles since they require a commitment to the village," Katherine said.

"As bored and worthless as they're feeling, I'm sure they'd welcome anything they could do to help," Rayne explained.

"Fine. I'll go tomorrow and work with all those in your camp to evaluate their skills and try to find a suitable place for each of them. I can't put them in some of the positions just yet, but I want that information ready so there are no more delays when Arthur's available."

"Thank you, Katherine. I appreciate the help. Do you need anything from me?"

"Now that you mention it, why don't we just start with you," she said as she turned to a fresh page in the book in front of her. She dipped her quill into the ink and looked up at him in anticipation.

Rayne sighed. "All right. I am proficient in Small Blades, Stealth, and Alchemy. At least, those are the skills I use most."

Katherine's eyebrows rose as he named his primary skills. "So, the leader of the refugees is a thief? How'd that happen?"

"I'm sure I don't know what you're talking about. I had a quest to help people and took the chance. I was an apprentice for an Alchemist before he died in the city riots," Rayne said as his eyes lowered to the table.

"Sorry to hear that. Meant nothing by the comment, it's just I couldn't think of any other reason you'd have skills in Small Blades and Stealth in a city."

"A man has to protect himself somehow," he said as he stood from his chair. "That's all I can offer you right now, but if you need anything else, feel free to ask. I'll see if I can make myself useful."

"Take care, Rayne," Katherine called as the mysterious young man walked away.


***


Samson spotted his target as he approached. The big man he looked for was arguably hard to miss. Rowan stood near one of his anvils with a piece of metal suspended in front of him. The now-familiar flow of magic was shaping the piece to his will. The display never ceased to fascinate him. He watched the spectacle as the magic drifted across the metal and the hunk of hot steel slowly took the shape of a dagger. The piece finished, and the heat dissipated as it softly clanged onto the anvil.

"Getting the hang of it?"

Rowan looked up and wiped the sweat from his brow. "Slowly, but yes. I don't know how Arthur makes it look so effortless. It takes some intense focus to complete the pieces, otherwise, portions of it warp and distort as the magic flows. What're you up to today?"

"Coming to bother you, of course. Had a chance to rig up some more armor for everyone? I don't like the guards being partially equipped after the last attack," he told Rowan.

"Almost done, actually. All the helmets and bracers are ready to go. I have a couple more breastplates left, but I don't think I can do those to match. The design Arthur used is too hard for me to focus on. I can get parts to look right, but then other sections end up looking like melted candle wax when complete. I know I'll eventually get it down, but I can't quite master it yet," Rowan told him with a sigh of resignation.

"No worries, had any luck rigging plates for the leggings? I'd like protection at least to the shins, although I'd really prefer all the way down to metal sabatons."

"You really don't ask for small things, do you? I can't make the sabatons, at least not anything near what Arthur can. His mind seems much sharper at focusing on mental images. I've got mock-ups of some of the plates complete so you can try them out," Rowan said as he motioned for a stack of metal pieces on a nearby workbench.

Samson nodded and walked to the bench. He hefted one plate, examined the curve of the steel, and pressed it against his thigh. The piece conformed nicely and didn't have any sharp edges he could feel. He repeated the process with another of the plates on his other leg and saw they matched perfectly. Tossing them back on the bench, he walked back to Rowan.

"Did you figure out the best way to incorporate them into leggings? Are you going to make full greaves like Arthur did, or do you plan to attach them to leather pants directly?"

"Probably both, to be honest. After considering the issue, I want your guards to have full sets of greaves for leg protection. I also plan to make a version attached to leather pants to protect only the shin and thighs with the lighter plates of steel. I want our scouting forces to use those. Being lighter won't affect their speed but will help protect them from attacks and dense foliage," Rowan answered.

"Excellent thinking. I need to make my rounds and check in on the guards. If you need anything just send someone for me," Samson told him with a nod.

"Will do."

Samson walked back toward the inn and then took the road, headed for the northeastern gate. Not far down the path, he heard footsteps approach him.

"How're you today?" came the sweet female voice.

"Ah, Lady Dalia, how are you? Is there anything I can do for you?" Samson asked as he spun to face the young noblewoman.

"No, Sir Samson, just walking around. I wanted to make sure nothing pressing needed my attention. How are you holding up after the battle?" Dalia asked.

"Faring well. Trying to establish a permanent guard force and ensure we're better prepared for events like this," he answered.

"I'm pleased to hear it. Have you heard from Arthur? I'm afraid I haven't talked to him much. The few times I have, he seems very distant."

Samson shook his head slowly, "The grief has taken him for now. Hopefully, he can shake it off and get back to normal."

"I hope he can do it soon. We need an active leader. Our village can't grow without him fulfilling his duties, and I'd hate to imagine having to replace him as Mayor," she said.

Samson raised an eyebrow at that, "You'd truly suggest the possibility of replacing him? Who do you think could take his place? You, my lady?"

A hint of anger flashed across her face so quickly he thought he might have mistaken it. "Of course not. I only wish to see the vision of our Goddess realized. We can't fulfill her glory without making the village a better place, and that requires a powerful leader. I merely wish for Arthur to recover quickly."

"I'm sure he will. I'm willing to give him time after the events he's suffered over the past few weeks," Samson said with a nod.

"I sure hope so, otherwise I might have to see if you'll take the job," she said with a laugh.

"Me, my lady? I don't think I'd be fit for such a position."

"Of course you would. Don't sell yourself short. You are a Paladin of the Goddess Lianna. I'm sure you would be up to the task if came to that," she said with a sweet smile.

"I'd prefer not to talk like that. Arthur will be fine, I'm sure of it."

"I hope you're correct. I have other matters to tend to, but I'll see you around," she said in a cheerful tone and veered away from him as she continued walking.

"That woman sure is an odd one," Samson muttered to himself.

# Chapter 20

*Re-awakening*

Arthur walked downstairs from his room. His mood was the same as every day this past week. He took his seat at a table and the meal appeared while he sat in relative silence. The food disappeared into his mouth as he slowly shoved it in. It had no taste and might as well have been ash.

He pushed back in his chair and stood from his seat. The idea of going back to his room and lying in bed appealed to him. His feet moved almost on their own toward the stairs before a last-minute urge turned his feet toward the back of the inn.

Stepping outside, he relieved himself and looked around. The weather wasn't bad, so he took a walk. The last week had been rough and people constantly tried to approach him with their condolences. He couldn't stand to hear it anymore. Nothing they said would bring her back.

Walking to the wall outside the village, he settled into a shaded area to sit. He leaned his head against the stone and enjoyed the breeze as his mind drifted and thought back on the battle last week. His progress in his different skills impressed him. The most important part was his level gain.

*You have gained a total of 29,000 experience.*
*You have gained a total of 3,600 experience in Swords.*

*Congratulations, you have been granted level 9 in Swords. Swing speed with swords increased by 24%. That new sword cuts great.*

*You have gained a total of 1,550 experience in Small Blades.*

*You have gained a total of 1,400 experience in Dual Wield.*

*Congratulations, you have reached level 6 in Dual Wield. Accuracy penalty with off-hand weapons decreased by 15%. Some enjoyable work in that battle.*

*You have gained a total of 1,950 experience in Medium Armor.*

*Congratulations, you have reached levels 3 and 4 in Medium Armor. Armor bonuses granted by Medium armor increased by 6%. That armor sure saved your life.*

*You have gained a total of 3,950 experience in Archery.*

*You have gained a total of 1,150 experience in Fire Magic.*

*You have gained a total of 3,880 experience in Earth Magic.*

*You have gained a total of 2,150 experience in Water Magic.*

*Congratulations, you have reached level 9 in Water Magic. Increases the effect of your Water Magic spells by 24%. That ball of ice was impressive.*

*You have gained a total of 450 experience in Dimensional Magic.*

    Between the raid kill experience and
turning in the quest for the completion of the
raid, his level advanced to twenty, almost
twenty-one. He subconsciously knew he needed
to work on unlocking his first class and
completing his Soul Bond quest, but he had no
willpower and couldn't gather any energy to
care.
    Arthur sighed as he realized he had a task
he couldn't keep putting off. He felt bad
about it since the little guy had saved his
life, but he didn't want Balair to intrude on
his feelings. It was finally time to bring him
back. *Boy, is he gonna be pissed with how long
it took.*
    Arthur activated his Summon Crimson Whelp
spell and waited for the cast time. The
familiar red portal appeared and the
glimmering ball of scales flew forth to land
on the ground in front of him. Balair looked
around the area in confusion. His gaze turned
to Arthur.
    *How long did you leave me in that place?*
    *It's been a week,* Arthur told him with a
sigh.
    *A week? I save your life and you wait a
week to bring me back?* Balair yelled at him
mentally.
    *Sorry. It's been a rough journey since we
last saw each other.*
    Balair carefully studied Arthur while
turning his head to each side, similar to that
of a dog. His master looked a little haggard.
Dark circles stood out under his eyes, showing
he had slept little. His hair hung low and
shaggy with hints of oil and grime. Usually,
Arthur took better care of himself. Balair
took a long, steadying breath, walked to
Arthur, and sat beside him.

*Tell me what happ…* Balair sent to him before light sparkled between his scales and grew brighter, enveloping him in a glowing ball of brilliant yellow. Arthur turned his gaze toward the dragon, but the intensity made it difficult to see. Balair's body seemed to stretch. His compact frame expanded and Arthur watched in fascination. The entire process took about half a minute but, as the glow faded from the creature, Arthur received a surprise notification.

*Congratulations, your familiar reached level 20 and evolved to a new form. Your Crimson Whelp evolved to a Small Crimson Drake. His base stats have increased to account for his new size. Your Summon Crimson Whelp spell has automatically been upgraded to Summon Crimson Drake (Small).*

The new and improved Balair sat next to him and admired his new physique. The little creature grew from the size of a medium-sized dog to that of a small pony.

*Uh, Balair, what just happened?* Arthur asked.

*I evolved, what else do you think happened? I know you can read,* Balair told him.

*I can read you stupid little rat. What I meant was what does that mean? I didn't even know you could evolve.*

*Fine. I guess you wouldn't know the details about any of it. Some creatures in this world evolve into larger and stronger forms as they grow. As a matter of fact, the dragons your family made their deal with were some of the original creatures to evolve fully. We evolve in tiers. Every twenty levels we advance to a new form. Once we reach that form, we get to stay that size permanently.*

*If that's the case, why haven't you evolved before? I know you're old and Calfuray seems to know you,* Arthur inquired.

*I always have unfortunate luck with masters being idiots and dying before I can gain enough experience. When my master dies, I am reset to the base experience level for my current evolved form. As a whelp, that's level five. As a small drake, it will now be level twenty.*

*But if you have to level with a master how would you ever gain a master if you've already evolved a tier? Wouldn't everyone start with the lowest level summon spell and advance it as they evolved their familiar?* Arthur asked.

*You'd think so, wouldn't you? Oddly enough, sometimes people don't learn their spells until later in their life. Summoning magic isn't as common as you may think. It's also possible to learn advanced summoning spells first. For instance, you may find a scroll that teaches you to summon a drake. When you use it, you would skip straight to one of that evolution and pass the whelps completely.*

*Ha, never thought of that. Well, looks like you have yourself a new form to play with. Anything special with it?* Arthur asked inquisitively.

*Of course. It's bigger and stronger, naturally. It also has one added benefit. It allows me to talk to others in mind to mind conversation.*

*Oh, no. Please don't go torturing people and forcing them to listen to your nonsense.*

*They could only be so lucky. I have countless years of experience to impart. Either way, it requires me to initiate a connection to them. If they accept the mental link, we can discuss things as you and I do now,* Balair explained.

*That could be helpful. It gets frustrating having to translate for you all the time. I'm sure it isn't much better for you.*

*Ain't that the truth?*

*You said the dragons are evolved as well. Do their babies become whelps when born, to join the pool of creatures as familiars?*

*Nope. As long as the parents are both fully evolved, it gives the babies free will to grow naturally with their bodies. Calfuray was one such dragon. If any of our kind mates that are a lower tier of evolution, their offspring joins the ranks of the familiars. It's part of why dragons look down on us. They see us as worthless usually.*

*That makes little sense. You'd think they'd feel sympathetic to you. They used to be you, after all.*

*No. Their ancestors used to be like us. None of the current dragons, except maybe one elder, were born into the life of a familiar. The current ones seem to have adopted the spoiled attitudes of kids of rich nobles. They believe they are above everyone and look down on others. That's part of why they forbid teaching magic to dragon familiars.*

*Huh. Never thought of that. Thanks for telling me. What caused you to evolve, anyway? Most of the fight was over by the time you saved me. There couldn't have been that much experience left to gain.*

*The quest. You accepted it while I was gone and it took a few minutes for it to assign all of my missing experience.*

*Good to know and thanks for saving me.*

*Humph. Don't mention it. I did it so Calfuray wouldn't skin me alive. It wasn't for you.*

The two sat in silence for a few moments before Balair looked to Arthur.

*Arthur, what's wrong with you? You don't look so good,* Balair asked with uncommon concern.

Arthur sighed. *It's a lengthy story.*

*I've got time. You look like you need to talk.*

*I guess.*

Arthur spent the next hour talking about the events with his mother. He needed to explain a few details about his life and his world before he left so the dragon could understand, but eventually, he finished his tale. He stared out toward the field ahead of him with tear-filled eyes when the story finished and rested his head back against the wall.

*I'm sorry, Arthur. I know it's not much consolation, but I truly am. She sounded like an exceptional woman. Although I'm kind of upset you didn't mention me. That, or you didn't tell that part,* Balair sent to him while trying to display a toothy grin.

Arthur couldn't help but chuckle at the creature's antics.

*It's been rough, but I'll eventually get through it. I know I've been struggling to cope with things around the village and have been neglecting my duties. I'm honestly surprised Allendria hasn't punted me across the inn as she did to you.*

Balair winced. *Don't remind me. I'm not sure my ribs ever straightened out when they healed.*

*I keep trying. I go out and attempt to do something to take my mind off things, and then I just can't focus.*

*Have you tried starting with mundane basics and trying to work your way back up to complicated things? Maybe just toss out some weak flames, or even just burn some raw mana?*

*Not a terrible idea.* Arthur focused on his hand and activated Weak Flame. The flame burst from his hand and almost instantly scorched him. He jumped up and ran around waving his hand trying to get the flame to go out but wasn't having any luck.

*What are you doing? Did you really cast a fire spell without building up your fire barrier? Idiot. You really are out of it,* Balair sent to him.

When the spell finally ended and his hand felt charred, Arthur looked it over. None of the damage looked terrible. Luckily, his Weak Flame spell didn't emit extremely hot flames.

Arthur looked at his stinging hand in disgust. *Can't even do a simple thing right.*

He shook his head in resignation.

*Enough of that for now. I'd tell you to run off and make yourself useful, but I'm worried your new and improved body would frighten people and they wouldn't recognize you were a friend. You may as well accompany me back to the inn.*

Arthur lazily strolled back toward the inn in a daze. Lots of quick movements to his left near the wall drew his attention. A glance in the direction showed a man running around and tumbling. Squinting, he recognized the figure as Rayne, the adolescent man who helped him kill Lyrinth.

The figure darted in motions quicker than Arthur thought possible. A quick scan of the guy told Arthur he'd gained two levels from the raid and was now level eighteen. Arthur guessed the young man was using magic since his mana wasn't full. Since he didn't recognize the structure of the power, it must be Air Magic.

Arthur watched in confusion as Rayne bounced around in quick, jarring motions. It didn't look like he'd cast any spells during the entire round of exercise. On a hunch, Arthur scanned him again. It confirmed his suspicion that he was just burning raw mana and not casting spells. Intrigued by this turn of events, Arthur changed direction and headed for Rayne.

When he was a dozen yards away, Arthur raised a hand and called to him.

"Rayne, right?"

Rayne looked up in confusion for the speaker. His mind intensely focused on combat, so the abrupt stop jarred his senses. His confusion shone in his eyes for a few moments when he looked to Arthur.

"Yes, Lord Mayor," Rayne said with a slight dip of his head.

Arthur chuckled at that. "Please don't. Just Arthur. You definitely don't need to bow. You saved my life after all. I'm sorry it took so long, but I want to say thank you for your help. My thoughts have been scattered lately."

"It's okay. Most know of the general issue. I don't know the exact details, but I know everyone deals with loss in their own way. If you don't mind me asking, what exactly are you doing out here?" Rayne asked.

"Actually, I was watching you a few minutes ago and had a question. Why do you waste all of your mana by burning raw mana instead of using spells?"

Rayne's mouth hung open a paltry amount as he stared at Arthur. "How'd you know that?"

"Well, I have a spell that lets me see basic information about people so I could see your mana drop over time. Any specific reason you were doing it that way?"

The question caused Rayne to shift nervously and tense up as if about to fight, or maybe flee.

"I understand if you don't want to answer. Everyone seems to be so secretive about magic, but I'm trying to change that," Arthur added when seeing Rayne's reaction.

"To be honest, I don't know any spells. A friend taught me magic, and she never learned any spells either. The only thing she showed me was how to burn mana to increase my speed."

Arthur smiled. "That would explain it. I learned my first magical ability from a tome and had the same issue. I didn't understand how to use the knowledge until I talked Allendria into helping me. Learning spells is both very effective and much more efficient in mana usage."

Arthur looked upward in thought. "I tell you what, I'll make a deal with you. If you agree to teach me Air Magic, I'll let you choose either Earth, Fire, or Water Magic for me to teach you, and I'll also teach you how to learn spells."

"How do I know I can trust you? The offer sounds too good to be true. I've never heard of someone willing to teach magic so easily," Rayne responded with squinted eyes, and his left eyebrow raised.

"Judging by your fighting style, I'm going to assume you had a rough upbringing. The skills I saw during our fight and the weapons you used hint at the life of a thief or even an assassin. I know that lifestyle can cause some genuine trust issues, so I'll agree to teach you the magic of your choice and how to use spells before you teach me Air Magic. Do we have a deal?" Arthur asked.

Rayne still looked skeptical. He barely knew Arthur, after all. Arthur saw the turmoil spin and could imagine him spinning the idea through his mind.

Arthur pictured the internal thoughts the man struggled with. *Would this stranger really think learning Air Magic was worth enough to trade for another magic and learning how to take advantage of spells? Training of this type would cost a small fortune for a noble in the city, and this man offers it as though it means nothing.*

The conflict of emotion warred on Rayne's face until Arthur finally noticed a hint of determination settle over the young thief. "It's a deal," he agreed before Arthur heard him mutter, "I promised her I'd do whatever it took to keep her safe."  "Fantastic, you want to start now or wait until later?" Arthur asked.

"I guess we could start now," Rayne drawled.

"Great. What would you prefer to do first? Do you want to learn new magic or would you like to learn how spells work?"

"Let's start with spells. I've done fine without them so far, but you seem to think they're important," Rayne told him.

"They're very important. The key benefit from spells is reducing mana cost and making set times for effects. It also helps your spells have mastery effects. The more you use a spell, the more you can increase its mastery. Each time you do, there is a bonus to the spell. Typically, it reduces the base mana cost. Is your speed boost the only thing you use your magic for currently?"

"Yeah," he said hesitantly.

Arthur narrowed his eyes and kept going. "Explain exactly what you do to increase your speed. I have a feeling you're missing just one minor detail for your ability to turn into a spell."

"Really? That close? Well, I envision the magic flowing around me and guiding my movements while pushing against my limbs for speed."

"Looks like you were so close to doing it yourself. The only thing your specific spell is missing is time," Arthur told him.

"What do you mean? I do it for an extended length of time. I can't do it for any longer than my mana allows."

Arthur laughed a little at that remembering his failure with time. "This is a different kind of time. When you create or learn spells, you have to picture your desired effect and manifest your magic for that effect. If I want to discover Weak Flame, for instance, I have to picture the fire extending from my hand at the size I want it to be. To learn it, I can then use the magic to push the flame away and let it burn as long as I wish. When I cancel the flow of power, I learn the spell."

"But, that's exactly what I already do. I heard nothing about time in that," Rayne said, exasperated.

"That's because you're casting something that's a boost to you that lasts for a length of time. If you wish to create a spell that leaves or augments your body, you have to picture the entire flight as it leaves your hand when envisioning the spell. You also have to picture things moving in the spell to help the magic understand the time it needs to persist. If not, it will fizzle out or explode as soon as it leaves your hand. Trust me, I know," Arthur said with a laugh.

"Your situation is similar because you want a specific effect to happen to your body but you want it to happen for a specified amount of time. Try to do your spell again, but this time, when you envision the speed increase, picture yourself or something around you moving for a set amount of time before activating the magic. You don't have to predict exactly what will happen. It's just a reference to judge the elapsed time. When you have your picture in mind, cast the spell and keep using mana for the time you specified in your original process. Then, when you reach the time you suggested with the movement, stop the spell and you'll learn it permanently."

Rayne looked confused at first but slowly smiled as the explanation concluded, "That sounds easy."

Rayne focused inward and Arthur watched faint hints of wind kick up around the young man. In a blur, Rayne dashed to the side and continued running. Arthur struggled to keep up with some of his movements, but he caught sight of Rayne's weapons as they blurred through the air in random patterns. He returned to his original position and slowed to a stop.

Arthur smiled at the wide-eyed expression he saw on Rayne's face. Judging by the look of shock, he succeeded in his spell.

"I guess it worked?" Arthur asked with a grin.

Rayne's gaze lifted to meet his, and he nodded. "That was amazing. The spell I learned was Haste."

"Let me guess, it increases your movement speed for a length of time and costs a lot less mana to use than what you spent learning it?" Arthur asked knowingly.

"Well, yes. It increases my movement speed by fifteen percent for thirty seconds and it only costs me forty mana to use. I used three times that before for the same effect."

"Did you see the Mastery listed? It'll be level one now, but the more you use that spell, the higher it goes. Each level changes something. When you reach level two, I have a feeling it'll drop your mana cost to thirty-five instead of forty. That's why spells are so important."

"Thanks. I never knew and honestly didn't think I ever needed to search for such knowledge. I used the magic without issue already. I can see how this is much more efficient, though."

"I'm glad it helps you. I want to stress that as long as you have enough mana, you can create any spell you imagine. Remember the difference in time. Anything that directly affects your body for a set amount of time or that leaves your body has to account for that. If you want to create a bolt of Air Magic that can fly from you and hit a target you have to picture the flight path of the missile. Unlike accounting for time, that has to be precisely where it will travel. Anything moving around it doesn't require you to picture exactly how they move."

"So, can I adjust the course of the magic in that case? For instance, make it fly around a corner?" Rayne asked.

Arthur chuckled, recalling he'd asked the same question himself. "Yes, you can. You still have to picture it hitting a specific spot behind the location for it to work, though. Also, don't turn the projectile too sharp or it's likely to fail."

"That's awesome."

Arthur smiled at the young man's enthusiasm. He felt drawn to him for some reason he couldn't explain.

"Rayne, I'm sorry for taking so long to talk to you and I know people have talked to me about you before, but what is your purpose here? How did you end up out here?"

"I'm surprised you remember that much with what you went through. I was actually given a quest to seek out this place. Needless to say, it was an odd one. Goddess Lianna signed the letter that granted the quest," Rayne said as he watched Arthur.

Arthur's shock was obvious. "That's an understatement. I guess she knew we needed your help. Without you, I would've died."

"I thought you might recognize the name. You can imagine it was shocking to me to find out she has a Paladin here in this village. I didn't know there were any worshippers of the old gods left in the world."

"Wait," Arthur said, "How do you know about the old gods? I haven't met anyone that recognized her name."

Rayne looked down for a moment. "Just something I heard in the city one day. I only know she was popular back when the Firebrand family was in charge," he said as he glanced at Arthur's hair, "that leads me to another question of my own. Your hair is an awfully unique color. I'd dare say it matches a bit of history myself. No one else here has mentioned it, but I'm a little more familiar with that specific segment of history."

Arthur grimaced at the statement. "Rayne, I'll be honest with you. I don't know you and don't have that level of trust with you yet to tell you much," Rayne began to speak but Arthur held up his hand, "but you saved my life, so for that I'll tell you I am, indeed, Arturian Firebrand. Before you pepper me with questions, I only recently learned this fact. There are very few in the village who know this truth and it must stay that way," Arthur finished with steel in his voice.

Rayne gulped at the glare and nodded. "Of course. My lips are sealed."

"Good. Now let's call it for the day. I'm sure you're eager to play with your recent spell and possibly try to make a few more. I need to get back to the inn and work on staying focused. Is there anything else I can help you with?"

"Actually, I'd like permission for the refugees with me to join the village officially. Katherine said that her authority was limited on the matter, but we really want to join this community and help in any way we can."

Arthur nodded. "I'll tell you what, meet me here tomorrow morning and we'll discuss it. I'll talk to some of the village leaders about this tonight and see where everyone stands on the issue. We can also work on teaching you the magic skill of your choice."

Rayne's smile was infectious as Arthur smiled right back with him. Arthur waved to the jubilant man and turned toward the village. It was time he finally rejoined the world of the living.

# Chapter 21



Arthur approached the inn to a scene of chaos. People ran out of the doors and screams echoed through the building. In a moment of panic, he dashed for the door and reached for his sword. His hand grasped empty air as he realized he wasn't carrying it. *Stupid fool. How have I not died from stupidity yet?*

Arthur burst through the door to see multiple people scrambling around the room and knocking over tables. They were obviously trying to circle the tables around the creature in the center of the room. It slightly amused Arthur to see Balair actually behaving and not harming anyone.

Two chairs flew across the room and hit the drake in the shoulder. He turned and hissed in the direction the chair originated. Arthur contemplated watching the show until he saw a man lunge toward Balair, holding a dagger.

"Everyone stop right now!" Arthur bellowed over the crowd.

All motion in the room froze, and the occupants looked toward him in confusion. Arthur's gaze swung toward Balair.

"What the hell, man? I thought I told you to stay near me for this exact reason."

*I got bored. You and that other guy were just standing around talking. I've been gone for a week and I'm starving.*

"I don't care! I told you to stick by me. I didn't want you scaring everyone and causing this exact scenario," Arthur hollered as he approached the small drake.

*Do I need to remind you of my majestic presence? I'm a dragon. Why would I worry about frightening people?*

Arthur's hand swung forward and hit the small dragon with a ringing slap against the side of his snout.

"I'm not having this conversation with you again. You will be civil and respect other people or I'll let you sit and rot in your own dimension. We clear?" Arthur asked.

Balair bowed his head in shame. *Yeah. Sorry about that. Forgot.*

"Everyone calm down," Arthur said at the looks of pure confusion around the room. "This is Balair. He's evolved since the last fight and is now a little bigger, but he's still the same little dragon we've always known."

*Little? Did you not notice I grew about 3 feet taller? How dare…*

*What did I say!*

*Sheesh, fine.*

Arthur did his best to help get everything put back in order and rearranged. He saw Daniel cleaning up as well and motioned for the man to meet him near the back.

"Daniel, thanks."

"Uh, okay, but what for?"

"For keeping things running while I've been out of it. I know you have a steadying influence over the people and I appreciate it," Arthur told him.

"Thanks. It's been a rough week for you and we've been trying to let you have the time you need."

"It truly means a lot to me. A little help from a young man and that worthless pile of scales there helped get me back on track. I know I'll still have days where I struggle to get out of bed and overcome my emotions, but I've gotta keep moving forward, ya know. It's what she would want me to do. Um… do you think we can get some of our village leaders together tonight? I need to get caught up on what's been happening around here."

"I'll make it happen. I suggest you find Allendria in the meantime. She'll be happy to see some of the old you coming back," Daniel told him with a slight grin.

"Thanks. I'll do that."

*And you,* he sent with a stern glance at Balair, *Stay out of trouble.*

*It wasn't my fault!*

*Sure it was. You didn't do as I told you.*

Arthur turned and walked out of the inn. He liked Daniel's suggestion and resolved to find Allendria. Knowing she'd taken the lead with the construction crews, he searched around the village for the projects currently being built. A quick question to a passerby told him the work still focused on restoring the wall, so he shifted direction towards the northeastern gatehouse. Arthur could make out small spots on the wall that looked like people working.

Arriving at the wall, he watched in awe as pieces of the wall expanded and blocks of stone rose from the ground to fortify it further. The construction crew was busy. The walkway behind the wall was actually wide enough to be a real wall-walk now. They had tied the spaces together between the platforms he'd created. He looked down the wall to see they hadn't replicated the platforms. Instead, they continued to expand the walkway but left off the stairs provided by his spell.

His gaze fell on the beauty standing at the base of the wall. She spoke with one worker and gestured toward something Arthur couldn't determine. He smiled and snuck up behind her. In a flash of motion, he leaped forward and enveloped the Elven beauty in a tight hug from behind. He smiled at his accomplishment for a moment until he felt an iron tight grip on his arm and he flew forward.

Allendria twisted as she grabbed him and used their momentum to bring him around her body. With a heavy thud, Arthur hit the ground and wheezed in pain. She looked down with her fist cocked back to attack.

"Arthur?"

"Good to see you too, beautiful," he said through gasps of breath.

She blushed.

"Remind me not to sneak up on you again," he told her.

"I thought you'd be smarter than that, but I should have known better," she told him with a chuckle.

Arthur slowly rolled over and pushed back to his feet. A quick pat-down knocked most of the dust off him. He saw many of the workers trying to hide their smiles at the turn of events and smiled inwardly at himself.

"Got some time?"

"Of course," she answered.

They walked away from the wall together, arm in arm. Arthur took in the view of the expanded wall as they strolled through the field.

"I'm sorry. I know I've been distant, and I appreciate you tolerating me. I'm super proud of everything you've helped get done while I've been useless," he told her.

A soft smile spread across her face as she put her hand on his cheek, "I knew you'd come back, eventually. Grief is a hard emotion. Everyone handles it differently. You just needed space. Some people are the opposite and need constant attention. The trick is being able to read the needs of those affected."

"Well, I appreciate the forethought, my princess," Arthur told her with a mock bow.

Her face darkened at the gesture until she saw his smile and she brightened up.

"I don't hold any ill feelings about you not telling me if you're worried about that. I'm sure you had good reason to keep it a secret."

She snorted at that, "I wish it was for some noble reason. To be honest, I didn't tell you because I didn't want to. I ran away from home and didn't know anyone. I had no idea where I was running to and had no friends to help me. Lo-and-behold, I stumble upon a goofy human who had no idea his kind are supposed to hate and fear Dark Elves. You offered me a choice but, more than that, you helped me without me asking. As we continued to stay together, I found a connection to you and I wanted nothing to come between us. I didn't tell you out of selfishness and not because of some higher reason."

"It's your choice, not mine. You didn't need to tell me and, as far as I'm concerned, nothing has changed between us. I may torture you with the occasional poor joke, but otherwise, you're still the woman I met and continue to stand by," he told her as he held her hands.

Tears formed in the corner of her eyes as she leaned forward and kissed him gently.

"Thank you," she whispered.

They embraced, and the feeling of their bodies entwined in the sunlight just felt right. They pulled apart and looked into each other's eyes.

"Your work with the construction crews is impressive. They've made significant progress this past week."

Allendria blushed at the compliment. "Thanks. They've really been working hard. I keep one crew busy doing repairs and construction in the village. The rest are focusing on the wall until it's complete. At this rate, we may need to recruit another team, especially with the recent wave of refugees."

Arthur winced at her statement. "Yeah, we need to come up with a plan for them. I won't turn them away without an excellent reason. It seems they have a divine calling to be here. Well, at least young Rayne does."

"He's very interesting to say the least," Allendria agreed.

"Have you met with any of the other refugees?"

"Only a handful. I've spoken with Rayne a few times, though."

"What's your assessment of them?"

"From the ones I've talked to, they appear to be exactly who he claims. A group of people who came on a journey with the promise of a greater future. I shudder to imagine living in one of those cities after hearing what they've been through."

Arthur's thoughts turned inward. He was skeptical about just allowing them to do whatever since he didn't know them very well, but they needed the help to get their village back on track.

*Can you help with this conundrum since you caused it?* He asked internally.

Allendria froze in place as a cool breeze rippled past. He looked around and the leaves on the nearby tree swayed in slow motion. A glance back at Allendria confirmed she too moved, but at such a slow pace it was hard to detect.

"Well, that's an awfully rude thing to say to someone who went out of their way to get you help," the Goddess responded in a playful tone.

Arthur turned to regard the Goddess. Her flowing strawberry-blond hair danced in the slow wind while her golden eyes stared into his.

"So you are still around. Nice of you to show up when convenient for you instead of when I needed you," he grumbled in a bitter tone.

Her eyes reflected a deep sorrow as she walked up to him. She reached out her hand and gently caressed his cheek, "I understand you being angry but you already know the answer. I have no power on Earth. The special circumstance of your birth was the only way I had any influence to help you when I did."

Arthur lifted his hand to touch hers. "I'm sorry. I shouldn't have said that. You've told me that, but in my panic, I tried to blame you. Would you be willing to help me with my current problem?"

She stepped back and laughed. "Of course. I wouldn't have made the trek down here otherwise. I can't stay for long lest my power be sensed by my sister. Anything specific you need to know?"

"Are any of the refugees spies?"

"No, that was a stipulation of my quest. If any had come with them, it would have meant a failure of the quest when Rayne finished it. Since he successfully completed it, that isn't the case."

"Well, that's a relief. That still doesn't answer if I can trust them, though."

"How about you take your own advice? You keep lamenting having to fight. Why not give them the chance they need? You need the help," she said with a wave.

Arthur sighed. "You're right. I'll talk things over with the other leaders and see what everyone thinks. Thank you, Goddess.

"Anytime," she told him before her figure faded from view, and the world popped back into motion around him.

Arthur turned toward Allendria as their walk resumed. "Lianna came to visit me just now. Needless to say, it was an interesting experience."

"So, what did she say?" Allendria asked.

"She told me there weren't any spies in their ranks but the ultimate decision is with us. I'm leaning toward giving them a chance. I want to do something other than fight. I'd like to help them," Arthur said.

"Then that's what we'll do," Allendria told him with certainty.

"I plan on discussing it this evening with the leaders of the village. You going to be there?"

"Yep. I need to get back to work with the crew here, so why don't you make yourself useful and help? Your mana pool is large enough to do much more than they can, anyway."

Arthur nodded in agreement. "Fine, even without my sword, I should have enough mana to power through much of the work here."

A glance at his mana pool showed his maximum sitting at 1,030. Combine that with the 10,000 from his amulet, and he could work a lot of magic.

Returning to the wall, he and Allendria split ways and Arthur set to work. Since the workers were expanding the short wall behind the main face, he assisted. His main spell was the archer platform spell, but he wanted to do much more at one time. With his sizable mana pool, this would be the perfect chance to create a larger spell.

He walked to a clear section of the wall further down. Interrupting the other workers while they were casting spells would merely cause a disaster. Focusing on the wall-walk, he extended his hands to help his concentration. He yanked the dirt from the ground and expanded it to the necessary twelve-foot height. He stretched it to six-feet deep so it would match the same depth as his archer platforms. With everything lined up, he pushed his magic and stretched this additional dimension far down the wall. He kept the magic flowing until half of his normal mana pool emptied.

Siphoning excess mana from his amulet to refill his pool, he focused on transforming the dirt to stone. The familiar power crawled over the face of the dirt as the long stretch spanned the distance. It continued to crawl until it reached the top of the dirt platform and melded the existing stone wall with the new stone section. With a quick breath, the magic ended and a new spell appeared.

*Congratulations, you have discovered the Combination Spell: Raise Stone Wall (Medium). You have gained 250 experience in Earth and Fire Magic for discovering a known spell.*
*You have gained 150 experience in Earth and Fire Magic for casting Raise Stone Wall (Medium).*

| Spell: Raise Stone Wall (Medium) | |
| --- | --- |
| Requirements: Earth and Fire Magic<br>Mana Cost: 80 MP<br>Cast Time: 16 seconds | Description: This spell draws dirt from the ground and solidifies it into a stone wall section spanning 6' x 12' x 200'. |
| Mastery Level: 1 | |

He felt a glorious sense of pride as he stood there admiring his newest accomplishment. That was a very impressive span of wall to complete at one time. He turned to look at the other workers with a smile. Every one of them stopped what they were doing and stared at the new stretch of the wall he finished. They'd have to toil for hours to create a section of wall that size and Arthur just did it in minutes.

Arthur secretly hoped many of the construction workers would focus their stat points on bettering their casting ability. The more that did, the more effective they'd be.

Instead of standing in place and basking in the glory of his underlings like a pompous jerk, he walked to the end of the stretch he'd just created and resumed casting his spell. He continued his work until he exhausted all of his mana in his amulet and personal supply.

A glance to the sky showed him the evening approached as he finished the last section of wall his mana allowed. Wiping sweat from his brow, he looked around and saw he stood alone without a soul in sight. His spell casting took him further down the wall than he'd realized and even allowed him to jump past a gatehouse. His stomach grumbled in protest and reminded him it was time for the evening meal. On his way to the inn, he glanced at the experience notifications from his spell casting.

*You have gained 18,450 experience in Earth and Fire Magic for casting Raise Stone Wall (Medium) (x123).*

*Congratulations, you have reached level 22 in Earth Magic. Increases the effect of your earth magic spells by 63%. A valiant effort, but not what you need to work on.*

*Congratulations, you have advanced to Mastery level 2 in Raise Stone Wall (Medium). This spell now costs 5 less mana to cast.*

While he walked, he dumped his two talent points into Earthen Assistants. He hadn't used them yet, but solely because their description didn't give him confidence they could work with stone. They would come in handy as the village tried to expand the planting fields, or when he dug a real moat of some kind.

It wasn't long before he walked into the common room of the inn. The emptiness of the place felt odd, but he remembered it was a village leader meeting. Daniel was good about keeping out the crowd during these get-togethers. He walked to their usual meeting table and grabbed a seat.

A bowl of food appeared on the table almost by magic, moments after his butt touched the chair. Looking up, he spotted a smiling Trisha.

"Thanks, Trisha. How've you been?"

"I'm doing great now. Thanks for asking. I hope you like it. Daniel has given me more freedom with the dishes now, and this one is something of my own creation."

"I look forward to it," Arthur said as he leaned over the bowl and picked up the spoon. The aroma wafting from the bowl enticed him, and the food slowly rose to his mouth. An explosion of sweet and savory flavor threatened to overwhelm his senses. Daniel's cooking was fantastic, but this dish was on another level.

"That is absolutely amazing, Trish!"

She blushed at the compliment. "Really? You truly like it? You're not just saying that to be polite?"

"Oh, I don't like it," he said, causing her cheerful expression to fade. "I absolutely love it. Definitely the best thing I've tasted in a long time.

"Don't tell Daniel I said that," Arthur
whispered to her.

She laughed and merrily scurried back to
the kitchen. Arthur sat in his chair, scarfing
down the food as quickly as he could manage
without burning his mouth. He was so engrossed
in his meal, he almost missed the other
members of the village leadership enter.

When Arthur finished, he stood up in front
of everyone. Allendria came up behind him and
put a reassuring hand on his shoulder. Dalia,
Daniel, Samson, Rowan, Vana, Katherine, Zeke,
and Corianne faced him. Balair slumbered in a
corner, and Arthur couldn't believe he'd
missed the creature when he walked in.

"Before we start, I have something to say
to all of you," he said as he looked from face
to face.

"I'm sorry."

Some people in front of him frowned in
confusion while others smiled.

"We faced an incredible foe and prevailed,
but instead of helping pick up the pieces and
getting the village back on track, I retreated
into self-loathing and failed in my
responsibility to you. All I can say is thank
you for keeping everything going without me,"
Arthur said as he lowered his head in shame.

"You've nothing to apologize for. You won
the fight for us. The least we could do is
give you the time you needed. You've given the
village a fresh life. It's only fair we help
in return," Daniel said reassuringly.

The other members in the room nodded in
agreement with Daniel.

"Thanks, Daniel. I appreciate all of your
work. Now I want to get caught up on what's
been going on this last week."

"We completed the cleanup on the site of the battle. All the enemy corpses were removed and burned. Much of the salvage from them is at the blacksmith waiting to be melted down. We have given the cloth from them to Katherine while the leather pieces are in the storage here at the inn," Samson summarized.

"Thanks, Samson. Is there anything the guards still lack?"

"I've been working with Rowan to get most of that done. The key things we need are breastplates," Samson answered.

Arthur turned to face the blacksmith, "You out of materials?"

"No," he responded in a defeated tone, "just can't quite get the process down with the detail needed in the breastplate. I've made progress and can do the others correctly, but I still lack the focus required for that specific piece."

"Hey, don't be that tough on yourself. No harm in that. Nothing a little practice won't solve. I'll come over and help make what you need when I can."

His gaze turned to face Daniel. "How are the food stores?"

"We're pretty steady for now but with the influx of refugees, we're burning through the supplies you brought back last time. Your storage method works fantastic and keeps everything fresh, but it won't be long before you need to organize another hunt," Daniel told him.

"Had a feeling that was the case. I can see the food in the storage the same as you, but you're a much better judge of how long that'll last. I'll see what we can do."

Daniel looked like he was about to continue but Arthur held up his hand. "If it's about the refugees let's hold off before we discuss all the other topics in the village. I plan on making a decision with them."

"Fair enough," Daniel told him with a nod.

"Allendria, I know you're not officially part of the village nor a village leader, but you run the construction crews. What update do you have?"

"The crews have been working nonstop to repair the wall and complete projects in the village. The wall is a few days from complete on the initial expansion and then I plan to run a rotation. I'll assign only one crew to the wall for constant improvements and expansion while the rest of the teams focus on the village infrastructure and housing. We've made quick repairs to most of the existing houses in the village and improved the roads. I've held off on completely redesigning the houses like you suggested until we got your feedback on the design. We built a few new compact stone houses as examples for you to look over."

"Terrific work. Since you're a natural with that, I bestow on you the title of City Planner," Arthur told her with a grin.

She appeared shocked as she stared at him in disbelief. "You want me to do what? City Planner? This isn't even a city."

"It's a title. It doesn't need to match the exact type of settlement. Whether it's a village, town, or city, the job remains the same."

"Uh, I accept, I guess."

Arthur pulled his gaze from a dazed but smiling Allendria to focus on Lady Dalia.

"Lady Dalia, how are the people in the village? Are spirits high?"

"The people are doing quite well. The victory over the raiders has them feeling invincible. I fear we will run into problems soon," she told him but was wearing an odd smile.

"A problem? Why would there be a problem?" Arthur asked.

"The stories of the battle circulated and after hearing of Paladin Samson's divine abilities, it sparked a surge in worship for our Goddess Lianna. I believe there will be urgent requests to construct a place of worship soon. If we don't, I believe trouble will erupt," Dalia explained.

"Whew, had me worried for a minute. That's something I'm sure we can arrange. Allendria," he said as he turned to face her, "can you assign one construction crew to Paladin Samson and instruct them to construct a temple to honor the Goddess Lianna? Samson should be able to consult on a proper building and we'll place it directly across the road from the bathhouse."

Allendria nodded at that.

"Any objection, Samson?"

"It would be an honor, sir."

"Good man. I'm sure our Goddess will give a little divine inspiration while you plan on the style," Arthur said with a smirk.

*Fine, I'll work with him on something suitable.* The voice called to him.

"Vana, anything of concern in our surroundings?" Arthur asked.

"None. We've been doing a rotating patrol but have seen nothing dangerous short of the occasional predator."

"That's wonderful news, don't look so glum," Arthur told her.

She huffed at him, but he continued his questioning.

"Zeke and Corianne, anything to report from you two? How's our supply of leather and archery implements?"

They looked at each other and Zeke motioned for Corianne to start. "I've cleaned all the salvageable leather recovered. I wanted to move it to the storage here from my shop, but I'm afraid space is limited. I dare say, we'll need a storage house soon."

Arthur watched as heads around the room nodded in agreement.

"Katherine, please add that to the list as a high priority," he heard her pen scratching furiously across the page.

"Zeke, how about you?"

"After the attack, we salvaged many arrows from the field. I've repaired almost half of what we found. Still working on them but would like to have somewhere to put these items when complete as Corianne mentioned. Village storage would be great, but an armory would be even better," Zeke suggested.

Samson cleared his throat. "If we are making suggestions, I'd like to request a barracks for the guard members. Isolating them from family while on guard duty helps keep them focused. They'd only need to stay there while on watch duty, but it would also be the perfect opportunity to incorporate an armory."

Arthur grinned. "Katherine, please add a barracks with attached armory to the list of important projects."

Daniel was the next to speak up. "Not trying to add to the pile, but you mentioned making space to store our food safely without resorting to your special storage. I appreciate the help but would like to have access to it without needing to hunt you down. If you run off on an extended hunting trip, we'll be without access for an unknown amount of time."

"Katherine, food storage to the list. Anyone have any other suggestions?" Arthur asked.

Everyone looked around, but no one spoke up.

"All right, now time to discuss the other issue. What to do with the refugees?"

Everyone started to talk but Arthur held up his hand again. "Please everyone, give me a moment first. I know we all have opinions on this, but let me lay out the details I know. I know the young man named Rayne led this group here. He is the very same man that saved my life," Arthur said and heard a huff from the side of the room.

"Sorry, Balair saved my life as well and as everyone can see has returned and evolved from the experience in our fight."

"I also know that the Goddess Lianna herself gave Rayne the quest to search us out. She confirmed to me that the group of refugees is free of spies from the evil Goddess or her minions. Now the question is, how do we handle them?"

Dalia was the first to speak up. "I feel sorry for them and I know we could use the manpower, but I don't think we can feed them. We've been doing well to take care of our own, but not sure the extra mouths to feed will be manageable."

"Lady Dalia is right. Our crops still need time to grow before they produce much of a yield. It would take a lot of hunting to supplement the food we need to provide for them. Our current storage is dwindling quickly," Daniel added.

"For what it's worth, I agree with you guys. There's one problem, though. I can't just let them suffer on their own. My primary goal here was to make this a better place. This village has come a long way since we started and there were plenty of times I didn't think we'd succeed, but we've pulled through each and every time. These people have suffered so long that I don't want to be responsible for any further suffering. It feels like I've done nothing but fight since I arrived here, and for once, I'd like the opportunity to help make people's lives better. I think if we do this right, we could even defeat King Wailyn and his group this way. Showing their citizens the utopia we create, will have them flocking to our cause and will remove many we'd otherwise be forced to fight."

Everyone looked around in thought. The silence was almost deafening as everyone contemplated his words. Eventually, Daniel lifted his head. "I'm willing to give them the chance if you are."

Everyone else slowly lifted their heads and agreed. Arthur wasn't sure, but it seemed Dalia was a little angry when her head came up, but she agreed nonetheless. Katherine took the moment to step forward and hand Arthur a sheet of paper.

"What's this?" he asked as he scanned the page.

"After speaking to Rayne yesterday, I took the time to visit the refugees today to get an accurate count of them and to list their available skills. It should prove useful, so we can decide what roles they may best serve."

"I don't want to force people into any specific role," Arthur started, but Katherine cut him off.

"I'm not suggesting you force them into anything, I merely wanted you to know their current skills so you could offer them something you think may fit them. If they refuse and wish to do something else, that's completely up to you."

"Thanks, Katherine. I forgot to ask. How's the day to day going in the village?"

"It's really busy. Work orders are a never-ending chore to deal with. I know you recently started the currency rewards for them, but it won't be too long before you need to create some commerce here if you plan to keep the program going with our new influx of villagers. The coin will all sit in pockets and never return if the villagers have nothing to spend it on."

"Damn," Arthur cursed under his breath. "I'll figure something out. There are plenty of useful items other than just their food I can make they will want. Even some of the small enchanted items would be a good investment for them. We need to issue work orders for items we can turn and sell. Daniel, can you look into items needed the most in the village and see what we can discover?"

"I'll get on it," Daniel confirmed.

"Any other concerns?"

Everyone shook their heads no and Arthur called out. "All right, meeting adjourned."

Everyone split directions while Arthur turned to Allendria.

"Care to join me in the bathhouse before we go to bed, my princess?"

"Of course, my prince," she returned with a mock bow.

Arthur grimaced. He forgot about his so-called nobility. It looked like Allendria would give as good as she got in this match. Locking hands, they strolled off to the thought of warm water and a warm embrace.

# Chapter 22



*Consolidating a Village*

Arthur arose early and in a pleasant mood for the first time in over a week. The events of yesterday were exactly what he needed to get out of the ever-sinking hole he'd dug for himself.

Breakfast was over quickly and he practically bounced out the door of the inn. He walked to the meeting spot and found Rayne waiting there for him.

"Up early, I see," Arthur called to the youthful man.

"Force of habit. Can't bring myself to sleep late."

"I feel sorry for you. I enjoy sleeping late when there isn't a fresh crisis to deal with. Unfortunately, it seems there's always so much to do and never enough time to do it all. I have some wonderful news for you, though."

"You've finally come to a decision about those of us who traveled here?" Rayne asked with a hopeful tone.

"As a matter of fact, we did. We decided to welcome y'all to the village. I'll make it official later today and invite everyone to become villagers and receive all the perks everyone else does. Until then, how about we teach you a magic skill?"

"Sounds great!" Rayne said with enthusiasm. "Do you recommend any particular one? I know you told me to pick one, but I'm not familiar with magic and hoped you'd help me decide what might be best."

*This kid shows wisdom well beyond his age.*

"That depends, I guess. I've seen some of your fighting, which is impressive by the way and I'd like to discuss some of that later, but do you have any other skills we may want to take into account?" Arthur asked.

"Actually, I was trying to get away from the fighting and apprenticed as an Alchemist. I was well on my way to becoming a professional in my own right before the riots broke out in the cities and rampant fighting took over. It caused me to revert to my other skills out of necessity."

"I wish it hadn't been so. I want you to know, here you don't have to fight if you don't wish. I'd be lying if I didn't say I think it would be a waste of the incredible gift you have, but I want everyone to be happy with their own choices. If you decide to lay down your weapons and become a tradesman, I'll not stop you," Arthur said.

Rayne looked teary-eyed for a moment before Arthur saw a flash of resolve pass over his features.

"I appreciate that. I saw what you had to fight against to protect your way of life here, and if it comes to it, I'll do the same. I have to for those who came with me."

"So you do some fighting and alchemy. It may be easier for me to tell you some of the basics of the magics and let you decide. Fire Magic is very useful for, well, exactly as it sounds. If you need to light something on fire, cook something, or even rapidly cool something, fire works great. It's an essential survival tool if ever stuck in the wild by yourself. Earth allows you to manipulate the ground and objects around you. It's how we built the wall surrounding the village. Water is great for irrigation purposes and tending to crops. It's also possible to filter out toxins or poisons from someone's body," Arthur told him.

Rayne contemplated the situation before asking a question.

"Can Earth Magic detect movement?"

"What do you mean?"

"Well, I use a lot of stealth and one of the biggest problems is detecting others with similar skills. So if I could use Earth Magic to help me sense people moving or even standing in certain places, it would further increase my skill," Rayne explained.

"It can't…" Arthur began but trailed off before he dropped his head and considered the question. The more he thought about it, the more he was certain it just might be possible. Detecting elements in the soil when he used his prospecting skill was possible, so why couldn't he use it to see if anything was standing on the surrounding ground?

"Now that you mention it, that may be possible. I've never tried it and want to kick myself for not thinking about it. I could try to do the spell if you want to know for sure?"

"I'd appreciate it if you don't mind… That would be a key factor in my decision. I like your reasoning for Fire, but if this is possible, I'll take Earth without further questioning." Rayne replied.

Arthur nodded, even more impressed with the intelligence he showed. He closed his eyes and pushed his power down below him. Reaching further into the ground, he expanded his sense further from his feet. It didn't take long for his magic to envelop a half sphere shape below and around him. To his disappointment, he couldn't detect anything on the surface. He could feel different minerals below him, similar to his prospecting spell, but nothing on top. Letting the power fade, he sighed.

Instead of giving up, Arthur thought the problem over some more. When his power seeped into the surrounding dirt, it felt like one solid piece of ground he was working with. Something that large and rigid wouldn't react to movements. It also didn't help that it was a hard and unyielding surface. He needed a way to sense movement. Something that could alert him to even the smallest of movement as someone crept along the ground.

On the verge of giving up, an idea struck him. A spider's web. Spider's detected movement on their web to alert them to something in it. His problem was, he enveloped a large, solid area. If he instead made a thin layer of magic along the ground and triggered it to respond to any changes in that area, it should serve his purpose.

Arthur sent his magic out again in a second
attempt. Instead of enveloping the ground
beneath him, he pushed the magic out as if
laying out a large blanket over the
surrounding area. When his magic enveloped an
area that was forty yards in diameter, he
stopped the flow of magic moving outward. He
pictured disturbances on the surface of the
ground. It didn't take him long to determine
that was a terrible idea. His mind was almost
overwhelmed by the massive amount of
information pouring into him as he felt the
movement of every tiny insect leg in the
space. It didn't take him long to figure out
how to get the spell to only alert for heavier
objects, and he set it so anything the size of
a squirrel or larger would send him the
information.

His gaze lifted to look at Rayne, and he
nodded his head. Rayne took the hint and
walked around Arthur. It thrilled Arthur to
feel the steps while he moved. With an
enormous sigh of relief, he released the
spell, and the notification he wanted popped
up.

*Congratulations, you have discovered the
Earth Magic Spell: One With the Ground. You
have gained 250 experience in Earth Magic for
discovering a known spell.*

*You have gained 80 experience in Earth
Magic for casting One With the Ground.*

Spell: One With the Ground

| Requirements: Earth Magic<br>Mana Cost: 1MP/sec<br>Cast Time: Channeled | Description: This spell extends a blanket of Earth Magic around you in a 40-yard diameter and will alert you to anything moving that is over your specified threshold.<br><br>Threshold - 0.45 kg |
| --- | --- |
| Mastery Level: 1 | |

"Outstanding! I figured it out. It works, but it's a channeled spell. Shouldn't be a problem if you only use it when needed."

"Channeled spell?" Rayne asked.

"Instead of a fixed mana cost, like the haste spell you learned, it costs a set amount of mana the longer you use it. It works more closely to the original way you used mana to increase your speed," Arthur explained.

"How much does it cost?"

"Only one mana per second. Not terrible since I have a sizable amount of mana available," Arthur told him.

Rayne hung his head. "I don't have a large mana pool like you. I invested in many other skills since I never used my magic correctly. If I can only use it for such a brief time, I'm not sure how effective it'll be."

Arthur smiled at the dilemma. He fished in his pocket for an item he brought for this very reason.

"Rayne, let me introduce you to your first perk as a villager," Arthur told him as he handed over the teardrop pendant.

Rayne looked at the item in confusion while he read its description. His face quickly morphed into wonder at the sight.

"You mean *I* get to use this?"

"Yep. We ask that everyone wear one. Even those who don't have magical skills use them to stockpile excess mana for our use. That's how we had enough to repel the attackers at the gate and to create the items we needed to succeed in such a short time. It was close, but it pulled us through. Do me a favor and don't show your fellow villagers yet? I plan on making enough this afternoon to present to each of them as a sign of their new status as villagers."

"Understood. I look forward to seeing their reactions when they receive them," Rayne said.

"So, Earth Magic it is then?" Arthur asked.

"Yep."

Arthur sat in the clearing and quickly realized the sun was wreaking havoc on his skin. They walked over to the bathhouse and sat outside the wall in the shade. He held his hand over to Rayne palm up and he quickly placed his hand in Arthur's. Arthur pushed the mana streams in and separated them.

"Whoa, those look different than I expected!" Rayne exclaimed.

"Sorry, forgot to explain. Since you have Air Magic I assume you learned the magic comprises three bands of power that are mixed in a specific pattern?" Arthur asked, and Rayne nodded in agreement.

"I've figured out it's much quicker to teach someone magic if I split the bands individually and get them to learn them first. Once you can mimic all three, I'll show you how they blend to finish learning the magic."

"Oh, awesome! Learning the first one took a while because I had to concentrate harder to pull the bands of power apart myself to recreate them. This should go much quicker."

A crease appeared in Rayne's forehead as he concentrated on the power flowing into his hand. Arthur relaxed and enjoyed the break. His thoughts drifted to the multiple things he needed to address, and he grimaced at the time this would take. There were arguably much more important tasks than this, and if he was being honest with himself, he should have asked Rayne to allow him to do this on a later day. Rayne's first band of power snapping into place quickly interrupted his train of thought.

The speed Rayne picked up on that first piece of the puzzle astonished Arthur. He'd never seen anyone form a band that quickly. Even Allendria took a little longer than that, and she was familiar with the process. Thinking it may have been a fluke, Arthur relaxed back into his thoughts.

Another twenty minutes later, and his concentration jolted again by him completing the second band. It was less than half an hour later when Rayne had all three ready. Arthur considered taking a break before they began the last part but, with how quickly he progressed through forming the bands, he was certain Rayne could finish the last part in no time.

Twenty more minutes and Arthur's assumption proved true as Rayne finished combining the powers and the skill snapped into place. The ex-thief's speed was astonishing. Arthur knew he had a truly gifted mind in his presence, but a notification he wasn't expecting stopped him short.

| Class:<br>Teacher<br><br>Rank:<br>Apprentice | The teacher is the backbone of civilization. Teachers help develop our future generations. The Teacher class grants the following bonuses:<br><br>• Increases the learning speed of any who learn directly from you by 10%.<br>• Allows you to teach any one spell from each school to an individual who has the necessary magic skill directly. (This effect can only be used once per person per magic school) |
|---|---|

<table>
<tr><td></td><td>Ranks: You are apprentice rank. Teach more people to increase the skill to the next rank and increase the benefits.</td></tr>
</table>

That was great. Another class on top of everything else. The second ability of the teacher class was the best part. Being able to teach anyone a spell instantly without having to go through all the motions was insane. He reached over to the excited Rayne and grabbed him by the hand. The spell knowledge for One With the Ground came to his mind and he willed it to flow to Rayne. Instead of the excitement expected, he received a message.

*Your recipient doesn't have the necessary requirements to use this ability. This requires Earth Magic level 7.*

*Well, damn. At least the spell transfer worked.* He turned his gaze toward Rayne.

"Well, good news and bad news. The good news is, I can teach you the spell directly. The bad news, you need to reach level seven in Earth Magic before I can."

"That's no problem. Surely there's a simple spell you could teach me so I can level up the ability?"

Arthur nodded and showed him the Earthen Wall spell. He explained the Flatten spell as well, so he could keep going back and forth to raise his level. Rayne nodded in excitement and dashed off. His feet slid to a stop, and he turned.

"My apologies. Are we done for the day so I can go practice, or did you want me to show you Air Magic first?" Rayne asked.

*Smart and polite, I like this young man more and more.*

"Have fun. I know the feeling of learning new magic. I'll find you at a later time regarding the Air Magic. Stay out of trouble," Arthur said with a slight chuckle.

Arthur watched as Rayne bounded away in excitement. He appeared to head for the refugee camp. Arthur's thoughts snapped back to the things he needed to do today. His first thought was of his promise to Rayne. Decision made, he left for the blacksmith. It was time to get some mana amulets made.

On his way, he realized he didn't know how many villagers arrived with Rayne. He stopped by the inn first to talk to Katherine. Finding her at one table in a back corner, he sat down beside her.

"Good morning, Katherine," Arthur said with a smile.

"Ah, Arthur, good to see you this morning. What can I help you with?"

"I realized during all the discussions, I don't know how many refugees are in the camp. I wanted to make sure I have enough mana necklaces made for everyone to have one. I'll call it a symbol of welcome from the village for them."

"Sounds like a splendid idea," she said as she ran her fingers across the one she wore around her neck, "they do make you feel special."

She then shuffled through her notes and finally settled on a page.

"I counted fifty-three adults and twelve children among the refugees," she reported.

"That many? Really?"

"Is that a problem? I spoke with many of them. Rayne initially left Seora with only about twenty people, but they picked up stragglers as they traveled who were tired of living in their hectic lives. The hope they offered them was too much to resist."

"No, no problem. Just surprised. When you put it that way it makes sense, though. It'll be fun finding stuff for them to do," Arthur said as he leaned back on the chair.

"Some are already skilled in different areas. There are a couple of cooks, a handful have martial skills that I think will take the chance at the guard, and some are even craftsmen. They should be a welcome addition to the growing village."

"That's good to hear. Can I count on you to help get some of them where they need to be? I have several projects to take care of here in the village and don't think I have time to work with placing each person in a job."

She sighed. "I guess so, you don't seem to appreciate the mountain of paperwork I'm already dealing with here, but I'll make miracles happen."

Arthur chuckled. "I knew I could count on you. How are we doing on resources for work orders?"

"As long as people keep taking the advice to ask for minimal coins to give them more experience, we'll be fine for a while. With our Quality boost to the village, the rewards are even better so many have been using that opportunity to work on skills."

"Wait, our quality level went up?" Arthur asked in confusion as he quickly opened the village control panel.

| Alem's Crossing Village Control Panel | |
|---|---|
| Village Rank: (1/5)<br><br>Criteria for Rank Advancement: (4/5) | Village Quality: Fair<br><br>Criteria for Village Quality Improvement: (4/5) |
| View Criteria for Rank Advancement | View Criteria for Village Quality Improvement |
| Create Work Orders | View Current Work Orders |
| Current Active Village Bonuses:<br>• 3% boost to stats of items made with Blacksmithing. | |

*Wow, they went up a quality level and almost had enough criteria for the next rank as well.* Thinking back on the old requirements, he realized the construction crew had done enough work to repair the four houses necessary. They completed far more than fifteen work orders. The village health probably rose exponentially with the new bathhouse. Both he and the construction crew had made progress on the roads, and he was sure the walls classified as village improvements. It must have advanced when he wasn't paying attention to events this week.

A check of the criteria for Rank made him giddy with excitement. The only item remaining to advance their Rank was increasing the village population, and that was about to happen this afternoon. The current bonus must be because of the Quality advancement. Arthur vaguely remembered from his village tutorial in which Quality ranks increased the experience gained from work orders and could grant village bonuses.

"Our village Quality improved and I'm sure you're currently checking the village control panel so you probably also noticed our village rank will rise later today," she told him with a grin.

"You're correct on all counts. I guess the experience boost was decent since you said more people have been working on work orders?"

"Sure is. Looks like about twenty percent more than before. Combine it with the experience boost from the bathhouse and it makes experience roll in quickly."

"Thanks for the help, Kat. You're a lifesaver!" Arthur told her as he stood from his seat. She smiled at the comment as he walked out the front door. His stride took him to the blacksmith shop so he could continue his original mission.

He fell into a methodical assembly process as he made the parts for the amulets. His magic flowed as the pieces of metal quickly formed into the familiar teardrop shape. Since he was so familiar with the piece, he could include all the enchanting script on them with the spell, so his time flew by. The amulets were small enough he could make multiple at once, similar to arrowheads, so he finished the entire process in just over an hour.

Rowan worked at his station crafting more arrowheads and various other pieces that Arthur couldn't identify because of their distance apart. Arthur wiped the sweat from his face and walked over to Rowan.

"How's the Arcane Smithing progressing?" Arthur asked.

Rowan started to answer and swore as the
magic ceased flowing over the piece he worked
on. The red hot metal landed on the anvil with
a clang. Arthur quickly reached his hand
toward it and used his Fire Magic to pull the
heat from the metal. The super-heated metal
resting on the anvil's face too long would
cause the anvil to soften.

"Well, I was doing fine until you
interrupted me," Rowan said grumpily.

"You're fine. It's easy to heat that metal
and cast the spell again. You should work on
your focus, though," Arthur said with a grin.

"Are you here just to bother me?"

"Possibly. I came here to make the
necklaces I needed, but that's done and I have
time to kill before I welcome the new
villagers. Did you still need those
breastplates made?"

"You finally going to take your head out of
your ass and get back to work?" Rowan asked
with a grin.

"Well, if you keep asking me so nicely I
may," Arthur chuckled.

Rowan gestured toward a stack of metal, and
Arthur walked over to toss the first piece in
the forge. He repeated the motions to make
identical pieces to the ones prior to the
raid. The pieces all needed to look the same,
so the guard force looked united and somewhat
intimidating. Warfare was partially
psychological, after all. His familiarity with
the pieces made the work pass quickly, and he
finished up the last of them in less than an
hour and a half.

"I made eight more so that should be enough
to outfit the rest of the guards and have a
few spares," Arthur told the smith.

"I don't know. Aren't you adding more people to the village today? I'd be surprised if a handful more didn't join the guard to take on a useful job," Rowan told him skeptically.

Arthur gazed to the sky as he thought over the problem. They had a surplus of metal after the raid, so there was no reason he couldn't help augment more of the pieces they needed. He could leave most of the armor for Rowan and his apprentices, but making the chest casings didn't take that long. He nodded to Rowan and walked back to the metal supply. By the time he finished, another ten complete breastplate casings sat on the table in front of him. Alex and Lana, Rowan's apprentices, approached and gathered the pile of metal to take them to fit the internal lining to them.

"That should do," Arthur said as he waved at the retreating apprentices, loaded with their new haul. "I doubt we'll need more than that anytime soon. I can't stick around any longer, though. I need to get to the inn and make sure I have everything in order to welcome the new villagers."

"Have fun with that. I'm sure I'll make an appearance when you get started. Now go do something useful, I have more work to do," Rowan told him with a shooing motion.

Arthur smiled at the man's antics and gathered the completed amulets. With a bit of devilish delight, he opened his small dimensional storage and tossed them in. It would make for a better presentation to open the door in front of the newcomers and hand them their prize from within a magical window in space. On his trip back, he looked over his gains during the work.

*You have gained 2,400 experience in Earth
Magic and Fire Magic for successfully casting
Crafting Spell: Arcane Forging (x48).*

*You have gained 8,700 total experience in
Arcane Smithing and Blacksmithing.*

*Congratulations, you have reached level 16
in Arcane Smithing. Increases the stats on
items created using this ability by 31%.
Finally thinking of others?*

*You have gained 10,050 total experience in
Enchanting.*

*Congratulations, you have reached level 14
in Enchanting. Your enchantments have a 39%
decreased mana cost. One day you'll get bored
with making the same thing.*

*Congratulations, you have successfully
created Intricate Mage-crafted Steel Mana
Amulet. You have gained 6,000 experience in
Jeweler for creating these items (x60).*

*Congratulations, you have reached levels 4,
5, and 6 in Jeweler. Increases the stats on
Jewelry you make by 10%. Yay, Talents!*

*You have gained 100 experience in
Dimensional Magic.*

The increases were welcome and soothing.
After a week of feeling utterly worthless, a
handful of stats could change a man. The bonus
of his Jeweler skill looked good as well. The
last of the amulets he made when he hit level
six were sporting a mana pool of 550 due to
the stat increase. The ones before were
slightly lower. Eager to see his new prize, he
opened the first tier of talents for Jeweler.

*You have 4 unused Talent Points.*

| Tier 1 | |
| --- | --- |
| **Talent** | **Description** |

| Steady Hand (0/10) | Improves your detail work. This gives you a 2% chance per talent to increase the Rarity level by one. |
|---|---|
| Magical Infusion (0/10) | Increases magical effects on Jewelry by 3% per point |
| Fit Testing (0/1) | This ability teaches an Enchantment that allows your items to size themselves to the wearer automatically. |

*Well, that's a no-brainer.* The Fit Testing talent was the obvious first choice for Arthur. Since he got his boots, he wondered how they automatically adjusted size. Despite his best efforts, he never could identify an enchantment anywhere on them. He assumed the crafter was smart enough to put it in the lining to protect their product, and he wasn't about to destroy his only good pair of boots to test that theory. This talent would've saved him a load of time when he was adjusting the armor to the guards to make sure it fit snugly. With that talent chosen, he checked the Tier 2 option before committing his next points.

*You have 3 unused Talent Points.*

| Tier 2 | |
|---|---|
| **Talent** | **Description** |

| The Power of a Gem (0/10) | Increases the effective boosts granted by incorporating gems into items by 3% per point. |
|---|---|
| Latent Quality (0/10) | Each point gives a 3% chance to increase 1 Quality rank when creating Jewelry. |
| Double Stack (0/1) | Typically, a person can only wear 1 ring on each of your four fingers. (Thumbs not included) This ability allows you to double stack one ring slot to add one extra ring to any finger of your choice. |

Arthur immediately chose the Double Stack. He didn't have enough jewelry to deck himself out yet, but now that his Jeweler skill was climbing, it wouldn't be long before he could put it to excellent use. The last two points were questionable. There were so many suitable options it was hard to decide. In the end, he put the two points in Magical Infusion. That would assist with any enchanted jewelry and not just those with gems.

With all of his notifications settled, he arrived back at the inn. Daniel was busy racing around the front and saw Arthur as he walked in. He swung his head toward the kitchen, and Arthur took the hint to meet him in the back. Daniel rounded the corner only a few moments after Arthur.

"Quite busy today," Daniel said with cheer.

"Seems to be. Did you need something? I was hoping to find Katherine and see if anything needed to be done prior to the meeting with the refugees."

"That's part of why I stopped you. Can we move it to tonight rather than this afternoon?"

"Any specific reason? I wanted to get it done and out of the way. They're getting restless with nothing to do."

"I understand that, but we wanted to have a feast for them this evening in celebration of them joining us. I've already started the meal preparation so it'll be ready by evening. Just need you to hold off until then."

"Sure," Arthur told him with a sigh. "I'll let Kat know and make sure they all come hungry and ready to eat."

"Thanks. I've gotta run. Too many people and not enough time," the man said as he hurried away.

"Daniel, one last thing!" Arthur called as the man was about to round the corner.

"Yeah?" he asked as he peeked his head backward.

"Is the plot of land south of the bathhouse vacant? I considered starting plans for my new home."

"Think so. No one has claim to any specific plots except those that already have buildings on them."

"Outstanding," Arthur said to a quickly fleeing back.

*Looks like it's time to play house.*

# Chapter 23

*Village Improvements*

Arthur walked over to the plot of land in question and looked around. There wasn't much in the area to get in his way, and the land was relatively flat. His mind started turning over the potential issues in building new-style buildings. He wanted something that mixed in modern amenities that he was used to, but he needed to accomplish them in a way that used magic from this world.

The problem of lighting was one he wasn't too concerned about. There was surely a way he could make rechargeable lights with his Enchantment skill. His Dimensional Disposal spell would be used to create a toilet in this place. That would also be a fairly simple task since he already knew the required spell. All he needed to do for that scenario was to make an activation panel of some kind that would power an enchantment to open the disposal portal and close it.

The part he wanted the most, which would also be the most challenging, was running water. The village used water from wells around the area. Coming up with a plumbing system would be a challenge, but if he planned to grow this village into something grand, it was absolutely necessary. Since they were trying to rebuild from the ground up, this was the perfect chance to start.

His access to Water Magic would allow him to create an enchantment to keep the water flowing. He already did that with the bathhouse filter. The piping itself was different. They didn't have nearly enough metal of any kind to make the plumbing system out of that. It also had the nasty side effect of rusting and corroding. The idea of making clay pipes came to him, but he knew of no body of water close enough that may harbor a deposit of clay near it.

This left him with only one proper choice, stone. It wasn't the best idea, but the Romans had a fantastic system using stone aqueducts. He didn't want to rely on an above-ground water system, though. With his access to Earth Magic, he should be able to create a solid system of stone tunnels under the ground and run them to and from the well to the houses and businesses.

A look across the village showed him the well in regard to his current location. It was a good hundred yards away, so he walked over to it. He kneeled to the ground and placed his hand in direct contact with the dirt near the well. Pushing his Earth Magic downward, he searched for the water. It took some time, but he finally brushed up against the water around the one hundred and fifty feet mark. He extended his senses another twenty feet lower, so he wasn't directly on the surface, and molded out a stone tunnel parallel with the well shaft. It took time to create the hollow space and then to solidify it into stone. After the first twenty feet were complete, the process sped up. It took him a solid hour to extend the pipe all the way until it was only four feet below his feet and turned to run parallel to the ground.

   With his muscles aching from staying in the
same position for so long, he collapsed to the
ground and sat with his back against the well.
The change in position felt fabulous, and he
stretched his legs out straight in front of
him to ease their tension. The effort of
extending that tunnel was far more than he
expected. Luckily, he had the foresight to do
the spell in increments, so he could learn the
spell as a scalable one. He also learned the
spell to make the ninety-degree portion of the
pipe. To his further delight, both spells were
new, so he named them.

*For creating the new Earth Magic Spell:
Stone Pipe (Scalable), you have been granted a
one-time bonus of 250 Earth and Fire Magic
Experience, 250 Personal Experience, and 1
Intellect. With great power comes great
responsibility.*
*For creating the new Earth Magic Spell:
Stone Pipe (90 Degree), you have been granted
a one-time bonus of 250 Earth and Fire Magic
Experience, 250 Personal Experience, and 1
Wisdom. Keep it up!*
*You have gained a total of 600 experience
in Earth and Fire Magic.*

| Earth Magic Spell: Stone Pipe (Scalable) | |
|---|---|
| Requirements: Earth Magic<br>Mana Cost: 60-240 MP<br>Cast Time: 8-80 seconds | Description: Creates a solid stone pipe for the desired length. The longer the length, the more mana and time required to cast. |

| | Dimensions: 2' Diameter x 5'-100' length. |
| --- | --- |
| Mastery Level: 1 | |

| Earth Magic Spell: Stone Pipe (90 Degree) | |
| --- | --- |
| Requirements: Earth Magic<br>Mana Cost: 60 MP<br>Cast Time: 8 seconds | Description: Creates a solid stone pipe in a 90-degree angle.<br><br>Dimensions: 2' Diameter x 5' length. |
| Mastery Level: 1 | |

He'd have to focus on creating this pipe as the main water flow line and then develop a smaller diameter version to feed the individual houses. Getting back to his feet, he dusted his pants off and focused on the task at hand. The work continued much faster now that it only required him to cast the spell and visualize the path. He created the network of pipes much as a city would have them arranged. The pipes followed along the edges of the road and led all the way to the front of his new property.

    With nothing else in the area, he could
make his house as big as he wanted to. He
didn't want it overly large right now, though.
The beauty of building with magic was he could
easily add on to the building. He pushed out
Earth Magic and used it to raise a small
platform above the ground. It only extended a
little less than a foot off the ground but it
would suit his purposes. His power crawled
deeper to envelop a larger area below, and he
wove in his Fire Magic to transform the area
into a solid stone slab.

    With easy steps, he walked out onto the
stone and looked around. The layout of this
house would be more challenging. He knew he
wanted to include four rooms in it, and each
set of rooms would share a bathroom. There
would need to be a kitchen area as well. With
the size of the stone slab, he could easily
put all of that on one floor.

    His first act was to use his magic to
create the four external walls. He carved the
front door out of the wall, and he turned to
the interior layout. A wall spanned the entire
structure on one side of the door to house the
living area. Walking to the middle of that
wall, he put another doorway in.

    Two more walls rose on each side of this
doorway, stretching the space. Now he had a
slab, almost split directly in half, with a
hallway positioned in the middle of this
segregated half. He created another doorway in
the center of each of these walls. These doors
would feed into the central bathrooms for each
of the bedroom sets.

Walking through the doorway, he imagined the space he would need to include a sink, something resembling a toilet, and a shower of some kind. He walled off this new bathroom area and focused toward the shower when he realized a problem. Drainage.

He worried about drainage before with his Dimensional Disposal spell because he needed somewhere for toilet waste to go. Now that he'd solved the toilet waste issue, he forgot about needing drains. Sadly, sinks and showers still needed some way to drain water away from them. The tricky part was wasting water. Theoretically, he could just put a disposal drain on each of these places, but that would lead to a host of problems.

Water needed to cycle through the ground to replenish the well supply. If they kept permanently getting rid of water and sending it to some unknown place, the water supply would diminish. He couldn't just let it drain somewhere outside the house either. Any soaps they used would be in the water when it drained out, and they might potentially damage the soil, not to mention all the houses draining into some unknown place would cause a marshy mess. The ideal situation would be to use it for irrigation, but the soap was the concern.

His mind fixed back on the filter, and his
solution was clear. He'd design a drainage
system that flowed to the fields but would go
through some enchanted filters before
irrigating the crops. The filters should be
able to dispose of the chemicals before it
reached their plants, and it would save a lot
of time on irrigation for the fields. It meant
a lot more piping, but that wasn't too bad.
They'd have to dedicate some of their magic
crew to monitor the upkeep and maintenance of
the pipes to prevent future issues.

His Earth Magic made quick work of a
shower. The base sloped slightly toward the
center as a drain and a stone grate covered
the hole. It was solid beneath, but Arthur
would fix that when he put in the piping. His
bench seat for the toilet rose with a quick
flex of his magic, and he even softened the
edges of the stone to taper it more like a
toilet seat from Earth. Finally, a vanity rose
from the stone and he placed a large basin
sink in the top. He left spots open on the
front so they could store items under the
sink. Wooden doors would cover the front at a
later time.

He quickly added doors to each of the rooms
that led directly to the bathroom and then in
the hallway, he added another door that led
directly into each room. The other side of the
hallway directly mirrored the first. The
bathroom and bedrooms were identical in layout
and design. He gave each of the bedrooms an
opening for a window in them.

    With this side of the house roughly laid
out, he walked back to the other side. The
middle of the house, directly in front of the
front door, would remain a large, open area
for a living room. On the side of the house,
he left the kitchen open to the living room
but placed a wall on the side of it. He
created another wall attached to the end of
that wall and extended it all the way to the
back of the house. This new walled-off area in
the back corner would become a small study and
a washroom. The doors for both of those
appeared in the stone and Arthur took the time
to add a window opening to each.
    Back in the kitchen area, he created an
extensive set of cabinets and countertops out
of stone and left the fronts open like he did
with the bathroom vanity. Stone would just be
too heavy to use as a door. He carved a large
kitchen sink into the stone top. With his mind
turned to cooking, he created a large island-
style cabinet in the middle of the kitchen but
made a large depression on the top. He would
need to get some metal to make a cooking grate
to cover this small fire pit. It would also
require an exhaust pipe in the ceiling above
it. An oven would eventually join the design.
Making something similar to a barbeque pit
should be relatively easy. He'd made plenty of
them back in shop class in school.

Looking around the area, the design impressed him. It would make a great and serviceable area, but man, did it ever look bland with no furniture of any kind. The plain stone walls also gave it a stark appearance. He'd burned through far more mana than he expected, and the time of the evening ceremony was drawing near, so he called it a day. There would be plenty of time to add in the plumbing lines. His next big issue would be temperature regulation. He needed an enchantment that would allow the building to be temperature-controlled and adjustable. He also needed the same solution to add to the pipes for hot water.

Shaking his head at the mountain of issues still left to solve, he walked from the building. Shortly after entering the inn, Daniel waved him down.

"Arthur, I need to get into storage to grab more food. We used almost everything we had out to organize the feast, and I don't want to hunt you down in the morning."

"Sure, let's walk out back and get that taken care of," Arthur told him.

As soon as he exited the back door, Arthur opened his Dimensional Storage. They both worked to haul out some of the supplies and move them to the storage location in the inn. The storage room itself wasn't large enough for Arthur to open the doorway any closer, so it required some manual labor. Once the crates rested in their new place, Arthur waved to Daniel and walked upstairs to relax in his room.

Arthur almost went to the kitchen instead, but he could wait just like everyone else. The amazing smells emanating from the space wafted clear up the stairs and made his mouth water even more. As soon as he walked into his room, a blur of purple assaulted him and he fell to the ground with his attacker.

The beautiful elf made a very unladylike noise as they fell, which caused Arthur to chuckle.

"What's so funny? That hurt," she mumbled as she tried to untangle herself from their bundle of limbs.

"Nothing. How was your day?"

"It's been quite productive. Construction has made significant progress. Where have you been?" she asked as she finally returned to her feet.

"Was working on our new house."

"A new house? The inn not working for you?"

"It's not bad but nothing like having a place of your own. I'm also trying to create a new lifestyle with some important changes to the way houses work. I think you'll love it," he told her with a smile.

"Fine, fine, I'll have to go check it out tomorrow when you go back. I'm assuming you'll be working on it tomorrow, anyway?"

"Probably. Need to do some experimenting with enchantments, though. There are a few I need to make the place functional and will have to figure out how to make them work."

"Mind if I tag along for that? I'd like to help with your enchantment work."

"Please, as if you even had to ask. Your insight is always welcome."

She smiled and hooked her arm in his.

"You about ready for the ceremony? I figured we should do one quick check on things before everything kicks off. There's always those last-minute things to address. It'd look good to see our fearless leader back in action," she told him with a mock salute.

Arthur sighed at her antics, and they walked downstairs together. The common room was far barer than he had anticipated. Many of the tables and chairs were missing, and only a few pieces of furniture remained. He spotted Daniel scurrying out of the kitchen.

"Daniel, what the hell? Where's all the furniture?"

"Outside, where else?" he asked in confusion.

"Why?" Arthur dragged out.

"You didn't think we could fit everyone in here, did you?" he asked as he looked around the room.

As a matter of fact, Arthur hadn't considered that problem. As soon as he said it, it made sense.

"Why is some furniture still in here, then?" Arthur asked in confusion.

"I thought you'd like to have a private meeting and meal with some of the refugee leadership after the ceremony is complete. They know little about how this village operates yet."

"I don't know how much I pay you, but it can't be enough. You think of everything," Arthur told him in excitement.

"Actually, it was Kat's idea," Daniel said as he motioned to the woman emerging from the kitchen carrying a bundle of supplies.

"Kat! I can't thank you enough for helping organize this and for the fabulous idea of the separate reception area," he told her sincerely.

She smiled at the praise. "It's my job after all."

"I feel bad I've neglected to ask how your Tailoring skill is coming along."

"Much better now that we gathered some more cloth. I wish you could have found cleaner material to work with, but I understand the situation."

"Sorry about that. I hope to find some flax or cotton plants eventually so we can start farming for our own supplies. Until then, we have to settle with what we have."

"I'll ask around and see if our rangers can keep an eye out. I'll make sure they know not to harvest it until you can cast Germinate on the plant," Kat told him as she continued carrying her burden to the door.

"Need any help with anything?" Allendria asked.

"No." Daniel waved off. "Go find yourself a spot outside to mingle. We are almost done setting everything up. Everyone should arrive shortly for you to start.

Arthur spent the next half hour walking through the crowd and making conversation with different villagers. Not many of the refugees were here yet, but Arthur assumed they'd arrive as a cohesive group together. His assumption proved correct a few moments later when they slowly filtered to the feast area.

Arthur spotted Rayne among the group and motioned for the young man to join him. Rayne brought two other women with him when he came forward. Both were middle-aged and had a no-nonsense look to them. He shook Rayne's hand as he approached and addressed the two ladies.

"Good Evening, ladies. My name's Arthur and I'm the Mayor of Alem's Crossing. I apologize for the delay in our meeting."

The first woman approached. She was short in stature, but her eyes held a deep fire.

"Name's Tina, Lord Mayor. I'm sorry for your loss," she whispered with remorse in her voice.

"Thank you."

He turned to the other woman. "And your name?"

"My name is Layla. Pleasure to meet you, Lord Mayor."

Arthur bowed to both ladies in turn. "Please join me as we make an announcement," he told the three of them.

"Ladies and Gentlemen, boys and girls, welcome to Alem's Crossing. I apologize for the delay and for keeping you sequestered in your camp near the wall. There have been many unexpected challenges lately. I stand before you after an impressive victory over a large invading force. I'm told you've come from an assortment of places between here and the city of Seora and I thank you for that," he announced to the gathered crowd.

"Our village is quickly changing and we've been working day and night to make it a better place for all. I'm sure you've noticed the abundance of construction going on around here, both mundane and magical. We decided to welcome any and all of you who wish to remain and become an official villager," he said to murmurs of excitement.

Arthur raised his hands. "I'm sure you have many questions and I can't blame you for that. I plan to convene with some of your leaders to discuss what this village truly means to its inhabitants, but I want to stress that all of you will have the same opportunities that every other villager has. I don't demand anyone perform any specific tasks, but we try to recommend jobs that might suit your skillset. Keep in mind, you don't have to take those positions if you don't wish to and no repercussions will come from those decisions," Arthur continued.

"We have many programs that some of you will be interested in so feel free to talk with your fellow villagers once we've concluded for the evening. One thing I want to stress is this place is one of magic. As such, I want to present each new villager with a token to commemorate your inclusion here," Arthur told them as he waved his hand dramatically and opened his Dimensional Drawer containing the amulets.

"Rayne, please step forward," Arthur called to the young man.

He nervously walked over to Arthur. Arthur reached out to him and held out the necklace.

"Welcome to Alem's Crossing," Arthur said with a smile as he sent a request for Rayne to join the village through the village interface.

The shadow of nervousness left Rayne's face as he saw what Arthur handed to him. He nodded with a wink and whispered, "I'll get it back to you later."

Arthur grinned. He'd already given Rayne one, but he needed to make a show of presenting the leadership first. He continued with Layla and Tina, who each took their necklaces with looks of awe. Continuing through the crowd, he handed out necklaces one by one as he accepted them into the village.

"Thank you for joining our family," Arthur said over the noise in the feast area.

"These necklaces are a symbol of the village, but they're also a line of defense. In emergencies, we may ask you to surrender them so we may use their excess storage. Don't worry, you'll get them back. You're also free to use them yourself to further your skills. Now, without further ado, I'm starving, so let's eat!"

The crowd cheered, and everyone found a seat at a table. They arranged the food in the center of the tables, and everyone dug in. Arthur and Allendria sat at a table with some of the other prominent figures. Vana, Samson, Rowan, and Dalia sat at his table along with Rayne, Layla, and Tina. Arthur made quick introductions before eating.

Everyone sat in relative silence as they ate their fill. The area buzzed with conversation and the overall mood had a giddy feeling to it. When those at the table completed their meal, they walked into the inn to leave the rest of the villagers to their celebration. All of them took a seat at the lone table in the now empty room, and Daniel and Kat joined them.

"Thank y'all for being here," Arthur started and quickly introduced Daniel and Kat. Rayne, Tina, and Layla smiled and nodded. They obviously knew the pair since they worked with them so often already.

"First and foremost, I'm not much on ceremony so let's dispense with the Lord Mayor nonsense. Just Arthur is fine. The only person here who truly has a title is the Lady Dalia," Arthur told them with a shallow bow toward Dalia.

She straightened in her seat and took on a more regal pose at the acknowledgment.

"I'm sure you have many questions but let me just give you a quick rundown of where we stand. Currently, we supplement most of our food with hunting trips into the forest. We've recovered seeds and plants through foraging trips and have crops planted, but they still need time to mature. Any estimate on that timeframe Kat?" Arthur asked as he looked at her.

She flipped through her notebook and looked at a page for a moment before answering, "Looks like two weeks until the crops start steady production."

Arthur nodded. "Until then, I'll continue to lead groups into the forest for hunting. We have construction running nonstop but with the added villagers will probably need at least one more construction crew, if not more. I'm working on some designs to build new housing throughout the village to accommodate all, but I'm also changing them to be more comfortable, so it's taking time. Until we have the housing available, I must ask you to remain where you've been. I promise I'll make it a top priority and you can freely move within the village as you wish. I also meant every word I said during the speech. Ensure those who came with you understand this is a fresh start for them. They can take any role they wish as long as they work for the betterment of our village. Any questions?" Arthur asked.

Tina quickly spoke up. "The housing. Do you have a rough estimate of how long it will take? Will we need to have multiple families under the same roof for a while until they can make enough?"

"I think I can have a design ready in a couple of days. Once I have it completed, the construction crews should make quick work of them. I estimate we could probably finish a house a day if we dedicate our time to it," Arthur told them.

"There's no way you can build an entire house in a day!" Layla spoke up.

"Magic, remember? There'll be some decorative pieces not finished in that time, but everything else should be fully functional."

Layla sat back with a look of shock on her face.

"Are there any jobs here that we are truly short on?" Tina asked.

"A few," Kat said. "We could use more people to tend the fields, especially as we expand them. We are also in need of more guards. That's a position that is volunteer only," she quickly added after seeing the looks on the ladies' faces.

"As Arthur mentioned, there will probably be plenty of positions in the construction teams available."

"Those are magical teams, correct? Do you need to have magical skills to join them?" Tina asked.

"They are magical teams but you don't have to have magical skills to join. If you join one of those teams, we teach you the magic needed for your job. You're required to only provide those services for the village for a specific stretch of time. After the time is up, you are free to pursue whatever you choose," Arthur explained.

"Truly? You'll agree to teach magic to anyone who agrees to the deal?" Layla asked in astonishment.

"Yep. Anything else?" Arthur asked.

"It looks like we'll just need time to get used to things and learn some more about the village," Rayne added helpfully.

Arthur nodded in agreement. "That's true. It's been a long and trying day, so I believe it's time I retire for the evening. Find me tomorrow if you think of anything else," Arthur said as he headed toward the stairs, "Oh, and be sure to try out the magical bathhouse."

Arthur heard conversation start up as all those remaining at the table continued discussing random things. He paid no attention and walked into his room. A pile of scales in the corner marked Balair.

*Been lazy all day?*

*I've been using my magic to help the construction workers. You build that maze of stone walls near the bathhouse?* Balair asked.

*It's the start of our new home. Trying to get the layout done before I continue working on it tomorrow.*

*Good. I'm tired of being cramped in this room with you two. Plus, you snore.*

*Hey, so do you!* Arthur huffed back.

*Doesn't matter. I'm going to sleep.*

*Goodnight,* Arthur sent before collapsing in bed himself.

# Chapter 24

*The Power of Thermodynamics*

Arthur and Allendria huddled over the bench in the blacksmith shop.

"So, you need to make a device that cools an area but also doesn't go past a certain level of hot or cold?" Allendria asked while scratching her head.

"Yep. Where I come from, the measure of hot or cold is called the temperature. We even assign specific numbers to them. For instance, water will freeze around the thirty-two-degree mark."

Allendria nodded. "Okay, so I got that part. Didn't you do something similar for the bathhouse already?"

"I did. I can use a similar design to that one for the cold storage room I plan to make for Daniel. The problem I have in the houses is, I need the temperature to be adjustable. Do you know of any control methods in Enchanting that can actively adjust an effect?" Arthur asked.

Her face morphed into a look of sheer concentration as Arthur waited on the answer.

"Now that you mention it, I may. In the Dark Elven city of Calzas, we have some old Enchantments from a forgotten time. One of them can regulate the speed at which water flows from one of our storage containers into the fields. The symbols used are these," she explained as she sketched out the symbols.

She pointed at one symbol and continued, "I don't know what that one is and we haven't been able to figure it out. We've tried it in other enchantments, but it never had an effect."

Arthur looked at the symbol and his special gift with languages came into play.

"That says 'Flow'," he told her with a nod.

"The only way it would work is to control another process. If you just tried to use the symbol by itself, it wouldn't do much. Was this symbol only used in that one Enchantment?"

"No. We found it on a few different pieces."

"Did the other items control water as well?" Arthur asked.

"Nope. They controlled many things."

"Good. That means the flow symbol was probably used to control the flow of magic and not the flow of the process itself."

"What's the difference?" Allendria asked, confused.

"To control the flow of each process individually would be difficult. Especially if it does something that has multiple effects. For instance, using Fire Magic to heat or cool a room. Both the heating and cooling aspects of the enchantment would need to be present, but if you tried to control the flow of one or the other directly, it's likely they'd counteract each other. If instead you merely change the mana flow so the aspect to remove heat received mana, the space would cool down and the element to introduce heat wouldn't fight against it because it'd be inactive. That's what I need to do! You're a lifesaver," he told her with a kiss on her cheek.

Arthur needed something easy to make that held a suitable amount of magic. To accomplish it, he used steel. He made a small disc of steel and then made another small wheel knob that fit on the disc. It looked like a miniature version of a combination wheel for a safe. Inside the knob, he left a slight depression to put one of his manufactured gems. These would not be useful if they quickly ran out of energy. He used tools to cut the runes into the outer disc to heat and cool the surrounding area. He then put runes on the knob with the flow symbol and tied them to the outer enchantments.

The piece looked fantastic and Arthur spent a good ten minutes checking every inch for any imperfections in the script or enchantment matrices. When satisfied it was ready, he pushed in the mana to enchant it. The expected rush of mana flowed out and then slowed to complete the enchantment. As soon as it finished, he added a Manufactured Sapphire to the piece with the storage rune on it and tied it together. The result was exactly what he needed.

*You have gained 100 experience in Earth Magic and Fire Magic for successfully casting Crafting Spell: Arcane Forging (x2).*
*You have gained 180 total experience in Arcane Smithing and Blacksmithing.*
*You have gained 205 total experience in Enchanting.*
*Congratulations, you have successfully created* Intricate Mage-crafted Steel Temperature Control (Sapphire Storage). *You have gained 180 experience in Jeweler for creating this item.*

| Item:<br>Intricate Mage-<br>crafted Steel<br>Temperature Control<br>(Sapphire Storage) | **Durability:** 100/100<br><br>**Rarity:** Rare<br><br>**Quality:** Well Crafted<br><br>**Weight:** 0.04 kg<br><br>**Slot:** Crafting Item<br><br>**Charges:** 2,800/2,800<br><br>*Area of Effect:* 20'<br>in all directions<br><br>**Traits:** A device that allows you to adjust the temperature of the surrounding room for up to twenty feet in any direction<br><br>Enchantment:<br>• Charges only deplete when temperature is far outside of the desired range. Once the temperature has stabilized in the given area, charges deplete very slowly to maintain. |
|---|---|

"We did it!" Arthur yelled in glee as he handed the device to Allendria.

She looked it over and smiled. "Sounds like exactly what you were looking for."

"Yep, I'll have to make a bunch of those and then I need to create a modified design that can heat and cool water as it flows through a cylindrical pipe, but this is the exact breakthrough I needed. I couldn't have done it without you," he told her with a quick embrace.

"Glad I could help. What's our next step?"

"I need to make one that permanently regulates cold for the storage room I have to build for Daniel. If I had the time, I'd just cut corners and figure out how to make a large dimensional bag he could store it all in preventing it from going bad, but this cold storage would be useful for all the villagers in the long run. Everyone can safely store all of their own food items in their homes."

"Well, as much fun as that sounds, I'm going back to the construction groups. You lost me with all the boring monotony you are about to embark on. If you need anything else, let me know."

He kissed her goodbye and turned his attention back to the project at hand. It took him three more full pieces before he felt confident enough to include the enchantments on the base and dial while forging. After that, the process flew by. He had to make some more gems with his Mineral Compression spell, but that didn't take long. He also made two quick Coldstones for the cold storage room.

His eighth piece completed with the infusion of mana, and a thought caused him to freeze in place. *Are there others here from Earth?*

He'd never considered that option before,
but this enchantment told him there may be.
Neither the device he created nor the
enchantment registered as a new or unique
item. The description of the item also used
the word temperature in it, which he doubted
was a common word in this world. The idea
nagged at him, but he couldn't dwell on that
right now. Maybe more information would come
to light later.

With enough of the temperature control
items completed, he used a quick enchantment
that mimicked the bathhouse one and set a
constant temperature around another disc of
steel to hold things right below freezing
temperature. At least, that's what he
pictured, and the description matched that,
but it didn't have an exact temperature level
listed. The air around the device was chilly
and made his breath show as fog.

The last pieces he needed to complete his
modern home were faucets and showerheads.
Since his Arcane Smithing could perfectly
mirror anything he thought of, he made the
faucets as a long steel pipe with a ball valve
style joint on it. He wanted a mechanical way
to shut the water flow but, in front of the
cut-off, he added another enchantment dial
that would adjust the temperature of anything
flowing inside the pipe. That was tricky, and
he failed five times before getting it right.
With the gem in place and the enchantments
finally correct, he viewed the item.

| Item: | **Durability:** 90/90 |
|---|---|
| Intricate Mage-crafted Steel Faucet (Sapphire Storage) | **Rarity:** Rare |
| | **Quality:** Well Crafted |

| | **Weight:** 0.03 kg<br><br>**Slot:** Crafting Item<br><br>**Charges:** 2,400/2,400<br><br>**Traits:** A device that allows you to control the flow of liquids through it. The enchantment allows you to adjust the temperature of anything flowing through it.<br><br>Enchantment:<br>• Charges deplete slowly because of the small area of effect inside the tube. |
| --- | --- |

The piece looked exactly as he pictured it. He wouldn't be able to test it until he had it installed in his house. He made four to use in his home. Once this proved effective in his house, he'd have to make more for everyone else. The showerheads he made in an almost identical method, but instead of just a pipe, he made them in the shape of a bell with the bottom capped off and small holes all over the surface. Rather than including the temperature control and the cut-off valve, he made a few of those by themselves. He needed to install them lower on the wall so anyone could reach them.

Arthur gathered all the completed pieces and stuffed them into his Dimensional Drawer. His work at the blacksmith shop left him in a pleasant mood as he returned to the inn. Finding the innkeeper scurrying between tables, he motioned for the man to meet him in the kitchen. Daniel acknowledged the gesture, finished up in the dining area, and then met Arthur in the back.

"What's up?" Daniel asked.

"I've got what I needed to make the cold room for food storage for you. Where do you want it? I plan to make most of it underground and then bring a doorway with stairs up to the ground level for entry. Do you want me to attach it to the wall in the back of the kitchen for easy access?"

"Uh, sure, why not?" Daniel asked with mild confusion.

"Don't worry, you'll like it. I'll start outside and get the primary part of it made. I'll connect it to the inn last." Arthur told him with a nod and walked out back.

Wanting to make a good-sized storage room, he focused on the area he'd be working with. This would be the central food storage for the entire village. His Earth Magic stretched out in front of him and he used the spell he used on the bathhouse to dig a hole in the ground that was twelve-feet deep. He wanted it deep enough to put a two-foot thick slab of stone on top and bottom and still have ten feet of clearance.

The entire floor of the new space transformed into a two-foot thick chunk of stone. Arthur raised walls that were two-feet thick around all four sides. With the room being thirty-feet on each side, having a solid stone roof concerned him. To mitigate it, Arthur lifted four giant columns to the height the ceiling would rest and then created the stone ceiling to cover everything but the area that would be the entrance.

With the room complete, Arthur added a staircase that led to the top. He couldn't enclose the top until he cut a doorway in the inn's side. Otherwise, he'd trap himself inside and have to waste magic to get out. He walked back to the bottom of the stairs and looked around. It was a little dark, but he could make out the general layout. He opened his storage and pulled out both of the temperature regulators for the space. Instead of placing them on opposite walls and risking them getting damaged by people carrying stuff around, he placed them on the ceiling on each side of the room.

As soon as the pieces fused to the stone, the room began noticeably dropping temperature. He walked back to the surface and into the inn.

"Daniel," he called to the man while he was carrying food from the kitchen, "do you have a saw anywhere here?"

"For wood? I don't think so. You can check the storage closet. It's possible there's an old one in there."

"Thanks," Arthur said and walked to the compact storage room.

Tucked away in a corner and covered in dust and cobwebs was a handsaw. It was a little weather-beaten and worn out, so Arthur used his Arcane Repair on it. When the blade emerged from the spell, it was sharp and shiny. He returned outside and peered at his next challenge, the doorway. The saw should make quick work of it, but he needed a starting point. He couldn't punch a blunt faced saw through a wall.

Walking back to the dirt area, he searched the ground with his magic. He identified some sand and extracted it from the dirt. He then created a small disc with the sand and sent it spinning with incredible speed. He slowly pushed this disc into the wall and sawdust filled the air. As soon as he had a hole big enough to fit the saw, he stopped the spell and let the sand fall into a pile on the ground. He finished cutting through the doorway and watched as the wall fell open.

Daniel's apprentices gave him shocked looks of confusion while they both brandished cooking pans in their hands, ready to swing.

"Sorry guys," he laughed, "didn't mean to scare y'all. I'm making a new opening to attach the cold room," he told them with a wave.

His focus turned back to the room, and he spent the mana to lift more stone to enclose the entire staircase and meld this into the inn wall. With the entire space enclosed, Arthur felt some of the frigid air seep up from the bottom. Finding some old tools in the storage area, he used his Arcane Smithing to make a pair of hinges, a simple latch, and a handful of nails. He attached the latch and the hinges to the door he cut from the wall and rested it back in its place. The thin crack around the edge let a negligible amount of cold bleed in, but it wasn't much.

"Finished the room," Arthur told Daniel as he walked around the corner and into the kitchen.

"That fast?"

"Yep, for now, you'll need to take some light in with you. I'll come up with some enchantments for light, but it'll keep everything so cold it won't go bad for a much longer time."

"We going to unload the food into it then?" Daniel asked.

"Sure. I made it big enough that I can open my storage directly into the space below. I will say you don't want to stay down there for prolonged periods of time. Temperatures that cold can damage you if you stay too long."

Daniel nodded and followed Arthur through the door and to the bottom. Arthur held up a hand and let Fire Magic flow out for light.

"Son of a bitch, it's cold down here," Daniel cursed.

"Yes, it is. Now you understand my warning," Arthur said with a chuckle.

Arthur quickly opened the storage room and the two men jumped in and unloaded the crates of food as quickly as they could. When the last crate fell to the floor of the chilly room, Arthur closed the door, and they both practically ran up the stairs.

"F… F… Fuck, it's s… s… seriously cold," Arthur said as he rubbed his arms furiously.

"S… S… Sounds like it almost t… t… took us too long," Daniel responded with a smirk on his face.

"Screw this, I'm going outside to warm up. I'll see you later," Arthur told Daniel as he walked out the back.

The sun on his skin quickly warmed him and the goosebumps vanished from his arms. With nothing else to occupy his time, he went in search of Allendria. It didn't take long to find her directing some of the construction crews, and he quickly convinced her to join him on a tour of their soon to be home.

As soon as they walked through the doorway, Allendria whistled.

"How many people do you expect to live here? Looks like we could house a quarter of the village in here."

"This is mainly just for the two of us. I made four rooms here, so we could have guests if we needed it. I figure Balair will stay here too. I plan on making a nice fireplace in the main room here," Arthur said as he motioned at the sizable space in front of them, "but haven't gotten to it yet. Knowing Balair, he'll prefer to curl up near it to sleep."

"This place looks a little bare," she said hesitantly.

Arthur laughed. "It's really nowhere near complete. There are many details I want to add to it. The most important will be the temperature controls and running water."

"Are you magically putting a waterfall in here or something?"

"Nope. I'll have to show you what I mean."

Arthur spent the next hour walking through the house with Allendria, explaining the unique features and how they worked. He had her watch with her magic as he made the piping through the walls to the different areas. His next enchanting challenge would be the toilets, but he was confident that would be easy.

He opened his storage and removed the new faucets and showerheads. The fixtures melded into the stone pipes he placed in the showers and the sinks. For the showers, he brought the pipe out of the wall to put the cutoff and placed the temperature control below it. Arthur then pushed the rest of the pipe back into the wall and moved it up to attach the showerhead.

Allendria followed Arthur as he ran the small diameter piping through the slab and to the front of the house. It surprised her to see the section of pipe sitting near the entrance.

"Where does that pipe go to?"

"I ran that to the well. I have to tie it into the well and keep an enchantment running that constantly forces water through the pipe to all the places it feeds. I plan on tying all the new houses into these larger lines so everyone can have these luxuries."

"So this pipe already feeds all the way to the well?"

"Yep. I can tie it in when I get the enchantment done."

She nodded as he finished connecting everything together.

"I saw some other pipes in the house that didn't lead this way. Where did they go?" she asked.

"Those are drains. When the water flows into the showers and sinks it has to go somewhere. Those pipes lead out of the house and I plan on making a network that goes all the way to the fields outside the village. I'll have the water go through some filters similar to the bathhouse and the farmers can use the water line to irrigate the fields. It'll save them a lot of time and hassle. It also ensures we don't waste water."

"Sounds good," she told him as she snuggled up against his arm, "I can't wait to live here with you."

"I'll get this done soon. I have a lot left to do, but my mana pool lets me power through quickly."

He continued around the building, making adjustments. He added sitting areas and Allendria helped with her stone magic to add things she thought the house needed. Since the roof was also stone, it required him to make adjustments to the building's structure. Arthur raised the walls on the house taller on one side and gradually sloped them down to the other. This would ensure the roof had enough of a natural slope to make any rain flow off. He attached a temperature control in each room and nodded in pleasure. There was still a never-ending amount of stuff to do, and the place needed some artistic decorations on the stonework, but it would be serviceable. Furniture was the next big problem.

The two of them left the structure and walked back to the inn. On the way, Arthur took a chance to look at the bundle of experience he'd gained through the day.

*You have gained 14,080 total experience in Earth Magic and Fire Magic.*
*Congratulations, you have reached level 22 in Fire Magic. Fire Magic spells now have a 63% increased effect. Becoming a plumber as well?*
*You have gained 1,800 total experience in Arcane Smithing and Blacksmithing.*
*You have gained 2,050 total experience in Enchanting.*
*You have gained 1,800 total experience in Jeweler for creating this item.*
*Congratulations, you have reached level 7 in Jeweler. Increases the stats on Jewelry you make by 12%. Fancy devices you have there.*

As they approached the inn, a breathless Vana approached him.

"Arthur, I'm glad you're here. I need your assistance," Vana told him.

"Sure. Allendria, you care to come help?" Arthur said as he turned to her.

"No! Err, I mean, we don't need to bother her with this. I need your advice on something. Can you walk with me?" Vana blurted.

Arthur took in her appearance and something seemed off, but he couldn't place what. Instead, he turned to Allendria.

"I'll go with her to take care of this. I'll meet you back in our room later," Arthur told her.

Arthur saw a look on her face he wasn't familiar with. He assumed it had to do with being excluded from the event, but he couldn't be sure. She nodded and calmly walked off, though Arthur spotted the tension in her stance.

"Vana, what the hell is that about? Why are you acting so odd?" Arthur asked.

"We've found something while scouting and I don't want Allendria to know. At least, not until I've discussed it with you," Vana explained.

"What is it?"

"More Dark Elves," she told him quietly.

# Chapter 25

*The Will of a Tyrant*

King Robert Wailyn walked through the castle. Attendants scurried from his sight as he went by. These poor excuses for people barely deserved to live, much less be in his presence. Finding useful people was becoming more and more difficult. *These fools are more trouble than they're worth most of the time. I should get rid of all of them. Can't they see I have bigger problems on my hands? I protect the lives of these people almost daily and they have no respect.*

His temper flared as a servant fell in front of him and didn't get out of the way quick enough. He flicked his hand and a fist of stone launched the servant down the hallway and out of his way with a scream. The wet thump he heard caused him to sigh. *There's another to replace.*

"Your Majesty," a guard called as he rounded the corner, "a messenger is here to see you."

"I didn't send for anyone. No one calls on the King!"

"Sorry, Your Majesty, but it is a delegate from the Dark Elves. He came in through the verified entrance," the guard said nervously.

*Damned Dark Elves are definitely nothing but trouble. Hopefully, their plan is well underway. If they could help him wipe out some of the sniveling fools in this world, it would help secure his position.*

"Fine, I'll meet him in my study in half an hour."

"As you say," the guard told him with a bow and ran to deliver the message.

All the peasants complaining about the lack of food grated on his nerves. They could either go with little food or die. There were no other options. He couldn't hold the vultures at bay any other way.

His path changed directions, and he headed for his office. The bare stone walls matched his attire. King Wailyn never cared to dress in what most considered a kingly manner. Most of the time he wore his plate leggings and plate and chain mixed breastplate. A helmet always annoyed him too much to mess with. Plus, it never looked right with his mustache.

His office was another matter. The large space shone with opulence. An assortment of armor and weapons lined the room, most were trophies from battles. His grand wooden desk was a piece of exquisite craftsmanship the previous fool of a king had.

King Wailyn felt no remorse for removing King Tristan. The man was on the path to have the entire world wiped out. No one could stand up to their kind of power. A knock on the door brought him out of his reverie.

"Enter."

A lone Dark Elf entered the room and walked up to the desk. He dropped into a deep bow and waited.

*At least the man knows the proper way to show deference.*

"Rise," King Wailyn told him and gestured for him to take a seat, "What can I do for you?"

"Thank you, Your Majesty. I'm here with some troubling news, I'm afraid."

"What happened?" the king asked with a
sigh. "Did they not get the goblin army moving
on time?"

"No, Your Majesty. The army started its
march as scheduled and began its conquest.
Much of the area in the northern part of the
kingdom is now completely 'sterilized' as you
put it. The problem was in the south. Our
southern army suffered almost complete
eradication."

"What!" Wailyn screamed as he slammed a
fist into the desk. The crunch of the fine
wood made him wince in regret.

"They encountered resistance in one
village. They destroyed the army and the three
Dark Elves directing them. Some goblins and
orcs escaped, but all the Dark Elves
perished."

"I don't give a damn that some of your
kindred died. I want to know what could've
possibly wiped out an army their size down
there. There's nothing down there worth
catching on fire, much less being useful in
any way."

"I'm told there was a village on the border
of the Forest of Nodara called Alem's Crossing
that was responsible," the messenger told him
with a hint of fear in his voice.

"Alem's Crossing? That place is a squalid
shithole like every other country village. The
army should have been able to walk right over
the place."

"Our reports told us the same, but when the
army arrived, they encountered a village
surrounded by a formidable stone wall. If
accounts are accurate, there was at least one
Dark Elf fighting for the village and even a
Paladin from a God or Goddess other than
ours."

"That's not possible," Wailyn seethed. "We eliminated the worship of the other deities years ago. Do we know which one the Paladin followed?"

"Not sure Your Majesty, but a few of the goblins said they heard the name Lianna mentioned," the messenger reported.

"That sneaky bitch is back again," Wailyn growled. *How'd she sneak a champion into a backwater place like that without anyone noticing?*

"So, a lone Paladin and a Dark Elf with a wall defeated the entire army? That sounds like a terrible excuse for failure."

"Not exactly Your Majesty, they had many defenders manning the wall, and all had weapons and some armor. They also used a lot of magic," he added.

"Look, if you're going to come report a failure at least make your report believable. There aren't that many magic users left, and I work to keep a tight rein on those. They wouldn't even be able to find magic that far away from civilization. Unless… are the Dark Elves betraying our deal! Did they provide the magical training with the fighter you saw?" Wailyn bellowed at the messenger.

The messenger cowered in his seat. "Of course not, Your Majesty. We recognize the actual threat the same as you. That doesn't change that there were confirmed sightings of Earth, Fire, and Water Magic."

"Well, at least the Earth and Fire would explain the appearance of the wall," Wailyn said as he tapped his chin. "But who could've taught them an advanced technique like that? Anything else I need to know?"

The messenger gulped, and Wailyn was immediately sure he wouldn't like the next bit of news.

"There was one other fighter that wasn't a Paladin but sources claim he must've been a Champion. He was the one that killed the three Dark Elves in command of the army. They say he had very unique hair and cast a spell that shouldn't be possible," the messenger drawled.

"Spit it out before I strangle you," King Wailyn warned.

"We think he is a Firebrand," the Dark Elf finished.

"A what?" King Wailyn roared. "I killed that family myself! None of them survived!"

"I do not doubt you, Your Majesty. I'm only reporting what information they gave to me."

King Wailyn sat back in his chair and felt his ears grow hot. His anger bubbled to the surface. They couldn't afford this kind of problem right now. Everything had been steady for so long, this could extinguish their agreement of peace.

"I want you to dedicate your resources to finding and killing that Champion along with the Paladin. I want him destroyed, quietly if possible, before his true heritage becomes common knowledge. The last thing I need is for dragons to return to the kingdom causing trouble. The army failed so try with more finesse this time," he said carefully.

"Of course, Your Majesty. By your leave?" the messenger asked.

"Dismissed."

The messenger darted around the chair and attempted to hide his haste as he reached the door and exited.

*Sniveling cowards. Just do your damn job.*

He leaned back in his chair and drummed his fingers along the desk. Those dragon loving fools almost destroyed this kingdom before with their constant resistance to the Ar'Tookuh. Had they reached an agreement like what was now in place, the fighting could've stopped. That foolish Tristan would've never agreed to the terms since it meant most of the populace would live almost perpetually hungry. *I had to show control over the kingdom somehow.*

Those worthless elves better hurry and fix this problem.

* * *

Arthur walked with Vana to the edge of the village.

"What do you mean, Dark Elves? Are they coming for a fight?"

"I don't think so," Vana intoned with a slight shake of her head.

"So what's the concern?"

"They look lost and hungry. I think they may be refugees from the civil war Allendria spoke of," she said carefully.

"Still not seeing a problem. Sounds like we needed Allendria for this meeting."

"Allendria has been working hard to keep her secret. What happens if refugees arrive and recognize her? Will it cause more problems? I want to go out and talk to them together. They're not far into the forest. I didn't want Allendria here in case they decide to keep traveling. If one of them spots her and tells the wrong people, it could bring even more trouble our way."

Arthur sighed. "Good thinking, but I wish I had my sword. I'll see if I can borrow one from a guard since I don't want to sneak into the inn."

Vana smiled and reached around the edge of the building she stood near. She pulled out a familiar weapon and handed it over.

"I figured you'd want it, so I grabbed it first. I had time to kill since I couldn't find you right away."

Arthur smiled and buckled it across his back.

"Great thinking, let's go."

They both dashed away from the village and continued into the trees. Their journey wasn't too far away, and they traveled swiftly. The entire trip took around an hour with quick breaks to walk and get a sip of water. Vana didn't want to arrive completely exhausted in case they weren't as friendly as she hoped.

"What's the plan?" Arthur asked.

"I was hoping you'd have one? Do we just approach and try to talk to them? Most of them are women and a few children. I only saw a handful of males in the group, and they looked older and a little frail. I'm not sure they could put up much of a fight."

"All right, let's try a straightforward approach for now."

Arthur and Vana walked carefully toward the party of Dark Elves. Arthur felt a little naked without armor on. He still wore his armor leggings and bracers since they were intact, but they destroyed his breastplate and helmet in the fight with Lyrinth. It helped that he planned to do this diplomatically, and the lack of armor would help assert his claim.

They wove through trees until he saw a clearing through the underbrush. Figures moved in the open space, but Arthur couldn't tell what they were doing. He took a deep breath and pushed through the tree line and into the clearing. Before he knew what was happening, two bows pointed in his direction, held by two older Dark Elves.

"What the hell, Vana? I thought you said they were unarmed?" he called over his shoulder.

"I never said they were unarmed, I merely said they only had a handful of Dark Elven males with them."

Arthur rolled his eyes at her smart ass remark and turned back toward the elves.

"Greetings. Does anyone here speak my language?" he asked. The chance he may offend one of them by speaking their language stopped him from trying. It also meant he could eavesdrop on their conversation since they wouldn't expect him to know it. A tense staring contest ensued until one of the older men spoke up.

"I am Daranth, and I can speak your language. What do you want, human?"

"I mean you no harm," Arthur told him while keeping his hands slightly raised and palms facing the elves. "My name is Arthur and I am the mayor of the local village nearby. My head scout Vana," he said with a nod her way, "told me she found you out here and it looked like you may need assistance. I just want to know if there's anything I can do to help."

The two elves lowered their bows with hesitation on their faces. They turned to each other and reverted to their native tongue.

"Are we really considering trusting a human?" Daranth asked.

"Do we have a choice? They are still on our tail and we haven't had any luck losing them," the other man said.

"Do we tell them about the threat? I doubt their village is very big on the edge of their kingdom. The group of Dark Elves after us could probably destroy the entire place," said Daranth.

"I don't see any reason to. It'll give us time to get away if they attack the villagers. There's a better chance our pursuers will avoid the village and not want to draw undue attention. Although, hiding among them may allow us to be invisible to our pursuers," the other added.

Arthur kept a calm smile on his face, even though he wanted to strangle the second elf for his callous remarks about the sacrifice of his own people. He understood there wasn't much trust between the races.

"I believe we don't have any other choice. The women and children," he said back in the common tongue as he nodded toward the group of huddled elves, "need a break and some time to recover."

Arthur nodded agreement. "You're welcome to anything I can offer in the village. Is there anything I need to know since you're out here? Y'all look like you're fleeing something?"

Daranth winced. "Since you are openly accepting us in, I feel obligated to let you know a Dark Elf hunting party is following us. If you wish to change your mind, I understand."

"How many are in the party?" Arthur asked.

Daranth blinked for a moment, taken aback by the question. "Four that I know of."

"Any of them have magic?"

"Only one."

"Okay. Take those with you and head northwest out of the forest. You'll find the village wall when you exit the trees. Approach the gate and ask for Paladin Samson. Tell him Arthur sent you and to provide shelter. Vana and I will take care of your pursuers. We'll catch up if we can prior to you reaching the village."

The elf stared at him, at a loss for words. His mouth moved a few times, but no sound came out. Instead, his attention snapped back to the moment and his face became serious. He nodded once and walked to the rest of the group, ushering the women and children to their feet and giving them directions. The group was back on the move in only a handful of minutes.

"Are you sure about this?" Vana asked as they watched the elves move closer to the village.

"Not at all, but I don't want their pursuers anywhere near the village. You have any of the good arrows left?"

"None of the exploding ones, but I have some of the excellent bodkin ones you gave me."

"Good, use those here. I have no issues claiming the lives of these elves. They're hunting innocents and are scouts for Allendria's Uncle."

Vana nodded and pulled out her bow. She rested an arrow on it and they crept forward. They had no idea how far away the targets were, so he let Vana keep the lead. She was far superior to him with scouting and detecting enemies.

Another two hours into the forest and the light was fading. The thought of hunting Dark Elves in the dark wasn't appealing, but Vana quickly held up her hand and they came to a halt.

She signaled in front of them and Arthur came up side by side with her. In the trees ahead, Arthur could make out four forms walking casually through the forest. They were keeping eyes on the ground and appeared to be looking for tracks.

"How hard can it be to find some women and children? They can't move very fast with the whiny brats with them," one elf grumbled.

"Shut up, this is easy work. We could be keeping the peace at home. All of those damn sycophants of the late king are still causing problems," another answered.

Two held swords, one had a mace, and the final only had a small dagger on his belt. Arthur was willing to bet the one with the dagger was the magic user, so he signaled to Vana that he'd take that target. With the target chosen, he activated the cast time on his Ice Spikes spell. When the spell completed, the shards of ice launched from his hand and hurtled toward his target. They shattered upon contact with the elf and he fell backward to the ground.

*You have dealt 10 HP damage to Dark Elf (1) (Level 18) with Ice Spikes (Barrier).*

The other elves quickly grabbed their weapons and charged toward their position. Vana didn't waste any time, and an arrow zipped across the space and sunk into one of the melee fighter's neck. He grabbed the protruding shaft and fell to the ground with a gurgle.

Arthur slid Ember from its sheath and ran to intercept the other fighters before they could close in on Vana. A sword hurtled for his head and he quickly ducked to the side. The mace of the other elf almost caught him in the jaw, but he picked up Ember and deflected part of the blow, causing it to glance off his unprotected shoulder. Arthur winced through the pain.

*Dark Elf (2) (Level 18) has dealt 20 HP damage to you with Iron Mace (Glancing Blow).*

With a roar of anger, Arthur spun to the side and sent a heavy overhanded counter strike toward the mace wielder. Arthur's face took on a manic look of glee as the elf lifted his mace and attempted to block it with the wooden shaft. Ember sliced cleanly through the shaft and continued to lodge itself into the enemy's face with a wet thump. He fell to the ground, and Arthur's blade slid free.

*You have dealt 200 HP damage to Dark Elf (2) (Level 18) with Ember (Mortal Blow).*

"You bastard!" He heard the other elf yell
as the sword came for him again. A quick jump
backward avoided the blow, but he lost balance
as he landed. The elf was quick to respond and
dashed in with another slice. Arthur blocked
the blow, but it rocked him back further and
he almost fell backward. The elf's sword was
on its way back for Arthur's head again when
an arrow sprouted from his bicep and he
dropped his blade. Arthur didn't waste the
chance and quickly slashed across the neck of
his adversary.

*You have dealt 220 HP damage to Dark Elf
(3) (Level 18) with Ember (Decapitating Blow).*

He turned to see the caster, and Vana
locked in a contest of speed. Vana released
arrows as quickly as she could and the caster
kept erecting some kind of barrier that the
projectiles crashed against. Arthur dashed
toward the caster to get to his side. Before
he reached his intended area, a compact ball
of fire zipped toward him. The trajectory
perfectly aligned with his path, so he dove to
the ground to avoid being set ablaze.
The ball of fire passed over him and he
felt the heat wash past. Jumping back to his
feet, he turned to face the elf. He activated
his Ice Spikes spell again, and the
projectiles launched from him. Instead of
another barrier, the elf responded by blasting
a stream of fire out and melting the missiles.

An arrow flew in and shattered against the barrier he held in place. Splitting his focus between the two of them must be taxing. Arthur couldn't do anything about the barrier because he wasn't familiar with how they worked. What he could do was to drain the caster's mana in a contest of wills. Instead of attacking, Arthur took on a defensive stance with Ember held in a guard position and waited for the caster to make the first move.

As soon as Arthur felt the stirring of the enemies' Fire Magic, he lashed out with his and grasped onto the elf's magic. He poured his focus into the contest and actively fought against the mage as he kept trying to change the pattern of the magic. Instead of trying to overpower Arthur with sheer force like Lyrinth, this mage tried to use finesse and wiggle the spell past. It didn't work.

The drain became increasingly obvious to Arthur as sweat began pouring down the elf's face. He started swaying back and forth and eventually collapsed to one knee while the power faded. Vana prepared to launch her arrow when Arthur held up his hand. He walked up to the elf and kneeled in front of him.

"Why are you pursuing unarmed people?"

"They belong to the king. He ordered us to bring them back."

"Are they servants? How do they belong to the king?" Arthur asked, confused.

"All Dark Elves belong to the king," the man said with a hint of confusion in his eyes.

"Has it always been that way?"

"No," the mage said as he shook his head. "The new king enacted that law. All Dark Elves serve him and belong to him. Those who don't follow reap dire consequences."

"I assume by the new king you're referring to the elf, Glirin?"

The mage's eyes narrowed in suspicion. "How do you know his name? He hasn't been king long enough for those out here to have heard it. Did the scum we're hunting tell you about him?"

Arthur's face grew dark and serious. "Those scum you're chasing are people who have every right to live as the rest. I don't care if they won't bend to the will of some power-hungry tyrant. Unfortunately for you, I can't afford to let you live and reveal what you know."

His hands came up in front of him and he activated a dual cast of Flamethrower directly into the elf. The smell of burning flesh filled the air and Arthur felt sick to his stomach. *I had to do it for the sake of those we found.*

He regained his feet and checked the other dead. They retrieved the elves' weapons to re-forge, and they salvaged some leather armor pieces, but none of them were wearing anything better than common gear. Vana spent a few minutes recovering any serviceable arrows she could find. When the two of them completed their task, they raced for the village.

The trip back took longer than their initial trip. The quickly fading daylight forced them to move slower than before, but they still made decent time and emerged from the tree line just in time to see the Dark Elven refugees cautiously approaching the wall. Guards dotted the gatehouse and Samson stood at the top. His imposing figure was hard to miss. They increased their pace and dashed toward the wall. Arthur didn't want any fighting to break out over the situation. He heard part of the conversation as he approached.

"We were told to search out Paladin Samson," he heard one elf say.

"I'm the Paladin Samson!" called the big man from the wall. "What can I do for you travelers?"

"Arthur told us to find you and ask that we be granted entry to the village," Daranth said.

"What are a bunch of Dark Elves doing this far from your home?" Samson asked.

"They're refugees fleeing their tyrant king!" Arthur yelled up to Samson as they closed the distance.

Samson's gaze swung to Arthur and Vana, and he nodded.

"Welcome back, Lord Mayor. Do you grant permission for them to enter?" Samson asked while gesturing to the crowd.

"Yes, Paladin Samson. They are under the protection of Alem's Crossing and by extension our Lady Lianna."

Samson nodded in reverence and waved a signal to guards behind the door. The creak of the locking timbers rang out, and the gates swung open. Arthur walked forward to stand near Daranth and led them through the gates.

    The Dark Elves looked nervous as they
walked through the gates with so many armed
humans nearby, but they followed Arthur
anyway. When everyone passed the gatehouse,
the doors banged shut, and the bar dropped
into place. Arthur quickly turned to face the
elves.

    "Don't worry. You're not prisoners here and
are free to leave any time you wish. We keep
them closed for the village's safety. If you
decide to move on, just ask a guard to let you
leave. You won't have any trouble. You're
welcome to stay here as long as you need."

    Daranth stepped forward. "Thank you for the
hospitality. Do you have anywhere we can
sleep?"

    "There's an inn in the village that has a
handful of rooms available. I'll put you up at
my expense for those that wish to stay, but
there aren't enough rooms for all of you,"
Arthur said as he took on a thoughtful
expression.

    "I have a sizable house I could let you all
stay in that would accommodate most of you. It
doesn't have any furniture yet, but we may be
able to scrounge up enough blankets for you to
all be comfortable."

    "I can't thank you enough, if there is
anyth…"

    "Arthur! Where the hell did you run off to
this evening? I thought you were supposed to
be returning to the inn much sooner than yo…"
Allendria started as she ran up to them. When
she spotted the people arranged with him, she
stopped dead in her tracks. Her eyes filled
with tears as she spoke.

    "Daranth? You're okay?"

"Princess Allendria," Daranth choked out as
he fell to his knees weeping. "We thought you
were dead."

She walked forward and laid a hand on the
older man's shoulder. "I'm sorry I had to flee
as I did. I couldn't risk telling anyone where
I was going. Not even you, old friend. Is my
father truly gone?" she asked quietly.

"He is. I'm so sorry," he said with a bowed
head.

She shook the tears from her eyes and
grabbed his shoulders.  "Stand up, my friend.
You don't have to kneel before me here."

He got back to his feet and looked around
in confusion, "How'd you end up in a village
of humans? They aren't holding you captive,
are they?"

She laughed. "No, my friend. As a matter of
fact, Arthur saved my life when I fled from
home and I've stayed here and made new
friends. This place is becoming a haven for
all kinds of people."

Allendria and Daranth were discussing the
state of things in their home when Samson
shuffled up beside Arthur.

"Uh… Princess?" he asked, confused.

"Yeah. Just found out about it at the
battle. Lyrinth let the cat out of the bag and
revealed it. Her father was the king and was
overthrown and murdered by her Uncle Glirin.
That was why she fled in the first place,"
Arthur explained.

"And you didn't tell me?"

"Sorry. It wasn't my secret to tell. She's been struggling with the two of us knowing as it is. I figured she'd tell you when she was comfortable," Arthur said as he scanned the area, "Make sure you keep the guards clear of them for now. They seem to be sticking to their posts, but I don't want anyone overhearing her true title."

"Will do," Samson nodded, and then his eyes narrowed, "and what do you mean by the two of us?"

"Vana was there and heard Lyrinth during the fight. She knows."

"Ah, makes sense. You three were in the thick of it during that fight. What are you going to do with them now?"

Arthur sighed, "I'll get them settled into rooms at the inn and give the rest my new house to stay in for now."

"You have fun with that. I'm gonna volunteer for a longer shift at the wall to avoid that headache. I'll see you later," Samson said with a clap on the shoulder and a chuckle.

The group wandered into the village with Arthur leading the way. It took some time, but Arthur got sleeping arrangements set up for all of them. Daniel put up as many as he could comfortably fit in the inn and helped gather blankets from those who could spare them. Arthur took careful note of those who donated to the cause and resolved to make it up to them somehow.

The remaining elves approached his new home with wonder on their faces. When he led them inside, they couldn't believe their eyes. Daranth was one who volunteered to shelter in the home, thinking it would be far less comfortable than the inn.

"This is your home? It is marvelous. It must have taken countless hours to complete such fine stonework. I can't even see the seams. Did you have dwarven workers construct this?" Daranth asked.

"Uh… I started building this a couple days ago. It's not quite done yet, but getting close. I've also never met a dwarf, so they had no hand in it."

Daranth walked to the nearest wall and felt along the construction. "You built this with magic?"

"Yes, I did. I've been working diligently to use magic to improve our village. The wall outside the village is also fairly new. My goal is to use some of the features in this house as an example of the houses we plan to build in the future," Arthur explained.

"Who would've thought humans were capable of this level of magic? I wasn't aware any of your kind even understood the skill of mixing magic anymore."

"As far as I know there aren't many, but I haven't met many other humans here personally. All that said, I'm afraid there isn't much in the way of furniture, thus the blankets. I'll do my best to see if we can enlist some crafters to do that work before long. If you wish to stay you're welcome to. As I said earlier though, you are all free to leave at any time, you only have to ask a guard to let you out of the gate. I'll have Daniel provide any food you need. We passed the local well on the way here for water. If you need anything else, let me know. Allendria can help if you can't find me."

"Young man," Daranth whispered, "I appreciate all you've done for us, but I noticed the looks the Princess sends your way. I don't object to it, but please be aware many of my kind frown upon that interaction between the races. Some may even take it as a personal insult. I tell you this because she seems truly happy for the first time in as long as I can remember. You take care of her or you'll answer to me," he finished with a grim tone.

"I swear it," Arthur intoned seriously.

"I'll get this lot taken care of. You need your rest. Goodnight, Lord Mayor."

Arthur smiled and turned to walk away. He waved back over his shoulder. "Still just Arthur," he reminded the elf.

# Chapter 26

*Unexpected Value*

Arthur spent the next morning at the blacksmith shop. He diligently worked to convert the iron ingots the apprentices made into steel. They'd used the last week wisely and actively salvaged all the metal from the battle. The task took a long time, but it was good to feel the heat from the forge. The monotonous work calmed him.

The most surprising turn of events was Balair. He used the morning to work alongside Arthur in companionable silence. Since he could use Arthur's spells and was proficient enough in the required magics, he also spent his time converting iron into steel.

A chipper Rayne approaching interrupted his work. The youthful man watched with awe as the magic worked across the metal. Arthur let him watch the show for a few pieces and finally turned to address him.

"What's up, Rayne?"

"First off, that was awesome. Magic is still new to me, but I'll be damned if that wasn't amazing. I came looking for you to fulfill a bargain," Rayne said in excitement.

"A bargain? What do you mean?"

"Wow, forgot already? The terms of our deal. You teach me how to use my magic and one magical skill, and I teach you Air Magic. I'm also finally level seven in Earth Magic so I can learn the spell you discovered as well."

"Oh, sounds great." Arthur spent a few minutes picking up the metal and stacking it near Balair.

*You got the rest of these?*

*Yeah, I'll do it,* the dragon grumbled.

*Outstanding work so far. Happy to see you doing your part.*

Balair merely huffed and went back to his work. Arthur turned to Rayne.

"Let's go find a suitable place in the shade."

They walked to a nearby tree and sheltered under its branches. The midday sun wasn't terrible, but sitting in it for a prolonged amount of time would burn.

Once seated, Rayne reached out his hand and Arthur laid his on the palm. Arthur smiled as the man had the forethought to split the power as he taught him. Arthur was quick on the uptake and had all three bands together within an hour. Once Rayne showed him the way they flowed together, it was only another twenty minutes to complete the skill.

*Congratulations, you have learned Air Magic for a 100 experience bonus.*

"Fantastic. Thanks for that," Arthur told Rayne.

The young man merely shook his head. "I can't believe how fast you did that. It took me what feels like forever to make that work. I admit your method of teaching makes it much faster, though."

"I assume your haste spell is just you channeling the Air Magic in the direction of your movements as you travel?" Arthur asked.

"Sort of. I actually wrap my limbs in a continuous flow of Air Magic and move the air at the same time I move my body. It took me a while to get working originally. You have to get the timing down right or you'll slow yourself down," Rayne explained.

Arthur smiled. "You don't say. Care to demonstrate? Can you cast your haste spell?"

Rayne stood still for a couple of moments and then dashed off. Arthur watched him run at top speed for a moment before he lashed out toward Rayne with his Air Magic. He began his continuous flow of air on Rayne's limbs but, to his amazement, Rayne sped up even more. Realizing the problem, Arthur directed the flow of air to wrap his limbs in the mana flowing the opposite direction. He quickly pushed against the body parts as Rayne traveled, and he watched the young thief slow down and look around in confusion. With his pictured effect actively working, he released the flow of the magic. The spell prompt he expected showed up.

*Congratulations, you have discovered the Air Magic Spell: Weak Slow. You have gained 250 experience in Air Magic for discovering a known spell.*

*You have gained 90 experience in Air Magic for successfully casting Weak Slow.*

| Spell: Weak Slow | |
|---|---|
| Requirements: Air Magic<br>Mana Cost: 45 MP<br>Cast Time: 3 seconds<br>Duration: 30 seconds | Description: This spell wraps the target's limbs in air and forcibly slows their movement speed by 15%. |
| Mastery Level: 1 | |

Rayne's look of confusion was comical, but Arthur explained what he'd done and how Rayne could do the same. Agreeing to be the guinea pig, Arthur jogged around the clearing until Rayne wrapped his limbs correctly and learned the Weak Slow spell himself. Rayne looked like a kid in a candy store with his quickly expanding magical knowledge. Arthur also took the time to learn the haste spell on his own and ensured he kept the power channeled for a longer period. He wanted the base time on his to last longer.

*Congratulations, you have discovered the Air Magic Spell: Weak Haste. You have gained 250 experience in Air Magic for discovering a known spell.*

*Congratulations, you have reached level 2 in Air Magic. Air Magic spells now have a 3% increased effect. Finally got the last one. Took you long enough.*

*You have gained 90 experience in Air Magic for successfully casting Weak Haste.*

| Spell: Weak Haste | |
|---|---|
| Requirements: Air Magic<br>Mana Cost: 45 MP<br>Cast Time: 4 seconds<br>Duration: 3 minutes | Description: This spell wraps the target's limbs in air and increases their movement speed by 15%. |
| Mastery Level: 1 | |

The leveling prompt of his Air Magic reminded him of something he'd been actively avoiding. His personal level was high enough to try for his first combat class. Now that he obtained Air Magic, gaining the necessary levels in the skill would be a simple task. The combat class was his last true hurdle to renewing the Soul Bond.

If he was being honest with himself, he could complete the skill challenge in a matter of days. The combat class would be the true test. He wanted the village in order before he embarked on the quest. Arthur resolved to discuss the matter with Allendria later that day.

A quick review of the quest showed him he was short two levels in Water Magic and eight in Air Magic. Since he only needed to reach level ten, that would take less than a day if he dedicated most of his mana to it.

"…never thought I'd be part of this," Rayne finished.

Arthur looked at him in confusion before he realized he had missed the rest of the conversation because of his internal conflict.

"Sorry, what was that?"

"I just never expected this big of a change when I accepted the quest from the Goddess Lianna. So far, I'm not disappointed, though."

"Glad to hear it. Are your people finding their way in the village now?" Arthur asked.

"Yeah. Many of them already have working positions. Some haven't been able to accomplish much. This place being so small makes it difficult to put their skills to use."

"What skills are we not utilizing?" Arthur asked.

"I'm not sure about all of them. I know we had a cartwright in the group who has no facilities to use here. There were also some chandlers, but no raw resources around here that I'm aware of."

"The cartwright is a position that doesn't do us much good at the moment. I'm not interested in traveling as a noble. Sadly, the chandler is about as useful still. I'm planning to use magic to change home lighting instead of the smelly tallow candles many of them make. I could offer to retrain them in the alternative method once I develop it. Would give them a viable job and save me a lot of time constantly making items," Arthur said thoughtfully.

"I'll leave those decisions to you. Most of the people are finding use with their skills. I'll admit, I'd like the chance to work on my Alchemy some," Rayne said.

"Why don't you?"

"Don't have the supplies or the tools. The drying racks for the herbs and the box to heat them in are essential to getting the maximum amount of potency. Some simpler potions I can make with nothing more than a grindstone and a bowl, but having real glass vials would be a lifesaver. Also, it's hard to carry a bowl into battle."

Arthur considered the problem. The boxes he referred to must be like a smoker on Earth. The drying racks he could get a general idea of since he knew the herbs needed to lie flat to dry.

"Can you draw?"

"A little. It's not very good," Rayne admitted.

Arthur led Rayne back to the blacksmith and a workbench. He fished out a small piece of coal and a scrap of old leather.

"Draw what you can remember of the drying racks and the boxes. Anything you don't think you can draw, try to explain to me how it looked," Arthur told him.

They spent the next half hour going over designs and discussing what the equipment should look like and how it worked. Arthur grasped the concept of both without too much trouble. When he was confident he knew what they should look like and how they worked, he tossed some steel into the forge. His spell activated, and the metal took shape. The drying rack materialized as a metal book. The book had thin metal pages made of small bands of wire mesh. The point was to ensure air could flow through the entire rack while it sandwiched herbs between the pages.

The process was similar for the drying box. He created it almost identical to a barbeque pit on Earth with a tiny firebox on the side and a larger box to hold the racks. He sized it to hold two of the racks at one time, so Arthur made Rayne a total of four racks. This would allow him to have two racks curing while he loaded the next two racks for use. Switching them out would be quick and easy.

Rayne profusely thanked Arthur for helping him get his work back on track. Arthur told him to speak with Daniel or Katherine about any herbs he could use. He also reminded him about putting the work orders to good use. Rayne was frantic with joy and ran off with the first two drying racks, headed for his camp. The man would need to make a few trips to haul the items.

With his own advice in mind, Arthur realized he hadn't been using the work orders to their full potential either. He created and turned in a work order for the armor, amulets, and the steel ingots. He inspected the experience totals for his day so far. Instead of breaking them down by individual turn ins, he had the information show totals for each skill.

*You have gained 11,800 total experience in Earth and Fire Magic.*

*You have gained 28,740 total experience in Arcane Smithing and Blacksmithing.*

*Congratulations, you have reached level 17 in Blacksmithing. You are granted a 48% bonus to forging speed. You need more hobbies.*

*Congratulations, you have reached level 17 in Arcane Smithing. Increases the stats on items created using this ability by 32%. More necklaces?*

*You have gained 14,040 total experience in Enchanting.*

*Congratulations, you have reached level 15 in Enchanting. Your enchantments have a 42% decreased mana cost. Power can corrupt.*

*You have gained 7,200 total experience in Jeweler.*

*Congratulations, you have reached levels 8, and 9 in Jeweler. Increases the stats on Jewelry you make by 16%. Pretty baubles.*

*You have gained 10,870 total experience.*

*Congratulations, you have reached level 21! You now have 5 available skill points. Just keep swimming.*

It wasn't a bad haul, considering it took into account all his work orders and the finished armor pieces. He dropped two points into Strength bringing it to an even 20 and another two into Agility lifting that to 30. His last point went to Intellect, making it 33.

Since he did his work here for the day, he went to check on the new Dark Elf host within the walls. His trip led him to his newly constructed house but, as he arrived, the sight greeting him shocked him.

Out in front of the building, elves lined the road, and all worked on a large assortment of wood pieces. Arthur couldn't guess where the wood came from, but he watched in fascination as they took small knives and furiously removed strips of wood from their individual projects.

A glance toward the opening showed some basic furniture pieces stacked inside the building. A couple of chairs and a low bed frame sat just inside the door. Rowan and Allendria stood nearby in conversation, so Arthur joined them.

"What's going on here?" Arthur asked.

"The elves wanted to help. I don't think I've told you before, but Dark Elves are pretty efficient with woodworking. Since this place is lacking in furniture, they wanted to put their skills to good use," Allendria explained.

Arthur nodded at the explanation and glanced at Rowan. "I guess you're responsible for their tools?"

Rowan smiled and nodded, "Allendria asked me about it last night so I worked early this morning to finish and bring them over."

"Explains why I haven't seen you at your shop all morning," Arthur said to Rowan before an idea struck him and he turned to Allendria, "do any of the people here know Earth Magic?"

"I'm sure some do. Magic isn't uncommon with Dark Elves. I know Daranth has Earth Magic. I can't be certain about the others. Why?" she asked slightly confused at the turn in the conversation.

"I might teach them magical woodworking. If they wish to contribute, we could use their help to get this done faster. When the construction crews get moving full speed, we'll need a lot of furniture to complete these places. We also need wooden doors for the buildings. I can teach them a much faster way to do it with Earth Magic."

"Something else you discovered on your own, huh?" Rowan asked, barely surprised.

"Kinda. We use a similar method where I'm from, but with machines instead. I just used magic to do the same thing. Turns out, it works."

"Of course you did," Allendria said with a sigh, "but why would you give up that information? You don't know these people?"

"Honestly? Convenience. No matter how many of these skills I find or learn, I'll never have enough time to do everything. Even with an infinite pool of mana, it's still not possible. I want everyone to feel welcome here, but I also want them to contribute toward the betterment of the village. It's one of the largest and most time-consuming aspects of the village and is one less thing I'd have to worry about."

"Seems like a lot of trust for people you don't know. Especially since they could take the new skill and just leave," Rowan mused.

"That's why I want to teach it to Daranth and let him and Allendria decide if others should learn this skill. I think Daranth will prefer to stay here with Allendria in residence, or do I miss my guess," he asked Allendria with a smile.

She took on a loving glow. "I think he'll stay with me. He's been a dear friend for most of my life. I almost regretted leaving him more than I did my own father."

Arthur nodded. "Thought as much. I'll let him decide, but I won't impose contracts on the Dark Elves. I don't want them beholden to a human city in any way. That could cause long-reaching repercussions if I'm correct?"

Allendria looked thoughtful for a few moments before nodding. "That would probably cause issues."

"Well, short of a trade treaty or diplomatic alliance, I don't see any way to hold them accountable without jeopardizing our position. Unless… you do it, Allendria!" Arthur nearly shouted.

"Yep, you lost me. I was following your trail of thought and then got lost in the brush," Allendria said, confused.

"Well, you *are* the Princess of the Dark Elves correct?" Arthur asked.

"Yes," she answered hesitantly.

"I'm sorry to say this so bluntly, but with your father gone doesn't this make you the Queen?"

"No," she said with a shake of her head, "a council appoints the king or queen from the available candidates."

"Well, dang. Do you lose your title as Princess?" Arthur asked.

"No. That's a title from birth."

"Well, are Princesses allowed to negotiate deals on behalf of their people?" Arthur asked.

Allendria yet again sunk into thought. It took her longer to reply this time. "Technically, yes. It's only happened a few times that I can recall."

"So, we can have you and I come to an agreement of terms for service. I'll offer to train those who wish to take up the position of magical carpenter, and in return, they'll provide their labor to build furniture for the village with materials supplied by the village. We'll pay them a fair wage and provide housing. In return, they agree to stay for a one-year contract term and are free to go after," Arthur explained.

"That is…" she began, "actually, that could work. It would separate the two nations, but still solve both problems."

"How about we discuss the idea with Daranth?" Arthur suggested.

She nodded and smiled. "That sounds great. He'll know the best way to do something like this. He was an advisor for part of his life."

"You two have fun. I'm headed back to the forge to get some work done. I've been wasting time most of the morning," Rowan told them with a wave.

"See you later. Everyone needs a break from time to time," Arthur told him as he left.

Arthur and Allendria approached Daranth and motioned for him to join them in a private conversation. When the older elf approached, Arthur broached the subject.

"I've been discussing an idea with Allendria this morning and we want to get your input on it. First, though, do you have Earth Magic?" Arthur asked.

"I'm fairly proficient in it," Daranth said amusedly.

Arthur assumed that meant the older man was a high level.

"Judging by the work I see around here, I guess you're also a Woodworker. Would you be interested in becoming an Arcane Woodworker?"

"I never picked up the skill for Fire Magic so…" Daranth began before he caught himself and narrowed his eyes, "How do you know about the arcane crafting skills?"

"Arthur's an Arcane Smith and an Arcane Woodworker already," Allendria mentioned in an off-handed manner.

Daranth's gaze swung from him to Allendria and back again.

"How?" was the only word he could get out.

"I come from another land and figured out both of them," was the only explanation Arthur gave.

Arthur could tell Daranth didn't quite believe his story, but the older man didn't press the point.

"Fine. Now what's your proposal?" Daranth asked in resignation.

Arthur and Allendria spent some time detailing out their thoughts. Daranth listened carefully and slowly nodded along. By the time they finished explaining, Daranth looked excited at the prospect.

"That could work. It will also be an excellent way for you to establish some independence here. I'd make one suggestion to go with it," Daranth told them.

"What is it?" Arthur asked.

"Build a diplomatic building for the Dark Elves here. You could even have this new building contain the living quarters of the elves who wish to take your offer. I'd suggest building it farther away from the village, though. If this place grows as you suggested, you may see an influx of elves, and having a section of the city dedicated to elven society would make others feel more at home."

"That's a fantastic idea." Arthur beamed. "We could set up an official Elven Quarter in the city and use the Embassy as the central building. You could even have the elves who stay in residence set up shops in the area. I also want to ensure that the elves can work on their own personal projects and sell them at their own prices so long as they didn't get the materials from the village. It'll give the people a chance to live a semi-normal life."

"Another good suggestion. I'd like to be the first to take your offer and learn this new skill. It sounds intriguing and with my years in politics, I can see your purpose behind it," he told Arthur with a wink. "Never enough time in the day to do it all, is there?"

Arthur chuckled at the clever elf and realized he was growing fond of him. He wouldn't wait for the official agreement and instead accepted Daranth at his word for now. He'd make sure the paperwork was in order for the rest of them, but Allendria could personally vouch for Daranth, so that was good enough.

He spent the next hour showing Daranth the way to control the sand in the earth and explained how the coarseness of the sand was used to smooth the wood. Daranth nodded like he already knew that, and Arthur assumed he did, truth be told. When Arthur activated his Cone of Sanding, the elf looked less than impressed.

"It's just a small whirlwind of sand?" he asked in confused tones.

"It may look like that but I have it solidified and spinning at high speeds. Watch this," Arthur said as he lifted a nearby stick and slowly fed it through the cone. As it emerged from the other side, he heard a gasp from Daranth. The finished piece floated over to him with his power, and he handed Daranth the perfectly smooth and straight piece of wood.

The elf ran his hands over the piece and marveled at it.

"That would have taken countless hours of work with a knife to trim that down to this size and we wouldn't have ever gotten the finished product this smooth," Daranth admitted.

Arthur spent the next few hours working with Daranth on forming the spell and unlocking his new Arcane Woodworking. Seeing the sheer childish glee on the older man's face was enough for him to know when he succeeded. He also showed the elf the Sanding Wheel spell and demonstrated how he could adjust the size of both spells to make rods of any size or cut small grooves into wood with the wheel. Judging by the fire in Daranth's eyes, the man was about to embark on a mission of crafting excellence.

Arthur and Allendria bid Daranth farewell as the sun fell and returned to the inn. They noticed Balair over by an empty corner booth, so they sat at the table near him. He informed Arthur that he finished the steel he left for him. Arthur thanked him for his loyal service and waved down Kat as she rushed by. The woman approached in a hurry.

"What can I do for you?" she asked in a slightly tense voice.

"Ouch, Kat, what's wrong?"

"I'm running so many ways trying to take care of problems that I honestly don't know anymore. I knew this job would be demanding but I didn't think it would require this much time. Hard to believe we just had the feast yesterday," she said with a dazed look in her eyes.

"Uh… Kat, that wasn't yesterday. That was days ago. Are you even sleeping?" Arthur asked in concern.

"I don't remember," she answered in confusion.

"Sit down over here," Arthur said as he motioned for a seat next to him. The frazzled woman mechanically obeyed.

"I need you to listen to me for a minute. Forget anything you currently have to do," he began.

"But I can't. So many people need stuff and I keep trying to make sure I take care of everything as you asked," she interrupted.

"Stop," Arthur told her forcefully, and she closed her mouth. "The only thing you'll do is go to your room and sleep. If I see you out of your room before tomorrow morning, I'll personally carry you to your room and have Balair block the door for an entire day. When you wake up in the morning, I need to meet with you. We need to draw up some documents for the village. After that, you will find at least one but possibly two others to be your assistants. It's obvious you need help with your tasks. I wish you'd come to me sooner."

He immediately felt guilty about that statement. Her stress was evident and had he not been in his melancholy state for so long, he might have noticed. Truth be told, he forgot about Kat most of the time and that just wouldn't do.

"Take care of yourself tonight. Anything you need to do can wait. Until you do as I've said, you're not allowed to work on anything for the village," Arthur told her sternly.

Small tears formed in her eyes as she got to her feet. She looked like a zombie as she half stumbled up the stairs to do as she was told.

# Chapter 27

*Classes*

Arthur and Allendria finished up their meal and took a quick dip in the bathhouse. Cleaning the sweat from the day always refreshed him, and the bonus experience from the bathhouse made it a necessity. When they returned to the inn and their room, Arthur sat with her on the bed. Since the battle with Lyrinth, Arthur avoided the topic but decided now was the time he needed to approach it.

"Allendria?"

"Yeah?"

"What do you know about classes?" Arthur asked.

"That's an odd question to ask. You already have a few of them yourself."

"No, combat classes."

"Oh, probably about the same as you. I know you need level 20, and they're triggered by the class menu. I'm not entirely sure which choice to make. I keep looking through the options but can't decide. I still think the Spell Blade is your best option, though."

"So, you've hit twenty as well?" Arthur asked.

"Sure did. Samson and Vana are also twenty. The raid did a number for our experience, and we've been grinding out work orders while you've been out of it, building up experience. I believe Rayne is also close to twenty."

"Well, damn, so what do these quests entail?"

"The hell if I know. It's different for every class. Have you not read your class menu yet?"

He opened his mouth to respond and closed it again and shook his head.

"Well, look it over before you ask questions."

Arthur nodded and focused inward. He thought Class Menu, and a message appeared in his vision.

*Congratulations, you've reached the milestone level to get your first combat class. You'll be given a list of options that reflect the skills you currently have. Picking a class to work toward will result in a quest or questline that will reward the class at the end. Each class has some basic information about their specific quest in the menu, but you won't know the full detail unless you accept the class quest.*

*You may only have one active class quest at a time. After you've unlocked your first combat class, you're eligible to find rare classes on your own. You can also attempt to gain another class through quests every ten levels.*

| Class Menu | |
|---|---|
| Current Class Quests: | Classes you're Eligible for:<br><br>• Spell Blade<br>• Water Shaper<br>• Terraformer<br>• Pyromaniac<br>• Frost Mage<br>• Rogue<br>• Ranger |

| | • Volley Veteran |
| --- | --- |
| Combat Class Bonuses:<br>• None | |
| Current Combat Classes:<br>• None | |

*Guess Allendria was right. This is pretty self-explanatory.* Looking at the menu options, he saw the classes he was eligible for. They made sense with the skills he had. This menu seemed to focus purely on combat skills, so it represented none of his crafting skills. He was sure he could switch the menu if he wanted but had no need.

Out of the options listed, he found the Spell Blade class the most intriguing. He could determine precisely what the other classes were about. Allendria told him what to expect from the Spell Blade class, and he thought it fit perfectly. He focused on that option, and another prompt appeared.

*To obtain the Spell Blade class, you must embark on a quest of mystery and danger. Enemies will be abundant. Recommended party size: 5.*

Based on what Allendria said. That was the extent of the information he would get until he accepted the quest. His attention returned to Allendria and his surroundings in the room.

"So a party quest of five people, huh? I wonder if it's another dungeon, like the beast one," Arthur said wistfully.

"Possibly, but no way to know. I looked over my options while you looked through yours and think I've decided. I plan to accept the quest for Pyromaniac. Fire is usually my best spell anyway," Allendria told him.

"Good to know. We should talk to the others in the morning. I'd like to ask Samson, Vana, and even Rayne about it. I think it's almost time for us to embark on some class quests. Hopefully, all of our quests will lead somewhere nearby. I'd hate for all of us to accept quests, and they all be in different directions. That'd take forever to do them."

"From what I've heard, most parties who embark on class quests can have all of their quests in a centralized location as long as they accept their quests while they're together."

"I hope that's true. We should all make preparations for our class quests. I want to see how far Rayne needs to go. If he's close, we can spend a few days letting him get the experience he needs before leaving together. I'd feel better having him around anyway," Arthur confessed.

"Sounds good to me. Let's deal with that in the morning, though. In the meantime," she said as she leaned forward to press her lips to his. He wrapped her in his arms, and they fell back on the bed together.

* * *

The following morning at breakfast, Arthur and Allendria sat downstairs for breakfast with Balair snuggled in the room's corner. There was a good crowd in the inn, and Arthur even spotted some of the Dark Elf refugees eating in there. They sat secluded together in the corner, but progress was progress.

Katherine met them for breakfast, and she looked infinitely better. She'd taken the time to fix her appearance and didn't look nearly as disheveled as she had the last couple of times Arthur saw her. She took a seat next to them and ate in silence. When they all finished, she looked at Arthur.

"Thanks," she said simply.

"No. I'm sorry," Arthur responded. "I should've seen what was happening to you and intervened sooner. You look refreshed this morning, though."

She nodded agreement at the statement. "Much better. What did you need me to help with this morning?"

Arthur and Allendria detailed out their plan with the Dark Elves, and she nodded along. She had her notebook out, jotting down details as they recited them. The only part that gave Arthur pause was when he had to detail his and Allendria's true identity to Kat. After seeing her dedication to her job and how close she'd come to doing serious harm to herself, he had no qualms in filling her in.

"How is that possible?" she hissed through clenched teeth.

"Long story. Don't really have the time to fill you in. Needless to say, it *is* true. Can you draw up the necessary documents for this agreement? As you can imagine, we need it kept quiet from the general populace."

Kat nodded furiously. "I'll write it up. I've dealt with some official documents before. When I have the paperwork complete, I'll let you know so you can both sign it and make it official."

"That's great," Allendria told her with a smile.

The woman practically leaped to her feet and barely stopped herself from bowing to both of them before she turned and scurried away.

"Hopefully, she remembers to find some assistants afterward," Arthur said with a sigh.

The three of them left the inn and walked to the blacksmith shop. Luckily, Rowan and Samson were both there.

"Mornin' fellas. Either of you seen Rayne or Vana?" Arthur asked as they approached.

"Haven't seen Rayne this morning, but Vana was at Bastion," Samson told him.

"Bastion? What's that? Is there a landmark I don't know about here?" Arthur asked, confused.

Samson chuckled. "No. That's what people call the northeastern gate. Its defense against two different forces gave it that particular moniker."

"Huh, well, it fits."

"Anything specific you need from them?" Rowan asked.

"Actually, I want to speak with those two and Samson," Arthur said as he turned to the Paladin. "It's time to discuss our class quest."

Samson's back went rigid, and he took on the guise of a professional soldier. "I'm glad you brought it up. I've been itching to come up with a plan. The quest I wish to undertake requires a party of five."

"Almost seems ordained," Arthur said wistfully with a look to the sky. "The quest that Allendria and I wish to undertake has the same requirement. I know Vana is high enough to earn her class, and I've been told Rayne is close if not already there. I'd like the five of us to make a plan and set a time."

"I'll walk with you. Let's go round everyone up so we can discuss it," Samson agreed.

"What about me? I get left in the dark here?" Rowan asked.

"You hit level twenty?" Arthur asked.

"Yeah. All those work orders add up over time."

"I'd love to help you out, but you do little fighting. You're far more valuable in the forge, Rowan. If you feel it necessary, we can work on yours at a later time," Arthur said in soothing tones.

"Yeah, guess you're right. Go have fun. I'll keep things running in the interim."

"Good man," Arthur called over his shoulder as the group walked to the gate. Balair got tired of the trip and leaped into the air. His patience was always short. Arthur told him he'd let him know when they found everyone.

Vana was easy to spot when they reached Bastion. She was consulting with James and Zeke near the gate.

"The ever valiant Ranger core. How are you guys holding up?" Arthur asked.

"Can't complain too much," Zeke said with a wave.

"Been pretty quiet," James told them.

Arthur spotted a rope with a few birds hanging from it slung over James's back.

"You guys doing some hunting?" Allendria asked.

"Pulled in a few so far in the woods. Nothing else roaming around. How're your fellow elves holding up?" Zeke asked.

"They're doing well. Looks like a few may be interested in staying in the village as carpenters."

"That's delightful news. Furniture is becoming a pressing issue with all the new bodies we gained. When the weather changes, the lack of housing will be rough," Vana mumbled.

"I'm working on that. The house I recently built is a design I'll have the construction crews start replicating as soon as the wall is complete. I'll have them make them as fast as they can and stick to a similar design for all of them. I have some improvements I can add to them later, but the basic house will work for now," Arthur told them.

"At least someone has a plan. You didn't come all the way out here to discuss housing and birds, though. Did you need me for something?" Vana asked.

"Actually, we do," Samson said. "We need to go round up Rayne, though. It's time we discuss our class quests."

Vana didn't bother arguing and just nodded her head. The group bid their farewells to James and Zeke and walked for the refugee area of the village. It took some questioning, but someone finally directed them to Rayne.

Arthur found the young man dutifully tending the drying box he made for him and asked Balair to join them. Old bowls lay scattered around, and a cracked pestle and mortar sat on a makeshift table. When they approached, Rayne didn't notice them until they were almost on top of him. His surprise was evident as he stumbled backward and nearly lost his footing.

"Arthur, Lady Allendria, Paladin Samson, and Ranger Vana, what do I owe the pleasure of your company?" he said formally, trying to recover from his surprise.

"I appreciate the tone but drop the titles. We're just regular people," Samson said with a chuckle.

"I'm also not a Ranger… yet," Vana added with a gleam in her eye.

"Sorry to appear so abruptly, but we wanted to talk to you about something," Arthur told him in a serious tone.

"Um, all right, did I do something wrong?" he asked as he scanned his surroundings.

The group laughed.

"Quite the opposite, we're here to discuss class quests. We believe you may be close to being eligible and wanted to plan a time to do the quests together," Allendria told him.

Rayne glanced back toward the small tent behind him. "I'm not sure I can leave for a quest."

The tent flap rustled, and a small figure stepped out.

"Who are these people?" the young girl asked with wide eyes.

"Libby, this is the Mayor of the village, Arthur. Beside him is the Lady Allendria, the Paladin Samson, and an archer, Vana," Rayne told the girl as he pointed to each one.

"Oh, thank you so much for helping us and letting us stay here," she said to the group. "Are they friends of yours?" she asked, swinging her attention back to Rayne.

"Sure are. Why don't you run and help Tina?" Rayne suggested.

Libby nodded and dashed off across the camp. Arthur caught Rayne's eyes for a moment and nodded to him.

"Hey guys, can you give Rayne and me a moment to talk before we get this conversation going?" Arthur asked the group.

They nodded agreement, and Arthur and Rayne walked to a more secluded area of the camp.

"I'm assuming you're somehow responsible for her? Is she why you were saying you couldn't leave?" Arthur asked, getting straight to the point.

"Yeah," Rayne breathed. His face played out a war of emotions that Arthur couldn't quite pinpoint. It took some time, but he eventually continued.

"You've done nothing but help me so far, and honestly, being alone for so long has been rough. Can I trust you to keep the information I tell you secret?" Rayne asked.

"You've held my secret without a word, and besides, you saved my life. It's a debt I'm not sure I can ever repay."

Rayne nodded. "Libby is my sister. We grew up with an abusive father. Eventually, both he and our mother passed away. We moved to Seora and found a great couple who became the family we never had. They died during the city riots. She's experienced more sadness and loss than anyone her age should have to endure. My one goal in life is to do anything I have to so I can keep her safe."

"I'm sorry, Rayne," Arthur said with remorse in his voice, "Loss is always hard. I'm glad she has you to look after her, but I'm also worried about you now. You know exactly who I really am. You know what's eventually coming here, and yet you stayed. Why?"

"Before we fled to Seora, I worked for a group in Esmere. We were actually a rebel force trying to fight back against the evil of King Wailyn and his cronies. We were actually a secret organization established under your parents' rule, known as the Shadows of the Flame. That was how I knew about your heritage. An unfortunate incident on a mission one night was how I gained my power. Long story short, I was already on the path to the same cause you stand for. Your presence just breathed life back into my purpose. I hate these corrupt fools and love what you're doing here. I'd do anything to give this life to Libby instead."

"Esmere? That's the capital city where King Wailyn lives, right?" Arthur asked.

"Yeah," Rayne answered, slightly confused.

"I think if you wish to protect her and give her this way of life, you must come with us. My presence will only go undetected for so long before more people come for us. The enemies are sure to be stronger each time until we can finally unseat Wailyn. We need you with us," Arthur said as he extended his hand.

Rayne stared at Arthur for a few long moments before he reached out and clasped his hand. "Hard to argue with the inevitable."

With the group back together, Arthur started off the discussion. "I plan on going for the class of Spell Blade. My quest says I need a party of five to complete. What does everyone else plan to do?"

Allendria jumped in next and told everyone she planned on Pyromaniac. Samson announced he was going for the class of Defender, and it also required a party of five. Vana chose Ranger, which also needed a party of five. All heads turned to Rayne to see what his decision was.

"I don't know what class I'll try for yet. I'm only level 19," he told them.

"No big deal. How far are you from twenty?" Arthur asked.

"I'm almost halfway there."

"That shouldn't take long. You think you could do it in a week?" Arthur asked.

"A week? Are you kidding me? I'd have to spend almost every day hunting animals in the forest for that much experience, and that's only if I'm lucky."

Arthur chuckled. "I guess you haven't discovered work orders yet?"

"What?" Rayne asked.

"You're officially a villager. Think *Village Menu* and see what pops up," Arthur told him.

Rayne took on a farseeing look, and his mouth hung open slightly. "I see the work order menu, but none of these orders are skills I have. How's this supposed to help me, anyway?"

"Work orders grant experience for skills
and personal experience when you turn them in.
I recommend you ask Kat to set your reward
low, like one copper, and it gives you even
more experience. In your case, make potions,
salves, whatever you can do and ask Kat to
make you a work order for them to turn in. We
can make them at any time. I want you to focus
on grinding through work orders and hitting
level twenty in a week. I want us to leave on
our mission three days after that," Arthur
told him.

"That might work if the work orders give
good experience," Rayne nodded carefully.

"That gives the rest of us roughly ten days
to get everything here progressing as smoothly
as possible. Samson, you need to appoint a
second in command. Vana set up some kind of
rotation schedule for James and Zeke and have
them report to Samson's second. I have Kat
finding an assistant or two to help with
village business, and Allendria, you need to
appoint someone to oversee the construction
crews. I plan to have them building new stone
houses before we depart. I'll spend my time
working on other building projects, and I have
some armor to make," Arthur said with a wink
toward Samson.

The big soldier grinned with a fiery light
in his eyes. Arthur's gaze turned to the side,
and he spotted a pile of reddish-orange
scales.

*When did you get here?* Arthur asked.

*About the time you and Rayne wandered off
by yourself. Are you going blind? You really
haven't noticed me?*

*Yeah, sorry about that. Super focused.*

*Whatever. I assume you want me to go on
this crazy quest, too?*

*Naturally, I need someone of your esteemed power to help on a quest this size.* Arthur mocked to the dragon.

*Fine, but I'm not dying for you again.*

Arthur could only chuckle as the group dispersed, and Rayne went back to his work. Vana and Allendria peeled off toward the Bastion, and Samson followed their lead. Arthur stood in the middle of the small clearing with only Balair as company.

*Well damn, everyone just up and left. Surprised you're still here.*

*What?* The dragon asked. *I was scratching an itch on my side. Where did everyone go? Well, if we're done here, I'm off too.* The dragon said and jumped into the air.

*Well, so much for that thought.*

Arthur wandered back toward the original part of the village. His mind turned over the different projects he somehow needed to finish in the limited time he had. Getting the Elven Quarter's Embassy would be necessary, so their agreement would be unquestionable, and he needed to complete the improvements on his house with the water and sewage flow. There was also the matter of armor.

The battle destroyed most of his armor in the fight with Lyrinth, so it would force him to make himself another set. He also promised Samson a new set of armor to go with his position as a Paladin. Arthur considered starting construction on the Elven Quarter, but decided against it and returned to the inn. It was time for him to consult with Daniel and Kat.

Kat was hard at work at a table, and two other people sat with her. It looked like she was talking to both of them. *Maybe new candidates?* Daniel was behind the bar, so Arthur gestured for him to join them at Kat's table.

"Hey Kat, can we talk for a few minutes?" Arthur asked when he reached the table.

She smiled his direction. "Sure, Lord Mayor. Ladies, we'll pick this up after I'm finished talking to the Mayor. You can sit at one of the other tables for now until we finish," she told them and returned her focus to Arthur.

The two women left their seats and walked to the other side of the common room. Arthur sat in one of their vacant locations, "New candidates?"

"Not candidates. I've already chosen them for the job. Just working on teaching them what their job will entail," she explained.

Daniel joined them at the table.

"Hey Daniel, need some advice from you two," Arthur told them.

Arthur explained the situation with the Elven Quarter and the Embassy and future plans for the village. He lightly discussed some of his infrastructure ideas, like the running water, but he could tell they didn't understand much of that. His concern was laying the place out properly and not just haphazardly building anywhere.

"We need to develop some kind of city plotting. We can assign basic lot sizes based on what currently exists and even draw in some roads for use as we build more housing. I'll also make sure we include the buildings you expect to see for the Elven Quarter. Is there any specific design you'd like to see?" Kat asked.

"Layout wise? Not necessarily. I want transportation of goods to be a major factor and don't want small crowded streets," An idea crossed his mind, and he added, "I also want the plots large enough so each person can plant a small garden on their property with their home. The homes will all end up being uniform in size."

That would help solve some of his problems with drainage. If he installed a small water filter for each house and let them use their water from the drains to water their gardens, it eliminated a lot of piping he would need. The gardens could all be on the backside of the houses, and they could dig a drainage ditch between properties to drain the excess water toward the fields.

"What about commerce?" Daniel asked.

"Let's try to separate the living areas from the business areas. I also want a separate market area. This should help keep everything organized and give us a set plan on how to expand each section."

"You better get Lady Dalia involved as you work on this," Arthur added, "I don't want her feeling left out since all of this is being done in what is technically her village."

They agreed, and Kat told him she'd get to
work on it. The three left their spots, and
Arthur rose. He considered starting on the
armor, but changed his mind and went to the
wall instead. He focused on spending every bit
of excess mana he could to help get the wall
as close to complete as possible. Deep down,
he knew they would continuously expand it, but
it was quickly becoming a very formidable
defense. The afternoon passed swiftly into the
evening, and before he knew it, he was clean
and in bed with Allendria for the night. He
took one last glance at his experience for the
day before closing his eyes to sleep.

*You have gained 31,500 total experience in
Earth and Fire Magic.*
*Congratulations, you have reached level 23
in Earth Magic. Increases the effect of your
earth magic spells by 66%. Back to walls
again?*
*Congratulations, you have advanced to
Mastery level 3 in Raise Stone Wall (Medium).
This spell now costs 10 less mana to cast.*

# Chapter 28

*Preparing a Village*

Arthur met the mass of people for their morning duty. With their timeline shortened, he asked Allendria to gather the construction crews so they could complete the housing designs and get to work. His help the previous day had helped them almost finish the work on the wall. The workers all gathered around the empty space.

"Good morning," Arthur called cheerily. "You've all done outstanding work getting the village walls in order, but I've brought you out here to discuss the next major project for all of us. With the influx of refugees and the condition of the existing buildings, it's time we focus on housing and other essential buildings."

"Katherine and Lady Dalia are working to come up with a village layout, but in the meantime, I want to show you all the design we'll be using for the houses," Arthur continued.

A younger woman raised her hand and said, "Um, Lord Mayor, there isn't anything out here to show us."

"Not yet, there isn't," Arthur told them with a grin. "I'm going to build it for you so you can see the method I want you to use."

"Are all the houses going to be the same? I know we have some families that are larger than others," someone said in the back.

"All the houses will have at least two dedicated bedrooms. We'll make larger houses for larger families. The only difference will be the addition of an extra bathroom and some bedrooms. The rest of the house will stay uniform for all," Arthur explained.

"Uh, what do you mean by bathrooms?" another worker asked.

"Bathrooms will be an addition to traditional houses that I'll be adding. It'll be a place in the house designed for taking baths and eliminating your bodily waste. I know you won't be familiar with it but just follow my lead. I'll show you this entire project from start to finish and detail how I want each of these features done."

Everyone nodded in agreement, as Arthur demonstrated. He started by quickly leveling the footprint of the house. Raising the foundation and transforming it into stone was quick with his arsenal of spells. He had all the workers join him on the platform as he created the exterior walls.

From there, he walled off one side of the structure to contain the housing area. He built this house in the same manner he did his own. The only difference was it was two bedrooms. On the side he walled off, he placed two bedrooms and a shared bathroom. This allowed him to use three doors on this wall. One for each room and link them together as well with their own entrances. The smaller size of the building allowed the perfect space needed on that half of the building for the three rooms.

He stressed the details on the bathrooms. The sink, shower, and toilet space designs he covered in detail. Arthur planned on doing the plumbing himself in these houses until everything worked as planned, and then he could train some of the workers in the process.

Minor things, like the placement of windows, he covered. Each room needed at least one window. The living room and the kitchen would definitely need a window or even two. He told them they could choose how to approach those themselves.

Avoiding his initial mistake, he stressed the importance of the different height walls to ensure a gradual slope to the covering roof. His last part was to show them the layout he expected for the kitchen. He sincerely hoped to replace much of the wood-burning style of cooking with enchantments, but that would have to wait.

More than anything, he made sure they each understood the importance of supporting walls and columns. If they made larger spaces without walls, he wanted to make sure they placed some decorative columns to help support the weight of the room. Villagers dying from a collapsed building would be a terrible fate.

The concept of running water registered with the workers, but they couldn't fathom his explanation on how it worked. They understood his example of how the water would flow from the sinks, even the shower, but explaining how the toilets worked or how the water would get to these devices alluded them. Arthur gave up on that particular path and asked them to focus on churning out buildings based on this exact model.

He waved Allendria over to him while the workers were examining the kitchen layout. "Do you have any you feel are exceptionally gifted among the group?"

"Actually, I was planning on placing Olivia in charge while I'm gone. She had some early problems adjusting but has been doing terrific work lately. Why?"

"I'd like to show a few of them the house I built so they can see what a larger version will look like. Mainly want to show them what it looks like with the faucets installed and the way I split the rooms."

"We can do that. I'll tell the others to take a temporary break while we examine the house. I can also use the time to talk to Olivia. I know two others who would be good to bring with us. The three of them should be able to keep everything on track while we're gone."

Vana dismissed the group to their work and had Olivia and the other two crew members join them as they walked to the house now occupied by the Dark Elves. Activity greeted them in abundance as they approached the building. Small piles of wood shavings littered the ground around the building, and many partially completed projects scattered the area.

Arthur spotted Daranth near a small pile of sawdust away from the others and approached. The elf focused on a rod in front of him and carefully used the magical sanding technique to taper the end of the pole. When he finished, his gaze found Arthur.

"Things are hopping over here," Arthur commented with a smile.

"They are happy to be of use. The last few
months have been nothing but strife and
conflict as the factions butted heads in our
home. The peace of this place helps them focus
on their passion for crafting."

"I wish my people didn't have to suffer. If
only I'd been powerful enough to oppose my
uncle," Allendria mumbled.

"None of that nonsense, Princess. You and I
both know you did everything you could before
you had to flee. What do I owe the pleasure of
the visit?" Daranth asked.

"We're actually here to show these guys the
house design," Arthur said as he waved at the
three walking with them, "They're part of the
construction crew that's been working non-stop
on improvements in the village."

"Well, you sure do impressive work,"
Daranth told the group, causing them to puff
up with pride. They all bowed slightly to the
Dark Elf.

"Thank you, Master Elf," Olivia told him
with pride.

The old elf smiled at the title but said
nothing.

"Olivia, can you take these two with you
and start your tour of the house? Allendria
and I will join you shortly to explain some of
the features you may not understand," Arthur
said to the woman with a nod toward the house.

Olivia took control of the other two and
proceeded to the entry and through the door.
Arthur and Allendria focused their attention
back on Daranth.

"Katherine should complete the document for
our agreement today. Allendria and I will sign
it this evening, and you can recruit any into
the positions you feel necessary," Arthur told
him.

"Good. A few have seen my work and keep asking how I've done it. I've been working to keep the magic unseen which is why I'm working farther from the others."

"I ask that you focus on doors and beds. Those will be the two most necessary furniture items. We also included the part we discussed detailing you being able to work on your own projects to sell in the market as long as you use your own sources or paid for materials. Luckily, the work orders have done a fine job of letting people build up small stockpiles of coins, and they've had little to spend it on," Allendria told him.

Daranth nodded and was about to respond before Arthur beat him to it, "We're also leaving in a little over a week. We don't intend the trip to be overly long, but we won't know for sure. Ideally, I'd like to have a lot of completed housing and furniture for them before we leave to keep tensions from rising. Would you be willing to accept the position of Village Carpenter? We need someone here to keep the work moving while we're gone."

"But, I'm an elf, one that you barely know?"

"Yeah? But Allendria knows you well, and I trust her judgment without question. I've also seen your work," Arthur said with a wave toward the pieces he worked on, "and I know it's far superior to anything I've seen here. Since you plan on staying here anyway, it seems like the perfect fit."

Daranth thought about it for a handful of seconds and finally responded, "I'll do it. I'm concerned your wood supply won't be sufficient, though. I'd like to source some better wood for the projects. What you have in the village isn't bad, but other hardwoods would work infinitely better for furniture. I don't suppose you have drying boxes, do you?"

"In response to your first statement, work with James. Daniel can get you in contact with him. James is our primary woodcutter. He can address your concern for wood supply and can probably help find the types of wood you need. The drying box isn't something we have. Just so we're on the same page, is this a normal wood drying room you're referring to, or do you use some type of enchanted item to help dry wood faster?"

"Well, at least you know what it is," Daranth said. "It is an enchanted container that speeds the drying process of the wood. We have two unique styles where we come from."

"Let me guess," Arthur said quickly with a smile. "You have one that uses a combination of Air and Fire Magic that uses heat to burn away the excess moisture quickly while the air keeps it from combusting. The other style uses Air and Water Magic that has the Water Magic pull the moisture out directly, and the Air Magic moves the excess out of the box?"

"So, you've used one before?" Daranth asked, surprised.

"Nope, but I'm familiar with the process. With some trial and error, I believe I can make one or both of those. If you know the runes used on them, it'll make it much faster for me to reproduce."

"I used them often enough that I can sketch the runes for you. I don't know what some of them are, but I know what they look like."

"That works for me. Just send a runner to the inn with the drawings when you're done. If you could draw me the overall design of the boxes, I'd appreciate it. It'll save me a lot of time. If I'm not there, just have your runner leave the notes with Katherine and I'll get them from her."

"Will do," Daranth told him.

"Anything else I can help with before we get back to our tour?" Arthur asked.

"I don't think so. I've got work to do anyway," Daranth said with a shooing motion.

Arthur and Allendria took the hint and joined the others in the house. It took some time to show them what the features would look like when complete. Arthur explained how the different faucets worked. He also showed them the temperature controls for the rooms. Those impressed them greatly. The sheer amount of wood it would save during the colder months was fantastic. Arthur was happy to see that the enchantment only dropped twelve charges since yesterday. It took four almost immediately when he set the temperature in the room before it leveled out. Since then, it only drained roughly one charge for every three hours of use.

The layout of the living area was the part he wanted them to see. They would design all the larger homes this same way. Arthur considered coming up with a plan for a three-bedroom house but figured with the ease of construction using their magic, it would be a pointless exercise. It took almost no more work to make a four-bedroom, anyway. If a family had a spare bedroom in the house, it might help in case of emergencies. When Olivia and the group were confident that they understood the expectations, they excused themselves to return to work.

"Any plans now?" Allendria asked while they walked back toward the inn.

"There are so many things I need to do, but I don't care to work on any of them. I need to make more enchantments for the houses, assist with building homes, start the elven district, build a new inn, and any other number of items to go over. Instead, I'll take the rest of the day to myself. I'm going to grind a few of my magic skills to reach my requirement for the Soul Bond quest," Arthur told her.

"That'll work. Since you're doing that, I'll go join the construction teams and make sure they aren't struggling with any of the work. If you need anything, come find me," she said and jogged off.

Arthur continued to the inn and found a quick bite to eat. While there, he spotted Balair lying in the corner of the room, being lazy.

*Hey, bum. You want to get out of the building today?*

The little drake huffed and rolled to his side. One of his back legs reached forward and scratched at the underside of his wing in a very doglike manner.

*Is that a no?*

*What for? I don't feel like doing a lot of work today.*

*I'm just going to enjoy the weather and do some magic. Need to increase the level of my Air and Water Magic. You can just lounge around near me and relax outside. Some fresh air might do your lazy ass some good.*

*Lazy? A creature as intelligent as I knows to conserve their energy until it's needed.*

*Sounds boring. You don't tire of doing nothing?*

*Well, sometimes. I'll tell you what, I'll go with you just to make sure you don't do anything too stupid and get hurt. I'm not answering to Calfuray when you kill yourself with a failed magic spell.*

*Oh, how noble of you,* Arthur told him sarcastically.

On the way out the door, Arthur saw Daniel come into the common room and quickly shifted his direction to catch him.

"Hey Daniel," Arthur waved as he got close, "got a minute?"

Daniel set down two bowls, wiped his hands on a rag on his waist, and walked over.

"Sure, what ya need?"

"Not really anything specific I need. I wanted you to know I've named Daranth as the Village Carpenter. I told him to find you to contact James. He had questions about sourcing wood for their furniture building. I have them focused on doors and beds for the new houses our construction crew started. Do you know if James has any help? I don't think he can cut the wood he needs by himself."

"I know he found a few of the refugees that volunteered to assist. They've been working to clear some of the closer trees. None of that will be ready to use for a little bit, though."

"Well, I'm working on that problem, so one thing at a time. Daranth's supposed to send a runner with some drawings for a solution to that issue. If you see a Dark Elf wandering around the inn with papers in their hand looking lost, please direct them to Kat or just take them yourself."

"Will do. Anything else you need?"

"Plenty, but only so much at once. Blankets, mattresses, and goods of that nature will become extremely scarce before long, so we need to figure out a solution for that. I also want to work on building your expanded inn. What you have now works, but I think you'll need more rooms before too long."

"I don't really want to see my building change, but I know it needs to. As long as we keep the layout the same, it should be fine. I want the wooden floors and the bar to stay."

"I agree. I'm only planning to change the walls and ceilings. We can use the extra wood in the current building to do the floors in the additional rooms."

"That'll work. We have one other concern. Samson told me you plan to leave in a week or so on your class quests? I'd like to ask that you make at least one hunting trip before then to help build our stockpile up. With the new influx of people, the food doesn't last as long. The fields will finally start yielding vegetables in a week or two, but we need meat."

"We'll take care of it. A hunting trip or maybe even two will be excellent practice for us while we prepare for our class quests. I'm going to do a little magical training on my own. I'll be on the southern side of the village if anyone needs me," Arthur told him as he walked toward the door.

Arthur exited the inn and felt the sun warm him up. The days seemed warmer. Arthur never asked what part of the year it was and if their seasons worked like the ones he knew from Earth. Judging from the temperature change over the last couple of weeks, he assumed summer must be approaching, or at least their equivalent to it.

Balair slowly tromped behind him and, when clear of the doorway, launched himself into the air.

*Thought you didn't want to work hard?*

*Flying takes infinitely less effort than walking. Have fun on your trek.*

Arthur grumbled at the thought and trudged along to his destination. With a flash of insight, he grinned and cast his Haste spell. He was here to work on his Air Magic, anyway. A small clearing with its lone tree on the edge marked his destination, and he came to a halt under the branches.

Arthur spent the rest of the afternoon constantly casting spells. His enormous mana pool could be both a benefit and a curse sometimes. He used a good chunk of it on the construction work that morning, but still had a lot left. For his Water Magic, he kept casting Gentle Rain along with his Ice Shards. Needless to say, something resembling a small tank formed in the field in front of him. With as dry as the surrounding area was, he wasn't too worried about it. The water would soak in before long.

His Air Magic consisted of renewing his haste spell and then casting his slow spell on top of it. Reflecting on his fights, he remembered a fundamental weakness of his was his squishiness to projectiles. With that thought in mind, he had Balair lob objects at him and practiced using Air Magic to deflect them. He discovered Weak Gust of Wind and Deflect during these exercises. The first was ideal for scattering small projectiles, like arrows, while the second was good to bounce larger objects in different directions. He was actually more excited about the Deflect spell because it looked like he could use it to deflect weapon swings.

The daylight started fading, so Balair and Arthur traveled back to the inn. Balair cheated and took to the air again, but Arthur used his Haste spell to make his trip a little quicker. He still arrived to find Balair already sound asleep in the room's corner.

To his surprise, the full party, including Rayne, were all seated at a table together and laughing heartily. He pulled up a seat with them.

"What's so funny?" Arthur asked.

Samson grinned. "I was telling Rayne about the time guardsman Paul shot you while we fought off the harpies."

Arthur grinned at that. "That was annoying at the time, but it's pretty funny looking backward. That poor man gets nervous every time I see him."

Everyone ate with light conversation around the table. When finished, Arthur raised a hand and spoke up. "I'd like to have us go on a hunting trip the day after tomorrow."

Samson looked toward the ceiling. "I might be able to muster enough guards for that. They need more training anyway."

"No," Arthur said as he shook his head, "I want only us to go. I want us to work together as a team to prepare for our upcoming quest. It serves two purposes for us."

"I'm game," Vana said with a cheerful tone. "I'll wager ten copper I kill more animals than any of you."

"I'll take that bet," Rayne chimed in from the side.

"So," Samson began with a glance at Arthur.

Arthur sighed. "Fine, I'll make your new armor tomorrow. I need to make some replacement armor for myself anyway after Lyrinth destroyed my last breastplate."

The look on Samson's face made Arthur picture the large man leaping in joy and running around like a kid with a new toy.

"Everyone else have what they need? If not, now's the time to speak up."

"I could use some better weapons. I've seen what you can make, and it's far superior to what I have. They don't have to be anything fancy, but my current weapons are only iron. Even just some basic steel ones would work better," Rayne spoke up.

"I can do that. You want the same designs? A swordbreaker and a stiletto dagger?"

"I'm surprised you know their names, but yes."

"They are very unique weapons and easily identified. I've been a fan of bladed weapons for a long time. You're honestly lucky. I'm guessing you haven't fought against many others who used steel?" Arthur asked.

"Ruined a stiletto dagger on steel once before. Another reason I'd like to get one in steel myself."

"I'll take care of it. I have an idea for your stiletto dagger. An enchantment I'd like to try."

"As long as it works, I'll be happy," Rayne agreed.

The group continued with idle chat through the evening until everyone called it a day. Arthur took the time to take a quick glance at his notifications for the day before collapsing into bed, exhausted but content.

*You have gained 8,900 total experience in Earth and Fire Magic.*

*You have gained 4,320 total experience in Water Magic.*

*Congratulations, you have reached level 10 in Water Magic. Increases the effect of your Water Magic spells by 27%. That's going to leave a muddy mess.*

*You have gained 3,410 total experience in Air Magic.*

*Congratulations, you have reached levels 3, 4, and 5 in Air Magic. Air Magic spells now have a 12% increased effect. That's a dull afternoon.*

# Chapter 29

*Back to the Forge*

The morning air was crisp as Arthur stood in front of a daunting pile of steel. He mentally went over all the unique items he needed to work on. *Armor for Samson, probably a new shield, and sword as well. Rayne's weapons. My armor. A metric butt-ton of temperature controls, and some faucets and showerheads.*

Temperature controls and household pieces would be quick and easy. The weapons and armor would command most of his time. The goal was to trigger his Arcane Artificer specialty when making his breastplate this time. Having a unique breastplate would significantly improve his chances of survival.

In the end, he worked on Samson's armor first. The man was the one that took the most damage during the fights and sorely needed an upgrade. Arthur wanted the Paladin well defended at all times.

Arthur sent one apprentice off to prepare the internal padding and straps for the pieces he would need. When the enchantments were complete, he didn't want to wait for them to make the lining to see a finished product.

His previous armor focused on weight reduction and durability. Now that a more advanced enchantment matrix was available, Arthur should be able to make armor that functioned better.

Deciding on the design was a different story. Arthur planned to make his armor very similar to the last armor. He wanted Samson's armor to be something more suited to his status as a Paladin. Now that Arthur knew the enchantment that allowed items to conform to size, he could focus purely on the design of the armor and not have to worry about the exact dimensions.

He started with a segmented breastplate that would allow Samson more movement. When he made the sabatons for Samson's original armor, he included clasps to help close the boots. Since that was much easier to work with, he incorporated clasps and hinges hidden inside the armor. Being able to suit up quickly could save his life.

The entire backplate of the armor hinged open so Samson could practically step into the piece. Arthur also included rounded pauldrons on the top. They looked like half of a dome on his shoulders. The embossed edges and intricate scrollwork added the flair to it. On the shoulder itself, Arthur embossed a Celtic cross symbol. A symbol of hope for the Paladin.

The enchantments took time to get right, but he included strength enhancements, durability boosts, and increased deflection chance. In a moment of insight, he realized he had a decent amount of spells that could benefit Samson in an emergency. Since he could create artificial gems to power them, there was no reason not to include some.

He slotted three tiny gems in the chest piece and dedicated one to store mana for the piece, one designed to hold the spell Weak Gust of Wind, and the last one was unseen on the inside of the armor. When Arthur originally figured out how to implant a spell into an enchantment, he needed to give it an activation word. In the heat of battle, that could be a problem. This enchantment he designed to activate if Samson pushed a paltry amount of mana into the internal gem. That would trigger the Weak Gust of Wind spell.

All of those additions, with the sizing enchantment included, were the ultimate design for the piece. The armor itself was a work of art, and Arthur caught himself chuckling when he saw the finished product. Figures. The damn shoulders look almost exactly like one of my favorites from an old Earth game. What can I say? The judgment armor looked impressive.

The enchantments cost a hefty amount of mana, but it was worth every bit. He barely took the time to check the enchanted shell before he quickly attached the interior lining that Lana handed over.

| Item:<br>Enchanted Masterful Mage-crafted Breastplate of Defensive Blast | Defense: 40<br><br>Durability: 320/320<br><br>Rarity: Epic<br><br>Quality: Exquisite<br><br>Weight: 6.0 kg<br><br>Mana Capacity:<br>800/800 |
|---|---|

**Slot:** Chest

**Traits:** A specially enchanted steel breastplate. Will release a defensive blast that can deflect weak attacks and temporarily stun opponents. This ability consumes 200 of the mana capacity each use.

**Enchantments:**

- 5% of damage inflicted is deflected from the wearer
- This armor grants +3 Strength to the wearer.

The result confused him a little. The ability sounded like his Weak Gust of Wind spell that he envisioned when he powered the enchantments. He expected it to be the standard name like everything else he created, but it had the unique title of Defensive Blast on it. The real question was, did it happen because the Rarity went up, or was it because of the advanced enchantment matrix styles he used?

Arthur carefully handed the piece to Lana, who took it with a sense of wonder. She reverently walked over to set it on a cloth-covered table, away from the dirty work, while Arthur prepared some more steel. The helmet was the next item on the agenda, and he liked the enchantments he used on his helmet. Samson's helmet would have identical enchantments, but he wanted to stick with the theme his pauldrons started and made the front of the helmet come down in a 'V' shape. He kept the barbute-style eye openings. Sleek eagle wings adorned the sides of the helmet and swept backward.

Samson's new greaves were plain in design, but he included another strength enchantment on them. Arthur also took the time to add three tiny gems to this one, too. They worked in the same way and were on one thigh of the armor. This time, he embedded the Haste spell into them. They only came out as Rare quality, but the effects were what Arthur expected, and the stats were far superior to what Samson wore now.

Arthur stuck with the standard enchantments he used before on the sabatons and then made matching gauntlets and bracers to complete the set. He even took the time to emboss a Celtic cross on each of the bracers to match the shoulders. With all the pieces complete, he received another notification that made him smile.

*Congratulations, you have successfully crafted a full set of high-quality gear. Due to the Rarity and the Quality of the set, it has been granted Set Bonuses. Your Mage-crafted Steel Armor Set has the following bonuses:*

*2 pieces - Increase base armor of all pieces by 8.*

*4 pieces - Increase HP of the wearer by 75.*

*6 pieces - Unlock Ability - Shield Wall - Allows whoever wears this armor to extend a shield of force across a space that spans ten feet in length and five feet in height. This shield can't be destroyed. Cooldown: 6 hours. Duration: 1 minute.*

With the armor finally out of the way, his attention shifted to Samson's sword. A standard arming sword was the design he settled on. A smooth fuller down each side of the blade decreased the weight. Arthur set another three tiny gems in this sword and used the Sheathe in Flames spell on the blade. Between his increase in smithing skills and the better materials, this new weapon sported an attack rating of 20.

The shield was the last item for Samson before he moved back to his own armor. The heater shield design still worked great, but Arthur wanted something more this time. He spent some time using his Mineral Compression spell, making gems until he received two larger manufactured rubies. With these in hand, he planned out his design.

Since he already put eagle wings on Samson's helmet, Arthur put the face of an eagle on the shield itself. The two rubies took the place of the creature's eyes and gave it a fierce look when the sun reflected off the piece. He used one of those gems as the storage piece and one to contain the spell Flamethrower. A smaller gem adorned the inside of the shield so it would be in contact with his arm while worn to allow him to activate the spell.

The Flamethrower spell was a powerful one, and it worried Arthur the enchantment wouldn't work and instead would turn into something else. He mumbled quietly, "Oh dear Goddess, please let this work," as he infused the mana into the piece. He held on tight while his mana plummeted, and a storm of raw mana floated around the shield. His will struggled to contain the blast of force and push the torrent of power into the shield. Tendrils of energy escaped the fury, and Arthur heard people yelling around him but couldn't make out the words.

With his strength sapped, he finally collapsed to a knee and released his hold on the errant power. The world slowed and he watched the abundant mana begin to explode outward. Before it touched him, a beam of light slammed into the object, and the raw power collapsed into the shield. The gong sound reverberated through his chest, and a gust of wind buffeted him, almost knocking him backward. The shield slowly fell to the ground and wobbled around like a coin spinning on its edge.

"Goddammit, Arthur! Will you warn people before you do that? I think I soiled my pants," Rowan yelled across the clearing.

Arthur's gaze turned to watch the man looking at the crotch of his pants.

"I didn't plan that. Happened by accident."

"Oh, well, that explains it all. Our all-powerful Mayor constructed another damn named item. As usual, he did it purely by accident. I really begin to question if you're smart or just incredibly lucky."

"Why can't it be both?"

Rowan just shook his head and walked toward Arthur.

"Fine, fine, what did you make this time?"

Arthur was still on one knee and merely motioned to the resting shield. Rowan walked over and picked it up. He studied the details of the eagle and ran his hands along the lines of the features. His gaze fixed on the rubies, and Arthur had to call his name three times to snap him out of his trance.

"What?"

"I want to see what I made. Quit staring at it like it's your first true love and give it here."

Rowan handed over the shield, and Arthur got his first glimpse at the piece.

*Hark and Rejoice, a named weapon has been created! Divine Fury joins the fray!*

*Congratulations, you have successfully created Divine Fury. This is a unique, named shield. You have gained 1,000 experience in Arcane Smithing and Blacksmithing for this feat.*

| **Item:** Divine Fury | **Defense:** 52 |
| --- | --- |
| | **Durability:** 385/385 |
| | **Rarity:** Unique |

**Quality:** Masterful

**Weight:** 4.0 kg

**Slot:** Main Hand/Off Hand

**Mana Storage:** 0/3,000

**Traits:** A named shield created by an Arcane Artificer. This shield is unique, and another like it has never existed in this world.

**Enchantments:**
- This shield draws in 10 mana per minute and fills its internal mana storage.
- Upon activation, the spell Divine Fury will bathe all enemies in front of the shield with divine fire dealing 30 damage per second for 10 seconds. If used on minions of evil or undead,

it will deal 60 damage per second. Cooldown: 5 minutes.
- Activation cost: 600 mana.
- This shield deals half its defense value as attack damage when shield bashing an enemy.

*You're welcome by the way,* he heard the voice of Lianna whisper in his mind.

*I was hoping my ability would trigger for my armor,* Arthur grumbled back.

*Well, it was either intervene to your prayer and save your life or let the piece explode and kill you. It would've probably destroyed a third of the village as well.*

Arthur gulped at that. He hadn't realized he'd come that close to catastrophe.

*That bad, huh?*

*I feel like the saying, duh dumbass, isn't forceful enough,* the soft voice responded in his head.

*Can you tell me what caused that?*

*You forget to obey the rules. You've been told before that particular materials can only hold a specific amount of power. That principle also applies to spells. More potent spells require more advanced materials to hold them. Your Flamethrower spell is too powerful for mage-crafted steel to hold. I know you like pushing boundaries, but please keep in mind limitations as well when you try unknown things.*

Arthur hung his head low at that. *I'm sorry, Lianna. Thank you for saving me.*

*Try not to make it a habit. Now get back to work. You have a lot left to do before your trip.*

Arthur spotted a telltale tremor in his hand and knew Lianna's message frayed his nerves. He carried the shield over to the bench holding the rest of Samson's new armor and sat down. His head just touched against the counter when he heard boots clomping toward him.

"What happened?" Samson called to him.

"Nothing. Just finishing your new gear. Perfect timing, actually. Do me a favor and check out what's on the bench," Arthur told him while he gestured to the bench behind him.

The shield lay behind the bench from where Samson stood so he couldn't see it from his angle. Arthur watched the ex-soldier carefully examine each piece of the armor.

"Is it ready to wear?"

"It is. Switch whenever you like," Arthur
said and trailed off. Samson didn't wait past
the first few words to ditch his old gear into
a pile. It took a little time for Samson to
switch everything out, but even Arthur had to
admit the man looked fantastic in the new
armor. The sizing enchantment that made it fit
him perfectly helped add to the regal
appearance of the armor itself.

"How's it look?" Samson asked.

Arthur chuckled at the question. That was
the last thing he expected the gruff warrior
to ask, "Looks good."

He swung his new sword, testing the
balance. His old shield was in his left hand
while he practiced some of his maneuvers.

"I guess you haven't had time to work on a
new shield?"

"Actually, I have. That's why I'm glad
you're here. I don't want your new shield out
of your sight," Arthur said as he regained his
feet and grabbed the shield from behind the
bench. The paladin's eyes sparkled when they
rested on the eagle's face embossed on the
shield.

"Congratulations, Samson. You're the proud
owner of the second named item in the village.
Now just make sure it doesn't leave your
side," Arthur said as he winced at the
statement. *Seems hypocritical since I keep
doing that myself and leaving Ember at the
inn.*

"I'll treasure it. You're sure I can keep
it?"

"Sure can. Consider it a gift from Lianna.
She had a hand in its creation."

Samson bowed his head. The silence stretched for a handful of seconds before he lifted his head again. Standing encased in his armor and hefting his impressive shield gave him an appearance that matched what Arthur thought of as a Paladin.

"How are preparations going for our hunt tomorrow? You have your second in command ready to fill in?"

"Yeah, he's ready to step up. We're set to go in the morning."

"Good. Now go show off your new armor and get used to the feel. I've got to get back to work on making the rest of the items we need."

Samson nodded in response and dashed off. *His speed is better in the new armor. The lighter steel must work in his favor.* Arthur looked back at the pile of steel and sighed.

Instead of reinventing the wheel and taking the chance of blowing himself up, he created duplicates of his existing armor. There were a few minor changes. He gave his pauldrons more detail on the wings, and the scales on the chest had more distinction to them. He did the enchantments with his new Expert Matrix, so they were stronger than his previous armor. He was even lucky enough for his helmet to upgrade to Epic rarity.

With his armor finished and re-equipped, he felt much more secure. The thought of Lyrinth's black blade shearing through his armor like butter still gave him chills. Hopefully, his other opponents wouldn't have that specific ability at their disposal.

    The faucets and temperature controls could
be mind-numbing work, so he took care of
Rayne's weapons first. He wanted them to
mirror the existing blades as closely as
possible so Rayne wouldn't need to get used to
any changes in his fighting style.
    The Stiletto Dagger was a simple creation,
but Arthur used his skill to make the handle
of the blade look like small metal bones.
Since the dagger was primarily a stabbing
weapon, Arthur wanted to build upon Rayne's
use of Air Magic and included a Haste effect
on the blade. The enchantment settled onto the
knife with no issues, but instead of embedding
a Haste spell onto the dagger, it added a
similar effect. When he finished the blade, he
took a quick look at the stats.

| **Item:** Enchanted Mage-crafted Steel Stiletto Dagger | **Attack:** 16-19<br><br>**Durability:** 140/140<br><br>**Rarity:** Rare<br><br>**Quality:** Well Crafted<br><br>**Weight:** 0.3 kg<br><br>**Slot:** Main Hand/Off Hand<br><br>**Traits:** A Steel Dagger, created using magical techniques. The thin, triangular design of this blade makes it ideal for puncturing armor. |
| --- | --- |

<table>
<tr><td></td><td>Enchantments:

- This weapon has a random chance to increase its movement speed and force by 15% when swung.
- This blade loses durability 10% slower.</td></tr>
</table>

Arthur thought back on his creative process and realized when he infused the mana for the enchantments, he pictured the weapon being constantly swung in a faster thrusting motion. He hoped this would grant it quicker swing speed, but it instead triggered this effect. It was nothing to complain about.

With the first dagger complete, he changed his focus to the swordbreaker. He wanted the theme of the weapons to match, so he used the small bone design on the guard. He made the cross members and the small ring on the side with the bone layout in mind. The pommel of the weapon was a small skull that capped it off. Arthur included the threaded design on this one so Rayne could take apart if needed. The blade was sturdy along the spine with the grooves cut in. He kept the tip of the swordbreaker spines as larger triangle shapes to help get a good grip on weapons. The blade side was thinner and razor-sharp. Arthur loaded this weapon up with a durability and agility enchantment. That should help make it functional for Rayne. Its attack was only 14-16 damage, but it was a slashing weapon and not a stabbing one. It was designed to deflect blows and destroy your opponent's weapon. The high durability of 200 would ensure this weapon would stay functional for Rayne for a long time.

Arthur was about to shift focus to the household items when a thought struck him. Vana still used the old enchanted iron dagger he'd made from one of their early hunts. Now would be an excellent time to make her a better weapon to carry. He needed to update Allendria's as well, but he had other ideas for her. Making Vana a standard steel dagger took no time at all, and Arthur used enchantments for durability and agility for the blade.

    His idea for Allendria was different;
Instead of a knife, Arthur planned on making
her a staff. She only used spells anyway, and
Arthur could build mana storage into a thin
steel staff. The staff itself was only a
couple inches in diameter and was hollow in
the middle to prevent it from being too heavy.
Its primary focus would be mana storage, but
Arthur wanted Allendria to use it defensively
and offensively to fend off attackers.

    When the core of the staff was complete, he
shifted focus to enchantments. He gave it a
durability and flexibility enchantment to keep
it from breaking, but he also added gems to it
to store mana and draw in latent power to
recharge itself. The mana left him, and the
finished weapon looked great.

| **Item:**<br>Enchanted Mage-crafted Steel Staff of Mana Storage | **Attack:** 10-12 |
| --- | --- |
| | **Durability:** 190/190 |
| | **Rarity:** Rare |
| | **Quality:** Well Crafted |
| | **Weight:** 3.2 kg |
| | **Slot:** Main Hand |
| | **Mana Storage:** 0/1,500 |
| | **Traits:** A steel staff created using magical techniques. This hollow weapon is light and durable. |
| | Enchantments: |

- This weapon replenishes 4 mana per minute until the internal Mana Storage is full.
- Critical damage will not bend or distort this item.
- This weapon loses durability 10% slower.

   With the crew all set with necessary upgrades, his mind-numbing work on household items took over. It took two hours, but a pile with an unknown number of temperature controls and faucets lay in a heap at his feet. He stretched backward with his hands on his hips, trying to relieve the cramp in his lower back. Deciding this work wasn't any fun, and he'd made enough progress for the day, he opened up his dimensional storage room and tossed in the staff and the weapons for Rayne and Vana. The doorway snapped shut, and he waved over an apprentice. Alex trotted over, and Arthur directed him to store the controls and faucets for use by the construction crews. He'd have Allendria tell Olivia where they were.

The work in the forge was complete, so he walked back to the inn. A relaxing lunch greeted him in the building, and Balair even sat on the ground near him, lapping at a bowl of stew. His pile of projects nagged at him after lunch, but he couldn't muster the drive to work on any of them. Instead, he talked Balair into joining him in the field for more magical work.

His afternoon passed quickly, and his magic experience ticked ever higher. The evening led him back to the inn, and all of his friends gathered at a table. Spotting them through the doorway, Arthur walked backward and quickly opened his storage to retrieve the weapons. There wasn't a lot of extra room in the inn for that spell during dinner. With weapons in tow, he walked over to the table. Samson's gruff warrior face was a picture of joy in his new armor. Divine Fury lay propped against his leg and within easy reach. Everyone turned toward Arthur to stare at the items he held in his hands.

"Sorry, guys. Samson had the luck of the draw with a named item. The rest of you get regular stuff, well regular for us anyway." Arthur grinned.

He handed Vana her new knife, and she took it gratefully. Rayne's look of boyish wonder when Arthur gave him the two daggers was worth the time they took to create. Finally, Allendria jumped up and wrapped him in a hug and a kiss when he gave her the staff.

"So, it just takes me making a weapon for you to get all riled up? I'll have to remember that," Arthur said with a chuckle.

She lightly slapped his cheek in response, and they all chuckled at his reaction of surprise. Their dinner was a boisterous one, full of friendly conversation. Arthur was pleased to see Rayne start to open up. The evening activities concluded, and everyone adjourned to their rooms for the evening with the promise of a morning meeting before their hunt. A glance at his experience notifications for the day prior to bed was the last thing he saw before the darkness overtook him.

*You have gained 3,300 total experience in Earth and Fire Magic.*
*Congratulations, you have reached level 23 in Fire Magic. Fire Magic spells now have a 66% increased effect. Getting fancy with the named items, huh?*
*You have gained 8,210 total experience in Arcane Smithing and Blacksmithing.*
*You have gained 5,080 total experience in Enchanting.*
*Congratulations, you have reached level 16 in Enchanting. Your enchantments have a 45% decreased mana cost. Trying to kill yourself?*

# Chapter 30



The group of companions quickly assembled in the common area shortly after breakfast. Arthur was happy to see the ever grumpy Balair tagging along with the group. They were all as prepared, fully geared with their armor and weapons. Rayne yet again looked intimidating with his leather armor and dark hood. The brace of throwing daggers on his hip reminded Arthur of Balair's words the night of their surprise raid.

"Rayne," Arthur called as he motioned for the man to join him.

"Yeah? You need something? Am I forgetting something?" He asked as he did a quick pat check of himself.

Arthur chuckled at his nervous antics. "Nothing of the sort. I know I've thanked you for saving my life in the battle with Lyrinth, but I just remembered that you saved our life one other time as well. Balair told me about your throw that saved us during the surprise raid. If not for you, I fear Vana or myself would've been in far worse shape. So thank you for that."

Rayne blushed, "I wanted to help, and you two seemed like the only ones trying to do anything. Wish I could've done more. Funny part is, I actually learned the Throwing Knives skill with that throw. Barely even damaged the caster I hit with it because I had no skill."

"Thanks for taking the shot either way. You ready to get this party started?"

"Kinda nervous, but let's do this."

Arthur motioned for the group to follow as they filed out the door. When they were outside, he gathered them together.

"We're going to have some fun on this trip, but I want us to practice our movements like we're on our real quests. Try to keep the movements clean and sharp. Samson, you have the lead on travel. Vana, scout our way as you can. We want to take out any animal we find and don't forget to keep a sharp eye out for useful plants."

"You said you're an Alchemist, right?" Arthur asked Rayne.

"Yeah, trained Alchemist."

"Does that mean you know Herbalism?"

"Not very high level, but I can identify many of the common plants."

"Perfect. You keep an eye out for them with us. I don't care what it is, spices, herbs, potion ingredients, anything, we keep it. Don't pick them if you can. I have an ability that lets me harvest seeds from them before we take the plant."

Rayne nodded his understanding.

"Samson, I'll pass the battle strategy to you."

The gruff Paladin nodded and faced the companions. "I'll take the lead to tackle any threats head-on. Arthur has backup creature control if we get into trouble. Rayne, strike and move as fast as you can. Try to stick to your strengths in the shadows. Vana and Allendria pick them off at range."

Everyone nodded in agreement, and Samson led the group out of the village. It wasn't long before they passed into the deserted outer ring of the forest itself and walked further into the vegetation. Vana dashed back from time to time with updates, and they continued unabated. The first sign of life they found was in a small clearing and was mainly small game animals and birds.

Since the threats were minimal, Samson stood guard for anything while the rest of the group waded through the clearing, spooking out animals and finishing them off one by one. A handful of squirrels and ducks littered the ground. Vana killed most of those with her archery. Arthur quickly realized he'd be at a disadvantage without his bow. Instead of making an issue of it, he approached Rayne again.

"Hate to ask, but can I borrow a couple of your throwing knives? I'll make you some nicer ones later. I forgot my bow, and it's honestly a hassle to carry with my new fighting style. I think the skill for Throwing Knives is exactly what I need."

"Ah, so we both get to suffer and look bad missing throws all day? That sounds perfect. Vana is making us all look like toddlers," Rayne said with a glance toward the woman. The look in his eyes showed his thoughts were far from her shooting ability. *Lord help that boy if he goes barking up that tree. Samson might just kill him.*

Rayne handed over two of his throwing blades, and Arthur tested them with a few tosses. He opened up his Dimensional Storage while the group tossed the animals in. He was about to close it when two more fell out of the sky and thumped against the ground in front of him.

*That was rude.*

*Hey, I caught those two trying to fly away. Vana was slacking on her job.*

*Don't tell her that. She's about the only one to kill anything. Plus, she can only shoot so fast.*

*She's no match against me,* the little dragon preened.

*I'm not even going to start on that argument. I've watched Allendria boot you halfway across the inn, and she was being nice. I'm sure Vana would just shoot you and be done with it. I'd hate to have to summon you again.*

*Fine. I'll keep playing cleanup.*

*Sky clear around us?*

*So far.*

The group continued their trek. They walked all the way to the cliff on the eastern side of the village. Along the way, they found multiple other clearings with various minor game. The second clearing echoed with a lot of swearing while Arthur kept throwing knives and horribly missing his targets. *It always looks so easy in the movies.*

Rayne missed a good amount of his throws but had some luck. Arthur almost gave up in frustration when one of his throws hit a duck in the back of the head, and it fell to the ground. The damned bird got back up after a few minutes and flew off. Apparently, hitting it with the blunt end of a throwing knife only stunned it. *Well, shit!*

*Congratulations, you have learned Throwing Knives for a 100 experience bonus.*

The cave they found in the cliff changed their plans. Initially, the group stayed away from it, but after some thought, Arthur talked them into checking it out. The last cave he'd explored in the section contained a wealth of resources. The village could use an influx of more metals and gems. The thought of loot drove his desire more than anything.

Samson led them into the cave with his shield at the ready. All weapons were out as they filed in behind the big man. The cavern opened into a vast space dotted with small tufts of moss. A few large rocks on the ground and a big open cave weren't very threatening. Two paths in the back branched off to places unknown.

"Which direction do we want to check?" Samson asked the group.

"Either is fine with me," Arthur told him.

The rest nodded their heads in agreement. Samson walked toward the one on the left until a crunching noise echoed in the room. Samson glanced behind him, trying to find which party member so carelessly allowed that loud noise in their travel. The group all looked around in confusion until movement caught Arthur's eye.

One stone in the middle of the room was much taller than he remembered. He pointed toward it while the others turned to follow his finger. The rock grew taller until it peaked around ten feet, and a face of black stone topped the monster. Two arm-like appendages ended in bowling ball-sized fists of solid stone. Green lichen dotted different parts of the weathered rock.

"Dammit, an Earth Elemental!" Allendria exclaimed.

Arthur gulped and activated his Scan ability.

*You have received 180 experience for successful use of Scan.*

<table>
<tr><td colspan="2">Name: Earth Elemental</td></tr>
<tr><td colspan="2">Level: 17</td></tr>
<tr><td colspan="2">Type: Elemental</td></tr>
<tr><td colspan="2">HP: 1310/1310</td></tr>
<tr><td colspan="2">MP: 150/150</td></tr>
<tr><td colspan="2">Stamina: 515/515</td></tr>
<tr><td>Strength: 22</td><td>Experience: N/A</td></tr>
<tr><td>Agility: 8</td><td>Skills</td></tr>
<tr><td>Intellect: 8</td><td>Combat Skills:</td></tr>
<tr><td>Wisdom: 2</td><td></td></tr>
<tr><td>Endurance: 33</td><td>? (???/???)</td></tr>
</table>

The group spread out, and Arthur watched as a streak of crimson passed him.

*What the hell are you doing?*

*I got this guy, don't worry.*

*He's as big as like six of you.*

*Size doesn't matter, well for me anyway.*

The little drake dashed across the space and dove at the elemental with claws extended. He quickly slashed and clawed at the monster, even scaling up its side and sinking his teeth into the unwavering stone that made up the face. Sadly, the creature barely gained a scratch. Eventually, Balair made a wrong move, and it swung out with one of its massive fists and sent him flying across the cave.

*He's all yours*, was the mentally anguished message Arthur received as the body of the drake flew by. Samson dashed forward and intercepted a swing of the golem's hand with Divine Fury. The reverberation from the metal on stone made his ears ache, but he gritted his teeth and pushed forward.

Arthur circled the side of the creature while Samson did his best to slash at its legs. The strategy was a sound one. If he could take out its legs, it would be immobile and they could pick it off piece by piece. Arthur activated his Haste spell and dashed toward the elemental from behind.

Samson took a step forward and slammed his shield into the gigantic creature, causing it to stumble. Arthur took that chance to dash forward and swing a full power blow into the back of its leg with Ember. The metal sparked when it made contact and stopped before cutting more than an inch in. A figure resolved beside him as Rayne appeared and leaped up to the creature's back. His stiletto dagger came down in a burst of speed, and a sharp *crack* resounded through the cavern. Rayne withdrew his blade, and Arthur could see a small puncture wound in the monster, but it didn't even flinch at the damage.

Rayne vaulted backward as the elemental's arms rose to pummel him. Arthur also dashed back to avoid the flailing of the monster. A ball of flame impacted a spot on its side, and the rock gained a black coloring to it. Out of instinct, Arthur dashed forward and swung Ember into the blackened place.

The sword dug in. Chunks of rock burst from the spot and showered the surrounding area. The elemental made a grumbling sound reminiscent of grinding stones together. Arthur leaped backward, but the creature's arm clipped his armor and sent him sprawling.

*You have dealt 25 damage to Earth Elemental (Level 17) (Crushing Blow) with Ember.*

*Earth Elemental (Level 17) has dealt 40 damage to you with Hammer Blow (Glancing Blow).*

The damage was minimal, but it was actual damage. The heat from the spell must've baked the stone and caused it to become brittle. Arthur got back to his feet and called over the noise.

"Samson, when we give the signal pull back. Allendria, bathe it in the hottest fire you can manage. Everyone else, when the fire retreats, rush in and bust him to pieces."

Vana nodded and stood back. She pulled one of the larger bodkin arrows from her quiver and nocked it. Rayne stood with weapons ready, and Samson danced on his toes to avoid the incoming strikes.

"Now!"

Samson dashed forward for a Shield Bash and
retreated before the creature could regain its
senses. Arthur focused on his magic and dual
cast Flamethrower. Before the Flamethrower
cast completed, it surprised him to see a
whirling ring of fire appear at its feet and
work its way upward. A quick look toward
Allendria showed the crease of concentration
on her brow from the whirlwind spell.

Arthur pushed the completed spell into the
vortex to feed the fire. He fueled the pure
fire while Allendria kept the vortex spinning
and building the heat inside. The cave got
uncomfortably warm, and sweat dripped down
Arthur's face. He wiped his face with his arm
and looked at the elemental. The stone
creature was a pile of blackened rock, and
tiny cracks littered its body.

*You have dealt 180 damage to Earth
Elemental (Level 17) with Dual Cast
Flamethrower.*

The heat emanating from the area was
oppressive, and the group couldn't get closer
to the husk of the creature. Arthur spotted
movement out of the corner of his eye and
turned just in time to watch a spinning bodkin
arrow flash from Vana's bow and slam center
mass into the elemental. The spinning head of
the bolt burrowed deep into the stone and sent
chunks of the monster flying. When all that
was visible of the arrow was the fletching,
massive cracks spider-webbed out over the
entire body, and the monster crumbled into
large chunks of rock.

*Earth Elemental (Level 17) has died.*

"Anyone hurt?" Samson called into the silence.

*Does pride count?*

Arthur chuckled at the small voice in his head.

*Hey, I tried to warn you.*

*Shut up.*

"I'm all good," Arthur called.

"Good here," Allendria echoed.

"Damn, it's hot over here," Rayne called from the side of the room.

"It's hot everywhere in here right now. Let's step back toward the entrance and let this place cool down before we continue. I'd say a fight like that calls for a break," Arthur told the group.

They walked back to the entrance, and everyone promptly collapsed in the slight breeze of the opening. Samson tried to stay standing and vigilant, but Arthur waved for him to sit down.

"You need some rest too. We'll all keep our eyes peeled while seated. Take a load off. You had the tough job of deflecting that things attacks. It barely clipped me and sent me flying. I don't know how your arms aren't broken."

"Proper deflection techniques. I've learned over the years to block a blow without taking the direct hit. Even a slight sweep of the shield to divert the momentum can diffuse a lot of force."

"Better you than me. I'm content to sit behind your shield and stab stuff."

Balair collapsed at Arthur's feet and grunted when his body hit the ground.

*Ouch, that wasn't the best idea.*

*Maybe a softer landing next time? Or don't crumple onto stone?*

Balair merely huffed and closed his eyes. The little dragon's breathing became steady and slow as he fell into a soft sleep.

"Allendria, have you seen one of those before?"

"Yes, but only from a distance. It traveled too close to our city, and the guards had to repel it. The walls made the fight much easier. I didn't see exactly what they did to beat it but remember seeing a lot of Fire Magic flying that day. Now I know why."

"Our weapons weren't doing any good, and none of us wield hammers. It was the best option I could see."

"That's all right, I'm claiming the kill," Vana said.

"Hey, now! That should be a shared kill count!" Rayne called back.

"But my arrow killed it. Besides, you did nothing but stab it once. Even that didn't do much damage at all."

"Fine, I concede. But it still only counts as one," Rayne told her with crossed arms.

Arthur laughed. The dwarf that came to his mind at the statement could very well be what the species would look like in this world if he ever saw one.

"I think we've spent enough time out here. Let's go find some loot."

The group got back to their feet and dusted themselves off. Allendria walked over to Arthur, pulled out a small cloth from her belt pouch, and wiped the ash from his cheek.

"Try not to smear dirt all over your face," she sighed at him.

"Sorry, heat of the battle and all."

They returned to a warm but tolerable
cavern. The pieces of the golem were still
exactly where they'd fallen. Arthur picked up
one and saw a green item box pop open.

| Item:<br>Mana Infused Granite | Durability: 280/280 |
| --- | --- |
| | Rarity: Uncommon |
| | Quality: Good |
| | Weight: 3.8 kg |
| | Slot: Crafting item |
| | Traits: A shard of granite, saturated in mana, from an Earth Elemental. |

Arthur wasn't sure what they could use it
for, but he hadn't seen a lot of Uncommon or
higher Rarity crafting items. A quick thought
popped open his Dimensional Storage, and the
group quickly tossed all the chunks into the
storage area. Instead of closing it, Arthur
left it open while he explored the first room
of the cavern. He hadn't been able to use his
prospecting skills in a while, so now would be
a perfect time.

Arthur circled the room and continuously cast his prospecting spell. He considered expanding its size to cover a larger area but quickly dismissed that idea. If he found something far from him, he'd be more likely to cause a cave-in while trying to get to it than anything else. His search yielded only one small vein of iron. Two casts of his Transform Stone: Gravel spell and the nuggets of metal fell to the floor. Those joined the assorted granite pieces in the storage room, and he closed the doorway.

The group got back into formation, lit some makeshift torches, and walked to the passageway on the left. The tunnel wound back and forth for a few hundred yards before spitting them back out into a small cavern. Stalactites lined the ceiling of the room, and water slowly dripped from some of them. A small pool of water shimmered in the room, and a low beam of sunlight drifted from the ceiling of the cavern. The group set aside their torches and surveyed the room. Small mushrooms grew around the pool of water and emitted a soft blue glow. Rayne let out an excited "Awesome" when he saw them.

"What are they?" Vana asked him.

"Blue Caps. They're an ingredient for mana restoration potions. Scarce in the city. Many adventurers cave dive for them."

"Before you pick them, let me try something," Arthur told him as Rayne reached for one, then stopped. He cast his Germination ability on the plants and observed. The disappointment set in for his failure until he saw a few insignificant specks of something on the stone near the bottom of the mushroom. He brushed his hand across them and looked closer. The box that popped up startled him.

<table>
<tr><td>Item:<br>Blue Cap Mushroom<br>Spores</td><td>Durability: 15/15<br><br>Rarity: Uncommon<br><br>Quality: Good<br><br>Weight: 0.01 kg<br><br>Slot: Crafting item<br><br>Traits: Seed spores of Blue Cap Mushrooms. Plant in a dark and shaded area with access to a water source to grow your own Blue Cap Mushrooms.</td></tr>
</table>

"Allendria, you have another extra piece of cloth or anything I can use to hold seeds in that magic bag of yours?"

She rolled her eyes at him but dug through the pouch and pulled out a small square cloth. Arthur carefully dusted the spores off of his hand and into the fabric. He repeated this process for every spore he found in the cave and, when complete, tied the corners of the cloth together to hold them tight.

Arthur considered putting them in his Dimensional Drawer spell but didn't want to take the chance of killing the spores due to lack of oxygen. Instead, he placed them in his pouch, and they harvested the Blue Caps. Rayne, Vana, and Arthur made quick work of the mushrooms with their experience in Herbalism.

With the task complete, Arthur turned toward a nearby wall and began his prospecting work. He'd only made it a third of the way around the room when the water in the pool began to bubble. Vana was the first to see it and shouted in alarm, drawing everyone's attention.

From the pool, a small fin emerged. The fin slowly rose from the water, and to their surprise, it connected to a humanoid head with scales. The creature's blue appearance and sharp teeth made it look alien to them. Before anyone could react, more fins popped up around the pool. The monsters all had the build of lithe humans, but small blue scales covered their bodies. Their webbed hands had sharp claws on the ends of their fingers. He couldn't see it under the water, but he assumed their feet matched.

An odd hissing noise emanated from the creatures, and Arthur's mind translated the sounds.

*"They destroyed our pretties."*

*"They must pay."*

*"We shall eat them in payment."*

Arthur gulped at the implications. "They plan to kill us. Keep on your toes."

With that warning issued, he didn't want to waste any more time. He activated Ice Shards and sent the spell hurtling toward one creature. The surprise attack was a success as the shards sank into its chest. The monster fell to the ground and ceased moving, but Arthur hadn't expected the fight to be that easy. He turned toward the next creature and activated Scan.

*You have received 160 experience for successful use of Scan.*

| **Name:** Blue-Scale Zhorian | |
| --- | --- |
| **Level:** 15 | |
| **Type:** Zhorian | |
| **HP:** 180/180 | |
| **MP:** 280/280 | |
| **Stamina:** 110/110 | |
| **Strength:** 12 | **Experience:** N/A |
| **Agility:** 12 | **Skills** |
| **Intellect:** 20 | **Combat Skills:** |
| **Wisdom:** 8 | |
| **Endurance:** 14 | ? (???/???) |

*Yikes, they must be casters.*

The thought had barely crossed his mind when a ball of ice soared through the air and slammed into Samson's shield. An arrow flew back in response and sunk into the eye of the offending creature.

*No more playing games.* He turned toward Rayne and nodded. Pulling Ember to the ready, he activated Haste and charged forward at full speed. His dash brought him to the first zhorian in line, and his sword flew directly for its head. Moments before it hit, a small glittering shield of ice formed in front of the creature. His sword smashed into the ice with a crunch, and the spell fell apart.

Someone dashed by as he swung Ember in a backhanded motion and caught the monster in the chest. He didn't bother to acknowledge the combat log and instead looked up to see Rayne dancing around two other creatures. Arthur wasted no time and charged the next target while ignoring the one he just damaged. Since it focused on Rayne, it didn't see Ember as the blade punched directly through its body and sprayed bluish-tinged blood out of its side.

Another hiss drew his attention, and he turned just in time to see two claws extended his way and another of the ugly zhorian on a collision course with him. Before the nails met his face, a ball of fire hit the side of the creature's face and knocked it off course. It stumbled past Arthur, and he shook himself out of the ordeal quick enough to slide Ember across its throat.

Another of the monsters flew across in front of him, and he watched as Samson charged through the group like a rampaging bull. Any he hit bounced off the metal shield and crashed to the ground. Some of them quickly sprouted arrows while others took a well-placed ball of flame to the face.

Rayne continued to slash and stab around the room and was barely even slowed down by the press of monsters. A dozen corpses littered the room, but more still emerged from the pool.

The big pile of scales symbolizing Balair landed on top of one creature and his teeth sank into the meaty flesh of their face. The fire that followed made Arthur wince in imagined pain at the ordeal.

*Well, if everyone else is going to go all out, I might as well do the same.*

With a thought, he activated Sheathe in Flame and charged forward. Before he hit the next in line, his Ice Shards spell activated and launched its barrage of projectiles into the second creature. His sword came around and found another Ice Shield blocking its way. Unfortunately for the zhorian, his Sheathe in Flame spell melted right through it and seemed to cancel the effect as the blade continued unabated into its skull.

Two fists of stone slammed into the next monster in line, and Arthur dashed forward again. Ember sliced through the next zhorian to interfere, and Arthur saw one about to attack Rayne from the side. He fished out a throwing knife and launched it. The blade caught the monster in the ribs, causing it to hiss and grab the knife. Its hiss drew Rayne's attention, and he swung around and jabbed his stiletto dagger into its throat. He nodded his thanks to Arthur, seeing the knife in its side, and continued with his fighting.

The enemies thinned and the room cleared out. Arthur turned in time to see three much larger fins emerge from the pool of water. Two of the zhorians that emerged were much larger than expected. They stood almost nine feet tall and were overly muscular. One held a large spear that vaguely resembled a trident, while the second carried a heavy-looking sword and a large shield that looked like a spiral shell. They were both strapped in leather harnesses, and bits of leather armor covered the more sensitive areas.

The figure in the middle worried Arthur more than those. She was a lithe creature that only stood a little over five feet tall. The scaly creature had a soft feminine face and wore a wide cloth strip that covered her upper chest. Soft cloth pants adorned her legs, and she sported wild blue hair. It spread out from her head like she touched electricity, causing it to stand on end. Her deep blue eyes seemed to sparkle with zaps of blue energy as he watched.

The female zhorian spoke up in her hissing voice. "You two take that Dark Elf. I want her head to decorate my trophy room."

"Yes, mistress," they both responded with a quick bow, "and the others?"

"Just kill them," she said as she gazed upon the assembled group. When her eyes spotted Arthur, she spoke again.

"Wait. Leave the one over there alive," she said, pointing at Arthur.

Arthur quickly relied on his ability with languages to turn this situation.

"What do you want with me?" was his question as he was supremely at odds with the hissing noises coming from his own mouth.

"You speak our language, human? Interesting," the female said. "What is your name?"

"I'm Arthur. Now, are you going to answer my question?"

"Well, Arthur, I suppose I can. I find you interesting. Your hair is an oddly unique color that I'm familiar with from history. I plan to kill you personally. The Firebrand family has always been a pain in the ass for my kind. I don't know where your dragon is, but I plan to finish you before they can come to save you."

Arthur noticed his friends looking at him with odd expressions on their faces. The few remaining zhorians all stopped fighting and watched the exchange with interest.

"Uh, what's up, Arthur?" Vana asked, confused.

"They plan to kill us. Nothing out of the ordinary. Continue as you were," he told them with a wave.

The action around went from zero to a
hundred in a heartbeat. Arrows flew, and a
fireball streaked past. The large zhorian
interposed itself with its shield and took the
blast. The flame washed over the surface of
the shell and didn't leave a mark. Arthur
quickly scanned the three larger enemies.

*You have received 600 experience for
successful use of Scan.*

<table>
<tr><td colspan="2">Name: Targan Shellbreaker</td></tr>
<tr><td colspan="2">Level: 20</td></tr>
<tr><td colspan="2">Type: Zhorian</td></tr>
<tr><td colspan="2">Class: Guardian</td></tr>
<tr><td colspan="2">HP: 390/390</td></tr>
<tr><td colspan="2">MP: 110/110</td></tr>
<tr><td colspan="2">Stamina: 300/300</td></tr>
<tr><td>Strength: 28</td><td>Experience: N/A</td></tr>
<tr><td>Agility: 13</td><td rowspan="2">Skills<br>Combat Skills:</td></tr>
<tr><td>Intellect: 6</td></tr>
<tr><td>Wisdom: 4</td><td></td></tr>
<tr><td>Endurance: 28</td><td>? (???/???)</td></tr>
</table>

<table>
<tr><td colspan="2">Name: Lothar Wavebreaker</td></tr>
<tr><td colspan="2">Level: 20</td></tr>
<tr><td colspan="2">Type: Zhorian</td></tr>
<tr><td colspan="2">Class: Spearman</td></tr>
<tr><td colspan="2">HP: 310/310</td></tr>
<tr><td colspan="2">MP: 120/120</td></tr>
<tr><td colspan="2">Stamina: 280/280</td></tr>
<tr><td>Strength: 27</td><td>Experience: N/A</td></tr>
<tr><td>Agility: 15</td><td rowspan="2">Skills<br>Combat Skills:</td></tr>
<tr><td>Intellect: 12</td></tr>
<tr><td>Wisdom: 4</td><td></td></tr>
<tr><td>Endurance: 23</td><td>? (???/???)</td></tr>
</table>

| Name: Ishmina Lightningscale | |
| --- | --- |
| Level: 20 | |
| Type: Zhorian | |
| Class: Sparkmancer | |
| HP: 230/230 | |
| MP: 530/530 | |
| Stamina: 180/180 | |
| Strength: 14 | Experience: N/A |
| Agility: 18 | Skills |
| Intellect: 24 | Combat Skills: |
| Wisdom: 10 | |
| Endurance: 16 | ? (???/???) |

*Well, shit.* Arthur leaped into motion and sent off a blast of Ice Spikes toward Ishmina. She smiled like a grandparent dealing with a troublesome grandchild and waved a hand. His spell shattered in mid-flight as the air currents shifted in the room. Arthur was about to strike again when the feeling of static filled the air, and the hair on his arms stood on end.

Before he could react, a blue flash lit the area, and a bolt of lightning zipped across the room and sizzled into his chest. Arthur flew backward and landed on the ground with wisps of black smoke curling from his breastplate. Part of the blast arced and hit Ember, which to his surprise, absorbed the energy and converted it to mana to fill its storage. Every nerve in his body felt like it was on fire. The power of that strike was far more potent than the harpy he faced could even imagine conjuring.

*Ishmina Lightningscale has dealt 110 HP damage to you with Lightning Bolt.*

Arthur struggled back to his feet as his muscles randomly spasmed. He fought his twitching fingers and forced them to tighten on Ember's hilt. Samson held Lothar back and Targan played defense for Ishmina. His shield deftly deflected Allendria and Vana's projectiles. Lothar pushed hard against Samson's defenses until a bright white flame erupted from his shield and bathed the spearman.

With everyone distracted by the spell, Arthur dual cast Flamethrower toward Ishmina. The spell activated, and flame burst across the gap. Targan quickly intercepted it with his shield, but the intensity of the fire was enough that it licked over the edges of the shell and burned into his flesh. When the spell ended, a giant zhorian with a burned face and legs stood in obvious pain.

*You have dealt 110 HP damage to Targan Shellbreaker (Level 20) with Flamethrower (Glancing Blow).*

*Well, some damage is better than none. He deflected a large amount of damage with that shield compared to what that spell is capable of.* Ishmina hissed her displeasure at the ability and moved her hands in an odd gesture. Water flowed from her hands and splashed Targan. Arthur paid close attention to what the magic did. He followed the spell as it used the Water Magic to replenish the skin and blood flow to the affected area.

*Great, she can heal.* The plus side was, Arthur thought he could replicate that ability since he carefully watched the magic work. This fight wasn't going how he wished. Lothar roared in pain, and Arthur turned to see Rayne standing behind him with both daggers punched into his back. Samson stepped forward and slashed with his sword. The blade dug into Lothar's chest and cut a deep gash across it.

"Foolish humans. I'll kill you all myself if I must," Ishmina hissed as she moved her hands in imitation of the earlier healing spell. Arthur immediately built up Fire Magic in front of him, pouring in a sizable amount of mana to fuel the spell. It was time to go big or go home.

The ball of fire in front of him was impressive, but he knew Targan could easily block it. Instead, Arthur began swirling and compressing the energy into a compact ball of spinning power. He squeezed the fire tighter and tighter until he looked at an orb of fire the size of a baseball. With a thought, he launched the ball toward Ishmina. Her eyes grew wide as she observed the spell, but Targan jumped into the path.

"No, Targan, don't!" she hissed out.

The compact ball of fire hit his shield and popped. At first, it seemed like nothing would happen, but a torrent of flame exploded from the small ball. The force of the explosion reminded Arthur of grenades from Earth, and the blast launched Targan into the wall at the back of the cave with a crunch.

*You have discovered the Fire Magic Spell: Fireblast for a 250 experience bonus to Fire Magic.*

*You have dealt 300 HP damage to Targan Shellbreaker (Level 20) with Fireblast (Crushing Blow).*
*Targan Shellbreaker has died.*

"You little bastard!" Ishmina screamed at Arthur.

She finished her spell, and the Water Magic shot from her and hit Lothar. His wounds quickly knit as he swung his trident in a broad arc to force Samson and Rayne to back away.

In her fury, she lost track of the battle and an arrow neatly sprouted from her right shoulder. The zhorian caster screamed in rage again and looked to Vana. The static built in the room and Arthur's hair stood on end again.

"Vana, run!"

A massive boom of resultant thunder accompanied the blue flash of light. The walls shook, and loose dirt fell from the ceiling. When his vision returned to normal, Arthur saw Vana lying on the ground with Allendria standing over her. Allendria was helping her back to her feet, and Arthur couldn't figure out how they were alive. He caught sight of an odd formation on the ground. He quickly realized it was the remnants of a shattered wall of stone.

Their survival made sense. Allendria must've quickly brought up a wall of stone to intercept the lighting. The lightning blasted the wall apart, but it negated any damage to the ladies. Arthur heaved a sigh of relief at that.

Arthur turned his attention back to Ishmina
to see her fury building on her face. He cast
Weak Slow on her and watched her anger morph
to disbelief. Her face turned to his, and he
just smiled a knowing smile at her.

"Hey, Ishmina, suck on this," Arthur told
her as he pointed Ember her way and activated
Dragonfire. The searing, fiery flame leaped
forward and engulfed the figure in a brilliant
fire. When it cleared, a thoroughly pissed off
Ishmina stood in her same place with a cracked
Ice Shield covering her body. The heat from
the spell scorched parts of her body, and she
had a look of discomfort on her face.

"You'll regret that young Firebrand."

Arthur felt the Air and Water Magic pouring
from her in waves, and oddly shaped black
clouds formed toward the ceiling of the cave.
They started swirling and sparked with flashes
of lighting.

"Everyone to me!" Arthur yelled over the
noise in the room.

Vana and Allendria dashed across the room
while still launching projectiles. One of
Vana's arrows sank into Lothar's side and
caused him to grip the wound in pain. With
Lothar distracted, Samson ran to Arthur. The
shadowy form of Rayne popped up near him to
mark the arrival of the last member.

With nowhere else to go, he cast his Dimensional Storage spell. The cast time started as they formed up, and the door swung open while the storm overhead built in intensity. Everyone jumped into the storage space and stood as far from the doorway as possible while stepping around the animal carcasses. Arthur and Allendria both looked to each other and nodded. They each pulled on their power and lifted a stone wall to cover the entrance of the space.

A few seconds passed before it sounded like artillery shells firing off in the room. The muffled *thumps* past the wall of stone were disconcerting. After a few moments, the rock shattered, and the blue flashes of lightning were visible all over the cave. The storm of mini lightning strikes was almost mesmerizing, if not for their situation. Ishmina stood in the middle of the storm with her arms spread wide, her eyes sparking with electricity.

"Damn, any ideas?" Arthur asked over the cacophony of noise.

"Against that? What do you expect?" Samson asked in disbelief.

"Can you counter it?" Allendria asked.

"I might be able to, but she is honestly far more powerful than me and has made me look like a child every time I use magic against her."

"How about Earth Magic?" Vana asked them.

"It might be possible, but I need to be close to the entrance to manipulate the earth outside this space. If I get too close, the lightning will arc to me," Arthur told them with hesitation in his voice.

Before any further arguing could happen, a throwing knife flew out of the space and headed straight for Ishmina. As soon as it left the confines of the dimensional space, a lightning bolt arced down and zapped it, sending it flying to the ground. Everyone turned to look at Rayne.

"What? No one else was doing anything. It was worth a shot," he told them, smiling.

"Well, that won't work. How long do you think she can maintain that spell?" Arthur asked with a nod toward the Sparkmancer.

"I'd guess about ten or so," Allendria responded with a thoughtful look on her face.

"Ten minutes isn't that bad. We can just wait here for her power to subside and then resume the fight," Arthur told them all.

Allendria shook her head. "No, ten hours. She's made the storm almost entirely self-sufficient now. It takes her almost no power to maintain it. She may even be capable of holding that for days. I don't know the extent of her power."

"So, that idea is out the window. Anyone else?" Arthur asked.

*Well, I'm not volunteering to do something stupid.* The voice in his head responded.

Arthur turned to see Balair lying in the back of the room. The little dragon watched the show outside the room with interest.

"We need to ground the lightning," Arthur told them resolutely.

"Uh, what?" Rayne asked, confused.

"Lightning is drawn to tall conductive structures," Arthur said as he scrambled around the room and grabbed the chunks of iron he extracted earlier.

He levitated the iron in front of him and used his Fire Magic to heat the metal. When it was hot, he activated his Arcane Forging spell, and the power flowed across the lump of metal and separated it into three metal rods the width of his thumb but eight feet long.

"I'll force these out of the entrance and embed them into the ground. I plan to stagger these so we can close the distance with her," he said as he pointed to Ishmina. "When we get within range, everyone hit her with everything you have."

The group nodded at his statement but were clearly apprehensive about the idea. Arthur held two of the rods in his left hand while a single rod rested in his right, with Ember resting in its sheath on his back. He gripped the lone rod in his Earth Magic and crept toward the entrance. When he was only a foot away, he launched the rod with his physical and magical strength. It soared like a javelin and the sharpened point embedded into the ground. Lightning immediately jumped to the rod.

The group ran while Arthur moved another rod to his right hand. This one flew in the same manner and landed another twenty yards away. Arthur was happy to see his plan was working until he glanced back at the first rod. The intense lightning and constant strikes had caused it to glow red. Before too long, it would melt or explode into metal fragments.

He increased his pace and launched the last
rod. It stuck in the ground less than fifteen
feet from Ishmina. The look of disdain,
coupled with the fear on her face, told him
everything he needed to know about how well
his plan was working. Another throwing knife
soared by his face and slammed into the
caster's right shoulder. An arrow followed
shortly after, and Arthur watched the quickly
spinning tip *thump* into her chest and burrow
deep. The hiss that emanated from the zhorian
reflected her pain.

Before Arthur could close the distance,
Lothar slammed into the group from the side.
The party went flying and landed in a
scattered heap.

*Lothar has dealt 40 HP damage to you with
Whirlwind Charge.*

Arthur heard a sizzling noise and felt the
hairs on his arms stand on end. The flashes of
blue near him drew his attention to the iron
rod, not ten feet from his spot on the ground.
He quickly rolled from the rod just as another
bolt slammed into it and sent little tendrils
of electricity across the nearby area.

Arthur renewed his Haste spell and charged
toward Lothar. The big warrior was quick, but
his speed couldn't match Arthurs when boosted
by Haste. The zhorian tried a downward thrust
that Arthur deftly avoided. The spear slammed
into the ground near his feet instead, and
Arthur responded by driving Ember to the hilt
in the creature's leg.

Lothar stumbled backward two steps, and then his eyes widened in alarm. The big spearman fell forward and landed on his face. Behind him stood Rayne, both of his blades dripping blue blood as he smiled ear to ear.

"Well done. Care to get her, too?" Arthur asked, nodding toward Ishmina.

"If no one else can, I guess I will," he answered with a smile, and Arthur watched as shadows exploded from him. His face, hands, and feet exploded with shadows, and Arthur stared at the mysterious form that had saved him against Lyrinth.

To his immense surprise, Rayne moved so fast he had trouble keeping track of him. The gain in levels coupled with whatever boost this form of Rayne's granted must have significantly increased his speed. Arthur turned and sent another round of Ice Spikes at Ishmina to distract her. She responded by raising a shield of ice, and the spikes crashed into the protection and shattered.

"I'm done playing with you, child. This ends now!" she yelled as the storm above them coalesced above her head. Bolts of lightning flew from the small storm, but Ishmina seemed to catch them and hold the power of these strikes between her hands. The new ball of energy built larger and larger as more bolts of electricity struck.

"Time to die, young Firebrand."

Her hand grabbed the ball of power like a basketball player palming a ball and moved backward in a throwing motion. She froze, and her mouth and eyes widened in shock. The energy in her hands unraveled, and small sparks of lightning shot across the room in all directions. Arthur raised Ember in front of him and caught one bolt. The sword absorbed the power, and the shock tingled his fingers but caused no damage.

The Sparkmancer slowly fell forward, and Rayne's figure stood behind her. His eerie blue jagged eyes looked like electricity shining toward them.

"Well, why the fuck didn't you do that a long time ago?" Vana screamed at him.

The shadows faded from him, and he grinned at the ranger. "I think I won," was his response as he sunk to a knee. Arthur rushed to his side.

"You hurt?"

"Not really. A few minor injuries. I try not to use that ability because it has an unpleasant side effect. I'll be fine once some time has elapsed," Rayne told the assembled group.

An unexpected message shocked the group.

*Congratulations, you have completed the Hidden Event – What Lies Beneath. You are granted 5,000 bonus experience, an advancement in level to a random combat skill, and a Large Loot Chest.*

"Everyone else get that message?" Arthur asked.

The slow nods of the group told him all he needed to know.

"A Large Loot Chest? I don't see a chest anywh…" Allendria started until a soft rumbling reverberated through the room, and a chest slowly rose from the floor near the pool of water.

The group approached the chest, and all looked in wonder at the intricate box. The wood was smooth and dark, banded in intricately designed metal. Arthur stepped forward and cautiously lifted the lid. Inside was a small collection of items.

| **Item:** Leather Breeches of the Fleet-footed Fox | **Defense: 18** |
|---|---|
| | **Durability:** 190/190 |
| | **Rarity:** Uncommon |
| | **Quality:** Good |
| | **Weight:** 2.0 kg |
| | **Slot:** Legs |
| | **Traits:** Leather breeches made from the softest of fox hides. This is imbued with the power of nature. |
| | **Enchantments:**<br>• Increases your speed through wooded areas by 10%.<br>• Increases your Agility by 1.<br>• Increases the |

| | chance for you to spot tracks from wild animals by 10%. |
|---|---|

| **Item:** Steel Vambraces of the Shade | **Defense: 22**<br><br>**Durability:** 210/210<br><br>**Rarity:** Rare<br><br>**Quality:** Good<br><br>**Weight:** 1.5 kg<br><br>**Slot:** Arms<br><br>**Traits:** Steel Vambraces of unknown origin, steeped in the power of a shade. The shadowy apparition grants this piece extra abilities.<br><br>**Enchantments:**<br>• You are 15% more difficult to detect when stealthed.<br>• Increases your Agility by 2.<br>• Damage done by you when attacking an enemy unseen increased by |

<table>
<tr><td></td><td align="center">15%.</td></tr>
</table>

| **Item:**<br>Ring of Minor Thought | **Durability:** 80/80<br><br>**Rarity:** Uncommon<br><br>**Quality:** Good<br><br>**Weight:** 0.2 kg<br><br>**Slot:** Ring<br><br>**Traits:** A ring of soft metal that emanates with power.<br><br>**Enchantments:**<br>• Increases your Intellect by 2.<br>• Increases your Wisdom by 1. |
| --- | --- |

*You have received Iron Ingot (x15).*
*You have received Gold Coin (x8).*
*You have received Silver Coin (x98).*
*Congratulations, you have been granted level 10 in Swords. Swing speed with swords increased by 27%. That was some clever work.*

"Not a terrible haul, guys. I think Vana should take the pants, Rayne the vambraces, and Allendria the ring. Any objections?"

None of them voiced an objection, so Arthur handed out the gear. Vana was not shy about stripping down and sliding her new pants on. It amused Arthur to see Samson paying very close attention.

Vana looked up to see the man watching her. "What?"

Samson cleared his throat and looked away. "Nothing. We about ready to go?"

"Let me check around here first for anything," Arthur told them.

He made his rounds and found some more iron ore and even a small vein of gemstones. Five opals, three rubies, and two sapphires fell into his hand and disappeared into his small storage. They dumped the iron into his still open storage room.

"Time to head back. We've had enough excitement for one day," Arthur told them.

Everyone nodded in agreement and left the cave. Balair quickly took to the air and flew back to the village.

*Not going to stick around and travel back with us? We may need your impressive bird-killing skills on the return trip.*

*Meh, I've done my part for the day. It's well past my nap time.*

The group bagged some more animals on their return trip, and Arthur was comfortable with the number of supplies they scrounged up. Vana and Rayne even spotted a few more useful plants. Arthur used Germinate on them before he let the two pick them. To his great relief, they also stumbled across a wild flax plant. He wasted no time in stuffing those seeds away. They were sorely in need of cloth, so linen would be better than nothing.

The party returned triumphantly to the inn and took their seats at a table. The odd blue bloodstains on their clothing drew the attention of those around them. A few people even asked for stories, and Samson told them about their exciting encounter. He was definitely a soldier through and through, though, as his story was very no-nonsense. The paladin would never make a useful bard.

Arthur took the chance to check over his notifications for the day while Samson continued his storytelling. He collapsed everything into just experience totals and levels.

*You have gained 560 total experience in Throwing Knives.*

*Congratulations, you have reached level 2 in Throwing Knives. You now have 3% increased accuracy with Throwing Knives. Can you please learn to use those before you continue bludgeoning poor ducks?*

*You have gained 11,750 total experience.*

*You have gained 3,830 total experience in Earth Magic.*

*You have gained 1,990 total experience in Fire Magic.*

*You have gained 480 total experience in Dimensional Magic.*

*You have gained 240 total experience in Air Magic.*

*You have gained 800 total experience in Water Magic.*

*You have gained 770 total experience in Swords.*

*You have gained 1020 total experience in Medium Armor.*

*Congratulations, you have reached level 5 in Medium Armor. You now have 12% increased defense on pieces of Medium Armor you wear. That was an impressive blast of lightning you took.*

*You have gained 150 total experience in Arcane Smithing and Blacksmithing.*

*You have gained 1250 total experience in Herbalism.*

*Congratulations, you have reached level 6 in Herbalism. You now have a 12% higher chance of identifying an herb successfully. I think you've been hanging around elves too long.*

*You have gained 1675 total experience in Farming.*

*Congratulations, you have reached level 8 in Farming. You now have a chance for up to 35% increased yield from plants. You need to show farming some love.*

"All right, guys. Fantastic work today," Arthur told them as he stood from his seat. "Now for the fun part!"

"Fun part?" Rayne asked in confusion.

"Yeah. Unloading and sorting all the stuff we found."

The table let out a collective groan as the group stood to walk to the back on the inn and got to work.

# Chapter 31


*A Questing We Will Go*

The morning dawned quickly and started with a hearty breakfast. The party gathered inside the inn and checking their equipment to leave. They handed all the affairs of the village over to their second in commands to prevent any issues while they quested.

Daniel approached the group with bundles in his arms. He handed one to each person as he passed. Arthur peeked inside the package, and the aroma of freshly baked loaves of bread and dried meats filled his senses.

"Figured you guys needed some food for the journey. Should be enough hard bread and dried meat to last you a little over a week. You'll need to supplement with some hunting if your trip takes longer," Daniel said.

The group showered him with thanks, and he returned to his work.

"Rayne, you ever decide on the class you'd like to pursue? I'm sure you hit the level twenty mark, or you would've said something by now," Arthur said.

"Yeah. I hit level twenty when we got that five thousand bonus experience from our event. I've looked over the available options and chose a class that seems somewhat unique to me. It's called the Shadow Walker class."

"Good to know," he told the young man and turned to face the group. "Let's get this party started."

They nodded, and all accepted their class
quests.

<table>
<tr><td colspan="2" align="center">Class Quest: Spell Blade</td></tr>
<tr><td>Requirements: Reach level 20. Have the Sword skill and Small Blades skill. Must have at least 20 Agility and 15 Intelligence.<br>Rewards: 18,000 experience, Unlock Spell Blade Talent Tree, Receive 3 skill points for Spell Blade Talent Tree.</td><td>Description: Proceed to Nightwatch and find the Armory.</td></tr>
<tr><td colspan="2" align="center">You have accepted this quest.</td></tr>
</table>

*Odd, not much information to go by. It's good to know the exact requirements for the class, though.*

"Everyone else's quest pretty vague in the description?" Arthur asked.

"Mine says I need to find the Shallow Bog and proceed to the Monolith Stone at the center," Vana told him.

"I'm supposed to go to The Tomb of the Lost and find the grave of Porthain Brightblade," Samson added.

"I need to travel to The Scorched Forest and find the Tree of Embers," Allendria said.

"I have to go to a place called Nightwatch and get to the Dungeon," Rayne told the group.

"Anyone know where any of these places are? Since we're grouped together, they should be relatively close to each other. I also have to go to Nightwatch, but I need to find the Armory," Arthur told them.

"I'm familiar with Nightwatch. It's an old, abandoned human fortress. It's on the northeastern border of the forest from here, a little over five days' travel. It got its name because it was used to keep track of the Night Elves movements. The Scorched Forest is close to that location. It was the site of a battle between humans and the Dark Elves. The forest hasn't stopped burning since the battle," Samson chimed in.

"I heard a traveler mention The Tomb of the Lost once. He sold some rare herbs to my old master in Seora. He told him it was almost ten days' travel south of the city, along the border of the Forest of Nodara. If I remember the last map I saw correctly, that places it within a day of Nightwatch," Rayne told the group.

"Anyone know of the Shallow Bog? I'd guess it's somewhere near the rest of those?" Arthur asked.

The group stayed silent, and no one had anything further to add.

"I guess we can ask along the way. Surely we'll find someone who knows," Arthur said with an upbeat tone to his voice.

The group checked their gear yet again out of nervousness. Arthur ran his hands over the brace of throwing knives now attached to his belt. He'd held up on his promise and made a new set for both Rayne and himself. As much as he enjoyed using his bow, it was too much of a hassle to carry with his other weapons.

The party took the road east out of the village and followed it until they reached Bastion. The gatehouse was back in perfect working order, and the construction crews were still making minor improvements. Samson took a few moments to confer with his second in command and bid a last farewell. They continued through the gate and out into the wide world of Dravincia.

* * *

Two days into their travel, the group stumbled upon a tiny village. The place looked worse than Alem's Crossing ever had. All the buildings were falling, and only one even had an intact roof. The one with the roof sported a sizable hole in one wall that gave an unobstructed view of the interior. Scorched wooden planks adorned the sides.

No one could recall the name of this place. The party walked through the wreckage of the village, investigating the homes. To neither their disappointment nor relief, they found no one and nothing of use, so they continued on their journey.

Their travel was uneventful until the morning of the fourth day. Another village dotted the landscape as they approached, but this one wasn't unoccupied. The group stopped just outside of it on a slight rise to watch the activity.

"More goblins? I thought we got rid of them all?" Arthur whispered.

"We made them all retreat, but that didn't mean they ran back to the forest. Looks like that place fell to a group of goblins while we were fighting the main army. Judging by those wooden pens," Samson said, pointing toward the edge of the village, "they keep prisoners here. I'm sure they have villagers from the surrounding area confined there. Well, those that survived."

"The orc force isn't that large. So we want to free them?" Vana asked in concern.

"We can't just let the orcs keep them locked away. As much as I'd like to say our mission is more important, I know it's not true. What's the point of the mission if not to gain the ability to save more people?" Arthur told the group.

"So, what's the plan?" Rayne asked, and the entire group turned to look at Samson.

"I wish we had more information. I need to know if they have anyone camped on the other side of the village," the soldier grumbled.

*Up for a quick flight?*

*Might as well.*

"Balair will fly over and check for us," Arthur said as the drake lifted off and flew toward the village.

The group waited for a good fifteen minutes before Balair returned. The small dragon thumped into the ground with his landing and turned toward Arthur.

*I counted twenty-five goblins and three orcs there. No one on the perimeter, though. I also saw roughly forty prisoners in pens. Some don't look like they'll survive much longer.*

"Samson, Balair's said he saw twenty-five goblins and three orcs over there but none on the perimeter."

"Fortunately for us, these orcs and goblins
can be lazy idiots. They have no sentries and
don't even appear worried about an attack. We
need to get in there fast before
reinforcements arrive. We can't assume they're
the entire force that's left here."

Samson crouched to a spot of bare dirt and
sketched a rough outline of the village. "Now,
here's what we'll do."

***

Arthur crept closer to one of the outer
buildings of the village. He paid close
attention to his surroundings to avoid bumping
into a goblin or an orc before the plan called
for it. When he reached the wall, he scurried
along the siding and pulled himself to the
roof. Crawling forward, he peeked over the
edge of the ledge and watched as the goblins
roamed through the village.

The ugly green creatures walked around
without a care in the world. Their dingy
clothing only further enhanced the putrid
smell coming from the small crowd. Arthur
hoped this plan would work. Otherwise, Samson
was in for a heap of trouble.

Arthur maintained his position on the roof
until he noticed a commotion in the milling
goblins. They scurried around and grabbed
random weapons before running toward the edge
of the village.

*Samson must've started.*

He crawled across the roof so he could get a good view of the action. In the distance, he watched Samson casually stroll across the field toward the village without a care in the world. The mob of goblins filtered out of the village center and approached him with confusion. *They must be freaking out with a lone armored man walking toward them without worry,* Arthur thought to himself with a smile.

Arthur watched the clearing near his building until the last goblin passed. He slid over the edge and quietly dropped to the ground. The movement in the corner of his vision told him he wasn't alone. Creeping forward, he closed the distance to the nearest goblin. Samson roared a challenge at the creatures, and their voices rose to join his. In the noise, Ember slashed forward and took the nearest goblin's head from his shoulders.

*You have dealt 210 HP damage to Goblin Raider (Level 18) with Ember (Decapitating Blow).*

The goblin's head fell to the ground and rolled away as the body fell to its knees and tipped forward. An arrow slammed into the next green creature in line, and it fell over with a grunt. Arthur dashed forward and slashed with Ember as fast as he could manage. The blade blurred from one goblin to another as it dug into flesh. The damage notifications scrolled past, and he pushed them to the back of his mind.

Arrows took down more enemies as they
closed on him and the figure beside him. Rayne
killed just as quickly, but with far more
finesse. His precise dagger strikes ripped out
kidneys and punctured hearts and lungs
everywhere he went. Anytime a goblin spotted
them and tried to attack, they ended up with a
feather shaft protruding from their chest or
face.

Flashes of red illuminated the area, and
Arthur looked up to see Allendria hurling
balls of fire at the goblins from the side.
Samson stood toe to toe with a crowd of
goblins and an orc as he deflected blows with
his shield and bashed enemies to the ground.
Within minutes, the group surrounded the last
of the enemies. A lone orc and four shaking
goblins stood inside the ring of friends.

"Why are you still here? Why didn't you
return to your homeland?" Arthur asked the
remaining orc in their harsh language.

The orc looked confused as he turned to
face Arthur. "You speak our language? Rare for
any not of the priesthood."

"I don't care how rare it is. Answer my
question," Arthur demanded with a threatening
glare while casually waving Ember.

A goblin gulped. "We not told to return. We
told to hold this location and collect
prisoners."

"What do you do with them?" Vana asked.

"We use for slaves. They work fields. Grow
food. When they get sick or useless, we eat
them."

Arthur grimaced at the statement. He
started to respond, but Samson beat him to it.
"If you eat the prisoners, why would you have
them grow food?"

The orc looked confused but answered anyway. "We not animals. We eat more than meat."

*Odd way of looking at that, but whatever.* Arthur thought to himself.

*I've spotted a goblin running from the village toward the trees. What should I do about it?* Balair asked him.

*Can you kill it?*

*Well, yeah.*

*Then don't let it escape.* Arthur told him before a thought struck him, *Actually, on second thought, let it go. I want someone to tell the goblins they aren't safe out here. I can't let these fools go now because they know I speak their language.*

*Fine, fine. I'll see what else I find from the air.*

"How many more of your kind are still in this kingdom?" Arthur asked.

"Not sure. We were huge host. I told that they killed many south of here in big battle. Not sure how many left."

"Then you're of no further use to me," Arthur said in the common tongue as he walked forward with Ember in front of him.

"Arthur, you can't just murder them," Rayne said from the side.

"Why not?"

"They're living, breathing people, although I use that term lightly here."

"No. They're evil creatures who've violated the people of this land for unjust causes, destroyed villages and homes, enslaved the people of the kingdom, and even ate those who fell ill or weak instead of trying to help. I declare them enemies of the land and sentence them all to death."

*You have made a decree! All lands under your influence have been given permission to inflict the death penalty on all orcs and goblins without reprise.*

*Hmm, I guess there aren't any local leaders still left anywhere nearby if my influence extends this far north.*

Samson nodded at Arthur's statement. "They've done nothing but commit evil. As a Paladin, it's also my duty to see them removed from the land."

"Rayne, if we let them go, they will come back again with more friends and do more harm. They're enemies of the kingdom. They started an unjustified war, and we're just trying to clean it up."

"I don't know if I can kill enemies who've surrendered," Rayne muttered.

"If your ideals are preventing you from executing enemies of the realm and a known evil, then I'll do it myself," Arthur said through gritted teeth.

Arthur walked to the orc in the front of the group, and the orc's eyes took on a resigned look. He slightly bowed his head forward when Arthur closed on him.

"I have sentenced you to death for your crimes," Arthur told him in their language, "do you wish to say any last words?"

"No," the orc mumbled quietly.

"I pray that whatever God you serve is just," Arthur said as he swung Ember and removed his head.

One goblin beside him dove toward Arthur, and he slashed his sword across them. The second goblin went down with an arrow, and Samson stood behind the final orc as it fell forward in death.

They shook off the effects of the battle and walked into the village. Two large cages butted up against one of the major buildings in the village, and the group walked up to the closest one.

"Who are you?" one nervous woman asked as they approached.

"Can you get us out of here? Where are the goblins?" Another villager called in a panic.

"Calm down," Arthur yelled over the noise, "I'm Arthur, Mayor of Alem's Crossing to the south. We've dispatched the goblins and orcs who kept you imprisoned. We'll open the cage shortly."

"We're finally saved. Where will we go? What will we do?" A scared female voice questioned from the front of the cage.

Arthur's gaze drifted to the speaker and spotted a youthful woman, probably in her late teens, on her knees and holding onto the bars with tears falling from her eyes. The disheveled clothing, or lack thereof, told him all he needed to know about the conditions here. The crowd's dirty and sometimes bruised faces showed the suffering they'd been subject to.

"You can gather any supplies or resources you find here and flee wherever you wish. I'm told the major cities survived the raids if you wish to take the chance at one of them. If you aren't happy with those places, you're all welcome to travel to Alem's Crossing to the south. We accepted refugees from the war and even fought back a large part of this raiding force when the invasion first started. I'll not force a decision on anyone, though. You can live your life as you wish."

Arthur stepped forward and brought Ember
down to shear through the locking bars holding
the prisoners in the different cages. The
crowd excitedly scrambled from the pens. Many
scurried toward buildings looking for anything
of use.

A thought struck Arthur as he watched them
run around, and he yelled over the group.
"Anyone here know where the Shallow Bog is?"

No one came by at first, but after a few
minutes of the crowd dispersing, a woman
approached. It surprised Arthur to see it was
the woman he noticed in the cage earlier.

"I know where it's at," she told them. "If
you head almost directly east of here, right
before you get to the forest is a small
valley. Follow that valley north, and it leads
directly to the bog. People avoid that place
because of the monsters it attracts. Be
careful if you go that way."

"Thank you. What's your name?" Arthur asked
softly.

"Prim, Lord Mayor."

"Nice to meet you, Prim. My friends and I
can't stay for very long. Make sure you let
everyone know we killed the goblins and orcs
on the outskirts of the village to the south.
They are free to take any of their weapons or
supplies they're carrying to see themselves
safely to their destination."

"Thank you, my lord," she told him with a
quick bow.

The party milled around the village for a brief time, ensuring all the people were free from their cages. When the ex-prisoners started gathering supplies and splitting into groups, Arthur and his fellow company bid their farewell. It disappointed the people to see them go, but the thrill of their newfound freedom overwhelmed their worry.

***

"Vana, duck!" Arthur yelled as he tossed a throwing knife in her direction. The agile woman dropped to the ground as the blade soared overhead and smacked into the chest of the gnoll behind her. The ugly creature with the face of a mangy dog yelped in pain and fell over.

"Thanks," she yelled to him and immediately shot right at him. The arrow passed within inches of his face, causing him to feel the air from its passage, and made a solid *thunk* into something behind him. He turned to see another gnoll holding its stomach with a fresh arrow sprouting from the wound. Arthur slashed Ember across its throat, putting it out of its misery.

He nodded his thanks to Vana and checked their surroundings. Rayne deftly finished a group of three gnolls and didn't even look to break a sweat. Samson pounded his sword against his shield, causing a loud banging noise that irritated Arthur. The gnolls must have sensitive hearing, similar to the animals their faces resembled because the sound seemed to cause visible pain to them.

Allendria held out her hands and did her best to maintain a wall of fire, separating her from their enemies. There weren't many of the creatures left, and the few remaining were dropping. The last furry creature fell to the ground with a bash of Samson's shield, and he stepped forward and stabbed it before it rose.

"That all of them? Anyone hurt?" Arthur asked as he scanned the surrounding figures.

"A few scratches. Nothing major," Samson said with a wave.

"I've got a minor bite on one arm, but it doesn't look like it's dangerous," Allendria said.

Arthur hustled to her side and checked the damage for himself. There was a small bite on her arm, but it barely bled. The damage was mainly superficial. The edge of her bracer absorbed most of the impact, and only the teeth on the outer side caught skin.

"Well, the girl wasn't kidding about the enemies here. No wonder people don't come here often," Vana said as she shuffled through the corpses.

The group split up and searched for anything useful on the gnolls. A handful of chunks of metal that looked similar to coins popped up. They didn't have any kind of emblem embossed on them, but he assumed the primitive tribe wouldn't mint their own currency.

The wooden weapons they wielded weren't anything special. Most were absolute garbage, but the few that were still serviceable flew into the Dimensional Storage space. The armaments joined the small pile of loot and items they'd stumbled across since leaving the village. All the scraps of cloth, leather, iron, wood, and anything they could repurpose lay in the center of the storage space. The only items that didn't sit in a pile were the seeds they'd gathered.

Rayne seemed thrilled with many of the herbs they'd found. The soon to be Shadow Walker chattered about the unique things he could make with each. His youthful enthusiasm made Arthur smile at his nonstop explanations. If Herbalism and Alchemy were what truly drove the guy, then Arthur would fully support his work. They needed an Alchemist, anyway. The right potion in an emergency could literally be life or death.

With the loot collected, they pushed further into the bog. Since it was in a valley, it was easy to figure out which direction to go. Vana moved ahead of them, carefully checking for enemies and scouting their destination. She called them to a halt before they crested a slight rise.

"Good news and bad news," she blurted.

"Fine, I'll bite, what's the good news?" Arthur asked.

"Found the Monolith."

"And the bad?"

"Guards."

"Of course, there is. Samson, want to take a look? See what we can come up with?"

The soldier nodded, and the group crept forward to the rise. They dropped prone and crawled over the high point to see the assembled force. A group of ten gnolls camped near the base of the imposing monolith. The solid black structure rose from the ground and had to be at least eighty feet tall.

The gnolls in question weren't the same ones they'd fought before, though. These were wearing real armor, and Arthur spotted actual metal weapons through the camp. Next to the gnolls were an assembled group of creatures that Arthur couldn't quite place.

"Uh, what are those?" he asked quietly.

"The little things? Hard to tell for sure, but I'd guess imps," Samson told him.

"You have demons on this plane?"

"No… well, not that I'm aware of. Why do you ask?"

"You said imps. The only imps I've ever heard of are typically minor demons."

"Oh," Samson said with a chuckle, "no, no. The imps here are small beastkin. They look like small goats with no hair that stands on two legs like people."

Arthur nodded at the very odd description. "They don't look that dangerous. This challenge doesn't look too bad. We'll have to be careful when we fight the gnolls since they look formidable with armor. The imps should go down fast."

Allendria shook her head at his statement. "I worry about you sometimes. If you don't know what they are, you might at least ask before you make assumptions."

"What? The imps?"

"Of course, the imps. They are the most dangerous part of this."

*Can never be easy.* "What do they do then?"

"Imps have a master level of control over Earth Magic. It is their native element, and it infuses their body with extensive amounts of it. They can use it to hurl magic at us, enhance their defenses, set traps in the ground, and many other uncomfortable things," Allendria explained.

"Anyone have any ideas then? There appear to be eight of them."

The party was silent as each person thought over the problem.

"Man, I'd kill for one of your hellfire arrows," Vana said under her breath.

"It sounds like an excellent idea, but if they can truly enhance their defenses, they may survive the blast with the delay they have."

"What about that new spell you did in the cave? Could you hit them with a dual cast?" Allendria asked.

"I guess I can," Arthur said as he pulled up the spell. He'd cast it mid-battle and never looked at the full spell description.

| Spell: Fireblast | |
|---|---|
| Requirements: Fire Magic and Air Magic<br>Mana Cost: 260 MP<br>Cast Time: 5 seconds<br>Distance: 100 yards | Description: Condenses a ball of flame and pressurizes it with air. The resultant orb of fire explodes on contact with its target for the following effects:<br><br>• Targets within 5 yards of the blast take 300 fire damage and |

|  | <ul><li>are knocked backward ten yards.</li><li>Targets between 6 and 10 yards of the blast take 180 fire damage and are knocked back 3 feet.</li><li>Targets between 11 yards and 14 yards take 80 fire damage and stumble, causing interrupt to any casting.</li></ul> |
|---|---|
| **Mastery Level: 1** ||

*It should do the job nicely.*

"What's the plan, then?" Arthur asked, turning to Samson.

"As much as I'd like to say there's some grand strategy, I'm afraid it isn't true. We'll have to rush them and kill as many imps as possible from the start. As soon as the battle starts, the gnolls will interpose themselves between us and the imps, allowing the imps to attack us without concern. We need to get rid of them at the beginning of the fight."

"Fine with me. I can still shoot them in the face, right? They aren't arrow proof or anything?" Vana asked Allendria.

She chuckled at the question, "They'll die by an arrow unless they cast stone skin before you shoot them. If they have enough time to erect defenses, this could turn bad fast."

"I'll dual cast my Fireblast into the center of them. Vana, you pick them off, starting at the left. Allendria, you do the same on the right. If luck holds, they'll all be dead before the gnolls can mount a defense. From there, we just have to fight them off."

Everyone nodded their agreement and turned to face the foe. Arthur judged the distance and realized he needed to be closer.

"This will be a running attack like the catapults. I have to be closer to hit them with my spell."

Arthur stood to his feet, and he heard the creak of armor as the others joined him. He took off in a sprint for the main group of the imps. He needed to make it sixty yards down the side of the rise to be within range. The group charged down the hill, wordless except for the loud clomp of their footsteps.

They were forty yards into their charge before Arthur heard one of the gnolls yell in alarm. Their camp quickly jumped to their feet and scrambled to find weapons. He passed the sixty-yard mark and activated the cast timer for his dual cast spell. They continued their charge until his counter was up, and he watched the swirling balls of power solidify in his outstretched hands.

His fists closed over each orb, and he reared back and launched the first with his right hand. It soared forward, and Arthur wasted no time in shafting stance and lobbing the second orb left-handed. To his shame, this orb didn't fly well. He expected the magic to take care of most of it, but apparently, your throw also mattered. The sphere still flew farther than one of his left-handed throws normally would, but it landed almost ten yards in front of the closest imp instead of in the center of the group.

The first orb struck true and sent four of the creatures flying while causing another two to stumble. The second one thoroughly scorched one imp since it caught him on the edge of both blasts, but it only staggered the others. He drew Ember as he continued his charge.

An arrow flew past, chased by a fire spell as the distance melted between them. A throwing knife sprouted from the chest of one of the small creatures as they continued their charge. They were twenty yards away when something hit him in the side and knocked him backward. The screeching sound of metal on metal echoed in his mind as he stumbled and regained his balance.

A gnoll stood beside him, bringing his sword around for another strike. It caught Arthur flatfooted, so he activated Passata Sotto. His body dropped to the ground, and Ember flew up toward the gnoll at an angle. The blade passed cleanly through the chain the creature wore and sunk into its abdomen. It gripped its stomach and doubled over.

Another sword was already on a collision
course with his head, and he quickly parried
the blade. The force of the blow surprised him
and knocked him off balance. His feet
scrambled to find purchase while another sword
swung for his chest, and he had no other
option but to dive into the attacker and
tackle them to the ground. His dagger found
the open area under their arm and punched into
their lung, causing a splash of fresh blood to
cover his hand. Arthur got back to his feet,
shaking off the excess fluid.

"Arthur, duck!" Vana's voice rang over the
field, and Arthur dropped to a knee without
question. A grunt echoed behind him, and he
spun to see a furry creature standing over him
with their sword held overhead, ready to
deliver a two-handed chop. The gnoll stood in
place with an arrow sticking out of their
right eye socket.

He nodded with a smile at Vana. *Guess we're
even.*

Arthur jumped back up to the feeling of
magic. He looked toward one of two standing
imps and felt the magic coming from them. Ice
Shards flew from his hand and slammed into the
small monster. It must've gotten its stone
skin spell in place because the magic knocked
it back, but the ice shattered on its skin as
though stone.

*You have dealt 0 HP Damage to Imp (Level
19) with Ice Spikes (Stoneskin).*

A ball of fire soared past and caught the second imp. The little creature went up in a ball of screeching flame. Arthur's original target turned his focus toward him and launched a volley of earthen projectiles at him. He let mana flow from him and ripped up a section of dirt to stop it.

Arthur ran around the newly formed mound of dirt and charged the remaining imp. He leaped into the air and came down with both blades pointed for the imp's face. His sword bit in but didn't go more than an inch into the skin. The dagger hit the imp's hide with an odd crunching sound and never even left a mark.

*You have dealt 0 HP damage to Imp (Level 19) with Enchanted Mage-crafted Steel Dagger (Stoneskin).*

*You have dealt 15 HP damage to Imp (Level 19) with Ember (Stoneskin).*

*That damn Stoneskin is getting on my nerves.* Pushing out both of his hands, he dual cast Flamethrower. The swirling red flame burst from his palms and slammed into the Imp. Like the golem, the little creature blackened. Unlike the golem, the fire did plenty of damage on its own and the little monster fell over as a charred heap.

*You have dealt 240 HP damage to Imp (Level 19) with Dual Cast Flamethrower.*

*Imp (Level 19) has died.*

Arthur watched as Balair dove on the last imp and bit into its skull with a crunch. The rest of the group dispatched the final gnolls with ease and took a deep breath. His gaze settled on the pile of imps. *They weren't kidding when they said those things could be dangerous.*

"Anyone hurt this time?"

"Got a deep gash on my left arm," Rayne told them.

Vana quickly assessed the damage. "This will take a little time to heal up," she told him as she pulled out a wad of the nasty salve she'd used on Arthur. Knowing the pain he'd endured from it, he stopped her first.

"Rayne, you want to try a different type of healing?"

"You're not a healer," Allendria said his way in a confused tone.

"Not technically, but when we fought those Zhorians, I watched Ishmina when she cast her healing spell, and I'm pretty sure I can mimic it."

"What he means to say is, he wants to experiment on you," Allendria whispered to Rayne conspiratorially.

Rayne gulped but nodded in agreement anyway after some initial hesitation. Arthur walked up to him and examined the wound. He let his Water Magic flow in the same way Ishmina had, but carefully guided it into the wound. All the dirt and blood from the cut washed clean, and the bleeding section of the cut shone through. Arthur focused on the water flowing over Rayne's body as he'd seen the Zhorian do. The water spilled all over the wound but seemed to do nothing but slosh bloody water.

He stopped the magic and examined the cut. Nothing looked different other than the cleanliness of the area. Arthur tried and failed three more times before he yelled in frustration. Allendria walked up to the two and asked what was wrong.

"Stupid thing refuses to work right. I'm having it flow over his body in the same way I saw the other caster do it."

Allendria chuckled. "You thought you could learn it by copying the outside pattern? Do you even know what the spell is doing? I can promise you it's not just flowing over the area. It's actively repairing the skin and tissue."

"Well, if you know that, can you tell me how?"

"I never took up that course of study. I know it's normally done by speeding up our body's natural healing processes. Had something to do with our bodies being naturally made of extensive amounts of water or something. Can't say I truly understand it," she told him.

Arthur smiled at the explanation. *Sounds like my biology class may be more useful than I thought. Judging on her statement, I need to use the magic to infuse the cells so they can heal themselves as an exponentially quicker rate. Bet I need to speed up the natural multiplication process while I pump Water Magic in.*

"Hold tight, I think I might know how this works now."

"Really? You expect me to believe you figured it out based on her vague explanation and her admission she has no idea how it works?" Rayne asked in disbelief.

"Possibly," Arthur answered hesitantly and let the Water Magic flow again. He pictured the water slowly trickling into the cells and imagined them splitting and multiplying. The flow of energy sped up, and Arthur happily saw pieces of flesh knit back together. The process was slow and arduous, but it undeniably worked as they watched in wonder. It took far longer than he expected but, when he finished, there wasn't a single mark left on Rayne's skin.

The young alchemist rubbed his arm in disbelief. "You did it."

Arthur smiled and checked the welcome notification.

*Congratulations, you have discovered the Water Magic Spell: Minor Heal. You have gained 250 experience in Water Magic for discovering a known spell.*

*You have gained 220 experience in Water Magic for successfully casting Minor Heal.*

| Spell: Minor Heal | |
| --- | --- |
| Requirements: Water Magic<br>Mana Cost: 110 MP<br>Cast Time: 4 seconds<br>Cooldown: 60 seconds | Description: Use the power of Water Magic to speed up the recovery process of the body. Heals target of 175 HP and closes minor wounds. |
| Mastery Level: 1 | |

*That'll be useful.*

"So, now that Rayne is as good as new, where to?" Arthur asked and turned his attention to Vana.

She looked around and faced the monolith.

***

Vana approached the imposing structure. The dark stone that comprised it felt like it ate any light surrounding it. When she was less than ten feet from the spire, a message popped up.

*Congratulations on reaching your destination, Vana! The last step of your class quest to obtain the Ranger class must be done solo. Are you ready to proceed? Y/N.*

Vana hesitated at the suggestion. Their journey had plenty of dangers in it, but the superior power of their group handled them well. She wasn't sure if she could go through that by herself.

"It says I have to do the last part of the quest solo," she told the group.

They all looked concerned with her answer.

"You sure?" Samson asked.

"That's what it says."

"Your choice. I think you can do it, but you have to believe you can do it first," Arthur told her with confidence.

"I'm going for it," she told them as she selected *Yes*.

A shimmering doorway appeared in front of her, and she slowly reached her hand toward it. Her fingertips brushed the surface, and she felt nothing. She turned toward the group. "I'll be right back," and walked through with a confident stride.

Her change in scenery was jarring. She went from a wide-open plain with an enormous monolith in the middle to a thickly wooded forest. The sound of insects almost deafened her.

*Welcome to your trial. There is an enemy hidden in the forest. Your job is to track it down and kill it. Use every skill at your disposal to make this happen. Keep in mind that skills useful as a Ranger will prove the most beneficial for this test.*

As soon as she finished reading the message, she slunk to the ground and assumed a stealth position. Her eyes darted across her surroundings. The woods seemed normal to her, and nothing appeared threatening here. If she needed to hunt, that's what she would do.

She pulled her bow off her shoulder and nocked an arrow. Without an idea of where to start, she picked a direction and slowly crept forward. Her eyes scanned the broad leaves of the bushes for signs of passage while also examining the treetops and ground for movement.

Her movement continued for an hour before she finally caught sight of odd tracks in the dirt. They were hard to make out from the dry ground, but she could see enough to know it wasn't an animal she knew. The footprint resembled a hoof print from a deer, but instead of the two cleaves a deer has on each foot, this track contained a large one in the middle and two smaller cleaves on the side.

She adjusted her position and scanned the ground to find more tracks. It took her a quarter of an hour to get her bearings and confirm the heading of the prey, but she resumed her trek in the direction the tracks led. The scenery changed drastically. The trail she now followed was much more vibrant and full of life. The plants along the trail were lush and alive. Flowers bloomed on many of them. The forest she'd traversed on her way here didn't look dead or dying, but it looked void of life and almost colorless.

She heard something pawing the ground ahead of her and stopped. Her senses came to high alert, and she ducked into a nearby bush. The scent of a clean forest filled her nose. *None of this scenario makes any sense. I'm told my prey is in here, but nothing so far seems like a danger to the forest. I sense nothing out of the ordinary, and the path I've followed actually looks to be helping the forest. Something isn't right.*

Her senses perked up again at a shuffling sound near her. An inky shadow passed near her, and she lifted her bow, preparing to shoot. A scent of fresh pine and wildflowers filled her nose, and she lowered the bow. *This creature isn't dangerous. Killing it would harm this forest. A Ranger should protect the woods.*

She stood to her feet and slung her bow over her shoulder, dropping the arrow back in her quiver. Her feet carried her along the path for one hundred feet until she came upon a small clearing. A solid beam of sunshine pierced the high trees with blinding light and illuminated the grassy field filled with wildflowers.

A large white creature resembling a horse stood in the center of the clearing. Its muscular legs and body displayed the power of the animal. A long, flowing mane lined the ridge of its neck and ended atop its head where a spiraled horn jutted skyward.

"A unicorn," she breathed in awe.

The creature heard her speak and turned to look at her. Instead of running away as she feared, the animal remained in its position and stared into her eyes. Her feet took her forward, drawn by the gaze of the majestic animal. When she was a foot from its face, she stopped in her tracks. She slowly lowered her head to the animal in a slight bow. It took a step forward and nuzzled her cheek with its face.

"I could never kill a creature as good and pure as you. I must give up this trial as a failure," she whispered as a tear fell from her face.

Her surroundings spun and the forest faded from view.

*Congratulations, Vana. A Ranger's job is to protect the forest. You must know how to take a life, but at the same time, you must also know when not to. Following directives blindly is not the way of the Ranger. You've now been granted the Ranger class. When you return, you will have access to the Ranger class tree, but you won't remember the full details. You will remember the lessons you learned and the critical decisions you made. The secrets of the testing must be guarded to prevent those not worthy from cheating their way through a trial. Good luck, Ranger Vana.*

The colors warped and twisted around her,
and she stood in front of the imposing
monolith again.

# Chapter 32



Arthur jumped to his feet when Vana appeared in the field.

"Vana! You okay?"

She looked around in confusion at first and finally turned toward the group. When she saw them, she smiled in response.

"Looks like I'm officially a Ranger now," she said with glee.

"Congratulations," the group called to her in unison.

"What was the trial like? Was it difficult? You've only been gone a half-hour, so we didn't think it was too difficult," Samson asked excitedly.

Her face took on a look of concentration. "I know it forced me to make a tough choice, and I chose correctly. Other than that, I remember little."

Arthur was about to comment on how ridiculous that sounded but stopped. *If the trials prevented you from remembering details, it would explain why so little information was known about the trials in general.*

"Either way, we're happy you're back and now have your class," Arthur interjected before anyone else drug the conversation out. Questioning her on something she obviously didn't remember would only frustrate her.

"Everyone else ready to get out of this horrible place? All the random rancid water standing around is making me queasy. I'm ready to be back on normal firm ground," Rayne quipped.

The group laughed and began their trek out of the bog. Their return trip was faster since they ran into no enemies on the way out. When they escaped the confines of the valley, they turned west and walked for the border. Once outside the range of the valley, their trek took them back to the north and toward the rumored location of the Tomb of the Lost.

They passed two more villages on their way north. The first of them was a tiny village and comprised only a handful of houses. This area looked like a small farming community that hadn't survived the raids. They checked the buildings for anything useful and survivors but found nothing.

The next village, they had a little more luck. It was a larger village, and Arthur saw a few people scramble for cover when they came closer. They approached the buildings, and a rock flew from somewhere amongst the buildings.

"Uh, who goes there?" Arthur asked in confusion.

"Village is closed. We're not getting taken away to some goblin camp," a boyish voice said from behind a building to his right.

"I'm a human, not a goblin. Surely you can see that much?" Arthur asked, confused.

"So what? I saw humans with the goblins and orcs in one of their armies. Fought side by side they did in my village north of here. How do I know you're not one of their allies?"

"What?" Arthur roared. "There were humans who sided with them? Who are they? Are they still around? Do you know which way that army went?"

The face of a young man popped around the corner. He couldn't have been much older than fourteen.

"So you're truly not with them?" he asked timidly.

Arthur turned a gentle smile toward the youngster. "No, young man, we're not. We've been fighting against them anytime we run across any of the goblin scum."

"The last group I saw continued west, but I ran into them in my hometown of Gael about three days north of here."

"What is the name of this village?" Vana asked as she examined the surroundings and watched the moving shapes in the shadows.

"We don't really know. The few of us left have never been here before, and none of us can read."

Arthur looked around the village. "I don't see any signs anywhere. What good would reading do you?"

"There's a map posted in what looked like the main hall of the village. None of us can read the words on it, though."

Arthur perked up at that. "Show me," he implored.

The group followed the kid to a nearby building. It looked to be in good repair. Its wooden siding had no noticeable gaps, and the roof looked old but sturdy. Inside was another story. Overturned benches and what looked like old bloodstains littered the area. The large map on the wall the boy led them to remained untouched. The details on it were remarkable. It included properly marked rises and falls for the valleys and hills. It also highlighted the boundaries and small forests correctly. Each location bore a meticulous label in fine print. Arthur carefully examined the document.

After a little searching, he found Alem's Crossing. It took him some time since he'd never seen a map of this world. Once he'd found the village, he could trace their travels. The village they'd found, where they liberated the prisoners, showed as Westerly. He followed the path they'd traveled and spotted the Shallow Bog. Tracing their route there, it surprised him to see a marker for the monolith. He followed their trail out and north. When he reached their current position, he saw the name Tartan.

"This is the village of Tartan," he said to the assembled group of ragged youngsters. They'd finally emerged from hiding as the party traveled through the village.

"I'd heard my Pa mention something about Tartan, but I'd never been there," one of the young ladies said.

The entire crowd of people here all looked to be in their teens. They must've banded together to flee and now didn't know where to go.

"What are you kids doing here? Why haven't you left?"

"Where are we gonna go? A few tried to leave. All but one came back because they ran into goblins. We don't know what happened to the other one. Just feared the worst."

"Can you give us a minute to discuss our plans?" he asked the youngsters. They all nodded and filed out of the building.

"Arthur, we can't leave them here. They'll die. They have almost nothing for food, and the goblins will eventually come by here and find them," Vana pleaded.

"I know. I know," he said heavily, "but what can we do? We can't bring them with us, and we can't turn around."

"We could give them most of our food to hold out while we are gone. Maybe pick them up and take them back to Alem's Crossing with us on our way back?" Allendria suggested.

"That's possible. We can head to the edge of the forest and hunt for food on our way north. I'm just worried goblins will find them," he said concerned until an idea struck him.

"You ready for a little Earth Magic work?" Arthur asked as he turned to Allendria.

"What you have in mind?"

"I think we could make an underground room for them to shelter in. I could even make a quick temperature control device to put in there with them to keep them comfortable. A few air vents disguised inside rocks would complete the room. Surely we can find a few buckets or a barrel to store some water in here in town. I know I saw a well when we walked in. Between our food rations and the room, they should easily be able to hold out for a week or two. Shouldn't take us longer than that to complete our quests."

The group all agreed to the plan and set to work. Arthur and Allendria led the kids outside so they could watch the work. They found a location behind the main building that was vacant and began work with the Excavation spell. Rayne, Samson, and Vana scoured the village looking for supplies they could use and some barrels or buckets.

The magical work took two hours to get everything sorted out. They dug the sizable hole and made a full room of solid stone. Arthur and Allendria tasked the younger kids with kicking dirt and dust over all of it to hide the stone. Arthur included a small room to the side for waste.

Arthur even figured out how to do the waste disposal enchantment in there for them. He tied the magic to a small disc of metal that covered the bottom of the stone toilet bowl. A little metal button on the front of the stone bench the toilet sat on caused the portal to open when pressed and immediately close when released. The kids were in awe of the building and the amenities.

The group of adventurers unloaded as much food as they could spare and stashed it on some small stone shelving on one wall. Vana, Samson, and Rayne brought in a large barrel of water and some smaller buckets filled with the precious liquid. They hid the entrance to the secret room with a rock. It'd taken some time, and Allendria finally figured out how to do it. They created a large flat rock that looked like an old piece of foundation and enchanted it to become almost weightless so they could lift it open. When the enchantment deactivated, it became its normal weight.

With the room set up, Arthur turned to address the teens.

"My friends and I have an important mission that can't wait. We'll be traveling northeast of here. We want you to stay down there. You must remain in this location until we return for you so we can take you somewhere safe."

"What if you don't come back?" one asked softly.

"If we haven't come back in two weeks, you can take your chances outside of the safety of the room. Just remember to be cautious when opening the place," Arthur told them.

The group waved goodbye to the kids, and they watched the youngsters shuffle into the underground room. Arthur turned and walked to the main hall. He'd decided he wouldn't leave such a valuable map behind. They carefully removed the map from the wall by pulling out the tacks that held it. Arthur folded it neatly and stuffed it into his Dimensional Drawer for safekeeping.

With all the tasks completed, they continued on their journey. The map was not only valuable in pinpointing their current path, but it also had the added benefit of showing all their destinations on it. The Tomb of the Fallen was the next closest target, so they made straight for it.

It was a full day before they saw the tomb appear in front of them. It looked like a small graveyard with one gigantic building in the center. They could only assume it was the crypt.

"Uh, any bets we find undead in there?" Vana asked with a gulp.

"Not taking that bet. I'd say the odds are about ninety-nine point nine percent in favor of that," Arthur chuckled.

"Anyone have any experience fighting undead?" Rayne asked.

"We saw them on campaign once. The sight of them and the stench is the worst part. They're generally weak and deal minor damage. They try to swarm you and bog you down with numbers. Tough to kill, though. Typically have to set them on fire or cut them into enough pieces that their body can't move anymore," Samson summarized.

"So Allendria and I will get a workout, got it," Arthur said with a cheer as he stretched his arms across his body.

"You must've forgotten I know Fire Magic as well," Samson grinned at him, "so I'll be joining that party. Divine Fury will also assist in the battle."

"Vana and Rayne, I guess you two get to play backup."

"I'll be having some fun here. I had the forethought to get Allendria to teach me Fire Magic weeks ago. I added in a Ranger talent and can now imbue my shots with magic power I command," Vana told him smugly.

"That's outstanding. Sorry Rayne, looks like you're watching everyone's backs this time."

"Fine, fine, guess I can save your asses from time to time. Should probably stick by you, Arthur, since you have a habit of getting hit more than the others."

The group laughed at Arthur's expense but trudged forward. The light slowly faded from the sky, and Arthur felt like a complete dumbass for entering a graveyard as evening approached. The longer they waited, the more dangerous it got for the village and the teens waiting on them.

They walked through the opening of the area
and passed the short rusted fence to enter the
raised walkway. They took extra care to avoid
the gravesites and only walked on the empty
walking paths. Their trip took them halfway to
the large central crypt when they heard dirt
moving around them.

"Well, damn," Arthur muttered.

Shambling forms materialized out of the
surrounding shadows. None moved quickly but
they advanced at a steady pace. Arthur reached
over his shoulder and grabbed Ember. He
planned to go at this fight all out, so he
activated Sheathe in Flames and stood ready
for the monsters.

The first came close enough, and he saw the
decayed skin hanging from its body. It still
resembled a human, albeit one with gaping
holes in its surface and missing its eyes. The
putrid stench that wafted from the creature
made him want to wretch. Arthur activated Scan
on the monster.

*You have received 180 experience for
successful use of Scan.*

| Name: Zombie | |
|---|---|
| Level: 18 | |
| Type: Undead | |
| HP: 200/200 | |
| MP: 150/150 | |
| Stamina: 200/200 | |
| Strength: 12 | Experience: N/A |
| Agility: 8 | Skills |
| Intellect: 6 | Combat Skills: |
| Wisdom: 4 | |
| Endurance: 18 | ? (???/???) |

*Those stats are odd,* was Arthur's first thought, then he cut a line through the creature's body with the flaming form of Ember.

*You have dealt 150 HP damage to Zombie (Level 18) with Ember (Burning Strike) (Elemental Weakness).*
*Your Burning Strike debuff has canceled Zombie (Level 18) Regeneration.*

*Ah, that makes more sense. They have built-in regeneration, so it penalizes their base stats.*

His attention turned to the next in line, and he continued his onslaught. Balair stopped his overhead scouting and joined in on the fun. He'd avoided the village for fear of scaring the youngsters and instead kept an eye out for trouble. Out here, he could go wild.

The party dashed through the undead with almost no effort. With nearly all members having innate Fire Magic, it practically nullified the undead's most dangerous ability of Regeneration.

Balair jumped on one undead and bit its head, preparing to douse it in fire as he had before, but leaped off the monster hacking and spitting.

*What the hell happened?*

*Those things taste horrible. I won't be able to get that taste out of my mouth for a week.*

*They are rotting undead, dumbass.*

Balair roasted the zombie who'd defiled his mouth, and Arthur continued the fight. With it being so one-sided, there wasn't much danger found, and before long, the scattered remains of the zombies littered the area, slowly smoldering.

The party checked the corpses for anything of use but didn't do an extensive job because of the level of rot and stench surrounding the bodies. They continued to the main crypt and stopped at the base.

Samson looked to the group. "You guys think it'll be a solo quest?"

"I'd say you can almost guarantee it," Allendria piped up with a broad smile.

"Good luck, Samson. You've got this," Arthur told him with a clap on the shoulder.

The soldier grinned and straightened his stance as he walked forward to confront destiny.

***

Samson approached the main entrance of the crypt.

*Congratulations on reaching your destination, Samson! The last step of your class quest to obtain the Defender class must be done solo. Are you ready to proceed? Y/N.*

Samson selected *Yes,* and the same portal he'd seen Vana walk into appeared in front of him. *Calm yourself. You can do this. Just like fighting a battle.* He told himself as he gritted his teeth and walked through.

His surroundings shifted to a vast
battlefield. Enemies fought from multiple war
fronts, and he could see at least three
different forces on the field based on their
colors and standards. The scent of coppery
blood wafted to him and brought back old
memories.

*Welcome to your trial. You must protect
King Tyran during the battle. Ensure he lives
to be victorious. Use every skill at your
disposal to make this happen. Keep in mind
that skills useful as a Defender will prove
the most beneficial for this test.*

Samson smiled at the message as he felt the
now familiar weight of Divine Fury in his
hand. The Paladin searched the battlefield for
his target. The surrounding action was hard to
sift through. People fought and bled
everywhere he looked. Horses crashed into
infantry with metallic shrieks.

A soldier galloped up to him. "Paladin,
aren't you supposed to be with King Tyran?"

"Yes, soldier. We were separated in the
battle. Can you give me his location so I may
join him?"

"Yes, sir," the soldier said with a quick
bow and pointed east. "Head east for a couple
hundred yards to get around the enemy line and
turn south. You'll find him on the other side
of the battle line. May the Goddess protect
you, Paladin."

Samson saluted the man and dashed for his target. He ignored the enemies fighting around him and curled around the enemy line. A few of them tried to slash out toward him, but he easily deflected their blows with Divine Fury. A man in a solid gold crown sat on horseback. His thick black hair curled out of the ends of his helmet, and green eyes stared at Samson as he approached.

"Welcome back, Paladin. Try not to get separated again. You have more important work to do."

"Of course, King Tyran," Samson said with a bow.

He turned and took a guard position with two other men near the king. The battle continued, and Samson ached to help. He'd never been one to sit on the sidelines while others fought. His fist clenched on his sword hilt.

"Calm yourself, Paladin. There will be plenty of fighting to come. This rabble isn't worth your time, anyway. All the peasants are good for is frontline soldiers to take the brunt of the damage," the king said with an offhanded wave toward the line of crumpling fighters.

Looking at the battlefield, Samson could see the truth of it. He'd been so focused on his task before that he hadn't noticed that most of the frontline fighters were barely armored and carried farm implements as weapons. The callous disregard for life from this king caused his blood to burn, but he swallowed his anger and remembered his goal.

*I can't kill the pompous fool, or I'd fail this mission.* Samson repeated this in his head over and over as he stood guard.

"Finally. Looks like the day is almost ours," the king said over the noise.

A small group of enemy soldiers broke from the main battle and fled.

"With me, men. We need to stop them."

The king trotted his horse forward, and the rest of the group followed. Samson stood shocked for a moment, but his military training kicked in, and he followed the order.

*This isn't right. I left the army because I was tired of seeing this. Most of these people don't even want to be here.*

He continued his trek until the king's horse smashed into the retreating enemies. Conscripted soldiers fell to the ground, trampled by the horse's hooves. The sound of cracking bones was impossible to ignore as the king used his horse to plow down the soldiers.

A man charged for Samson with fear in his eyes and weapon raised. He pulled up his shield and stopped the attack. His arm moved forward to retaliate but froze due to the sheer terror reflected in front of him. They stared at each other for a few moments without movement until a sword punched through the man's gut, and blood splashed out of his stomach to adorn Samson's shield.

"Heads up, Paladin. You're moving awfully slow today. Not feeling well?" another of the guards asked him.

"Just a bad day," he grumbled out, not knowing how to respond. The violence around him felt wrong in every way. *Why would I ever defend someone so unworthy of the task?*

"Your Majesty, Duke Trawl has fled the battlefield. Only remnants of Count Stonel remain. Do we round them up?"

The king flashed a cruel smile. "Round them all up for me and divide them by type. I'll personally see to the peasant militia."

The soldier who'd delivered the message bowed and rode off to his task.

"Let's finish this fight."

The king rode toward a gathering of soldiers, ringing a ragtag bunch of peasants. Pitchforks and scythes riddled the surrounding ground, signs of their surrender.

"Orders, Your Majesty?" the captain of the assembled guards over the prisoners of war asked.

"Execute half of them and leave the other half to work my fields as slaves."

The guards nodded at the order and turned to face the crowd. A sea of terror reflected in the eyes of those in the ring of soldiers. Samson couldn't take the looks any longer. *To hell with this quest. I'll just have to go without a class.*

Samson dashed forward and slammed his sword into the back of the guard captain.

*You have dealt 235 HP damage to Guard Captain (Level 19) with Enchanted Mage-crafted Steel Arming Sword (Heart Strike).*

*Guard Captain (Level 19) has died.*

He continued around the edge of the prisoners until he found the next one. This one watched him kill the captain and was already on the offensive with a sword flying for his head. Divine Fury met the blow, and sparks flew from the contact. Samson stepped into the guard and bashed him. The snapping of ribs echoed off the shield, and Samson kicked out, sending him flying.

A gleam of metal flashed in the corner of his eye, and he quickly turned and brought up Divine Fury. Something hit the shield, and he watched an arrow fall to the ground with a newly flattened metal tip. Without understanding why he reared back with his left arm and slung Divine Fury forward. The shield slipped free from his arm and spun as it crossed the distance. The archer stood in place, a look of absolute shock plastered on his face, as the shield smashed into him and fractured his skull. The power of Earth Magic flowed from Samson, and the shield changed course and flew back to him. When it was close enough, it stopped spinning, and Samson held out his arm as the shield carefully slid back into place.

*Congratulations, you've unlocked the Ability Shield Throw.*

"What's the meaning of this?" the king roared over the crowd but, before anyone could answer, two more soldiers rushed Samson with weapons drawn. *Good. If they focus on me, they'll leave the peasants alone.*
He caught one sword on his shield and parried the other with his sword. Spinning to the side caused the first attacker to fall off balance from trying to push down on his protection with pure brute force. This one stumbled past him, trying to regain their footing before Samson swept his sword across the soldier's neck. A fountain of blood spurted from the wound, and they collapsed.

Samson ran at the other attacker and leaped into the air. Instead of coming down in an overhanded chop, he braced himself against the back of Divine Fury and let the weapon lead the way. The guard was foolish enough to remain in place, and his shield hit the guard with a meaty *thump*, followed by crunching bone and a wet gurgle.

More guards converged on his position. The peasants behind him picked up their weapons and prepared to fight again. *If only I could do more to help. I fear I've only doomed myself along with them.*

"Bring me that paladin's head, now!"

The outburst drew Samson's attention. *The worthless excuse for a king is the reason for all of this. His callous behavior toward commoners is probably what started this entire war.*

There was no way he could win the fight against all of them. Even with his advanced armor and weapons, he'd eventually fall to a concerted attack from that many. Instead, he decided to take out the worst problem of all. *If I can kill the king, it should save countless lives, especially if it takes a while to replace him.*

Samson dashed for the king perched on his horse. One of the other guards jumped in to intercept him, and he leaped forward, placed his shield against the man's face, and flipped over him to continue dashing forward. The king watched his approach and noticed he had no one between him and the irate paladin. In a desperate bid, he kicked his horse into action, and it galloped toward Samson.

Just before they met, Samson dove to the side and let the horse pass. He didn't want to injure the horse, so he swung his shield into the animal's rear leg as it passed, causing it to stumble and trip. The king fell from his saddle, and the horse regained its feet and trotted off. Samson approached the king as he lay in a daze.

"What is the meaning of this? You're here to protect me," the king mumbled in confusion.

Samson couldn't explain it, but his response came from his soul. "I'm a Defender. My job is to protect those who need and deserve it."

His sword came down and plunged directly into the king's chest.

*Congratulations, Paladin Samson. A Defender has to stay true to themselves. Remember your journey here today and the lesson you've learned. To defend is a glorious gift and one to be used for worthy causes. You've now been granted the Defender class. When you return, you will have access to the Defender class tree, but you won't remember the full details. You will remember the lessons you learned and the critical decisions you made. The secrets of the testing must be guarded to prevent those not worthy from cheating their way through a trial. Good luck, Defender Samson.*

His surroundings distorted, and he stood outside of the crypt again.

# Chapter 33



*A Trial by Fire*

"So, how'd it go?" Vana asked Samson when he reappeared in the graveyard.

"Looks like it went well. I'm officially a Defender."

"Fantastic news. I'm guessing you don't remember much of the trial itself?" Arthur asked.

Samson stared off in concentration for a few moments and shook his head. "No, I only remember a few details. I know I learned a new skill, though. Pretty awesome."

"Oh, really?" Allendria asked, intrigued. "What skill is that?"

Samson grinned at her and turned to a small sapling. He activated his new Shield Throw ability, and his shield flew from his arm as a spinning disc. It snapped the little tree and came flying back toward him. When it was about to hit the former soldier, it slowed and stopped spinning. The shield came to a rest back on his arm.

"That is totally bad-ass," Arthur shouted.

The group took their time congratulating Samson on his new ability. The paladin preened in the limelight at the attention. It didn't take long for the smell of the decay to waft by and remind them they still stood in a graveyard. The group quickly left the area and retreated a far distance away before stopping for the night.

Their journey continued full swing in the
morning. Arthur pulled out the map from his
Dimensional Storage Drawer and spread it out
so they could see the complete picture. They
traced the route they needed to take to reach
the Scorched Forest. With their trip planned
out, Arthur returned the map to the safety of
his storage.

The trip itself was uneventful, as much of
their journey thus far. They ran into one
group of goblin scouts that Vana had the good
grace to dispatch before any of the rest even
saw them. She told the group about finding and
ridding the area of them. They only stopped
for the occasional rest. The group was all in
agreement about the need to make this mission
quick. Everyone had responsibilities to worry
about back in the village.

They knew they headed the right way because
the temperature in the area slowly rose. It
was barely noticeable at first but, as they
got closer to their destination, it became a
stifling heat.

"Allendria, if I die of a heat stroke, I'm
blaming it on you," Rayne said in mocking
tones.

"I might let you. This is getting
ridiculous."

*I feel fine. You guys need to stop whining.*

*You're dragonkin. You live around heat and
breathe fire. Of course, you're fine.*

*That just sounds like an excuse to me.*

*How about we go hiking to the snow caps in
the mountains? You think you'll be fine up
there? Maybe you'll slow down like lizards.*

*That's all I need is to be on a mission
with a bunch of human popsicles.*

*Got a point there. Would definitely have to
invest in heavier clothing.*

Flames licked the horizon as they approached. The haze made it look like a mirage in the desert as the air rippled. Skeletal trees, blackened by fire, dotted their line of sight.

"Uh, Allendria. I know you've said this place has been burning a long time, but how is that possible?" Samson asked.

"How should I know? I'm not some elven scholar. I only know it was the aftermath of some battle. I don't know how this can happen, either."

The group approached cautiously. The heat was still oppressive, and the warmth on their skin was uncomfortable. They trudged forward so Allendria could finish her task. Arthur examined another burning tree as they approached when an arrow zipped past him and hit with a resounding thud.

Arthur fixed on the arrow's destination and saw a lizard pinned to the base of a tree. The hissing creature tried to rush toward them. Its size was an astonishing thing. Arthur couldn't figure out how he'd missed a lizard the height of a Labrador and nearly twice as long.

It tugged a few more times, and the arrow slipped through its hide. The creature charged for them and Arthur saw the blood dripping from the fletching of the shaft now embedded in the tree.

"More around us. Keep your eyes peeled," Vana called to the group.

Arthur activated his Ice Shards spell, and
the crystalline projectiles hit the charging
lizard broadside. The shards dug deep into
flesh and hissed from the difference in
temperature. The ice shards melted and turned
to steam while the lizard still limped
forward.

Ember slid free, and Arthur watched Samson
charge one lizard. His shield came down in a
heavy blow and drove the creature's head into
the ground, stopping its charge. Arthur saw
Vana shoot another and slow it, so Arthur
launched two Throwing Knives at the target.

*You have dealt 50 HP damage to Fire
Salamander (Level 18) (Critical Hit) (x2).*

The creature collapsed and slid to a stop
with one last arrow to its face. Arthur rushed
to Allendria's side. He swung Ember into the
ribs of one of the creatures attacking her
while she fended off the other. Her blast of
fire only seemed to strengthen the lizard as
it continued to chase her.

"Allendria, use your Fire Magic to pull the
heat from the area. Those lizards are gaining
strength when you hit them with fire," Arthur
told her.

They both used their Fire Magic to chill the air by extracting the heat. They pushed the hot currents of air they siphoned off, upward and away from the battle. The lizards in the colder area noticeably slowed their speed. By the time Arthur and Allendria finished siphoning the heat away, the creatures were almost moving in slow motion. Arthur charged at the group in the now affected area and quickly removed all their heads. Their reaction was so sluggish, they had no chance of resisting their own demise.

*Fire Salamander (Level 18) has died (x8).*

The group stared at the dead lizards. A look around revealed none left standing. They didn't have any kind of loot on them, but they might prove useful in other ways. Arthur opened the Dimensional Storage and tossed them all in with the rest of the loot. Since Rayne desired to become an Alchemist in the village, they would try to get him ingredients to work with.

They all checked for damage and only had some minor wounds. Most were still close to full health, so they formed back into a group and continued on their journey. They observed the trees and their surroundings for more hidden enemies but found none. As they continued forward, the air grew even hotter.

Arthur grabbed at the edges of his armor and tried to pry it away from his skin, hoping to get any fresh air to flow in. Sadly, it didn't work, so he resorted to using his Fire Magic to increase his resistance to fire in the same way he did while forging. Some of the uncomfortable heat fled after that, but it was still uncomfortable breathing the hot air. They hadn't traveled more than a quarter of an hour before the others spoke up.

"Don't, think, I, can, go, much, farther," Vana said through heavy breaths.

"Same," was all Rayne could force out of his dry mouth.

"Damn. The heat will finish us off. Allendria, we need to fix this. It appears the hardest challenge here isn't enemies like the other places but an environmental challenge. The lizards we fought give me an idea, though. Let's create a dome around us to regulate the temperature. Everyone hold up while we get this sorted."

Everyone collapsed and stayed seated where they fell. They withdrew water skins and gulped down mouthfuls of the precious liquid. Arthur approached Allendria, who also used her Fire Magic to avoid some of the uncomfortable heat.

"We need to create a dome around us by removing heat and having the area regulate a temperature similar to what you did with the lizards."

"Fine. That shouldn't be hard, but how are we going to walk like that. It'll burn through far too much mana if you have to keep actively using mana to keep the surroundings cool. I definitely don't have the mana to do it and don't want to use all of what I have before I get to my quest."

"I agree, but I think you should learn the spell as well when I make it. I'll grant you the knowledge with my new Teacher class," Arthur told her.

"Wait, you got another class?"

"Oh, yeah, sorry, forgot to tell you. Got that one when I taught Rayne his Earth Magic."

"Fine, Fine. What's your plan?"

"I helped Rayne figure out how to do an active spell that tracks movements called One With the Ground. I'll adapt some of the principles from it to develop a spell that will create a dome over us and actively regulate the temperature. If done right, its spell cost should be low enough for me to maintain for an extended time."

Allendria nodded at the explanation and stood back to let Arthur work. He turned inward and focused on the way he'd done his One With the Ground spell. The initial problem with the earth spell came when he couldn't get it to work right when picturing the energy like a dome. Luckily, this would work more like one of his Temperature Control devices than a regular spell.

Arthur tried pushing out his magic into a dome-like area and pulled out the heat. The space gradually cooled, and he concentrated on correctly picturing his time changes for the spell. It was a relatively straightforward process since he'd literally done this multiple times, making the Temperature Control devices already. It surprised him that he hadn't already learned this spell by accident from the Enchantment process. The magic snapped into place, and he checked the requirements.

*Congratulations, you have discovered the Fire Magic Spell: Heat Control. You have gained 250 experience in Fire Magic for discovering a known spell.*

*You have gained 80 experience in Fire Magic for successfully casting Heat Control.*

| Spell: Heat Control | |
|---|---|
| Requirements: Fire Magic<br>Mana Cost: 1MP/3 sec<br>Cast Time: Channeled | Description: This spell regulates the temperature in a dome centered on the caster. This dome extends twenty feet in all directions.<br><br>Threshold - 85 degrees Fahrenheit |
| Mastery Level: 1 | |

*That should work.* Arthur deliberately set the threshold a little higher so it would take less mana to maintain. Something in the mid-seventies would've been far more comfortable but also more mana intensive.

He walked close to the group, and they all perked up as the air shifted around them.

"That's much nicer. Man, I'm glad you pulled that off," Samson said as he tried to push his breastplate from his body to suck in air. "Pretty sure I was getting close to well done."

The group laughed good-naturedly at the jest. Arthur walked to Allendria, laid a hand on her shoulder, and used his ability from his teacher class to teach her the Heat Control spell.

"Thanks," she told him with a kiss on the cheek. "That's awesome being able to teach like that. The best part is I understand some of the more advanced things you did to make that work that I didn't before. Using that ability to teach more advanced spells would help many people break past barriers like that to their progress."

Arthur hadn't considered that before. With the progress happening in the village, he'd considered starting a magical school at some point. That school could use abilities like that to a great extent.

"I'll keep that in mind," he told her with a smile.

Arthur walked over to Rayne and laid a hand on his shoulder.

"You've been working on your Earth Magic, right?"

"Yep, been training it often along with my Air."

Arthur just nodded and used his ability to teach Rayne One With the Ground. The youthful man smiled at the spell.

"You weren't lying. That's some impressive magic the way you did that spell."

"No big deal. Let's get this quest done," he told Rayne as he spun to see the rest. "Let's go. I'll keep this shield up as we travel. Stay within twenty feet of me at all times, or I fear you won't like the consequences."

The group wore nervous looks on their faces but continued on with him. It took another two hours of travel from that point. After the hour and a half mark, the heat outside their bubble of protection looked unbearable. He and Allendria could probably withstand it with their Fire Magic for a brief time, but Rayne wouldn't survive. They could easily show Vana and Samson since they had Fire Magic.

Out of curiosity, Rayne grabbed an old arrow out of Vana's quiver and snapped off the tip so as not to waste good metal. He tossed the shaft and fletching outside his area of influence. The feathers almost immediately caught on fire, and the wood darkened. Within seconds, the wood turned black and lit on fire.

"Yep, definitely stay near me."

The biggest surprise came at the two-hour mark. The swirling fire and heat caused rippling distortions in the landscape. When they first saw their destination, they were all convinced it was a mirage. Ahead of them stood a circle of perfectly preserved green trees. The landscape on both sides was still a raging inferno, but these trees looked untouched.

They approached cautiously but everything appeared safe as they neared. When they entered the area of influence around these preserved trees, Arthur felt the heat lessen on his dome. Since Vana had plenty of subpar arrows to spare, he snapped another and tossed the shaft outside his area of influence and observed. The shaft landed on the soft green grass and sat there untouched. The fletching remained perfectly intact, and it didn't catch on fire.

Arthur carefully dropped his shield and
felt a cool breeze on his warm skin. The rest
of the group let out loud sighs of contentment
with the change in temperature. They walked
past one stand of trees, and an unexpected
message popped up.

*You have entered the Tranquil Sanctuary.
This place is a haven for those on a quest. Do
not defile this place with fire.*

*Well, not sure it can say it more plainly
than that.* In front of them stood their
target. There was no doubt that it was their
destination. A towering tree stood in the
center of the glade with nothing growing
around it. The monstrosity had to be fifty
feet tall, and glowing lines of fire that
looked like pulsing veins covered every
section.
"Think we found the Tree of Embers," Vana
said with a smug smile.
The group walked to the edge of the scorch
marks on the ground near the tree and stopped.
The party all spread out to rest and relax
while Allendria nervously checked everything
she was wearing.
"You'll be fine," Arthur told her while
pulling her into a tight hug. "I have faith in
you. I know you'll beat this."
Allendria smiled and rested her forehead on
his. "Thanks. Just nerves, I think."
"Understandable. Take the time you need.
This glade is a comfortable resting place. We
can stay as long as necessary. There's even a
small spring over there for water," Arthur
said, pointing at a corner of the glade.

"I won't keep you waiting long. We have things to do," she told him confidently with one last kiss before she rose to her full height, straightened her back into a regal stance, and walked to the tree.

***

Allendria approached the tree with her head held high, but her nerves were an absolute mess. *Should I do this? Can I really do this alone?*

Those two thoughts warred with her emotions until she came within a dozen feet of the tree and received a message.

*Congratulations on reaching your destination, Allendria! The last step of your class quest to obtain the Pyromancer class must be done solo. Are you ready to proceed? Y/N.*

She gulped at the message but selected *Yes.* A swirling, blue portal appeared in front of her, and she stepped through with a confidence she didn't genuinely have. Her surroundings warped and spun until they resolved into her standing near the edge of a small village.

*Welcome to your trial. Wildfires are sweeping through the land, and they approach this village from all directions. Protect this village from fiery annihilation at all costs. Use every skill at your disposal to make this happen. Keep in mind that skills useful as a Pyromancer will prove the most beneficial for this test.*

*Odd. I would've sworn this test would ask me to go crazy and burn things to the ground, not put it out.* She shook off the feeling and walked toward the small village.

There was nothing out of the ordinary about the appearance of the place. The buildings all looked well maintained with their wood plank walls. Some even had some beautiful pieces of trim around them, giving them just a bit more style. Come of the locals spotted her approach and an older gentleman approached.

He looked ragged and tired as he hobbled her direction. His walking stick was a finely carved staff of wood that Allendria would swear was oak of one variety or another. His eyes and cheeks had a sunken and haunted look to them.

"I don't think we can help you, Lady. We're preparing for a horrible fire headed this way. We hope to flee to the south before it arrives," the older gentleman told her.

She flashed a kind smile toward the gentleman. "I'm here to help with that. I think I can quell some of the fire and help save the village for you."

"You're just one person, and while I thank you for the concern, we can't ask you to help us. We've already begun packing to flee."

Allendria then noticed a circle of wagons in the middle of the village being loaded with household items of all varieties. Oddly, no one seemed to move very fast, and almost all of them looked as bad as the gentleman in front of her.

"I plan to do what I can, anyway. My name's Allendria."

"I'd say thank you, but you may regret that in the end," the man started before delving into a horrible coughing fit. When his coughing stopped, flecks of blood adorned his hand, shocking Allendria. The older man quickly wiped it on the side of his pants before continuing, "My apologies about that. I forget my manners. Name's Hank."

Allendria walked closer, but he merely nodded at her and stepped backward.

"No disrespect, Lady Allendria, but I haven't been feeling the best lately and don't want to risk my illness on you," he breathed before another fit of coughing took him.

"I appreciate your honesty, Hank. I still plan to help. Do you mind if I look around to see what I have to work with when the fire arrives?"

"We still have a lot of work to do. I only ask that you don't get in anyone's way as they prepare to leave," Hank said with a wave. "Good luck."

Allendria only smiled and dipped her head before she walked away from the conversation. She made a beeline for the wagons and got a closer look at the people loading them. All of them looked terribly sick, as did Hank. *These unfortunate people are being uprooted while trying to fight disease.*

A young girl running around the corner interrupted her train of thought. She ran headfirst into Allendria and fell to the ground with a whimper. Allendria bent over and helped the little girl to her feet. Crouching down, she looked the small child in the face and brushed back a stray piece of hair. The youngster didn't look as bad as the rest, but her red, swollen eyes told a different story. Allendria also noted her skin was hot to the touch when she brushed her hair away.

"You okay, dear?" she asked in a comforting voice.

The little girl sniffled for a moment before answering, "Yes, Ma'am. Wasn't looking where I was going. Sorry bout that."

Allendria smiled at her. "You worried about the fire?"

She didn't answer but nodded her head in a solemn gesture.

"Don't worry," Allendria told her with a wink, "I'm here to stop the fire and keep the village safe."

"Really?" she asked excitedly.

"Really, really. Why does everyone here look sick?" Allendria asked, trying to shift the topic.

The child looked at her feet and kicked at the dirt. "We don't talk about it much. Everyone started getting sick a couple weeks ago. Some didn't make it."

"Do you not have a healer here in the village?"

"No ma'am. We have none who can do magic here. We sent someone for a healer when it first started, but they never returned."

Allendria nodded. "Sorry to hear that. Hopefully, everyone else will recover soon."

The little girl had an odd expression on her face, but she just nodded and continued on her path around the building. Allendria stood to her feet and dusted off her pants. She spotted the telltale glow of orange on the horizon to what she assumed was the west. She ran for that side of the village and took stock of her options.

She could see flames consuming everything through the trees in front of her. Her first instinct was to run at the fiery inferno to divert the blaze, but she needed a plan. *I can use the dome spell Arthur taught me to shield myself from the fire, but it would drain mana fast and not protect the village. I need something to wall off the village. A wall of stone, maybe?*

It would be an unorthodox method to get around the problem, but why not try it? It was a trial for her class that required Fire Magic. That didn't mean you couldn't solve the problem with other magic. She examined the area in front of her and called into mind her largest stone wall spell. She activated the spell, and a message startled her.

*This zone is restricted. You're unable to cast any spells but those in the Fire Magic skill in this area.*

*Well, damn. So much for a clever way around the problem. It makes sense, in a grim way.* She took stock of her resources. Her mana pool, when combined with her amulet, was an impressive 910. It wasn't nearly as remarkable as Arthur's reserves with his fancy weapon. She then realized she'd forgot to add her new staff, bringing her to 2,410. *Not too shabby.*

I need to clear a safe zone around the village. The most dangerous part was the embers from the leaves and branches. The trunks of the trees would be green enough to resist much of the flame. If the leaves and smaller branches caught on fire and drifted on the wind into the village, it'd spell disaster. She could handle a stray ember here and there, but many of the trees butted up directly to a structure. She'd watched Arthur cut wood using Earth Magic before and even knew how he'd managed it. Since that was out of the question, she had to do it with Fire Magic.

She focused on a tree that was some distance from the village. She didn't want to catch the village on fire accidentally. She focused on a thin line of fire burning across the trunk of the tree. She angled it so the tree would fall away from the village after the spell finished. She watched the line burn and sputter as it slowly ate through the wood. It wasn't more than an inch through when the unexpected happened. The entire tree lit on fire in an instant.

Allendria panicked and fell backward onto her butt. She rolled over and crawled away from the tree until she was a safe distance away. Turning around, she focused on her Fire Magic again and withdrew the heat from the burning tree and directed it away. The tree slowly stopped burning until all that remained was a charred husk.

*Why didn't that work? Was the temperature too high in that large of an area?* Her thoughts shifted to the problem. *Maybe try a smaller line of fire and move the flame? If I keep it a direct stream of highly concentrated fire and then move it back and forth along the trunk, that may allow enough heat to dissipate as I burn through.*

With the new idea in her mind, she changed focus to another nearby tree. This time she created a highly condensed stream of fire that flew in a straight line. It immediately burned into the tree in rapid succession. Allendria watched as it looked on the verge of turning to a full-fledged inferno again, so she slid the beam side to side along the trunk.

The fire ate through quickly, and it wasn't long before her back-and-forth motion paid off. Right before the beam cut all the way through, she heard a loud *Crack!* and it toppled in the direction she wished. She walked up and saw the burnt portion of the tree sitting smooth next to the splintered section that broke loose. Her notifications surprised her a little.

*Congratulations, you have discovered the Fire Magic Spell: Searing Beam. You have gained 250 experience in Fire Magic for discovering a known spell.*

*You have gained 60 experience in Fire Magic for successfully casting Searing Beam.*

| Spell: Searing Beam |
|---|

| Requirements: Fire Magic<br>Mana Cost: 30 MP<br>Cast Time: 2 seconds | Description: This spell creates a beam of fire that can burn through flammable objects and quickly heat any non-flammable objects. |
| --- | --- |
| Mastery Level: 1 | |

*Congratulations, you have learned Woodcutting for a 100 experience bonus. Unconventional, but I like it.*

*Congratulations, you have learned the hidden subskill Arcane Woodcutting for a 500 experience bonus.*

Allendria laughed to herself at the notification. *I've so got to rub that in Arthur's face. Finally, learned a hidden skill that he hasn't yet.*

Equipped with her new spell, she went to work. She quickly felled tree after tree and was careful to keep them falling away from the village. She cleared everything within one-hundred yards of the buildings. The trees she left lying where they fell since she couldn't use Earth Magic to move them. Even if they burned, it should be easy for her to control the fire.

Her attention turned to the rapidly approached fire, and she waited. Sweat beaded on her forehead as the flames grew closer. The uppermost branches of the trees she felled lit on fire and the flame crawled down the tree trunks. The fire moved slowly, and she quickly snuffed out the fire on the logs once the upper limbs and leaves combusted. Luckily, with the trees lying on the ground, facing away from the village, none of the fire caught in the wind. Before long, the blaze steadily died in front of her, and the main inferno jumped from tree to tree, circling the village. There wasn't much foliage on the ground, and only small tufts of grass and fallen leaves ignited before quickly burning themselves out. *If nothing else, these villagers did an excellent job of keeping the forest floor clear.* Allendria thought to herself.

The little time she spent examining the village told her the next place in danger was to the north. There weren't many trees near the village to the south. She sprinted for the northern side and quickly overtook the fire as it jumped from tree to tree around the perimeter.

Without delay, she cast Searing Beam to drop the trees near the buildings. She'd felled another five before something caught her eye. Through the trees, she spotted the little girl from earlier kneeling down next to some kind of dip in the ground. In a moment of fear, she dashed for the child to get her away from the fire. When she reached her, she grabbed her and saw her crying.

"What's wrong? You can't be out here. The fire is almost to this part of the forest."

"I don't wanna leave without momma," the little girl cried before she broke into coughing.

It stunned Allendria. She didn't look terribly sick before.

"Well, go get her and get out with the rest if you must," Allendria told her.

"I can't. She's down there," the child told her, pointing to the side.

Allendria turned and finally looked into the sizable hole beside her. She'd been so preoccupied with the child and the fire, she'd somehow missed it. The sight in the place brought tears to her eyes and caused her to fall to her knees.

Bodies lay sprawled in the crevice. All looked in rough condition, and some even oozed nasty looking fluids. Many had black splotches on their skin that looked like infections. All stared straight ahead in death.

"Dear Goddess," she breathed.

She quickly turned her attention to the child. "Have you heard the villagers call this a plague?"

The little girl didn't answer and merely nodded her head yes.

*Oh, no. I can't deal with this. Dad warned me how bad the last plague was, and it happened two-hundred and thirty years ago.*

In total, that plague killed half the population of the Dark Elves and about sixty percent of the humans. Her father forced her to study the event because it was strife with systematic failures across the leadership. No one isolated the infected. They allowed them to roam and search for help, spreading it farther and farther. Some places with magical healers stopped the spread when it reached them, but they were few and far between.

She still remembered the one thing her father told her on that day after her lesson.

"Being a leader can leave you with some of the toughest decisions imaginable. How do you justify life? Would you kill one person to spare ten others? How about fifty? A hundred? What if you had to destroy an entire village to protect the rest of the kingdom?"

She ran through scenarios over and over in her mind of what to do about this. *I can't cure them. I only have access to Fire Magic and don't know any healing spells, anyway. I could try to heat their bloodstream to burn out the disease, but I'm sure I'd just end up killing them that way.*

Her gaze swept past the child to the rest of the villagers, still packing carts to leave. *I can't allow them to leave this village. If they take this disease out of here and spread it among the populace, it will quickly multiply through the countryside.*

"Lianna, please help me," she softly whimpered as she covered her face with her hands and wept.

A soft touch brushed against her shoulder, and she looked up. A radiant beauty of a woman stood in front of her. Her flowing strawberry hair only accented her smooth skin. When the Goddess smiled at Allendria, some of her anxiousness melted away.

"Goddess?" she asked in disbelief.

"Yes, child. I see you're troubled."

"How are you here?"

"Come now, my dear. You know I've visited Arthur personally. My influence and power grow by the day with him leading the charge. It allows me more freedom to intervene. It also helps this realm is closer to my level of existence. Class quests are really quite unique," the Goddess explained with a wistful tone. "Now, what can I help you with?"

Allendria's eyes filled with tears again at the thought of the decision she needed to make.

"I don't know if I can do it," she mumbled softly under her breath

"So, by that logic, you already know what you must do."

"I do," she told her with her face down in shame.

"So why ask for my help? I can't directly interfere with a class quest. I've merely slowed time around us so we can speak," Lianna said with a gesture around.

The flames burning in the forest flickered in slow motion, and the people running about the village moved slower than a snail.

"Are you ever forced to take lives?" Allendria asked carefully.

The Goddess adopted a regretful look and crouched down to join Allendria. She wrapped an arm around the Dark Elf before finally answering her question.

"Some things are inevitable. I've been around longer than you can fathom, and yes, I've had to take lives. Being a god has its struggles. Some of my brethren have no issue killing and destroying. I'm not one of those. I've made those decisions before, and each one of them hurt my soul, but there comes a time in every person's life where they have to make a choice. I fear your choice is destined to make you a leader. The role of a leader is arguably the toughest one. Life and death decisions may become far more common than you wish to deal with."

"But I'm a nobody now. Just another Dark Elf and a friend to some humans."

Lianna looked at her and cocked an eyebrow. "You can't be that dense, girl. You're still the Princess of the Dark Elven nation. You also seem to be quick on the way to adopting a title of queen for another kingdom," Lianna told her with a wry grin, "that boy sure loves you."

"I have no authority, though. My words have no power."

"Only because you let it be so. People listen to you and follow your commands."

"Of course, but it's because Arthur appointed me in charge of them."

"Did he now? I could've sworn you took that job on your own. You even voluntarily helped them when you didn't need to. They look up to you. Now the Dark Elves in the village have already begun to see you as the rightful Princess. It's not that you have no power, it's only that you haven't learned to exert it."

"That doesn't give me the right to murder an entire village!"

Allendria's mind snapped to the young girl as images of people on fire and screaming flashed through her mind. *I can't do it. Her soft smile and innocent behavior. She did nothing to deserve the hand fate dealt.*

Lianna's response snapped her out of her dark thoughts, "Leaders don't just take one thing into consideration. As you've no doubt already thought of, what happens if they spread this disease?"

Allendria's head dropped to her chest. "It'll start another wave of the plague similar to what my father warned me of."

"Yes, it will."

She pictured the old man in the village as his eyes melted, and skin shriveled in the fire. The young girl stared at her as her hair lit on fire, and she screamed for her mother. Random faces of those she'd seen as she traveled through the town reflected similar scenarios in her mind.

"How do you do it? How can I sit here and watch them burn by my own hands?"

"You don't. Whatever you do, don't close your eyes. The sounds and smells will wreak more havoc than anything. Stare blankly as you do what you need to and picture all those you care about. Make sure you understand you're doing it to save their lives."

"And that works?"

"A little, but nothing will completely fix the pain."

"Thank you, Goddess Lianna."

Lianna reached over a hand and brushed Allendria's hair back over her left ear. "Stay strong. You can get through this trial, and it will help you prepare for the future."

The touch on her hair caused her mind to
race back to the young girl again. The images
of death returned in full force, and she could
only squeeze her eyes shut against the tears.

Before she could respond, the surrounding
space blurred back into full speed, and she
couldn't find Lianna. Her face morphed into a
mask of determined resolve, and she turned to
the pit of the dead.

"Little one," she said to the young girl,
"it's time to say goodbye and head back to the
village. I have to send them on their journey
and will do it with fire."

The small child walked to the pit, and her
tiny mouth opened. "Love you, Mom. The
friendly lady said she's going to send you to
the afterlife. Please wait for me when you get
there."

She scrambled away from the pit and walked
back toward the village. Allendria hung her
head, and the tears wouldn't stop. *She won't
have to wait very long. I'm so sorry.*

Allendria tugged at her Fire Magic and
swirled it in a whirlwind of force until it
surrounded the pit. The heat grew in
intensity, and with one last pull, the ring of
flame condensed and fell into the hole. Skin
charred and peeled as the fire consumed all in
its path. The sharp tinge of copper and burnt
hair filled the area as the flames continued
to devour their prey. The fire continued until
the skeletal faces stared at her and seemed to
mock her very existence.

Allendria turned to look at the village and
then checked on her reserves.

| HP: 340/340 |
| Mana: 205/410 |

She still had mana siphoned away in her staff and a little in her necklace, but she'd burned through a good chunk of it. With the number of buildings present, she wouldn't have enough mana to do the job.

*The part that takes the most mana is drawing the heat and getting it started. Once the fire is established, it works faster and for less mana.* Then a thought hit her. *I have a ton of fire around here. I should be able to channel power from it directly and amplify it for my spells.*

She focused on some of the flames approaching the village and walked closer to them. Opening herself to her Fire Magic, she drew on the currents of fire and pulled the power into the space between her hands. Feeding trickles of her mana, she shaped the power and condensed it to a more lethal version. When satisfied with her work, she launched the ball of flame at the nearest building.

*Congratulations, you have learned the subskill Fire Amplification for a 100 experience bonus.*

It impacted the wooden siding, and the ball burst through the wall and splashed fire across the entire ground level. Allendria heard screams over the raging fire, and the heat licked away her flowing tears. Without stopping, she continued forward.

Fire seemed to follow her in a wall as she advanced. Her power fed the flames and pulled them along with her. It didn't take much of her mana to fuel the fire. She continued launching balls of fiery energy and the village became a blazing inferno of its own.

She approached the last building in the village. The main hall was where most of the villagers were gathering supplies and loading wagons. The villagers sat huddled outside the building and wept in fear as the old man who welcomed her approached.

"Why are you doing this?" the old man asked. "You said you were here to save the village."

"My goal was to save the village. I just hadn't realized what that meant until now," she told him with a sad smile. "I can't let you spread the disease to others. It could destroy the world as we know it. I'm sorry. If it brings you comfort, I'm sure this will haunt me for the rest of my life."

She pulled with all her might and drug the wall of fire forward. With one final push of her mana, she enveloped herself in the magic of Fire to resist the heat and slung the wall of flame at the last building. The screams of the villagers assaulted her ears as they quickly burned and fell to the ground. The structure went up in flames, and everywhere she looked, red and orange light greeted her vision. She stood in the middle of the inferno as steam rose from her eyes. *Oh, Goddess, what have I done?*

Her surroundings vanished, and she stood in a clear forest meadow with nothing else around.

*Congratulations, Allendria. A Pyromancer is the embodiment of flame. Fire is used to both fight and to cleanse. Sometimes a forest needs to burn to grow anew. You've now been granted the Pyromancer class. When you return, you will have access to the Pyromancer class tree, but you won't remember the full details. You will remember the lessons you learned and the critical decisions you made.  The secrets of the testing must be guarded to prevent those not worthy from cheating their way through a trial. Good luck, Pyromancer Allendria.*

The air distorted around her, and she appeared back in the meadow facing the Tree of Embers.

# Chapter 34



Arthur walked up to the standing form of Allendria. He reached out his hand and brushed a tear away from her face. "You okay?"

She seemed confused for a few moments before finally shaking her head up and down.

"I think so. I'm not sure why I was crying."

"The tests seem to be brutal. I'm sure it was something you faced. No one seems to remember much from them, so the magic of the quests must do it to keep people from learning the secret of how to complete them," Rayne chimed in from the side of the group.

"I think he's right," Arthur agreed.

The group took the time to relax for once. They'd been traveling non-stop with little rest and even less sleep. Being surrounded by this expanse of burning wilderness gave them an odd sense of security. With the amount of effort it took them to reach the place, they took the chance for a long rest.

Everyone found them a soft spot on the thick grass to bed down. Samson volunteered for the first watch, and Arthur curled up with Allendria to sleep. Vana bedded down near Samson's choice for the watch, and Rayne slept by himself to the side. The entire group took their turns, rotating through the watch, and all woke up the next morning refreshed and ready to continue.

The first item on the agenda was something to eat, and consulting the map quickly followed. The large scroll showed them the path from the forest. It depicted this place on the sheet by an almost perfect circle, so as long as it was accurate, they should be able to travel due north to exit and continue their journey. It was only a day and a half to Nightwatch, judging by the map.

The group checked all their weapons, and Arthur readied his spell. He cast the Heat Control spell, and they all walked back into the inferno. A little over two hours of travel brought them back to the fringe of the Burning Forest, only this time in an unfamiliar area. They all breathed an audible sigh of relief when they were clear of the heat, and Arthur dropped his spell.

"Remind me never to go back there," Rayne said in a sour tone with a glare at the forest.

"I'm with you there," Arthur agreed.

They continued on their way when a large thump sounded near them. The group all spun and drew swords, only to see a large ball of reddish-orange scales staring back at them.

*Should've known your lazy butt would stay out here.*

*Hey, I'm resistant to heat, but even that kind of fire would hurt me. I was confident you had this handled. I've mentioned I hate walking, right?*

*Could've used my spell slacker.*

*I don't have the mana capacity you do. Also, wouldn't do to be drawing double the mana just for each of us to fuel the spell.*

*Whatever. Anything dangerous around?*

*Not really. I ate a goat earlier, but I wouldn't classify him as dangerous.*

*A goat? You didn't kill someone's goat, did you?*

*No, no… I don't think so. It was over to the east on some foothills, so I think it was wild.*

*Any other game around? We'll need some more food at our current pace. We gave most away to the kids and have only grabbed a couple of things here and there.*

*You guys like goat? I'm sure I can find you one.*

Arthur grimaced at the thought. *I'm sure goat will do if you can't find something better. If you see a deer, get it immediately.*

*Balair, the Huntsdragon to the rescue,* the ball of scales told him as he flapped his wings and took off again.

"Being his normal lazy self," Arthur told the others as the dragon flew off. "On the bright side, he agreed to keep an eye out for some game for us to replenish some of our food supplies."

"About time he does something useful," Vana murmured under her breath.

The group continued on their trek before Samson came to stand by Arthur.

"You ready for your quest?" the paladin asked.

"A little. I think I'll be fine, but only time will tell."

The ex-soldier nodded in understanding. "You scared about finishing your quest, then?"

Arthur's mind turned for a few moments, thinking about the question.

"Pretty sure that's the same question as before."

"How so? Your Soul Bond quest isn't the same thing as gaining your class," Samson asked, confused.

*Ah, leave it up to me to make that mistake and look like a fool.*

"My fault. Brain shut off for a bit and thought you were referring to the class quest. I honestly don't know how to feel about the Soul Bond quest. It hasn't really sunk in yet and doesn't feel real."

"Well, right now, it isn't. It might be in a few days, though."

"I guess I'll deal with it when the time comes. I know I should be excited that I'll have a powerful new friend but the drawbacks worry me. It is also a little concerning since she told me not all of her kind agree with the decision she made."

Samson perked up at that, "Strife with the dragons? People rarely see them anymore. They stay to themselves mostly."

"Calfuray told me some of the dragons thought they should ignore their contract with me and stay away from human affairs."

"Think it'll cause trouble?"

"Goddess, I hope not, but that seems to be my luck. It also puts the uncomfortable issue of another person's life in my hands, and this time literally. If I die while bonded, so does she."

Samson looked down in sorrow. "So not sure if it's worth the price?"

"She seems to think it is, but I'm not sure. With our situation, I'm not sure I can afford to turn down the help," Arthur said with regret.

"We'll figure something out," Samson responded with a clap on his shoulder.

The group continued on their trek across the grassy plain. The weather held, and they made excellent time. Their camp that night was a simple affair. They cooked a meager meal of a simple stew from two rabbits that Balair dropped to them. The morning rose cloudless, and they continued their journey.

The day sped past as their feet carried them. Some black clouds on the horizon worried Arthur. Flashes of lightning illuminated the gloomy clouds. As their trip progressed, Arthur was sure the storm was heading their direction. They considered stopping to hunker down when the sound of thunder reached them but pushed a little farther.

A fort came into view as a reward for their efforts. The stone walls surrounding the building stood out, although they weren't very tall. An enormous stone tower jutted from the ground and connected to a manor house of similar stone near ground level. The entire area was devoid of most life. Even the green grass seemed to fade and turned a brittle yellow as they closed the distance.

The group walked toward the gate, wary of their surroundings. When they were within throwing distance, an unexpected message startled Arthur.

*Warning: You are about to enter the Dungeon of Nightwatch. Ancient evil stirs in this place.*

"Damn it, how did we end up with a dungeon for our class quests?" Arthur asked as he turned to look at Rayne.

The young man's eyes were wide with surprise at seeing the same message himself. "Just crappy luck, I guess."

"Must be why both of ours are in the same place."

Arthur looked around to the rest of the group. Samson looked anxious and ready as his hand kept squeezing and releasing his sword hilt, and Vana had an evil grin on her face that almost frightened Arthur. Allendria wore a wry smile before turning her attention to the building in front of them.

"So, we ready for this?" Samson asked.

The group nodded in agreement, and everyone assumed their fighting positions. Samson took the lead and advanced through the small gate. The broken, rusted hinges and the wooden gate barely hung by a sliver of metal. He crept forward with his shield up as they entered the courtyard. Piles of refuse and trash littered the ground around the small clearing. Old boards and busted metal tools jutted from the collections.

Rayne was at the rear of the party, and when he crossed the threshold of the gate, it swung shut and slammed with a resounding thud. The party spun to stare at the closed door while the rusted metal groaned and protested.

*Greetings, mortals. You were foolish enough to enter my domain, and now it will be the last mistake you ever make. Minions! Make quick work of these intruders.*

The voice intruded on their thoughts, and the rough, gravelly voice grated on Arthur's senses. The piles of refuse around them shifted and moved. Arthur looked to one and saw a skeletal hand pop from the dirt and grab a broken scythe blade jutting from the pile of trash.

"More undead?" Arthur asked in a resigned tone.

"Afraid so," Samson replied as he took a step forward. He shifted his stance, and Arthur watched him thrust his left arm forward, launching his shield. The large chunk of metal spun and slammed into a skeleton. The head exploded into pieces as the spinning shield struck it. It returned to Samson, and he dropped into a ready stance, waiting for an enemy to approach.

An arrow flew across the battle and knocked a skeleton down. The shaft protruded from the skull of the creature, but it still rose back to its feet. Arthur drew Ember and activated Sheathe in Flames. He dashed for a skeleton that approached Samson on his flank. His sword came down in an overhanded chop, but the creature turned to him with a grin and raised its weapon.

Metal sparks flew from the impact as Ember met the broken scythe blade he'd seen earlier. The fact that Ember didn't slice right through it baffled him, but there was no time to dwell on it. Arthur lifted his sword and swung again from the side, but the skeleton was efficient and caught that strike on its scythe as well. Arthur expected a counterattack, so he observed the weapon. To his surprise, a skeletal fist slammed into his chest and knocked him back a step.

*Skeleton Warrior (1) (Level 20) has dealt 25 HP damage to you with Punch.*

So they develop a better fighting style the higher their level goes, Arthur thought ruefully.

Most of the monsters he'd fought since coming here used fundamental fighting tactics. This one had already proved to be an exception.

Shaking himself out of the reverie, he jumped back on the offensive. He swung at the creature and stayed on his toes to keep moving. The monster deflected the attacks until Arthur outpaced it and skirted around its side. It finally missed a strike aimed for the back of its shoulder, and Ember drove into the skeleton. The weapon flared and flames engulfed the monster. Arthur jumped back to avoid the conflagration.

*You have dealt 200 HP Damage to Skelton Warrior (1) (Level 20) with Ember (Critical Hit) (Burning Strike).*

A cry of pain behind him caused him to turn to see Vana with blood running down her right bicep. The skeleton in front of her held a rusted dagger with a line of blood dripping from the edge. Arthur activated his Ice Spikes spell and launched a volley of crystalline spears at it. The ice smashed into different body parts, causing bones to crunch and snap.

*You have dealt 210 HP Damage to Skelton Warrior (2) (Level 20) with Ice Spikes (Critical Hit) (Shattered).*

The skeleton wobbled as it continued its assault on Vana, and its speed slowed considerably. Vana capitalized on the opportunity to dash forward and smash her dagger into its skull.

Arthur heard a footfall near him and turned to see another skeleton walking toward him. A sizable chunk of metal was already en route to his head, so he activated Passata Soto and dropped to the ground as the weapon flew over him. Ember stabbed out and crunched into its ribcage. Fragments of bone rained onto the dirt, but the skeleton never stopped moving.

*You have dealt 110 HP Damage to Skelton Warrior (3) (Level 20) with Ember (Critical Hit) (Shattered).*

It continued its assault with another strike, but Arthur was better prepared. He caught the misshapen hunk of metal on the flat of his blade and pushed it off balance with a well-timed parry. He fished out his dagger with his left hand and slammed the hilt of it into the skeleton's skull.

*You have dealt 240 HP Damage to Skelton Warrior (3) (Level 20) with Enchanted Mage-crafted Steel Dagger (Critical Hit) (Mortal Strike) (Pommel Strike).*
*Skeleton Warrior (3) (Level 20) has died.*

Arthur ran over to Samson while the paladin held off three different enemies. All three were similar in appearance to the ones he'd fought already, and all carried oddly shaped chunks of metal.

Ember swung around and quickly separated the head from the one nearest him. A shadow shifted into visibility near another, and Rayne's stiletto dagger slammed into the back of its skull while his swordbreaker chopped into the skeleton's neck. Samson used the attack effectively and stepped forward to slam his shield into the last and knock it to the ground. A quick stroke of his sword finished it.

A flare of orange drew his attention, and he watched as Allendria roasted a skeleton. The area quieted, and Arthur looked around. The smoldering corpse of the one that Ember lit on fire lay near one of the refuse heaps, and the rest of the twice-killed bodies littered their surroundings.

"Could've been worse," Rayne said optimistically.

"Skeletons are still skeletons. Don't like the damn things. Undead make my skin crawl," Vana complained.

"I agree wholeheartedly," Arthur chimed in.

The group looked around and walked toward one corpse to check for loot when a loud scraping noise echoed through the clearing. They all swung to look at the mansion door as it creaked open. Three creatures shambled from the doorway toward them. They looked like humans at first, but their bumbling way of walking set them apart. Arthur spotted chunks of flesh hanging from one of their faces and noticed some gruesome looking wounds on some of the others. He activated Scan to see what they were dealing with.

*You have received 190 experience for successful use of Scan.*

| Name: Ghoul | |
| --- | --- |
| Level: 18 | |
| Type: Undead | |
| HP: 260/260 | |
| MP: 420/420 | |
| Stamina: 200/200 | |
| Strength: 16 | Experience: N/A |
| Agility: 6 | Skills |
| Intellect: 20 | Combat Skills: |
| Wisdom: 12 | |
| Endurance: 14 | ? (???/???) |

*Damn, a caster.* A streak of orange and red descended on the trio, and flames burst from Balair's mouth, headed for the lead ghoul. It turned to see the small drake and lifted an arm. A shield of eerie green light formed over the creature and absorbed the flame. It hissed in protest at the bright light from the fire as it sizzled against the shield. Balair twisted out of his dive and flew toward the party.

*Didn't faze them. Casters of some kind.* Balair sent his way.

*Guessed as much from my scan showing their mana pool.*

*No warning?*

*You tend to dive in before getting the information you need. I scanned at the same time you dove. How about you try some patience next time?*

*Can we get back to the fight before they get to us? What's the plan?*

"Fire?" Arthur asked Allendria.

"Might work, but they could also deflect it with their magic. Depends on how we do this. I'm sure we can overpower them through sheer mana. Eventually, they will run out using their shields while we can keep casting with our reserves."

"Don't like the idea of wasting mana. Surely we can come up with a better plan. We may need that mana later."

She gave him an odd look. "You really think you can burn through your entire mana pool? You do realize you couldn't even do that with the battle at the village. What makes you think three ghouls can do it?"

"Better safe than sorry? If you know they are ghouls, do you know if they have weaknesses?"

"I'm tired of telling people I'm not a scholar. Just because I have a long lifespan doesn't mean I dedicate my time to learning about every stupid monster I probably won't ever see," she huffed at him.

"Fair enough, sorry. Anyone else?"

The party glanced at each other, and everyone shook their heads.

"Rayne, think you can get close? Try not to go all out. You need to save your best abilities for your class quest."

"I'll see what I can do."

"I'll hit them with Divine Fury. It has a damage bonus against evil. I think those count," Samson said confidently.

"Sounds good."

The group hunkered down in defensive
positions and waited for the approach. Arthur
spotted a faint shadow walking around the
group and knew Rayne had made his move.
Without delay, he activated Ice Spikes. The
spears of ice flew from his hand and smashed
into the lead ghoul's green shield. Samson
stepped forward and roared at the group. They
all turned to face him, and he smiled as the
eyes on his shield glowed. A burst of searing
hot flame shot forward and slammed into the
ghouls.

Low pitched moaning noises echoed from the
ball of fire until the flame cleared. When the
heat dissipated, all three ghouls still stood
in their place. One of them couldn't move
because his legs melted to the ground in a
puddle of burning flesh. The other two looked
like they'd been in the sun for too long and
had a slight red tint to their otherwise pale
skin.

A barrage of arrows flew by and crashed
into the creatures. The glowing green energy
stopped most of the projectiles, but some
slipped through and caught a shoulder or a
hip. They typically did nothing but stagger
the monsters, and they didn't react as if
pained at all.

The lead ghoul lifted its arm, and a
swirling ball of black energy formed. The ball
shot toward them. Arthur grasped at his mana
and ripped a chunk of earth from the ground.
The black sphere hit the dirt, and it
immediately changed to a pale gray and
disintegrated.

*Thank god that wasn't my face.* Arthur almost returned fire with his Fire Blast spell before he saw the flicker of movement behind the ghouls. That spell would likely harm Rayne with its blast radius. The young thief materialized behind the ghouls, and his blades cleanly stabbed into the back of the closest one. It arched its back and its mouth opened as if to scream, but no sound came out.

Rayne dashed backward as the creature turned to grab him. Arthur cast his Stone Fist spell and hit the monster as it advanced on Rayne. The magic hit with a heavy crash and the creature flew backward into its two companions. Rayne gave Arthur a grateful nod and ran from the fight.

*You have dealt 80 HP damage to Ghoul (Level 20) with Stone Fist (Crushing Blow).*

Arthur activated Fire Blast, and the ball of fire swirled in his hands. It slowly condensed more and more until it burned with concentrated power. He dropped Ember and used a trickle of Earth Magic to keep it near him as he grasped the ball of fire in his right hand and launched it with all of his strength. As soon as it left him, he surged his Earth Magic to bring Ember back to his hand. To his surprise, it caused a notification.

*Congratulations, you have discovered the Earth Magic Spell: Telekinetic Retrieval. You have gained 250 experience in Earth Magic for discovering a known spell.*

*You have gained 80 experience in Earth Magic for successfully casting telekinetic Retrieval.*

<table>
<tr><td colspan="2" align="center">Spell: Telekinetic Retrieval</td></tr>
<tr><td>Requirements: Earth Magic<br>Mana Cost: 40 MP<br>Cast Time: 1 second<br>Cooldown: 10 seconds</td><td>Description: Use the power of Earth Magic to lift an object and quickly return it to your hand.</td></tr>
<tr><td colspan="2" align="center">Mastery Level: 1</td></tr>
</table>

The ball of fire floated in an arc toward the monsters, and the lead ghoul raised its shield. When the ball of energy touched the surface, it no longer mattered. The orb expanded quickly, and the burning flame exploded from the point of impact. It blew the three ghouls in three separate directions as the fire caused damage to each of them.

*You have dealt 450 HP damage to Ghoul (Level 20) with Fire Blast (Critical Hit) (Burning Damage) (x3).*
*Ghoul (2) (Level 20) has died.*

The ghoul with the melted legs never returned to its feet, but the other two somehow managed the feat. It riddled them in burn marks, and the smell of burning flesh filled the area and made Arthur a little queasy.

The leader of the group reached a hand toward Arthur, and he flinched. No energy swirled in its outstretched arm, but an odd sensation filled him. The feeling of something grabbing at him itched in his mind until the ghoul forcefully pulled its hand back to itself. Arthur felt a jarring sense of power leave him as a trail of blue energy leaked from him and hit the ghoul. Its eyes glowed blue for a few moments before it flashed what Arthur would swear was a grin from its deformed mouth.

He reeled from the experience and quickly saw his mana flashing at him. It was almost empty, and it had just been over three-quarters full. The understanding dawned on him.

"They can drain mana!" he shouted to Allendria.

Her face went pale, but she nodded in response. Arthur pulled mana back into his pool from his necklace just as the creature that stole his mana outstretched both arms. A giant ball of swirling black energy pulsed over its head, between its outstretched arms. The power built and condensed until the swirling vortex seemed to suck in the light of the surrounding area. The ghoul's gaze focused on Arthur, and it leaned forward to launch the energy when the tip of a blade punched through its face and sprayed black blood.

The power above its head warped and distorted before folding in on itself and disappearing with a pop. The other creature was on the verge of attacking Rayne when Balair returned and laid into it with another breath of fire. The monster was only concentrating on Rayne, so it didn't notice the small dragon dive in from behind. The stream of flame ignited the flesh, and it toppled over, the last of its HP draining away.

The group breathed a collective sigh at the stillness in the air. The corpses still smoldered, but nothing moved any longer. They hesitated to try to search the bodies again, but after an extended amount of stillness, took action.

All the metal the skeletons used, they set to the side. The ghouls themselves were a little better in the loot department. One of them had a small rod of wood, no longer than his forearm. Arthur picked it up and looked at the item.

| Item:<br>Unknown Magic Wand | **Attack:** ?<br><br>**Durability:** 63/75<br><br>**Rarity:** Uncommon<br><br>**Quality:** Well Crafted<br><br>**Weight:** 0.5 kg<br><br>**Slot:** Main Hand/Off Hand |
| --- | --- |

| | **Traits**: An unknown magical wand made of yew. Either use a skill to identify this item or find someone who can identify it for you to discover its potential. |
| --- | --- |

*Been a while since I've seen an unidentified object.* Arthur activated his Identify skill and received a disappointing message.

*Your skill is too low in Identify to reveal the secrets of this item.*

*Of course, now I need to find someone to identify it for me.* He shook his head at the luck and tossed it into his Dimensional Drawer. The larger items all joined their pile of loot in the Dimensional Storage. They saw one other thing on one ghoul and it started his gag reflex again. Melted into the flesh on one of the ghoul's hands, sat a ring. Rayne was kind enough to sever the finger and use his blade to pop the ring off before Arthur lost what little food he still had in him.

After a thorough cleaning, he looked at this item to see its properties.

| Item:<br>Ring of Wisdom | **Durability**: 50/55<br><br>**Rarity**: Uncommon<br><br>**Quality**: Well Crafted<br><br>**Weight**: 0.02 kg<br><br>**Slot**: Finger |
| --- | --- |

| | **Traits**: A ring that increases the wearer's Wisdom by 1. |
|---|---|

"Allendria, you want the ring? My regen is already higher than yours."

Her face took on a sickly green look for a moment before she carefully nodded. Arthur assumed she envisioned it trapped on the ghoul's finger as she gingerly grabbed it with two fingers. She looked the item over and even took the time to sniff it before finally sliding it onto her finger.

The last item they found was an iron key that reminded Arthur of old skeleton key designs. Its name showed as Key of the Damned and went into Arthur's pouch. He was sure they'd need it before this was all over.

The group checked all of their gear. A few dents and dings were all they had to show for the battle. They were tired and had minor scratches, but nothing that wouldn't heal quickly. The hit to his mana concerned him, but he still had a large pool available.

"Damn things took almost all of my mana. Had just enough left in my staff to fill it back up, but I have no further mana stored," Allendria grumbled.

Arthur walked over and handed her his necklace. "Put that mana back in your staff and siphon some from here. You need to have at least double your normal mana available for an emergency."

"I can't, you have your quest coming up next," she protested, but he held his hand up to stop her.

"I don't think I could use that much mana. Take what you need. Ember still has some as well."

She nodded at that and slipped the necklace over her head. A few minutes of concentration and she took it off and handed it back.

They returned their focus to the mission at hand. With the useful items secure in the Dimensional Storage, he cut the spell off, and the room disappeared. They hefted weapons into ready positions and followed Samson to the front of the building.

The wooden door looked surprisingly sturdy for the age of the building, but the metal hinges sported a dense layer of rust. Instead of trying to show finesse, Samson lifted his leg and kicked the door as hard as possible. It rocked on its hinges but swung open to reveal a building marred by age.

Tears and scratches adorned the walls, and a few threadbare tapestries remained. A multitude of stains marked the floor, but the craftsmanship and quality of materials proved it was a work of art before it fell into ruin. The fresh hardwood planks would've been the envy to every home improvement TV show host.

A spiral staircase of jet black metal, untouched by rust or the elements, sat in the middle of the common room. It curved gently upward to stop at the top level of the building. More troublesome was the curve downward that led further into the ground.

"Ideas?" Arthur asked.

"As much as I hate to say it, down," Samson grumbled.

"I was afraid you'd say that," Vana gulped. Buildings weren't quite her thing anyway, with her skill in archery.

They walked toward the staircase when a
door burst open on each side of the room. Four
skeletons and a ghoul emerged from the doors.

"I've got the ghoul. You guys deal with the
skeletons," Arthur called.

"Vana with me, we've got the left. Rayne
and Allendria, the ones on the right are
yours," Samson called.

Arthur watched Samson charge headfirst into
the skeletons in front of him. He was lucky
the sizable man attacked the side that also
had the ghoul. It allowed him easy passage to
his prey, with Samson clearing the way so
effortlessly.

The ghoul took stock of him as he
approached, but Arthur didn't care to waste
time. If he could overpower it quick enough,
this should be an easy fight. He activated his
Haste spell and dashed the last few feet.
Ember and his dagger were ready to strike when
he also added Sheathe in Flame to the mix. The
flare of the weapon as it flew toward the
creature's head caused it to shirk back and
hiss from the light. With the surprise attack
and the speed in which he delivered it, Ember
crunched into its left collarbone, sinking
into its chest.

The flame on the blade caused the withered
skin around the wound to char black and light
on fire. His dagger followed with a thud into
the monster's right eye socket. He removed
both weapons, and the creature dropped to the
floor.

*You have dealt 200 HP damage to Ghoul
(Level 20) with Ember (Critical Hit) (Burning
Strike) (Mortal Blow).*

*You have dealt 60 HP damage to Ghoul (Level 20) with Enchanted Mage-crafted Steel Dagger (Critical Hit).*
*Ghoul (Level 20) has died.*

Arthur spun to see Samson swinging at a skeleton as Balair charged into its legs and knocked it to the ground. Samson stepped forward and removed its head from its shoulders. Rayne deftly attacked another and used his daggers with masterful style, as he inserted the blades into joints and applied force to pop them apart, effectively dismantling the creatures.

Allendria was far more reserved as she took careful shots of concentrated power with her Fire Magic. Being indoors, she didn't want to chance lighting the entire building on fire. The fight preoccupied Arthur, so it surprised him when Samson seemed to blur across the room to stand right next to him. Arthur heard a clang from the man's shield and turned to see he'd caught the sword of a skeleton, initially intended for Arthur.

"What was that?" Arthur asked as he jumped forward to assist the man.

"New class skill. Worked like a charm. Points come at a premium for the classes, but they are ever useful. Without my new Intervene skill, I would've never got to you in time," the Guardian answered.

"I owe ya one," Arthur called to the man as they expertly hacked together and took down the monster.

Arthur looked around with a sigh and wiped his forehead. The skeletons were all dead, and the quiet returned to the room. They deposited the few useful scraps in his storage room and continued to the stairs. Samson led the way as they carefully wound down the stairs. They passed one doorway that led into an empty room. Nothing stood out, so they kept moving farther down. They spotted another door farther down and headed for it before Vana told them to halt.

"I sense a secret room here," she told them with a wave to a blank section of wall.

"You have the Detect Hidden skill?" Arthur asked.

The ranger shook her head. "No, I spent my class point on a True Sight ability. It lets me see hidden places, traps, and enemies. Essential for scouts. It shows a secret door over here."

She walked to the blank wall and felt around the stonework. After a couple of minutes, an audible click echoed in the stairway, and a panel of the stone swung open. Samson took the lead, and the group walked through the entrance. Arranged on neatly organized shelves, the room's contents made him smile.

*You have found Iron Ingot (x15).*
*You have found Gold Coin (x328).*
*You have found Silver Coin (x511).*
*You have found Copper Coin (x1,143).*
*You have found Sapphire Chip (Medium) (x2).*
*You have found Snapdragon Root (x14).*
*You have found Direscale (x4).*
*You have found Primrose Petal (x31).*

The find was great for the coins alone. He could melt them down and forge them into new currency for the village to continue paying people. The herbs excited Rayne, so Arthur agreed to give them to him when they returned to the village. The iron would go to the blacksmith shop, and he placed the Sapphire Chips in his Dimensional Drawer for necessary enchantments.

They continued down the stairs until they reached the bottom floor. A single doorway greeted them on the level. With a nod to the group, Samson walked forward and gently tugged on the door. It didn't budge. Arthur walked over and saw the door had a keyhole on it. He inserted the key they found, and the lock softly clicked as he turned.

The door swung open, and a long corridor greeted them. Three doors lined the right-hand side while a single door occupied the left. Not sure where to start, they went to the first door on the right and the closest one to them. Inside was another hallway. With no better option, they followed this hallway, but Vana put location marks on the stone walls so they could backtrack if needed.

The hall ended in a door with an iron grate on the front at face level. Arthur peeked inside and saw two guards sitting at a table with two doors behind them. He backed up to address the others.

"Looks like we may have found the dungeon. Two guards inside the door."

"Fine, let's get this over with," Samson said in a serious tone as he approached the door. He pulled on it with slight amounts of pressure to see if they locked it. It didn't budge, so Arthur stepped forward and discovered that his key unlocked this room as well. Samson glanced at the group one last time before swinging the door open and charging in.

The guard tried to jump from their seats, but the party rushed in so fast all they did was fall over the chairs as they panicked to stand. Dispatching them both took only moments. Arthur looked around in a flash of confusion. *Why does an abandoned fort need guards for its dungeon?*

Arthur walked over to peer inside one of the doors and got his answer. A hallway of cells was visible, and inside each was something that used to be a human but had conduits of magical energy flowing into them and pumping some form of evil magic into them. Their bodies morphed, and skin rotted. It was apparent the leader of this place used the dungeon to create more of their minions.

They walked through the first door and glanced around. The vile magic at work made Arthur sick to his stomach, and he walked down the cells and strategically burned each of the corpses until the magic stopped flowing, and it fell to the ground. They walked through the second doorway and did the same thing. After they completed the gruesome task, they returned to the guardroom and gathered their items. Two iron daggers and a handful of coins ended up in their storage, and they tossed the guard's bodies into one of the hallways.

"You ready, Rayne?" Arthur asked.

# Chapter 35

*Trials and Tribulations*

Rayne felt the wrongness of the dungeon's rooms as they entered. The malevolent power spoke to the inner demon in him.

*It time to feed?*

*No. This isn't the time for you.*

*But the power is so tempting.*

*We have an agreement now stop the foolishness.*

The group returned to the guardroom while Rayne shook off the voice. It hadn't bothered him in a long time. Even when he used the power during the fight with the Dark Elf, it hadn't bothered him. *Why would this place stir it up?*

"You ready, Rayne?" Came Arthur's voice.

The noise amidst the silence startled him at first. Standing up straight, he looked at the firm man and nodded. A glowing scroll on the table in the room's corner drew his attention. He was sure it was the quest marker for him. Walking to the table, he sat in the chair. The tightly rolled scroll sat, so Rayne removed the ribbon and carefully opened it. A notification greeted him.

*Congratulations on reaching your destination, Rayne! The last step of your class quest to obtain the Shadow Walker class must be done solo. Are you ready to proceed? Y/N.*

He selected *Yes*, and the world blurred. As his vision cleared, he stood in a city, surrounded by buildings. A glance around showed him standing in an alley.

*Welcome to your trial. You've been hired to steal a rare ruby from the Intriel Estate and deliver it to dock warehouse number five. The benefactor of this mission may change the details of this quest as necessary. Use every skill at your disposal to make this happen. Keep in mind that skills useful as a Shadow Walker will prove the most beneficial for this test.*

*A thief quest, huh? Shouldn't be too bad. Rayne took stock of his surroundings.* If he needed to find an estate, he'd have to find the fancier part of the town. He hid all his weapons out of sight and walked into the city. The crowds seemed somewhat tame compared to most major cities he'd seen. It might be because of the goblins and orcs invading, but he couldn't be sure.

A glance up and down the street gave him an idea of where he was. The broken dirt road and dilapidated buildings told him he must be in the poorer section in a city this large. His gaze searched the horizon until he spotted the direction the more beautiful buildings resided. He lifted his hood and walked toward his new destination.

The crowds were odd to his senses. They didn't move and bustle like he expected them to. He didn't have to weave through like normal, and they almost seemed to part for him as he neared anyone. Brushing it off to his time in the countryside, he continued on his path.

    His trip didn't take as long as he
expected, and he stepped onto a solid
cobblestone street. An inn caught his eye, and
he ducked inside. The patrons looked better
off than the people he'd passed since coming
here. Luckily, his well-made armor fit in just
as well here. Armor was universal in style. As
long as he wasn't attending court, he'd be
fine.

    It took some time for him to work the room.
He ordered drinks for people and nursed an ale
to look like he was almost drunk. His
questions turned to the houses until he
finally had someone slip up and tell him which
of the mansions belonged to the Intriel
Estate. Some more time visiting was necessary
to not raise suspicions, but he eventually
excused himself in a loud drunken bid to go
pee.

    As soon as he exited the building, his
demeanor shifted right back to himself, and he
rushed to his target. Nothing said he had a
time limit on this quest, but he didn't want
to leave his friends trapped in the dungeon of
a Dungeon any longer than necessary.

    When the building the man described finally
came into sight, Rayne ducked into a nearby
alley and shimmied his way to the roof of the
adjacent building. When on top, he lay prone
and observed the structure. The layout was
standard for many of these manors. It reminded
him of the mansion he'd robbed to gain entry
to the Shadows of the Flame. With the layout
being similar, he would bet his target would
be somewhere upstairs near the noble's office
space.

The guards in the place were a
disappointment as well. Half of them seemed to
be sleeping while standing. The other half
weren't paying attention to anything and
looked to be daydreaming. With a sigh, he
determined he needed to get this over with.
The guards were so pathetic he could just
overpower them and steal it, but he wanted to
make a challenge for himself. This was a
Shadow Walker quest, after all, so he should
be use skills how he thought a Shadow Walker
would. To him, that meant stealth.

He circled the small wall around the estate
until he found a space free of onlookers and
activated one of his skills. In a running
sprint, he leaped on the wall and kept
bounding higher until he reached the top. *That
Wall Running skill is super useful in a city.*

Dropping over the edge of the wall, he
looked around. The area was clear, and there
was only one guard visible near his
destination. The one lone window on the back
of the building was his intended target. If
his luck held, it'd be a guest room.

Rayne quietly moved toward the guard near
his target. The man never noticed his
approach. Whoever owned this mansion should be
ashamed of their guard force. He stepped up
behind him, wrapped his hand around the
guard's face to cover his mouth, and plunged
his stiletto dagger into the side of his neck.
The guard tensed and went limp.

*You have dealt 230 HP damage to Guard
(Level 20) with Enchanted Mage-crafted Steel
Stiletto Dagger (Critical Hit) (Mortal Blow).
Guard (Level 20) has died.*

Rayne lowered the man to the ground and drug his body to the wall. He carefully propped him up and made it look like he was sleeping. *This shouldn't be too hard for these lazy guards to believe.*

He examined the window and found it unlocked. *Yet another disappointment to add to the list.* Rayne was feeling bad for whoever was in charge here. They must be incompetent. The room on the other side was indeed a bedroom. He slipped through the window and walked to the door. He cracked it open slowly and peered out into the hallway. It was clear in the direction he could see, so he pushed the door open a little more and checked through the slight crack on the hinge side to see in that direction. *Not a soul in sight.*

He pictured the layout of the building from his view outside and walked out the door and into the hallway to his left. This direction should lead to a staircase near the central area of the building and allow him to reach his destination on the second floor.

Rayne stuck to the edges of the hall and dashed through the lit areas. One guard sat at the base of the staircase, and Rayne swore the man was sleeping standing up. Rayne smirked and decided to test his skill and sneak past the sleeping man without alerting him. Killing him would be far too easy and would set off alarms if someone found him. They were far less likely to discover the guard he'd killed outside than one in the middle of the manor.

The guard stood near the entrance to the stairs and thankfully didn't block the doorway. Rayne walked forward on the balls of his feet to reduce sound. Choosing his foot placement carefully, he continued toward the guard. When he was within a few feet of the man, the guard snorted and grumbled while raising his free hand to scratch at his face. Rayne froze in mid-stride and stood perfectly still until the guard lowered his hand and drifted back to sleep.

When his foot landed on the stairs, he walked up with the same careful steps. At the top of the stairs, he peered around the exit to the staircase, looking for enemies. He felt the same sense of utter disappointment as the hallway was empty. The hall had one door on each side and a final door at the end of the hallway. If the layout held the same, the room he needed was the one at the end of the hall.

He ignored the doors on the sides and went straight to the end of the hall. He almost felt foolish as he carefully opened the door and checked inside. *At this point, what are the odds anyone will be guarding anything in this place correctly?*

The room inside was the office. A large wooden desk with intricate scrollwork on it sat in the center of the room. An equally ornate chair with a padded leather cushion rested at the desk. A large bookshelf lined the wall to his right, packed to the top with a variety of unique works.

On his left was the window visible from the outside. Hanging on the wall behind the desk were two jewel-encrusted swords and a large heater shield. An oddly placed painting hung on the back wall near one of the swords. Its appearance immediately drew Rayne's attention. There was no reason someone would hang a picture in such an odd location and with no discernable spacing with the rest of the items on the wall. The swords and shield spaced out evenly, but this was just jammed in-between the sword on the left and the shield in the center.

He made sure the door was closed and locked before walking over to examine the painting. Reaching up, he grabbed the edges, and it moved with ease. He lifted it and set it to the side against the wall. The space behind it looked like every other section of the surrounding wall. Nothing stood out or immediately caught his attention. He carefully examined all the seams in the wall behind the painting. It took a few minutes, but he finally spotted a tiny seam along the bottom edge of one of the bricks.

When his vision caught on the seam, the entire square lit up blue on the wall in his sight as his Detect Hidden skill triggered. With the hidden compartment highlighted, he ran his fingers along the edges. Feeling every crack and lightly pushing on each tiny section as he passed until he covered the entire area. His luck finally kicked in when a finger on his right hand felt a small part of the stone indent in as he put pressure on it. A soft *clunk* drifted to him, but nothing happened.

Rayne looked around the room for anything that may have shifted. A book on the bookshelf stuck out farther than it should. *I'm pretty sure those were all lined up when I walked in.* Walking to the book, he grabbed it and pulled. It slid out without resistance, and a small piece of stone sticking jutted from the wall. A quick tug on it set off a grinding noise, and he turned in time to watch the stone panel swing open.

A large ruby sat in the opening, surrounded by piles of gold coins and smaller gems. *That's more like it.* Rayne strode to the opening with confidence and grabbed the ruby. In a flash, he dropped it into his pouch and looked to the rest of the treasure.

*No. Remember your training. You steal only what the mission requires and nothing more.* Rayne sighed and pushed the panel shut. It snapped closed, and he turned in time to hear the door to the room emit a *click* and creak open. He unsheathed his daggers and froze in place, unsure of what to do until a familiar face entered the room. Her porcelain white skin, with raven black hair and eyes the color of honey, bore into his soul.

Rayne's knees wobbled as he stared at the beautiful woman he'd seen oh so many times in his nightmares. Tears welled in his eyes, and his daggers clattered to the floor as he dropped to his knees.

"R… Rose? It can't be, you're dead," he breathed softly.

"Oh, you mean when you killed me? Luckily for me. The shadow that took you also snared me and saved my life. Took you long enough to finish your mission. At least you didn't fall out of a tree this time," she told him with a smirk.

The tears ran down his face in streams. "This can't be real. You're not here. What nightmare is this?"

Rayne watched as Rose's face morphed to one of compassion. She walked to him and kneeled in front of him. Her hand reached forward and cupped his cheek.

"It's okay. I understand it wasn't your choice. I know you weren't in control, and I forgive you. I could never stay mad at you anyway," she said with a smile.

Rayne's shoulders shook with his sobs as Rose leaned forward and enveloped him in her arms. The touch of her skin comforted him. They stayed that way for an unknown amount of time until Rayne's emotions settled. Rose pushed away and looked him in the eyes.

"Now, it's time to work. I need your help. We have an important job to take care of."

"What do you mean? I'm here to complete a quest."

"Oh, I know," she waved off, "who do you think the benefactor is, anyway?"

Rayne fished in his pouch and pulled out the ruby. "So this was for you, then?"

Rose chuckled at the ruby and walked over to the wall. She quickly pressed the first stone and walked directly to the bookcase to pull the stone lever and open the panel. Rayne watched in fascination as she walked back to him, took the ruby, and placed it back in the secret space.

"Come now, surely you haven't forgotten your initial trial test?" She asked with a hint of amusement in her voice.

Visions of his first solo mission flashed before his eyes. He even winced as he remembered falling through a tree. Realization struck him, and he understood what she was saying.

"This is your mansion?"

She nodded, pleased he understood.

"So, what's the actual mission then?"

"I need your help to rid this city of its lord."

"So, an assassination mission then?"

She nodded.

"Wrap yourself in your shadows and let's move. I don't want to alert people in the building to your presence. I'll explain the plan as we move," she said as she glanced out the open window, "the sun is setting, and our moment of opportunity is quickly approaching."

Rayne watched her turn toward the door in surprise, utterly confused by what she was referring to. She spun back to face him and saw the look on his face.

"What's wrong?"

"I don't know what you mean by wrapping myself in shadows."

Rose's face morphed into an expression of disbelief. "How not? You have the same soul inside you as I do? Have you not fed it and grown its powers? Surely you have at least the shroud ability?"

"It can feed? I've only ever had one ability from it granted during our bond."

She shook her head and turned back to him. "This won't do. How have you never figured out the abilities of your shadow soul?"

"I'd guess because I locked it into a deal and don't communicate with it. You mean it can strengthen?"

"Of course it can. It just requires spiritual energy to become stronger and unlock more of its power."

"That sounds, I don't know, evil," Rayne said in concerned tones.

"Why would it be evil? You're just pulling out spiritual energy from those people and creatures who die and using it to boost your own power. The process itself isn't inherently evil," she explained.

"Wouldn't that trap their soul?"

"No. Spiritual energy is distinct energy altogether. It's the same energy they base some of the shamanistic magic on."

*Shamans are primarily seen in the orc and goblin tribes, so not sure that argument would hold weight. I guess I'll just have to trust her.* Rayne thought.

"Fine, how do I do this then?"

She stood in front of him as shadows crawled across her body and covered her completely. It took all of his focus to look at her. His attention kept drifting to other things in the room, and he struggled to return to Rose.

"Tough to look at me, isn't it?"

"Yea," he grumbled in frustration.

"That's how the magic works. It hides me in the shadows and forces attention away from me. You can only look at me because you can harness the same power."

"That still doesn't explain how I do it."

She huffed at him and walked over to lay a hand on his shoulder. "Take this, and you'll see."

Shadows poured from her hand and into his body. The soul inside him came alive at the power.

*Ah, it feels so good to feed after so long.*

When the flow of shadows finished, he saw a strange notification.

*You have absorbed 5,000 Spiritual Power from Rose (Level 20).*
*Congratulations, your Soul Bond with the Soul of Shadows has advanced to Level 2. A new ability has been unlocked.*

| Soul Bond Ability: Shroud of Shadow | |
|---|---|
| Requirements: Soul Bond with Soul of Shadows Level 2<br>Cast Time: Instant<br>Effect Duration: 2 minutes<br>Cooldown: 5 minutes | Description: Shadows surround you, making you harder to detect by enemies and decreasing all noise you make.<br><br>Effects:<br>• Makes anyone without an affinity for Shadow Energy to look away from you.<br>• Decreases all noise of anything within ten feet of you by 98%.<br>• The shroud breaks if the caster attacks anyone or takes damage. |
| Mastery Level: 1 | |

"Wow, that's a rush," Rayne commented, feeling slightly lightheaded at the power flowing through him.

"Intoxicating, isn't it?"

"Sure is. You ready to get moving now? I have friends waiting on me to finish up this quest," he said and froze in his thoughts. "Rose, are you going to come back with me?"

"I'm sure we can work that out. I've missed my clumsy little thief. You always were my best student," she smiled as she walked over and tussled his hair.

Rayne nodded, and they separated to activate Shroud of Shadow. The purple energy flowed over him and coated him like an extra set of armor. His surroundings even took on a purplish glow, and the dark spots of the room were now as easy to see as anywhere else.

He looked and saw Rose cloaked in the same way. It no longer tore his gaze from the sight of her enveloped in shadow, and he assumed it was because he was holding onto the same power. She dashed out of the room, and Rayne enthusiastically followed.

They ran through the mansion and out into the courtyard. The two of them only passed a handful of people, and none of them so much as looked his direction. The sleeping guard at the base of the stairs stood in the exact same spot. Rayne almost knocked him over because of his laziness as he passed, but didn't want to break the shroud.

Rose wound through the streets and eventually scaled a wall to a rooftop. Rayne deftly followed and kept pace with her stride for stride.

"So, the target?" Rayne asked.

"City Mayor. I'm tired of his pontificating and am ready to change leadership. He's been in my way for years."

"Is he part of the evil goddess' group?"

"This fool? No. I'm just tired of having to listen to his posturing about the peasants and the need to loosen restrictions on them so they can be more prosperous. I didn't fight my way back from death just to be content with the life of a thief. I'm a noble now and will be treated as one."

"What about our mission? What about the Shadows of the Flame?" Rayne asked.

"I don't have time for that anymore. This is my new life, and I won't waste it."

*This can't be Rose. She would never resort to this. She lived for the goal of the Shadows of the Flame. She died fighting for that cause.*

Rayne remained silent and followed behind her. They continued along the rooftops until coming into view of a clearing near what Rayne assumed was a meeting hall. A small crowd stood outside and listened as a man on the balcony of the building spoke.

"Fellow citizens, it's time to look out for the prosperity of this nation. For too long, working people have been downtrodden and degraded. You starve and have nothing to show for your work. The nobles take everything from you by force and give nothing in return. I plan to put an end to this. I'm convening a special tribunal tomorrow and will begin prosecuting these nobles for their crimes. They have no authority to treat you like they do. Stand behind me, and we'll return this nation to peace and prosperity!"

"The fool. Definitely have to kill him now. I'm sure my name is on his list."

"He's fighting for the same thing we fought for? What are you doing? What have you become?"

"I told you. That Rose is gone. There are more important things to worry about. Help me get rid of this fool, and we can rule this country together. We can do everything we once strove to do."

*My mission says I must help her complete her task. Let's get this over with, so I can go home. Home, huh? I wonder when I started thinking of the place like home? Haven't even been there that long.*

Rayne simply nodded and remained silent. The crowd dispersed, and the man walked back into the building. The sun was almost entirely below the horizon. Rose took a seat and motioned for him to do the same. They remained seated, relaxing as the light faded from the sky. When darkness ruled the night, Rose got back to her feet.

"Time to go. Let's finish this mission."

Rayne rose and followed her as she jumped from the low rooftop and landed in the street. Shadows enveloped her body, and Rayne activated his Shroud of Shadows as well. They moved toward the building and dodged a patrol of guards. She took him to the side of the meeting hall and motioned toward a window. They walked to the window, and Rayne glanced inside.

Dozens of people stood around the room in conversation. Most were smiling and looked to be enjoying themselves. He didn't see their target anywhere in the group, so he looked to Rose and shook his head. She motioned again and pointed toward a second-story window. Rayne sighed and agreed.

Rose backed up and took a running approach to the wall. Rayne watched her Wall Running skill kick in as she bounced from the surface of the wall and kept going higher. She grabbed onto the ledge and hung for a moment while using one of her hands to force the window open. She hoisted herself up and rolled through the window.

Rayne backed up and took the same approach. His Wall Running was a little rusty, but he got to the windowsill. Hoisting himself up, he rolled into the room on the other side. No one was visible in this room, and it looked like sleeping quarters. A plain bed and dresser sat in the room, as well as a small washbasin to clean up before bed.

Rose crouched at the door and motioned for him to come closer. When he approached, she slowly cracked the door, and Rayne saw their target sitting at the desk on the other side. He looked tired as he sifted through the different papers. She slowly slid the door shut and turned to him.

"Ready?"

"You're set on this course of action?"

"Absolutely. Now complete your mission. I expect better of you. I trained you to be better than that."

The biting words stung but set off more alarms. *Rose was never a callous person. The only thing she hated was evil and people who did evil.*

Rayne pulled his daggers, and she nodded in approval. She withdrew blades of her own and Rayne frowned. *Rose never dual-wielded daggers before. Why start now?*

Before his thoughts went any farther down that rabbit hole, she started counting down from three on her hand. When her fist closed, she yanked the door open and dashed into the room. Rayne was hot on her heels, but the space on the other side was empty.

Rayne stopped and looked around in confusion. The problem baffled him until he heard cheering downstairs.

"He must've gone downstairs to join the celebration. We want to wait back in the room for him?"

"No, we end this now. I'm past caring who sees. They can't do anything to me, anyway."

Before Rayne could protest, she dashed for the stairs. He stood shocked for a moment before gathering his wits and following her. He'd only made it halfway down the stairs when the screaming started. When he dashed out into the crowded room, he froze in shock.

Rose ran through the crowd and lashed out at every person she passed. Rayne watched as energy swirled from each person and entered Rose. *She's killing them all and taking their spiritual energy.*

He couldn't wrap his head around the problem. *Rose wouldn't do this. She was a kind woman. She'd do anything to fight evil, but she'd never stoop to this, not even in death.* With that final thought, the situation clicked into place. He understood the task he needed to complete. *She never came back. The shadow possessed her, and she wasn't fortunate enough to subdue hers as I had mine.*

With grim resolve, he chased after the woman who was once his best friend in the world. She stopped and stood in front of the Mayor as he faced her with defiance.

"Showing your colors already. I'm almost relieved you were the first on the list for judgment."

"I'm flattered, but when you die none of that will happen. I'll be in charge of this city, and neither you nor any of the fools here can stop me."

Rose turned to Rayne. "Finish your task."

He nodded slowly and walked toward the mayor. When he passed beside Rose, he pivoted and thrust his stiletto dagger directly into her stomach. She looked at him in shock that quickly morphed into anger.

"What are you doing? He's the enemy, not me. I'm your friend."

"No, you're not," he whispered, "you're the shadow who took control of my friend. Rose would never do the things you have. It's up to me to end you for good."

He withdrew his dagger and stabbed forward again, aiming for her heart. Rose turned to the side and avoided the blow. Her foot lashed out, and Rayne leaped backward to dodge the kick. He watched in disbelief as the shadows swirled around her and filled the hole in her midsection. The energy spun faster and faster until it dissipated and left behind a smooth patch of skin with no visible damage.

"A good try. I'm surprised you figured out the truth. Now it looks like I'll have to kill you and the mayor," she said as she dashed forward and swung a dagger at his face.

Rayne lifted his swordbreaker and caught the blade in the grooves. He twisted his weapon, and her dagger flew from her hand and buried itself in a nearby wall. Her other blade thrust forward, and Rayne twisted to dodge it. It scored the front of his armor but didn't penetrate.

Rayne's stiletto dagger punched forward toward her midsection again, and she used her now empty hand to slap his hand to the side and knock the blade off course. She kicked out, and he wasn't quick enough to avoid this attack. Her boot smashed into his midsection and caused him to stumble back, gasping for air.

*Rose (Level 20) has dealt 30 HP damage to you with Kick (Winded).*

Her dagger swing that followed caused him to stumble back further as he gasped for air. He fished a throwing knife free and launched it in her direction. She brought her dagger up and deflected it, but it nicked her cheek as it passed. The anger in her eyes worried him.

The first big breath of air he sucked in felt like a cool breeze on a scorching summer day. Rose had always been better than him, and it seemed no exception now either. Rayne activated Shadow Form.

*Ah, so you wish to fight another of my kind. This should be interesting.*

The shadows enveloped his face, hands, and feet, as his bonus to speed kicked in. His eyes and mouth illuminated in the darkness as blue electricity and a devious smile formed. The smile quickly faded as shadows exploded from Rose, and the same energy wrapped her in a cocoon of power.

"You think I wouldn't have the first ability you get already unlocked? Come now."

Rose dashed forward at him again, and the match remained a stalemate of speed and power. Blades danced and clashed. She still fought with only one knife while Rayne barely kept pace with two. He needed to tip the balance somehow. *She doesn't know I learned the Haste spell.*

*How do I beat her? The shadow in her healed the damage I did to her.* Rayne asked the soul he'd made a deal with so long ago.

*A contest of wills. If you can stab her again, pull the shadow from her. You have to overpower the soul inhabiting her. If you can absorb its energy, it'll have no choice but to flee or die.*

Rayne dashed forward and activated Haste. He worked hard to keep his same pace to throw her off guard. To Rose, it would look like nothing changed. She still battered at him, and he let her get close to hitting him every time. Her movements were much slower than his now, but she wasn't aware of it. Rayne waited until the opportune time hit. Her attack came at the perfect angle for him to catch the blade with his swordbreaker again. At the same time, he thrust forward his stiletto dagger, and its unique ability activated. The combination of his Haste spell and the ability caused the blade to move forward so quickly the eye could only register a flash as it sunk into her chest.

Her eyes widened in shock, and Rayne felt her pool of shadow energy. He reached out with his mind and forcefully ripped at her power. Her mouth opened in a gasp as energy flowed from her chest wound and absorbed into his hand. Rose's eyes narrowed, and she focused on Rayne.

"You can't have my power. It's mine!"

He felt the stream of power slow down as she struggled to hold on to her power. A tear ran down his cheek as he lived through his worst nightmare again. Few people ever needed to kill someone so close to them twice in one lifetime.

"I'm sorry," was all he could choke out before he violently ripped the power out of her grasp and absorbed it all. Blood flowed from the wound, and her eyes reflected pain. She tried to speak, but the words never came out as she collapsed on the ground. Rayne fell beside her and reached out to lift her head. His tears flowed as he rested her head on his lap.

"Goodbye, Rose. I'll find you again one day, the real you."

"I'll wait for you," was her whispered response before her head lolled to the side with a dying smile on her face.

The surrounding area turned solid black, and he looked around to a sea of nothingness. Standing up, a notification flashed into his view.

*Congratulations, Rayne. A Shadow Walker is a unique calling. It requires you to remain true to yourself. Good or evil doesn't apply. You must be willing to do whatever is necessary, no matter how hard it may be to accomplish your goals. You've now been granted the Shadow Walker class. When you return, you will have access to the Shadow Walker class tree, but you won't remember the full details. You will remember the lessons you learned and the critical decisions you made. The secrets of the testing must be guarded to prevent those not worthy from cheating their way through a trial. Good luck, Shadow Walker Rayne.*

The world shifted, and the blackness took on streaks of gray as the surrounding air swirled. He stumbled forward and was back in the dungeon with his companions eagerly watching him.

# Chapter 36

*The Power of Disruption*

Arthur watched the now familiar portal pop open, and Rayne emerged. His face wore a look of confusion and sorrow, but his eyes frantically searched as though he didn't know why. *His trial must've been rough as well.*

"You get your class?" Vana asked.

"Yeah. Guess you guys are right, I can remember just minor pieces. Something about a mayor and an old friend. I have a new ability and learned even more about my soul bond but can't remember how I figured it out."

Arthur perked up at that statement. "What do you mean by your soul bond? Are you bonded to a dragon? I've never seen it around. I thought only my family could?"

Rayne shook his head. "I have a soul bond with a shadow spirit. It happened years ago because of an accident. It's where my shadow form ability comes from. It appears I can evolve it and gain more abilities. Didn't know that until now."

"That definitely answers some questions," Allendria said.

"Anything happen while I was in there? Any more monsters show up?"

"Quiet out here. I think Balair was snoring earlier, though." Samson quipped.

*Hey, I was meditating. There's a difference.*

*Sure, sure.*

"You need any time before we move on?"

"No, I'm fine. Let's get going. You still
have a quest of your own to complete."

The group all rose from their resting
places and readied weapons. Samson hefted his
shield and took the lead. They walked back to
the initial hallway they'd found when reaching
this level. The door on the far end of the
hall on the right was the only room that went
anywhere. The other two doors led to large
storage rooms with nothing of interest to the
party. Rotted or deteriorated objects littered
the floor in those rooms.

The hallway they found led straight for a
hundred yards before coming to another
staircase going down. The group continued down
the steps, and Arthur examined the wall as
they descended. Rivulets of water ran down the
stone at intervals. The bottom of the
staircase came into sight, and Arthur saw a
puddle of water near the corner of the room.
Since the pool wasn't very large, he assumed
it must leak out through the stone floor to
drain.

The torchlight in this part of the fortress
spluttered and didn't illuminate as much of
the hall. Arthur couldn't even hazard a guess
about how the torches stayed lit. They also
didn't put off smoke or cause soot stains on
the wall. It left an eerie feeling.

They finally approached a door at the end
of the lower hallway. It was a stout door,
banded in iron, and in perfect repair. Arthur
stepped forward and inserted the key into the
door. It swung open, and the group walked
inside. The room was an expansive affair with
shelves lining the walls on all sides.

A few thick oak tables sat throughout the room that sported ceilings almost fifteen feet tall. A few old and rusty looking weapons and pieces of armor decorated the shelves and tables. Nothing in the room appeared to be in usable condition. The group walked through the room and surveyed the area. A large rusty gate sat at the end of the room and looked barely hung to the wall.

"You know, I find it very odd an armory would be this low in the basement. Wouldn't you want it near the main entrance so guards could quickly arm up during an attack?" Samson asked.

"It's very unusual," Arthur agreed, "Nothing here looks usable. There is so much rust on these pieces I don't even think I'd get much metal from them if I tried to re-forge them. They must have put this room down here for a reason, though."

"I'm guessing it has something to do with that gate," Allendria said with a nod toward the expanse of metal.

"Well, whatever the reason, I guess I'll do my class quest while you guys figure it out. Search around the room while I'm gone, if you wish."

The members of the party mumbled their agreement, and Arthur spotted a shining point on the wall near a shelf. Walking over to it, a closer inspection revealed it was a small ceramic disc. A smooth glaze covered the piece, and the picture of a regal man embossed the front. Arthur reached out and touched it.

*Warning! You cannot proceed on your class quest with enemies nearby.*

*Enemies nearby? Where?*

"I tried to enter my class quest, but it says I can't because enemies are nearby," Arthur said cautiously.

The entire party slowly turned to stare at the grate on the far wall.

*It's right. I sense something behind that gate, headed this way.* Balair told him.

"Attacker incoming!" Arthur called to the group.

Everyone pulled out their weapons and readied for the assault. They felt the group tremble. The vibrations signaled something large approached at a relatively quick pace. When the monster's head drifted through the shadows of the passage beyond the gate, the friends all tensed up, and one of the ladies, Arthur thought it was Vana, let out a slight squeak of surprise.

The beast's head was the size of an enormous dog and covered in scales. Its long, serpentine body slithered behind it as it approached the old gate. The giant snake's cat-like eyes bore into the group. It slithered up to the gate and coiled up. The large tail of the green creature whipped out and slammed into the barrier, sending it flying across the room in broken pieces.

"That's not good," Samson commented.

"No shit, now we have to kill it. That thing's massive," Arthur responded.

*That's what the ladies tell me too. It happens when you have such a prestigious form to fly around in.*

*You're not helping this situation.*

*What? Need me to kill it for you? This is your quest, after all.*

*I need you to distract it with your so-called impressive presence.*

*I don't appreciate your attitude, but I'll do it.*

"Samson, any ideas?" Vana asked.

"Sure, I'm going to walk up to it and slam my shield into its nose. You guys can join the fight if you wish."

"You're gonna do what? That thing has to be over twenty feet long," Arthur asked in disbelief.

"Well, sure," Samson replied as he eyed the length of the creature, "but the head is the part more likely to kill us. Just avoid the fangs and the tail, and we'll be fine."

"Do you even hear yourself? That doesn't seem possible. That's pretty much all a snake is, a head and tail. It's also still coiled up."

"Fine, do me a favor and blast it with some arrows and spells so it will uncoil and come to us. Then I'll bash it in the face."

Arthur just sighed. The Paladin was becoming bolder and bolder as time went on. *Not exactly a terrible quality to have for his role, but definitely a dangerous one.*

"Fine," Vana quipped as she pulled free an arrow and loosed. It flew across the room and bounced off the scales on its body.

"Well, that might be a problem."

Arthur fished out a throwing knife and launched it at the creature. It rolled end over end until it hit the creature, causing it to fall to the ground with a clink.

"Definitely a problem," Arthur said.

Arthur made a decision that would either work great or possibly collapse the entire place. He activated a Dual Cast Fireblast. Balls of fire swirled in both of his hands as they condensed further and further with compressed air. When they were down to baseball size, he grabbed them both and flung them at the snake. They arced across the room and landed in the middle of the coiled body.

The ground rocked and caused the party members to stumble. The snake hissed and flew backward, quickly unraveling and landing against the wall of the cavern on the side. Black scorch marks covered its body, and smoke curled from some of the burns.

*You have dealt 300 HP damage to Cavern Adder Boss (Level 22) with Dual Fire Blast.*

"Excellent shot. That was a lot easier than it looked. I really was looking forward to bashing it in the face, though," Samson said with a hint of regret in his voice.

"Uh, I think you'll get your chance," Allendria chimed in as she pointed to what they believed was the corpse of the snake.

The eyes on the creature stared at them with a promise of a slow death. Its body crawled along the ground, and it rose back up to peer down at them.

"All right. New plan. Samson, you charge it and hit it in the face. Rest of us will throw whatever we can at it," Arthur said.

Samson grinned at the prospect and charged forward with a roar. As he approached, a blur of orange and red darted by, barely clearing the ceiling, and unleashed a small torrent of flame at the snake. It hissed again and reared back, allowing Samson the chance to charge unabated.

After the fire cleared, the snake spotted Samson only feet away, and its head darted downward, mouth open and fangs exposed. The Paladin lifted Divine Fury, and the right fang slammed into the shield with a screeching noise. The left fang passed over the back edge and nicked Samson on the forearm. He grunted at the hit but pushed upward with the shield.

An arrow flew past and struck the creature in the head, but it fell away again. Another arrow followed shortly after, but this spun at high speed and slammed into the top of its head with a wet thump. The snake reared back with a loud hiss of agony. Samson tried to swing his sword at the exposed front of the creature, but his arm spasmed and would not cooperate with his effort.

Arthur dashed forward while a blur of shadow near him marked Rayne. As they moved farther, a shadow enveloped the young man, and he disappeared from Arthur's sight altogether. Arthur lifted Ember and brandished his dagger in a defensive position.

The snake's head darted down again, and Samson barely got his shield in the correct path to stop the blow. The ordinarily stalwart Paladin fell to a knee and sweated profusely. Damn, *it must've poisoned him.*

Arthur lunged at the monster with his blade extended and felt the tip slide between the scales and dig into flesh. His dagger came around in a follow-up swing and punched a smaller hole near his sword wound.

*You have dealt 110 HP damage to Cavern Adder Boss (Level 22) with Dual Strike.*

Arthur watched as and Rayne materialized in midair, leaping for the monster. His flight carried him high, and he plunged both of his weapons at the base of its skull. He held on tight as gravity pulled him down, causing long gashes to slice through the hide as his blades carved furrows.

The snake turned to look at Rayne as he stumbled away from the attack and tried to regain his footing. The young man was open to an attack and off-balance. The creature reared back to strike when a ball of fire hit its head on one side and caused it to recoil away from the blow. Before it could recover, Balair slammed into the other side of its face and dug furrowing grooves into the snake's scales. He bounded away before the snake could retaliate.

The creature looked around in confusion and finally focused on Arthur. He stood sure of himself with both weapons ready, although the enormous monster terrified him. It reared back one last time, but before its head came forward, he heard a loud bellowing roar. The noise drew the snake's attention, and it turned to eye Samson. The man stood on shaky legs with his shield raised high.

"I'm not done with you yet. Feel the wrath of my Goddess," he told the monster as the eyes on the shield lit with a fiery light. The blast of flame that emanated from the shield slammed into the beast, and it shrieked and writhed, trying to get away from the fire. Samson followed its movements with the shield, and the rest of the party vacated the area as quickly as possible.

The thrashing finally ceased, and the body eventually crashed to the ground. The charred flesh cracked in places, and blood leaked from the damaged portions that hadn't completely cauterized.

Samson smiled in triumph and promptly crashed to the ground with a clatter of armor. Arthur ran to the big man and saw his health was down to 120, which should have left him fine, but the damage must be primarily from the poison. *The venom must act fast to drain health that quick.*

Arthur saw the puncture wound on Samson's arm. It landed on the lower bicep and didn't penetrate far, but he could see sickly looking lines of black crawling from the wound. He placed his hand on Samson and used his Water Magic to sense the man's blood in the same way he had his mothers. He could feel the vile poison as it flowed into Samson. Without delay, he traced it to the end of its travel and worked frantically to cast his filtering spell ahead of the poison.

Arthur quickly learned his weak filter spell wasn't quite up to the task with just one filter and needed to stack multiple in a line. Each progressively removed some of the poison as it passed through. After some time, Arthur finally breathed a sigh of relief and sat next to Samson. He cast his healing spell as his final act to restore some of the lost health. With a sigh, he stood back to his feet.

"I think he'll be all right. I isolated the poison and got as much as I could. There may be trace amounts of it left, but it shouldn't be anything he can't recover from in a short amount of time."

The group stood around him, listening to his words, and he heard a collective sigh of relief. They all took the time to relax and take a breather until he heard Balair in his head.

*Hey, I know you guys are tired and all, but there's a small chest back in the entrance to this cavern. I think it's your prize for winning.*

Arthur bounded to his feet. "Balair says a chest is over near the gate," he said as he motioned in the direction. "Looks like we got some loot."

The party stood back to their feet, casting wary glances at the resting paladin. His eyes remained closed, but he was breathing steadily. They walked over to the small wooden chest, banded in metal. Arthur reached forward and flipped the small latch on the front. The top popped open as if spring-loaded and revealed the treasure.

*You have found Gold Coin (x310).*
*You have found Silver Coin (x402).*

*You have found Copper Coin (x1,027).*
*You have found Deathstalker Root (x10).*
*You have found Lionsbane Rose (x8).*
*You have found Venomhide Boots of*
*Detection.*

| Item:<br>Venomhide Boots of<br>Detection | Defense: 8<br><br>Durability: 69/75<br><br>Rarity: Uncommon<br><br>Quality: Well Crafted<br><br>Weight: 0.4 kg<br><br>Slot: Feet<br><br>Traits: Boots made from the hide of a Cavern Adder and cured in its venom.<br><br>Effects:<br>    Allows the wearer to feel vibrations in the ground around them for ten yards in all directions. |
| --- | --- |

"The boots aren't bad. I don't think Rayne or I really need them. We have a spell we can use to do something similar. Vana, you want them?"

"You sure know how to treat a lady," she said with a smile as she walked over and plucked the boots out of his outstretched hands.

"Let's plan to camp here for a while until Samson recovers. We can push some of these old tables over here to cover the entrance to this cavern. I don't think we should go any farther down for now," Arthur told them.

"You need to get your class quest done. We shouldn't have you wait," Allendria protested.

"Samson's more important. I'll worry about my class quest when he's back on his feet. You'll need my help if something else shows up."

"Don't be ridiculous. As long as you don't get the danger message when you try to start it, you should be fine to go to your quest. None of us were in danger on any of the other quests," Vana said as she walked over and put a hand on his shoulder.

"Fine, I'll help you guys get the tables over to the cavern and barricaded against the doorway, then I'll go to my class quest."

The group worked quickly as they pushed the long tables across the floor. The grinding noise of the wood on stone made Arthur's ears hurt, but they managed the task in short order. When everyone finished their work, they all collapsed and pulled out little bits of food and water skins. When Arthur finished his morsel of food, he stood back to his feet and nodded to the group.

"Wish me luck," he told them as he turned and walked for the spot he'd identified earlier.

A resounding "Good Luck" echoed as all of them responded in unison. The small ceramic piece sat in front of him, and he reached out to touch it again.

*Congratulations on reaching your destination, Arthur! The last step of your class quest to obtain the Spell Blade class must be done solo. Are you ready to proceed? Y/N.*

He selected *Yes,* and the swirling portal appeared and pulled him in.

* * *

Arthur stepped out to a scene of disgust. Broken bodies decorated the landscape around the castle in front of him. Blight and rot infested most of it, and the stench of death hung heavy in the air.

*Welcome to your trial. An evil creature has taken up residence in the castle. This magical creature can only be killed by someone who understands magic, and a Spell Blade is uniquely suited to deal with them. Harness the ideals of the Spell Blade to complete your challenge. Use every skill at your disposal to make this happen. Keep in mind that skills useful as a Spell Blade will prove the most beneficial for this test.*

*That's an odd message. A creature uniquely suited for a class I haven't earned yet is my target? Seems kinda one-sided.*

Arthur just sighed in frustration and
pulled out his weapons. A quick inspection of
both showed they were in excellent condition
and ready for a fight. He crept forward
through the rot until a corpse moved in front
of him. Before it did anything else, he dashed
to the monster and sliced it into pieces with
Ember. The body fell still, and Arthur
frantically searched the area for anything
else moving.

Nothing else stirred, so he resumed his
trek toward the central castle doorway. The
door was ajar, and he could see a dim green
glow coming from inside. With a deep breath,
he stepped forward and gently pushed the door
on the right. The high pitch squeal that
emanated from the door caused the hair on his
neck to stand on end.

*So much for a stealth approach.*

Arthur peered around the corner and spotted
a rotted corpse sitting on a throne in the
middle of the room. Green light emanated from
its eyes sockets and poked through some of its
clothing. A small golden crown sat on the
creature's head, and a jeweled blade hung at
its hip.

Arthur rounded the corner and strode toward
the monster with confidence. The ghastly green
light shifted to focus on Arthur. The gaze
felt like it tugged at his soul as he
approached.

"My name is Arthur, and I'm here to put an
end to you."

The creature stared at him, and it looked
him over but never moved or responded.

"You hear me? I'm here to kill you."

"I heard you, impatient human. You think you're the first to come for me?" it asked as it motioned around the room. Arthur looked around the room he'd mostly ignored until now. Piles of bones and bodies, some still partially armored, adorned the room.

"Probably not, but I'll definitely be the last. I have too much at stake to lose to you."

"Ah, a man of ambition and purpose. I was once like you. I was a King. Don't be like me. I delayed. I sat around. I ignored the warnings. I told myself I imagined things. I was far too indecisive while those around me plotted and schemed. Now, because of my folly, I am stuck here, cursed for eternity to rule over a kingdom of ruin. Don't be like me. Don't wait for life to happen to you. Take control of it."

The creature's reaction surprised Arthur. He seemed genuinely remorseful. The toll this curse had taken was a heavy burden, and the previous king's voice sounded tired and worn. The words rang even heavier to Arthur. He'd spent so much time letting things happen to him since he'd arrived. He'd refused to take control of his destiny. He'd merely reacted.

*If I make it out of here, I'll change. I'll take the fight to them,* he resolved to himself.

"Then I'll have the honor of ending your curse and putting you to rest."

The creature finally stood and gestured with its hand. Multiple spots around the room rattled and moved until pieces of solid black armor shot from them and smashed into the figure on the pedestal. When all the pieces settled into place, a regal-looking monster, decked out in black plate armor with green edges, stared down at him, as though he was an insignificant insect.

"I'm afraid it won't be that easy," the monster said before a glowing ball of green power swirled in its hands. It pushed the energy forward, and the power surged for Arthur.

Arthur violently ripped up at the stone with his Earth Magic, and the green orb sizzled into the rock, corroding the area.

"Fantastic. You have some talent. If nothing else, this may prove interesting."

Arthur ran toward the creature with both weapons ready and closed the distance. Another pile rumbled, and a massive two-handed sword flew from the edge of the room, and the king caught it. The undead monster pushed his attack to the side with the new weapon, but Arthur slammed his dagger into the creature's side.

*You have dealt 10 HP damage to Death Knight King (Level 22) with Enchanted Mage-crafted Steel Dagger (Ethereal Power).*

An odd feeling swept over him as the dagger sat inside the monster. The sense of magic permeated the blade. *Why is the damage so low?* The thought barely registered before the foot of the death knight rose and planted firmly in his chest, sending him flying back down the pedestal.

*Death Knight King (Level 22) has dealt 40 HP damage to you with Kick.*

Arthur cringed as he slid back to his feet. The kick sure was painful. *Fine. If a regular blade doesn't work, let's try a spelled blade.* He thought to himself as he activated his Sheathe in Flame spell that lived on Ember.

*This zone is restricted. Spells enchanted on weapons may not activate.*

*What the hell?* Another ball of green fire interrupted his thought process. He dove to the side and rolled, careful to keep his weapons out of the way to avoid cutting himself. When back on his feet, his mind searched his options.

*I can still use Sheathe in Flames, I just can't use the one built into Ember. That spell definitely seems like something a Spell Blade would use, and the quest told me any skills used by them would be beneficial.*

With that in mind, he cast Sheathe in Flame on Ember. The blue fire crawled along the blade and beat back some of the eerie green glow with its clean blue light.

"Now we have ourselves a fight," the undead king quipped before launching another blast of power.

Arthur pulled up another chunk of stone and intercepted the missile. Running toward the monster again, he readied himself for an attack when the ground around the death knight bubbled and churned. Green bubbles floated up from the surface of the ground and popped, releasing a thick black goo. Arthur wasn't about to run into that mire and came to a screeching halt.

Another spell activated, and Arthur waited patiently as the swirling ball of fire built in his hand. He tossed the ball at the knight, but it sent out a blast of black energy that snuffed out the Fire Blast spell as though someone blew out a candle.

Limited on options and without a bow, Arthur pulled out a throwing knife and cast Sheathe in Flames on it. The blade lit up blue, and he hurled the projectile at the Death Knight. It soared, end over end, until it sunk into the knight's left bicep.

*You have dealt 40 HP damage to Death Knight King (Level 22) with Throwing Knife (Status Weakness).*

*Never seen a status weakness before. Is he weak to weapon enchantments?* That was when it clicked. The quest told him that a Spell Bade needed to deal with this monster. A Spell Blades' key advantage was their ability to infuse weapons with power to disrupt and harm.

Arthur needed to close the distance to get a good hit with Ember to end this. Throwing knives wouldn't cut it. He cast Haste on himself and looked at the area around the death knight. Nothing the creature had done so far led him to believe it could work elemental magic, so Arthur focused his Earth Magic and dual cast his Stone Fist spell. The magic built under the ground near the knight, but he noticed it too late. When the creature finally took his eyes off of Arthur long enough to look toward the building power, the fists emerged from the stone floor and smashed into his armor. The knight flew backward and landed on the ground away from his protective spell.

*You have dealt 10 HP damage to Death Knight King (Level 22) with Dual Stone Fist.*

Arthur used that chance to launch into action. A full-speed sprint brought him to the death knight, who fought his bulky armor to get back to his feet. Ember came in from the side, but the creature lifted his plated arm to intercept. The sword cut through the plate armor and stopped in what passed for flesh.

*You have dealt 50 HP damage to Death Knight King (Level 22) with Ember.*

Arthur brought his dagger around for a thrust into the creature's midsection, but to his utter shock, the Death Knight reached up and caught his arm. Burning power emanated from the undead hand and seared into Arthur's wrist. It felt wrong even through his metal bracer.

Arthur clenched his teeth and kicked outward. His boot connected firmly with the center of the knight's armor, and the grip loosed as the monster stumbled backward.

"You insolent worm! How dare you!" The king yelled as power surged around him. The eye sockets of the scattered skulls in the rooms all glowed green and energy swirled around the room in a vortex. The power coalesced over the Death Knight and siphoned directly into his chest. His eyes shone green, and Arthur gulped. He activated Scan.



| Name: Death Knight King | |
| --- | --- |
| Level: 22 | |
| Type: Undead | |
| Class: Death Knight | |
| HP: 450/450 | |
| MP: 300/300 | |
| Stamina: 400/400 | |
| Strength: 24 | Experience: N/A |
| Agility: 10 | Skills |
| Intellect: 17 | Combat Skills: |
| Wisdom: 8 | |
| Endurance: 18 | ? (???/???) |

*What the hell? He was full health and mana despite the spells and damage he'd taken.*

"Play time's over," the undead monster growled out.

He pulled his arms to his chest and energy built up around the knight. Power blasted from the creature in all directions, and a wave of green power battered at Arthur and knocked him to the ground in a clatter of armor.

*You have taken 110 HP damage from Death Knight King (Level 22) with Eldritch Nova.*

Arthur clambered back to his feet and saw the monster drawing in more power. Black energy swirled in front of him and launched toward Arthur. Arthur dove to the side as the spell passed.

*I can only damage this thing when I use enchantments on my weapons. It must be susceptible to magic. It can also heal its damage. I have to find a way to kill it while also disrupting its magic.*

With that thought in his mind, he changed focus to his weapons. The Sheathe in Flame spell was still active. The burning fire lit the blade of Ember. Mana of some kind must hold the death knight together, so he needed to counter that magic. He would have to do this on the fly to get it right.

He charged forward and launched his Ice Spikes spell. A green shield of energy formed in front of the knight, and the ice shattered to pieces. Arthur used that time to close the distance. He began pouring mana into his left hand and made it crawl across his dagger. Before long, the entire blade had a thin coating of constantly moving mana.

He thrust forward with Ember, and the Death
Knight swept the blade to the side with his
great sword. Arthur grinned at that and used
the chance to punch his dagger into the
knight's chest. When the edge entered, Arthur
could feel the odd mana powering the death
knight. He couldn't describe what the power
felt like, but he felt the way it moved.

A swirling pattern steadily flowed in the
creature's chest. Arthur focused on the power
and pushed mana through his dagger and into
the energy. The raw mana surged into the
swirling vortex, and the death knight
screeched in pain. Arthur watched the swirling
power fall apart and slow its spin.

*You have dealt 100 HP damage to Death
Knight King (Level 22) with Enchanted Mage-
crafted Steel Dagger (Disrupting Blow).*
*You have learned the Spell Blade ability
Disrupting Blow.*

The creature fell backward, and his blade
came out. The green light in its eyes
flickered like a candle going out before it
regained its feet, and the light blazed back
to life. It lifted its hand to draw in power,
but the energy wouldn't coalesce. Shadows
swirled and then faded, only to surge back
again. The creature tried to force power out,
but Arthur could see the struggle on its face.

Arthur didn't give it enough time and stepped forward with Ember. The blade pierced into the chest of the knight, and it roared as the flame poured in. Arthur brought his dagger down into the creature's neck and felt the swirling power beginning to spin again. With a massive push, he blasted more mana into it, causing the spinning energy to grind to a halt.

*You have dealt 300 HP damage to Death Knight King (Level 22) with Ember (Critical Hit) (Mortal Blow).*
*You have dealt 50 HP damage to Death Knight King (Level 22) with Enchanted Mage-crafted Steel Dagger (Disrupting Blow).*
*Death Knight King has died.*

"Sleep, fallen king. I'll not repeat your mistakes."

"Please tell Allendria I miss her. She was the light of my life and the cause of this ruin. When you propose to her in the near future, make sure she knows that. Her loss was too much to bear. Please protect her. Don't make my mistakes. Watch out for treachery." The light faded from the Death Knight's eyes as it finished. "Thank you for ending my curse."

The visage of the monster faded, and the soft lines of its face came into view. Arthur stared in shock as he looked into his own face, only slightly older.

His surroundings faded into gray nothingness before a message appeared to him.

*Congratulations, Arthur. A Spell Blade
wields significant power. You must correctly
harness your skills to overcome complicated
tasks. First and foremost, you are the front
line against spell casters. You've now been
granted the Spell Blade class. When you
return, you will have access to the Spell
Blade class tree, but you won't remember the
full details. You will remember the lessons
you learned and the critical decisions you
made. The secrets of the testing must be
guarded to prevent those not worthy from
cheating their way through a trial. Good luck,
Spell Blade Arthur.*

Blackness swirled on the edges of his
vision, and he emerged to a familiar scene.
His friends arrayed in the Armory, waiting on
his return.

# Chapter 37



Arthur emerged from the portal to a chorus of clapping.

"I guess we all succeeded?" Vana asked.

Arthur confirmed it with a nod, and they all cheered.

"Now what?" Rayne asked.

At that moment, a message appeared in their vision.

*You have completed your objectives in this dungeon. You are free to leave if you wish. For those brave enough, one ultimate challenge awaits. On the upper floor, at the main entryway, lies the actual boss of this dungeon. You may overcome it for incredible rewards or return to your life outside this place.*

"Well, that's not ominous at all," Allendria mumbled.

"Suggestions?" Arthur asked.

"I don't really need anything else here, but I'll go with whatever the others want," Samson said.

"I'm fine with what we have, but I'll admit the idea of some awesome gear sounds great," Rayne added.

"I do love shiny things," Vana agreed.

"Allendria, anything to add?" Arthur asked.

The Dark Elf sighed and waved her hand. "Fine, let's go kill a boss."

Arthur took a moment to cast his healing spell on himself, to recover his HP from his class quest. An inspection of his gear showed everything was still in good repair. He also took this time to look over his new class talents.

| Class Quest: Spell Blade | |
| --- | --- |
| Requirements: Reach level 20. Have the Sword skill and Small Blades skill. Must have at least 20 Agility and 15 Intelligence. Rewards: 18,000 experience, Unlock Spell Blade Talent Tree, Receive 3 skill points for Spell Blade Talent Tree. | Description: Proceed to Nightwatch and find the Armory. |
| Quest has been completed. | |

You have 3 Unused Spell Blade Talent Points

| *Spell Blade* | |
| --- | --- |
| *Tier 1* | |
| *Disrupting Blow (1/1)* | *Coat your blade in magic and deliver a surge of raw mana on impact to disrupt spell casting and magical regeneration.*<br><br>*Mana cost: 50*<br>*Duration: 2 minutes*<br>*Duration of Disrupt Effect: 30 seconds* |

| Spell Edges (0/5) | Increases the strength of your weapon enchantments when used on bladed weapons by 10% per point. |
| --- | --- |
| Spell Faces (0/5) | Increases the strength of your weapon enchantments when used on blunt weapons by 10% per point. |
| Shiv (0/1) | A quick, thrusting attack that can only be used when blocking or parrying with your main hand. The ability causes your off-hand weapon enchantment to deal 10% more damage and guarantees at least one status effect is applied when an enchantment that has status effects is used.<br><br>Mana Cost: 30 Stamina<br>Cooldown: 30 seconds |
| Mana Channeling (0/10) | Boosts the duration of enchantment spells you cast on weapons by 25% per point. |
| Imbue (0/1) | Permanently affix weapon enchantments you cast to their designated weapons for the duration of their respective spells. Enchantment won't fade when you drop the weapon. |

The options were intriguing, to be sure. The abilities themselves primarily drew his attention. Imbue and Shiv were both chosen immediately. Being able to keep enchantments on his weapons if he dropped them would be vital if he was ever low on mana. Shiv sounded like an instant counterattack and a fantastic chance to get in a status effect. He put his last point in Spell Edges before turning to their task.

The group formed up behind Samson and began their slow trek back to the main entrance. Just because the dungeon told them it was safe to leave didn't mean it told them the truth. They returned to the main hall without running into anything and looked around one final time.

"We sure about this?" Samson asked.

Everyone nodded their head in confirmation. The Paladin hefted his shield and walked toward the staircase, headed up. The idea of fighting something on the second floor of a manor was a little unnerving. If the battle turned magical, it could quickly become a problem.

They slunk forward with careful steps until they reached the top of the stairs. A wide hallway ran directly down the center and ended in large double doors made of what looked like bronze. Each entry had a skull embossed on the front, and the eyes on each one glowed a familiar eerie green, although Arthur couldn't place why.

Samson walked up and gently nudged the door open with his shield, unwilling to touch it with his hand, even while wearing a glove. The door swung open silently, and the group walked into a room filled with bookshelves. An endless sea of books littered the shelves. A raised platform with a sturdy wooden chair stood in the center of the room. Someone sat hunched over in the chair, making it impossible to see their features.

Samson turned to look at Arthur, but he only shrugged. They turned back to the form in the chair and walked forward. They hadn't made it more than a handful of steps in when the door behind them slammed closed. Arthur spun and watched a shield of red energy shimmer across the entrance to the room. *No turning back now.*

The figure in the chair slowly rose and hovered. The body stretched out until it looked like it was being pulled on a torture rack. Green and blue power swirled around the body, and it changed. The shape shifted, and the eyes on the person glowed with dull blue flames. The legs disappeared, and a large robe shimmered into place over the figure to envelop their frame. The floating apparition looked like death incarnate with its enormous scythe weapon that appeared in its hand. Arthur activated Scan.

*You have received 220 experience for successful use of Scan.*

**Name: Lich Lord Ravenfall**
**Level: 22**
**Type: Undead**
**Class: Lich**
**HP: 500/500**

| MP: 700/700 | |
| Stamina: 300/300 | |
| Strength: 18 | Experience: N/A |
| Agility: 10 | Skills |
| Intellect: 28 | Combat Skills: |
| Wisdom: 12 | |
| Endurance: 19 | ? (???/???) |

"Looks like it's time to stop holding back. Hit it with everything you have!" Arthur yelled.

The eyes on Divine Fury lit with ruby light as a blast of fire spewed forth. Arthur pulled in mana and dual cast his Fireblast spell. The twin orbs formed, and he launched them into Samson's inferno. He watched flames from Allendria join the conflagration in front of them. Vana and Rayne waited nearby to see the damage.

The fire cleared, and the lich floated in the same position he had before. An orb of green energy covered him, and he appeared to have no visible damage. Infuriated, Arthur dug into his Divine abilities and activated Retribution. The pillar of light slammed down into the undead creature while the green shield cracked and crumbled. An audible pop echoed through the room, followed by the screams of the undead monster.

*You have dealt 350 HP damage to Lich Lord Ravenfall (Level 22) with Retribution (Resisted 150).*

When the light cleared, a smoking lich floated nearby. The edges of its robes singed and blackened, while a thin layer of ash covered its skin. Its eyes flared brightly, and flames danced around the room. Blue balls of fire emerged from numerous locations and coalesced on the undead lich. Afraid of what he may see, Arthur cast Scan again and confirmed his worst suspicion.

"The damn thing just healed all its damage. It's at full health and mana again."

"How are we going to kill it?" Vana asked.

"Apparently, we get to do it multiple times," Rayne quipped.

"I have to kill it," Arthur told them. "A Spell Blade's primary use is to kill casters. I have an ability from my class quest that allows me to disrupt his magic. It should give us the chance to finish him."

"Ah, you brought a Spell Blade with you," the floating apparition hissed out. Its gaze focused on Arthur, and chills ran down his spine.

"Guys, remind me not to speak our plan out loud next time. I forget human-style creatures can understand us," Arthur told them.

*Dumbass,* was the only response he got from Balair.

The little drake sprung into the air and landed on top of the bookshelf closest to them. He ran across the top toward the monster and flung fire toward the undead. Vana rolled to their right and shot arrows toward the monster while Rayne slunk into shadow. Samson charged forward, shield raised, straight for the lich. A ball of green power smashed into his shield and brought Samson's charge to a screeching halt. The energy pushed him back a few steps, and he tried to brace himself.

Arthur pulled out both weapons and launched an Ice Spike spell at the lich. He didn't expect it to do much damage but needed a distraction. This fight wouldn't end unless he could get his disrupting spell into the monster. The lich brushed the attack away and threw a return orb of green at him. Arthur leaped over the projectile in a forward dive and rolled back to his feet.

Samson used the distraction to close the distance, but the metal scythe was on a collision course with him. He spun his shield into place, and the point of the scythe hit in the dead center of the shield. While the attack didn't damage the shield, the power behind the enormous weapon sent Samson tumbling away.

A ball of fire hit the side of the undead creature and sizzled against its flesh. It turned to face Allendria and launched a volley of three green shots, forcing her to duck and dive to avoid. Arthur slipped through the next wave of green energy headed his way and was within striking distance of the creature.

Fires sprouted from Ember as Sheathe in Flames came to life, and his dagger appeared to drip thick mana. The scythe came down in a vicious arc, and Arthur barely avoided it. In his hop backward, he activated Haste. When the blade whizzed past, he jumped forward and stabbed with Ember. The edge hit the creature high in its left shoulder, and he quickly followed with a thrust from his dagger.

The blade flew forward at incredible speed until a firm grip locked on his arm. He looked down and saw the ghastly arm of the monster holding onto his own. The dagger stopped short and hovered inches from the creature's chest.

"Not today, young Spell Blade. I know which one is more dangerous," it hissed.

Arthur jerked backward, but the grip of the lich was too strong to break. The monster's eyes flared a bright green, and a wave of power pulsed from it. Arthur felt the green energy hit him, and he immediately gagged and vomited on the ground.

*Lich Lord Ravenfall (Level 22) has dealt 80 HP damage to you with Repulsive Wave.*

Arthur wobbled backward, but the creature's grip held him firmly in place. Power built in the lich's other hand in a steady flow. The orb of energy grew larger and larger, only inches from Arthur. He'd have no way to dodge an attack that close. The creature in front of him grinned, but the sight quickly morphed into an open mouth scream as Rayne's figure materialized behind it. He pulled both daggers free and struck forward again.

The grip on Arthur's hand loosened, and he used the distraction of Rayne's attack to push forward his own blade. The dagger struck solidly, and he pulsed in the disruptive mana. A beam of fire crossed the room and burned a small hole through its head while an arrow thunked into one of its empty eye sockets. Samson dealt the last attack as his sword hammered into the neck of the creature and ended the fight.

*You have dealt 100 HP damage to Lich Lord Ravenfall with Enchanted Mage-crafted Steel Dagger (Disrupting Blow).*

The chopped and burnt remnants of the monster fell to the ground, and the scythe followed with a clatter of metal. The party all breathed a sigh of relief and walked back toward the entrance of the room.

"That thing sure was nasty," Vana commented. She visibly shivered at the memory of the monster.

"Where is that sweet reward the dungeon promised, anyway?" Rayne asked as he surveyed the room.

"Not sure," Arthur said as he looked around. "Anyone hurt?"

"Just a bit of a stomach ache from that nova spell. Nothing terrible," Allendria said.

"That was a nasty bit of work," Samson agreed.

They cut their search around the room short when blue dots of light materialized in the room. They came from scattered little objects around the room, from jars and candles to pieces of jewelry. The motes of power converged over the dead form of the lich, and the remnants of the body rose again in the swirl of energy. It reassembled itself and stared back over the group with the flames in its eyes burning bright.

"Well, damn. How do we kill it now?" Samson grumbled.

"I'm immortal, you fools. You can't kill me," the lich called to them.

"Allendria, I know you're not a scholar and all, but any ideas?" Arthur asked.

"I only know they are some of the most powerful undead creatures. I can't tell you much more. They're pretty rare."

*Kill its container,* Balair sent to him.

*It's what?*

*The container. The lich locks its soul away in an external container. It's how they never age or die. Destroy that, and their soul flees this realm.*

Arthur slapped himself on the forehead. *A damn phylactery, of course.* It was common for liches to work that way in many games from Earth, but he assumed this was real and not just a game. If the same criteria held true, they needed to destroy the containers until they found the right one.

"Start destroying all the items that glowed blue earlier. One of them contains its true soul and is the only way to kill it," Arthur called to the group.

They all turned and dashed around the room. Arthur made a beeline for the nearest shelf and quickly slashed into a ceramic jar that crumbled to dust. Nothing happened, so he moved to the next. He turned toward the lich to see Samson engaged in combat with it, trying to keep it distracted. An arrow flew across the room and smashed another jar to pieces. A beam of fire melted a small necklace on a bench in the back of the room. Rayne ran along the bookshelves, striking everything he could.

When Rayne was within a few steps of his next target, a blast of black energy forced him to retreat. He must've gotten close if the lich intervened. The young thief moved toward the goal again, but more blasts of power cut him off. Vana and Allendria both shifted their focus to the area. Only three objects were near Rayne's location, and Allendria melted through a bracelet while an arrow from Vana snapped apart a necklace.

The last target was a metal vial, standing on a broad base with a fluted and tapered top. Vana activated her Drill Shot, and the arrow spun while Allendria built up her fire spell. The shaft and beam launched at the target at the same time. The arrow clinked against the vial and fell to the ground while the flame split around the bottle and had no effect.

"Damn, he must've warded it. We need to disrupt the magic on it. Rayne, take this," Arthur called across the room as he fetched a throwing knife and imbued it with the disrupting spell. He threw it toward the young man, and it tumbled end over end. It hadn't made it halfway there before green fire enveloped the blade, and it flew to the other side of the room.

"I'm done playing games with you, vermin. It's time to end this!" the lich roared.

Orbs of green and black formed all around its body and launched in all directions. The party did everything they could to dodge the power, but three of the blasts still connected to Arthur.

*Lich Lord Ravenfall (Level 22) has dealt 150 HP damage to you with Death Orbs (x2).*
*Lich Lord Ravenfall (Level 22) has dealt 60 HP damage to you with Eldritch Fury.*

*Yikes. That hurts.* He took a quick glance at his stats.

| HP: 260/550 |
| --- |
| Mana: 660/1,080 |
| Stamina 200/550 |

His health had taken a severe blow in a very short amount of time. If this fight drug on much longer, it could be bad for them all. Vana kneeled on the ground, trying to stand, but not having much luck. Samson stood stalwart behind his shield, but the heavy heaving of his chest and shoulders told Arthur it exhausted the man.

Arthur grabbed another throwing knife and imbued it again. He tossed it toward Rayne with the same result. The lich blasted it out of the air with a casual glance before turning its focus on him. Its hand came up to cast another spell, but divine Fury clanged into the side of its head. Samson took that chance to close the distance again.

He ran toward the container, but the lich wouldn't relent. A wall of green fire rose in front of Arthur, causing him to come to a halt. With nowhere left to turn, he charged to Samson to help the man fight. They tried to coordinate their attack together, but the lich wasn't having any of it. It gestured quickly with its hands, causing spells to launch in rapid succession and throw them off balance. Its scythe took turns cutting back and forth through their attacks, forcing them to dodge and stay on the defensive. Another explosion of energy caused Arthur and Samson to fall backward and land in a pile together.

*Lich Lord Ravenfall (Level 22) has dealt 80 HP damage to you with Repulsive Wave.*

Arthur looked over his shoulder to see the smiling image of the lich. He turned back to Samson and whispered to the Paladin. Grabbing his last throwing knife, he imbued it with power and carefully slid it under the shield. Jumping back to his feet, he turned and charged the lich. Samson rose shortly after and hefted his shield as he activated his Shield Throw ability and launched it toward the undead. It spun past the undead, missing him by inches, but it wasn't his intended target.

The shield spun until it slammed into the bookshelf near the metal vial. It fell to the ground with a clatter that thoroughly confused Rayne, standing nearby. Usually, Samson returned it to himself so he wouldn't leave himself open. The young man glanced down and smiled. The gleaming blade of the throwing knife shone through. He reached down and plucked the blade from the straps of the shield and charged the vial. It took him three steps to close the distance before the knife crashed into the jar. A pulse of power from the enchantment was all it took to shatter the container, and swirling angry power burst from the vial containing the ghastly figure of a screeching soul. The black energy surged and squealed until it slammed back into the chest of the lich.

"What have you done?" the lich demanded.

"Ended the threat you pose on this world," Arthur shot back before he turned to face Allendria. "Firestorm?"

"Let's do it!" she yelled.

Arthur thrust forward one last time and smashed his dagger into the lich, unleashing a storm of mana and disrupting its magical energy. He dashed backward, out of range, and activated the cast on his dual cast Flamethrower. The eyes on Divine Fury lit with fire, and Vana outstretched her hand as she remained kneeling. Fire spewed from all of them and hit the lich. Allendria focused on the flames and used her Fire Amplification to swirl the fire and build their power ever hotter. A hole scorched through the roof of the building, exposing the party to a sky of stars.

The fire reflected in Allendria's eyes as sweat poured down her skin. The purple tone shimmered in the moonlight while reflecting the fiery blaze in front of her. She finally slumped forward, and the flame quit spinning. It slowly sputtered out, and a charred corpse and soot-stained flooring were all that remained. The floor in that area was probably unsafe to walk on since it showed signs of extensive fire damage near the concentration of the flames.

*You have dealt 120 HP damage to Lich Lord Ravenfall (Level 22) with Dual Flamethrower.*
*Lich Lord Ravenfall (Level 22) has died.*

*Congratulations, you've successfully completed Nightwatch. You are each eligible to take one book from this library as your reward. Many works here are scarce and may not exist elsewhere.*

The group stared around the room at the selection and gulped. *That'll take some time.* Arthur began his search and looked across everything he could see. Luckily for him, his ability allowed him to read all of these, even if he didn't know the language. His heart skipped a beat when he ran across an extraordinary book.

| Item:<br>Tome of Dimensional Rift | Durability: 110/110<br><br>Rarity: Artifact<br><br>Quality: Unrivaled<br><br>Weight: 0.8 kg<br><br>Traits: This book contains the knowledge to use the Dimensional Rift Spell if you have the requisite skill in Dimensional Magic.<br><br>Requirements:<br>• Dimensional Magic Level 10 |
| --- | --- |

*A rift spell! I recall seeing someone use one of those when I learned Dimensional Magic from the tome. That would allow me to create small portals that connect two different locations instantly. I'm betting with a high enough skill I could also use it to bridge one place to another for people to travel.*

His mind spun with the possibilities of this spell until he saw a book two places over. His thoughts came to a screeching halt as he gazed at the spine.

"Allendria, can you come here for a minute?"

Her footsteps approached, and when she walked up beside him, he pointed toward the book.

"Can you read what's on the spine?"

"No. I don't recognize that writing at all. Is it a form of runes? Something to do with Enchanting?"

"No. It's not of this world. That is the English language where I'm from," he whispered.

Her gaze spun to meet his. "I thought there was no one else from your world here?"

"I thought the same thing."

He hesitantly reached out and grabbed the book labeled Diary of Bartholomew Baker. He flipped it open and examined the last page.

*Dear Adventurer,*

*If you're reading this, then I've finally died. I've waited for months for Tristan to come to save me, but to no avail. He's always been such a wonderful friend. No one else cared to listen to me when I rambled on about the first automobiles we ever saw as they trundled down the road. He laughed when I described the fad of the young men trying to steal young ladies' hairpins without their knowing.*

*Tristan is an honorable man, and I can't imagine why he hasn't come to get me. A group of rebels captured me on the way to the capital. Our king and queen, and their young son, Arturian, were due to have a meeting with the council of nobles to discuss the unrest. Rumors swirled of a building army preparing to invade the country.*

*To anyone who finds this and can read it, I was Bartholomew Baker and came from Chicago, Illinois, in the year 1919. My life has been turbulent in this unknown world, but I wouldn't go back if given a chance. The Goddess abandoned me and left me here to rot. Don't trust the deities. They have been plotting and scheming their entire lives. They're all two sides of the same coin.*

*To no regrets,*
*Bart*

Arthur felt a tear run down his cheek. This man was friends with his father. Judging by a rough estimation of the timeline, they captured him during the rebellion. *I wish dad would've been able to save him. I hope he didn't die thinking his friend abandoned him.*

He slowly closed the book and placed it back on the shelf. There was far more to the story. He'd only glanced at the last page. The man's life story could've been an exciting read, but practicality brought him back. There wouldn't be a lot that book could offer that would be worth him choosing it over the rift book.

The group all stood around with smiles on their faces and a book under each arm. Arthur pulled in power and created a Dimensional Pocket that was the size of a standard bookshelf. He labeled the pocket as Dimensional Bookshelf and carefully placed his book in it. He told the others they could store theirs in the space as well if they didn't want to lug them along. Everyone quickly agreed, and Arthur spotted some interesting titles in the group. Samson had picked up a book of martial skill training. It looked more like a book for small unit tactics, probably to help him train guards. Vana found a large tome that was a bestiary and an herbalist compendium combined. Rayne chose an Alchemy book. Arthur was sure it was full of rare potions and ingredient listings. Allendria opted to hang onto her book. She said she'd like to read some of it as they traveled and dropped it in her bag. Arthur watched the cover of a book titled Comprehensive Lore of the Dark Elves drop into the pouch.

They turned as one to leave the room, with Allendria lagging behind. When they reached the staircase, they had to wait a few moments as Allendria came rushing back to them.

"Had to fix my bracers. One was coming loose," she told them while waving and pointing at the offending piece.

The others all nodded and trudged downstairs and out of the building. It was finally time to head home. Arthur smiled when he saw he'd reached level 11 in Swords and Level 6 in Dual Wield during their recent questing. *Progress is always good.*

# Chapter 38

*The Return*

The trip back to Alem's Crossing took less time than their questing. They ran across one roving band of goblins, only ten strong, and quickly wiped them from the countryside. The lower level goblins stood no chance against a party of their skill and gear.

Since they didn't have to go back through the different quests and zigzag across the map to hit their determined spots, it only took them a couple of days to reach the village of Tartan and a group of frightened refugee kids. They'd packed into the hiding place but looked in good condition. They hadn't left a lot of food, but these kids had done well to keep everyone alive and somehow ensure they had enough energy left to still travel.

The trip across the countryside took a little longer. With the new refugees in tow and the need to keep them fed, they had to dedicate a little more time to feed them. The first time Balair swooped past and dropped three rabbits amidst the group, the kids, young and old, all screeched in terror and took off running.

While Arthur had to admit it was funny, he
still scolded Balair in front of the children
as he introduced them to his familiar. Mind to
mind, though, they laughed at the joke. Over
the next couple of days, Balair split his time
in the air and on the ground. The kids
immediately took a liking to him, and the
ordinarily grumpy and lazy dragon seemed to
relish in their attention. The younger ones
all wanted to ride the dragon and pretend they
were a fearsome knight on a quest while the
older ones were happy enough with the
occasional pat or scratch on his snout.

When they crested the final rise and Arthur
saw the gleaming stone of the walls come into
view, he took in a giant breath and released
an audible sigh.

"Ladies and gentlemen, we're home," was his
only pronouncement as they walked toward the
walls.

The massive structure in the distance
fascinated the children in the group. Arthur
noted the wall must've grown at least another
few feet since they left. *Olivia must have
them rotating a shift on wall construction
duty still.*

The wide-eyed faces of the children brought
joy to Arthur, and he even caught Allendria
admiring their looks of awe when she didn't
know he was watching. The kids all muttered in
excitement as they approached. When within a
hundred yards, the gates swung open, and Toren
emerged flanked by Zeke, James, Daranth, and a
company of four other guards. It amused Arthur
to see Paul in amongst them.

"My Lord Mayor," Toren said as he brought
his fist to his chest in salute. "The village
welcomes your return. It looks like you even
found some new additions."

"Good to see you, Toren. Any trouble while we were away?"

"None, sir."

"Just the way I like it. It's good to be home."

Arthur strolled through the gates while the crowd followed him back through.

"I don't mean to be rude, but we've had a very long journey. I plan on conferring with each one of you tomorrow, but for today, I plan on a hot bath and a warm meal with a long nap."

The crowd laughed at that, and everyone scattered to go back to their work. The kids looked confused but continued to follow. They walked into the inn, and Arthur made a line directly for the bar. A smiling Daniel stood there to greet them.

"The brave adventurers have returned from their valiant quests. I see everyone here, so it must've worked out." Daniel called over the crowd.

The noise in the room went silent as everyone turned to look at the party.

"All sporting our new classes, as well. Was a hell of an adventure. Care to have a seat with us and talk about it? Have a favor to ask first, though."

"I guess the favor has something to do with those half-starved kids following behind you?" The innkeeper asked with a broad smile.

"It does. They're all orphans from the war with the goblins that we found holed up in a village. Can you get them fed and settled?"

"As if you need to ask. Go take your seats and I'll send Trisha over with your food. I'll get these young ones situated and join you."

    The party walked to their usual bench, and
everyone collapsed into their customary seat
with a collective groan.

    "Man, it feels good to be back here," Vana
commented while rubbing her shoulder. "It's
been far too long."

    The food came in quick order, and the
conversation picked up throughout the inn.
Daniel finally came and joined them at the
table. They recited the tale of their journey
to him. No one could describe their class
quests, but they talked about everything else,
including the battle with the lich. The crowd
in the inn gathered closer to the table as
each person took turns recounting parts of the
story. The trials of the Scorched Forest awed
everyone. They were even more impressed by the
battles with the undead and the party clearing
out a dungeon. Everyone in the inn was on the
edge of their seats when Arthur took up the
tale about battling the lich.

    When he recounted them killing the lich the
first time, everyone cheered until he revealed
it wasn't yet dead. This led to a chorus of
gasps around the room while he finished the
story. When he talked about everyone's work to
distract the monster and Samson's throw that
delivered the weapon needed to Rayne, the
crowd cheered and hooted again. They stayed up
throughout the evening as the crowd came and
went. The entire party spent the night being
congratulated until Arthur was ready to call
it quits. He stood and dragged Allendria away
and to the bathhouse and then quickly retired
to their room. They both walked through the
door, and Arthur barely had the strength to
latch the door behind them before they both
collapsed in bed and were sound asleep before
their heads even hit their sheets.

★★★

Arthur approached the location of the Dark Elf woodworkers. Pieces of furniture lay strewn all over the area. Piles of sawdust sat to the side, and Arthur noticed a couple of wooden wheelbarrows propped to the side. A younger man scurried around, shoveling up sawdust and loading it onto the wheelbarrows.

"Daranth, how have things been?" Arthur asked as he walked up to the older elf.

"Things have been good. Your woodcutter, James, has done a fantastic job of finding the correct wood for our projects. We've been working nonstop to build the necessities. I think our last two beds will be complete today, which will make sure almost everyone has one available. Some of my people have been working on common eating tools and selling them on their own. Others have even taken out time to carve again and sell some of their figurines," the old man beamed with pride.

"That's marvelous news, but I'm afraid you may need some more beds."

"The kids, I guess?"

Arthur nodded. "I plan on making a place for the orphans to live similar to what I've done with the place you now inhabit. You have any paper? I'd like to discuss a distinct style of bed for them."

Daranth perked up at that and fetched a small piece of coal and a slip of paper.

"Something new again?"

"Yep. Since it will be a bunch of younger kids staying together, I'd like to make the most of the space. I have a sinking feeling we'll find more like them before long," Arthur said sullenly.

Arthur grabbed the coal and quickly scratched out his design. When he finished with his picture, he handed the completed drawing to Daranth. The older man studied it carefully. He spun the page to look from different angles before placing it on the bench in front of him.

"I think I can make this. What is it called?"

"Where I'm from, we call them bunk beds."

"Bunk beds it is then. I should be able to make one of these a day with sufficient lumber."

"Anything you need from me?" Arthur asked.

"Don't think so. I'll let you know if I run into anything."

Arthur traveled to the blacksmith shop and immediately opened up his Dimensional Storage. Without delay, he walked in and grabbed scraps of metal from their trip and tossed them out. When Rowan's apprentices spotted him at work, they hurried over and grabbed the pieces of metal and hauled them off to the shop to re-forge into useful metal. Rowan walked over to join in on the action.

"A decent haul, it appears."

"Wasn't bad. As usual, everything seems to be cast-offs and scraps. I find it very hard to imagine a kingdom that knows steel and even had something as powerful as Magesteel, reduced to so poor a state. I even asked Rayne about it once, and he told me most of the guards in the major cities only sported iron weapons. Only a handful of mercenaries ever carried steel," Arthur confided.

"Something strange happened, but I can't pinpoint exactly when. I recall my father mentioning something about it. Steel used to be widespread, and so was magic. Magesteel was always rare, but it wasn't unheard of to see one or two pieces in the city from time to time. When my father was a young man, the lords swept through the land and confiscated almost all of it. Most of the people who created it also disappeared at the same time."

"Sure is an odd mystery, but nothing we're gonna figure out today. Anything to report? Things have been progressing nicely since I left."

"Nothing really. Been working on common items, mostly. Farming implements, hinges, nails, and the like. Those Dark Elves are consuming nails like nothing I've ever seen. Keeps me busy. With my new Arcane Smithing, it makes it easy. I feel sorry for poor saps who still have to make those tedious things by hand."

Arthur chuckled at that. "I completely agree. The guard fully armed?"

"Armed and ready. Even have a few spare sets. We still need us a barracks and armory, though. I can't keep extra weapons just lying around the shop taking up space."

"I'll take care of it. It's on the never-ending list."

Arthur said his goodbyes and headed for the sound of construction. Allendria had left early this morning, headed for the construction crews. She was eager to see how the work progressed, and Arthur had to admit he was as well. When they'd returned yesterday, they stuck to the main road and walked straight to the inn, so he'd only seen glimpses of the recent work done.

Rounding a corner, he came to a halt. In a long row in front of him, sat ten perfectly formed houses in his newest design. A street in their standard cobblestone design stretched the lengths of the buildings. A small drain culvert ran alongside the road to carry water away from the street. He wasn't sure whose idea that was, but he wanted to shake their hand.

Arthur watched Allendria walk out of the last house down the line and turn toward him. She enthusiastically waved him over. Olivia stood next to the Dark Elf with a look of pride plastered on her face.

"Arthur, Olivia has done some amazing work here while we were gone," the Dark Elf gushed.

"I can see that. The amount of housing you finished thoroughly surprised me. Ten of them in such a brief time is impressive," he agreed.

"Well, there are actually thirteen finished and two more nearing completion. We have another row started behind this one," Olivia said with a wave at the house they stood near.

"That's even better news. How's the design been working? You making mostly the smaller houses?"

"So far. We hope to make a handful of the larger ones before long. We don't have many large families in the village, so the smaller houses work out great. The elves have beds and basic kitchen tools ready almost as soon as the buildings are complete. They have truly been wonderful in their skill."

"I'll let Daranth know you appreciate the work. A craftsman always likes to hear it."

Olivia blushed. "You don't have to, but thank you. You have far more important things to do."

Arthur saw Allendria grinning out of the corner of his eye and turned to see her amused expression. He caught on quickly and just nodded to the young lady.

"Mind showing me some of the work?"

"Of course, Lord Mayor," Olivia said with a bow.

Arthur let it go. He was tired of trying to correct people. They walked through the houses, and Arthur admired the work done on them. He quickly noticed minor things here and there. Small details carved into walls on both the outside and inside that weren't part of the original design. The counters in the kitchens were often more ornate and had unique patterns to the stone and trim styles around them. Details were not something he would harp on, and he preferred to let his construction crews do what they thought best and what helped fuel their creativity.

Olivia was in her element as she walked them around and spoke of the slight design changes and showed them the newly furnished rooms. Most were still almost empty, but nearly every bedroom they walked into had a bed. The few that didn't Olivia promised had one of the way soon.

Arthur took the time to discuss the idea of the orphanage with Allendria and Olivia. They were both smitten with the thought, so Arthur agreed to work on it tomorrow. The kids needed a safe place to stay until they could figure out what to do with them and how to help them get their life on track. *Maybe a school is in order,* Arthur mused to himself.

    With the afternoon fading into evening,
Arthur and Allendria walked back to the inn.
He hadn't found time to speak with Daniel much
yet. Last night was mainly a celebration, and
they discussed almost no business. He needed
to see the genuine state of the village.

    They entered the bustling inn to people in
loud conversation and the smell of food
wafting through the air. Their usual table was
empty in the corner, so they took a seat.
Arthur spotted Katherine as she walked down
the stairs and waved her over. Daniel joined
them not long after for their discussion.

    "How have things really been going? I know
everything looks great out in the village, but
you guys are the backbone here. Any major
issues?" Arthur asked.

    "Actually, no. Everything has been
surprisingly calm and quiet. Everyone has been
working together without issues. A few good-
natured arguments between craftsmen from time
to time, but nothing that escalates to
anything dangerous or out of the ordinary. If
we don't get commerce running in the village
soon, we may have a problem, though. Our
supply of coin is dwindling, and we won't be
able to pay our promised wages before too
long. The work orders have been strengthening
our village, but no one is spending what they
make because they haven't really needed to.
The only thing any of them pay for is food. We
have no real consumable market yet," Daniel
summarized.

"I was afraid we'd come to that. Money has no value if you can't use it for anything. Food will help that, and hopefully, when our crops start yielding, that can help drive some spending. If our new carpenters in the Dark Elf camp finish their creation of beds, I'm certain they will turn to making things that people wish to purchase instead. That will also help money flow, but then the Dark Elves also need stuff to buy. I'll talk to Rowan about selling more items. Pots, pans, utensils, cups, and the like. Stuff like that draws in spending."

"We're hoping when the village becomes a town, the ability to generate real quests will be helpful for some of this," Katherine said as she nodded agreement to his summary.

"Wait, are we close to that?" Arthur asked as he quickly checked the control panel. To his surprise, the village was rank 4/5 on its way to a town.

"I guess we are," he mumbled under his breath. Arthur turned to look at the others, and they all grinned at him.

"He's getting really good about not checking things, isn't he?" Daniel asked the two ladies. Both broke into laughter at his expense.

"Fine, I've been busy. What do you mean by towns making their own quests, though?" Arthur asked.

"Well… you know that you can issue work orders that work similarly to quests. When villages become towns, they advance so the villagers themselves can issue quests. For instance, if someone says they want a shed built but don't have the time. It can issue you a quest to build them a shed if you wish. The town automatically assigns it experience boosts, and it determines a fair price the requester should pay for the work," Katherine explained.

"I was wondering about that. For instance, Rowan just mentioned we needed a barracks for the guards and an armory to store the spare weaponry, and it surprised me a quest didn't accompany that."

"If we were a town, it would be possible. It doesn't do it automatically, though. If a person suggests something like that, the village will prompt them to see if they wish to create a quest for it."

Arthur pulled up the Rank Advancement screen for the Village Control Panel to see what was missing.

| Criteria for Rank Advancement |
| --- |
| Current Village Rank: (4/5) |
| Current Criteria for Rank Advancement:<br><br>1) Increase Village Population by 40. (40/40)<br>2) Build 3 Additional Houses. (2/3)<br>3) Have at least 75% of your buildings connected by roads. (100/75)<br>4) Increase Village Defenses by 150 points. (5,400/1500)<br>5) Establish 2 Official Industries in the Village. (2/2) |

So they were only one house short. Judging by what Olivia said, we should complete the next house tomorrow.

"So, we should be a town by tomorrow, then?" Arthur asked.

Daniel and Katherine both nodded in agreement. Arthur took the time to steer the conversation back to their finances and then opened his smaller storage space and removed the coins they'd found during their trip. The assortment of coins clinked onto the counter and left both Katherine and Daniel wide-eyed.

"That's far more than I expected to see anytime soon. It does eliminate much of our short-term problem. Could I ask you to re-forge them before we start to issue them? I'd like to keep all of our coinage unique and easier to identify. It'll help us determine if any coin is entering from outside the region," Katherine suggested.

"Great idea. I'll work on it before I turn in for the evening." Arthur agreed as he scooped the coins back into his Dimensional Storage.

"I still can't believe you guys fought off a lich…" Daniel began before James and Zeke entered the room and made a direct line for Arthur.

"This can't be good," he breathed as the group turned to face the two scouts.

"Arthur, we have some news we felt urgent," Zeke said as they approached.

"What is it?"

"We've spotted multiple groups of people approaching from different directions while out scouting. Almost all of them are within a day's travel."

Arthur jumped to his feet, "Are we under attack?"

James motioned for him to calm down and take a seat. When he was back in his chair, James answered, "No. They appear to be groups of refugees. We haven't wanted to get too close, but we've seen them from a distance. I can confirm they all look road worn and weary. I spotted seven distinct groups, all of close to twenty."

"I saw eight groups of about the same size. Two groups appeared to be nothing but kids when I saw them. Every traveler looks to be in rough shape," Zeke agreed.

Arthur ran his hand over his face. *Just when we start catching up, this has to happen.*

"I need Samson here," Arthur breathed out in exasperated tones.

"You call for me?" Samson answered back as the door to the inn swung open.

"You have impeccable timing. Need your help with an issue."

"The refugees coming this way?"

"Naturally."

"They filled me in on the situation when they returned from their scouting. I sent them here to get you up to speed. Had a suspicious feeling you'd want to see me, so came over myself after I arranged the guard."

"We face a dilemma again. A whole new set of refugees. Do we accept them? Turn them away? Could we possibly take all of them in? So many unanswered questions," Arthur groaned.

"You tend to attract problems. Daniel, how are we doing on supplies?" Samson asked the innkeeper.

"We are well stocked. James and Zeke have done a wonderful job of hunting in the immediate area in shifts while you all went gallivanting off. The big hunt before you left stockpiled an appreciable amount of food. Our first waves of crops should be in this week. That's a hefty amount of villagers, though." Daniel said.

"We must decide on this. Daniel, can you send for Dalia and Daranth? Also, please gather Rayne and Vana. We will eventually have to set up an official council for the village," Daniel nodded and rushed to the back.

"We can't leave the kids out there," Allendria said to him in pleading tones.

Arthur reached over and caressed her hand. "I promise you the kids will come in. We just need to come up with a plan for the adults. Some way to incorporate them into the village gradually."

She clasped his hand tightly, and they sat back down to wait. One by one, the others from the village joined them in the inn. Lady Dalia was the last to arrive at the impromptu meeting.

"For those unaware, Zeke and James have spotted no less than fifteen groups of refugees headed our way. Each of these groups has around twenty people in it," Arthur recited.

A few gasps of surprise told Arthur not everyone heard the news yet. They had said nothing to anyone as they entered the inn, so that wasn't an enormous surprise.

"I wanted all of you here because I want your opinion of what to do with them. I have been told that two of the groups are nothing but kids. I've already decided to take in any orphan children up to the age of sixteen without question. I need to know where all of you stand on the adults."

"I may be a little biased here," Daranth began, "but you took us in when most wouldn't have. For that, we are ever grateful. If things in the human kingdoms are as bad as they were in our home, I think they'll need all the help you can give."

"I appreciate that," Arthur told him with a nod of his head.

"I'm leery of letting too many in at once. We've been here for some time now, and I imagine we've drawn a hefty amount of attention. Some of them may be spies for the king as much as I hate to admit it. I know many of them legitimately need help, but can we take that chance?" Vana asked.

"I doubt the king would know anything about our small little village yet." Dalia waved away. "The regional lord at most might know us, but with the assaults by the orcs and goblins, it'd surprise me if that were true."

"Your reasoning is sound," Samson agreed with Dalia.

"I'm sorry milady, but I think you're wrong," Rayne chimed in, "I watched those men for a long time and know Lord Preston is fantastic at learning information. I have no doubt that he knows what's happening down here, and he is always steadfast in his duty to inform the king of threats. I wouldn't count out the idea he already has people on the way here."

"I want to clarify that I don't want to turn anyone in need away, but I also don't want to invite danger into the village. Can anyone think of a way we can work this out?"

"Maybe do it in groups? Have all the orphan children come in immediately, followed by families with children and then the couples and single people? Stagger them out so we can build shelters for them. Have them camp outside the village until we are ready for them to join us. We can still provide food to them, and we could let them stay inside the wall like we did with Rayne's group," Allendria suggested.

"So, let's put it up for a vote," Samson suggested.

"I like it," Arthur called as he raised a hand to quiet the murmuring in the room. "All those in favor of allowing the refugees in all at one time like we did with Rayne's group, raise your hand."

Arthur put his back down, but James, Zeke, and, surprisingly, Dalia all raised their hands.

"All in favor of allowing them in, but in waves as Allendria suggested?"

Those three hands went back down, but Allendria, Arthur, Samson, Daniel, and Daranth's rose.

"It's settled. Samson, get us a plan together on how to get them settled. The orphaned children will come into the village as soon as they arrive. The rest can enter the safety of the walls, but I want them camping separately and to have guards watching them. You don't have to have people patrolling the camps to make them nervous, just keep them in sight. Allendria, tell Olivia we need to ramp up production. I'll work on the orphanage first thing tomorrow and, if luck holds, might have it finished before they arrive. I'm guessing with how late it is and how tired those groups will be, they'll stop for the night. Should give us some time to prepare."

"Are we sure we want to go through that trouble?" Dalia asked. "Seems like an unfounded worry right now, and the extra hands could help get production moving. We'll also need to get more hands to pick crops soon."

"We have decided. We'll stick with it," Arthur said as she pursed her lips at his response. "That reminds me, though. Samson, assign at least one guard to watch the crops on rotation at all times. I don't want to believe our new refugees will be a problem, but desperate people can do crazy things."

The big man nodded.

"If that's all, I think we can call this meeting adjourned. Oh, and one last thing. It's come to my attention that the village of Alem's Crossing will probably become a town tomorrow at some point. Be careful what tasks you assign to others, or they may become quests," Arthur said with a smile.

Looks of astonishment filled the room before all quickly morphing into joy. Some high fives rang out around the room, and even a good-hearted whoop echoed in the space.

The crowd dispersed, and everyone rushed to take care of their new tasks. Arthur headed for the back of the inn when Dalia caught up to him.

"Arthur, a word?" she asked.

"Yes, Lady Dalia. What can I do for you?"

"I feel there is an issue of authority here. I'm the noble lady of the village, and my decisions should hold more weight. To be outvoted on something by simple villagers seems wrong," she said with a grimace.

"I understand your concern, but you named me as Mayor of this village. As the Mayor, it's my decision on how we handle business. I chose to vote on the matter and give everyone an equal say. I'm sorry you feel the way you do, but this decision affects all of us, so I felt all of them deserved a say," he explained carefully.

"I'm in charge of this village," she demanded. "I have you to help manage the day to day, but this village is mine."

Their conversation rose in volume, so Arthur ushered her out the back door and into the cool night air.

"Lady, I hate to say this, but your title really doesn't mean much out here. You have no power of your own and no direct followers to assert that power," he said as she narrowed her eyes and flushed with anger. "Also, need I remind you who I truly am? You and I both know that I still have more power than you, that's just the reality of it. I won't tolerate a noble who has a crisis because she feels she should get to make all the decisions and ignore those whom she makes decisions for. I promise you will rise as I rise, and when I finally take back my throne, you'll be there by my side. Until then, we do things the way I've outlined them."

"How dare you! I should just remove your title of Mayor," she spluttered.

"You could," Arthur agreed, "but then you'd just force my hand and make me announce my true identity. I'd rather not do that until absolutely necessary."

Red flushed her cheeks, and she turned and stomped off in anger without another word. *Spoiled little nobles. Didn't take her long to adopt that attitude.*

Arthur found a secluded spot to sit and dump out the coins. He would be far too busy tomorrow to worry about re-forging them, so he decided to take care of it tonight.

It took a solid hour of work, but melting the coins in batches and re-forging them worked much better and much faster than trying to do them one at a time. He'd only lost a handful of coins in the process, but that was because of impurities in the original coins he'd removed and not because of failure. Dusting himself off, he returned to the inn and found Daniel.

"Finished reworking those coins. Anywhere you want them stored?"

"We really need a good strongbox to hold them in. Wish we had a locksmith in the village," the innkeeper lamented.

Arthur knew how locks worked on Earth, but he wasn't knowledgeable about how to make them. The simple locks common to this time probably wouldn't be too difficult to reproduce with his Arcane Smithing, but he needed someone intimately familiar with them. He was pretty sure he knew exactly who to talk to.

"I'll see what I can do. In all reality, we need a functioning building for the village to use as a village hall and not the inn, but we make do with what we have."

"True enough. Follow me."

Arthur followed the innkeeper, and Daniel directed him to stash the coins in the boxes he'd previously used and, when they were full, put the rest in the corner of the old storage room in some old canvas sacks. It would work for now, but he added this problem to his ever-growing mental list of issues to resolve.

A glance at his experience for the day showed good increases in Earth and Fire Magic and some small gains in Dimensional Magic, but nothing advanced him a level, so he dismissed it.

His final task of the day brought him to his room at the inn, and he sat on the bed. Allendria walked in shortly after him and closed the door.

"Mind keeping an eye out for me?"

"Sure. What's up?"

Arthur waved his hand, and the Dimensional Bookshelf appeared. He grabbed his Dimensional Rift book and closed the bookshelf portal. Allendria nodded in understanding and took a seat near him as he cracked open the book.

When his eyes latched on to the page, the words swirled and reformed until he could read them. As soon as he mumbled the first few words, the pages began turning on their own, and the words bled from the pages and flowed directly into his mind. As before, he lived through the experiences of others. Unfamiliar people used small portals, mostly while fighting. They summoned portals to allow them to strike someone from behind while standing twenty feet in front of them. Redirect projectiles so they'd travel elsewhere instead of at themselves. The possibilities were fantastic.

*Congratulations, you have discovered the Dimensional Magic Spell: Dimensional Rift. You have gained 250 experience in Dimensional Magic for discovering a known spell.*

| Dimensional Rift | |
| --- | --- |
| Requirements:<br>Dimensional Magic<br>Mana Cost: 160 MP<br>Cast Time: 2 seconds<br>Duration: 8 seconds | Description: Create a small portal in space that connects to a location of your desire. Any object sent through the portal will reappear out of the second portal in the direction you selected it to face. |
| Mastery Level: 1 | |

The book crumbled to dust and then disappeared altogether. This new ability would be difficult to adapt to his fighting style, but if he could do it correctly, he'd be even more dangerous.

# Chapter 39
## Betrayal

Arthur focused on the work ahead of him. The extensive building he planned for the orphanage spanned over one hundred feet long. He ensured each half of the building only joined at the kitchen and living area. One side would be for the boys and the other for the girls. They had all the same amenities as the mock-up houses. Arthur also installed new toilets like those he'd designed for the orphans in Tartan.

His mind came back to the problem of plumbing. If he could just get the enchantments right, completing the entire system would be simple. There was just too much construction to complete to worry about the plumbing just yet. He'd spent the morning getting the orphanage up and off the ground to prepare for the arrival of the refugees.

Arthur left the new building and found Daranth hard at work. Beside the elf stood three fully assembled bunk beds, just as Arthur had drawn them. All the Dark Elves in the area worked feverishly on pieces for the structures.

"I thought you could only do one of these a day? I just drew that for you yesterday and not even halfway into today you have three complete?"

"I recruited the entire group to help assemble them. We've come up with a method of each making a specific piece over and over and then fitting them all together. Makes the work go much quicker since we are intimately familiar with our pieces. I made seven of the sections myself for each of those beds. I handle some of the more intricate ones on the rails because they'd take far too long to make by hand. I've also recruited two others and taught them Arcane Woodworking," Daranth said as he waved toward two elves to his right. Each concentrated on their pieces as the swirling sand carefully ground away at the wood.

"So, you've set up an assembly line then. Good thinking. Is your production speed still rising, or has it leveled off?"

Daranth looked surprised. "It's still rising as we get more familiar with it. I'm surprised you know the method."

"I've seen it used before but never took part in one. What do you think your final production speed will be?" Arthur asked as he waved at the full assembly group. He could swear a haze of floating yellowish dust filled the entire area.

"I think we can pull off almost two beds every three hours. It'll be close."

"Marvelous news. I'll have Daniel find someone to haul them to the new orphanage. I just completed it a few minutes ago in preparation for the arrivals."

"You're a good man," Daranth whispered. "I don't know many who would go out of their way to help people they don't know. You'll make a fine leader one day."

Arthur swelled up with pride. Compliments usually sounded empty, but coming from someone of Daranth's age and professional knowledge, he felt it was sincere and not just flattery.

"I appreciate that. I need to get moving. More to do, and never enough time. If you need anything, let Allendria or I know."

Daranth nodded his understanding as Arthur turned and continued on his way. This time he aimed for the construction area. He was only a few steps away from rounding the corner to the street of new houses when a noise stopped him. A clarion blast echoed through the streets, and a notification popped up on his screen.

*The Village of Alem's Crossing has evolved to the Town of Alem's Crossing. Townspeople can now generate their own quests within its boundaries.*

A broad smile formed on Arthur's face. *About time.* The place remained eerily silent before he heard a raucous cheer ring out through the town. Apparently, all the others received the same message.

He rounded the corner to see the construction team members cheering and high-fiving in the street. Allendria stood with them. Her eyes glistening at the joy of the townsfolk. When he approached, she met with him but let them continue their celebrations.

"Guess you saw?" Arthur asked.

"No, I can't see it, silly. I'm not officially a member of the town, remember? They told me what happened," Allendria said with a laugh.

"Oops, sorry. I never asked you about that.
With you being a Princess, would you be able
to join the town without renouncing your
claims elsewhere?"

"Technically, yes. It might make it
difficult for me in the future, but I can be a
member of cities and towns in addition to my
titles. I couldn't do it with villages,
though," she told him with a sparkle in her
eyes.

"So, I take it you're ready to join Alem's
Crossing?"

"For you, of course."

Arthur sent her the invite to the town, and
she smiled and accepted.

"Now you're stuck with me," she teased him
as she ran her nails through his hair.

"You say that like it's a bad thing."

He leaned over and kissed her softly. "I
love you, Princess Allendria."

She pulled back with wide eyes before tears
puddled in the corners. Her mouth split into
an enormous grin before she answered back. "I
love you too, Arthur Firebrand."

They stood in each other's arms, enjoying
both the celebration of the town and the next
step in their relationship. The commotion
continued for what felt like fifteen-minutes
before everyone finally put their heads back
to their tasks.

Arthur split from the group and walked
toward the newly planned Elven District. They
had things well in order, so it was time for
him to begin the next item on his list. He
wouldn't lie and deny that part of him really
wanted his house back.

The work on the main embassy building dragged well into the noontime hours and comprised the base foundation and all the supporting walls before James trotted up to him.

"Refugees are within sight of the wall. So far, two groups are visible," the man reported.

"Thanks, James. I'll come to the wall immediately. Is Samson already there?"

James nodded, and Arthur walked after the woodcutter. Now that he was spending more time on scouting, Arthur wondered how he'd kept the Dark Elves supplied with the wood they needed. It was a question for another day, though.

The wall came into sight, and Arthur saw it bristling with guards. He imagined that virtually every guard they had was present for this. Samson stood near the gate, eagerly awaiting his arrival.

"You ready?" Samson asked.

"As ready as I can be. All the guards know their orders? The watches assigned?"

"Yes, sir. You need anything from me?"

"Now that you mention it, I want you with me when I address them. I want them to see the Captain of the Guard standing with me. You look rather intimidating in that armor," Arthur commented with a glance.

"Do we really want to intimidate them?"

"Not really, but sometimes intimidation can warp into admiration with the right words. Hopefully, I can find the correct ones."

One group must have come within earshot of the gate because Arthur heard a guard call for them to halt until someone emerged to greet them. The guard signaled something down to Samson, and he nodded.

"He wants us to wait for a little while. Another group isn't far behind, and it's easier to address two groups rather than just one."

Arthur agreed, and they waited in the stillness. He took the chance to refresh his Haste spell as often as possible. For added benefit, he cast it on every guard in the area. Building up his Air Magic was the final task that remained for his Soul Bond quest.

The guard repeated his original message as the second group approached, and this time Arthur and Samson walked to the gate. The large locking bar lifted from its position, and Arthur used his Earth Magic to set it to the side. Three guards stood behind them in a row and two more in front. The two in front shoved the gates open while Arthur, Samson, and the three guards walked through to greet the refugees.

James and Zeke had definitely downplayed the scenario. These people looked horrible. Their feet were mostly bare and lined with blood and dirt from the extensive travel. Arthur could swear most of their clothing was as torn and ragged as the orcs and goblins they'd fought. The scenario made his heart ache at the hardships they'd endured.

"Ladies and gentlemen!" Arthur called over the crowd of assembled people. "My name is Arthur, and I'm the Mayor of the town of Alem's Crossing. I greet you in these tough times. We've seen the orcs and goblins that ransacked much of the countryside and have defended our very walls against them."

The crowd mumbled at that. The story must've gotten out somehow because most of it sounded like people confirming something they'd been told and not hearing something for the first time.

"I can understand the hard times you've endured and can doubly understand the tough decision it must've been to seek out an unknown location with little hope. I'm prepared to offer you shelter here," Arthur told them.

The crowd grew anxious and mumbled prayers. Some openly wept, and one woman even fell to her knees and cried.

"I have conditions, though," he said as he raised his hands. "I won't ask for much. I only ask that you stay camped outside of the town itself until we can slowly integrate everyone in and provide housing. We'll provide food and necessities to your camp for you. I'm taking all orphans from the war first. We'll accept any children who no longer have parents or caregivers into town immediately. Once we have them settled, I'll start bringing in families with children and then finally incorporate everyone else."

"That's not fair," one voice called from the crowd. "Why would kids make a difference? Some of us are important craftsmen who are far better for a town than children."

Arthur's anger flared briefly before he calmed himself. "It's fair because that's how I've determined this will happen. Let me make this clear, you do not have to stay here, you can leave and find another place to shelter. If you choose to stay, you'll abide by these rules, or I'll have you removed from the town by force. Anyone who stays is free to leave at any time. Still, if you leave without sufficient cause or because of an emergency, we will not allow you to return until the surrounding area has stabilized, and trade returns to normal. Have I made myself clear?"

The crowd quickly bobbed their heads in agreement. A few still looked upset, but no one questioned him again. Arthur and the guards carefully escorted the group of people through the gates. The full company of guards manning the walls surprised the newcomers as they passed through the structure. For many, Arthur could almost watch some of the tension fade the moment they walked through those gates.

They sorted the orphans out of the group and gave them into the care of Allendria and Olivia. The rest formed a small group to the side. Another casual wave and he refreshed Haste spells on the guards to grind some more Air Magic experience. They'd noticed when he'd started earlier, so took precautions to move slower, so they wouldn't frighten the refugees.

The group formed up into a solid formation, and guards flanked both sides as they marched together toward their new campsite on the edge of town. Arthur traveled alongside the group, hoping to ease tensions if the mayor walked with them.

Arthur watched one man sliding through the formation to reach the outer edge. The guard near the man's location didn't see him since he focused on the path ahead. Arthur increased his pace to get closer to the guard without going full speed. He needed to know where this was going first.

The ragged man with streaky black hair and a bushy beard broke from the edge of the crowd and snatched the guard's dagger from his belt. He raised the blade to plunge it into the guard's back, but Arthur had been paying close attention. As soon as he broke ranks, Arthur dashed forward at full speed. Ember came free of its scabbard, and when the man reared back, he brought Ember around and removed the refugee's hand.

Women in the crowd screamed, and those with children clutched them close and covered their eyes. Men in the group took firm stances in front of the women and children and looked around in confusion. The guard spun around quickly with his Haste fueled steps and saw the aftermath of the attack. When the guard spotted his own dagger in the man's hand on the ground, a look of humiliation spread over his face.

"Sorry, Lord Mayor. I should've been watching the crowd closer," the guard said as he hung his head in shame.

"Yes. You should have, but you weren't the cause of that man's actions. Don't forget he made that choice himself, and that's not on you," Arthur told him as he clapped him on the shoulder.

The guard merely nodded, and Arthur turned to look at a group of frightened refugees. Arthur turned to look at the assailant as he squirmed on the ground, clutching his stump.

"You have attempted to murder a guard of my town. As such, I declare the death penalty for the attempted murder of someone who has only tried to help you," Arthur pronounced and brought Ember down one last time to separate the man's head before turning back to the refugees.

"I told you from the start. Obey the rules, and this place will be a welcome haven for you. If you try to harm others like this man," Arthur said with a wave toward the dead refugee. "This is the punishment that awaits. If that's too much for you, remember you're free to leave if you wish, just remember there are no second chances to return."

It took some time for word of precisely what happened to filter through the small crowd, but the sight of the dagger proved the actions of the man in their minds. The guard finally retrieved his weapon after Samson joined them and told him to pick it back up.

"Clean this up. I'll cover your spot the rest of the way. Try to be more vigilant next time," Arthur told the now nervous guard. Samson's imposing shadow hovered near the man, and he waited for the dressing down sure to follow.

"You heard the Mayor, now get moving," Samson yelled as he turned and resumed his spot near the front of the line.

The crowd continued forward until they reached their new campgrounds. Luckily, the previous refugees were kind enough to bring all their old supplies out here and set up a makeshift camp for them with what was available. A few long tables were already out, and Daniel stood nearby with pots of stew.

    The kids in the group jumped excitedly and dashed for the food. The parents, now nervous after the event earlier, yelled after them frantically. When the kids stood in the food line, many of the parents looked frightened as they cast a glance at Arthur.

    Arthur only waved them on with a good-natured grin. *Kids will be kids.* The smell of the food quickly filled the air and the obviously malnourished adults swiftly joined the kids in line.  It wasn't long before the sound of wooden spoons clunking on wooden bowls was the only noise in the area. Arthur left them to their meal and walked back to the wall.

    The rest of the day proceeded in the same fashion. Arthur spent his time at the wall, casting Haste and Slow spells to pass the time. He even occasionally had a guard lob rocks at him so he could practice his Gust of Wind spell.

    He'd greet newly arrived groups of refugees and give the same speech. They brought them into the town, and then sifted them into groups. Finally, they took them to their new camp. Luckily, there wasn't another incident like the first. They had to escort out a handful of people for fighting and causing trouble in the refugee camp. They had immediately tried to assert dominance over their fellow refugees and bully them out of their food or few meager belongings. Arthur quickly marched those people to the gate and pushed them back out. He told them if they returned to the village, they would be subject to immediate imprisonment. They didn't know the town had no prison, and Arthur wouldn't tell them.

The best part of the day was when he looked at his experience notifications. His morning mana usage on the embassy building was a good chunk of experience, but the refugee's arrival pulled him away from that work. His Air Magic experience, on the other hand, was far better. He hadn't realized just how much he'd been using it until he saw the notifications collapsed together.

*You have gained 2,300 total experience in Fire Magic.*
*You have gained 2,300 total experience in Earth Magic.*
*You have gained 1,150 total experience in Dimensional Magic.*
*Congratulations, you have reached level 12 in Dimensional Magic. Decreases the mana draw of Dimensional spells by 33%. Better practice your rift spell.*
*You have gained 120 total experience in Swords.*
*You have gained 15,300 total experience in Air Magic.*
*Congratulations, you have reached levels 6, 7, 8, 9, and 10 in Air Magic. Air Magic spells now have a 27% increased effect. Now to finish that pesky quest.*

The last message confused him for a moment before a quest box popped up in his vision.

| Power of a Bond |
| --- |

| Requirements: Gain Level 20, Learn One Combat Class, Reach Level 10 in Earth, Fire, Air, and Water Magics. Reach Level 10 in Dimensional Magic.<br>Rewards: 10,000 experience, Unlock Dragon Bond Skill. | Description: Calfuray has agreed to renew your soul bond with her if you can meet the necessary requirements. |
| --- | --- |
| You meet the requirements of this quest. Do you wish to complete? Yes/No | |

Arthur mentally selected *Yes,* and the experience flowed into him. He neither saw nor felt anything of the dragon bond itself, but figured it may take time. Calfuray said she'd find him when he completed the quest.

*Congratulations, you have reached level 22! You now have 5 available skill points. Thank you for protecting the orphans.*

A careful look over his stats led him to put 2 into Agility, bringing it to 32 and then 2 into Charisma, causing it to settle at 12. The last point he put in Luck, bringing it to 11. He really hoped he could resolve more of the problems with diplomacy instead of fighting. The Charisma may help.

***

A figure slunk through the darkness toward the edge of the camp. This upstart Mayor tried to keep them from joining the population. He was either smarter than he looked, or he just had excellent advisors. The man crept around a corner until he reached the very edge of the camp. Two guards stood watch between him and the actual town of Alem's Crossing.

Their silhouettes stood out against the moonlight as they shuffled from foot to foot. If he could get past trained guards in cities, these fools definitely shouldn't trouble him. He activated his stealth skill and, for a bit of extra caution, added in some of his divine power to fuel a shroud. He couldn't risk the mission being compromised.

The guards never noticed his passing as he slunk through the field and hid within the shadows of a sizable stone building. The size of the building in this compact town surprised him. The size of the structure would classify it as a nice property in most of the cities he'd visited. Judging by the smooth seams and the lack of mortar joints, he deduced they must have at least one Earth Magic user sufficient in stone. That was a rare skill, even in the city. The lords of the realm personally employed the few living people still knowledgeable in the craft, but they didn't allow them to work their magic often.

He sat in the building's shadow and scrutinized the road. *Our contact was supposed to get us access to this town as soon as we arrived, but this recent development has thrown off our plan.* Now he waited patiently for a sign.

Moonlight reflected from a space between two of the buildings down the road. He almost dismissed it at first, but noticed it flashing in a pattern. Creeping around the corner, he stuck to the side of the building and stayed low to approach the target. When he neared the entrance the light reflected from, he withdrew his dagger and dashed around the corner. A hooded figure stood waiting for him, knife extended toward his face. The man came to a sudden halt and held his arms to the side.

"You're not that good. Is the full group here?" the hooded figure asked.

"All here, Mistress. I thought you were getting us into the town?"

"I can only override so many people. We will delay the plan. I want to wait until everyone has time to get in clean. We can't afford for someone to make a mistake and be detected trying to sneak in. Bide your time and wait until they lift the restrictions. When the entire group gets in, you can launch the attack."

"Very well. You couldn't have sent me a message instead of making me slip in here?"

"I can't risk exposing myself. They know me and would ask too many questions. I also don't have the blessings of Goddess Isabell as you do."

The man merely nodded and backed out of the alley. He glanced both directions and dashed back toward their camp.

The Mistress sighed. "They better not screw this up."

* * *

The next week was a whirlwind of activity.
They got the rest of the bunk beds made they
needed and installed in the new orphanage.
Arthur also took the time to figure out the
plumbing design. The water flow was the tricky
part. He kept picturing it like an Earth-style
system of constant pressure with a standard
cut off. When he shifted his focus to having
the faucets slow the water down before
stopping it, he avoided some of the leaking
issues he experienced from the start. The
stone pipes developed cracks and leaks when
constantly pressurized.

It meant he had to change some of the
enchantments throughout the plumbing system,
but once he had it working correctly, the rest
moved swiftly. When finally complete, he
showed Allendria, and she was ecstatic. She
couldn't wait to force, well politely
relocate, the Dark Elves out of the house so
they could live there. *She is still a
Princess, after all,* Arthur thought.

After he got the plumbing working and
showed Allendria, he grabbed Olivia and one
other person. He explained what he did and how
it worked. He carefully walked them through
the process. The new showers and faucets with
their now running water fascinated them almost
as much as Allendria.

When all of them were efficient at the process, Arthur started running the stone pipes to all the new houses. It wasn't strenuous work, but it was time-consuming. He also had to extend the drain lines out to the fields. That was a grueling afternoon of walking and casting. It took him less than an hour to enchant a large filter to end the line and cleanse the outgoing water. He created a metal spout that burrowed into the ground and connected to the stone pipe underground. The stone opening dumped the excess water, now cleaned by the filter, to the elevated spot above the fields.

Arthur could swear he saw tears in a couple eyes. Even the Water Mages in the field sent nods of thanks. They taxed their mana reserves daily, casting Gentle Rain through the area. The Earth mages in the field wasted no time digging trenches from the discharge pipe that branched through the crops and delivered the water to the plants along the rows. As the water usage increased in town, it would water more and more of the plants naturally.

Arthur spent his fourth day finishing the Dark Elven Embassy. This was the first building to boast a second floor built by magic. The living quarters were upstairs, and the plumbing snaked through the entire building. A small toilet space attached to every other room on the floor, ensuring each room had access to a personal toilet. Each end of the hallway contained a larger room for showering. Allendria told him Dark Elves weren't shy about their bathing and didn't adhere to the same customs some humans did. The two large communal showers each had five bathing stalls with partial walls between them.

The Dark Elves were in awe of their new home. Allendria had the honor of presenting them with their new living quarters and displaying the features. The ordinarily stoic Dark Elves all showed a wide variety of emotions on their faces. Most wore looks of disbelief while others had looks of pure joy. Each of them personally walked up to Arthur and thanked him while shaking his hand in the human custom.

That simple gesture told him how much they cared. One thing he'd learned about Dark Elves so far was they avoided customary greetings from other kingdoms and typically stuck with only theirs. For them to show him thanks, using human gestures was significant. When their tour completed, they returned to Arthur and Allendria's home.

"Mayor Arthur and Princess Allendria, we thank you both for your wondrous gift at our new embassy. In return, we wish to show you your new home," Daranth told them with a smile as he ushered them through the door.

The couple walked through and the sight astonished them. Wooden furniture of multiple styles decorated the entire home. A large wooden construction that resembled a couch sat in the center of the living room. A glance at the kitchen showed an assortment of wooden bowls and utensils, as well as some beautifully crafted cutting boards. They took them into the bedroom to show them the sturdy bed and matching set of dressers. A large armoire sat in the corner to hang up more official clothing. Two armor racks adorned one wall to hang their battle armor. They decorated the furniture in the room with flames and dragons crawling over the trim pieces. Arthur and Allendria were utterly speechless at their new home.

"You'll need these far more than we do in your new home," Arthur protested.

"We can make our own beds. For a craftsman of wood, it's a tradition for us to make our own furniture. It helps improve our craft while simultaneously displaying our quality of work," Daranth argued.

"I can't thank you enough," Allendria squealed as she dove into Daranth's arms with an enormous hug.

The Dark Elf merely smiled and wrapped his arms around her.

"This is thanks enough, I assure you," he told her and then turned to Arthur. "I thank you as well. You've given us more than a building. You've given us the start to a new home of our own."

"Happy I could help. When I have time, I'll work on more buildings in the new Dark Elven quarter. I'd like to get some storefronts and a workshop made for you, so it's easier to keep your work together and sell it to townsfolk."

"I look forward to it."

The next day they organized another hunt with the guards to supplement their new numbers. They had to leave enough behind to both guard the town and the refugees, so they only took three with them. Even with the small number of guards, both Zeke and James, more than made up for the loss. They filled the storage room full of ducks, squirrels, rabbits, and even a few hogs and deer.

The newfound stockpile thrilled Daniel when he laid eyes on the stack of corpses in Arthur's storage room. He was confident they'd be set for some time with the fresh meat and their crops finally yielding food.

Balair spent his time running and playing with the refugee kids. Every now and then, he'd join Allendria or Arthur in one of their building projects, but usually, he just ate, slept, and played with the kids. After seeing the joy on the children's faces after what they'd been through, he couldn't even chide the little dragon about being lazy and dodging work.

Arthur spent time in the blacksmith churning out some of the typical items such as nails and hinges for the cabinets and doors. He ensured he repaired all their gear and weapons from the quest. The durability dropped on most of their items while fighting.

This time also allowed Arthur to catch up on some promised tasks. He found Samson at the blacksmith shop and conferred with him about the other items they needed.

"Any idea where you'd prefer to build the barracks and armory?" Arthur asked the soldier.

He reflected on the question before finally answering, "I'd suggest you build them outside of town toward Bastion. It needs to be far enough away that the town won't swallow it anytime soon. Also makes it easier to train guards without others nearby."

"You want a pretty simple design? Common area and kitchens downstairs with living quarters upstairs? Do you want the armory nearby?"

"Actually, you plan on using your new plumbing there for water, right?"

"I do. Why?" Arthur asked.

"Can you put the living quarters downstairs and the eating area upstairs? If you do that, we can attach the armory directly to the side. In emergencies, they could wake up and rush through the armory to get suited up and out to assist."

"I like it! Now to the important one. Goddess Lianna's Temple. Any ideas?"

The Paladin shook his head. "I wish I had. I'm sure you can think of something. If she could offer us some guidance, that would be fantastic."

A flash of light temporarily blinded both of them, and when the light faded, they spotted the radiant beauty of the Goddess herself. Samson sunk to a knee and bowed his head immediately. Arthur merely offered a coy smile. Lianna walked over to Samson and laid a gentle hand on his shoulder.

"Rise, Paladin Samson," she intoned.

The man stood to his feet. He fought to hold the tears back as his eyes glistened with moisture.

"You've done well, my brave champions. I hear you have a dilemma for me?"

"I wouldn't exactly call it a dilemma. We are planning to build a temple dedicated to you. We just can't seem to settle on a design," Arthur said sheepishly.

"I'd be more upset, but a temple is a huge step for me in this world. I've always been fond of some of the temples on your home world, Arthur. How about you make one in the style of a cathedral on Earth?"

"Any specific one in mind?" Arthur asked.

"I was always fond of the gothic style cathedrals. Maybe something along the lines of Notre-Dame? Not nearly as large, of course. A nice size area for the congregation and a bell tower. The design elements would make it stick out, though."

"You're lucky. I had to write a thesis paper about its design during college for my architecture degree. I should be able to get some of those elements you wish for."

"Luck has nothing to do with it. I already knew about your study of that style." She told him with a wry smile, "I do have a favor to ask you, though. Make me a flat disc of your mage-crafted steel that is twelve feet in diameter. I plan to imbue it with my power, and you can inlay it at the entrance. It will prevent any of another god's minions from entering."

"That's a fantastic idea," Samson beamed.

Arthur hurried to the nearby shop and grabbed a few ingots of steel. He finally noticed the slow effect on the workers in the area as he raced back to the Goddess. A quick burst of Fire Magic heated the ingots, and then he cast Arcane Smithing. With a sly grin, he added a unique design element to the face of the piece. When the magic finished, a glimmering disc of steel clattered to the ground. An almost perfect image of Lianna's face embossed the disc.

Lianna laughed at the display but walked over and touched it, anyway. A surge of light passed from her, into the disc. When the light faded, she disappeared, and Arthur examined the piece.

| Item:<br>Divine Symbol of<br>Goddess Lianna | **Durability:**<br>5,000/5,000<br><br>**Rarity:** Artifact<br><br>**Quality:** God-touched<br><br>**Weight:** 12.0 kg<br><br>**Traits:** The Goddess Lianna blessed this disc. It will deal extreme damage to any that sets foot on it if aligned against her. |
| --- | --- |

    They both stared at it in shock before
shaking out of their reverie. Samson walked
around in a stupor for the rest of the day
while Arthur continued work on the remaining
tasks. He finished the barracks and armory
first. It took him two days to get those in
working order, and Rowan recruited people to
transfer extra equipment to the armory for
storage. The new living quarters completely
enamored the guards.

    Building the church took longer. He even
screwed up on one portion of a ceiling and
caused a small section of the building to
crumble and collapse. It didn't take long to
fix with his magic, but he had to redesign
that portion to make it more stable. Three
days of solid work and the building was
complete. He had Samson help him get the disc
in the entryway and mounted on the floor.
Daranth and the elves brought in wooden
benches, similar to church pews. Arthur made a
free-standing Celtic cross on the dais in
front of the building that reflected the ones
on Samson's armor. Additionally, a small bowl
of steel sat in the front for offerings.

    The townspeople gathered in front of the
church to commemorate the opening, and Samson
led them in prayer.

"The Goddess Lianna works to protect us through these dark times. This world has fallen under dark and terrible influences. People are suffering, and the kingdom is collapsing. Lady Lianna promises to protect all who show their faith in her. Rise from the ashes of despair and embrace Goddess Lianna!" he shouted over the crowd. The clouds parted, and a beam of golden power bathed the clearing in its light. Everyone felt an immediate sense of relief and comfort at the gesture and then slowly filtered into the building. Arthur watched the townspeople with a great sense of satisfaction. They could only get stronger by embracing the light.

The remaining work progressed quickly. After they settled the orphans in, they moved in families with children. There weren't many of those, so they quickly moved to families without children and single adults. Since Olivia and her crews worked tirelessly to make more housing, the refugees were all brought into the town within a week and a half. The night the entire town became one, Arthur declared a festival and a large communal dinner.

Arthur finished his work at the anvil and laid the last piece aside. With the festival approaching, he cleaned up his area and walked to the bathhouse. A quick scrub refreshed him and got him ready for the dinner. He gathered outside the inn where every table and chair available in the town sat in the clear area around the cobblestone road.

Daniel, Trisha, and Paula all worked tirelessly to shuttle food around the area and prep the tables. Arthur even spotted a handful of unfamiliar faces assisting with the work. Many of the new townsfolk already found useful positions of employment. They now had a far larger farming group and a full team of loggers that worked to keep their woodworkers supplied. Two more construction crews had signed their agreements and were being trained.

They had more than enough construction to last for a long time. Arthur didn't worry about them being out of work anytime soon. If the work in town came to a halt, he could transition them to maintenance on the streets and buildings. They could also use them to build in other villages and towns when his campaign officially started to get rid of the usurper King Wailyn.

People filtered into the area, and the conversations grew louder. Knots of people formed, and Arthur walked over to join Rayne.

"Enjoying yourself?"

"I am. It's been so long since I've seen people just mingling and enjoying themselves. Life in Seora was a constant struggle to stay alive. It was all I could do to keep Libby and me safe."

"You always have a home here with us. I'm happy to see your business get off the ground. I noticed a few potions at your place when I strolled by."

"It was a great feeling. I owe so much to Gerard and his wife Greta for teaching me an actual skill. Something other than fighting, anyway. I feel he'd be happy with my choice."

"I don't know them, but I believe you're correct. I look forward to seeing what you can do with your Alchemy," Arthur said before spotting Allendria across the crowd. She stood with Daranth in conversation, and Arthur got a wicked idea.

"Watch this," he told Rayne as he cast his new Dimensional Rift spell. One end of the portal was directly behind Allendria while the other sat right beside Arthur. When it snapped into place, he reached his hand through his end, and it popped out of the other portal directly behind the Dark Elf. He reached farther in until his hand was within reach and tapped her on the shoulder. Quick as a flash, he withdrew the hand and closed the portal.

The look of confusion on Allendria's face was humorous until she heard Rayne chuckling and turned toward them. Arthur stood there with a goofy grin and eyes gazing toward the sky, while Rayne bent over laughing. Realizing she'd been the brunt of the joke, she stormed over to him.

"Mister all-powerful wizard. You really think practical jokes are a good way to waste mana?" she asked with a dangerous look.

"You've got to admit, it was good," Rayne chuckled before he looked up to see the seriousness in her face. Silence overtook him in a flash and he quickly disappeared into the shadow.

"Traitor," Arthur whispered to the now empty air.

An evil grin split Allendria's face before she reached out and put a hand on his waist.

"One day you'll learn never to mess with a Pyromancer," she whispered as his side began to burn.

He squeaked in protest and jumped away from her. The burning pain quickly subsided, and she held up her slightly glowing red hand for emphasis.

"Sorry. I'll keep that in mind," he told her as she nodded and turned back to Daranth. "Love you."

"Love you too. As long as you remember the warning."

The rest of the evening continued smoothly. The older townsfolk demanded a retelling of the class quests. They wouldn't relent in their demands until they gave in, so the party complied. The chanting finally died down as Samson began the story. It was humorous to see the reaction of the orphans they'd saved from Taranth when he mentioned them in the story. Their look of awe at being included in a story of this proportion dwarfed most of the story for Arthur.

The night finally wound down with the food platters mostly empty and the townspeople back in their homes. Allendria and Arthur finally retired to their home. Since the Dark Elves now took up residence in the embassy, their house was finally theirs. They'd enjoyed the new privacy, and the new showers quickly hooked Allendria.

His sleep was restless, and his dreams haunted until a shrill cry woke him up with a jerk. He sat up in their bed for a moment and felt Allendria stir next to him.

"What's wrong?" she asked.

"Not sure. I could've sworn I heard a scream," he told her before another one rang out through the room.

Both of them launched out of bed and scrambled for their armor on the bedside racks. They'd become so accustomed to wearing it they could dress quickly. The two of them left the room and dashed to the entrance of the house. Walking outside, Arthur watched a guard run by.

"Paul? What's the screaming about?" Arthur asked.

"We have reports of an attack on the edge of town. Paladin Samson has ordered all guards to the location."

Arthur nodded and waved the man to continue.

"Let's go check it out," he told Allendria.

They jogged down the pathway before something brought Arthur up short. A flash of metal in an unlit space between two buildings caused him to stop and put an arm out to catch Allendria.

"There's something in that space between those buildings ahead of us," he whispered to her.

Arthur cast Haste on both of them and pulled Ember and his dagger out while Allendria readied her staff. The two crept toward the hiding spot. They were only twenty yards away when a knife flew from the location toward Arthur's face. He ducked under the blade as it flew by.

A man in black leather armor launched from
the concealed spot straight for him with a
dagger in each hand. Arthur didn't wait for
him to approach and instead charged right
back. He waited for the initial thrust and
spun to the side. He brought Ember up in a
vertical position and caught the backhanded
swing of the other dagger. Arthur activated
Sheathe in Flames, and the burning blue fire
caused the assassin to stagger in surprise.

Arthur kicked out and caught the person in
their thigh, sending them stumbling backward.
A cry of alarm from Allendria shifted his
focus, and he saw another man fighting her
while a third stood on a nearby roof about to
jump on her from behind.

He fished out a throwing knife and launched
it at the man on the roof. His focus on
Allendria distracted him, and the knife buried
in his right shoulder. Arthur started to cast
a spell when a sharp pain stung his side. He
looked back at his original attacker and the
blood now covering his blade.

*Assassin (Level 22) has dealt 50 HP damage
to you with Iron Dagger of Agility.*

Arthur quickly cast his Minor Healing spell
on his side and it knitted back together. The
assassin frowned under his hood before dashing
back at Arthur.

*How are you getting hurt in the middle of
the night?* a voice asked him in his mind.

*Assassins in the town. The attack on the
outer parts must be a diversion to draw away
the guards.*

He heard nothing else as his attention
snapped back to the fight at hand. Ember rose
to deflect the incoming dagger and he
activated Shiv with the successful parry. His
blade flew forward at lightning speed and slid
into the assassin's side. The enemy jumped
backward, and blood squirted from the wound as
he reached down to cover it with his hand. The
moonlight revealed the matching blood on his
own dagger.

*You have dealt 110 HP damage to Assassin
(Level 22) with Enchanted Mage-crafted Steel
Dagger.*

Flashes of fire lit up his surroundings, so
he knew Allendria held the others at bay, but
she still had two of them near her, even if he
had injured one of them. Arthur dual cast
Stone Fist and crushed his assassin between
the stones as they emerged. The crunch of
bones was audible through their surroundings,
so Arthur turned to the other two.

*You have dealt 220 HP damage to Assassin
(Level 22) with Dual Stone Fist (Crushing
Blow).*

Allendria spun her staff to keep the
remaining assassins at bay and launched minor
fire spells to scare them anytime they got too
close. The man he'd hit with the throwing
knife stood with a knife in his left hand
while his right arm hung limp. The other
displayed a fresh burn across part of his
face, and he flinched every time Allendria
cast another fire spell.

Arthur crossed the distance on his toes, trying to stay as quiet as possible, but the man nearest him seemed to sense him and turn. Ember slashed toward the man with the burn on his face, but he lifted his daggers and caught the blade in a scissor style block. Arthur merely activated Sheathe in Flames and watched the fear dance in the man's eyes as he stumbled backward. A quick step and a thrust brought his dagger directly into the assassin's chest.

*You have dealt 165 HP damage to Assassin (Level 22) with Enchanted Mage-crafted Steel Dagger (Critical Hit) (Mortal Blow).*

The man fell to the ground, clutching the wound in his chest when a flash of fire drew Arthur's attention. Allendria poured flame at the remaining assassin, and he buckled under the pressure. He fell to the ground, writhing and screaming before the sound died, and Allendria dropped the spell. A blackened corpse was all that remained.

Arthur turned to look at the last surviving assassin. "Who sent you?"

"The king," the man muttered.

"I'm almost disappointed. It shouldn't be that easy to get answers, should it?" Arthur asked Allendria.

"It's a strange thing."

"There's no reason not to tell you. You already know who ordered this attack. There's nothing you can do to stop him anyway," the assassin said and coughed. A small trail of blood leaked from the corner of his mouth.

"How many of you are in the town now?"

"That, I won't tell you," the man said with a hint of defiance back in his eyes.

"Why can't the king leave us alone?" Arthur asked in low tones.

"You upset the balance. You flaunt the limits he has imposed on the populace and bring magic back to the kingdom in abundance," the assassin answered as he tilted over sideways.

"You endanger the entire kingdom," were the last words from the dying man before he fell to the ground.

Arthur walked over to examine him. He didn't stand out in any way. Nothing about him screamed assassin or dangerous, but Arthur assumed that would defeat the point. He searched the man and found a small slip of paper. The writing resolved itself, and Arthur stared at a list.

*Arthur*
*Allendria*
*Dalia*
*Daniel*
*Daranth*
*Katherine*
*Rowan*
*Samson*
*Vana*

The part that disturbed Arthur the most was the inclusion of Daranth on the list. The Dark Elves hadn't been here that long. This was a recent list, which meant they either had spies watching the town or someone inside the town worked with them. Neither option was good, but there wasn't time to dwell on that now.

*They've targeted the leaders of the town. Tell Samson that Dalia, Daniel, Daranth, Katherine, Rowan, and Vana are their actual targets. I'm sure he can handle himself. Allendria and I are closest to Dalia right now. We'll go check on her and then head for the inn.* Arthur told Balair.

*I'll let him know,* was the only response he received.

"Dalia is the closest on the list. We need to go check on her and then head for the inn," Arthur told Allendria. She grimaced at the suggestion but knew it was the right thing to do. Allendria wasn't overly fond of Dalia, to say the least. The two ran for the minor noble's house and rushed inside.

"Dalia, are you okay? Assassins are in the town," Arthur called into the darkness of the house.

"Help! Assassin in my room," Came Dalia's voice from the back.

Arthur entered the room to see Dalia standing in front of the attacker with a dagger out and a trickle of blood on the blade. A nasty cut marked her bicep, and the assassin stood in front of her with two knives drawn.

A thin beam of fire shot from Allendria and seared a small hole in the man's arm, causing him to drop one of his blades. Arthur threw one of his throwing knives, and the blade sank into the assassin's back. A hiss of pain escaped the man, and he turned to face Arthur. When he saw who stood in front of him, he cursed. "Damn, they failed. Screw this."

Writing shadows lifted from the assassin's feet and enveloped him in a cocoon of power. The energy swirled until it disappeared in a flash of power. The space stood empty when the energy dissipated.

"You okay?" Arthur asked Dalia as he walked over to examine the wound.

"Yes, I'm fine. He got a lucky shot out of surprise. I kept enough distance to stay safe, but had you two not shown up, I'd surely be dead. Thank you both," Dalia said with a glimmer of tears in her eyes.

"You're welcome. Let's fix this up real quick," Arthur told her as he cast his healing spell on her arm. When the magic took hold, some of the strain in her face eased.

"We have to keep moving. I think you best come with us. We're headed for the inn. One assassin had a list of targets, and both Daniel and Katherine were also on that list," Arthur told Dalia.

She agreed and they ran from the building. When they approached the inn, a loud ruckus came from the building. The sound of furniture overturning and wood smacking on wood was audible from outside. A man flew from the door of the building and landed in a heap outside. Balair leaped from the doorway and on top of the assassin. His teeth shone as his mouth opened wide and he clamped his jaws over the man's face. A quick burst of fire ended that threat.

*Nice work. Anymore left in there?*

*He was the last. Had to chase him around the room as he kept knocking over stuff, trying to slow me down. I think Daniel may be pissed at me for breaking some of his stuff.*

*I'm sure it'll be fine. You saved him and Katherine after all.*

*I did, but I fear the assassins got to Paula before we could get rid of them. She didn't make it,* Balair told him solemnly.

"Bastards," Arthur swore.

"What's wrong?" Allendria asked.

"Balair let me know that Daniel and Katherine are fine, but the assassins killed Paula during the struggle."

She covered her mouth and shook her head in disbelief. They walked into a scene of sorrow. Daniel sat on the ground with Paula's head in his lap. A bloody knife lay by his side, and the body of another assassin adorned the floor not far away.

"Daniel, you okay?" Arthur asked hesitantly as he approached the innkeeper.

"She jumped in to save me and took the knife meant for me," he said with tears falling from his face. "I'm supposed to protect them, not the other way around."

Allendria walked over to the usually jovial man and kneeled in front of him. She reached out and gently closed Paula's eyes and then leaned forward and wrapped her arms around Daniel. His sobs echoed through the building and into their very souls.

Samson dashed into the inn with a clank of armor, pursued by two other soldiers. Vana and Rowan were hot on his heels. When they saw the scene, everyone stopped.

"Another casualty," Samson said in heavy tones, and he lowered his head.

Arthur looked toward the Paladin. "What do you mean another?"

"The attack in the outer section of the town was real, even though it was mainly designed to pull my guards from the town proper. Seven people died, two of whom were children," the ex-soldier said with the stoicism of a veteran of battle.

Arthur's face fell from the news. *Children dead? Who would do such a thing? Why torture these people more? Will it ever end?*

With that last question came a resolve. *It will end when I make it end. Enough is enough.*

# Chapter 40

*Declaration of War*

Arthur spent the next two hours walking through town with Samson and assessing the damage. There wasn't any property damage anywhere. Since the town consisted of mostly stone buildings, there wasn't much to set on fire. A few charred items littered the streets, but primarily scraps of furniture. His steps brought him to the bodies arrayed in the street.

Seven figures lay on the ground with their eyes closed and arms crossed. Each of these people trusted him to keep them safe, and he let them down. When his gaze landed on the last two, his breathing halted, and his chest constricted. The two children's lives had barely started. He turned toward Samson.

"Have them arrayed for a funeral pyre. We'll build it outside of town. I want the ceremony inside the wall. Make sure everyone is present," Arthur told him as his face morphed to one of anger.

"Arthur?" Samson asked carefully. "What are you going to do?"

"I'm tired of sitting back and doing nothing. We've been trying to turn the lives of this town around, and people keep interfering with it. We've spent this entire time just reacting. I'm done with that. I've sat back and reacted long enough. We're taking the fight to them."

"We don't have the men to do that," Samson reminded him.

"I'll do it by myself if I must. Just have everyone ready for a funeral this evening. I'm going to get some sleep before the day begins. I'll see you in a little while."

Samson reached out and grabbed his shoulder. "You know this isn't your fault, right?"

Arthur could only shake his head. "It both is and isn't my fault. I appreciate it, though."

Arthur continued back toward his home. Allendria met him at the entryway and walked forward to embrace him. He could do nothing more than rest his head on her shoulder and squeeze her tight. The two stood together for a while before both walked inside and laid in bed. Neither bothered to take off their armor but both were asleep almost instantly.

The morning didn't fare any better. The sorrow of the attack reflected on every face they passed. The inn didn't have the life to it they'd grown accustomed to. The typical jovial environment was now quiet. Daniel shuffled around and delivered food but was silent and didn't speak while he walked around. Some helpers from the feast picked up the slack and served food around the inn.

Arthur couldn't focus on anything else. Instead of going to work, he took Allendria by the hand and walked to one of his favorite places to mull over problems and practice magic. They sat near a tree on the edge of town before Balair wandered over to join them. The small drake only laid down near them and rested, also uncharacteristically silent. When the silence dragged on too long, Arthur finally spoke up.

"It's time for a change," he breathed.

Balair turned to look at him from the simple statement while Allendria grasped his hand tighter and said, "How so?"

"I'm going to make the announcement tonight," he told them both.

"What announ…" Allendria began before going silent. "So you've finally decided to take matters into your own hands?" she asked.

"The threats will never stop. The attacks won't stop. None of this will stop until we get rid of King Wailyn. I can't continue letting people die if I can do something to stop it."

"People will die trying to get rid of him," Allendria reminded him.

"They are. But his policies are sure to kill at least that many people by next year. This kingdom is on the verge of death and ruin, anyway. If I don't do something about it now, it'll be too late."

*I was wondering how long it'd take you to figure that out,* Balair huffed.

"Not all of us are as old and as intelligent as you," Arthur said with a smile.

*It's time. Are you sure they'll follow you?*

The response from the drake shocked him for a moment without some kind of snippy comeback accompanying it.

"I don't know. I hope they'll follow, but I don't know if they'll believe my story."

"They'll believe it because they need something to believe in," Allendria assured him.

"I hope you're right."

They sat and enjoyed the breeze as it blew across their skin and scales. The sun shone brightly, but the shade of the tree blocked most of the heat. They all lay down and drifted off to another round of sleep.

A grunt caused Arthur to scramble to a sitting position and check his surroundings. Samson stood over the group with an eyebrow raised.

"Going to sleep all day? The ceremony you requested is due to start soon."

"Thanks. I needed some time to clear my head."

"You still plan on going through with it?"

Arthur merely nodded, and Samson shook his head as he turned away.

"I'll have all the guards on alert near the people. I don't want this getting out of hand."

"Good thinking. I'll see you down there."

Allendria was up and brushing grass from her hair. The conversation with Samson woke her, and Balair slowly stretched each of his legs in turn. The creature looked like a dog as he yawned, and his tongue rolled out. The three got to their feet and walked back to the inn.

A quick bite of food settled their stomachs then Arthur found Daniel.

"I'm making an announcement tonight. I need everyone at the ceremony, and I mean everyone," Arthur told him in low tones.

"I understand. Samson and the guards made the rounds today, informing everyone."

"I'll see you down there," Arthur told him.

Their walk started at a leisurely pace, but Arthur felt like the weight of the world settled on him as they neared their destination. It felt harder to trudge down this hill as he walked, but he kept pushing forward. Eventually, he stood in front of a gathered crowd with the funeral pyre of bodies on top.

Many tearful faces littered the gathering, and he felt a tear escape the corner of his eye as he watched the last of them gather from the town. When all were finally present, his attention snapped into place, and he turned to address the crowd.

"My fellow townspeople. Last night we were attacked. For those of you who've been here since the beginning, this isn't the first time this has happened recently. The people who lost their lives last night were precious souls we can never bring back. I promised to do my best to keep this town safe and feel I've failed in that assignment," he said as he lowered his head.

"We're with you, Mayor," one man called from the crowd.

"It wasn't your fault. You've saved many of us already," a woman said from the back.

"Please, please," he called as he waved them to stop. "I've not been completely honest with you so far. I fear they have targeted me because of who I am. I don't know for certain, but I think the danger you're in is entirely my fault."

"We tried to do this the nice way. We tried to make a better life for everyone here. We've worked hard to get food and supplies that the people need to keep everyone alive. All of this has made us a target for King Wailyn and his cronies, and I'm sick of it!" he yelled the last as an angry pronouncement. His gaze locked onto Dalia, standing nearby, and she wore a look of worry etched on her face.

"I am Arthur Firebrand, true king and son of Tristan and Violet Firebrand. I name this the Kingdom of Fire, and I declare war on King Wailyn!"

His pronouncement rolled across the gathering as everyone stared in shock with mouths agape. The sound of beating drums filled the area before a notification popped up in everyone's view.

*King Arthur Firebrand from the Kingdom of Fire has declared war on King Wailyn. Any battle between the forces of these two nations will be immediately classified as an active raid zone.*

"That's not possible," a voice rang over the group. "They died a hundred years ago. You'd be a crippled old man if even still alive."

"He's right. He can't be the lost prince," another voice joined.

The commotion lifted as countless voices rose to argue about the announcement. A look of anger covered Dalia's face as her eyes practically pierced through him. *In hindsight, I probably should've warned her.*

The crowd continued for a few moments before an earth-shattering roar echoed over the clearing. The group immediately stilled and looked around for the source of the noise. Arthur recognized it immediately and looked skyward. A violet creature descended toward the town. Her eyes stayed glued onto Arthur the entire descent until she landed with a thud to his side, away from the pyre.

"A dragon!" a woman yelled from the crowd. Screams echoed through the clearing, and people scattered.

"That's enough," Calfuray grumbled over the crowd.

The shock of a dragon appearing and then somehow talking to people silenced them and brought most to a halt. A few nervously shuffled backward, trying to distance themselves from the situation.

Arthur walked toward the dragon with a smile. Her scales shone in the fading sunlight, and she focused on him as he approached.

"It's good to see you, Calfuray."

"Hello, Arthur. You've met my terms. Now I've come to fulfill mine," she said in her low grumble.

"It'll be good to be with you again," he told her and walked straight to her. She didn't hesitate this time or try to pull away. She stretched her head forward, and he reached out and touched her. A mental command brought up a notification.

*Do you wish to initiate the Dragon Bond with Calfuray? Yes/No.*

Arthur selected *Yes,* and a storm of mana exploded around them. An enormous wall of raw energy burst out of both of them and spun like a vortex around their location. The energies mixed and melded as the power continued to spin. Streaks of purple and red energy mixed with dull gray and resolved into a single storm of an almost burgundy color before it collapsed back into them, and mana flowed back into each.

*You and the dragon, Calfuray, are now Soul
Bonded. You have access to the Soul Bond
Talent tree, and you can share your mana pool.
The dragon Calfuray now has access to use any
spells you know and can cast any as long as
she meets the magical level required.*

Calfuray roared in triumph. *Welcome back,
young Arturian.*

Arthur chuckled and told her, *It's Arthur
now. Just Arthur.*

Arthur turned to face the now stunned
crowd.

"The dragon bond is renewed. My family yet
again stands with the dragons. This marks a
new day in our kingdom. A new day should have
new beginnings. Since this town is where it
all started, I feel an alternative name is in
order. From now on, this town is no longer
Alem's Crossing. I declare it to be Alurian,
the capital of the Kingdom of Fire."

A few slow claps started in the crowd, but
before long, everyone shook out of their daze
and shock and joined in. It didn't take long
for the volume to skyrocket and the cheering
to begin in earnest.

"We shall honor the dead tonight. They paid
the ultimate price for our freedoms, but
tomorrow we prepare for war. Any who wish to
fight, meet at the blacksmith in the morning.
Everyone else can help prepare supplies."

*Would you do the honors?*

Calfuray merely snorted and turned to look at the pyre. A jet of flame flew from her mouth, and the fire burst to life. Flames devoured the dried wood and quickly turned the bodies to ash. Arthur stood next to Calfuray with his hand on her leg. The warmth of her scales and the rhythmic beating of her heart helped calm his soul.

Arthur looked across the crowd and spotted Rayne. He motioned him to come over, and the young man gulped at the thought. Arthur insisted, and when Rayne walked his way, he scanned the crowd for the rest of his friends. He motioned Vana, Samson, and Allendria over as well, and they all gathered near Calfuray. Most of them shuffled from foot to foot nervously.

"Everyone, this is Calfuray. Calfuray, this is Rayne, Samson, Allendria, and Vana," he told her as he pointed to each.

"Pleasure to meet you all," Calfuray said with a slight bob of her head.

"Am I the only one who finds it incredibly odd talking to a dragon?" Rayne asked hesitantly.

Calfuray chuckled, which sounded a little like a grumble from her and caused Rayne to take a step back. "I'd be more surprised if it didn't feel odd. My kind have kept to themselves for a long time."

Allendria walked up to the dragon. "You're beautiful," she breathed as she reached out to caress her scales.

*You picked a good one,* came the thought to him.

*I wholeheartedly agree. Did the situation ever get solved with the dragons, or are you pretty much on your own?*

*It got resolved, but I'm afraid it wasn't
how anyone wanted. There are now two factions
of dragons, and I'm worried we may run into
trouble with the other side at some point.*

*Why can't it ever be simple? Always
something else.*

*That's the way of life I fear.*

*Is there anything you can tell me about my
parents? I know you said you were young, but I
hoped you might remember something since our
last encounter.*

*I'm afraid there's nothing else I can tell
you. I only met them during the bonding
ceremony. You weren't old enough yet for me to
stay with you permanently, so I was still in
the land of dragons when you disappeared.*

*I just want to know who they were,* Arthur
thought as he hung his head in disappointment.

*I remember they were wonderful people. If
you'd like to distract yourself, I'd recommend
you check out your Soul Bond tree. Nothing
starts off a relationship like new stuff.*

Arthur perked up and brought up his Soul
Bond talents.

*You have 2 unused Talent Points.*

| **Soul Bond** |
| :---: |
| **Tier 1** |

| Shared Mana Regeneration (0/1) | Combines the mana regeneration of both parties to create a higher mana regeneration rate for both. Both mana regeneration rates are added together and then multiplied by 0.8 to reach your final mana regeneration rate. |
|---|---|
| Dragon Healing (0/5) | Grants you the ability to heal HP like a dragon does. Each point after the first increases the healing speed by 10%. |
| Hard as Iron (0/5) | Each point increases your base defense rating of all pieces of armor by 15. |
| Feed the Flames (0/5) | Increases the effectiveness of your special dragon bond abilities by 10% per point and reduces their cooldown by 3 hours. |

The selections were impressive. If these were only the first tier options, Arthur was excited to get farther in the talent tree. Arthur's mana regeneration was nice, but with his shared mana pool and his large capacity, he took the Shared Mana Regeneration skill first. He tossed his second point into Dragon Healing to allow him to regenerate health when injured.

*How do I get more talent points in the bond?* Arthur asked.

*You gain more by completing hidden quests. I can't tell you exactly what they are since the criteria are unknown until you complete it. I've heard others mention things like kill so many of a specific type of monster together, or cast so many of a particular magic spell together. I can't say for sure if those are correct.*

*So, don't plan on gaining a lot of them.* Got it.

*We might be able to rake in a suitable amount in the beginning, but I have a feeling the points will be harder to come by the longer we're together.*

They both remained silent after that and watched the pyre burn. Samson, Vana, and Rayne still stood nearby, watching the fire dance while Allendria fussed over the dragon and carefully stroked her scales. After the pyre finished burning to ash, everyone dispersed and returned to town.

***

"I have no food coming in from the fields," Lord Quintin protested. "They promised us food in return for our cooperation with the plan of the Dark Elves. I think we've been double-crossed."

Lord Quintin sat in the enormous meeting room of the castle at Esmere. Lord Preston and Lord Brayson sat across from him while King Wailyn paced the edge of the room. Lord Brayson fidgeted in his chair, obviously uncomfortable in the predicament they found themselves in.

"The problem will be resolved soon. Our fancy little upstart down in his backwater village interrupted the plans and took out the larger portion of the goblin raiding force. Because of that, they haven't had many extra hands to make deliveries as promised," King Wailyn grumbled. *These whiny nobles really grate on my nerves. The entire world is at stake, and they wish to complain about trivial problems.*

"Do we know when our minor infestation problem might be solved?" Lord Preston asked diplomatically.

"Should be any day now. The assassins should have arrived a week ago. It'll take a little time for the reports to trickle back. In the meantime," he emphasized with heat in his tone, "we keep to our plan."

"Our next shipment is due any day now. Do we have the resources ready to meet the deadline?" Lord Brayson asked.

"Just barely," Lord Quintin conceded. "The mixture of the sanctions and the requirements makes the process exceedingly difficult. I'm not sure how much longer we will survive at this rate."

"We'll make it happen. We…" King Wailyn began, but a notification cut him short.

*King Arthur Firebrand from the Kingdom of Fire has declared war on you. Any conflict between your two forces will be automatically treated as an active raid event.*

"Firebrand," King Wailyn muttered. "I guess the rumors were true. That Dark Elven scout heard correctly."

"The boy," Lord Preston reminded him. "We never found him."

"It's been a hundred years. Without the agreement we have, there's no way he could be alive unless he was old and crippled. How is this possible?" Wailyn asked.

"Is this our mysterious threat we've been half ignoring? Was it the son of the late king all along?" Lord Quintin asked.

"Damn. All the spies in this kingdom and we couldn't verify his identity? How's that even possible?" Lord Brayson added.

"It's because he's hiding away on the edge of the kingdom in some no-name village. He's been outside the edge of our notice. A scout reported they believed he may be a Firebrand, but I dismissed it as impossible," the king said as he clenched his fist around the hilt of his sword.

"He still can't have a large enough army to be a problem, right?" Lord Quintin asked.

*The Dragon Pact is renewed. The house of Firebrand has bonded with a dragon.*

"Damn it!" King Wailyn yelled as he smashed his fist into the wooden table. Splinters flew into the air and landed back on his armored gauntlet with slight clanking noises.

"What is it?" Lord Preston asked.

"The upstart renewed the Dragon Pact. He bonded with a dragon. It's a kingdom level event, so all kings and queens of the land would've received the message."

Lord Preston stood slowly and dusted off his tunic with a flick of his wrist. "I'm afraid that means I need to return to Seora at once. I'll be his first target."

"Get rid of him. He needs to die before he destroys everything," the king confirmed.

"I know we aren't supposed to, but can I
get access to the armory? I want to use some
of the better steel and enchanted weapons to
end this threat once and for all. I believe we
still have an Ice Lance hidden away?" Lord
Preston asked cautiously.

"Do it. Get rid of him and kill the dragon.
Bring the armaments back as swiftly as you
can. We don't want them to find out we
violated our agreement. The consequences would
doom us all."

Lord Preston bowed slightly and turned to
leave the room. His steps gradually increased
in speed as he headed directly for the armory.
Time was not on his side.

***

The town of Alurian was a beehive of
activity. People hurried everywhere they went,
and there wasn't a single person not doing a
task.

Following the declaration of war, the town
spent the night at the funeral pyre in
remembrance. When the following day dawned,
preparations began. Full teams of woodcutters
left to harvest wood for weapons and arrows.
Rowan and both of his apprentices worked at
full speed to churn out arrowheads and
weapons.

The morning revealed forty men and women
eagerly waiting at the blacksmith. Many of the
men gave the women wary glances. It wasn't
uncommon to see a woman adventurer, but a
woman soldier was an entirely different
matter. Arthur wasn't about to discriminate
and took them all. He joined his efforts with
Samson to get the full contingent armed and
armored.

The construction crews continued working around the clock to improve the defense of the town, making the wall grow both taller and wider. A few large lookout towers dotted the wall near the gates. Two of the construction crews volunteered to accompany Arthur on his conquest, which secretly pleased him. If he could show how they wanted to change the world, it would help sway some of the populace to his side. The ordinary farmers and craftsmen didn't care about wars. They wanted to make a living. War only seemed to interrupt that.

Hunting parties ranged out almost daily to stockpile on necessities. Birds fell from the sky like rain to have their feathers stripped for arrows. The wild hog population took a good hit as they continued their quest to build up their food supply. Arthur even used the town's new ability and assigned some personal quests of his own. He had enough wealth from his journeys that he could afford to back tasks to give people some extra experience.

Most of his quests involved people finishing something he started. For instance, he assigned the blacksmithing apprentices the task to attach the lining to the pieces of armor he made. It was something they would do anyway, but it had the added benefit of granting them extra experience and a little coin.

Arthur also created more enchantments. He wanted to ensure they had plenty of spare faucets and temperature controls so they could continue building when he left. He created some of the toilet enchantments and showed two of the construction people how to set them correctly for them to work.

The problem of logistics set in, since typically an army would need some kind of supply chain to keep them fed. With their ability to preserve food longer by freezing it, it negated much of this, but they still needed to transport it long distances without it thawing. He approached Daranth with the conundrum and consulted him about building wooden wagons. The elf immediately latched on to the idea and set to work.

Within a week and a half, four full-sized carts sat in front of the Dark Elven embassy. All stood almost twelve feet tall from the top of the cart to the ground. Arthur spent some time inside these new wagons with his enchanting. They designated three of the carts for food, so they received a temperature regulating device in them to keep the inside at a freezing temperature. The Dark Elves included shelving inside all the carts to allow them to stack items for easy access.

They designated the last cart for spare armor and weapons. Ingots of metal lined the floor of the cart for last-minute repairs or additions. The biggest problem he saw was pulling these things. Loaded down with supplies, they'd be far too heavy for the soldiers to tow. Instead, he turned to a spell he'd never used. His Earthen Assistant talent granted him the chance to make an earth elemental that would assist him. These creatures would be strong enough to pull a cart of supplies without a problem. The drawback was he only had three points in the talent so he could only make three at a time. A look at his talents showed him he had two free unspent points. He dumped one more in Earthen Assistants, bringing it to 4 and placed the other in Earthen Will bringing it to 2, increasing his overall power of Earth Magic spells by 10%.

To test the spell, he cast it and watched a misshapen lump of Earth rise from the ground before slowly melting and distorting until it took on a humanoid form. The creature stood eight feet tall and looked as immovable as the dirt that made it. Arthur examined the elemental carefully until he identified how it functioned. The Earth Magic was a constant swirl of power that tied to him as a tether. The creatures drew magic from him but would also absorb magic from the ground and feed the excess back into him in a never-ending pattern. This made the overall cost of the spell small and allowed it to continue for a much longer time.

He instructed the creature to grab a cart and walk with it. It complied and moved with ease. It didn't appear phased by the weight at all. Hopefully, the same would hold true when it was full. He instructed the elemental to work out in the fields and help clear new planting areas for the rest of its duration.

It took a solid two weeks of preparation, but the town was finally as ready as it would ever be. Samson used the time to take those who volunteered to fight out to train in the forest. It helped both forage for food and supplies and gain them the necessary skills. He also made sure every member knew both Earth and Fire Magic. If they planned an assault against superior numbers, they'd need the magic to tip the scales in their favor.

"You think they're ready?" Arthur asked the Paladin.

"Hells no! We're stuck in an awful situation and don't have the luxury of time. It'll have to do. Do you even have a plan?"

"Kinda. We can't possibly attack head-on. Even the guard force of Seora outnumbers us. I plan on taking the city by surprise. Our fighting force will mainly serve as distractions. I want to see if Calfuray can get me and possibly Rayne into the city and drop us off at Lord Preston's manor. We can deal with him and capture the city while you lead the force against the wall and keep their attention on you. Play it safe, avoid bow range when possible, and launch as much magic as you can to spook them. I want every eye in the city, concentrated firmly on you."

"That might work. It'd help if I had more people. Even with lobbing magic, the small size of our fighting force will only intimidate so much."

"Let me see what I can do. Surely a clever application of magic could solve this problem," Arthur said.

Arthur rolled the problem through his mind as he walked. He needed something like a Mirror Image spell. That would allow him to make copies of the people in the army and increase their size in the field. He didn't even need the copies to do damage. Their people were becoming proficient enough in magic that each one could put on a show to appear like multiple mages. If he could also find a way to combine this new spell with an enchantment, he could tie it to enchanted items for them to use during the battle so no one would need to waste their mana maintaining the illusion while fighting.

*Lady Calfuray, you busy?*

The dragon somehow projected a snorting sound to him, *Lady, huh? What? I bond with a king and just magically gain a human title? All kidding aside, I'm assisting with the defenses. I'm not sure how you got the lazy Balair to do work, but you might indeed be capable of divine miracles. It doesn't help that I have to try to keep some distance. The townsfolk are still leery of me, it seems.*

*Can you meet me in the clearing on the southern side of town? Want to consult with you about a magical dilemma.*

*See you there.*

Arthur turned toward the clearing in question and cast Haste to boost his speed. Calfuray would make it there fast since she could fly, and he didn't want to keep her waiting. Even running full speed, he still arrived to the sight of her curled up on the ground, breathing deeply.

*Still too slow.* She huffed.

*One day I'll find a way to move faster than
you.* Arthur shot back.

*Doubt it. Now, what's this magical issue?*

*I have a small army that'll march on the
regional capital of Seora. I need them to look
like a much larger force. I considered using a
spell like Magic Mirror but honestly don't
know how it works. I know you don't have the
spell, but hoped you might understand how it
works?*

*You're fortunate some of our knowledge is
hereditary, and the dragon families believe
strongly in passing on knowledge. My bloodline
has bonded and worked alongside many mages
over the centuries and learned a great deal of
human magic. While I don't know exactly how
the spell you describe is done, I can tell you
it requires you to use Air and Water Magic.
Searching my memories shows Water Magic making
reflective surfaces to mimic the copies of the
target, and the Air Magic confines the Water
Magic and allows it to remain stable. I don't
hold out much hope you'll be able to figure it
out with that negligible amount of
information,* though, the dragon told him with
a puff of smoke from her nostrils.

*I've done crazier things. If it's truly a
mix of Air and Water Magic, that isn't
impossible to do. Learning how to do it
correctly is really going to suck. Sounds like
I need to do it in steps. I need to learn how
to create a reflective surface out of water.
Then I need to learn how to create multiple to
reflect images while not being visible.
Knowing the Air Magic works as a container
helps tremendously.*

The dragon shifted and rolled on her side. She lifted a front claw and scratched along the scales on her side and let out a sigh of relief.

*I'll be interested to see if you can try. I recall my mother telling me your family was always good with magic. You may have the natural family talent, after all.*

*Thanks for the help. I think I've pulled you away from far more important work for too long. I want you to help as much as you can. The people need to feel safe around you.* He told her before she shifted. *Yeah, I know, it'll take time. Just do what you can, please?*

*Yes, Your Majesty,* she sent as she executed a mocking bow in front of him. A toothy grin appeared on her face, and she launched back into the air.

*She'll be the death of me one day, I just know it,* Arthur thought with a shake of his head.

Arthur made one more stop before calling it a day. Daranth stood amidst his workshop, covered in a layer of dust and wood shavings.

"Got a minute?" Arthur asked the elf.

"Sure do, Your Majesty," Daranth said with a quick bow.

"Come now, none of that. Still just Arthur."

"You realize that title doesn't go anywhere just because you ask people not to use it? The more popular you become, the more that title will be forced upon you. The weight of it will never fade."

Arthur felt the words ring true. It was an aspect of his life he'd have to get accustomed to bearing. Still, his friends need not pander to the title.

"Thank you for the advice. I'd still prefer
friends to call me Arthur."

"What can I do for you, then?"

"What are Dark Elven marriage customs
like?" Arthur blurted out.

"I was wondering how long it'd take to
reach this question," Daranth said with a
knowing smile.

"I can't imagine life without her. I don't
want to lose her. I know it'll be tough,
especially since we're different races, but
I'm determined to make it happen."

"Good to hear. You'll have a lot of
opposition, but in terms of the marriage
customs themselves, the most important for you
is the engagement. For a Dark Elf, you have to
craft something for them to symbolize your
love. It's common to use jewelry or pendants.
The most important part is to ensure it has a
personal connection with her."

"That could be challenging. I'll have to
give it some thought."

"Good luck. The item can be the deciding
factor for many couples. Think long and hard,
and choose wisely."

Arthur returned to the inn while
contemplating the issue. It would take some
time to figure this out.

The following day brought the start of the
march. A total of sixty-four people marched to
war. Only about fifty of those were fighters,
while the rest were construction and support
staff. Arthur walked to the side with Vana,
Rayne, and Allendria while Samson led the army
from the front. Rayne was weary about leaving
his sister yet again, but her identity was
safe within the town. To everyone else, she
was just another member of Alurian.

Arthur spent the first three days of their journey experimenting with his magic. Allendria hounded him about his spell work while she tried to assist him with his endeavor. Balair spent the time soaring through the skies with Calfuray but never could quite keep up. She seemed to enjoy teasing the little drake and really loved to dive bomb him and send him tumbling through the air. She was a valuable asset, scouting their path as they traveled. She could fly uncommonly high and had incredible eyesight. This allowed her to see vast distances and inspect large swaths of ground quickly.

While not an overly large force, they were both big and well-armored enough to prevent anything from interfering with their march.

They passed many tiny villages on their way to Seora, but most were nothing but ash. Arthur felt the spread of the kingdom's borders as they marched farther along the path. The lack of anyone or anything to prevent his dominance over the area was both a comfort and somewhat depressing.

It wasn't until the fourth day of their march that Arthur finally figured out the trick to creating a mirrored surface with his Water Magic. It involved a tight structure of air to both contain and block outside interference. His biggest problem making the spell was keeping the surface smooth. He'd make the pane of water, but it would continuously ripple from the slightest air. When he used the Air Magic to act as a barrier, the problem resolved itself. A new spell joined his repertoire.

*Congratulations, you have discovered the Combination Spell: Reflection. You have gained 250 experience in Air Magic and Water Magic for discovering a known spell.*

*You have gained 80 experience in Air Magic and Water Magic for successfully casting Combination Spell: Reflection.*

| Spell: Reflection | |
|---|---|
| Requirements: Air and Water Magic<br>Mana Cost: 40 MP<br>Cast Time: 4 seconds | Description: Creates a pane of water that reflects the image of anything in front of it. |
| Mastery Level: 1 | |

With the first step out of the way, he showed Allendria the spell and explained what he wanted to do. His idea was to create a set of mirrors through a specified area that would reflect a singular image of a soldier to multiple places at once. He didn't want the copies to appear side by side, or it'd be too easy to determine it was the same person.

Arthur's primary problem, though, was figuring out how to spread the images without someone else blocking them when standing nearby. It took a consultation with Samson to figure that out.

"You want to do what?" the Paladin asked in disbelief.

"I want to create mirror images of the army, so it looks like there are far more people assaulting the city. I need you to provide the distraction while we sneak in and get rid of Lord Preston and capture the city," Arthur explained.

"So what's the problem? Wave your hands, do your fancy magic, and let me be your distraction," Samson said in confusion.

"We don't want them side by side but rather spread apart so it won't be obvious they're the same person. If anyone steps in between the reflective path, it'll cause the image to fail. Makes it hard to create a unified force that way."

"Use slants in a formation then," the ex-soldier said with a wave of his hand.

"You mean make the projections be in diagonal? Won't the images be too close?"

"If I have everyone stand in a single row and you make slanted projections of them, they'll each have staggered versions of themselves. I've never known a military force that could recognize that detail when our entire army is wearing pretty much identical armor."

*Damn. Is it really that simple?* Arthur thanked the big man and hurried to join Allendria at the edge of the formation.

Their trek led them through four more villages and what used to be a town although they were in such terrible shape Arthur didn't even bother consulting the map to see their names. Whatever their names were before was irrelevant when no one lived there, and barely any buildings remained standing. Almost none of the ones standing were occupied, short of a couple of stragglers that looked like skin stretched taut over bare bones. The few people they ran across joined the procession since they were kind enough to feed them, and when they were strong enough, they assisted with tasks around the camp.

It took him another four days to get the images arranged correctly. They had plenty of time since the trip took around three weeks in total to reach Seora. When the spell finally snapped into place, Arthur jumped up in excitement. He was pleased to see the copies of himself do the same.

*Congratulations, you have discovered the Combination Spell: Mirror Image (Diagonal). You have gained 250 experience in Air Magic and Water Magic for discovering a known spell.*
*You have gained 180 experience in Air Magic and Water Magic for successfully casting Combination Spell: Mirror Image (Diagonal).*

| Spell: Mirror Image (Diagonal) | |
| --- | --- |
| Requirements: Air and Water Magic<br>Mana Cost: 100 MP<br>Cast Time: 8 seconds<br>Duration: 5 minutes<br>Cooldown: 3 minutes | Description: Creates two copies of the caster on two sides of them in a diagonal pattern. These copies will move in the same way as the original. |
| Mastery Level: 1 | |

With that hurdle out of the way, he turned his focus to Enchanting. This part was even more troublesome. He didn't have any material capable of holding a spell that powerful that he was aware of. He almost died enchanting Divine Fury with his Flamethrower spell, and it wasn't even a dual element spell.

A far more straightforward solution finally came to mind. He just needed someone capable of refreshing the spell on the army while they fought. One of the support members would make the perfect candidate. It came down to a woman named Chloe, who was in charge of one of their construction groups. Arthur pulled her to the side and discussed the issue. It took some convincing, but Arthur talked her into duty. Two days of work later, and she'd picked up Air Magic. She already knew Water Magic because she used it for some of the construction work.

While they traveled, he allowed her to wear his necklace to draw extra mana. When the pendant was low on mana, Arthur would put it back on and siphon some of the mana from his sword back into it so she could continue. They were only a few days from Seora when she reached level ten in both Air and Water Magic. Arthur was confident she'd be high enough in her skills to learn the spell. He placed a hand on her shoulder, and the message appeared, but there was something different.

*Do you wish to teach Mirror Image (Diagonal) to Chloe? Note that doing so will use up the one spell slot you can teach for both the Air and Water branches for this person.*

So there was a drawback to teaching
combination spells. It made sense to Arthur,
but he just shrugged off the message and
taught the spell. Chloe jumped in excitement
with a squeal and immediately cast her new
spell. Five Chloes ran across the open area in
an almost perfect diagonal before they finally
returned to talk to Arthur. He had to admit
seeing all five of her forms looking his
direction and moving their mouth while talking
to him was very unnerving.

"This is great," she told him as she looked
to her clones and watched them mimic her
movement. "Kind of creepy, but great."

"Glad to hear, because you'll get to cast
that spell a lot. I need you to keep the spell
cast on the army while we work to get rid of
their leaders. I plan on making some pieces of
armor to help you with mana. They'll be ready
before we reach the city."

She bounced with joy and ran up to Arthur
and gave him a hug, "Thank you," she said
before she got really nervous, backed away and
bowed slightly. "Sorry, Your Majesty. I
forgot."

Arthur just laughed and waved a hand at
her. "None of that, Chloe. You're doing me a
big favor, after all. I take no offense at
your excitement. Keep practicing your magic
until we get there. The higher your level, the
better you'll be with your spell. You may get
some useful talents to help with the cost or
duration of the spell if you're lucky."

She nodded and ran over to her group of
friends. She'd spent so much time working with
Arthur and Allendria lately that she had spent
little time with them. Allendria turned to
look at him with a quirked eyebrow.

"Getting awfully friendly there," she commented with a wry smile.

"She did that, not me. I've got work to do, anyway. Have some armor to make."

Allendria giggled. "What do you plan on making now?"

"Mainly accessory pieces. Some bracers and a necklace. As a matter of fact, I'll make her a necklace similar to mine and bracers with some manufactured gems to store mana. I just worry it won't be enough. Even if I only have her multiply twenty of the army at once, that'll cost 2,000 mana every five minutes. That doesn't give me long to get rid of this Lord Preston before she is out of mana."

"Can you have her use their mana instead?" Allendria asked.

"No, I ca…" he began before stopping. *Is it possible? Can someone contact another and use their mana if allowed? What about an item? If I upgrade all their necklaces with manufactured gems, it should give them enough reserve mana to use the spell multiple times. I can make plenty of the manufactured stones. We brought an ample supply of charcoal with us stashed in my dimensional storage with a handful of other somewhat essential supplies.*

"Can you use the mana from one of my objects while I wear it?" Arthur asked Allendria.

"Never tried. Not sure it will work."

"Give it a shot."

She walked to him and stared him in the eyes. She carefully placed her hand on his necklace and extended her other hand to the side. He felt mana stir inside her before a notification appeared in his vision.

*Do you wish to allow Allendria access to the mana storage in your Intricate Mage-crafted Steel Mana Amulet (Sapphire Storage)? Yes/No.*

He mentally selected *Yes,* and he felt the mana pull from the amulet and swirl into Allendria's palm. A small burst of flame exploded from her outstretched hand before she cut the fire and looked him in the eyes again.

"Guess it works."

"Yeah, I got a message asking if I wanted to let you use it. Did the job when I confirmed."

"Now that you have your answer. What's your plan?"

"I have a lot of gems to manufacture and a lot of amulets to modify. Will probably make some bracers as well to give our casters some extra firepower."

She laid her hand on his shoulder and spun him to face her, "Good luck," she told him quickly before bounding off and making a beeline for Vana. *Leave it up to her to ditch work.*

Arthur focused his attention on the armor. It took him two full days of travel to make enough gems and approach each person about modifying their amulets. He also made ten mana bracelets and gave them to those Samson said had the best command of their magic. He explained why he was changing their gear and what the mana was for. He brought Chloe with him to introduce her to everyone so they'd be familiar with her face.

With all the gear changed and everything handed out, the final day allowed him to do nothing but relax. He spent the day enjoying the weather and daydreaming until a message came to him.

*We're not far. I can see the city getting closer. The walls look formidable, and their defenses are ready. I think they know you're coming,* Calfuray sent.

*I know I should've asked this earlier, but will you be able to get Rayne and I inside the city and to the manor of Lord Preston?*

*What do you think I am? A horse? You're asking me, a majestic dragon, to ferry you two humans around like a common beast of burden?*

*Uh, maybe? I don't care if you carry us in your claws as long as you can hold on and not drop us. I don't want you to attack much. I mainly want you here with Samson and the army to keep the guards distracted and occasionally breathe fire on the walls. I don't want you in too much danger, and I can't let you loose on the city for fear it'll cause the death of far too many innocents.*

*Fine, but you owe me for this. I'll figure out exactly how later,* she sent with a projection of a feral grin.

*Damn. Probably going to regret that, but too late now.* Arthur walked to the front of the army and matched stride with Samson.

"Almost there. Calfuray tells me she can see the city walls approaching. You ready for this?"

The paladin flexed his hand in front of him and rolled his shoulders.

"It's been a while since I marched to war, but I imagine I'm as ready as I'll ever be."

Arthur laid a hand on the big man's shoulder. "I truly appreciate everything you've done. I'm sure Lianna is proud."

"Maybe I'll get lucky and get another champion point for this battle. If Lord Preston ends up a Champion of Isabell, I'd say it's an excellent chance," Samson replied excitedly.

"Another point?" Arthur asked before bringing up his Divine Power Skill Tree.

You have 1 unused Divine Power talent point.

| Novice Skills | |
| --- | --- |
| Divine Fury (1/1) | Channel a raging storm around your body that deals 25 HP/s damage to enemies. Lasts for 30 seconds.<br><br>Mana cost: 600<br>Cooldown: 3 days |
| Nurtured Growth (0/1) | Infuse plant life in a 100 square yard space with the power of divinity. Plants will grow 150% faster and produce 100% more usable food.<br><br>Mana Cost: 800 Mana<br>Cooldown: 2 Weeks |
| Call Wrath (0/1) | Marks a target enemy for wrath. All damage you do to a marked enemy is increased by 100% for 5 minutes. |

| | Mana Cost: 150<br>Cooldown: 1 Day |
| --- | --- |
| Retribution (1/1) | Call upon holy fire to bathe an area and deal damage to all enemies in the space. Cast range of 200 yards. Deals 50 HP/s damage for 10 seconds.<br><br>Mana Cost: 500 mana<br>Cooldown: 5 days |
| Blessing of Salvation (0/1) | Send out waves of healing energy to revitalize allies near you. This ability will restore the health, mana, and stamina of all nearby allies by 40%<br><br>Mana Cost: 200<br>Cooldown: 7 days |

Since he hadn't advanced tiers in his Divine Champion skill, he still only had the same abilities to choose from, but defeating Isabell's champion had granted him one point to use. He must've missed the notification during mourning his mother. The options remained the same, so he chose Call Wrath. Unlike last time, for this fight, his goal was to kill one man. He was sure there'd be others that had to die first, but that one man was the tipping point to his control.

He'd gained large swathes of experience over the last few weeks and took a chance to look at his latest stat sheet. He hid all but the combat and magic-related skills he typically used. He also dropped out the individual spells and their mastery levels.

**Name:** Arthur Firebrand
**Faction:** Kingdom of Fire
**Level:** 22
**Age:** 26
**Race:** Human
**Class:** Spell Blade
**HP:** 530/530 (550)
**MP:** 780/780 (1080)
**Stamina:** 530/530

**Strength:** 20
**Agility:** 32
**Intellect:** 34
**Wisdom:** 16
**Endurance:** 26
**Charisma:** 12
**Luck:** 11

**Experience:**
8745/63000 (0 stat points available)

**Skills** (225% boost to any skill for level up)
**Combat Skills:**

**Archery:** 10 (5170/6000)
 - **Aim Shot:** 7 (1695/3200)
**Block:** 3 (330/1000)
**Dual Wield:** 6 (2190/2500)
**Medium Armor:** 5 (800/1900)
**Parry:** 4 (370/1000)
**Scan:** 5 (1640/1900)
**Small Blades:** 8 (830/3800)
**Spears:** 2 (450/750)
**Stealth:** 4 (470/1400)

**Swords:** 11 (2095/7200)
**Throwing Knives:** 3 (480/1000)
**Unarmed:** 1 (275/500)

**Magic:**

**Air Magic:** 10 (1680/6000)
**Dimensional Magic:** 12 (1700/8500)
**Earth Magic:** 23 (52210/69000)
**Fire Magic:** 23 (31615/69000)
**Water Magic: 10** (3790/6000)

He couldn't ask for much more in the limited time he'd spent here. His combat skills needed work, but city management usually took up most of his time. He needed to help the people and couldn't waste time fighting monsters all the time.

This fight would be the tipping point in this struggle. It was time they stood up and took back this kingdom.

# Chapter 41

*The Assault on Seora*

Their army stopped inside the tree line outside of the city. They didn't want to expose their exact numbers before the fight. They needed to ensure their illusion spell was active when they marched out and revealed themselves.

Samson, Allendria, Rayne, and Vana joined him in an impromptu meeting. Samson invited two other soldiers to join the conference. Both had previous experience, and one even served with Samson in the army before. Neither would discuss the specifics of their service with anyone, but Arthur had no reason to doubt either man. The first soldier was Parthain, and the one Samson served with before was Kiernan.

Samson introduced them to the group and let Arthur know they were his lieutenants and would help keep order along the fighting lines. Arthur nodded and motioned for the two to join them as they seated themselves around a small fire.

"Tomorrow is the day. I'll confer with Calfuray, and when she's ready, she'll take Rayne and me into the city. I'll fly with her over the city and make a pronouncement telling them the rightful King has returned, and we'll spare any who lay down their weapons. Following that, we'll return here and give them time to decide. I truly doubt anyone will change their minds, but it may get the citizens riled up and cause unrest to further distract the guards," Arthur told them all before turning toward Rayne. "Can you draw us a rough map. I know you're somewhat familiar with the city."

Rayne nodded as Arthur opened his Dimensional Drawer. He'd managed to sneak a few pieces of parchment from Katherine for a situation like this and handed a sheet to Rayne with a small stick of coal. Rayne took the items and set to work. While he drew his sketch, Arthur continued.

"Chloe will walk through the army, constantly refreshing the images. I want you to focus on a distance battle as much as possible. Light them up with bows and spells. Target their archers first. Calfuray will make sweeping attacks on the wall, but I don't want her near the city proper. If she lights something on fire, it could destroy the entire place, and trap the people inside. We want as few casualties as possible," he said as the people nodded along at his explanation. "When the attack has begun in earnest, Calfuray will drop us near the manor of Lord Preston. I expect us to meet stiff resistance from his personal guards. When we defeat him, I can declare the rightful rulership of the city. We will then make a sweep of the remaining guards that refuse to bow down. It won't be easy, but we can do it."

Samson shook his head. "You make it sound so simple, but we both know that's not how the fight will go."

"Oh, I'm fully aware that no battle plan ever survives contact with the enemy, but that's our general idea. I rely on you, Kiernan, and Parthain to do whatever necessary to keep their attention. Calfuray will also be here to help."

"What about us?" Vana and Allendria asked in unison and then looked at each other and laughed.

"You do what you do best. Keep Samson alive and wreak havoc," Arthur responded with a chuckle of his own.

"I want to go with you," Allendria said, and Vana agreed.

"I'd love to have you both with me, but Calfuray can only carry two of us. I've chosen Rayne because I know he is familiar with the city and is excellent at sneaking around one. This mission will be just as much stealth as it is combat."

Both women huffed but didn't object farther. Allendria wore a look that told him he would regret that decision later, but Arthur would take that look if it kept her safe and away from the battle he feared waited for them when they found Lord Preston.

Rayne looked up from his work and motioned for Arthur and the group to look. Everyone leaned forward until they could see the drawing he'd created. It was a crude affair, but definitely did the job. He'd done a rough sketch of the wall with a solid line and then drew the major roads that wove through the city. He marked the critical buildings along those main roads and lightly shaded everywhere else buildings sat. He pointed to the house near the back corner of town from them and said, "That's Lord Preston's Manor."

The group took time to digest the information on the map, and Samson traced out routes through the city roads. Arthur looked at the map and spotted two large buildings not too far from Lord Preston's house.

"What are those buildings?" he asked while pointing them out to the young thief.

"Warehouses for goods. They store the upper market items for the wealthier parts of the city. Few people are ever around there anymore since most of the luxuries faded away."

"I think we found our point of entry," Arthur told him with a smile.

"I'm not sure Calfuray can land on one of those. They may not be sturdy enough to hold her," Rayne pointed out.

"It'll be fine. If she can't land, I'll have her fly slowly and low to the buildings, and we can jump."

"Do you hear yourself?" Rayne asked in disbelief. "You want to jump from a dragon onto a warehouse mid-flight?"

"Yeah," Arthur said with a shrug. "Shouldn't be too hard."

Rayne merely shook his head and muttered, "What have I signed up for?"

"Any questions?" Arthur asked.

"Fallback plan?" Samson reciprocated.

"If the worst happens, get back to Alurian. The defenses are sturdy enough, and with Rowan still manning the forge, you should be fine. Continue as you have been and try to make this a better place. Name a leader and forge ahead."

The group nodded, and everyone walked away to visit with friends. Allendria remained behind with Balair.

*Am I coming with you?* Balair asked.

*Not this time, my friend. I have a job for you.* Arthur told him.

*Sounds like something I won't like.*

*Actually, I just want you to guard Allendria. Keep her safe for me, okay?*

The little dragon turned to look at the Dark Elven Princess.

*I'm not sure she needs it, but I'll do it. She's not going to kick me again, right?*

Arthur giggled a little, which caused Allendria to turn toward him. Her eyes narrowed in suspicion as she looked at his smiling face.

*Just don't piss her off and you should be fine.*

"I'm going to take care of a few things before we call it a night. You need anything?" Arthur asked.

"I think I'll go chat with Vana. She's been nervous about Samson. It looks like she's growing closer to him."

"He's an honorable man. She also helps keep him on his toes," Arthur agreed as he watched her walk away before scurrying off to a hidden part of the forest.

He wanted to do some work and needed it to be secret. His Dimensional Drawer opened up, and he removed a small stack of his gold, silver, and copper coins he'd gathered. He'd squirreled away some for his personal use and never gave them all over to the town.

His mind spun with the possibilities. His engagement gift would focus on Allendria's calling. Since it needed to resonate with her, a pendant designed to display her Pyromancer class was his intended item. The gold and silver were much easier to work with than steel so he could melt and mold small pieces of it with raw mana.

The design used the silver as the base of the pendant. After a careful application of heat, an oval the size of his palm formed from the silver. He allowed some more flame to melt some of the copper, and he dribbled it on the surface to create a rough outline of a person. Finally, he melted some gold and surrounded the copper. With all the metals needed on the disc, he summoned a small orb of fire and pushed the medallion in using his Earth Magic. When it looked soft and pliable, he cast his Arcane Forging spell.

The beam of magic worked just as well on
this soft metal as it had on steel. The line
of power moved across the surface, and the
rough disc with the splotches of other metals
took shape. It formed the image of Allendria,
her skin accented with the copper metal while
silver embossed her clothing. Gold swirled
around her hands and accentuated her eyes
while an aura of golden flames surrounded her.
When the spell finished, he quickly extracted
the heat before it melted again.

He took some more of all three metals and
made a small rope of each. Those three ropes
wound together in a braid to form a rough
necklace. With some heat and another cast of
Arcane Forging, the power enveloped it as
well, and the regular ropes flowed and
reshaped to look like tree branches
interweaving with a multitude of colors.

When both pieces were complete, he could
only stare at them. They were fantastic and
just what he hoped for. He spent some time
carefully etching the symbols on the necklace
and the medallion to enchant it. He wanted
this to be a flashy piece, so he gave it a
small manufactured gem on the back to store
mana. He used an additional enchantment to add
some flair. When he combined the two enchanted
pieces, the end result was better than he
hoped.

| Item:<br>Pyromancer's Embrace | Durability: 140/140 |
| --- | --- |
| | Rarity: Epic |
| | Quality: Exquisite |
| | Weight: 0.4 kg |

| | **Mana Capacity:** 1000/1000<br><br>**Slot:** Neck<br><br>**Traits:** An amulet and chain made of gold, silver, and copper, designed for the Pyromancer Allendria.<br><br>**Enchantments:**<br>• When the user casts the enchantment on this item, it causes the golden flames on the face of the amulet to dance like actual fire and the vines that make up the necklace appear to crawl. This effect lasts for five minutes. Cooldown: 30 minutes. |
|---|---|

*She'll love it.*

Arthur cleaned up the rest of the metal and tossed everything but the necklace back into his Dimensional Drawer. He bounced along the ground as he returned to camp and sought out Allendria.

*Calfuray, can you meet me outside of camp on the eastern side? There's a clearing there you should be able to land in.*

*You need something?*

*I know you haven't known us long, but I plan on proposing to Allendria and would like you to be present. She'll be a big part of both of our lives.*

*That explains the emotions I kept getting from you. I'll meet you there.*

Arthur found Allendria and led her away to the clearing. He told her he wanted to show her something, and she followed along, infected by his giddy attitude.

When they arrived, she spotted Calfuray sitting in the knee-high grass. The stars shone, and the moon's full light bathed the clearing in a peaceful calm. They walked to Calfuray, and Arthur turned to her and took her hands.

"Princess Allendria," he began with a smile which grew even larger when he watched her face morph into a lopsided grin. "We met in a forest, and I had the honor of saving you. Since that day, you've been my best friend in this world. You've stood by my side every step of the way and even went along with some of my more foolish and not well thought out plans."

Arthur moved his right hand to his side and fished out the necklace while keeping his focus on her eyes.

"We may not have known each other a long time by some standards, but I can't imagine my life without you," he said before sinking to a knee. Her mouth quickly opened in shocked surprise as she figured out what was happening. Tears puddled on the edges of her eyes as Arthur lifted the necklace to her. "Will you marry me?"

She gently ran her finger over the intricate designs of the necklace and the image of her on the face. "Of course I will! I love you too!"

They embraced and kissed deeply under the moonlight.

"I'm happy for you both. Even in tough times, you must remember why it is you fight. Never forget this," Calfuray rumbled into the clearing.

Allendria walked over and outstretched her arms. She reached across the chest of the dragon and squeezed up against her as much as possible. The size difference in the two made it almost comical, but the dragon took the gesture seriously and snaked her head down to wrap around the Dark Elf's back and hold her firmly.

"You're family now too, Calfuray. Never forget that," Allendria told her.

*Yeah, you can keep her. I like her,* the dragon sent to him mentally.

The two spent some time together in the clearing while Calfuray returned to the sky. She needed to find something to eat before the fight tomorrow. The newly engaged couple celebrated their new arrangement before returning to camp. It may have been a reckless action in unknown territory, close to a city they planned to siege in the morning, but neither of them cared.

When they returned, Vana, Samson, and Rayne waited close to where they emerged from the trees.

"Congratulations!" they all called in unison.

"How did you guys know?" Arthur asked.

Balair stood nearby and strutted forward. *I told them.*

*How did you know?*
*Calfuray told me.*
*Of course she did.*

"Balair told us," Vana answered. "Your celebration must've been something else. I think half the people on this side of camp heard part of the…" she continued before a grunt from Samson made her realize what she was saying. She quieted down as her face took on a deep shade of red.

"Well, I'm glad you guys know. Hopefully, everyone else will take it as well as you have."

"I'd like to think so," Rayne started, "but I've seen far too much irrational hatred to believe it'll be that easy. We've fought with her and know her personally. While most in town respect our Dark Elven friends, many of them will object to their new king marrying someone of another race."

"They'll get over it." Samson waved off. "I'd love to stay and celebrate, but we have a fight in the morning, so I'm going to get some shut-eye before my next rotation comes up."

"Good night all," Allendria told them, "and thank you."

The following morning dawned with a cool breeze. The sun filtered through the trees, and the camp stirred to life. Everyone ate a hearty breakfast before checking their equipment and preparing for the fight. Rayne approached Arthur before the assault started and handed him two small vials.

"A healing potion and a potion of fire suppression. I haven't had a chance to make many yet. It takes a long time to prepare and dry the herbs, and I still have limited supplies. The fire suppression potion breaks and creates a large blanket of thick foam to suffocate flames. That's a weak healing potion, so it only heals 75 HP. It's only for an emergency," the young thief stressed.

"Thanks. You have some of your own, right? You're coming with me into the maw of the beast."

Rayne pulled out a handful of vials from his pouch. "I have a few for myself. Only one healing potion, but I have some others that might prove useful."

"All right, let's get this show on the road."

Arthur walked toward the gathering of soldiers. They all shifted nervously from foot to foot and turned to watch him as he approached. He came to a stop in front of them, and every eye in the crowd fixated on the new king.

"Good Morning. Today, we embark on a new beginning. Today, we take our first step toward freedom. We've worked hard to breathe life back into the people of this region. Despite all of our efforts, the traitor King Wailyn constantly seeks our destruction. Now it's our turn to fight back. I'm counting on you to hold the line. I need every eye in the city focused here. Rayne and I," Arthur said with a wave toward the young thief, "will enter the city to eliminate Lord Preston and gain control from the inside. Keep the guards on the wall away from us. Many are just people following orders. We don't want unnecessary deaths."

Arthur slowly pulled Ember from its scabbard and raised it above his head. "I have faith in all of you. It's time to feed the flame. For the Kingdom of Fire!" Sheathe in Flames activated on Ember and lit up at his final pronouncement. The men and women in the clearing cheered, and most of them drew their weapons and held them skyward.

The crowd finally quieted, and Samson walked through. "You heard the King. Everyone get into ranks and set your position. Chloe will be through to activate the spells, and we can march out. Maintain your spacing, so the illusions don't distort."

Arthur conferred with the two lieutenants, Parthain and Kiernan, about the status of the fighters. He had them point out some of the better mages in the group in both Fire and Earth Magic. Arthur used his Teacher class skill to grant the fire mages his Fire Blast spell since they needed a powerful spell to assault the wall. He gave the earth mages his Stone Fist spell. That spell could wreak havoc on a wall if used enough.

When everyone was ready to go, Chloe zipped through the lines and activated the Mirror Image spell. The force of fifty changed into a force around one hundred. They decided she'd only spell twenty of the people to help conserve mana.

The new force stood eerily still until Samson yelled out a command to march. They advanced through the trees, and Arthur watched the trunks distort some of the mirror images until they passed through and solidified again. Luckily, they didn't break when something interfered with them.

The army cleared the trees and formed up on the rolling expanse before the walls. Arthur could see guards atop the wall with spears held high. It gave the appearance that the wall itself had a spiked top. Calfuray touched down near him, and he turned to her.

"Thank you for doing this," he said as he ran his hand over the scales on her jaw.

"Don't get used to it. I'm still not a horse," she huffed before lying flat and allowing Arthur to climb to her back. He seated himself behind two spike ridges ahead of her wings, and she stood back up. The quick motion almost knocked Arthur to the ground, but he held onto the spike in front of him.

*Better hold on tight. That would've been embarrassing to have the king fall off his mighty dragon right before the big battle,* Balair sent to him. Arthur glanced to the side and spotted the little dragon with a smug grin on his face standing near Allendria.

Calfuray crouched down for a moment, and Arthur felt his stomach drop as she launched off the ground. They slowly rose until he could see the layout of the city. The map Rayne roughly sketched out was eerily accurate in terms of the general design. There were a few places he had buildings shaded in that were bare now, but Arthur saw scorch marks near those areas leading him to believe a building burned down there.

They flew toward the city, and Arthur could barely see the people in the crowds below. When they spotted them descending, he heard screams of alarm drift up and the streets emptied quickly. They gradually lowered until they were almost within bow range and held their position. Arthur looked to the city and gulped. He'd never been very fond of heights and instantly regretted this decision.

His Air Magic stirred in him as he readied himself to talk. This high up, it'd be hard for anyone to hear him, so he would use his Air Magic to amplify his voice as he spoke.

"Ladies and gentlemen of the city of Seora. I am Arthur Firebrand, the son of Tristan and Violet Firebrand, and the true king of this land. The traitor, King Wailyn, murdered my family and took their throne. Any who do not wish to take part in this fight remain indoors, and I'll ensure your safety. To the guards on the wall, lay down your arms, and walk away. No harm will come to those just doing their jobs. If you stand with Lord Preston and his corruption, I will deal with you after this fight. Lord Preston, I'll give you this chance to surrender the fight, and I'll let you live. The city has one hour. After that time, we will attack."

Arthur finished speaking, and Calfuray turned back toward the army when he saw a figure walk to the balcony on Lord Preston's manor. They carried a long gleaming spear mounted through the center of a shield. It sparkled like crystals in the sunlight, and Calfuray stared at it in suspicion. It only took her a few moments before she quickly dove.

A bolt of icy power burst from the weapon and caught her on the back right leg as she dove. She roared in pain and continued her fall before pulling out of the dive and soaring over the buildings. She banked hard to one side as another burst of ice smashed into the rooftop below them, and she made a beeline for their army. As she flew over the wall, she released a torrent of flame in protest. Men screamed, and weapons fell with a clatter as they passed into the open field. They reached the army, and Calfuray landed and gently put weight on her injured leg.

"You okay?" Arthur asked frantically as he slid to the ground and ran to examine her leg. A slight trickle of blood ran from her scales at the impact area.

"I'll be fine. It was a glancing blow, or it would've been much worse. There aren't supposed to be any Ice Lances left. Your parents worked hard to find and destroy every one of them that still existed."

"I guess they missed one. I'm surprised ice can hurt you so badly," Arthur remarked.

"Ice itself wouldn't hurt me that much. Those weapons were designed to kill dragons. They use ice, but their enchantments allow that ice to do incredible damage to dragons. If you were hit with it, the damage wouldn't be any different from taking the blow of a normal ice spell. It has a racial boost to damage against dragons and can puncture scales."

"Then I need to get it and destroy it," Arthur said with finality, "I hate to ask, but can you still get us into the city?"

"I can, but you won't like it. It'll have to be a quick drop for you two. I can't slow down too much. Luckily, the place you want to land is opposite his house from that balcony. You'll have to jump to the warehouse as a fly by."

"Great, let the guy scared of heights jump from a flying dragon onto a building," Arthur grumbled to himself.

"You're free to sneak in on your own," she told him in a dry tone.

"No, it's fine, thank you. I still plan to give them their hour I promised, so rest up and recover."

Arthur filled Rayne in on the plan, and the thief nodded but looked a little pale at the thought of jumping from a moving dragon. Balair flew high above the army and kept watch of the movements in the city. He never slowed his flight and didn't come close enough to the city to be a target. Guards scrambled along the wall, and the charred patch was quickly cleaned of bodies. When the space was clear again, and no more fire burned, another set of guards took the position, although, Balair noted they kept nervously glancing at the scorch marks around them.

When the hour passed, Arthur nodded to Samson, and the Paladin called the order to march. Their force trudged forward in a neat line. The soldiers on the wall scurried from place to place while they continued their steady walk. When they were just outside of bow reach, Samson called a halt.

"Care to do the honors?" Samson asked him.

"Would be my pleasure," Arthur said before turning to the army.

"For the Kingdom of Fire!" Arthur yelled before building a ball of swirling flame in each hand and launching them with a combination of Air and Fire Magic and his own throwing force. The balls arced over the open field. One landed on top of the wall and burst into flame, engulfing the nearby guards. The other orb fell short and smashed into a crenellation on the wall.

*You have dealt 720 HP damage to City Guard (Level 18) with Dual Fire Blast (x6).*

Arrows flew from the wall in response, but they all fell short. Arthur watched an arrow fly from their side, bathed in fire, and impacted the chest of a guard on the wall to send him flying back into the city proper. He looked over to see Vana with a malicious grin.

"What? I'm a better archer than they are. Ranger, remember?" she told him.

For good measure, Arthur also cast a Dual Stone Fist that slammed into the base of the wall and caused many of the guards to stumble and struggle to keep their balance. Bits of stone and dust fell from the wall in response to the attack.

After that, spells flew from their side of the fight. Compact balls of fire soared across the sky and hit the wall. Some splashed with little power left in them from the flight. A few others hit like this, and Arthur knew they were the casters he taught his Fire Blast skill. Earth spikes flew from their army and peppered into the wall and smashed into some of the guards not smart enough to take cover.

    With the battle in full swing, Arthur
turned and found Rayne standing near Calfuray.
He nodded to them both, and the dragon
crouched down. The two men scurried up on her
back and took a seat. She launched off the
ground and quickly gained altitude.

    Calfuray banked in the air until she lined
up with their target building. Her head dipped
down as she gradually dove and picked up
speed.

    "You two get ready. This is going to be a
rough stop. I'll try to slow down as much as
possible without placing myself in too much
danger," she roared over the wind as they
dove.

    Arthur tensed up and waited for their
moment. Right before they reached the
building, Calfuray arched her back and flared
out her wings. They caught the air like an
unfurled sail and slowed her flight. The quick
stop almost unseated Arthur, but he held on,
and when the building was below them, he
launched off of her back and fell to the
ground. She'd stayed close to the building,
but the fall was still a good fifteen feet.

    Arthur's feet hit the roof, and he
immediately rolled forward. The impact of the
roll on his back brought a sharp pain as he
fell to the roof with a flop and stopped. He
stared at the sky as the ache in his back
slowly subsided.

    *You have taken 60 HP of falling damage from
(Warehouse Roof).*

    "I'll take falling out of a tree any day to
that," Rayne groaned beside him, and looked to
see the thief in a similar position.

"I assume there's a story behind that remark?" Arthur asked in amusement.

"Actually, yes. I'll have to tell you about it one day."

The two eventually regained their feet and looked around. They couldn't hear anything in the surrounding area. The sounds of the battle at the wall filtered through the buildings, but the nearby area was eerily quiet.

Rayne took the lead and scurried to the edge of the roof. He waved Arthur over, and they hopped to a landing below used for loading. From there, they jumped a little farther down and landed on the broken cobblestones of the street below.

The buildings near them were in poor repair, and the streets had small weeds growing between some of the stones. *That shouldn't be possible in a city this size,* Arthur thought to himself. *How is there so little traffic on the streets that plants have time to grow?*

He followed Rayne as the young man dashed from building to building, constantly hugging the edges and carefully peeking around corners. At one point, the thief stopped and turned to Arthur.

"I fear it's worse than I thought. This city is dying and quickly. Even before I left, there was activity here, albeit not much, but now it looks like this part of the city has been abandoned for some time," Rayne mumbled as he gestured to a few different spots around them.

Grass and weeds grew along the edges of the streets, and a few discarded items lay everywhere. Those items were in various stages of decay. Two cloth animals with missing eyes leaked straw stuffing. An old chair with a broken leg lay toppled on its side. Some wood turned an ugly brown color and looked brittle.

"How can it come to this? Surely the people would do something?" Arthur asked.

"They tried. The riots claimed many lives. In the end, no one had anything to fight with. Guards put down the riots, and it appears things have gotten worse."

Arthur could only shake his head and motion for Rayne to continue. They slipped through more of the city and gradually crept closer to Lord Preston's manor. When they were within sight of the small wall surrounding the manor, they saw their first signs of life. Two men stood guard near one entrance. They appeared to be hired killers, but that wasn't what stood out the most. Arthur inspected them and saw they bore what he could swear were steel weapons.

"Steel? On the guards? Is that common since we're in the city?" Arthur asked.

"No," Rayne answered with a shake of his head, "I've only seen steel a handful of times. Usually, only the highest members of the guard can carry it. Even then, it's rare to see."

"We going to take them out, or do you have another way in?" Arthur asked.

"I'd say we could find another way in, but we are running out of time. They can only maintain their illusions for so long, right?"

"I guess that means a head-on assault?"

"I'm not a brawler. You can run at them head-on if you want. I plan on sneaking up on them."

"Fine, I'll rush them and you stealth behind them for the attack."

Rayne nodded, and shadows wrapped around him as the magic drew Arthur's attention elsewhere. *That's still unnerving.* Arthur pulled Ember and his dagger free and took a deep breath. He charged around the corner and ran straight for the two guards.

Both stood unaware for a few moments before one caught sight of the crazy man charging them with weapons drawn. He drew his blade, and the noise startled the other guard. That man noticed Arthur approaching and also lifted his blade as they braced for the attack.

Fire swirled along Ember as he channeled Flamethrower through it. With less than ten feet between them, he pointed the sword, and flames exploded from the end. One yelled in fear and fell backward while the other raised his sword in front of his face to try to deflect the flame. When the fire dissipated, the man stood standing with the blade in front of his face, but his skin was crispy and scorched. He fell to the ground, causing his skin to crack and blood to leak from the wounds before succumbing to his injuries. The fighter on the ground sported red welts on his face from the heat burning past him, but none of it touched him directly. Before Arthur could even close the distance, Rayne appeared behind the man, and both daggers fell to slice into each side of his neck. Blood poured down his collar and he fell to the side.

*You have dealt 220 HP damage to Guard (Level 18) with Flamethrower (Critical Hit).*

*Guard (Level 18) has died.*

"Care to warn me next time?" Rayne hissed. "You almost caught me in that spell."

"Sorry," Arthur told him, "I didn't think you'd get here that fast."

Arthur looked at the weapons the men held and confirmed they were steel. He quickly opened his Dimensional Storage and tossed them in before shutting it. Rayne looked around the corner and scanned the courtyard beyond the walls. He quickly ducked inside before turning to Arthur.

"Looks like your flame drew attention. Four more guards are headed this way. The good news is, I didn't see anyone else in the courtyard, so we might have an empty path to the manor if we can beat them."

"Fine, I'll handle it," Arthur told him as he sheathed his blades and formed small balls of fire in each palm. The orbs solidified, and he dashed around the corner, lobbing both balls directly at the incoming guards. They stumbled to a stop as the spheres soared their way and landed amidst them with a *Whoosh* of power. The orbs turned the area into a swirling inferno of fire until all that remained were black tendrils of smoke rising from the scorched grass.

*You have dealt 400 HP damage to Guard (Level 18) with Dual Fire Blast (x4).*

The blast scattered the four guards around
the clearing, and all had visible burns on
them. The hands on one guard were so badly
burned he couldn't grab his weapon. Another
merely laid on the ground and held his hand
over his left eye as he screamed and blood
leaked down his face. The two others slowly
rose to their feet and patted at the burning
pieces of their clothing. They both drew
swords and charged at Arthur with a roar.

Arthur brought his weapons back to the
ready and braced for their rush. A throwing
knife flew forward and took one of them in the
shoulder, causing them to grimace in pain and
slow his charge. The other continued forward
and took a leaping downward slash at Arthur.
He calmly sidestepped the attack and flicked
Ember out in a quick motion, removing the
man's dominant hand. The guard looked confused
for a moment before he fell to a knee and
gripped the stump of his arm. Blood flowed
between the fingers of his remaining hand as
tears ran from his eyes.

*You have dealt 75 HP damage to Guard (Level
18) with Ember (Severing Blow - Hand).*

The second guard saw his fellow guards on
the ground and stopped his charge. He turned
to flee when Rayne flickered into existence
behind him, and a stiletto dagger slammed into
his left eye socket. The guard twitched for a
moment and then slid from the blade and fell
on his back. Arthur walked closer to the guard
with no hand and finished him with a stab to
the chest. He then walked to the last two and
ended their misery.

"Couldn't you have let the man with the burned hands go? He wasn't a threat," Rayne asked, uncomfortable with the killing of an unarmed man.

"I could have, but he's guarding the personal manor of Lord Preston. That leads me to believe he is directly tied to them and their activities. I can't let him live and heal up to return and fight us another day. If it had been a normal city guard on the wall, I would've left him and returned to assist him after the fight. There's no mercy for anyone we find in here," Arthur said sternly as he gestured to the manor.

Rayne looked at him in disbelief before slowly nodding. Arthur repeated his process and opened his storage to stash the guard's valuables and weapons. They joined the small stack of items, and he closed the doorway. Rayne resumed his lead, and they crossed the courtyard to the front entrance.

"You ready?" Rayne asked.

"Let's go."

# Chapter 42


*The Power of Evil*

Rayne slowly pushed the door open and peeked inside. The entryway inside was clear, so they slid the door wider and slipped inside. Rayne turned and gently closed the door while Arthur kept watch of their surroundings.

"Think he'll be upstairs?" Rayne asked.

"I don't know. Your guess is as good as mine."

The two walked forward and did their best to stay quiet. Rayne did a much better job of it than Arthur. The thief glanced at him from time to time with exasperated looks on his face as they moved. Arthur could only shrug in reply.

The two walked up the stairs and entered the main hallway. Two guards stood near a door in the back and called out an alarm when they spotted them. Everyone drew their weapons and dashed for each other. Arthur fished out a throwing knife and threw it. The guard he launched it at spun his sword and deflected it out of the air.

Arthur closed with him and caught the guard's sword with his dagger. The man struggled to push against him, but Arthur swung Ember at his midsection, causing him to jump backward.

"You've gotta show me how you deflected that," Arthur told him excitedly before the guard just grunted and slashed toward him again. Arthur pulled his sword across his body at an angle and caught the blade. With a gentle push, he slid the blade along his own until it neared the hilt and then forced it away from him.

The guard's momentum kept moving with the parried blade, and Arthur stabbed his dagger into the man's side. Hot blood splashed from the impact and dripped to the ground before the guard took a step back and clasped a hand to the wound.

*You have dealt 80 HP damage to Guard (Level 18) with Enchanted Mage-crafted Steel Dagger (Critical Hit).*
*You have inflicted Minor Bleed on Guard (Level 18).*

Arthur turned just in time to see Rayne catch the other guard's blade with his swordbreaker and jerk. The blade flexed and then shot from the man's hand before the thief stepped forward and planted the stiletto dagger in his side.

Arthur's opponent roared and drew Arthur's attention as he charged back at him. The man's rage made his already clumsy fighting even worse, and Arthur used his Deflect spell. The power surged out, and the man's blade rebounded from empty air, making him stumble off-balance. This time, his dagger found the neck of the guard, and he stumbled to the ground as blood leaked from his mouth. The man tried to move and rise, but his strength failed him, and he gradually sunk to the floor.

*You have dealt 80 HP damage to Guard (Level 18) with Enchanted Mage-crafted Steel Dagger (Critical Hit).*
*Guard (Level 18) has died.*

Rayne's guard was already on the floor with two additional puncture wounds in him. The storage room popped open, and their belongings flew in before Arthur quickly shut it. Arthur wouldn't allow them any further access to these weapons. If they didn't succeed in their mission, at least they wouldn't have access to the steel anymore to go after Alurian.

The two checked themselves one more time before wrenching the door open at the end of the hall and dashing in. The room they entered was one of fanciful design. Tapestries adorned the walls with scenes of battles of past ages. A few weapons hung on racks around the room, and most looked old with a coating of patina on them.

The two slowed their charge and halted. The room was empty of people. Decorations were all that littered the space. A chest, roughly four feet tall and six feet wide, sat in the middle of the room. The thought of all the treasure it could hold forced Arthur's feet forward. He subconsciously walked forward until he was mere feet from the box. A hand on his shoulder wrenched him backward, and he heard Rayne's voice.

"That's not a normal chest."

"Yeah, I know. It's a big-ass chest. Should have a lot of good stuff in it."

"No," Rayne said with a shake of his head, "I feel the power of shadow on it. Something is wrong with it."

With that final pronouncement, the chest
rattled and bounced in place. The lid popped
open, and it revealed a maw of sharp teeth.
The outline of a shadow formed around the box
and the face of a demonic creature hovered
directly above the lid.

"What the hell?" Arthur asked.

"We're screwed. That's a mimic!" Rayne
yelled.

Arthur activated Scan.

*You have received 210 experience for
successful use of Scan.*

| Name: Demonic Mimic | |
|---|---|
| Level: 21 | |
| Type: Demon | |
| Class: Mimic | |
| HP: 800/800 | |
| MP: 200/200 | |
| Stamina: 400/400 | |
| Strength: 26 | Experience: N/A |
| Agility: 7 | Skills |
| Intellect: 12 | Combat Skills: |
| Wisdom: 7 | |
| Endurance: 26 | ? (???/???) |

"So, it has a lot of health. It's still
just a demon trapped in a box," Arthur said in
confusion.

"They're hard to kill and can use Shadow
Magic."

"Nothing a little fire won't fix," Arthur answered as he pointed Ember at the monster. His Flamethrower spell poured from the end of the blade and crossed the distance. Before it hit, the creature opened its mouth, and a portal of shadow swirled in front of it. The flames hit the swirling disc, and the shadows pulled the fire into it before the portal closed, leaving the mimic untouched.

"That could be a problem," Arthur commented.

The mimic bounced forward with the lid continually opening and closing. The slamming of its mouth caused Arthur to wince, but he activated Sheathe in Flames and dashed forward. Ember came around and struck the side of the chest, only to stop less than an inch into the wood. The flame on the blade blackened the nearby wood, but a quick hop from the mimic and the sword fell free.

*You have dealt 15 HP damage to Demonic Mimic (Level 21) with Ember.*

The monster hopped forward one more time and bit at Arthur. He pulled back, but not before the giant teeth punched through the bracer on his left arm and into the flesh below. The wound ached as he jumped back and dislodged the tooth. A glance at the wound showed bright blood leaking from the puncture wound.

*Demonic Mimic (Level 21) has dealt 45 HP damage to you with Bite.*

A throwing knife hit the box and stuck into the wood but did minimal damage. Arthur looked over to see Rayne shrug. "Had to try something. All I have is a dagger and throwing knives. Not sure I can do much to it."

Arthur dashed forward again but switched his enchantment on Ember. He used his disruption enchantment instead, and his sword bit into the rim of the lid. The area where his attack landed lost its shadowy appearance and the blade dug deep into the wood. He had to lift and push on the weapon in quick motions to dislodge the sword.

Arthur dove out of the way of the thing's attack and rolled to a stop near Rayne. He reached his hand out, and Rayne placed a dagger in it. His disrupting spell enveloped both of Rayne's knives.

"Go for the hinges. If we can separate the top from the bottom, it should render it helpless," Arthur told him.

Rayne nodded and melded into the shadows. The mimic advanced toward Arthur, but before it came close enough to attack, it stopped. It quickly spun and snapped at the air, and Rayne flew backward to land against a desk. His arm had a deep gash down the side, and he stood up on shaky feet.

Arthur ran forward and swung toward the exposed hinge on its back, but the monster was too quick and spun again with a bounce. His sword crashed into the lid of the chest and stuck again, but this time, Arthur channeled his Flamethrower spell through it. The wood caught on fire with ease without the mimic's protective layer of shadows.

The shadowy face erupted in screeching before two arms of swirling purple power appeared in the air, one on each side of the chest. The left arm swung forward and hit Arthur in the center of his chest, causing him to stumble backward and lose his grip on Ember. The hand reached up and grabbed hold of his sword to wrench it free. The creature popped the sword into its open mouth and it clanged to the bottom of the chest.

*Demonic Mimic (Level 21) has dealt 30 HP damage to you with Backhand.*

"You bastard! That's my sword!" Arthur protested.

The creature merely bounced toward Arthur again as he brought his dagger in front of him and coated it in the disruption effect. A shadow blurred in the air, and Rayne landed on top of the lid with a thud. The mouth slammed closed from his weight, and Rayne stabbed his swordbreaker into the hole in one latch, pinning its mouth shut. A shadowy hand came around and swatted the thief off of the lid, and he rolled to the ground nearby.

Arthur charged in and jumped. He soared over the lid and bounced off the wood near the back to land directly behind the chest. A quick spin allowed him to smash his dagger into the hinge of the box. A sharp metallic *clink* echoed through the room as the pin in the hinge snapped and slid free. The top and bottom brackets remained affixed to the wood, but the lid bounced freely. Arthur saw both of the hands reaching toward him, so he dove away to put distance between himself and the box.

*You have dealt 70 HP damage to Demonic Mimic (Level 21) with Enchanted Mage-crafted Steel Dagger (Broken Hinge).*

"You need me to get the other one or think you can handle it?" Arthur asked Rayne with a confident smirk.

"You're welcome for closing its mouth so it wouldn't eat you with your foolish stunt."

Rayne dashed forward with Haste fueled steps and slashed at the remaining hinge. The blade clanged against the metal, but the stiletto dagger didn't have the power to break it. He needed a solid hit with the swordbreaker.

The lid rattle more, and a shadowy hand reached forward to wrench the swordbreaker free. The appendage stretched forward and plucked Rayne's swordbreaker from its hinge and tossed it in its mouth to join Ember.

"Great, now you have nothing to hurt it with," Arthur commented to Rayne.

Rayne only stuck out his tongue, and Arthur just sighed. He cast a Weak Firebolt at the monster, and the swirling portal of shadows appeared again and swallowed the fire. Arthur noticed that the portal appeared directly in front of the creature's mouth, and that gave him an idea. *A foolish idea, but an idea, nonetheless.*

Arthur used his Earth and Fire Magic to pull a layer of stone from the nearby wall and pressed his arm into it. *Thank god they made the walls of stone.* The stone grew to encase his arm until it layered four inches of solid rock in a ring around his forearm. The weight was difficult to move, but he needed the protection. This monster would have to die from the inside.

He ran forward and used all his strength to
punch his encased arm toward the creature. It
jumped forward and slammed its jaws shut on
the stone around his arm. The impact jarred
Arthur and the teeth of the beast dug deep
enough to puncture skin, but the stone held.
Before the creature could try to bite again,
Arthur channeled flame into his exposed palm
and cast his Flamethrower spell into the heart
of the chest.

Fire exploded out of all sides of the lid,
and the monster's shadowy face screeched in
agony. Rayne ran up to the creature and
plunged his dagger into the edge of the chest,
and Arthur watched the dark power from the box
gradually fade and flow into Rayne himself.
The energy slowly faded until Rayne stood up,
and his eyes flashed a hazy purple for a
moment before returning to normal.

Arthur used his Fire Magic to pull the
flames off the chest and keep it from burning
down the rest of the room. A small layer of
smoke collected along the surface of the
ceiling. He walked over and kicked the bottom
half of the chest to tip it over. Ember and
Rayne's swordbreaker dagger clanged out onto
the stone, but a few more goodies joined them.

*You have found Small Pouch of Coins.*
*You have found Sentient Soul Stone (x3).*
*You have found Skillbook of Shadowstep.*

Arthur grabbed his weapon and tossed Rayne
the swordbreaker. Since they were in the
middle of enemy territory, they gathered the
extra pieces and threw the entire chest and
the prizes into his storage. The remnants of
the mimic's chest may prove useful if any
residual energy remained. Arthur grabbed a
small chunk of metal from the storage and cast
his Arcane Repair to fix the holes in his
metal bracer. A quick healing spell took care
of his wounds and another sealed Rayne's arm.

His storage space closed, and they checked
their weapons. Nothing in the room looked
useful, so they turned to leave when clapping
sounded near the balcony. A man rounded the
corner with jet black hair, cropped short in a
military fashion. He continued to clap as he
walked into full view and stopped near the
entrance.

His hawk-like nose stood out and his smooth
voice rang across the room. "So good of you to
join us, Arthur Firebrand. I'm Lord Preston
Wayne, and I have to admit I was skeptical you
were who you claimed to be, but the dragon,
the Dimensional Magic, and now your appearance
itself tells me the truth. I see your mother's
face when I look at you."

"How dare you speak of my parents,
traitor."

"Your parents were kind people with
misguided goals. They would've destroyed us
all," the noble said with what sounded like
regret in his voice.

"You mean like King Wailyn is doing? People
starving and living in horrible conditions is
what you consider saving everyone? You're as
foolish as he is."

"I'm not really here to argue with you," Preston told Arthur, and the noble's gaze moved to Rayne. "Ah, you've even brought the Shadow Assassin with you. I wondered where you went. You caused quite a stir in this city before you disappeared."

"We're finally going to put an end to you," Rayne gritted out slowly.

Lord Preston brought his hands together in two hard claps, and people appeared all around the room. Rayne and Arthur couldn't explain how they showed up as they did, but the outlook was grim.

"Stick close to me. When they charge, I'll hit all of them at once," Arthur whispered to Rayne.

The thief brought his blades up and stood back to back with Arthur.

"I don't know if you brought enough. You do know we beat almost the entire horde of goblins and orcs you foolishly allowed the Dark Elves to raid the country with? There aren't nearly enough people in here," Arthur said confidently, even though he didn't feel that confident.

"I could find more people. Or I can just rely on better people," Preston said as he snapped his fingers.

Every person in the room vanished into shadows as the two watched.

*Well shit! Just had to get cocky, didn't I?*

"You didn't think you were the only assassin around, did you?" Lord Preston asked Rayne.

"Can you see them?" Arthur asked the thief.

"Barely and only in glimpses."

"Let me know when most of them are close to us."

Rayne nodded, and they waited as they slowly spun in a circle while remaining back to back. The air felt suffocating with the dread that permeated the room. Rayne yelled out, "Now!" and Arthur cast his spell.

His Divine Fury spell roared to life, and the area erupted into yells and screams. Flashes of light lit up empty locations and caused the assassins to flicker into view before they faded again. The spell's effect kept slashing into them and temporarily causing them to blink into existence. Rayne and Arthur both took the chance to launch throwing knives when they appeared out of the shadow.

Some of the thieves had the presence of mind to dodge through the pain, while others usually ended up with a blade in the chest or arm. Within fifteen seconds, most of the assassins had fallen out of their stealth and collapsed to the ground. Arthur and Rayne charged forward into the remaining assassins and struck. Their blades danced across flesh as they flashed into view. A few of the killers slashed out with a knife, and two of them caught Arthur on the arm. Rayne took a shallow wound to his side, but nothing that slowed him down.

With all the assassins in the room incapacitated, the two turned to look at Lord Preston with malicious grins on their faces. The lord looked unfazed by the development.

"Divine spells, so you truly are a champion," Lord Preston sighed. "What is Lianna thinking?"

"I'd guess she's not happy you killed my father. They were allies after all," Arthur said in disgust.

"Oh, that's not it. We couldn't have done that without some divine help, after all. I just don't know why she's trying to change the balance."

Arthur's anger flared at the statement. *Is he implying Lianna helped them kill my parents? Surely that isn't true?*

"Isabell is the real poison of this world. One way or another, we'll make sure her influence dies here," Rayne told him in defiance.

Rayne's statement shook Arthur out of his dark thoughts and returned him to the mission.

"Let's see how you measure up then," Preston said as he held his arms to the side, and two more people emerged from the balcony. On his left stood a man of middling age with barely visible streaks of gray in his short beard and mustache. The contrast of the ebony hair with the gray made him stand out, along with his dark purple robes which worried Arthur. On his right was a beautiful woman in her mid-twenties with flowing blonde hair. The purple robes she wore billowed around her form and had silver trim around the sleeves and neck. Arthur scanned all three of the enemies.

*You have received 860 experience for successful use of Scan (x3).*

<table>
<tr><td colspan="2">Name: Lord Preston Wayne</td></tr>
<tr><td colspan="2">Level: 32</td></tr>
<tr><td colspan="2">Type: Human</td></tr>
<tr><td colspan="2">Class: Wizard, Traveler</td></tr>
<tr><td colspan="2">Title: Champion of Isabell</td></tr>
<tr><td colspan="2">HP: 620/620</td></tr>
<tr><td colspan="2">MP: 780/780</td></tr>
<tr><td colspan="2">Stamina: 620/620</td></tr>
<tr><td>Strength: 18</td><td>Experience: N/A</td></tr>
</table>

| Agility: 18 | Skills |
| Intellect: 30 | Combat Skills: |
| Wisdom: 16 | |
| Endurance: 29 | ? (???/???) |

| Name: Khaldur Quinn | |
| --- | --- |
| Level: 27 | |
| Type: Human | |
| Class: Geomancer, Pyromancer, Stonebreaker | |
| HP: 500/500 | |
| MP: 800/800 | |
| Stamina: 500/500 | |

| Strength: 17 | Experience: N/A |
| Agility: 12 | Skills |
| Intellect: 27 | Combat Skills: |
| Wisdom: 17 | |
| Endurance: 25 | ? (???/???) |

| Name: Laulin Dinsur | |
| --- | --- |
| Level: 27 | |
| Type: Human | |
| Class: Assassin | |
| HP: 620/620 | |
| MP: 300/300 | |
| Stamina: 620/620 | |

| Strength: 18 | Experience: N/A |
| Agility: 26 | Skills |
| Intellect: 12 | Combat Skills: |
| Wisdom: 6 | |
| Endurance: 29 | ? (???/???) |

"The woman's an assassin and the other two are casters," Arthur hissed at Rayne. The thief's face took on a grim expression, and he hunched down lower with his weapons out front.

"May have to let your friend out to play," Arthur told the thief quietly.

Rayne nodded. "When the time is right, he will. Just remember, I'm useless for a while afterward."

Arthur wanted to start this fight before they got the chance to react. He dual cast his Fire Blast spell and launched the two orbs of fire toward the three members. Laulin dove to the side and melded into shadows while Preston and Khaldur just stood with a smile plastered on their faces.

The fire exploded and swirled over them. When the spell cleared, both stood precisely where they'd been and didn't have so much as a singed hair. Preston ran his hand through his hair and stared at Arthur.

"I'm a Wizard, boy. That won't hurt me. You do know what a wizard is, don't you?" Preston asked.

When Arthur didn't answer, he just continued. "The Wizard class is only available when you've reached level twenty in the four base elements. Too bad you'll never make it far enough to see the class yourself."

Rayne dashed in front of Arthur, and blades rang beside him. He turned in time to see Rayne locked in combat with Laulin. She'd almost caught him with her knife before Rayne intervened. *Fine, they want to play dirty, I'll play dirty.* He poured in the mana and cast Retribution. The beam of searing power slammed into Preston and Khaldur's position on the edge of the balcony.

The two men buckled down under the power as it pummeled into them, but Preston eventually lifted his hand, and a translucent dome of energy pushed back the beam of light. He stood with his hand in the air and stared daggers at Arthur, promising his retribution. The spell ended, and he lowered his hand. Khaldur finally regained his senses after the damage from the magic. The reprieve from Preston's dome aided in his recovery.

*You have dealt 300 HP damage with Retribution (x2).*

The sound of blades ringing near him continued to echo through the room. Power built in Preston's hand, so Arthur readied for the spell. Preston pushed his hand forward, and Arthur activated his own spell. A rift of magic formed in front of the Wizard and sucked in the spear of ice he launched. The projectile appeared from the rift Arthur placed beside Khaldur and sunk into the man's side. Rivulets of blood ran down the length of the ice and dripped to the floor. Preston looked on in disbelief.

"You couldn't have figured out that spell already."

Arthur only snapped the portals closed and stared into the man's face as Khaldur slowly extracted the ice spear. When it fell to the ground, it shattered, and Khaldur covered the wound in a thin layer of stone. Power built from the Geomancer and numerous shards of stone rose from the ground and hovered near him. With a gesture, they launched toward Arthur.

Arthur cast a combination of Gust of Wind and a dual Cast Deflect to knock the missiles out of the air. A grunt of pain drew his attention to Rayne, and he saw a shallow stab wound on his side.

Arthur needed to help Rayne, so he waited for the thief to strike again. When he saw his left arm dart forward, Arthur opened a small rift in its path and redirected it to a portal directly behind Laulin. The blade sunk into her back and she arched forward with a surprised expression on her face.

His attention snapped back to the men in front of him as both wound up spells. Arthur dove to the side to dodge the ball of fire that Khaldur threw at him, as he opened a rift and redirected the fireball Preston launched at him toward the Geomancer. The flame splashed over the man but caused no harm.

Shadows flashed through the room, and Arthur turned to see Rayne transform into his Shadow Form. The young man launched forward at incredible speed and struck at Laulin with precise stabs. The woman did her best to dance and dodge backward, but the blades continually found flesh. Her skill and speed were enough to allow her to avoid most of the damage, but her arms became a mess of small bleeding cuts, while a few thick lines of blood adorned her ribs.

Arthur pulled his weapons free, cast Haste, and ran at the two casters, He'd figured out he couldn't beat them in a one on two magical fight. Preston smiled and the Geomancer chuckled at his dash. They both raised a hand, and fire blossomed in their palms. Arthur waited for the cast and instantly dove to the side while maintaining his own fire barrier. The flames swept past him and narrowly missed while his fire barrier protected his skin from the blazing heat.

Arthur bounced back to his feet and charged for Khaldur. The caster pulled a small blade from his belt as Arthur closed and lifted it to intercept Ember as it swung for him. Arthur's sword bounced off of the dagger and caused the man to stumble. He stepped forward and thrust his knife at Khaldur's chest, and the man twisted. The blade scored a deep gash across his chest, but the twist saved him. The stone under his feet rumbled, and a fist emerged to send Arthur flying backward.

*Khaldur has dealt 50 HP damage to you with Stone Fist.*

*I have got to stop getting hit with that spell.* Arthur rose to his feet amidst the protestations of his ribs and locked eyes on his targets. Shards of ice and stone hovered near Preston and sped forward. Arthur activated Passato Sotto and dropped to the ground below the projectiles.

Arthur grabbed a throwing knife and palmed the blade while pushing mana into it. The knife swam with the power of his disrupting spell, and he launched it toward Khaldur. The mage's eyes went wide as he lifted his hands to push the blade off course, but the disrupting spell prevented the magic from moving it enough. The blade sunk deep into his chest, and the Geomancer finally stumbled away from the fight before his leg caught on the short balcony rail, and he tumbled over it backward. A heavy thud quickly followed his muffled scream.

Preston glared at him. "It's hard to find good help. You know how long it took me to train him properly?"

Arthur merely shrugged. "He was on the wrong side."

Arthur chanced a glance toward Rayne and watched as the thief struck a solid blow into Laulin's shoulder. The assassin stumbled backward, warily casting glances at the evil visage on the thief's face from his ability. She sunk her head in resigned fate before shadows swirled around her. When the swirling violet energy collapsed back to the woman, she was now a foot taller and bulging with muscles. Her skin shone with glowing purple veins and took on a gray hue.

"What," emerged from Rayne in distorted tones before the creature darted forward and smashed into the thief with its shoulder. The shadowy form of Rayne flew backward and crashed into a nearby table. The young man rose from the splintered wood and dusted off his clothes while the power of his form held him together. Arthur knew Rayne's time was almost up, so he ignored Preston and dashed to save him.

He struck at the unfamiliar form of Laulin
with both weapons, and they rang against her
skin like striking stone. Neither damaged the
assassin. A fist lashed forward and launched
Arthur backward to land on the pile of
splintered wood near Rayne.

Arthur rolled back to his stomach and
pushed himself to his knees before he turned
to regard the thief. "Any ideas?"

"Disruption," was the only word that leaked
from his mouth.

Arthur leaped to his feet and placed a hand
over both of Rayne's daggers. The spell coated
the blades again, and the thief sprang to
action. His incredible speed helped him dodge
some of the blows from the monstrous woman,
and his knives punctured and dealt damage.
Arthur coated both his blades in the same
spell and rushed to help.

A blurring effect in the air near him
caused him to dive to the ground and land on
his stomach. A burst of Air Magic flew over
his head and hit the chair to his right,
causing it to explode into a shower of
splinters. He rose to his knees to see Lord
Preston with his hand extended again. *Time is
ticking,* he reminded himself and jumped back
to his feet.

He dashed around the fight with Rayne and crept behind the woman. Rayne pushed the attack and drove her toward Arthur. When she was within striking range, Arthur thrust forward again with both weapons. Ember slid into flesh and stopped after a foot of the blade sunk in. His dagger punched in a few inches before it also halted. The heavy sword's thrust was enough to push past the defense, and Arthur sent an additional burst of raw mana into the assassin to disrupt her energy pattern even more.

The purple muscles bulged and shrunk in rapid succession. Laulin seemed to shift back to herself and then quickly back into the enhanced form. He pulled his sword free and swung it at her neck. The blade hit right as she shifted back into her woman form and cut cleanly. It stopped at her spine, and he pulled it free. The woman's shape-changing halted and settled on a body that was half demonic and half woman. The lifeless form was a grotesque aftereffect of her gamble for power.

Arthur saw Rayne down on a knee in front of her. The shadows retreated, and his eyes reflected a look of pain. *His power is taking its toll.*

Arthur detected Earth magic to his side and saw the spell flying for Rayne. He opened a rift in its path and redirected it to strike Preston from directly over his head. The projectiles smashed into him but didn't do any damage. They only caused him to stumble. Arthur ran for the lord with his weapons drawn.

Lord Preston calmly drew a sword at his approach and waited. Arthur slowed as he neared and struck out with short testing blows. Preston easily batted them aside and looked almost bored. At one point, he even lifted his off-hand to cover a yawn. Arthur renewed his Haste spell and pushed forward. The speed of the attacks increased, and the lord finally got serious. No matter how hard Arthur tried, he couldn't land a blow on flesh.

Lord Preston pushed back and went on the offensive. Arthur struggled to keep pace as the lord danced him across the room. Swords rang, and Arthur lost almost all sense of proper form as he struggled to keep up. Preston's blade slipped past his guard and scored a long cut across his bicep. The cut burned but he cast his healing spell. The blood ceased flowing and the wound knit shut. Lord Preston disengaged from the fight and looked at his opponent in a new light.

"You're far better than I expected for someone who hasn't been here long. It's almost a shame to get rid of you. You'd make a fine addition to the group. Sure you don't want to switch sides?" Preston asked.

"Not a chance in hell."

"Thought you'd say that. Now it's time to stop that pesky healing magic of yours," the lord said as he deftly slipped a dagger free from his belt. The serrated knife shone with a dim purple light on the blade.

The lord ran forward and continued his assault. Arthur had enough trouble with the man when he used only one weapon. With both of the blades, Arthur could do nothing but stumble around the room and haphazardly dodge. The sword glanced from his pauldron, and the dagger rang off his bracer. Arthur played on a gamble and waited for the sword to return. When it came at him, he lunged forward with Ember and cast his Deflect spell. The blade bounced away from him and Lord Preston twisted. The sword bit through his robes, and blood welled up on his side.

Lord Preston grunted in frustration and continued his assault. The strikes continued to fall until the dagger finally found purchase in his shoulder. A feeling of unease settled over him, immediately followed by a pulse of magic that rattled him to his core.

*Lord Preston has dealt 80 HP damage to you with Manastrike (Disrupting Blow).*
*Your flow of Mana has been disrupted and will not recover for 5 minutes. Unable to cast any spells for the duration.*

*Crap.* Arthur was fortunate it didn't cancel active spells, so his Haste was still in effect, albeit only for another three minutes. When it wore off he'd have no chance to avoid the damage.

Lord Preston's sword smashed into one of his pauldrons and bit through the metal. The blade dug into his shoulder and caused him to drop his dagger.

*** 

"Samson, they're pulling back on the eastern portion of the wall!" Allendria called to the Paladin.

His gaze moved to that section, and he called back, "Appears so. Care to make one last concentrated attack? If we can get them to abandon the wall, we can take control of it ourselves."

"Casters, prepare your best fire spells, but don't cast them at the wall. Cast them at me," Allendria told them as she walked into the open field in front of them.

"Lady, we can't do that. You'll die," one soldier said carefully.

She sent him a cocky smile. "You're not that good. Now, just do as you're ordered!"

"You heard Lady Allendria. Give her all you've got!" Samson roared over the gathered soldiers.

Fire Magic swirled down the line as power built in the hands of each fighter. Many looked apprehensive at the idea of launching them toward Allendria. The Dark Elf stood with arms forward as the flames soared her way. She caught the balls of fire as they approached and mixed them in streams of power. She wove the threads of energy together and stretched it into a lengthy line of force. She closed her eyes and lifted her hands to the sky with a yell as a giant ball of power soared for the wall.

As soon as it hit, the power unfurled and laid out across the wall in one long line of blazing fire. Soldiers leaped from the wall as the fire spread across the battlements. When the flame died down, no one remained on the wall.

"Good enough?" Allendria asked Samson with a grin.

"That'll do," he told her with a slight bow.

"Soldiers! March for the wall! We are taking the city!" Samson called to the assembly.

The army moved forward in unison until they neared the wall, and then two of the earth mages worked in concert to lift a ramp directly to the top of the wall. The forces stepped foot on the wall and spread out as their illusions broke. Samson ordered anyone who surrendered to be detained. They fought any who resisted to the death. Allendria stood atop the wall and observed the roundup.

"I wonder how Arthur is doing? I didn't think we'd be able to force their guards off the wall," Vana quipped as she came to stand near Allendria.

"I hope he's all right," she said as she turned to look toward Preston's manor.

A loud thud shook the ground near her, and she turned to see Calfuray staring at her. Balair hovered near her.

"Get on. We have to go!" Calfuray rumbled at her.

"What's wrong?" Vana asked.

"Arthur's losing. He needs help," she told them as she frantically shifted from foot to foot.

"Samson!" Allendria yelled at the soldier standing down the wall.

The Paladin turned to look at the elf. "What is it?"

"Rescue mission. Let's go!"

Samson left in a sprint and ran straight for them.

"Calfuray, can you carry all three of us?" Allendria asked.

"I must. It's not a very long trip," the dragon said as she gazed toward the manor.

The dragon lowered her bulk as Vana, Samson, and Allendria scurried onto her back.

"I thought you weren't a horse?" Allendria quipped with a wry grin.

"I'd rather be a living horse than a dead dragon. Hold on!"

The dragon hunched her legs and jumped with one massive thrust, carrying them into the air.

* * *

Arthur collapsed to the ground while blood welled from his shoulder. He stared into the face of Lord Preston with resignation.

*Sorry, Balair. Don't think I can beat him. Tell Allendria I love her.* Arthur sent to the drake.

*Tell her yourself,* came Balair's voice as Calfuray's roar echoed through the room. Samson, Vana, and Allendria dropped to the balcony and sprung to action. Fire danced around his fiancé's hand and splashed across Lord Preston. Samson charged forward and smashed his shield into the noble, while Vana launched an arrow that sunk into his shoulder.

Vana spotted Rayne on the ground and ran to check on him while Allendria ran to Arthur. Samson stood toe to toe with Preston and stared the man down.

"You okay?" Allendria asked.

"Not really. Getting really tired of getting my ass kicked."

"That's what happens when you don't train your combat skills," she said with a smirk.

Arthur stood with shaky legs, and Vana brought Rayne over to the group.

"Time's up, Lord Preston. You can't beat us all," Arthur told him. "Surrender, and I'll make your trial quick."

Lord Preston merely smiled, "It's not over. It's only just begun."

The man's eyes lit purple, and energy rolled over him. The power spun around him with that same purple hue, but flashes of black lightning crackled through the surface. Dreading what they'd see, the energy faded, and Lord Preston stood in his same place, seemingly unchanged.

A shadow covered the man, and he disappeared. Arthur stood confused for a moment until a sharp pain smashed into his side.

*Lord Preston has dealt 80 HP damage to you with Manastrike (Disrupting Blow).*

*Your flow of Mana has been disrupted and will not recover for 5 minutes. Unable to cast any spells for the duration.*

Before Arthur could comprehend what happened, shadows swirled around him, and he disappeared again. This time Vana jumped backward and caught a slash across the midsection that left a thin line of blood before Preston vanished again.

"Damn, he can transport himself. Everyone get back to back! Leave no space uncovered!" Arthur called.

The party pressed themselves in a loose circle, leaving barely any gap between them, and waited. The form of Preston appeared and disappeared in rapid succession. He'd show up, dash in with a slash, and move again. Their new strategy seemed to work but he was so quick it was hard to block the blows. Rayne and Arthur were already running out of Stamina, and he was sure the others had used a fair amount of power during their fight at the wall. Arthur fished out the small healing potion Rayne gave him and downed it. As the liquid flowed into his mouth, he felt some relief as minor wounds stopped bleeding and his HP rose by 75 points.

Another blade slipped through and caught Arthur while he heard the occasional grunt of pain from others in the circle.

"Allendria, can you Firestorm? He cut me off from magic with his dagger."

"I'd need help with the flame."

"Samson, can you help out?" Arthur called.

"It'd be my pleasure," the warrior replied as the eyes on the shield lit up. Fire exploded forward, and Allendria grasped it with her magic. She turned the blazing inferno into a whirlwind of fire around their position. Preston appeared inside the flames the next time he stepped from the shadow and immediately regretted the decision. He slunk back into shadow before the fire could do too much harm.

"Allendria, stop the flame. Samson, next time he appears, I want you to strike forward in a direct thrust. I don't care where he shows up at."

Allendria let the fire die, and Samson looked confused but Arthur saw the man's head bob. Arthur reached behind him with his left hand and grasped Allendria's hand. The message appeared in her vision, and she smiled.

When Lord Preston emerged, Arthur cast his spell using the stable mana of Allendria. The rift formed in front of Samson as he thrust his sword forward. Arthur arranged the other portal so it would emerge directly beside Preston. Samson's blade punched through the black vortex and emerged from the other side to sink into the ribcage of the lord. The man froze in his attack with his sword mere feet from Arthur's head. He looked down at the weapon stuck through his chest and stumbled back. The sword slipped free, and blood spilled to the floor.

"Well played. You may be what the world needs after all. I concede defeat today, but you may not be so lucky next time."

Preston's form turned ethereal, and the man stood straight, as though nothing hindered him, and pain didn't exist. His body darted through the wall and out of the castle in the general direction of the capital of Esmere. Arthur received a notification.

*The Kingdom of Fire has successfully taken the city of Seora. All loyal to King Arthur of the Kingdom of Fire can lay down their arms and surrender. Any who do not are subject to death.*

The battle was over, and now it'd be time to clean up the city.

"Thank you all. What about the battle on the walls? Whose keeping them focused there?" Arthur asked.

"The defenders on the wall surrendered. We control the city wall near our initial assault location. The spells were too much for them to handle. We sped this way when Calfuray detected your life was dropping dangerously fast," Allendria explained.

Arthur walked to the balcony and looked into the sky. Calfuray soared through the air with sunlight sparkling from her violet scales. She opened her mouth and roared as a plume of flame filled the sky in a vibrant display.

*Thank you, Lady,* Arthur sent to her.

*Again with the title? Hummmm...I guess I'll accept it, My King,* she sent back in mock tones.

Arthur finally sunk to the ground and relaxed. There was much left to do, but he was weary from the fighting. Rayne plopped down next to him, and the two sat back to back, each supporting the other's weight.

"Looks like they'll be useless for the rest of the day," Vana quipped.

"Figures, he becomes a king and thinks he can have everyone do the work for him," Samson prodded with a teasing tone to his voice.

Arthur didn't care. They were one step closer to their goal, and it would mean a better life for those around here. That thought crashed into him like a ton of bricks. *That means I have to find a way to feed these people now.* The groan that escaped his lips this time was one of dread and not one of pain.

# Chapter 43

Ambassadors

The day drug on as their forces and the newly converted city guard patrolled the city looking for enemy forces. All those who switched sides reported to Arthur at Lord Preston's manor and pledged their swords to him and the Kingdom of Fire. He accepted their oath and turned them back toward weeding out the corruption in their ranks. The soldiers seemed ever so eager to comply.

A thorough search of the manor found more guards with steel weapons that resisted and died shortly after. All the new weapons and armor adorned his storage space. The raid on the city also helped boost his experience.

*You have gained 120 total experience in Stealth.*

*You have gained 1,525 total experience in Throwing Knives.*

*Congratulations, you have reached level 4 in Throwing Knives. You now have 9% increased accuracy with Throwing Knives. Getting better with those.*

*You have gained 1,100 total experience in Dual Wield.*

*You have gained 1,100 total experience in Small Blades.*

*You have gained 480 total experience in Block.*

*You have gained 300 total experience in Parry.*

*You have gained 600 total experience in Air Magic.*

*You have gained 610 total experience in Dimensional Magic.*

*You have gained 880 total experience in Medium Armor.*

*You have gained 1,250 total experience in Fire Magic.*

*You have gained 240 total experience in Earth Magic.*

*You have gained 310 total experience in Water Magic.*

*You have gained 1,250 total experience.*

*You have gained 3,480 total experience for raid kills.*

They spent days going through the city in search of anything they could use to keep the citizens alive and fed. Arthur ordered every noble manor emptied of food and took control of all the supplies personally. He sent out teams of hunters and foragers to scour the nearby land in search of food. This sent murmurs of awe and disbelief through the citizens of Seora. Apparently, hunting and foraging the landscape was forbidden, and the threat of the orcs and goblins made the prospect too scary for most to even consider.

A small cache of food they found made large meals that stretched the supply longer. They fed everyone in the city at least once a day. Members of the construction crews traveled the streets with armed guards and used their magic to repair roads and fix structures. They brought many of the older wooden buildings on the verge of collapse down, and the workers built nice stone houses in the design used in Alurian. It would take time to get a proper water and sewer system in place, but food was far more critical. Balair and Calfuray helped with this task by scouting for them and chasing wildlife back toward their general direction.

Now and then, Calfuray would drop off a deer or wild hog as she flew by, insisting she'd already eaten and didn't need that one. The soldiers running the cooking camp grabbed them without complaint and began skinning them and removing the meat.

Arthur and Allendria stood on the balcony of Lord Preston's manor and watched the sun fade on the horizon.

"You're making a difference," she told him with a soft touch on his cheek.

"I just hope it's not too late," he breathed.

* * *

King Wailyn stood from his desk and paced in anger. He glanced back at the notification he'd received.

*King Arthur Firebrand has captured the City of Seora for the Kingdom of Fire.*

*That fool failed me! How could Preston lose to this new upstart?*

His anger boiled over when a knock rapped on the door.

"Go away! I'm not available!" he roared.

The door slipped open, and the king readied fire in his hand to launch at the foolish human who dared enter his office without permission. The purple skin of the intruder caused him to stamp down his power as he regarded the form of Glirin, the King of the Dark Elves.

King Wailyn returned to his seat as the Dark Elf King strolled to take the chair on the other side of the desk.

"Well, Glirin, what brings you all the way out here?" Wailyn asked.

"It seems you failed to rid yourself of the pest problem. Now we have the son of the late king and queen to deal with. Not only that, but he's also already taken Seora from you."

"I'll take care of it. I'll remind you he's the same person who wiped your raiding force off the map."

"I'm not here to point fingers. I'm only here to tell you I've taken steps of my own. Our Goddess has made it abundantly clear she wants this issue resolved, no matter the cost."

"Oh, really? What steps have you made?"

"I've sent him a message. One I'm sure he'll not like," the man said with an evil grin.

King Wailyn fetched one of the few bottles of wine he had left from the drawer of his desk and poured two glasses. King Wailyn lifted his glass and said, "To our Goddess."

★★★

"Your Majesty," a guard called as Arthur walked down the street.

"Yes?"

"There's a delegation for you at the main gate. They look like a party of Dark Elves and declare they are ambassadors from the Dark Elven nation."

"I'll come immediately," Arthur said, and followed the guard through the winding streets back to the gate. He trudged to the top of the wall and looked out through the crenellations. A party of four dark elves stood with stoic faces in front of the gate.

"I'm King Arthur Firebrand. Can I help you with something?" he called to the group.

"Your Majesty, I'm Ambassador Finthra, and I've been instructed to deliver a message. King Glirin from the Dark Elves of Calzas declares war on King Arthur Firebrand and the Kingdom of Fire for the kidnapping of Princess Allendria!" The declaration rang out over the clearing, shortly followed by the notification.

*King Glirin and the Dark Elves of Calzas have declared war on King Arthur Firebrand and the Kingdom of Fire. Any battle between the forces of these two nations will be immediately classified as an active raid zone.*

*So they finally step forward,* Arthur thought as he gazed to the southeast where the Dark Elven city of Calzas sat and then glanced back toward the northeast, toward Esmere. *Fine, I'll get rid of you both.*

# Epilogue

*A Clash of Sisters*

Lianna watched the conflict with interest. That little weasel Preston would pay for divulging information he shouldn't even know. She'd need to dig deeper and see what he knew.

Without the timely arrival of Arthur's friends, he would have died, and her plan would have failed. *That boy needs to work on his combat and quit playing with crafting.*

"What the hell is wrong with you!" the familiar voice rang across the wide-open expanse of white.

Lianna sighed. "You really have to stop bothering me, especially unannounced, Bell."

"Don't play that game with me. Of all the people you could find, you had to bring back the son of those two! We had an agreement. You knew they would send this world to its doom and helped me fix it. Why would you jeopardize it all now?" Isabell fumed.

"Because, dear sister, look at the world now. It might as well be dead. You've destroyed it on your own with your misguided attempts to save it. I plan on fixing it. Arthur will get rid of your blight, and then we can see if he is up to the task of fighting the bigger threat. You hid and cowered from the true enemy while supplicating to them. Maybe the people would be better off dying on their feet than dying from starvation."

"You would rather the Ar'Tookuh invade and destroy this world then? How is that any better?" Isabell asked, exasperated.

"Who's saying they can't be stopped? They are a mortal race, albeit a very advanced one."

"You really think your young Firebrand will be able to fight against their power?" Isabell asked, intrigued.

"You forget, sister. I brought him back because of a very special skill that I knew lived in his family. Who better to resist an army that spreads through the universe like a plague than a man who can jump through the dimensions? He's a smart one and comes from a world that is also technologically advanced. He'll figure out how to make the best use of his skills."

Isabell regarded her sister's words before slowly shaking her head. "I guess we'll have to see. I might believe he has a chance if he can ever best my real champion. Until then, I won't relent."

"I'd expect nothing less," Lianna confirmed with a nod of her head.

Isabell turned and stormed away, only to disappear a few steps into her walk. *Leave it up to her to make a scene instead of just disappearing.* Lianna was glad her sister was so easy to manipulate. Arthur would never grow into the man he needed to be without the threat of her attacks. She'd do far more damage just leaving him be and allowing him to become complacent and fall into his obsession with crafting and building.

Despite her bravado in front of her sister, the state of the battle concerned her. Enemies surrounded her champions. The threat of the Dark Elves from the southeast, King Wailyn from the northeast, and the splintered dragons from the west troubled her more than she'd like to admit.

*Arthur, you better think of something fast.*

# End Notes

Thank you for reading The Dimensional Wars, Book 2: Soul Bond. I've worked hard to improve my craft since the start of the book. I thank all of my fans who've stuck through the series with me so far.

Reviews are the lifeblood of many authors. I highly encourage you to post a review for the book when you've finished. Love it or hate it I'd still like to hear about it to see what I did right and what I may have done wrong.

This is a work of fiction. Names, characters, places, and events are either the products of the Author's imagination or used in a fictitious manner. Any resemblance to actual persons, living or dead, is purely coincidental.

## A Young Thief

If you enjoyed the character Rayne in this book, I highly encourage you to read Rayne (The Dimensional Wars Origins) to see how he became the young man he is here.

## The Dimensional Wars

Book 1 - Dravincia
Book 2 - Soul Bond
Book 3 - Regicide (Release TBD)

   If you are looking for more book
recommendations, or if you feel like chatting
about books you have already read. Go to the
LitRPG Books group on FaceBook.

 If you want to see updates on The Dimensional
Wars or if you have any questions or comments
you wish to share with me let me know on The
Dimensional Wars FaceBook page. I'm always
willing to talk to anyone.

If you want updated news about releases please
visit my website at
http://thedimensionalwars.com.

To see new releases as well as any LitRPG
books that are on sale, visit the LitRPG
Releases FaceBook Page

Finally, if you're looking for a new book to
read but can't decide what to try next, pop on
over to the LitRPG Amazon Storefront.

To learn more about LitRPG, talk to authors
including myself, and just have an awesome
time, please join the LitRPG Group.

# Final Stat Sheet

**Name:** Arthur Firebrand
**Level:** 22
**Age:** 26
**Race:** Human
**Class:** Spell Blade
**HP:** 530/530 (550)
**MP:** 780/780 (1080)
**Stamina:** 530/530

**Strength:** 20
**Agility:** 32
**Intellect:** 34
**Wisdom:** 16
**Endurance:** 26
**Charisma:** 12
**Luck:** 11

**Experience:** 14895/63000 (0 stat points available)

**Skills** (225% boost to any skill for level up)
**Combat Skills:**

**Archery:** 10 (5170/6000)
  - **Aim Shot:** 7 (1695/3200)
**Block:** 3 (810/1000)
**Dual Wield:** 7 (1190/3200)
**Identify:** 1 (75/500)
**Light Armor:** 6 (700/2500)
**Medium Armor:** 5 (1680/1900)
**Parry:** 4 (670/1000)
**Scan:** 6 (810/1900)
**Small Blades:** 8 (2330/3800)
**Spears:** 2 (450/750)
**Stealth:** 4 (590/1400)
  - **Detect Hidden:** 1 (50/500)
**Swords:** 11 (2745/7200)
**Throwing Knives:** 4 (1005/1400)

**Unarmed:** 1 (275/500)

**Magic:**

**Air Magic:** 10 (2280/6000)
**Dimensional Magic:** 12 (23100/8500)
**Earth Magic:** 23 (53210/69000)
**Fire Magic:** 23 (33615/69000)
**Water Magic: 10** (4100/6000)

**Professions:**

**Barter:** 3 (100/1000)
**Blacksmithing:** 18 (1365/38000)
  - **Alternate Heating:** 1 (160/500)
  - **Arcane Metal Construction:** 3 (300/1000)
  - **Arcane Smithing:** 17 (23985/30000)
  - **Metal Construction:** 3 (300/1000)
**Cooking:** 2 (400/750)
**Enchanting:** 16 (5605/15000)
**Farming:** 8 (1635/3800)
**Firemaking:** 2 (700/750)
**Herbalism:** 6 (10/2500)
**Jeweler:** 9 (1500/4600)
**Leatherworking:** 7 (195/3200)
**Mining:** 6 (2400/2500)

| | |
|---|---|
| | - **Magical Mining** 6 (2025/2500)<br>**Skinning:** 4 (175/1400)<br>**Woodworking:** 1 (395/500)<br>  - **Arcane Woodworking:** 1 (355/500) |

www.ingramcontent.com/pod-product-compliance
Lightning Source LLC
Chambersburg PA
CBHW070918100726
47908CB00001B/21